Yes, most marriages ended up like hers – it was a truth universally acknowledged. Perfection only existed in books. Maybe the only lasting friendships were between females. She recollected the golden days of her teenage years spent with Jude. There was nothing like the feeling of having a best friend, a partner in crime, someone whose thoughts you shared, and who would see everything from your point of view. Just as Jude did.

Sherry Ashworth is a teacher, freelance journalist, radio broadcaster and author of five previous novels. She lives in Manchester with her husband and two daughters.

# Just Good Friends

## Sherry Ashworth

CORONET BOOKS

Hodder & Stoughton

First published in Great Britain in 1998
by Hodder and Stoughton
First published in paperback in 1999
by Hodder and Stoughton
A division of Hodder Headline PLC

A Coronet Paperback

10 9 8 7 6 5 4 3 2 1

ISBN 0 340 68200 0

Typeset by Palimpsest Book Production Limited,
Polmont, Stirlingshire
Printed and bound in Great Britain by
Clays Ltd, St Ives PLC, Bungay, Suffolk

Hodder and Stoughton
A division of Hodder Headline PLC
338 Euston Road
London NW1 3BH

For Sally Convey

## Acknowledgements

Thanks to Colette, Libby, Tony, Lorraine and little
Shug, who helped too.

## Acknowledgments

Thanks to Glenn Libby, Troy Bethune, and Steve Chase, who helped me...

# Chapter One

'Not far now,' Jude said cheerfully.

In response there was a blood-curdling yell.

'I fail to understand your objections, Aida. It's not as if you were happy in the old place. They never took to you next door, especially after you nicked their roast chicken.'

A louder, increasingly demented wail was joined by a lower pitched miaow, *sotto voce*.

'You too, Ludmilla? Come on! My driving isn't that bad!'

Jude heard a vociferous howl of protest. Quickly she angled her driving mirror to see what was going on in the cat travelling box in the back seat of the car. Aida was standing rigid on all four paws, her eyes glittering with terror. Ludmilla sat on her haunches, in a position all too familiar to Jude.

'Oh, bugger!'

Jude tried not to inhale the pungent aroma of cat wee.

'Really, Ludmilla! You could have waited. Ladies aren't supposed to relieve themselves in public. Ah, look! Here we are. Just over the brow of this hill, and you'll see a row of cottages on your right. Stone cottages. Ours is the one on the end. Ah – the removal men are here already.'

In front of her Jude saw the lorry with the words Fielding's Removals painted in white at the back. It was almost blocking the lane, as the cemented parking space opposite her new house was far too small for it. Jude had to drive a little further on before she found a grass verge where she could leave her Micra. Finally she got out of the car, pushed back the passenger seat, and extracted the cat box, careful not to sway it too much. The capacity of Ludmilla's bladder was remarkable.

The removal men were sitting in the cab, Frank, the large one, smoking and Terry reading the *Sun*. Jude hopped on to the step and rapped on the glass. Frank stubbed out his cigarette and wound down the window.

'Lunch break,' he said.

Jude bit her tongue. She didn't want to get on the wrong side of the removal men, but it infuriated her, the little tricks that men had to make you dependent on them. All morning Frank and Terry had been heaving and sighing and making out that lifting her furniture was some sort of Herculean labour only to be attempted by men soaked in testosterone. She'd have done anything to hire a women's removal company, but there was none in the *Yellow Pages*.

But Jude Jackson was not given to sulks. She would make the best of a bad situation. The gap in proceedings would allow her to enter her new house herself, and carry the sopping wet Ludmilla and Aida over the threshold.

There was a long garden leading to her front door, over-grown now, although in the past someone had attempted to plant a rockery. Her cottage was semi-detached, with two mullioned windows and some sort of climbing plant festooning the doorway. It was almost twee, but it was redeemed by the roughness of the grey stone walls. It was because the cottage was both pretty but no-nonsense, that Jude had fallen for it. That, and the price.

She unlocked the door.

Immediately she was in the front room. There was of course a smell of damp, as the property had been empty for so long. She paused for a moment to listen if there was any noise from next door. She'd enquired of the estate agents about her neighbours, but she'd drawn a blank. Each time she'd come for measuring up and such like, no one had been around. Jude rather hoped she'd find herself living cheek by jowl with a woman like herself, single, professional, with a life, just like her friends back in Manchester.

Meanwhile there were poor Aida and Ludmilla, still imprisoned in their travelling box! She walked briskly with them into the kitchen, plonked the box on the floor and set about turning the water on. Then she unlocked the box. Aida was out first, ears pinned back, cautiously sniffing about. Ludmilla edged out as if she was in a western, expecting a stray bullet to get her at any moment. When Frank and Terry knocked at the door, both cats froze at the sound. Jude went to let the men in.

'Shall we make a start?' Frank asked.

'I'll give you a hand if you like,' Jude said. 'To get the show on the road.'

Frank gave a sidelong glance to Terry, a twist of amusement on his lips.

'We'll manage between us.'

Jude bridled, but restrained herself. She knew she had the power to reduce men to quivering wrecks, should she choose to do so. She decided to bide her time.

'Shall I put the kettle on, then?'

'Now you're talking, love.'

Jude smiled to herself, and went outside to set about emptying her purple Micra. There was a lot of work to be done. She sniffed the air appreciatively. It was fresh and wholesome. She had never lived in the country before. The novelty of it was appealing. There were actually fields opposite the house – a real view – and a sense of space. A breeze played with her hair as she opened the boot to get out the box with the kettle and coffee things. Jude felt happier than she had for a long time.

It was a busy afternoon, a blur of packing cases and Frank and Terry with their big boots and beer bellies traipsing in and out of the cottage, the cats almost getting out once or twice, Jude changing her mind about the positioning of the sofa repeatedly, the bed almost scraping the wall at the turn in the stairs, setting up the music system, and then finally, as if by magic, Jude was bringing the men their last mug of tea.

'That's about it,' Terry said.

'Aye,' Frank concurred. He looked speculatively around Jude's living room. 'Not a bad job, even if I say so myself. A nice place for a little woman like you.'

Jude watched him sip at his tea, and wince.

'Tooth bothering you?' she suggested.

'Now and again.'

'Here. Let me have a look. I'm a dentist. I've just bought a practice in Mytholm Bridge – it's why I've moved here. Sit down and open your mouth and I'll give you a free examination. Not a usual perk, I know. Come on now, you're not scared of a little woman, surely? Oh dear, I can see what's causing the trouble. You've not had a check-up for a while, have you? There's quite a bit of decay at the back. Someone will have to take a drill to that, or even yank it out.' She turned to Terry. 'And don't you snigger – your front tooth looks a bit suspect too.'

Terry shut up instantly.

'No hard feelings.' Jude fetched her purse and handed the men a generous tip. 'You'll be needing this. Even treatment on the NHS costs a packet these days.'

She watched them return hastily to the van and went to get her car keys so she could move her Micra into the parking space they'd vacated. Men amused and irritated her by turn. She had discovered that it was perfectly possible to live without them, and she was happier that way. Her friends who were in relationships had their freedom curtailed, their lives were a series of compromises, and for what? Love? It was temporary. Companionship? Cats provided plenty. She locked the car, patted its bonnet, and made her way back to the house.

Back inside, Jude surveyed her living room. There wasn't much more to unpack. She was essentially a minimalist, wanting few possessions, enjoying space, peace and order. One of the advantages of living alone was that she had these things in abundance. Another was that you didn't have to share your booze.

Jude moved rapidly towards the kitchen. One of her first acts on entering the cottage had been to pop a bottle of Moët et Chandon into the fridge. Now she took it out, seductively cool to the touch. Gently she began to prise the cork out.

'It's a shame that cats can't drink alcohol,' she said to Aida and Ludmilla, who were watching her closely. 'It's about your only design fault. It's going to have to be a tin of tuna for you. Now I wonder where it is? Silly me! Must have left it in Didsbury. Only joking!'

There was a satisfying pop as the champagne cork somersaulted into the air.

'Cheers!' cried Jude, and drank straight from the bottle.

Revived immediately, she set about feeding the cats, humming the march from *Aida*. She set their bowls on the floor.

'Welcome to your new home, my cherubs.'

She carried the bottle into the living room and looked around her again. Despite the profusion of packing cases and the smears on the walls where the previous owners had removed Blu-tacked posters, she liked this place. Something in it felt right to her. She drank some more champagne, courting intoxication. She liked the off-white walls with their hint of peach, the small diamond-paned windows and the open staircase. She loved the way the fireplace was the central feature of the room. It boasted real Victorian tiles and had a substantial mantelpiece above it. As a cloud moved from the face of the sun, the rich, golden light of the late afternoon filled the room, making the packing cases seem to glow. Jude turned and saw the empty mantelpiece.

'I know what goes there,' she said to herself.

She rooted around in a crate to the left of her and extracted a photograph. The face that grinned from the brass frame was that of a woman in her sixties, her face weather-beaten, heavily lined, with sharp, intelligent eyes, and greying, dishevelled hair. In the brightness of the eyes, the combative jut of the chin, there was more than a passing resemblance to Jude.

'Your new home,' said Jude to the photograph, and placed it on the mantelpiece. 'And OK, it's in one devil of a mess, but what the hell, I've only just moved in. And I know I'm drinking in the middle of the afternoon, but look who's talking!'

Jude remembered smuggling some whisky into her mother's room in the hospice so they could have an illicit drink together. Somehow it tasted better like that. Not that the nurses would have disapproved. They respected Phyllis's wish never to concede one inch to the cancer that was co-habiting with her. She refused to give up smoking too. 'I don't see the logic,' she'd said. 'I mean, if I'm going to die anyway I might as well continue. I can't believe there's not a smoker's corner in heaven.'

Jude studied her mother's photograph, solemn for a moment. But only for a moment. With sudden decision, she delved into the packing case again, found her CD of *The Barber of Seville*, and put it in her hi-fi. The overture immediately filled the room with colour. Jude lifted the bottle to her lips again.

'To me!' she declared.

And then there was a rapping at the door. Jude was still for a moment. Surely none of her friends had followed her here for a surprise visit? Perhaps it was a neighbour. A new friend. With a rush of warmth for the person who was so keen to welcome her to Mytholm Bridge, she made her way to the front door, still carrying her bottle of champagne.

She opened the door and was confronted by a middle-aged man in a lovat green pullover with leather patches on the sleeves. He was tall, lanky and Jude watched him pause to take her in, and all the chaos behind her. She held on to her bottle as if it was a weapon.

'Ian Fulwell,' he said, as if in answer to a question. 'I live next door.'

'Jude Jackson,' she replied. If he could be brusque, then she could be brusquer. Anything you can do, I can do better. She saw his eyes stray into the interior of the cottage and she guessed what, or who, he was looking for.

'There's no one else here,' she said. 'I live by myself.'

'So the Micra is yours.'

'Well observed,' she commented.

'I'm afraid there's a problem.'

'You've not pranged it, have you?' He shook his head. 'Men drivers!' she said jokingly.

'The problem is you've parked it in my space.'

'No. I've parked directly opposite my own house.'

'Come with me.' Ian Fulwell's invitation was more of an order. Jude was reluctant to obey it, but could see that this situation needed sorting. She followed him out of the house and through the garden. Directly in front of her was a large maroon Discovery half on the grass verge, half on the road. Her Micra was comfortable in the cemented parking place on the opposite side of the road.

'Perhaps I should explain,' her neighbour said. His tone bordered on the amenable. He ran his fingers through his hair, and attempted a smile. Jude stood with her arms folded, unconsciously adopting the pose of her mother in the picture of her in the *Rochdale Observer* heading a picket line. 'The previous occupants parked a little further up, and let me cement this verge for my Discovery.' He waved his arm in the direction of Jude's Micra.

'That was very good of them.'

'You can fit your car on the verge, along the lane, whereas I can't.'

He sounded eminently reasonable, as if he was explaining a maths theorem to a class of twelve-year-olds. Jude resented the tone of instruction and wished she were a little taller. It was hard to be assertive with a man who towered over you, but she was damned well going to try.

'According to the deeds, that parking space is on my land.'

'*I* paid for it to be cemented over.'

Jude's veins thrilled with the combat.

'Technically, it doesn't belong to you.'

'It was an established principle that the space was mine.'

He was taking refuge in the impersonal, like most men; Jude knew she was winning. She could afford to be generous.

'I tell you what. We'll operate on a first come, first served basis. Whoever gets there first can have it.'

Jude saw him swallow hard and his nostrils dilate. She had made him angry. But then, she often made men angry. Men rarely expected opposition.

'You're being unreasonable,' he said.

'Me?' said Jude.

She heard the sound of barking coming from the Discovery.

'So you have dogs?'

He nodded. Did she detect a menace in that nod? She hoped not. She could hardly retaliate by threatening to send her cats out at him. For a moment she felt vulnerable, standing alone on the road outside her new house, dusk falling, in conflict with a stranger – a stranger whose house adjoined hers. She wished they could have got off to a better start. Perhaps it was not too late to be friendly.

'If you leave your dogs outside, you're welcome to come in for some champagne.'

'I'd be glad to, if you move your car.'

He was smiling at her; he'd interpreted her invitation as a climb-down. This would never do.

'I tell you what. You go and park down the road, and I'll come into your place for a cup of tea.'

His eyes narrowed as he tried to piece together what Jude had just said. For one moment she thought he was about to smile and concede defeat. Then he turned on his heels and strode off to his Discovery without a word. He climbed into it, revved the engine as loudly as he could, and drove off. She watched until the vehicle had gone round the bend in the road and was out of sight. Then she walked back down the garden path.

'Bugger, bugger, bugger!'

Jude felt her pulse racing. She'd won; that was important; that was the main thing. But what bad luck, that her neighbour should turn out to be so bloody-minded and dictatorial! The last thing she wanted was to be on bad terms with the people around her. And yet what choice did she have if her rights were trampled on?

Jude knew better than to blame herself for this conflict. How dare he greet her with the command to move her car? What sort of control freak was this man who like some power-crazy traffic warden came barging down people's front paths telling them where they could and couldn't park? Obviously some sort of emotional cripple who could only relate to women by giving them orders. She wondered if there was a Mrs Fulwell and pitied her. *'You've placed the salt-cellar too near my plate; it was established that the cruet set was to sit exactly in the middle of the table, Mrs F!'* Jude smiled to herself. *'You've rolled over on to my half of the bed, Mrs F. I'll thank you to move over to your side.'*

And that Discovery, and those barking dogs! All the external trappings of masculinity. No matter — she was more than a match for him. The last thing she would do was let him spoil her pleasure in moving to Mytholm Bridge. She walked over to her hi-fi and turned up the Rossini until the music bounced off the walls. It was Rosina's aria.

> *'Ma se mi toccano*
> *dov'è il mio debole,*
> *sarò una vipera, sarò,*
> *e cento trappole*
> *prima di cedere farò giocar.'*

That's good! I shall be a viper, and I'll play a hundred tricks before they'll have their way. Most appropriate. She took another swig from her bottle and began to unpack in earnest. If you can't make good friends to start with, you might just as well make do with good enemies. It was a sentiment of which her mother would have approved.

*'Jane, will you marry me?'*

'Yes, sir.'

'A poor blind man, whom you will have to lead about by the hand?'

'Yes, sir.'

'A crippled man, twenty years older than you, whom you will have to wait on?'

'Yes, sir.'

'Truly, Jane?'

'Most truly, sir.'

'O my darling! God bless you and reward you!'

The words misted in front of Becky's eyes, so she took off her glasses and raised her hand to brush away the tears. She could never read the end of *Jane Eyre* without crying. You'd think that over the years, seeing those words approaching, knowing that Jane and Mr Rochester would finally come together, realising that she would have him, blind, crippled, that a person would be able to choke back the tears, feel a little detached – but no. Becky sniffed loudly and luxuriously. This was true romance; despite his infirmities, she loved him. In fact, she loved him more.

There was one more liquorice all-sort left in the bowl. Becky had stopped eating them because she had become so carried away with the book, but now the climax had been reached, she would celebrate with one final sweet. This was the time of day she liked best; mid afternoon, when Amy was at school, Paul at work, and most of her house chores almost done. If she couldn't have some private time now, when could she? Her enjoyment of the moment was so exquisite that she decided to stop reading, reserving the last few pages of the book for another time. She marked her page with a leaflet she had picked up from the library.

She had turned up the fire, because there was a fair old wind blowing up outside. She had shut the door of the lounge so no heat would escape. She was curled up on the armchair, her feet tucked under her, having kicked off her shoes that lay forgotten under the settee. It must be wonderful to be Jane, finally to come home to the man you loved, and to know he loved you. That night Jane would prepare for bed, secure in the knowledge she and Edward Rochester would be married at last. Where would she sleep in Ferndean? Becky tried to visualise a bedroom, with a small, four-postered bed, with a white, virginal counterpane, and Jane asleep on it. Becky closed her eyes. Some stray thoughts about collecting Amy and making dinner occupied what was left of her conscious mind as she drifted into a comfortable doze, giving herself up to the luxury of uninterrupted solitude, floating, drifting, on the white counterpane . . .

At first she thought the bleeping was from Amy's virtual pet, which she had promised to baby-sit. Surely it didn't need feeding again? But it was louder than that, and more irregular. Becky opened her eyes. What could the noise be? It was coming from the hall. She opened the door of the lounge and then she knew what it was. The smoke alarm. And there was smoke too – billows of it. Bitter, metallic smoke, wreathing in dark clouds around the ceiling.

Now panic took hold of her. She made her way to the kitchen, which seemed to be the source of the smoke. Immediately she knew what had happened. She had forgotten all about the eggs! An hour ago she'd put some eggs on to hard-boil for Paul's sandwiches tomorrow. Then she'd sat down with *Jane Eyre* and promptly forgotten all about them. The saucepan had boiled dry and the eggs were charred and blackened.

What did you do in a situation like this? Ring the fire brigade? She wished that Paul was there – men always knew what to do in these situations. She ought to put the fire out straightaway. She switched off the gas cooker but smoke still billowed from the saucepan. So she lifted the kettle and poured the water over the eggs.

In the same instant there was an almighty explosion. Becky jumped back from the cooker. There was egg everywhere, over the cooker, on the work surface, on the floor, on the ceiling. The sulphurous smell of egg mingled with the smoke.

Horror and amusement fought for supremacy. Becky wanted to laugh at her own incompetence – but just look at the mess! She began to assemble cleaning materials and hoped that when she had scraped the eggs off the walls, Paul wouldn't notice. Only a few weeks ago he'd re-painted the kitchen, and he would be livid to see what she'd done to his handiwork.

She scrubbed away furiously. If she could get the kitchen cleaned and the house aired before he came home there might not be any need to tell him about it at all. She knew what would happen if he found out. He would take on that look of exasperation – or should she say eggs-asperation? – and she would feel six inches small. Only it was true; she shouldn't have fallen asleep with the eggs still boiling away. She rather wished Amy had been with her so they could have had a laugh about it. She attacked the surface of the cooker with vigour.

Amy was great at keeping secrets, despite being only thirteen. She'd never breathed a word the time Becky had answered the phone leaving the hot iron sitting on Paul's pyjamas. In fact she'd taken them round to Karen's to throw them away. Nor did she complain when Becky inadvertently hoovered up a favourite pendant – perhaps because she'd bribed her with another. Amy was thoroughly used to her mother's domestic mishaps.

Becky looked up and gazed out of the kitchen window, which gave on to the back of the house where there was only room for a small patio, because of the hill. She'd planted some shrubs and flowers so there was something pretty for her to contemplate when she stood at the sink. At the front of her house the road was not made up as it was a private cul-de-sac which she shared with Karen, her next-door-neighbour. Thus it was that Becky was unaware of the car that drew up and stopped outside her front door.

She started at the ring on the doorbell. Her first thought was that it was Paul and she would be caught red-handed – or yellow-and-white-handed. But if it was Paul, why wasn't he using his key? Mystified and slightly anxious, Becky wiped her hands on the tea cloth and tried to waft the smoke away.

She opened the door to Denise.

'Becky – hi! What on earth is that smell?' Denise wrinkled her nose in distaste.

'A nuclear explosion in a chicken roost.' Denise looked bemused. 'Only joking. I forgot I had some eggs boiling. They're absolutely everywhere.' Becky continued to scrub at the cooker.

'Oh dear! Would you like me to go?'

'Please don't. It won't take me long, and then we can have a natter.' It occurred to Becky briefly that Denise might offer to help, but then, aliens might descend and take over Mytholm. 'What's brought you here?'

'I was just passing. You are in a mess, aren't you?'

'Yes. I was in the lounge, reading, and I fell asleep.

'It's all right for some. *I've* been rushed off my feet all day. A client in Halifax, and another in Ripponden.'

Denise gave aromatherapy massage. She was very good; Becky had paid for her services once or twice and come home smelling like parma violets. Denise didn't need to do it for the money, as George brought home more than enough, but she claimed she valued the independence it gave her.

'Would you like some coffee?' Becky asked.

'Love some.'

Luckily Becky had just about finished her mopping up operations. She switched on the kettle, got out two mugs, and cursed silently that Denise should find her like this. Not that Denise would be unkind, but her house was always so immaculate. She was immaculate too. Even now, in her late thirties, Denise looked as if she could have stepped off the pages of *Vogue*. Becky knew she was the sort who would have slipped on the pages of *Vogue* and grazed her knees. The coffee was ready, and Becky took it into the lounge, Denise following her.

Denise made for the armchair and picked up the book that

was lying there. In her 501's and white Moschino sweatshirt, she had a studied elegance. Her hair was glossy, brown and shoulder-length. Her features were regular – at least, they began to be so once Becky had put on her glasses; until then Denise was just a blur. It was rather better like that.

'Is this what you were reading? *Jane Eyre*?'

'That's right.'

Denise opened it casually, and as she did so the page marker fell out on to the carpet. It lay there, un-noticed. Becky settled herself on to the settee. She was glad Denise had called. Although she could be irritating at times, she was probably Becky's closest friend in Mytholm. They had known each other since they were pregnant together twelve years ago. Becky was astonished that Denise had wanted to cultivate the friendship as she was the image-conscious, glamorous type; Becky was dizzy, disorganised, disaster-prone. Yet perhaps it wasn't so strange after all. Ever since she was a girl Becky had ended up with friends who had complemented her. They were the actors and she was the audience. She was happy to live vicariously off them, free of envy. Besides, Denise was fun. For all her moments of vanity, and that tendency to see the world only in reference to herself, Denise knew how to enjoy herself. An afternoon spent with Denise was as wicked as chocolate, whereas two Beckys together could bore for Britain.

Denise sniffed. 'I can smell the eggs from here.'

'Yes, and the smoke alarm was louder than you would believe. Anyway, it's a comfort to know they work. I'm glad I insisted my father had one installed. Lucky Karen wasn't in, else she would have—'

'Karen's at my house this afternoon.'

Karen, Becky's next-door neighbour, cleaned for Denise.

'I think she's been looking a bit more cheerful lately.'

'Do you?' Denise's eyes gleamed. 'I think I might know why. When I picked Rowan up from school the other day, I saw her talking to none other than Jim Ferguson – the builder.'

'She would do. She's having her front room re-decorated.'

'Becky! There's talking . . . and there's *talking*.'

Becky was pleased. Karen was a divorced single mother, whose first husband had been none too good to her. If anyone deserved a bit of flirtation, Karen did. But trust Denise to be the first to know about it. Her friend continued.

'But I wouldn't have said Jim was the right one for her. He's the same type as Steve. A bit of rough. Did I ever tell you that Steve had a criminal record?'

'No.'

'Don't tell Karen I told you. It was to do with car parts. He received stolen goods and sold them on. I suspect that was one of the things she found attractive about him. There's a part of her which is self-destructive. I'm sure women with violent husbands bring it on themselves. Or maybe—' she paused – 'maybe it's a sexual thing. According to the psychiatrist Clement Freud—'

Becky did not bother to correct her.

'—if you have an idea that sex is wrong, somehow, you can only end up having it with criminals.'

'I've never heard of that before!'

'Or to you, a real man is someone who's threatening. Someone powerful, someone who grapples with you for control, the Stallone type,' Denise informed her. 'Don't you ever fantasise about being totally overcome by a man, so that you have no choice? No choice whatsoever?'

'Do I have any fantasies? Well, I used to like the Bay City Rollers, but that's not what you mean. Tartan scarves still send me weak at the knees. No, seriously, I suppose I like the Mr Rochester type, someone who's seen more of the world than you, but needs looking after.'

'Mr Rochester? I don't think I know him. Is he local?'

'No, silly. He's a character in *Jane Eyre*.'

Denise looked daggers. Then she examined her fingernails which were painted a rich brown. There was a pause.

'You ought to get out more, Becky. Then you wouldn't have to fantasise about people in books.'

Becky felt that was a bit unkind. Perhaps Denise was riled

because she had exposed her ignorance about literature. She decided to change the subject.

'I took Amy to the orthodontist the other day. Do you remember I told you I was going? He was absolutely awful to her! He told her she needed four teeth out and two tram-line braces, and it wasn't so much that, but he was so callous. He could see she was upset and he—'

'That reminds me. I'm considering having my hair taken shorter. What do you think?'

Becky gave her a critical look. 'It's up to you. I like it the way it is, but then, I never was one for change.'

'Quite,' Denise said.

Becky was silent for a moment. There was something different about Denise today. She seemed a little on edge. Perhaps it was the smell of the eggs. Becky watched her looking around the lounge, and saw her eyes alight on her wedding picture, her and Paul outside St Margaret's, the sun shining brightly, all of fifteen years ago. Becky studied the picture too, and for some obscure reason it made her sad. That was the high point of her life. And there she was, captured under glass like the fishing fly in the paperweight on Paul's desk. Heavier than you'd think, and her only function being to keep everyone else in order.

Becky felt uncharacteristically gloomy. She wondered why. Was it Denise who was making her feel this way? Was it her accident with the eggs? Was she pre-menstrual? The last was probably true. She resolved to shake herself out of her melancholy.

'How's Paul?' Denise asked.

'Fine. How's George?'

'Fine.' Well, that was the men dealt with. Denise continued.

'Why don't we go out some time, Becky? We've not had a girls' night out for ages.'

'I tell you what. I've been meaning to invite you, George and the children over for Sunday lunch. You must come. Amy would love to see Petra.'

Denise looked a little alarmed. 'Are you sure? It's such a lot of work.'

'Not for me. It's not as if I do anything else. It'll give me something to get on with.'

Once again Becky was swept by a feeling of meaninglessness. Yes – she was definitely pre-menstrual. It was back on to the Oil of Evening Primrose for her – intravenously, if needs be.

'That would be lovely, Becky, but I was thinking more that *you* ought to get out. You should.' There was a decided emphasis in Denise's voice. It was amazing! It was almost as if she had been reading Becky's mind. Becky would have never put Denise down as the empathetic type, but she was happy to be proved wrong.

'You ought to get out and meet people,' Denise continued. 'I've been thinking that for some time. Even if you don't want to go back to work, you could always take a class or something.'

Becky felt she was meant to hear this. It was fate. Or rather, it was a good friend who had the courage to help her face the truth. She saw Denise pick up the leaflet that had fallen on the floor.

'Look at this! Here are this term's classes at the Community Centre. One of these would be sure to suit you. There's flower arranging, beauty therapy – hmm–' Denise glanced at Becky critically and frowned – 'local history, only for old fogeys, I guess, tips for a better sex life – no, don't look like that – just my little joke . . . how to fill in your self-assessment form . . . line dancing for beginners, intermediate line dancing, advanced line dancing, creative writing – no – you'd be better off getting a job after all.'

'Creative writing,' Becky interrupted. 'Tell me what it says about that.'

'Not a lot. "Writing for profit and pleasure. For those with a serious interest in the power of the written word."' Denise yawned.

'I quite like the sound of that.'

'Too much like school.'

'Oh, I don't know. Barbara Taylor Bradford came from these parts, and look at her now. Living over in the States, a household name. And I read in the papers the other day about some girl who'd sold the idea for a novel to a publishers and then some Hollywood producer got wind of it, and she was a millionairess overnight.'

'Do you know what I love about you, Becky?' Denise reached over and tapped her on the arm affectionately. 'You have a touching belief in fairy-tale endings. Which paper was it? Was it recently?'

Becky shrugged.

'Not that I believe you. Still, a creative writing class might suit you, I can see that. But knowing you, you won't want to go alone. Tch, tch. I suppose I can give up one night a week. George can always take Rowan to Cubs.' She grinned at Becky. 'But look, I must be going. I want to get home before Karen leaves. And I'm expecting – but never mind. Give me a ring and we'll arrange about lunch.'

Denise took her hold-all from the back of the chair on which she'd hung it. She air-kissed Becky, and hurried out of the house. Becky stood by the lounge window and watched her depart.

The pungent smell of the burnt eggs was still omnipresent. There would have to be some explaining to Paul. Not only that, but she would have to broach the subject of the creative writing class. It wasn't the cost he would object to – in fact it was unlikely he would object at all – but she just knew he would pass a comment or two. It was affectionate teasing really, only it got out of hand occasionally. Men were like that. They didn't always know what they were saying.

Unlike women. It was truly unbelievable, the way Denise had sensed her mood, and provided her with the ideal solution. Becky felt a warm rush of gratitude to her. Although Denise had a bit of a reputation in Mytholm for being loose-tongued – and it was true – she almost made the *Mytholm Times* redundant – Becky was glad she'd stuck with her.

Denise was loyal – she would always look out for her, like a true friend.

She returned to the kitchen and saw some eggs she had missed on the top of the food processor, and scrubbed away with renewed vigour.

Denise wound down the window of her silver Brava and inhaled deeply with relief at getting out of Becky's house. It had taken all her self-control not to complain out loud about the disgusting smell of burnt eggs. Still, one had to be kind to one's friends, especially right now. And she was satisfied she had been kind to Becky. It had been her intention, and she had fulfilled it. Someone had to look after Becky. She wasn't going to do it herself.

Denise withdrew her mobile phone from her bag and turned it on, placing it on the seat beside her. Only then did she start the engine and turn the car in the direction of Mytholm Bridge. She mastered the descent carefully, her foot hovering near the brake. She stopped just before the centre of Mytholm, and looked in her driving mirror to check on her appearance, and made some slight adjustment to her hair. As she drove off again, she glanced down again at her mobile.

The centre of Mytholm was full with traffic. Mytholm linked Halifax and Rochdale, and many cars used it as a through route. It was also becoming a popular tourist destination because of the clog factory, the back-to-earth houses that stood sentry-like, four storeys high, the craft museums and barges on the canal.

Nipping through some amber lights Denise left Mytholm and began her homeward ascent. She passed small terraced cottages with washing hung on lines criss-crossing small front gardens. There was the Clough Inn on her right. She drove automatically, reviewing what Becky had said. She had not realised that it was possible to make so much money from writing stories. She was lost in thought, thinking about how it would be when she signed her contract with Spielberg or Tarantino. Thus it was that she was distracted when her mobile began to ring, but only momentarily. Quickly she pulled into the verge, licked her lips, and answered the caller.

'Hello?' It was her chocolate-brown voice, reserved for the telephone and the bedroom. Finding out who her caller was made her smile to herself. She listened for a while and then interrupted.

'No, I can't. You know why I can't. It wouldn't be right.'

She continued to listen, settling back in the driver's seat, idly watching a lorry with the words Fielding's Removals on the side rumble past her on the road. She pushed her hair behind her ear.

'There's nowhere we can meet that would be safe,' she told him.

She widened her eyes at his description of what he would like to do with her. It occurred to her that she could certainly use it in her bonkbuster novel.

'No, I shouldn't be listening to you. I'm going to cut you off!' Her tone was playful. He would know she didn't mean it. She moved her head slightly so she could see herself talking in the driving mirror.

'I'm sorry. What did you say? Yes, I do wear silk stockings, when *I* want to.' She laughed. 'That depends.'

It was almost time to pick Rowan up. She threatened her caller that she would cut him off, and finally she did so, happy with the turn the conversation had taken.

Denise started up the engine, enjoying the nervous excitement his call provoked in her. Knowing all this, having spent most of the day awaiting this call, it had taken all her best efforts not to tell Becky. Becky would hardly approve. Denise knew she had to tell someone, or she would burst. What else were friends for? She pressed her foot down on the accelerator. If she hurried, Karen would still be at her house.

# Chapter Two

Karen thrust the vacuum cleaner repeatedly across Denise's carpet to the rhythm of an artillery of expletives, of which 'bloody' was the least offensive. The vac roared in protest and refused to pick up the piece of thread that lay in its path. Eventually Karen had to bend down and pick it up herself, firing a final salvo of obscenities. She straightened herself and downed tools.

'I know why you haven't had the bloody thing fixed,' she muttered aloud. 'Because you never bloody use it yourself.' Then she shut up, aware that she was slagging off Denise in her own house. For a moment she felt contrite. Then seeing the portrait of Denise that hung over the fireplace, the one she had commissioned from the artist in Mytholm, she stuck out her tongue at it. She resumed hoovering, rehearsing her grievances as she did so.

Denise took liberties with her. It wasn't just the cleaning she had to do. She'd put on the dinner before now, sewn name tapes on Rowan's clothes and even changed the bed linen. And whereas most of her other customers tidied round before she got there, Denise had a habit of kicking her frilly knickers under the bed and leaving them there for Karen to find. Not to mention all the dirty tissues down the side of Petra's bed. God knows what she's been doing with them! All of that for four pounds an hour!

The vacuum hoover swallowed something too large and roared with indignation. Karen switched it off and up-ended it to see what was wrong. It was then that she heard the sound of a key in the lock. It was obviously Denise, although half an hour early.

'Karen?'

'Hi, Denise!' Karen shouted cheerily.

Denise entered the lounge.

'Something wrong with the hoover?'

'It think it's taken up something it shouldn't.'

'I know. You've got to be careful with that vac. It's so sensitive. But leave it now. I came back early because I've had enough today. I've done three whole bodies. I'm knackered. Do you fancy a coffee?'

'I've still half an hour left to do.'

'Forget the housework, Karen. Let's just have a natter. You know I feel uncomfortable being your employer. I'm not the sort of person who enjoys giving orders. Go and put the kettle on and bring out the low-fat digestives.'

Wondering what she had up her sleeve now, Karen unbuttoned her housecoat and made her way to Denise's kitchen. It was a deliberately traditional farm kitchen, with a big oak table in the centre, quarry tiling on the floor, and little hooks in the beams for the copper utensils that hung from them. The wooden chairs bore a stencilled design of tulips. There was an old-fashioned dresser with a willow pattern dinner service.

The jug kettle had a pattern of roses round the base. Karen opened the cupboard to look for the low-fat digestives. There they were, next to a half-opened packet of some Italian double chocolate biscuits. Karen's mouth watered. Had Denise forgotten they were there, or was she saving them for a private binge? One doesn't waste one's best biccies on one's cleaner, evidently. One palms her off with low-fat digestives.

Karen took off her housecoat. Beneath it she was wearing an old T-shirt, and some black denims. She looked good in jeans and she knew it. With men and with money she was very unlucky. But she had a figure to die for, and a face that wasn't too bad either. She had the elfin look – large eyes, high cheekbones, a heart-shaped face. She came across as vulnerable and it wasn't always an advantage.

She put the two mugs of coffee on the tray, opened the biscuits, and put a few on a plate. She took it all in to Denise, who was now reclining on the settee, a bright orange settee with cushions in a jazzy fabric.

'I'm all in,' she said.

Karen put the tea tray on the ebony coffee table. She helped herself to her coffee and went to perch on the armchair.

'Me too,' she replied.

'Any reason in particular?' Denise asked.

'I had both kids off on Monday with streaming colds. I couldn't go down to the shop and I stayed in with them all day. They did nothing but fight so I couldn't even get on with the typing I've taken in.'

Denise nodded sympathetically. 'I know what you mean. Rowan gets headaches and becomes really clingy. I have no time to myself in the evenings. And that's when I need to do my paperwork. It's no joke being self-employed. And George is never around when I need him.'

It was the opening round in their favourite game of one-upmanship – who has the least time. Karen took a deep breath. She was playing to win.

'I was so desperate I sent the kids into school on Tuesday, running noses and all!'

'I thought Rowan's headache was a symptom of an infection; do you think he could have picked it up from Seth?' Denise enquired softly.

'There's a lot of it about,' Karen said, stalling, and helped herself to a biscuit. Round one to Denise. The cow.

'I saw you talking to Jim Ferguson the other day,' Denise began.

''S right. Did I tell you Bobby flooded my living room?'

'He didn't!'

23

'He did! They've been doing Noah in school, haven't they, and he decides to do a full re-enactment in my bathroom. He wanted to see what would happen if the bath overflowed.' Karen sighed. 'Yes, I spoke to Jim Ferguson yesterday – Ferguson's are making good the damage. I'm going to need the room re-plastered and re-decorated. And he reckons I should have a new damp course. God knows how I'm going to afford it. Jim's coming to look at the house tonight and give a formal quote.'

'Lucky you!' Denise said. 'Jim Ferguson all to yourself. I'd watch him if I were you, Karen.'

'Oh, I don't think he—'

'He knows you're on your own, doesn't he?'

'With two little boys, I'll have you know.'

'If he's interested in you, the boys won't put him off.'

'I think you're wrong, Denise. He can't be interested in me. He's known me since the Infants'. And he's a decent bloke.'

'I'm not sure there's such a thing as a decent bloke, thank God. Which reminds me, I've just come from Becky's. I thought she seemed a little down to me.'

'Does she? I've not noticed anything.'

'She fell asleep reading this afternoon and some eggs boiled dry and nearly set the house alight. That sort of absent-mindedness is often the first sign of depression.'

Karen gazed at Denise, not encouraging her, not discouraging her.

'To be truthful, I feel a little sorry for her. In fact I suggested she should do a little more for herself. It's OK for you and me – we work – but Becky does nothing all day. It's as if feminism passed her by. Yes, I said I'd go with her to a creative writing class at the Community Centre. Just for support.'

'That'll be nice for her.'

Denise kicked off her shoes, and drew her legs under her on the settee.

'Yes, she ought to do something for herself for a change. She's always running around after Paul and Amy and that father

24

of hers. She goes over to Rochdale two or three times a week to see him. Between you and me, I worry that our Becky's made herself into a doormat.'

'Not a doormat,' Karen said disapprovingly.

'Oh no, not a doormat! Did I say doormat? What I meant was, she always puts herself last. When she has so much to offer. I don't blame her. I get the impression that Paul can be a bit of a trial.'

Karen breathed more easily. She hadn't enjoyed listening to Denise badmouthing Becky, but Paul was fair game. She wasn't too keen on Paul.

'I heard him shouting through the walls last night. He can be a right bastard at times,' Karen supplied.

'Do you know what he was shouting about?' Denise asked.

'Not really. But sometimes when I've been round there he demands things. Like asking for the newspaper and insisting she gets it for him straightaway.'

Denise tutted and shook her head.

'Now this is just what I mean. Paul can be very forceful and I'm not sure that being submissive is the best way to deal with him. I think if she stood up to him a little, he'd respect her more. Men think they want passive women, but really they're searching for an equal. I wouldn't be surprised if he provocates her just to get a response.'

'He provocates her?' Karen repeated, gently emphasising Denise's error. 'So is that why you think Steve hit me?'

Denise had the grace to blush. 'Oh, no! It was different with your Steve. He had a vicious temper. In that case, it wasn't your fault. It was the drink's fault. Paul isn't violent—' she paused. 'He just has high standards.' Karen said nothing. Denise added, 'I happen to know this is true.'

'Do you? How?'

'I shouldn't be telling you this.'

Karen was curious. 'You can tell me. I won't say anything.'

'I know. No – forget I said what I did. I'm so indiscreet sometimes!'

Karen knew the rules of this game. 'All right. We'll drop it. So tell me how the children are? Is Petra behaving herself?'

Silence. The clock ticked audibly and the wind rattled the windows.

'Karen – I think I'm going to *have* to tell you. I've got to speak to someone, I really must. But I want you to promise me you won't tell a soul.'

'I promise.' It was a promise Karen had no intention of keeping. It was likely Denise did not want her to; Denise was the main means by which news was transmitted in Mytholm Bridge. On the other hand, if the confidence really was private, then Karen would have the greatest delight in telling all and sundry.

'You see, I've been talking to Paul. That's why I know he finds his marriage difficult.'

'Talking to *him*,' said Karen, wide-eyed. 'How did that happen?'

Denise hugged herself. 'I spent a day in Manchester – do you remember? I was looking for some duvet covers in the sale at Kendals'. I bumped into him outside Waterstone's and he said he'd give me a lift back home. I thought it was because I was Becky's friend. I did – honestly.'

Now Karen was genuinely curious. 'What happened on the journey?'

'Nothing! That is, we talked. We got on well. He has an amazing sense of humour, which is something I'd never realised before. You wouldn't guess, from the way Becky talks about him, but then she never gets the point of jokes. No, really, Karen, we just got on well. That was all. And he said that if I was ever going into Manchester again, to let him know. It was all above board. I even told George.'

This was not the first time Denise had confided in Karen that some bloke was giving her the eye. It was another of their games. Denise would tell Karen about the man who tried to pick her up at her Halifax exercise class – *when I was drenched in sweat after the jogging machine!* – and Karen would counter with the nineteen-year-old lad who tried to pull her at the bus stop. *Young enough to be my son. I had to tell him how old I was, and he didn't believe me!* This time Karen had nothing to say in return. Paul was Becky's husband. This wasn't a game after all.

'So you've only seen him the once?'

'Well, I did take him up on his offer of a lift – Becky knew! She must have known – I mean, I rang in the evening when I knew she'd be there.'

'Dangerous.'

Denise tossed her head. 'We're just good friends. Becky is my friend, and so is Paul. At least, I thought that was all it was . . .' Her voice faded as her eyes met Karen's. Karen's expression was stony.

'So what else has happened?' she asked.

'Nothing. Really nothing. It's just that he rings me up from time to time and we talk. I feel so dreadful about this. I know he's Becky's husband and I never intended any of this to happen. It's why I know they're not happy. Paul has no one else to talk to except for me.'

Karen realised that there was no point in taking the moral high ground. She wanted to find out more. Denise would yield information much more easily if she thought was doing it to impress.

'Well, at least he hasn't made a pass at you. It happened to me once. I was at a party when my cousin's husband started smooching and said he wanted to go to bed with me.'

Silence again. Denise took a deep breath.

'He does want to go to bed with me.'

'Denise!'

'His phone conversations are full of what he wants to do with me. He just won't give up, even though I've told him categorically that there's no future. Flirtation is one thing, but I would never have a relationship with my best friend's husband. No, I wouldn't. But it's such a relief to tell you.'

'I'll bet.'

'Promise me you won't tell Becky.'

'Of course not.' Karen shifted uncomfortably in her chair. She tried to take a sip of her coffee, but it had gone cold, and she didn't want it now anyway. No, she would not tell Becky. There was no point. To tell Becky would be to make her miserable needlessly, because it wasn't as if Paul had been unfaithful – yet.

'And the awful thing is that she's invited us all over for Sunday lunch. Becky insisted and I didn't feel as if I could say no. "No, sorry Becky, but since your husband fancies me, I think it's better that I stay at home." But it's going to be an ordeal.'

Dislike of Denise rippled through Karen like indigestion.

'Just make sure you're not alone with him,' she said.

'Why? I can assure you I won't do a thing. To tell you the truth, I think he's rather creepy! And he has thick black nostril hairs! I could never go to bed with a man who had visible nostril hair.'

Karen giggled in spite of herself.

'Yeah – and and a sweaty top lip – that's what I can't stand. Little beads of sweat on their top lips.'

'And men with thinning hair and dandruff, so the flakes are visible!'

'Greasy thinning hair and dandruff!'

'And hair around their navel!'

'Damp armpit shadows on their shirts!'

'Gruesome!'

They both laughed, Denise with the ringing tones of a victor, and Karen rather guiltily. Somehow she thought she ought not to be laughing. Becky would not be laughing. She hated the way Denise brought out the worst in her. Denise was a cow. And the worst thing was, she had succeeded in telling her something that she really could not pass on to anyone. Anyone at all. Poor Becky. Poor old Becky.

'I feel so much better now, Karen. And I must let you go. Your bus will be due in five minutes.' Denise got to her feet and walked over to the sideboard where she had put her handbag. As she fished around in it for some money Karen went for her things.

'Here we are, Karen.' Denise handed her some coins.

'Cheers, Denise. And be careful!' Karen waved as she walked out of the courtyard and down the lane to the bus stop. Once away from the house she examined the money in her hand. Six pounds. Six bloody pounds. Denise had only gone and docked her pay for their half-hour chat. Karen fizzed with indignation. And then the bus came trundling along the road.

Karen did not notice the look of interest that the bus driver gave her. She was engaged in a feat of mental arithmetic. Three times two hours was twenty-four pounds which she didn't declare to the tax man. Twenty-four pounds, every week. Twenty-four times fifty was one thousand two hundred pounds. She had to go on cleaning for Denise. Only next time she wouldn't stop to talk.

The bus took a breath-taking dive down the steep hill into Mytholm town centre. Karen was accustomed to it, as was the old lady with a shopping trolley in front of her. She wondered now if she ought to say something to Becky? Warn her in some way? Or perhaps she should speak to Paul? At this thought, something recoiled in Karen. It was possible he'd make a pass at her. She disliked the semi-flirtatious manner he adopted with her, and knew it would be a mistake to have a private conversation with him. If she spoke to anyone, it would have to be Becky.

It would be easy enough. Becky was always popping in to chat, happily looked after the boys, and occasionally employed her too, on generous terms. Becky was one of the most approachable people Karen knew. On her behalf, she seethed with anger. She decided she would have to say something. The bus stopped to pick up some more passengers.

But if she told Becky, she would be finishing off Denise's job for her. Denise only wanted to prove she was the more attractive woman – she couldn't possibly want to sleep with Paul. Nobody could want to sleep with Paul. Even his duvet. As she passed old Mr Slater's dental surgery on top of Smith's newsagent she decided at that moment to bury her clandestine knowledge; what you don't know, can't harm you. More than that, what you don't know, doesn't exist. In a manner of speaking.

Karen got to her feet. The next stop was Seth and Bobby's school. One thing she was certain about, Becky's interest came first. Becky was her friend. She'd been there for her when Steve had been pestering them last year, and Karen wanted to return the favour. Silence, she decided, would be the best way to do it.

The door to the surgery was at the side of the newsagent's window. Jude paused to admire the new brass plate with her name engraved upon it. On the door itself were painted the letters 'Crown Street Practice' which had amused Jude the first time she'd seen it. Bridge Street would have been just as good. But then, she was at college with a girl called Sally Payne, which was just about the best name for a dentist you could think of.

Smiling, Jude ascended the stairs. She was pleased to see that the glass door leading to the suite of rooms that comprised the practice was slightly ajar, which meant that someone had come in early. She liked enthusiasm in her staff.

'Hello! It's me!' Jude called out. There was no one behind the desk, but in the little ante-room to the toilet, where the kettle and coffee things were, Emma, the dental nurse, was making a drink.

'Do you want a coffee?' she returned.

'If you think I've got time.' Jude took off her coat and hung it on the coatstand behind the desk.

'Oh sure. Your first patient isn't due for fifteen minutes.'

Jude stood behind the desk, looked at the appointments book and saw how full it was. It would be non-stop today, just how she liked it. This moment, just before all the patients arrived, was her favourite part of the day. A lot of her colleagues complained that dentistry was tedious – working in confined spaces, the backache, the way half your patients were terrified of you – but it wasn't like that for Jude. She enjoyed the contact with the public, and loved the way each day took on a different shape depending on the work, depending on the people she met. Three days into her new practice, every patient was new. She had been waking early, partly because the thin curtains in her bedroom let in the light, and partly because she couldn't wait to see what each day would bring.

'Here we go,' Emma said. Carefully the nurse brought out two coffees. Jude found that again her eyes were drawn to Emma's stomach. Her pregnancy was quite clear now. That was something Mr Slater had not mentioned as he was preparing to hand over the practice to Jude. Not that it mattered, as Emma intended to return after her maternity leave. Jude was pleased, as she was an excellent nurse. Except it would have been nice to have had some warning, if only to prepare herself – first-time pregnant mums could make tedious working companions. Then, as if to cue, Emma started to speak.

'Gavin felt it kicking last night.'

'Did he?' Jude sipped at her coffee.

'Yes. Just as we were getting ready to go to bed. He put his hand where I thought the baby was and it gave a little kick. The baby must have known it was his daddy! Then Gavin carried on talking to it for a whole half hour!'

'How nice,' Jude said.

More footsteps on the stairs. Sheila walked in. She was the hygienist and had the room by the side of Jude's.

'Morning!'

She put her empty shopping bags behind the reception desk.

'I took the kids in early today,' she said. 'Hello, Jude! Hi, Emma. Is it today you've got your ante-natal?'

'Yes, that's right. Just a routine appointment with Dr Sutcliffe.'

'Oh, so it's not your hospital one?'

'Not for a few weeks. Then if I'm lucky they might give

me a scan. I know some people say they're dangerous, but I love seeing the baby. It brings it all home to you.'

'I know what you mean. The first time I saw Adam on the screen it brought tears to my eyes. You think, that's my baby!'

'Yes! My cousin has a picture of her scan. She bought a frame and—'

Jude could take no more.

'My first appointment is Amy Howarth, right?'

'Actually, no. There was a call this morning – been up all night with toothache. I hope you don't mind me fitting him in early.'

'No problem,' Jude said.

She turned the lights on in the waiting room and walked through to her surgery, overlooking Crown Street. The strip lighting flickered into life and Jude breathed in the familiar smell of surgical spirit.

She wondered whether to give her hands an extra scrub before she started work. This morning when she had walked into the kitchen, bleary-eyed, she had been greeted by a headless shrew, its intestines artistically arranged outside it, in a mannner worthy of Damien Hirst. It was the cats' contribution to the weekly housekeeping. Perhaps she could flog it to the Tate. It took Jude some time to clean the carpet tile it was laid on, and she resolved that as soon as possible she'd replace the carpet tiles with some smart ceramic ones. She'd noticed a flooring shop a little way out of Mytholm Bridge.

Otherwise, the house was wonderful. In the evening the wall lighting and the glow from the fire was rich and soothing; in the morning the view from her bedroom window was of fields and hills and hills and fields – there were even some sheep quite nearby, looking a bit shop-soiled, but real sheep. And there was sky, too. Back in Didsbury her bedroom window gave on to chimneys and roofs only. For the first time Jude was beginning to notice the weather, and the difference it made to every day. Yesterday she had taken her Micra for a spin on the moors, had stopped the car, and walked for a while, revelling in the fresh air and rolling hills. When she had got home, the Discovery was parked outside her house. She'd smiled to herself. It was a fair cop.

Since moving in, she had seen no evidence of a Mrs Fulwell. Either she'd done a runner, or he'd buried her in the back garden. She suspected that when she began to meet more people, she'd find out a little more about her taciturn neighbour. She knew she ought to start making herself a social life. This was the week she had earmarked for finding out what was going on in the town. It was all too easy to work all day and then do nothing in the evenings, to retreat into an effortless solitude, and then discover emptiness. But that wasn't Jude's style.

She heard the sound of someone walking up the stairs, and guessed it was her first patient. She dried her hands and came out from the surgery to greet him.

'Oh. It's you,' she said.

'Where's Tony Slater?' asked Ian Fulwell.

Jude consulted her watch. 'Given the time difference, I should say he'd be fast asleep, tucked up with his wife in the luxury suite in the hotel in Trinidad where they're celebrating his retirement. Obviously you've not been to the practice for a while, else you would have known he was selling up. I bought him out.'

Ian Fulwell cleared his throat. 'Given the change in ownership, I'm not sure that it's professional for you to treat a neighbour.'

'Nonsense! You're scared, aren't you?'

The dents of either side of his nostrils dilated with anger.

'I am not scared.'

'I dare you to let me have a look inside your mouth.'

Tight-lipped, Ian Fulwell made his way to the chair. Emma came in and fitted him with a blue plastic bib.

'Very fetching,' Jude said, her eyes dancing. 'Now open wide. Aah. Are you ready, Emma? Eight absent, seven, six,

OK, five severely broken down, possible abcess. I'd say some root canal therapy was needed here. I'm surprised you haven't had more trouble with this little beauty. What I'd like to do is take a periapical X-ray and examine the root. It might just be possible to save the tooth.'

Jude noticed how her neighbour's hands made tight fists on the sides of the chair, but whether from fear or anger, she didn't know. Perhaps he was right and she ought not to treat him. The temptation of being so close to him with her array of drills and other implements of torture was quite overwhelming. She smiled, and saw that he was looking directly at her. Their eyes only being a foot apart, Jude stepped back.

'First off, you'll need some antibiotics to reduce the inflammation. Then we can get you back for a course of treatment. It's all right, you can shut your mouth now.' Jude set about preparing for the X-ray. Ian Fulwell was silent, and Jude felt herself grow more and more self-conscious. Now she would have done anything for Emma to witter on about her foetus. The trouble with servicing the public was that you never knew who might turn up in your surgery. She remembered the story a teacher friend of hers had recounted: at a parents' evening she'd found herself face to face with her gynaecologist, who she'd only visited the day before. Compared to that, this was nothing.

The X-ray completed, Jude wrote out a prescription for her neighbour. As she did so, and he got up from the chair, he attempted some polite conversation.

'I hope you've settled in.'

'I have, thank you.'

She wasn't going to help him any more. She handed him the prescription and explained briefly how he should take the pills. Unexpectedly, on leaving, he thrust his hand at hers. At first Jude thought he wanted to indulge in a spot of arm wrestling, but she realised instantly he was attempting to shake her hand. She did so, pressing his hand as firmly as he did hers. A spot of aggression was good for the adrenalin levels.

She returned to the sink to scrub up for the next patient. She knew it was unlikely that Ian Fulwell would return for the rest of the treatment; it would be relatively easy for him to find another dentist more kindly disposed towards him. Jude was surprised to find she was just a little disappointed at the thought.


Amy sat in the front seat of the car staring straight ahead of her. Contempt and exasperation were written all over her face. Becky glanced at the mulish set of her mouth and exhaled sharply. Her daughter slowly and purposefully turned her head and looked out of the window at Mytholm Bridge Community Centre, formerly the Infants' School.

'*You've* got no right to be angry.' Becky spoke sharply.

No response.

'You had the whole night to do your homework. You shouldn't have been on the 'phone to Sophie for so long.' Still no response. Becky turned her head quickly to glance at Amy. She hated having to tell her off. On one hand, the girl needed firm boundaries, but on the other, she needed unconditional love. How can you give someone both? Especially someone as difficult as Amy.

'As I said before, I'm not prepared to write a note to your form teacher which doesn't tell the truth. You'll have to explain to her yourself.' Becky heard Amy give a sniff. She wondered why. She turned into the car park by the canal, and as she slowed down she glanced at her daughter again. Now Amy turned a tragic face towards her, two large tears making their way down her cheeks.

'What is it now?'

'You don't understand! I'm so scared!'

'Scared? Scared of what?'

'Of the dentist! He'll say I've got to have a brace.'

Checkmate, thought Becky. How can I tell her off about homework not done when she's terrified of the consequences of her dental appointment? Or were the tears a front? Impossible to know. You can bring someone up, even mould their character, and still not know what they're thinking.

'Come here, Amy.' Awkwardly Becky stretched over the gear stick and gave Amy a hug. Her daughter felt limp in her arms. 'The dentist won't be doing anything to you today. And if you really don't want a brace, you don't have to have one.' Amy leant her head on her mother's chest. Becky knew it would be wrong to bring up the homework again.

'Can we just go on to school? Because if we decide I'm not going to have a brace there's no point in seeing the dentist, is there?'

'Yes, but you promised me you'd have a chat with Mr Slater about it.'

'I'm not going.'

'Coward!' Becky was losing her patience.

'Well, then, I get it from you. *You* hate going to the dentist.'

She probably does get it from me, Becky thought. Why is it that children can be counted on to inherit only your worst characteristics?

'Look, I'll tell you what. You go to the dentist, and then we'll see about a new pair of jeans on the weekend.'

'And a Kangol T-shirt to match?'

'I said we'll see!'

They got out of the Fiesta and made their way across the car park to Crown Street. Amy linked arms with Becky in a gesture of forgiveness. It was moments like this that made it all worthwhile.

Amy was nearly as tall as her now. She was fair, too, her hair tucked behind her ears. The navy blue blazer she wore did not suit her, but then, school uniform rarely suited anybody. Becky remembered her own maroon blazer with loathing. They were approaching the dentist, and Amy's grip on Becky's arm tightened perceptibly.

'I'm not having a brace, you know.'

'I know,' Becky said, thinking to herself that if the dentist was able to confirm the orthodontist's findings, Amy would have to have one.

'The lads call you names. And Sophie said her cousin had a brace and it didn't work.'

'You promised me you'd wait and see what Mr Slater said.'

'I'm not having a brace!'

Children were so awkward! Becky decided she'd probably have an easier time as leader of the Conservatives. She pushed open the door of the surgery. Kids pulled against you all the time, and brought out the worst in you. For example, the art of bribery.

'Come on, Amy! Be brave, and I'll let you invite Sophie round one night. She can even sleep over.'

'All right,' Amy said grudgingly.

At the top of the stairs the dental nurse was behind the appointments desk. She smiled at Becky.

'Amy has an appointment with Mr Slater to have a second opinion about a brace.'

'Mr Slater's retired now,' the receptionist told her. 'We have a new lady dentist!' This last comment was addressed to Amy, who stood a little way from the desk, looking slightly alarmed. 'She's very nice,' Emma added. 'I'll take you in now.'

'I'll go with her,' Becky said. Dental surgeries always made her feel nervous and her legs go weak, and she knew Amy would be feeling just the same.

'Just remember what I've told you – the dentist won't be doing anything to you today,' she whispered to Amy as she crossed the empty waiting room.

It was Amy who entered the surgery first and stood by the chair hesitantly. The new dentist was standing a little behind the chair, and as Becky looked at her preparatory to explaining Amy's problem, she realised that she knew her from somewhere. Those questioning brown eyes were unexpectedly familiar, and there was something in the whole cast of her face that was completely disorientating. Becky frowned for a moment, trying to recollect where they had met.

'I hope you don't think I'm rude,' the dentist said, 'but I've met you before.'

'Yes. I know you too.'

Feeling she had permission to do so, Becky gazed at the dentist for a few moments. Her hair was dark, short, with a side parting and there was a rash of freckles on the bridge of her nose. Her eyes danced; her wide, expressive mouth was breaking into a smile.

'Becky!' Jude said. 'You haven't changed at all!'

Becky panicked. She still hadn't recognised her. She looked at the face above the white coat and wondered again who it could be. As she looked, Becky remembered just such a pair of laughing brown eyes, the same snub nose and mobile mouth on someone much younger.

'It's not Jude?' she said, putting her hand to her mouth in surprise.

'I just do not believe it!' Jude said.

'I didn't know you became a dentist!'

'BDS, King's College, London. I've been working in Manchester, but I've moved here.'

'This is where I live,' Becky said. 'And this is my daughter.' She gestured at Amy. 'Amy – this is Jude Jackson. She used to be my best friend.'

Jude laughed the same infectious chuckle that she had when she was twelve.

'When we were at school,' Becky continued. 'And then we lost touch. But you've not changed a bit.' Becky looked Jude up and down. She hadn't put on weight. Nor was she wearing a wedding ring. She looked older and even more sure of herself, but that was all. Looking at Jude made Becky feel as if she herself was twelve again.

'Hi, Amy!' Jude said. 'So you're married?' she asked Becky.

'Yes. Fifteen years. After I finished secretarial college. His name's Paul.'

'I always knew you'd marry,' Jude grinned at her. 'And I always knew I wouldn't.'

Now Jude stepped from behind the chair and faced Becky. Impulsively they both hugged. Becky broke away, eager to explain it all to Amy, who stood by the door, grinning stupidly.

'Amy – don't you remember me telling you about Jude? I met her the first day at junior school. She went round the class introducing herself to everyone, saying "can I be your friend?" and then we were sat next to each other. And we just hit it off!'

Jude's eyes sparkled with delight.

'And your mother copied all my answers in maths – she always forgot to do her homework.'

'You never had any dinner money,' Becky rejoindered. 'I was on a forced diet because I gave you half my lunch most days.'

'Of all the surgeries, in all the world, you have to walk into mine!' Jude mugged.

Becky laughed with delight. She remembered how they used to fool around together.

'Jude. You must come over! We'll have so much catching up to do. You will visit me, won't you?'

'Just try and stop me. Let me tell you – I've bought a house on Whitestone Edge.'

'Near Denise!' Becky exclaimed. 'I must introduce you. And to Paul. Can you come over this Sunday for lunch? Everyone will be there.'

'Damn. Not this Sunday. I've promised to visit some friends in Manchester. Besides, I'd like to have you all to myself.'

'On Monday, then.'

'Sure. You'd better explain where you live. Becky King!'

'Howarth now,' Becky reminded her.

'I'm looking forward to meeting your husband. Is your Dad nice?' Jude asked Amy.

'All right,' Amy said, looking embarrassed.

Becky had opened her handbag during this exchange and was drawing a map of the whereabouts of her house. 'I can't wait to tell Dad about meeting you. Mum's in Canada, of course. Did you know she went there after the divorce? How's your Mum?' Becky remembered her well. She was always in the papers. She was a local councillor, notorious for her stroppiness. She was the one who was responsible for getting all the local playgrounds recovered in wood chips, and refused to let the Lord Mayor get a new Rolls.

Jude didn't reply so Becky looked up. Jude shook her head, not trusting herself to speak. Becky realised immediately.

'Cancer,' Jude said briefly. 'Nine months ago.'

'Jude, I'm sorry!'

Jude shrugged. 'And young Amy!' she announced. 'What can we do for you?' She hasn't altered a bit, Becky noticed. She still changes the subject when her feelings are roused. At that, her heart warmed towards Jude. She was thrilled to have found her again, dying to tell everyone – Paul, Denise, Karen, everyone.

Amy looked at her mother, who seemed to have rather taken over *her* dental appointment.

'I'll explain to Jude,' Becky intervened. 'The orthodontist said she need a fixed brace and four teeth removed. But Amy's not too happy. I think she's scared of the extractions – aren't you, Amy – it's all right – Jude will understand – and the brace can be such a nuisance. I told her that most children have them nowadays but she refused. So we agreed to have a second opinion and—'

'Hop on the chair, Amy. That's it. Now open your mouth. Aha!' Becky watched Jude having a good look at Amy's teeth. Her best friend Jude looking in her daughter's mouth. Something in the scene moved Becky. She was no longer afraid for Amy. Amy held on tightly to the sides on the chair.

'OK. You can close now. Amy, listen. There is a bit of crowding at the sides on the top and bottom, OK? That's why the orthodontist suggested you have a brace. If you don't have a brace, you won't look bad, because no one will be able to see the crowding, but there is a heightened risk of decay later on. I can arrange for you to see another orthodontist – a friend of mine. See what she says. But remember – they're your teeth, and it's your decision. Whatever you do, that's fine.'

'What do you think I should do?' Amy asked her.

Jude smiled. 'Just like your mum,' she remarked. 'Seriously, wait and see. Get another opinion. Relax in the meantime. Having teeth out isn't so bad. It doesn't hurt. And most kids have braces these days. We'll see if we can't arrange some designer braces, with a little tag saying Armani.'

Amy laughed, infinitely relieved.

'But as I said, it's up to you. No one's going to force you either way.'

Amy gave her a brilliant smile as she got up from the chair, went over to Becky, and linked arms.

'Look at you both,' said Jude.

Emma popped her head round the door.

'Your next patient's here!'

Becky thrust a piece of paper towards Jude.

'Here's a map for you. There's a turning circle just after the town centre where you can position yourself to turn right, as otherwise you'd have to double back on yourself – then you carry on up the hill—'

'Oh yes – I know where you are. I looked at a house up there. Is half seven OK?'

'Perfect.'

They hugged again, to Amy's acute embarrassment. So she left the surgery and stood by the desk, reading the notice listing the duty dentists. Jude was OK. She was cool. It was funny to think of Mum being young and having another life. Like it was weird. She hoped that when she got back to school somebody else wasn't sitting next to Sophie. She hated being on her own. If you were, you got teased, by Petra and everybody. She wished her Mum would hurry up, and she was glad when they finally left the surgery.

# Chapter Three

'Mum. Can I ring up Sophie?'

'Again? You were only speaking to her an hour ago!'

'Yes but I don't know whether I've got to do the fourth question for maths and I'll get in trouble if—'

'Yes, all right, but be quick because I need your help here.'

Amy vanished from the kitchen. Becky just hoped that Paul wouldn't catch her on the phone again, or else he'd blow. Which in a way he had a right to. That child was never off the telephone. Recently she'd started ringing every time there was a competition on the TV, not that she'd ever won anything. Becky threw the prawns on to their lettuce beds. At least she could have a good moan to Denise when she got here. But then who said motherhood was meant to be easy?

'Amy!'

No reply.

Now with firmness.

'Amy!!'

Still no reply.

Now with desperation.

'Amy!!! I need your help.'

'Go and help your mother!!' echoed a deeper voice from the lounge.

Amy bounced into the kitchen. 'Guess what! Alex – that's

Sophie's Mum – she's bought her a Fimo kit and she's making a set of little animal ornaments and she said she'd make me a pony or a dog and then she said we could sell the others at school for charity. Isn't that brill? I like Sophie. We can sell them at break to the other second years. Then we can—'

'Amy! You're not dressed yet!'

This was true. Amy, who was peering in the saucepans on the stove, was clad only in an over-large Mickey Mouse T-shirt.

'Denise will be here soon!' Becky warned her.

Amy vanished again, Becky sighed, and got on with the prawn cocktails. Evidently there would be no help. Not that it mattered. Lunch was almost ready and the sherry trifle was setting in the fridge. The sherry had come out of the bottle rather too quickly, and Becky had to admit there was a chance it wouldn't set at all; she hoped her guests would be too inebriated to notice. The joint was roasting in the oven, and even Becky would be hard pressed to sabotage a prawn cocktail.

It was somewhat ironic that she should be so hopeless in the house when she was a full-time housewife. Becky put this anomaly down to her lack of organisation; one day, when she'd sorted herself out, taken a cookery course, and when Amy was off her hands . . . Her mind drifted. She noticed the sun had come out and there was a fresh wind blowing the budding branches of the trees. It was a beautiful spring afternoon. To celebrate, she picked up a prawn and popped it in her mouth.

'Mum, I'm dressed now.'

Becky glanced at Amy as she returned to the kitchen.

'Oh no, Amy, you can't wear that!'

Amy had on a tiny denim skirt that hugged her bottom, then stopped. Her legs were bare and slightly mottled. Above the skirt was a crop top reading 'Babe' that revealed a good few inches of midriff.

'I can wear what I like.'

Becky shuddered inwardly. How do you tell your own daughter that she looked like an under-age prostitute? She wondered what Amy saw when she looked in the mirror. She knew she ought to be tactful.

'I think you'll be cold later on. We're all going for a walk.'

'A walk!' Amy wailed with distress.

'Yes, a walk. Put on some leggings and a sweater.'

'But leggings are so sad! Nobody wears leggings!'

'Sophie does. She wears them all the time.'

Amy shifted her weight from one leg to the other. 'I know Sophie does, but . . .'

'Don't stand arguing with me. Go and put something warm on.'

Amy gave one loud exasperated tut and slouched out of the room.

A squirt of thousand island dressing, and the prawn cocktails were ready. As Becky was carrying them carefully out to the dining table, Amy came slowly down the stairs, stopping midway. She now wore a creased pair of jeans with the same crop top.

'Oh, Amy. You can't wear those. They're dirty. You've got them from the laundry basket!'

'I'm not wearing leggings!'

Becky stiffened with frustration. Why was Amy so unreasonable? What did it matter what she wore? She was only a child and it wasn't as if she was going out anywhere. It was only Denise and her family coming round – they were hardly strangers.

'Wear those jeans if you like!' Becky shouted, the tone of her voice denying Amy the permission she gave.

'All right then, I will!' shouted Amy.

The air was live with sparks. It was just then that Denise and George's car drew up in front of the house. Amy ran down the rest of the stairs to the kitchen, and held open the door as Denise, George, Petra and Rowan came in.

'Hi,' she said shyly.

Becky encouraged everyone to take off their coats.

'Shall I take them upstairs, Mum?' Amy asked sweetly.

Overloaded with Denise's fake fur, George's overcoat, and Petra and Rowan's anoraks, Amy struggled upstairs.

'Your Amy is so well-behaved!' Denise declared.

Becky didn't feel she could contradict her.

She ushered her guests into the lounge to say hello to Paul. Her husband was seated on the sofa surrounded by the Sunday papers. A small glass of whisky was by his side. Becky found herself wishing that he would have at least cleared the papers away and waited for the guests before helping himself to a drink, but she was grateful for small mercies. Paul seemed in a fairly affable mood, and had raised no objections to this dinner party that had been thrust upon him on his only free day of the week.

He rose to his feet. He was a tall man, broad-shouldered, with a bullish face. His nose was large and squat, his eyes slightly protuberant. His thinning hair was cut close to his head and emphasised his bulging temples. Altogether he had the appearance of an off-duty army major. He shook hands cordially with George. The contrast between the men was almost comic. George was short, cherubic with a beaming smile, and a somewhat nervous manner.

'Can I get you a drink?' Paul asked.

He walked over to a small sideboard against the conservatory window and poured George the gin and tonic he'd asked for.

'And you, Denise?' he asked, his back towards her.

'The same for me, Paul.'

'Me too,' Becky added. Paul did not respond. Either he had chosen to ignore her, or he didn't hear her. Either way, it was best she went back to the kitchen.

Petra and Rowan were standing self-consciously by the door of the lounge.

'Amy! Look after Petra and Rowan! Show them your computer!'

'D'you want to come upstairs?' Amy asked them diffidently.

It was strange, Becky thought, as she opened the oven to look at the roast, which was well done now, that Amy and Petra weren't better friends. They'd played with each other since they were small, and had been at the same schools all the time. Now they were even in the same class, but kept a distance. A pity. It would be so nice if the girls were as close as she and Denise. But children deliberately set out to cross your expectations.

I'll get my drink now, Becky decided. The lunch was as good as ready, and the lunch party was her idea after all. She switched off the oven and returned to the lounge.

She was pleased to see that George and Paul were getting on well. They were sitting on either side of the settee, each with a drink in their hands. There was no drink for Becky, and she suppressed the annoyance she felt. Now was not the time to express it. Becky was amused to see Denise standing with her drink at the bookcase, examining the books. This interest in literature was somewhat sudden. Had she been inspired by her encounter with Mr Rochester the other day? Maybe not; Becky could see now that her friend was only contemplating her reflection in the glass. Not that she needed to. In her cream pullover and long brown skirt with a slit up the back, she looked enviably well groomed.

She observed that Paul glanced at her from time to time, as he conversed with George. She wondered whether to go and join them, but it seemed a shame to interrupt, as they were getting on so well. Instead, she went to pour herself the drink she so richly deserved. She noticed that Paul's voice was dominant.

'I think you've got to have one these days. It's a fairly thorough old rigmarole, and you've got to make sure the staff are well briefed. The logo looks good on your notepaper.'

Becky realised they were talking about Paul's recent Investors in People award. She smiled brightly to hide her lack of interest. Paul was rather self-important at times. Becky decided it fell to her to introduce a new topic of conversation, and there was something she was dying to tell Denise and George.

'You'll never guess what happened when I took Becky to the dentist the other day. We found out that the new dentist was an old school friend of mine – Jude Jackson. I've not seen her for over twenty years. It was an amazing coincidence.'

'She's been going on about this all week,' Paul interjected waggishly.

Becky shot a warning glance at him.

'I'd better go and get the vegetables started.'

'I'll come and help you,' Denise said, and walked over sinuously to Becky. 'Then perhaps the men can wash up after,' she added, smiling at Paul. He clicked his tongue disapprovingly but smiled back at her.

One thing that Becky appreciated about Denise was that she was good with Paul. And it would be nice to have a natter in the kitchen. Becky's spirits rose. Perhaps it was the gin, but she had a good feeling about today. Despite Paul's habit of using her as a butt for his humour, they'd have a lovely, idyllic Sunday.

She turned to Denise with a smile.

'Shall I show you where the plates are?'


'Somebody must finish the wine,' Paul announced. He lifted the bottle of claret to examine how much was left.

'Denise?' Paul asked, and as he asked he poured the remainder of wine into her glass.

'I won't able to drink it,' she said.

'You should really have dessert wine with that trifle,' Paul continued. 'Is there any?' The question seemed to be addressed to Becky.

'I don't think so.'

'Go and have a look.'

'I mean I'm sure there isn't any.'

'*Say* what you mean.' Paul laughed. 'I can't stand people who don't say what they mean.' He laughed again. 'That's just me, I'm afraid. Straight. Straight down the line. What you see is what you get.'

Paul was drunk, and Becky loathed him like that. Whenever he had too much wine he got unbearably full of himself. The broken veins on his cheeks seemed redder than usual, his jowls had swollen and his eyes seemed to pop out from his face. There was a story book she used to read to Amy with a picture of a troll under a bridge, with staring, malevolent eyes. He was Paul to a T.

Everybody had finished their trifle but there was still some in the serving bowl.

'Any more trifle?' she asked.

Everyone declined. It was rather soggy.

'Then I'll call the children.' Becky stood up. 'Amy! Do any of you want more trifle?'

There was a stampede down the stairs. Rowan appeared, a smallish boy with shoulder-length hair and Denise's eyes.

'Find your bowl, Rowan, and you can have some more trifle.'

There were a few muted giggles, and Amy and Petra appeared. Amy's face was flushed and her eyes were shining. There had been too much sherry in the trifle after all. Perhaps that was why the girls had been getting on well. Petra was grinning; they had been sharing some joke.

'More trifle for you, girls?' Amy and Petra consulted each other with a look.

'No, it's all right, Mum? Can we go upstairs again and can you make Rowan stay downstairs?'

'He's no one else to play with.'

'He can be a nuisance,' Denise proffered. She sipped at her wine.

'He keeps coming into Amy's bedroom when we're trying to talk,' Petra whined.

Amy burst into infectious giggles.

'I understand,' Becky said. 'Why don't you let Rowan play on the computer in your room, and you two girls go and talk in our bedroom?'

The suggestion was greeted with delight and the children

disappeared. Becky was happy that Amy was having such a good time. She was looking forward to finding out what it was they had been talking about.

Paul was holding forth again.

'They're all Glenlivet malts,' he was saying, 'but there's a difference between the ones higher up the Spey valley—'

'Like the Glenmorangie,' George suggested.

'No, no; that's a Skye malt. There's a world of difference. Now when I took a party of Japanese business men round the distilleries the manager told me the secret is in the water.'

'So should you drink water with single malts?' Denise asked.

'Absolutely not. Unless you're like Becky here and choke every time you try a whisky.'

Becky attempted a smile.

'You need a mature palate, to be able to dishtinguish – distinguish between the peat smoked malt and the – I can place a single malt within five miles. I've got the Aberlour here, and the Ben Rinnes. Now—'

Becky hoped her guests weren't as bored by him as she was. She could cope with him when Paul displayed his less attractive side behind closed doors. In public he was somewhat embarrassing. She decided to cut him short.

'Paul knows a lot about whisky,' she said. 'He took a course a year or two ago.'

'*We're* taking a course soon, aren't we, Becky?' Denise announced demurely.

'This is the first I've heard of it,' Paul said.

'I haven't had a moment to tell you,' Becky said untruthfully. 'It's only a creative writing course.'

Paul didn't look remotely interested. She had been worried about nothing.

'Creative writing?' he asked. He laughed. 'Going to be the next Barbara Cartland, are you?' He glanced at Becky, indicating to George and Denise that they should join in his mirth. 'The only writing I've ever seen her do is the shopping list. So what's brought this on?'

'I thought I'd do something different.'

Paul turned to Denise. 'And what are *you* going to write about?'

'Wouldn't you like to know!'

Becky admired the way she handled him. Paul looked quite nettled.

'I bet you've got a good imagination,' he said to her.

'I imagine all sorts of things.' Denise drained her wine glass.

Paul laughed, and belched accidentally, and laughed some more to cover it up.

'Write a bestseller and I can retire,' he said to Becky. 'But first of all you can get the coffee on.'

Becky had got away with only the minimum amount of ribbing. She rose from the table.

'After coffee maybe we can go for a walk. I think I need to clear my head.'

'Me too,' said George. 'A walk would be just the thing.'


There was quite a wind up, and it ruffled Becky's hair, blowing it in her eyes, so that every so often she had to push it back, because she had to watch her footing. The path they were walking on was pitted with puddles of rainwater and mud, and she didn't want to get her boots too dirty. Every so often she looked up, over the dry-stone wall on their left, to catch the view of Mytholm Bridge below them, nestling between all the hills. She could see the pattern of all the streets as in an aerial map. As the path became muddier she stepped on to the line of grass between the ruts worn in to the path. She was the last in the party, just behind Rowan, who was swinging a dead branch he had found on the path in front of him, and muttering to himself. George was with him. She had been having a conversation with George about Mytholm High. It was interesting to hear what another parent thought about the school. He told her he was intending to help out in the Christmas pantomime. The church bells from the village chimed five.

Paul was walking ahead with Denise. Frankly, she was glad to be rid of him. Theirs was the sort of marriage that thrived on absence – his absence. Recognising that was part of the art of staying married. Even the most loving couples could have enough of each other. She guessed that even Jane Rochester would get irritated with the tapping of her dear spouse's stick after a while. Elizabeth Darcy would get fed up to the back teeth with Darcy's sulks and his refusal to help in the nursery. Emma would find Mr Knightley a know-it-all.

Yes, most marriages ended up like hers – it was a truth universally acknowledged. Perfection only existed in books. Becky smiled wryly to herself, then looked ahead at Amy and Petra. They were in close conference, bumping against each other as they walked, matier than they'd ever been. Maybe the only lasting friendships were between females. She recollected the golden days of her teenage years spent with Jude. There was nothing like that feeling of having a best friend, a partner in crime, someone whose thoughts you shared, and who would see everything from your point of view. Just as Jude did. Becky was filled with happiness as she anticipated tomorrow evening. She would be able to be her old self again. She would liberate her inner teenager. Those were the days. We were so innocent then.


'I hate her!'

'Yeah – me too!'

'You know, she never washes her hair. She told me that if you don't wash your hair it never gets greasy. And her school blouse is dead grubby.'

'Yeah, and I saw her out shopping with her Mum and she was like dead scruffy in one of them dead old green and purple jackets.'

'Yeah, she's such a bitch.'

'What do you think of Tracey?'

'I can't stand her. Always sucking up to the teachers. She fancies old Greenlees and she sent him a Valentine's card. Honestly! I saw her put it in his locker! It said, "I want to shag with you."'

Amy screamed with shock and delight.

'Yeah, and she never got into trouble so I reckon he didn't tell on her, which means he's going to do it!'

'Oh, that is like so sick!'

'Tracey's a slag anyway. Like Sian. She smokes twenty a day. Do you smoke?'

'No.'

'Nor do I. It stinks.'

Amy was glad she got the right answer.

'You can hang round with us if you want,' Petra said.

Amy was so excited she was lost for words. It was important to choose the right words.

'Oh, cool!' she said.

Everything was swimming with bliss. Amy looked ahead, and there was her Dad with Petra's Mum. And she knew her Mum was behind with Petra's Dad. The whole world was making friends. It was brilliant!

Denise looked down and saw that there was mud on the hemline of her skirt. A walk was a daft idea, and had it not been for . . . She needed to get out of Becky's twee little house and just now the chill air was a relief to her. Walking just a little ahead of Paul she did not have to talk to him. Yet.

His closeness made her tingle, as it did on the several occasions he had given her a lift. She didn't fully understand why that was so. It wasn't as if she found him very attractive. She preferred younger men. There seemed to be so much of Paul – he was powerfully built and his face seemed to swell when he talked – she didn't like that so much. But then there was something in the way he looked at her, something lustful, that reflected back her own attractiveness. When she was with him she felt vampish, and she liked that. Not like a mother uncomfortably close to middle age. Paul connected with her secret, internal life.

That touch of aggression he had – much of it was frustration with Becky, she was sure. She heard the trudge of his boots as he walked behind her. Living with Becky would be enough to drive anyone insane. Paul would be different with her. Not that for one moment did Denise contemplate having any sort of illicit relationship with Paul. That wasn't what she wanted.

No. What she wanted was the chase, the confirmation that she was irresistible. That Paul was Becky's husband added spice. That was all, and it was innocent. She could still bathe Rowan at night, cook George's dinner, and hold to herself the knowledge that Paul wanted her, and feel innocent. She had done nothing. Even if she did, no reasonable person would blame her. Being married to George was as exciting as watching paint dry. Yet for the sake of the children, the sake of the money, the sake of the house, and of her reputation, Denise was happy to stick with him. Provided she could have the life of her own that she knew she so richly deserved, her secret life. George, in tacit admission of his own failures, never questioned her too closely on what she did with her time. It was better that way. She heard Paul advancing on her.

'Don't walk so fast.'

'I'm sorry. I was thinking.'

'What were you thinking about?' Paul panted in between his words. He was evidently unaccustomed to exercise.

'None of your business.'

'Come into Manchester next week. I'll take the afternoon off. I've got to see you again.'

'Next week is difficult.'

'Don't mess me around. I've been wanting to get you alone all afternoon. It's been driving me mad, seeing you there and not being able to touch.'

'How do you think I feel? Knowing about us, and seeing Becky calmly eating Brussels sprouts.'

'Sod Becky!'

'She's my friend.'

'I'm your friend.'

Denise found that she was breathing hard. It was fear; it was excitement; it was a kind of sexual excitement. Whatever it was, she liked it. When she glanced at Paul, she could see that there was something indisputably manly in the set of his head on his shoulders, his whole stance. He *was* a sort of over-ripe Sylvester Stallone.

In front of them was a stile, and then a barn. The footpath seemed to end there, and Denise wondered if they would turn back. Then they would meet the children and Becky and George as in some bizarre country dance, in which you seamlessly exchanged partners.

Paul stopped at the stile to help her over. In order to climb up, she had to lift her skirt over her knees. Immediately Paul put his hand on her thigh and quickly slid it up her leg. And as quickly removed his hand, so she could almost think she had imagined it. Standing on the cross-plank of the stile, she was a little taller than him, and looked down on his thinning hair, his bulbous features, and experienced a moment of repulsion. Perhaps repulsion and attraction were closely related.

Paul climbed the stile after her, and together they looked around. The grass was flattened along the side of the barn, and Denise could see that this path would lead them back to the main road. Perhaps it would be a good idea to walk along it. As she thought that, she felt Paul's hand on the small of her back, and its pressure made her stiffen.

'Come here,' he said thickly.

She turned, and he pulled her to him. Before she had a chance to object he was kissing her, rubbing his face against hers, his cold, rough skin moving over her, his tongue pressing at her mouth. Denise was shocked, and aware that at any moment somebody could cross the stile, turn and see them. It was the most exciting thing that had ever happened to her. Her mouth opened against the pressure of his. For one moment she gave herself up to his insistence, and then broke away.

'How dare you!'

'I'm sorry. You make me – I can't control myself. Christ – if it wasn't for the rest of them I'd take you now.'

Denise thrilled to his words. She repeated them to herself internally. She would remember them. She tingled with an electric excitement. Then there were voices at the stile. She wiped her mouth and Paul took a few paces back. Amy and Petra appeared.

'This way,' Paul declared.

'And then we're back on the main road,' Denise said cheerfully. It was important to sound normal so no one would suspect anything. Rowan clambered over the stile, and finally came Becky and George.

They all set off in the direction of the tree lined road in the distance. Denise hung back a little, thinking perhaps she'd better speak to Becky. They needed to talk about Thursday. She'd offer to pick Becky up, and Paul would be there. She was flushed from his kiss, but knew that the unaccustomed exercise would be a good cover-up. Unaccustomed exercise indeed.


Becky, Paul and Amy watched George start his Peugeot, and they waved at the Clarks as they reversed down the track.

Amy was thoroughly happy. Petra was really, really nice and dead funny and everything. They were a bit mean about Sophie but – oh well, Sophie would never know. And Petra said that Amy could sit next to her in English tomorrow. The rest of the class would be bound to notice.

'Glad that's over,' Paul said. 'I'm going to have a shower.'

Becky exhaled softly. There was a lot of mess in the kitchen and evidently she would have to clear it herself. But it had been worth it. Everyone had had a lovely day. But it was over now, and a wave of sadness engulfed her, the same sadness she used to feel on Sunday afternoons when she was Amy's age, knowing the weekend was over and there would be school in the morning. A sense that special times were only fleeting interludes.

But no, she told herself. Jude had arrived, and there was the writing class on Thursday. There were still things to look forward to. Including pans to scrub and the dishwasher to fill.

'Come on, Amy. This time I really do need your help.'

'OK, Mum,' she said brightly.


Karen unlocked her front door with some trepidation, hoping Jim Ferguson hadn't made too much of a mess. She had prepared the room last night by carting the telly, the video, and a canvas-back armchair up to her bedroom, and covering the rest of the furniture with old blankets. So her bedroom became their temporary living room, and the boys had spent the evening jumping on the bed and causing havoc. She had to scream until she was blue in the face to get them into their room, and even then they weren't asleep until past ten.

It wasn't all bad; having the telly upstairs meant that she could watch it in bed, and she lay there, under her sloping roof with the little skylight above her, tucked up watching some seventies costume drama with Tom Courtenay and fell comfortably asleep.

The morning had been a nightmare. Jim had promised to arrive early so she could let him in before taking the boys to school, but he never arrived, and so the boys were late, she missed the bus up, and didn't get back home until half ten, and Jim was waiting outside in his van. As soon he got started, she had to rush back into Mytholm again to Sun Wholefoods, and apologised profusely to Eleni, who insisted she went to sit in the back room and chant for a while to regain her sense of calm. In actual fact Karen went into the yard for a quick fag, which was much more effective.

Then there was a delivery from Suma, a rush on the ginseng,

no time for lunch, and another dash back home, just catching the bus this time, to see what Jim had been up to. As she opened her front door, there was the sound of Radio One and a strong aroma of stripping solution, cigarette smoke and male sweat.

'I'm back!' Karen announced.

'Oh, aye.' As Karen entered her living room, Jim turned off the radio, and faced her, greeting her with a smile. He'd been working hard. Half the walls were bare now.

'Do you want a brew?' Karen asked him. That was only polite, and even though she felt dubious about being alone with Jim, it was only right to make him a cup of tea.

'Wouldn't say no.'

She walked through the living room into the kitchen at the back. It was a narrow galley kitchen with an old linoleum floor. A calendar from the local Chinese takeaway hung on the wall by the kettle, and on the fridge were coloured plastic alphabet letters that Becky had given her for the boys. Behind them were various notes, telephone numbers and reminders. Karen felt the weight of the kettle and decided there was sufficient water. Just then Jim appeared in the entrance.

'All right?' he asked her.

'Not bad,' Karen said. 'Tea or coffee?'

Jim wrinkled his nose in a gesture of dissatisfaction.

'I've got some Norfolk Punch here,' she said nervously, getting a bottle from her Sun carrier bag. 'Eleni gave it to me. It's very good for you. A mixture of natural fruit juices and other extracts.'

'I tell you what,' he said. 'I could do with a pint.' He glanced at his watch. 'I'll run you over in the van to the Robin Hood and treat you to a pub lunch.'

The thought of the food tempted Karen. If only she could be sure that lunch wasn't a euphemism for something else. She hoped to God that Jim wasn't interested in her. She wished that Denise hadn't been so insinuating the other day. Her comments reminded her that he used to have a bit of a reputation with the girls. She eyed him, trying to size up his intentions. He grinned at her disarmingly. He was hardly dressed for the pub; his denims were stained with stripping fluid and his black vest-type T-shirt revealed surprisingly muscular arms with an eagle tattoo.

'I've got a shirt in the van,' he informed her. 'Come on – I'm parched.'

It was the casual matiness in his tone which disarmed her. That, and her rumbling stomach. Within a few minutes she found herself next to Jim in the van, careering round the bends of the hill down to the Robin Hood.

She followed him into the pub feeling rather dissolute; pubs were for the evening, not Monday lunchtime. But there was an inviting menu chalked up on the board and the delicious smell of real ale.

'Just a half of Timothy Taylor's,' she told Jim. 'And a steak and kidney pie, chips and peas.' Her mouth watered at the thought. He indicated a table close to the fireplace, and she sat there, watching him carry over the beers. She felt moderately safe; they were in public, and he could hardly make a move on her in the lounge bar of the Robin Hood. She didn't entirely trust him; perhaps it had something to do with the pin-ups of girls with impossibly huge breasts that she'd noticed in the back room of his office. Jim came to sit down beside her.

'I deserve this,' he told her, as he downed his pint.

'Working hard?' she asked.

'I've spent all weekend down the Clough Hall Health Club, doing it up. Do you remember my sister Shirley? She's the owner. She got a loan out from the bank.' Jim spoke with deference.

Karen took her Silk Cut from her handbag and offered Jim one. He took it, got out his lighter and went to light hers.

'I remember Shirley. She was two years above us, weren't she?'

Jim nodded. Karen recalled a tousled little girl, notorious for taking on and clobbering the boys in playground fights.

'Cheers,' she said. Then there was silence. Karen became

aware that Jim was looking at her and it made her feel uncomfortable. She put her arms over her chest defensively. She would not help him out with the conversation. The minutes ticked by. Every so often he lifted his glass and drank some beer. Eventually he spoke.

'So you work down at the health food shop?'

'Yeah; four half days a week.'

'Right.' He took a puff on his cigarette. 'I don't go in there.'

He took another pull on his pint. Karen was damned if she was going to help him out. She watched the illuminated display on the fruit machine dance in front of her. Then someone put a record in the juke box. It was 'Wonderwall'.

'D'you like Oasis?' Jim asked her.

'They're all right,' Karen replied. Evidently Jim had not grown into one of the world's greatest conversationalists, she thought. Just then their food arrived. Her mouth watered. The pastry was light and crisp, and there was a huge portion of chips. Karen ripped open the little packets of brown sauce and vinegar that came in a little straw basket, and set to with vigour. So did Jim. They ate in silence. Karen forgot about her taciturn companion as she gave herself up entirely to the food. She felt the tension ebb out of her as she ate; she couldn't remember the last time she'd had a decent pub meal.

'Another half?' Jim asked her.

'Wouldn't say no.'

He got up from the table and went to the bar. Karen studied his broad back and the way it tapered to a neat waist. It was odd the way he had no effect on her. Perhaps it was because she could remember him in the playground pretending to be a Dalek. Or perhaps it was because Steve had put her off men for good. Just then, she felt glad not to have to feel anything. She watched him come back with the drinks.

'Cheers,' she said.

'Cheers,' he said.

They sat in a companionable silence. Karen ridiculed herself for thinking that he fancied her. Like everything else, it was Denise's fault for putting ideas into her mind. Jim Ferguson just didn't fancy going to the pub by himself, which was — She felt something cool and soft probing her thigh. She blanched in horror and looked up at Jim. He was staring ahead fixedly at the darts board.

'Lay off, will you?' she told him.

'Lay off what?' He looked puzzled. And Karen looked down and saw a black mongrel puppy eagerly gazing up at her, hoping for some titbit from the table. She laughed despite herself.

'It's the bloody dog. I thought you were touching me up.'

'I wouldn't do owt like that,' Jim said.

'I'm pleased to hear it.'

Both of them were blushing.

'I don't make passes at customers,' he said.

Karen smiled at him tentatively.

'I just thought we could be mates,' he continued. 'And you looked like you could do with a square meal.' Jim put two cigarettes in his mouth, lit them both, and handed her one.

'Cheers,' she said.

'Cheers,' he replied.

They listened to the juke-box while they smoked. Jim's inability to hold a conversation was in its way quite soothing. Finally he looked at his watch again.

'Best be getting back now.'

'Good idea.'

'Tell you what,' he said. 'Come round one evening and say hello to Shirley. I know she's looking for staff at Clough Hall. Are you interested?'

'Might be.'

'I'll arrange something.'

He stood up first and moved the table back so she could get out. She followed him to the van, enjoying the lightheadedness that came from unaccustomed daytime drinking. Monday wasn't turning out so bad after all.

\*　　\*　　\*

Karen was lying on her bed watching *Home and Away* when Jim shouted up to her from the living room.

'Karen! You've got a visitor!'

Damn, she said to herself, as she left the bed and turned off the set. She made her way down the stairs, and saw Denise standing at the door.

'Denise!'

'I'm so glad you're in. Can I drive you down to pick the kids up?'

'It's rather early.'

'I know, but I thought I'd take you out to tea first.'

Karen laughed inwardly at the thought of two treats in one day.

'Well, all right. Will you be here when I get back, Jim?'

'Aye.' While Karen put on her coat and checked her handbag she observed Denise, whose eyes lingered on Jim's physique. It gave her an idea. Karen smiled to herself.

'Right – let's go. See you later, Jim!'

The triangular slice of chocolate fudge cake looked like the prow of a steamer, and the swirl of cream on top like a a puff of smoke. Karen was still full from her lunch, and wasn't altogether sure she could manage it, but she ordered it on principle. It was the most expensive item in the tea shop, and Denise was paying. Denise had not bought herself a cake, indicating her cast-iron will when faced with gâteaux; Karen, on the other hand, enjoyed eating in front of Denise, demonstrating that whatever she ate, she never put weight on.

'I need to talk,' Denise said.

It was the kind of line they came out with in bad soap operas. Karen speared her fudge cake with her fork, and supplied the next line.

'Is something wrong?'

'No – not exactly. It's Paul. Oh, Karen, I'm so glad I have you to talk to. I know you'll understand.'

'What's happened?'

'Nothing. That is, I saw him yesterday. You know, I told you. We went to Becky and Paul's for lunch. All the time I was conscious he couldn't keep his eyes off me. I was so scared Becky would notice I could hardly eat. I haven't eaten properly for days,' Denise said, glancing at Karen's fudge cake.

'Did she notice anything?'

'Oh no. Not Becky. She just fussed around us as she always does. And then she suggested we all went for a walk. I tried to avoid him, but he caught up with me. He told me how much he wanted me, how I drive him mad with desire. He said he couldn't control himself. He said if it hadn't been for the rest of them, he'd have taken me there and then. He's such a passionate man, Karen!'

'But he didn't make a pass?'

Denise lowered her eyes to the table, and traced the floral pattern on the tablecloth with her finger.

'He kissed me. I couldn't stop him. We'd got ahead of the others – no one was around – Paul is such a romantic!'

Karen mentally substituted the word 'ratbag'. She seethed with disgust. The cake lay forgotten.

'And then?'

'The others caught up with us. And I went home in such a state. I couldn't sleep all night. He seems to obsess me, Karen. Not that I would ever have an affair with him – I couldn't do that to Becky – but it's so hard not to respond to the needs of a man. And not to meet your own needs. Why is something that feels so right condemnated by the world?' She sighed. 'Perhaps it's jealousy.'

Condemnated, wondered Karen? Denise's malapropism had momentarily distracted her. Now she looked at her friend with loathing.

Some time ago she had told off Bobby when he put some food on the edge of his fork and flicked it into Seth's eye.

Presently she felt an overpowering desire to do the same to Denise. But there was a better way of avenging Becky.

'It must be hard for you,' Karen said, 'having all those feelings and not being able to do anything about them.'

'I knew you'd understand!'

'It's not like that for me and Jim.'

Denise looked at her quizzically.

'No, not at all. When I came back this morning from the shop, he wasn't in the lounge. I would have thought he'd scarpered except his van was there. I called for him, and he answered from upstairs. I thought he was in the bathroom, but when I went up to check, he wasn't.'

'Where was he?'

'In my bed – starkers!'

'Karen!'

'He was sitting up with my duvet only just covering his you-know-what. He said, d'you fancy joining me?'

'I don't believe you.'

'It's true as I'm sitting here. At first I was that taken aback, and I would have run out, but I did rather fancy him, and we were at school together – did you know that? – so it wasn't as if we were strangers. So then while he was watching me I began to take my clothes off – slowly, you know – and I could hear his heavy breathing. By the time I got in the bed he could hardly restrain himself. In fact I thought I would just have to make do with a quickie. But do you know, he was ready again in half an hour. The younger they are, the shorter time it takes them to recover. And don't you believe what they say in the magazines – size *is* everything.'

Denise's eyes were wide with amazement. Karen revelled in her triumph, but quickly remembered to add a few corroborative details.

'And then he said he were that parched we'd better go down to the Robin Hood for a pub lunch and a pint.' She paused. 'And it's going to take him more than a week to finish my living room.'

With that Karen recommenced eating her fudge cake.

'This'll replace some of the calories I've burnt up,' she added, like a prima donna unable to resist coming back for encores.

'I'd be careful if I were you, Karen,' Denise said warningly. 'I hear he's a bit of a jack-the-lad.'

'Yes, but he's met *me* now.'

Denise finished her coffee, and Karen sensed victory. She had trumped her. It had been remarkably easy – perhaps it should be her who was going to the creative writing class.

'Do you not think,' said Denise, 'that perhaps you've become less choosy about men since Steve left you? That's nothing to be ashamed about. It's quite understandable.'

Karen wanted to reply that Denise was so desperate that she nicked her friends' husbands, but bit her tongue. For Becky's sake she needed to keep an eye on the situation. She could not afford to alienate Denise entirely.

'So what are you going to do about Paul?'

'I think I need to see him again alone – just to talk. I need to explain to him that nothing can ever come of his infatuation with me. As flattered as I am, I don't accept invitations like Paul's. I am a married woman.'

Karen thought fleetingly of George and his gentle, angelic face, and wondered about Denise's marriage.

'But now it's time to pick up the boys. And look, it's started to rain. Let's go quickly – I don't want to get caught!'

I bet you don't, thought Karen.

# Chapter Four

As Jude's car began to strain with the effort of climbing the hill that led to Becky's house, she slipped into second gear. She reflected that since arriving in Mytholm Bridge she had become expert in high altitude driving. Everywhere she went was either down a hill, or up a hill. She passed a row of stone terraced houses grimy on the outside, but uncurtained windows gave views of well-lit clean pine interiors, Habitat furniture and well-stocked bookshelves.

Jude wondered if Becky's house would be like that. In fact, it was impossible to imagine what Becky's house would be like, or for that matter, what Becky herself would be like. Yet apart from her mother, Jude had been closer to Becky than anyone else, ever. Would it be possible to forget what drove them apart?

At the top of the hill Jude looked on to the passenger seat to follow Becky's map. It took her two attempts to edge the car round the sharp corner, almost doubling back on itself, to get to the lane in which the house was situated. And there it was – just as Becky had said – the end house with a glowing conservatory. Out of the corner of her eye Jude caught some movement there, and anticipated Becky meeting her at the door.

In fact it was Amy who ran round the side of the house to greet Jude.

'You can come into the house through the back – only visitors use the front door!' Jude passed a little rockery on her left, and Becky was there to greet her at the kitchen door. Jude hugged her with real feeling.

'I'll take your jacket upstairs,' Amy said. 'Give it to me.'

Jude did so.

'Look at this,' she declared to Becky, gesturing around her. 'You have a real house.'

She knew it was an absurd comment, but she wanted to express her surprise that Becky had grown up. Jude guessed that never having married, never having had children, time had stood still for her. Inside, she still felt eighteen. But here was Becky in her late thirties, in her own house.

'Come in and have a look!'

Jude took in the busy kitchen, with the mug tree and filter coffee machine on the work surface, and walked into the dining room, with its square table, its fireplace stuffed with honesty, the bowl of fruit with some apples and two badly speckled bananas and the prints on the wall of various rural scenes. The room was rather too untidy for Jude's tastes, but undeniably comfortable. An elderly armchair by the window had an antimacassar thrown over it, which was slipping off. By its side was a magazine rack with that day's *Daily Mail*, and *Hello* magazine.

'And the lounge is through here.'

Becky took her into the next room, where there was a gingham settee, a coffee table with more magazines, two armchairs and a drinks trolley, a small television and hi-fi. Amy's school books were scattered on the rug in front of the fire.

'Nice,' Jude said. The warmth of the room enveloped her. There was the faint memory of the smell of their dinner, and the whirr of the video recording something. Outside small lights dotted the hillside opposite, and the sky was a deep navy.

Just as Jude was about to comment on the conservatory, she noticed a figure rise from a tall cane chair within it and she realised this must be Paul, Becky's husband. She was consumed with curiosity, and turned to greet him. He was a big, bear-like man, with large features. Jude immediately imagined him in the middle of a rugby scrum. She put out her hand to shake his. He looked a little taken aback at that, but gave her his hand and allowed her to shake it.

'And so you're Paul,' Jude said, smiling at him.

She was aware that she was being examined, and held his gaze boldly.

'Pleased to meet you,' he said. 'It's . . . ?'

He seemed to be struggling for her name, so Jude supplied it.

'Can I get you a drink?' he said, walking over to the trolley. 'We have the usual sort of things, sherry, gin, whisky—'

'Do you have a can of beer?' Jude asked. She was thirsty.

'Becky will get you one from the kitchen.' Jude noticed her run out. 'So they tell me you're the new dentist. Did you know Tony Slater? Friend of mine – keen on golf. He was chairman of the golf club for a number of years. They wanted me to take over, but I didn't have the time. Working in Manchester means I have to travel.'

'What do you do?' Jude asked him, as he sat down on the armchair.

'I have my own firm – a mail order company. When I took it over eight years ago it was a tiny concern. Doubtful if it could keep its head above water. But I've turned it right round. We employ upwards of forty staff, mainly part-timers. I get more flexibility that way. I've got to be able to respond to changing conditions. These days you can't afford to stand still.'

Jude nodded, and noticed that a button had popped at the bottom of his shirt. Her eyes were drawn to the inch or two of midriff that was exposed, and she saw how substantial and fleshy his stomach was. This was the man Becky had chosen. Extraordinary!

'Of course, it's a lot easier getting in of a morning now they've improved the M66. They're extending it all the way to Ashton-Under-Lyne. That'll open up some new opportunities. Most mornings I've got to get on the road before seven if I'm to avoid the worst of the traffic.'

Becky came back and gave Jude a glass of beer. She sat by her on the settee.

'It's the bottle-neck at the Halfway House – that's what I've got to watch. You can have a tailback there for a mile or so on a bad morning. But I cut through the pub car park and I can skip the lights that way. I can gain a good four minutes doing that.'

'Jude is living on Whitestone Edge,' Becky supplied.

'Bit out in the wilds. But then you only have to get into Mytholm. I looked at property up there but it's a bit remote for me. Living here I can be on the main road in two minutes.'

Jude noticed that Paul was no longer looking at her. In the beginning he observed her narrowly, and she had felt a little uncomfortable. There was something insinuating in the manner he used with her. But now he had clearly written her off as a woman; she could tell she was being treated as an honorary man. Becky seemed happy saying little. Jude became aware that Paul didn't look at his wife once, although she monitored him with the occasional glance. She clearly realised how he was hogging the conversation.

'So how did you meet our Becky?' Jude asked him.

'She worked in my old firm. A haulage company in Denton. I was assistant manager.'

'I was a secretary there,' Becky added.

'It was taken over in the end, but I got wind of it and managed to get myself another position in Littleborough.'

What *does* Becky see in him?

'I left suddenly and the firm was in a bit of a pickle. Amy – check the video!'

Jude's eyes travelled to the video, that was quiet now.

'It's stopped recording, Dad.'

'Bloody hell – right in the middle of a match. I told you to ring Lewis's, Becky. I knew it was playing up.' He sighed dramatically.

'We don't mind if you watch the match here,' Becky said.

'We'll go and have a chat somewhere else. Shall we go in the conservatory, Jude?'

'That's fine by me!'

Thankfully Jude got up and carried her beer into the conservatory. She liked the room as soon as she walked into it. There were plants everywhere in large clay pots. A pair of standard lamps cast soft shadows. Relieved to be out of Paul's reach, Jude settled herself comfortably in a cane chair, her legs crossed under her. Becky came to sit next to her, and Jude was flattered to see that Amy had followed them, and settled herself on the floor with some school books.

'Shouldn't you be doing your homework in your room?' Becky asked her.

'This is only geography. I've just got this map to trace and colour in.'

'As long as you don't make any silly mistakes.'

Amy grinned at Jude in happy complicity. She was a gawky-looking girl, with Becky's soft prettiness, but her father's height. One day she would be attractive; now she looked as if her individual features were at war with each other. Her chin was too long for her small mouth; her eyes were pale but her nose rather prominent and there were a few angry spots on her forehead. She lay herself flat out on her stomach to trace her map. Becky was watching her too. Jude was aware how womanly Becky seemed now; her arms were rounded, her bust was full, and her face, although as pretty as ever, looked slightly careworn. There were faint shadows under her eyes and the suggestion of tension in her face. Jude was pretty sure what the cause was. Becky's husband was unspeakable. Why on earth was she still married to him? What hold did he have over her? Jude began to feel the stirring of a mission. Fate had clearly brought her here as rescuer. Just then Becky pointed at Amy engaged in her homework on the floor.

'I'm pleased I've left all that behind,' Becky said.

'Come on! It wasn't that bad!'

71

'Not for you. You always did so well at school.'

'Were you a swot?' Amy asked Jude, not taking her eyes off the tracing paper.

'Me? A swot?' Jude gave a wicked laugh. 'Who was it who asked the new biology teacher what an orgasm was?'

'She thought you meant an organism!' Becky laughed at the memory.

'What is an orgasm?' Amy asked.

'Ask your mother later,' Jude declared. 'She's busy now because she's going to tell me everything that's happened to her since nineteen seventy-seven – that was when we left school.' Becky chuckled. It melted Jude. It was the same laugh she'd always had.

'There's not a lot to say. You know I didn't want to go to university, so I went to secretarial college. I did quite well, actually, and I got a job almost straightaway. I was living with Mum then, but after a while I moved out and shared a house with some friends. I met Paul in the early eighties and we married in nineteen eighty-three, all of fifteen years ago. It doesn't seem like it. And then Amy came along.' Becky lowered her voice. 'But I had a difficult time with her – a bad pregnancy. I was advised not have another.'

'So what do you do now?'

'You mean, do I work? Not any more. I don't think I'd like to go back to being a secretary. I'd like to do something more interesting.'

Jude stroked her chin.

'I know I ought to go back to work,' Becky added quickly. 'But there's my father who's virtually housebound now, and relies on me, not to mention Amy and Paul. Come on, what about you? What have you been up to?'

'Five years in London learning dentistry. Unbearably hard up – worked as a barmaid in a sleazy pub in Camden Town and had more propositions than you've had hot dinners. Amy – you can also ask your mother what a proposition is. Then what? Ah yes – came back up north to live with mum and worked in

Longsight. Until just recently.' Jude held up her glass. 'Do you get refills in this establishment?'

Amy scrambled to her feet.

'I'll get you some more.' She left the conservatory.

'Are you living alone?' Becky asked. Jude knew this was a tactful way of enquiring about her love life.

'Not alone,' Jude said. 'You see, one wasn't enough for me, so I've settled down with two. Cats, that is. No, I wouldn't recommend dentistry as a way of meeting men. Well, you meet them, but they run screaming from your clutches.'

'Are you lonely?' Becky asked.

'Here's Amy back already. You're a star,' Jude said to her. 'There's a bit of a head on this.' Most of the straight glass consisted of foam. Amy look abashed. 'But this is just how I like it!'

'Amy!' said her mother, with fond exasperation.

Jude decided to come to Amy's defence.

'Becky – do you remember my mother's birthday?'

'It was the ninth of March.'

'I know, but I'm thinking about the time we decided to make a party for her. When we typed out a little menu and I asked you to get some cocktail biscuits from the cupboard—'

'And I didn't know what you meant and found a brown paper packet of little fish-shaped biscuits and even though I thought they smelt a bit stale—'

'You put them out in a little glass bowl. And the Director of Education ate the lot—'

'And they were the cat biscuits!'

Becky laughed uproariously at the memory. Amy had stopped working to listen to them.

'I used to love going to your house, Jude. Your mother used to fascinate me – I never knew a mother who swore before. But when I came home and said in front of my Dad, "Bugger! I've missed Blue Peter," he grounded me for a week.'

Jude smiled, and recalled how Becky's family used to appear to her in the beginning. 'Your family was like one in a story book. Or that *Janet and John* reader we had at school. There was a mother and father, a child of each sex, and even a dog.'

'We weren't as boring as that!'

'I can remember that three-piece suite your mother bought – the one in gold Dralon – and she was so worried that it would get dirty, that she didn't take off its plastic cover for a year.'

'That was understandable,' Becky said. 'We weren't that well off!'

Jude could hear that Becky was hurt, and she could have kicked herself for her tactlessness. Fortunately Amy intervened.

'I saw Nana three years ago. She came over for a holiday with Aunty Eileen and they bought me a Walkman.'

'Lucky you!' Jude said, deciding to chat to Amy for a while instead. The past was proving rather treacherous. 'So Amy, tell me. Do you have a best friend?'

'Kind of.'

'You do,' prompted Becky. 'There's Sophie.'

'I know, but . . . Sometimes she gets on my nerves. I've been sitting next to Petra. She's fun.'

'Petra is the daughter of a friend of mine,' Becky explained. 'Denise. We're going to start a creative writing class this week. Would you like to come with us?'

Jude considered the possibility. She knew she ought to start getting herself a social life. But not creative writing – she was a factual person, and preferred it that way. A little imagination could be a dangerous thing. Jude paused just long enough for Becky to pick up her doubt.

'But then you never liked English at school. You were a scientist. But do you have any hobbies, Jude? Because hobbies are a wonderful way of meeting people. Of course, I'll introduce you to all of my friends, but they're all women.'

'And what's wrong with that?'

It was Becky's turn to look uncomfortable now.

'Well, it's nice to meet men. You might as well enjoy the advantages of being single,' she said.

'Hold on – I don't follow your logic. The advantages of

74

being single seem to be that you're free to pursue men in order not to stay single, which argues that there aren't any advantages after all. Q.E.D. *Quod erat demonstrandum.*'

'Don't be so clever,' Becky said. 'You ought to join something in Mytholm in order to meet people of both sexes.'

'Tell you what – let's cut corners. I'll leave it to you to find me someone suitable. At least five foot nine, able to hold a decent conversation, dress sense not important – it's what's underneath that matters. Oh, and good teeth. He's got to have good teeth.'

Amy looked up in astonishment.

There was a cry of 'Becky!' from the living room. Becky quickly rose to her feet.

'It's Dad,' Amy said unnecessarily.

Jude watched Becky scuttle into the living room, and could hear Paul quite clearly through the glass partition.

'You can put the kettle on. I want a cup of tea. Haven't you had enough wittering for one evening?'

'I've not seen Jude for over twenty years,' Becky said defensively.

'And I'll have a couple of slices of toast while you're at it.'

Jude was pleased when Amy spoke. She didn't want to hear any more. She didn't trust herself to stay quiet. Privately she decided that Paul needed throttling. And why was Becky taking it all so meekly?

'Why did you and Mum stop being friends?'

The sudden question from Amy distracted Jude. She had to ask Amy to repeat it.

'Why did you stop being friends? You must have, because you haven't seen each other for so long.'

'We grew apart after a time – we had different interests.'

'Like me and Sophie.'

'Maybe. Perhaps I was a bit of a swot after all. I used to stay in and learn my physics notes, and your Mum was more of the party animal.'

'But you're not like that now. You're cool.'

Jude recognised the strength of the compliment; she was flattered.

'And your Mum's cool too.'

'We-ell . . .'

'You don't know her as well as I do.'

'Who dumped who? Did Mum tell you she didn't want to be friends any more?' Jude registered the intensity of the question and felt a little sorry for Sophie, whoever she was.

'You don't do that with your friends. You might sometimes have to dump boyfriends, but it's different with mates. You just find you spend less time together.'

'Did Mum carry on hanging around you even though you had other friends?'

Jude began to feel uncomfortable. She did not want Amy to probe any further. Of course she remembered why she and Becky had ceased to be friends, and she preferred not to just now. Jude wondered how she could change the subject. There was no need. Becky returned. Jude rose to her feet.

'Paul doesn't seem too keen on my being here,' she said. 'Tell me if you think I ought to go?'

'Perhaps it would be better if . . .'

'I know,' she said. 'Come to my house instead. Now, if you like.'

'Oh!' Becky seemed grateful, but uncertain.

'Can I come too?' piped up Amy.

'Another time,' Jude said quickly. 'I bet it's your bedtime soon.'

'Yes – you have your homework to do. And she'll never do it without me pushing her, Jude. She leaves everything to the last minute. I don't know whether it's her age or what.'

'Mu-um!'

'I know what, Jude. You can come into the kitchen with me while I prepare Paul's supper.'

'Let him make his own supper. I want you to come back to my house.'

Colour flooded Becky's cheeks. Jude walked into the living room and addressed Paul.

'United are two up, are they? I'm a City fan myself. Listen – Becky's coming back home with me. I need her advice on a couple of matters.'

Paul regarded her for a few moments, and then scratched a spot on his chin.

'Women's stuff, is it?'

'Come on, Becky,' Jude called.

Avoiding her husband's gaze, Becky hurried to the back door, where her jacket was hanging on the peg. She kissed Amy goodbye with a reminder about her homework and dinner money. She followed Jude around the side of the house and waited while the passenger door was opened for her. Jude settled in the driver's seat.

'Was I wearing a jacket when I arrived?' she asked.

Becky thought for a moment. 'Yes. You were. I know because I noticed how much it suited you. A dark green combat-style jacket.'

'Amy took it away and that's why I've forgotten it.'

'Shall I go and fetch it for you? She will have left it on the bed.'

'Give me the key. I'll get it. I'm not risking you changing your mind.'

Within a moment Jude was out of the car and opening Becky's front door. She walked through to the living room to find Amy. As she got there, Paul turned to see who it was, the telephone receiver held tight to his ear. He looked shocked – obviously she should have announced her presence more effectively.

'I left my jacket,' Jude explained.

'I'll ring you back,' Paul said, replaced the receiver, then shouted 'Amy! Our visitor wants her jacket.'

There was an uneasy silence until Amy appeared with the jacket and Jude slipped it on.

'Thanks, Amy. 'Bye!'

77

Amy responded by reaching up to Jude and giving her a kiss. She was surprised, but realised instantly that this was what children did. The softness of Amy's lips on her cheeks revived far-off memories. Meanwhile Paul watched them, unsmiling.

Becky was certain that she would have to pay the price for her adventure. It would mark the end, no doubt, of the period of peace they had been enjoying. But she wouldn't allow these thoughts to trouble her now. Tonight she was off duty, and on her way to Jude's house.

'It's the end of the terrace,' Jude said, as they reached the crest of the hill.

'You've got such a long garden!' Becky exclaimed. 'Do you like gardening?'

'I quite like watching other people garden. Really I chose it for the cats. I'm going to let it grow into a wilderness so they can play at being in the jungle.'

'Let's hope your neighbours don't object.'

'Actually, I rather hope they do.'

'Jude!'

'I've already had a run-in with my next-door neighbour about parking, Aida's had a close encounter with his Hound of the Baskervilles, and to cap it all he plays the piano really badly every evening. I'm sure he does it on purpose.'

'How awful! What's his name? Do I know him?'

'Ian Fulwell. A graduate of the Count Dracula charm school. But enough of him. Here we are!' Jude switched on a light and Becky looked eagerly inside.

There was no hallway; they walked straight into the capacious, meticulously tidy, square living room with its oak beams and large fireplace. There was a staircase on Becky's left, and the kitchen was through the back. It was just the right size for a single person. Jude's settee was navy, set off with a few carefully positioned cream cushions. Newspapers and dental catalogues were stacked to one side. A large, gleaming, black hi-fi dominated one corner of the room. As Jude switched on the various lamps, more of the room became visible. Becky saw the photograph of Phyllis Jackson, and then a tall phallic-shaped object covered in hessian.

'What on earth is that?' she asked.

'Cat scratching post. Not one of my most successful purchases. They still prefer the back of the settee.' Now Becky saw a small, long-haired cat peering at them from one corner of the settee.

'Aida,' supplied Jude. 'Ludmilla's over there.' She pointed to a low bookcase and another large tabby-and-white cat was lying on top of it, her tail hanging down one side. 'Now what's it to be? I have some vodka, some tonic, and some cans of beer in the fridge. Or we can be really boring and have some coffee.'

'I wouldn't mind some coffee,' Becky said.

Jude disappeared into the kitchen. Becky hesitated; she wasn't sure whether to follow her. She didn't want to impose herself. And yet it wouldn't be imposing herself. Jude was her oldest friend and she felt as close to her as ever. They could almost be sisters – *were* sisters, in effect. They more or less grew up together, and you never lose that, Becky thought, as she moved around, casting her eyes over the objects in Jude's living room, her copy of the *Guardian* with its half-full crossword, an empty CD case, a terracotta oil burner. Meeting Jude again had made her feel authenticated. The memories of her childhood were so distant now they seemed like stories she told herself. Jude coming back like this proved they weren't stories.

It pleased her also that Jude still looked young. Recently Becky had been forced to deal with several stray grey hairs, extracting them with eyebrow tweezers, and it had hurt like hell. She called the lines around her eyes laughter lines, but knew a euphemism when she heard one. Since she and Jude were of an age, and Jude looked good, it was conceivable that she still looked good too. Not that looks were at all important. It was a shame it was all other people had to judge you by.

The other cheering thing was how her attraction towards

Jude had not faded. She remembered how exciting it was when they first made friends, and Becky could hardly believe that Jude had chosen her, out of everyone. She was content to be her sidekick, to bathe in her reflected glory. It was odd that she should still feel that way. She couldn't wait to introduce her to Denise and Karen. It was going to be wonderful, having Jude back again.

At that moment she appeared, holding two mugs of coffee. She placed them on an occasional table and went over to the hi-fi to put some music on.

'Anyone for tenors?' asked Jude.

Soon the ringing sound of Pavarotti filled the room. She turned him down a little and came to sit on the settee. Becky drank her in with her eyes. When she was young, Jude used to be a gawky little thing, always dressed in hand-knitted cardigans buttoned up tightly. Now her gawkiness was fashionable, and Jude had accentuated it by her urchin-style haircut. Becky envied her that fine bone structure and the bright intelligence in her eyes. How strange that she should still be single! She was dying to find out why, and began to cast about for a question that would prompt her friend, but not sound too rude. *How come you're still single?* might be as good a start as any. Jude interrupted her train of thought.

'So what do you think of my house?'

Becky looked around and thought the lounge looked something like one of those model rooms in IKEA, very stylish, but not suggestive of life. 'It's beautiful,' she said.

'Yes; I fell in love with the place as soon as I saw it. It really was a "got-to-have". I didn't even risk trying to negotiate a lower price.'

But Becky wasn't listening. She was trying to imagine what it would be like to live in this house, and thought it could be quite pleasant, if the fire was blazing, and a good film was on the TV, but it would be lonely. Becky couldn't imagine living without anyone else. You would think of something to say, and there would be nobody around to say it to. You would end up talking to yourself. You would spend your time thinking why it was you were living alone, and feeling none too good about it. The way that Jude pretended to be happy was impressive, but it had to be an act. Just had to be.

'I'm going to have to do some things to the kitchen when I've settled in a bit more. I'd like to re-tile – both the floor and the walls.'

'By yourself?'

'I can't afford builders.'

'I'm sure Paul will give you a hand.'

Jude looked at her blandly and Becky felt a little uneasy.

'Do you ever go back to Rochdale, Jude?'

'Mum lived there right up until she went into the hospice. Then I had to sell the house. So I've seen quite a bit of the old place. It's changed a lot, and not necessarily for the better. The town centre is pretty dead.'

'It wasn't that lively when we were there,' Becky added.

'That didn't bother me,' Jude said.

Becky knew what she meant. The truth was, Becky was the lively one. *She* went to parties, to the clubs, had boyfriends. She was the one who read *Jackie*, followed the advice given, experimented with dieting and false eyelashes, studying every aspect of her appearance. Jude just stayed at home and studied. Full stop. Becky often had to defend her to the other girls, although there were occasions when it was difficult to do that, and she'd just stood by when people joked about Jude. Remembering that made her feel awkward. She would make up for it now.

'I bet you have an exciting time now – being independent and single.'

'Never a dull moment.'

Was Jude being sarcastic? Becky wasn't sure. She remembered Jude asking her before to find her a man. Becky became unbearably curious.

'Do you have a boyfriend now?'

'No,' said Jude. 'No one in particular.'

'So you do have men friends?'

'Difficult not to, when fifty per cent of one's acquaintances are male.'

'Is there anyone who stands out?'

'I once knew a three-legged sailor with a hare lip—' Jude stopped as she saw the expression on Becky's face. 'Sorry. I know you want me to be serious. I have had the odd relationship. Number one lasted until he discovered he was allergic to cats; two was good looking but knew it; three was addicted to breath fresheners – he was certainly bracing to kiss; four—'

'Have you ever been in love, Jude?'

'There isn't such a thing.'

'I was in love with Paul.'

Jude looked incredulous and Becky felt defensive.

'How can you say there isn't such a thing as love when so many books and stories have been written about it?'

'Let's get real. Love is just an amalgam of the sex urge, the desire to procreate and the fear of loneliness. I don't have any of those.'

Becky didn't believe her. 'Well, I've been in love lots of times. When I first met Paul, he swept me off my feet. It felt so wonderful to be wanted in that way. I had to have my tonsils out about three weeks after we met, and he came to see me every visiting hour, bringing me so many flowers I had to share them with the other patients. The fact I was in hospital and barely able to croak a greeting didn't put him off. He loved me too. I knew deep inside that we would end up married – I had a premonition. It was as if it was all meant to be.'

'This thing is bigger than the both of us,' Jude mugged.

'I'm just a girl who can't say no!'

'One enchanted evening—!' Jude broke into song now. 'You may see a stranger . . . across a—'

'—crowded room. And suddenly you find – how does it go after that?'

'That men are such a bind? Sorry, Becky. Ignore me. I'm just a crotchety old spinster at heart.'

Becky forgave her instantly. She couldn't remember a time she'd felt less inhibited. Being with Jude again was wonderful. 'Anyway, you're not a crotchety old spinster. You're young and more attractive than ever. You ought to be in a relationship.'

'But I am. I'm in a relationship with you, and there are several other women back in Manchester who are good friends, who you must meet as soon as possible. There's Alex who I play squash with, Laura who I met at Dental College, and Ann—'

'That's not what I meant.'

'I know. But believe me when I tell you I prefer my women friends. They're loyal, uncritical, with no hidden agendas, unlike the men I know. Don't look so headmistressy at me, Becky! I do know what I'm talking about. Oh, all right, men do have their uses, but once you've got yourself a DIY manual and an implement to help you unblock the toilet—'

'Jude!'

Becky was delighted at her irreverence. It reminded her of a time when she was irreverent too.

'My dear, I am a lost cause. Now let's talk about you. Are you happily married?'

'As happy as most people. Paul is the dominant type, and I'm relatively easy going. It works after a fashion. At least it's a stable environment for Amy, and financially we're all secure. These things do matter. You see, a workable marriage is all about learning to be tolerant.'

'So what exactly do you have to tolerate?'

'Well, like all men, Paul's a little short-tempered. All that travelling at he has to do, and the responsibility of running his own business – I don't envy him, I can tell you. And he has a way of teasing me, but that's just his sense of humour.'

'And what does he tolerate in you?'

'Quite a bit. I talk too much, I'm constantly worrying about Amy and I'm hopeless in the house – a sort of female Frank Spencer.'

'And he tolerates all that? I'm impressed!'

Becky felt decidedly ill at ease. Jude's comment seemed

barbed. She wanted her to stop probing. There were certain stones better left unturned. If Jude was married herself, or even in a relationship, she would understand this. For now, she would deflect the conversation back to Jude.

'I'm so glad we've met again,' Becky said. 'Let's not talk about men and talk about us.'

'Hear, hear!' said Jude.

'Are you happy being a dentist?'

'Pretty much. It's harder work than people think, but it's useful work. I like the contact with the public.'

'Did you ever want to be a doctor?'

'My father was a doctor,' Jude said laconically. 'I suppose I had the feeling that my mother would have preferred me to do something different. Becky – just listen to this!'

Jude swept her arm in the direction of the hi-fi, and Becky heard Pavarotti sing something or other with a thrilling resonance. The music sounded familiar and she wondered if it had been on an advertisement.

'Do you like opera?' she asked Jude.

'I adore it. All that power and passion – when you listen to opera singers, you *know* that there's hope for the human race. Whenever I feel too jaded and cynical, I listen to Kiri te Kanawa or Placido Domingo.'

'I don't remember you liking opera at school.'

'I didn't see my first opera until the sixth form, and we didn't hang around together then.'

What Jude had said was true; their friendship hadn't survived their third year at secondary school. Something rather unpleasant had happened, and Becky felt its presence in the air between them. Ought she to defuse the situation by referring to it?

'You never liked classical music – you were a David Bowie fan, weren't you?' Jude continued. 'You bought the Ziggy Stardust album, but your parents wouldn't let you play it when they were around. So you had to come to my house.'

It was strange to think that Jude still remembered that. Becky was flattered. She couldn't think of anyone else who took such a degree of interest in her that they would remember any of her preferences. She knew with utter certainty that she must not let Jude go again. This time she would put Jude first.

'Is there anything I can do to help you settle in?' Becky asked, wanting to put her resolution into effect immediately. 'If you need to go shopping for things, I can go with you, or if you have anything delivered when you're working, you can give me the key and I can let people in.'

'That's great,' Jude said. 'I think I'll take you up on that.'

'And I'll introduce you to my friends, and if you want to go to an opera, you can take me. That's if you explain it all, of course.'

'I'd love to, Becky! I tell you what – I haven't thrown out the Sunday papers. I'll have a look to see if anything's on in Leeds or Manchester. And if there is, I'll book for us.'

Jude bounded off the settee, and the little cat poked her head out to follow Jude with her eyes. The cat raised itself, stretched into an arc, then sprung off the settee to follow her owner.

Becky felt happy. She and Jude would be friends again; she wanted it, and clearly Jude wanted it too. She took up her suggestion of the opera immediately. Becky could not help but compare her to Denise, who made out that she was doing her a favour by agreeing to go on the creative writing course. Jude acted simply as if she wanted Becky's company.

She would pursue this friendship, no matter what Paul said. It wasn't as if she were a child. She was a child when she had that disagreement with Jude, and perhaps now was the time to deal with it. Then they could start with a clean slate. Jude returned, reading aloud from a paper.

'Yes. *The Marriage of Figaro*. At the Palace. The second week in June. Thursday, Friday and Saturday. Thursday is your writing class – which day shall I try for?'

'Saturday would be nice. Tell me as soon as possible and I'll let Paul know, so he doesn't book a match at the golf club.'

'You do that,' Jude said.

'I hope he won't mind spending an evening without me.

I've learnt you shouldn't always put men first. I've grown up since we were fourteen. I remember when Joe from the fifth year asked me out, and we'd arranged to go for a Wimpy. I couldn't get in touch with you to explain what had happened, and I stood you up. I'm sorry.'

Becky felt nervous. This was why their friendship had suddenly ended. At the time she thought Jude was unreasonable – surely anyone would prefer a *date* to an evening with a girlfriend – even Jude herself would. Becky had thought it was tight of Jude to drop her so suddenly. But now she was prepared to take the blame, as long as they could exorcise this particular ghost.

'You did let me down, rather,' Jude said, her voice neutral.

'The funny thing was, I didn't even like him that much. But I was so thrilled at being asked out by someone, I couldn't bear to say no. It was very immature of me, but I wasn't the brightest of things. I'd have had a much better time if I'd have gone with you to the Wimpy Bar.'

Jude looked impassive. Was she thinking about something else, or was she still upset? Surely not – it was well over twenty years ago!

'I did ring you – every half hour, but there was no answer at your house. You hadn't told me you were at your grandfather's. I was selfish, wasn't I? I should have told Joe that I couldn't go out with him that night. But I didn't have his telephone number, so it would have meant standing *him* up.' Becky realised she was becoming defensive, and it was so silly, because she'd only been a child then, and everybody makes mistakes.

'You forgive me, don't you?' she asked.

'There's nothing to forgive,' Jude said. 'How much can you afford? Circle is best, but the tickets can be pricey. It's rather cramped up in the gods.'

'I'm happy to pay around twenty pounds,' Becky said, feeling as if she had been gently moved on.

'Excellent. Me too. If I finish work early we can eat beforehand.'

'Would you like me to cook?'

'No way. We'll go out and find a good café-bar.'

'But one that serves banana milkshakes.'

'You remember I used to like those!' Jude exclaimed.

'Of course. Whenever I make one for Amy, I think of you.'

'Does she like them?'

'Loves them.'

Jude grinned from ear to ear, and Becky was glad to have made her happy. The evening had only just begun, and she knew now they would have so much to talk about. She could hardly wait to start.


Jude lay in bed, her head propped up on a cushion, her knees bent, and a biography lay by her side, abandoned. Her thoughts interested her more than other people's printed words.

She had come to Mytholm Bridge to make a new life for herself, and yet she had found her old life. All the world's religions had got it wrong; God wasn't love, but the mistress of irony. She was a trickster. Jude's eyes strayed to where her two cats lay entwined together in their basket, and for a moment she wished she could be a cat herself, and get down amongst them and burry herself in the rise and fall of their warm, furry bodies.

Seeing Becky again brought all of her childhood back. It brought her mother back, it re-animated Rochdale, it made Jude feel whole. Becky was part of her, and all the more so because there was no one else now. She loved her gentleness and eagerness to please, but it irritated her too. Becky always needed some sort of prop or crutch. She was the same old Becky – loyal, affectionate, attentive. She was wasted on that bastard of a husband.

Jude's mind filled with a series of exclamation marks. It was hard to believe men like that still existed. The way he gave her orders! The way he ignored her! The way she took it! What power did he have over her that she should submit to being treated like that? Was it his sexual prowess? Disgusting even to think of Paul in that context. Did he frighten her? Did she fear being alone? Jude vowed to find out.

And what effect did all of this have on little Amy? Jude admitted to herself that she had taken to the girl. Becky was lucky to have had a daughter. There's nothing as special as the relationship between a mother and a daughter. One day, Jude thought, I would like to have a daughter. Technically, she told herself, I could. There's no reason to suppose I'm not fertile. But until someone perfects the science of parthenogenesis, I'll have to do without.

Or perhaps, she thought, switching off her bedside lamp, and curling up in her bed, I shall get a virtual daughter on my computer. You can get virtual pets, so why not virtual kids? They could be programmed to interrupt you during work and demand to be fed, or ask for help with a French translation. Until you got heartily sick of them and grounded them in a corner of your screen. Perhaps I'll patent it, she thought.

It was the sort of joke that Becky would enjoy. Jude was glad she'd found her again. She'd not changed. Still apologising for everything. She'd apologised for the time she'd stood her up for Joe Patterson. Jude reluctantly recalled that time; it had been a chilly November evening, just after the clocks had been put back. They'd planned to meet outside the library. At first she wasn't worried; Becky was often late, and the steps of Rochdale library were perfectly familiar to her, even if it was dark. Her grandfather had offered to wait with her, but Jude had refused. She was on home territory, and her grandfather's Morris Minor stunk of Dutch pipe tobacco, and it made her feel rather ill.

After half an hour, she began to get concerned. Some boys passed her and called out something she couldn't decipher, but it succeeded in making her feel uncomfortable. She wondered whether Becky was ill, and had been unable to contact her since

Jude had been at her grandparents' in Alderley Edge all day. There was a phone box opposite the library and Jude quickly crossed the road to use it. She rang Becky's number but there was no answer. Jude was puzzled and couldn't think of an explanation to fit the facts. So she decided to ring home and see if her mother was back from London. No reply there either.

Jude replaced the receiver and opened the door of the telephone box, eager to see if Becky had arrived in the meantime. There was no one on the library steps. At least it wasn't raining. Jude decided she would wait a little longer. And then—

Jude opened her eyes with a start. She didn't want to think about it – certainly not now, when she was trying to fall asleep. With an effort of will she brought herself back to the present. There was a patient coming in tomorrow with a crown on her front tooth, and the x-ray had shown that the post had broken. That was why the crown kept coming loose. Now, she could try to drill the post and loosen it further, although there was a risk – Jude yawned – there was a risk she would go through – or she could take out the tooth – she'd need to think – and she drifted into sleep.

# Chapter Five

On Thursday morning Becky unlocked her father's door with the usual amount of trepidation. One worried so much about elderly relatives living alone. You never knew what you might find when you arrived. This time it was the sound of gunfire; Dad was watching an old western. He twisted round in his chair as she entered and smiled at her.

'How are you, Dad?' Becky asked, taking off her coat and putting it over the back of a chair.

'You get out of this town for good, and you're not taking her with you!'

'Turn it down.'

His eyes still on the screen, Becky's father lifted the remote control and switched off the sound. The picture still flickered in the shady room.

'Not so good,' he replied.

'The arthritis?' Becky looked around the house to see what needed doing. Certainly the front room would benefit from a hoover; all around the sides of the armchair were sweet wrappers where her father had discarded them. It was painful for him to bend down, but he enjoyed his barley sugars. There was a thin layer of dust on the mantelpiece and dirty dishes on the table.

'Aye. I'm stiff this morning. Right stiff.'

His eyes still scanned the set absently. Becky began to clear the table and thought that she might take the tablecloth with the rest of the washing. If only it didn't smell so badly in the house. There was a musty, dusty smell, mingling with the sweetish aroma of old food. The little back kitchen was plain, with a cooker and fridge that looked as if it had come from a second-hand furniture shop, although Dad had owned them as long as Becky could remember. She found her father's house depressing, and it always made her appreciate her own home the more. She felt guilty because she had not suggested to Paul that her father move in with them, although he'd veto the idea immediately. But at least, she thought, he wasn't in a home. That was what he dreaded most of all. The fact that her visits helped keep him out of one assuaged her guilt. So she did not resent the frequent trips to Rochdale to see to his needs.

'Guess who I've met up with?' Becky announced, as she brought the duster in with her from the kitchen.

'Aye?'

'Jude Jackson! Do you remember Jude? She used to be my best friend – Phyllis Jackson's daughter.'

'Oh aye. Those meals-on-wheels lasses – they're no good, the ones who do it these days. I were upstairs when they called yesterday, and I couldn't get down, and she went away and left it on the doorstep. On the doorstep.'

Becky carried on dusting. She'd rather hoped that talking of Jude would take her father out of himself, but like most old people, his horizons had narrowed, and his bodily needs were all he ever thought about. This had the advantage of meaning that he was never bored; every twinge in his joints was fascinating to him, every meal that he ate was of all-consuming interest, and if she didn't stop him, he'd have regaled her with the details of his bowel movements.

'Do you want me to hoover now, or shall I do upstairs?'

Her father's eyes were still focused on the TV. 'Aye. Do upstairs. There's some clothes as needs washing. Then you can make me a brew.'

'I've bought you some Bakewell tarts,' Becky said.

'Good lass.'

He still had a sweet tooth, Becky thought, pleased to receive approbation from her father. She was a daddy's girl. Always had been. Perhaps it was the result of her parents' arguments. So many of these could have been avoided if Becky's mum had tried a little harder to please her husband. It wasn't as if Dad was impossible to manage. As a girl Becky knew her father's little ways, would anticipate when he wanted a cigarette and look for his lighter; she'd fetch him the evening paper as soon as it arrived because she knew he liked to look at it before anyone else; she took pains to be quiet in the morning because he always woke in a bad temper.

His bedroom smelt even worse than the rest of the house. That was partly because he left his dirty washing lying around. The first thing Becky did as she got into the room was to heave open the window, and breathe in some fresh air. Now to work. Into the bin liner that she'd brought with her she scooped up Y-fronts discarded on the threadbare carpet, an old shirt and some Argyle socks.

Years of doing this had taught Becky how to cope. She waved goodbye to fastidiousness and distracted herself by thinking about something else entirely. Jude had had her in stitches last night over the phone, with her account of the nervous patient who'd come into the surgery with a hypnotherapy tape made up especially for tooth extractions. As she was yanking out a molar, a voice was leaking from the Walkman intoning 'You are a calm person. You are not afraid.' Becky had attempted to defend the patient, but Jude had said it was incredible, the things that people believed. Typical Jude. Always the realist.

Becky entered her father's bathroom and set about with the bleach and J-cloths. The seat in the bath needed a good scrub. Becky wondered what the creative writing class tonight would be like. Now it was so close, she felt somewhat presumptuous for signing up, when she hadn't so much as written a word for years. Except, of course, the story about a lighthouse that Amy was asked to do for English homework, and was in tears over. Becky had written a page or so in the style of an eleven-year-old, and was rewarded with a B-. It was a blow to her ego from which she had not yet recovered.

What I shall do is write a romance, she suddenly decided. In the style of *Jane Eyre*. I can set it around Mytholm. The walk she had taken with Denise and everyone came back to her and she imagined the same location, but with herself and her hero, tall, classically good looking, firm jaw, tender expression, his hand grasping hers – she squirted the Toilet Duck under the rim of the toilet – and then he stops to kiss her.

*'I love you,' he says to her.* Becky straightened herself, pressing the Toilet Duck to her bosom.

*'The rest doesn't matter,' he says. 'My life is meaningless without you. I want you for my own.'*

*'Yes,' she said simply, trembling, aware of the significance of the moment. There would be no going back.*

*'O my darling! God bless you and reward you!'*

Becky put down the toilet duck, and wiped a tear from the corner of her eye. Of course, when she got home and tried to write this down, it would all have fled from her mind, and there would just be shopping lists there. Yet she was gripped by a desire to use writing as a way out of the present; the idea of getting so wrapped up in a story that you forgot everything – yes, that was what she wanted.

She returned to the bedroom to change the sheets on her father's bed, still lost in a reverie of an alternative life for herself. It was like a fragrance that loitered in the air, sweetening the present. Not sweetening it quite enough; her father's bed reeked of the musty aroma of sweat and God knows what else. She worked quickly now, keen to get out of the room. She emptied the vanity bin by the bedside table into a black bin liner and carried it downstairs.

'Tea and cake now,' she announced to her father. 'And I've brought you a steak pie for your supper. I'm putting it in the fridge.'

Back in the kitchen she opened it, and was greeted by the smell of sour milk. She identified the rogue carton, and threw the contents down the sink. The difficulty for her father after the divorce was that he had never been used to looking after himself. Most of his generation was like that. Her father was in his seventies now, and what did he know of equality of the sexes? And did it matter? Becky was able to care for him.

'Here we are, Dad. Come here – give me that remote control!'

Becky switched off the set, and brought her father a cup of tea, accompanied by a side plate with two Bakewell tarts, each with a little glacé cherry in the centre. She placed them on a little table by his side. He bit into the tart and ate noisily.

'So what have you been doing with yourself?'

'The chiropodist came,' he muttered, spitting out cake crumbs. 'She's been seeing to my in-growing toenail.'

Becky nodded approvingly. 'And have you been out?'

'Aye. To the corner shop and back. That's as far as I can manage. I can't get to the Over Sixties.'

This was the club he went to, in the Methodist Hall. Becky was troubled that he'd been missing meetings.

'Now that won't do. I don't see why you can't get a taxi. I'm going to leave you a fiver, Dad, and I want you to use it for the fare. I don't want to think of you staying in all the time.' Becky opened her bag and took out a note. Her father watched her, and stretched out his hand to take it.

'You're a good lass. You're the only one left who cares about me. All the others have scarpered. I don't know what I'd do without you.'

'You won't have to do without me.'

'Thank the Lord you're not like your mother. I think of her and it gives me grief.' He took the second Bakewell tart. Becky thought it was sad that he still dwelt on his failed marriage. She decided to distract him.

'Amy's made a new friend. A girl called Petra. She's the daughter of a friend of mine. Amy's been a lot more cheerful lately. And she didn't do too badly in her maths test, either.'

'You should bring her round more. Why don't you bring her round? She's a pretty young thing.'

Becky was delighted at this praise of Amy. 'I will do. It's just we've been busy lately, what with one thing and another. Did I tell you I'm starting a writing class tonight?'

'Oh, aye? What's that in aid of?'

'Just a bit of fun.'

'Fun. I don't know what that is any more. I've not been to a match for I don't know how long.'

'Isn't there a way we could manage it? I'd go with you, and Amy too. I can ring the ground. Do you remember the first time you took me to the Wanderers?'

Her father nodded. Becky remembered it vividly. She couldn't have been more than ten. Stuart, her brother, had been away at Scout camp, and so Becky used his season ticket. She'd sat with her Dad in the stands, wearing a Wanderers scarf, and it was cold, so she put her hand in her father's big coat pocket. She was the only girl for miles and she felt like an honoured guest. When the Wanderers scored for the third time Dad had lifted her up in the air and everyone had cheered. She still supported them, even though Paul and Amy laughed at her. Her father was quite a romantic figure of a man in those days. It saddened her to see him now, but she would be true to him, even if no one else was.

'All those stairs,' her Dad said. 'I couldn't manage all those stairs.'

'They must have provision for disabled spectators.'

'Aye, but what if I had one of my turns?'

'They have the Saint John's Ambulance.'

'I wouldn't want to be treated by one of that lot.'

'They're properly qualified.'

Becky's dad raised his eyebrows. 'Oh, aye? Like those jumped-up nurses they have at those homes? I were speaking to Walter Holland t'other day, and he were telling me about a chap who'd been just three weeks in one of them places – aye, just three weeks – and he were found dead in his bed. A heart attack, and nobody had read the signs. He were all alone when he died.' Her father's voice quavered. She didn't want him getting maudlin. Becky changed the subject again.

'Jude Jackson is a dentist now – she's Amy's dentist. Amy might be needing a brace.'

Becky could see her father feeling his teeth with his tongue.

'They don't fit as well as they used to,' he said. 'I get crumbs underneath them.'

'Would you like me to take you to the dentist?'

'How do I know they won't make them worse?' he said suspiciously.

'Well, as long as you can manage. Look, Dad, I'd love to stay and chat, but I promised Amy I'd pick her up from school.'

'You've not been here five minutes.'

'Come on! I've given your upstairs a thorough spring clean, and I'll be back again on Monday.' Becky picked up her coat. 'Tell you what – I'll bring you up to my house for an afternoon. It'll be good for you to have a change of scene.'

Her father gave her a pathetic look. Becky grinned at him, opened the front door, and breathed in the fresh air with gratitude.

'Bye!' she called.


'I only have another five minutes,' Denise said. 'I promised Petra I'd pick her up from school.'

Karen didn't mind. There was a lot one could pack into five minutes.

'I've never been to bed with a painter and decorator before. It's the foreplay, Denise. That's what's so exciting. He brought round these body paints and drew two huge sunflowers on my breasts. The brush he used was so ticklish! And then, below, he painted a face – he used my navel as the mouth, did a nose and eyes below it, and said there was no need to do the hair—'

'I don't know how you can tell me about that while you're waiting for your boys to come out of school.'

Karen chose to ignore that remark.

'He couldn't even wait for the paint to dry before adding the finishing touches – if you catch my drift. Talk about a multiple orgasm – I had to use a calculator to keep track. By the time we'd finished, the paint was getting everywhere. So we went into the shower together to get rid of it all. Now the shower attachment—'

'I'm so glad for you, Karen. I think there's a stage in every woman's life when those sort of sexual gymnastics fulfil a need. I think maturity comes when you learn to control those animal impulses.'

Karen shot Denise a covert look. So she hadn't been to bed with Paul yet. That was all to the good.

'So have you decided what to do about Paul?' she asked her.

'I'm going to talk to Becky.'

'You can't do that!'

'Don't worry. I won't tell her everything. But I've been thinking, Karen. I was thinking all last night, in fact, instead of sleeping. I can't sleep while I'm living in this emotional maelstrom. I watched dawn break and tried to balance everyone's needs – Paul's needs, Becky's and lastly mine. Oh, and George's. And I realised finally that my relationship with Paul is going nowhere. That was what I was trying to explain when you began to tell me all about Jim.'

'I'm sorry,' Karen said. She was. At any moment the headmistress would ring the bell, and Seth and Bobby would come racing out across the playground, she would have to leave Denise's Brava and take the boys with her to the Co-op to get something for supper. She didn't want to do that until she'd found out what Denise was up to.

'I can't betray Becky. She's my best friend. We brought up our children together. It would almost be as if I was being unfaithful to myself. I just couldn't do it. I made myself think how I would feel in Becky's position.'

This was a new Denise. Karen's brow furrowed in puzzlement. What had brought this on? Had Paul given her the boot?

'In Becky's position, I think I would like to *know* that my husband was unhappy. I'd want to be able to do something about it. I think I have to find a way of implying to Becky that Paul has needs that are being overlooked. It's what a true friend would do.'

It was the same old Denise.

'Be careful. Don't hurt her.'

'You can trust me, although it may be difficult. We've planned to go out after this writing class tonight. We'll be alone as luckily this new friend of hers isn't coming.'

'Yes, Jude. Becky mentioned her to me. She's a dentist, isn't she?'

'Sounds dull. Have you met her?'

'Not yet. Here come the children. Thanks for the lift, Denise. 'Bye! Don't do anything I wouldn't do!'

'Is there *anything* you wouldn't do?' Denise muttered.

What does one wear for a writing class? Becky opened her wardrobe and looked at it in despair. Everything she owned was so mumsy and conventional. There comes a point in a woman's life when Marks and Spencers has everything that you need – knickers, separates and ready-made desserts. There was nothing that Becky could wear that hit the right note of eccentricity or creativity that she thought might be suitable for the occasion. If only she had one of those fisherman's smock tops, or a long floaty skirt and Isadora Duncan-style scarf. Even a pair of gold-framed bifocals would help. Becky's glasses – a special offer from Specsavers – were depressingly ordinary.

Becky smiled to herself. She cornered the market in ordinariness, she knew. She stepped out of her jeans and into a Black Watch tartan skirt, and teamed it with a roll-neck black sweater. She sat down at the dressing table and opened her cosmetic pouch. Some make-up would probably be in order, especially since she'd suggested to Denise they should go to the pub afterwards. Some eye-shadow and—

'Mum! Where are you?'

'In here.'

The bedroom door was pushed open and Amy appeared.

'Can I come in and talk?'

'Of course. But don't mind me. I've got to get ready to go out.' Becky found a brown mascara at the bottom of the pouch, investigated it to see if it was still working, then took off her glasses in order to apply it. Meanwhile Amy stood by the dressing table and began to finger the make-up that Becky had laid out in front of her.

'Stop fiddling!'

'Sorry.'

'It's just that it puts me off. I can see you out of the corner of my eye. What's wrong?'

'It's school.'

Becky tensed slightly. Amy found certain subjects difficult, and she dreaded it when her daughter came home and reported lower than average marks.

'What about school?'

'Well, it was after games. There was like this awful smell in the changing room. Everyone was looking round – it was ever so embarrassing. I was getting changed with Petra – she's in the netball team although she said she wasn't going to carry on with it because the teacher won't let her play in attack where she's best, and—'

Becky switched off. As long as the problem wasn't academic, it couldn't be that important. Most afternoons Amy came home and rabbited on about school and Becky only listened with half an ear. Not that Amy ever guessed.

'She's very good at acting too and she could have a part in the play if she wanted. She said she'd only audition if I did and—'

Becky put her glasses back on, found some peach-coloured lipstick and applied it carefully, then looked at herself in the mirror. Something wasn't quite right. Perhaps it was just because she wasn't used to wearing make-up. She blinked with the unaccustomed weight of the mascara.

'You look nice. Like I was saying before, there was this awful smell, and Petra whispered to me that she knew who it was. It was Sophie. And it was, because Petra told me to walk over to her and it was stronger in her corner.'

Did writers wear make-up? Jackie Collins certainly did, and so did Joan Collins. But maybe if you were a very serious writer, you didn't.

'Petra said I should tell her but I didn't want to. But I said we should write a letter to a problem page about what to do if your friend smells so we wrote it at break.'

Becky stood up and slipped on her shoes. She looked at herself in the mirror. She would have to do. She needed to leave in the next few minutes.

'Sophie came in and she said, what were we doing? Petra tried to cover it up, but she read the letter. It didn't have her name in it or anything, but Petra was giggling so much I think she must have guessed. I said it wasn't her, though.'

'You must be kind to Sophie, pet,' Becky said. 'I've really got to go now. You must go to bed when Daddy says. Paul! I'm off. Amy must go to bed at nine.'

Becky hoped that penetrated into his study.

'You must go to bed at nine,' she told Amy.

'I don't have to be Sophie's best friend, do I?'

'Of course you don't. It's not as if you're married to her. At your age you should be friendly with a lot of people. Petra is a nice girl.'

'I know. Have a good time.'

'I will.' Becky kissed her daughter goodbye and flew down the stairs.

Becky arrived at the Community Centre with only a few moments to spare. It was better that way, because being in a hurry stops you being nervous. She made her way to the lounge unbuttoning her jacket and hoping Denise hadn't let her down.

But there she was, sitting at one end of a long, conference-style table, in a clingy black dress and an expensive scarf draped round her neck. If Becky was a potboiler, Denise was definitely sex and shopping. There were a few other would-be writers seated around the table and Becky scanned them to see if there was anyone she knew. Surprisingly there wasn't. There were a couple of elderly ladies, an old man, a couple of younger ones and two or three women of her age. None of them looked like writers at all, except possibly for the young man who had his hair scraped back in a ponytail and had just the expression of brooding intensity that denoted a potential literary genius. Becky took a seat next to Denise and hung her jacket over the back of it.

'What a shower!' whispered Denise.

Then there was another latecomer. Becky looked up automatically. Her heart missed a beat. There was something about this man that was unutterably familiar. No – it wasn't that. She quickly lowered her gaze. This new student was just one of the most attractive men she'd ever seen. It wasn't because he was conventionally good looking. On the contrary; there was almost an ugliness about his features – his nose was a fraction too large, his mouth wide, but his eyes – they were what drew Becky – his eyes were alive. Brown, intelligent, laughing eyes. A Booker prize winner at least. She glanced at Denise to assess her reaction to this literary god, but her friend was searching through some papers in her attaché case.

The new arrival made his way to the top of the table and placed on it a shabby brown leather briefcase.

'Hello. I'm Chris Scott,' he said. 'I'm your tutor.'

Her tutor!

He looked around the table and did Becky imagine it, or did his eyes rest on hers for one delicious moment? She imagined it; for now he smiled, but it was at one of the other women.

'Hello, Ann!'

Becky felt jealous of her.

'Well, since it's past eight, we might as well begin. I know a couple of you, but for those of you who don't know me—' His eyes met Becky's – 'I've taught creative writing in a number of places and I write short stories, including one that was broadcast on Radio Four not too long ago. I'm working on my first novel. I've heard it said you can't teach creative writing, but—'

His voice was deep, cultivated, but with a trace of a Yorkshire accent. He wore a navy sweater. His presence was utterly compelling. Becky found herself tracing the lineaments of his face, her gaze travelling over the contours of his chin, his cheekbones, the jut of his eyebrows. Then the class laughed. He had made a joke and Becky had been so engrossed in her perusal of him, she had stopped paying attention to what he had been saying!

This discovery brought her to her senses. She was surprised at herself, a wife AND mother, giving a man the eye. What on earth had got into her? She was only here to learn to write. But he was gorgeous and she wasn't disposed to be too hard on herself.

'Those of you who have been to my classes before know that I like to begin with hearing a little bit about your aspirations, or preferably something you've written, to give me an idea of what you can do. Perhaps if we—'

The old man to Becky's left cleared his throat deliberately and began to speak.

'Eric Brakewell, that's me. I want to put my war reminiscences into shape.' Becky noticed there was a pile of notebooks in front of him. 'Like that *Bravo Two Zero* chappie. If you like, I'll read you a bit about when I was stationed in Selby in the RAF barracks. Or what about when I was sent down south to Canvey Island? Now I would have seen some active service but a bout of pneumonia left me a bit wheezy and I was given sick leave. I've got it all down here. If I can just find it. And I have a nice little anecdote about an evening in our Andersen shelter, and how my grandfather taught me cribbage. Or would you like—'

'Tell you what,' said Chris, grinning at him. 'You select

your favourite, and meanwhile we'll go round the rest of the group. Is that all right?'

Eric nodded, and began to search through his notebooks.

'Ann!' Chris said to the woman he knew. 'How's the novel coming on?'

'I've finally got a version of the first chapter I'm happy with.'

'Is that the version we worked on at Woodvale last year?'

'No. I've gone back to the opening I had at the Mill Bank course in 1995.'

'It had its strengths,' Chris commented.

The young man in the ponytail was a poet. He explained that he'd been working on haiku but they seemed so cluttered to him. He was looking for something simpler.

'I'll read you something I've written,' he said.

Chris nodded. The poet fixed his eyes into the middle distance and Becky was impressed to see that he'd committed his poem to memory. There was a pregnant pause.

'*Time.*' Another pause. The poet visibly relaxed. 'That's it,' he said. 'A minimalist poem. It's the space around the word that does the work.'

'Do you have any more?' Chris asked.

'I have a work in progress,' he said.

Then out of the corner of her eye Becky saw Denise raise her hand. 'I'm hoping to write a novel. I've made a beginning especially for tonight. It's not very good. I don't really think you want to hear it.'

'Please go on,' Chris said.

'It really is quite amateurish. You'll be used to hearing much better.'

'I'm sure you're wrong.'

Denise shook her head, then drew out a notebook from her bag.

'Well, here goes.

'*Diana – I can't control myself. Christ – if it wasn't for the rest of them, I'd take you now.' Phil cupped her petite, youthful face roughly in his strong, manly hands. Diana removed them. In the next room, Phil's wife, Betty, sat completely unaware, presiding over the boring, tedious dinner party. Diana could not help but remember how, the previous afternoon, Phil had come unannounced to her house, and painted her lithe, supple, naked body with a sunflower until she wriggled in ecstasy, and then he ravished her with wild, passionate abandon.'*

The two elderly ladies clapped loudly.

'I like that,' one of them said. 'I'd like to able to write like that. Wouldn't you, Vera?'

'Did that take you long to write?' Chris asked Denise.

'No. That's the amazing thing. It just came to me. It came to me in the middle of the night and I had to get up and write it all down.'

'Clearly something inspired you. Have you worked on the plot?'

'I'm trying to. At the moment I'm not sure what comes next.'

'And you?'

Becky was momentarily confused, as she had been so caught up in Denise's new-found talent. Then she realised Chris Scott was talking to her. She blushed, and wished she hadn't. He gave her an encouraging smile.

'Well, I haven't exactly written anything yet. I'm Becky. But I know what I'd like to try to write. A romance. Like Charlotte Brontë. Not that I'm comparing myself to her.' Becky stopped, feeling self-conscious.

'There's always a market for romances,' Chris said. 'How far have you got in your plans? Do you have a heroine? A hero?'

Becky was silent. She wondered if he would notice if she based her hero on him? Those lively eyes, those jutting eyebrows.

'A setting?'

'I thought I'd use Mytholm.'

'Good idea. Write about what you know. And what obstacles are your lovers going to overcome?'

Becky nervously twisted her wedding ring. 'Do they have to have an obstacle?'

'There won't be a story if they haven't. *Jane Eyre* had the first Mrs Rochester.'

'I've got a lot of thinking to do, haven't I?'

'Don't be downhearted. You've got to start somewhere. I'll show you how.'

He came from behind the table over to where Becky sat, with a sheet of paper. She felt her pulse rate increase.

'All of you will find this exercise helpful,' he said. 'Becky – take this sheet of paper and write down something your heroine says to your hero.'

Becky picked up her biro; she wrote:

—*I know I shouldn't feel this way, but I can't help it.*

Chris took the paper. 'Now I'm going to write the next line.' He wrote

—*You won't look at me. You're trembling. Have I upset you?*

'Now it's your turn.'

Becky wrote:

—*Yes. You have upset me.*

—*What is it you want to say? Don't be afraid.*

—*I love you. I've loved you from the first time I saw you. But it makes no difference. We must part.*

'Well done!' Chris said. 'You're off and running. You can all try this now. Pair up and develop some dialogue.'

As he moved away from her Becky saw that they had just been demonstrating a writing exercise. That was all. And besides, she had no right to drool over him in this fashion. It was disgraceful. She ought to put a stop to it straightaway. She'd even sneaked a glance at his fourth finger, left hand, to see if was wearing a ring – he wasn't. What on earth had got into her?

It was then that she had the idea. There was Jude instead. In jest, she had promised to find her a man. Here were the fates providing her with the choicest specimen imaginable. Right age, creative, intelligent, kind, but unashamedly masculine – he was meant for Jude. Greater love hath no friend than this. Jude should have him.

The plot. How about the plot? Obviously the hero and heroine have to meet. It was up to the author to write the script, name the place. She would do that. It was essential that she speak to Chris later, not too obviously, bring Jude into the conversation, oh, ever so subtly, intrigue him, hook him slowly in. Then a few words to Jude, not saying too much about him, and hey presto! Perhaps if she stayed behind after the class . . .

Nearly everyone had gone. Eric was putting his notebooks back into his Tesco's carrier bag, and Ann was talking to one of the other women about a writer's conference she'd attended. Chris opened his briefcase prior to putting his files away. Becky approached him.

'Time is the problem, isn't it?' she said conversationally. 'A novel takes so long, and I'm so pressed for time, what with my husband and daughter – is it the same for you? I mean, are your wife and children demanding?'

He paused, and then smiled at her with an expression that she could not understand.

'I'm not married.'

'But you're in a relationship?'

'Not at present,' he said. Becky could have punched the air with glee. Jude would have him. Then a thought struck her? What if he was gay? Most of the best-looking men are. How could she broach that subject? Ask if he was a Shirley Bassey fan?

It was at that point Denise joined them.

'Coming for a drink, Becky?'

'In a moment.'

'Where are you off to?' Chris asked.

'Where do you drink?' she countered quickly. If he said the

King's Arms, she would give up immediately. It was Mytholm's only gay pub, notorious for the types it attracted.

'The Wheatsheaf,' he told her. 'Why don't you both come along with me?'

Denise shook her head. 'Becky and I—' she began.

'We'd love to,' said Becky.


They found a table in the Wheatsheaf that wasn't too near to the juke-box and settled down with their drinks.

'It must be so difficult for you,' Denise said to Chris, tossing back her hair from her face, 'teaching a class when you know so few people will ever write anything worthwhile.'

'Worthwhile in what sense?' he asked.

'Surely you'd like to see some real success. I was wondering—' once again she tossed back her hair – 'do you think it's too soon for me to start looking for a publisher? I would hate anyone to steal a march on my ideas!'

'You'll need at least three chapters and a synopsis. You don't sound as if you've planned your novel through to the end.'

'I suppose I must.'

Chris turned to Becky. 'Are you also hoping for commercial success?'

'Well, I—' Becky began.

'Would you advise me to get an agent or go straight to a publisher?' Denise asked.

'I'd do a bit more writing first, if I were you.'

Becky was getting annoyed with Denise. Usually she tolerated her self-absorption, but now she was in the way. Feeling unusually determined, Becky seized the initiative.

'There are things that happen in life that you wouldn't believe if they were in a book,' Becky intervened. 'Just recently my best friend Jude turned up again after twenty years!'

'Had she been abroad?' Chris asked.

No. We'd just lost contact. But she's come to live in Mytholm Bridge. I tried to persuade her to come to your class, but opera is more her thing. And she's busy too – she's a dentist. She has the practice in Crown Street.'

'I think you must have a streak of sadism to want to be a dentist,' Denise interjected.

'No,' said Becky emphatically. 'Not Jude. She was wonderful with Amy and her brace. She was so gentle and reassuring. And she has such a good sense of humour.'

Denise winked at Chris. 'Jude is quite a polygon.'

'Do you mean paragon?' he suggested.

Denise laughed, but she did not sound amused. Becky thought she seemed in rather a bad mood. When Denise began to excuse herself on the grounds that she was starting work early in the morning, Becky was secretly relieved.

And then there were two.


As Denise stepped outside the Wheatsheaf, it began to rain. She scowled in irritation. It was a rotten ending to a dismal evening. She felt as if she had wasted her time; it seemed to her that if this Chris Scott knew anything about successful novel writing, he wouldn't be earning his keep by teaching creative writing in a one-horse town like Mytholm. He'd be sailing on his own yacht in the Med with the likes of Jeffrey Archer and Salman Rushdie. She was not surprised he couldn't recognise her talent.

She walked quickly towards her Brava. She thought how transparent Becky's behaviour was. She was slavering after him. Then Denise's brow cleared. All the scruples she had been having about Paul were pointless. Becky was every bit as bad as she was.

An idea was forming in Denise's mind. As yet, she was only working out its justification. Not only was Becky a flirt, but their so-called friendship was nothing but convenience. Becky had called *Jude* her best friend. It was weakness to feel so beholden to Becky.

Across the road from the car park stood a telephone booth,

unoccupied. She ignored the faint smell of cigarettes and disinfectant and pressed out the number quickly. The line was not engaged. Paul answered.

'It's Denise. I've decided. Yes. Karen will provide me with an alibi. It's what friends are for.' She laughed at something he said. 'Be good, or I might change my mind.' She replaced the receiver.

Research, she told herself. That was what it was. Her best-seller needed just the right note of authenticity. She imagined telling Melvyn Bragg all about her affair on her *South Bank Show* Special.

'My first class?' Chris pondered. 'That must have been for the Workers' Educational Association, oh, about eight years ago. Until this summer I was teaching part-time at West Yorks University – used to be the Poly.'

'So you must be a graduate then?' Becky asked, her chin propped on her hand.

'Yes. That's right. I was at Oxford.'

'Posh!' she announced, to cover her delight on Jude's behalf. He was her intellectual equal.

'I wasn't one of the posh ones,' he said, laughing. 'I was just a northern grammar-school lad. Flat cap and whippets.'

Becky laughed too, joining with him in complicity against southern stereotyping of northerners.

'No,' he continued. 'I joined the Labour Party and worked hard so as not to waste my parents' money.'

The Labour Party! Jude's mother was a Labour councillor. 'Do your parents live nearby?'

'They're both dead,' he said, in a matter-of-fact tone.

Becky tried to look sober for a moment, but it was an effort. Both of them orphans – if ever a match was made in heaven, this was it.

'They haven't died recently?' Becky was worried he might not be ready for romance, if this was the case.

'Some years ago. But I have a sister who I'm close to. She reminds me a bit of you. She was good to me when my partner left me last year.'

'Your partner? Male partner or female partner?'

'Female.' Chris looked surprised. 'My fault, I suppose. But the word "girlfriend" seems so twee when you've just turned forty.'

Becky hoped she hadn't dented his masculine pride. It was important to restore it.

'I think any woman must be mad to walk out on you!'

The smile he gave her in return made her feel quite weak. If only Jude knew what she was sacrificing for her! Becky felt a little guilty. She had not mentioned Jude for a bit.

'My friend Jude lives alone too – that is, except for her cats.'

'I have a cat,' he said.

'Really? Then you must meet Jude. Do you like opera?'

'I don't know much about it.'

'Jude will explain it to you. She loves to talk about opera. Now look – I'm having a dinner party soon. Not this weekend coming up, because I have to see my father, but the next. Jude will be there. You're invited too.'

Chris looked a little surprised, but pleased.

'Are you sure?'

'Absolutely. I'll give you all the details next week.'

'What's on the menu?' he asked, as they both rose to get their coats.

Jude, she thought, and smiled as she imagined how splendid it would be if she could wheel in a huge cake and Jude could pop out, just as in the films.

'Italian, probably,' she said.

'I'll bring some Chianti.'

'Ciao,' replied Becky, and waved as she went off towards her car.

*　　*　　*

Chris walked to the town centre, where his bus stop was situated. He joined a queue consisting of two bedraggled teenage girls. He was humming to himself.

He was feeling good. Last week he'd finally landed an agent for his new novel, and then he'd been offered some reviewing in the Yorkshire Press. Things were finally looking up. He had enjoyed himself tonight, most definitely. Becky had lifted his spirits, not the least because of her transparent attempt to match him with her friend. It was good to go out with a woman again. After Laura's sulks and vindictive farewell, Becky's sunny good nature was like spring following winter. Something about her appealed to him. It had clearly appealed to someone else too. It did not surprise him that she was married.

No, there was no harm in going to her dinner party and meeting her friend. If Becky was strictly out of bounds, this Jude wasn't. He wasn't the sort to look a gift horse in the mouth. And then his single decker bus turned into the main street.

# Chapter Six

Denise Clark stood at the turning circle with her overnight case, under a tree just breaking into blossom. She scanned the traffic anxiously. So far, all had gone according to plan. At 1800 hours she had left George with the children, explaining that Karen wanted her to stay the night as Seth was running a high temperature and she needed help – and not to ring, as Karen's phone was out of order; at 1815 she parked close to Karen's to allay suspicions, then walked down to the turning circle. She was to be picked up by Paul at 1830 hours. And there, just as he had promised, was his Mondeo. He pulled up with a squeal of brakes and she got into his car. He explained that he had told Becky that he needed to start work early on Monday, and so he was spending the night at Clive's place in Salford.

That much was true. Clive, a colleague of his, was in Singapore on business and Paul had the keys of his flat. It was all wonderfully convenient. Denise stole a glance at Paul's manly profile as she sat by him in the front of the Mondeo. So this was it. She had embarked on her affair.

Paul had turned up his tape of Meat Loaf so loud that there was no need for either of them to talk. Denise was glad, in a way. There had been more than enough talk, and she wanted time to prepare herself. This was actually the first occasion she had been unfaithful to George. This was not to say there hadn't been any other opportunities. Until now no one had tempted her this far.

Tempted seemed the wrong word. What surprised Denise as she was driven past the inner city shops with their metal shutters, and the numerous Indian restaurants, was how right and natural this seemed. Why shouldn't she decide to go to bed with whoever she wanted to? Her body was her own. Marriage vows were about staying together, but implicit within them was that one partner could not meet all your needs. George played bridge with cronies of his, she gossiped with Becky and Karen, talked about the children with her mother, and by extension, there was no reason why she shouldn't have sex with Paul. It might very well strengthen her marriage; she would be happier, and so she would treat George with less contempt, and he would be happier. No one need ever know the source of her energy. And by the same reasoning, she was helping Becky cope with Paul. She guessed he could be difficult. In fact, the more she thought about it, the more virtuous her adultery seemed. It rather spoiled the fun.

Then, not for the first time, she wondered what Paul would be like in bed. Would he be so desperate for her that he tore off her clothes as they entered the flat? Would he tell her how sexy she was and lie there lost in admiration as she divested herself of her clothing? Would he have any particular fetish? She'd heard of men who liked to be tied to the bedposts, or even dressed in nappies. Perish the thought! Denise devoutly hoped that he was perfectly normal. The idea of sexual deviation disgusted her. Thank God Paul lacked the imagination to be anything but normal.

They left the main road and Paul guided the car into a small courtyard in front of a block of flats. They looked fairly modest. Denise was a little disappointed. She had hoped for a waterside apartment on the Quays, perhaps. These flats looked dreadfully suburban. A line of wheelie bins stood sentry on one side. She waited by the car as Paul took her case from the back seat, and his from the boot. She linked arms with him as he led her to the entrance lobby.

'You don't know how long I've been waiting for this,' he told her, and squeezed her arm. It hurt her.

The lobby of the flats was bare, with rows of pigeon-holes for letters. There was a smell of other people's dinners. Denise scrunched up her nose. She followed Paul up the stairs, and he came to a halt on the top floor, where he quickly unlocked a door and held it open for her.

Denise walked in and turned on the light. It was obviously a single man's flat. There was a black leather settee in front of a large television; a sideboard with bottles of spirits; blue velvet curtains (a mistake, she thought) and a small table against a wall by what was evidently the entrance to the kitchen. A small passageway led to the bedroom. It would have to do.

Paul closed the door, came to her and pushed her head back with the ferocity of his kisses. She felt a little panicky; it wasn't meant to happen quite like this. She hoped he wasn't going to take her here and now. His hands wandered down her back and cupped her bottom and pulled her fiercely to him. She pushed herself away.

'Not yet, Paul. Give me a little time.'

He laughed but broke away from her, and instead ate her with his eyes. Aware of his gaze, she took off her coat and found a peg on the back of the door. She wore a pink angora sweater and a black calf-length skirt. Denise realised she felt unaccountably nervous. What seemed natural before now seemed unreal, as if she had stepped into somebody else's life. The fact she was in a stranger's flat added to this sense of dislocation.

'I'll take my case to the bedroom,' she told him.

'I'll get us both a drink,' Paul said, moving over to the sideboard.

Denise walked through to the other half of the flat. She noticed the functional bathroom, and a small box room kitted out as a study with a large computer. She pushed open the remaining door. There was an exercise bike on one side, and a double bed in the middle of the room with a Manchester

United bedspread. It was reflected by the mirrors on the doors of the fitted wardrobe, and the mirrors on the ceiling. Mirrors on the ceiling! Now that would be something to tell Karen about. She put her suitcase on the bed, then turned and opened the wardrobe to look for some hangers. She was greeted by the pungent aroma of old trainers. Quickly she shut the door and decide to hang her change of clothes over the side of a chair. On the bedside table she saw a well-thumbed paperback, and a framed photograph of two children. She placed that face down. She wanted no witnesses.

Then Denise looked at herself in the mirror and as usual was pleased with what she saw. She did not look her age; that was part of her attraction. There was something in the pout of her lips, the curve of her cheekbones and the fall of her fringe on to her chiselled forehead that pleased her – always had pleased her. She pulled down her angora sweater to accentuate the shape of her bust. With her brassière on, it was firm, round and womanly. She had been sensible enough not to breast-feed her children. She inhaled, then pulled in her stomach. Her bust looked even larger now. She could understand why Paul was so besotted with her. She pouted sulkily into the mirror, and loved the woman who pouted back at her. Not for the first time, she thought it a pity that she hadn't made it into the cinema. Tonight, however, she was acting in her own adult movie.

There was a small rap on the door.

'Would you like your drink in here?' Paul asked her.

She smiled inscrutably at her reflection.

'It's all right. I'll come out.'

'No need.'

She turned and watched as the door opened and Paul stood there with her gin and tonic, completely naked. Her hand flew to her mouth. He grinned at her. She saw the redness of the skin of his chest, the protuberance of his stomach and the little thing below that seemed to wave at her in greeting. This was not so much *Last Tango in Paris* as *Carry On Bonking*. Paul placed her drink on the dressing table and advanced. Denise had the very

strange sensation of being hugged by a naked man and she hoped
to high heaven that he wouldn't stain her black skirt, which
could only be dry cleaned. With his stubbly face he nuzzled
at her neck, fumbled at her breasts with his large hands and
pushed himself repeatedly against her. Denise glanced in the
mirror. She certainly looked a lot better than he did. The bald
patch at the back of his head was reflected in the mirror like a
monk's tonsure.

He lifted her sweater off her head and revealed her black
bra. He pulled it over her breasts, not waiting to unfasten it
and mauled her with his hands. He was murmuring her name
repeatedly. She cast another look in the mirror and the cameras
rolled. A man was about to make love to her. He was wild
with lust for her. Now his hand was sliding up her thigh. She
closed her eyes automatically. Then opened them again to look
in the mirror.

Now he eagerly unfastened her skirt, pulling down the zip.
He tugged at her slip, her tights, her knickers and now she was
as naked as him. She looked in the mirror. She saw and loved
the curve of her back and the swell of her thighs. Now he took
her to the bed, pushed her on to it and lay on top of her. The
soundtrack would be Celine Dion. Cut!

'You're not wearing a condom!'

'I've had a vasectomy,' he told her. 'Becky insisted. The
doctors warned her against having another baby.' His hand
was meanwhile investigating her. The talk of Becky both
sobered and excited her. Here was Becky's husband stroking
her, fingering her, and Becky didn't know. At that moment
Becky was the other woman; she was the one who'd been
sidelined. Denise felt triumph and a vague sense of pity. For
that matter, Becky was perfectly welcome to George, if she
could stand him.

Take Two. Paul had decided she was ready. He rolled on
top of her and lunged at her, pushing himself in with deep,
panting breaths, and Denise lay back and looked at the mirror
above her and thought how funny he looked, heaving away like

that, his bottom bouncing. That needed to be edited out. She liked the way her hair was spread out on the pillow, and then she moaned a little to create some atmosphere. She wondered about pretending to orgasm, but guessed that Paul would not be too long, and she was right, for he gave a deep, rumbling sigh, and fell on top of her, squashing both her breasts. He groaned again and his pants of breath came more slowly, and she felt him shrivel inside her.

Denise smiled to her reflection above. It was lovely to be able to reduce a man to this, to have him utterly prostrate on her, to know that she had this effect. It confirmed everything she thought about herself. And yet this was worth nothing if no one knew. If they continued to have this affair, and Denise was nothing loth, then she needed an audience to make it all worthwhile. The première would be at one of those big cinemas in Leicester Square. But for now, there was Karen. She only partly listened to Paul's protestations that she was gorgeous, sexy, her body like silk. She knew all that.

With a little flatulent plop Paul withdrew himself.

'Christ, Denise!' he said. With his thumb and index finger he tweaked her right nipple. She winced with the pain.

'Was it all right for you?'

She smiled her inscrutable smile.

'Did you come?'

'Several times,' she said. She took a last lingering look at her reflection above. 'I'd better go and wash now. Then maybe we can eat.'

She would insist they went somewhere swanky for dinner tonight. He could afford it, and more importantly, she deserved it. She was a star.


There were times when Jude's heart sang with the pleasure of being free. Times such as now, when it was her half day, the sun shone enticingly through the windows of the Crown Street practice and all she had to do was switch on the alarm, run down the stairs and head back home, to spend all afternoon doing nothing. Emma and Sheila had a list of domestic tasks as long as your arm but Jude only had her own pleasure to consult. She knew they resented her a little; she was acutely aware that they exaggerated their chores to elicit sympathy from her. More fools them, she thought to herself.

Once in her Micra, she turned her Maria Callas tape on loud, and drove home. The warmth of the sunshine through the windows caressed her skin and made her feel languorous. She wondered whether it would be warm enough to sit in the garden and read. It was certainly tempting; at that time of day no one would be around. She could even turn on her stereo and listen to some music, and perhaps drift off to sleep in the sunshine, Aida or Ludmilla on her lap. Thinking of that, she came round the bend in the road to her cottage.

And there it was. In her parking space was the Discovery. Jude cursed aloud. It irritated her beyond measure that she could not always park outside her front door. Even more galling was the view from her front window when *he* was in – not fields, but the bloody Discovery! And triply maddening was the fact that she would not be alone on the terrace this afternoon.

*He* would be next door, playing his blasted piano. Jude had even considered becoming the anonymous donor of piano lessons for him. Anything but have to put up with those repetitive chords and scales. No wonder his wife left him. Jude admitted to herself as she got out of the car that she didn't actually know that his wife had left him, but she'd established that he lived alone. Not only that, but he was visited occasionally by a rather glamorous young woman in cut-off denim shorts and cropped hair. He had the temerity to kiss her in full view of the terrace; frankly, it was obscene. And puzzling too; what could his girlfriend see in him?

When she unlocked her front door, however, all was quiet. Motes of dust floated on the sunbeams that pierced the mullioned windows, and Jude smiled to see Aida stretch ecstatically before padding over to greet her. Jude crooned some words of endearment and walked into the kitchen to throw some dry food into the cats' feeding bowls.

She thought then about feeding herself, as she was rather peckish. I know what, she decided suddenly. I'll have a picnic! She quickly opened the fridge, checked that she had some cheese, and a can of lager. There was bread in the bread bin. Excellent. All she needed to do now was to get changed. She dressed formally for work and couldn't wait to get out of her skirt and blouse. Jude took the stairs two at a time and went into her bedroom.

It wasn't quite warm enough for shorts, she thought to herself, as she went to her wardrobe. Some denims and a T-shirt would be ideal. She took off her day clothes, and stood in her bra and pants surveying the row of T-shirts. She selected a tie-dyed orange, and turned to pull it over her head.

At that moment she saw him. He was directly opposite her, outside her window, his ladder propped against the birch tree in her garden. His face met hers with horror. At first an electric shock of fear convulsed Jude; then she came to her senses. Ian Fulwell was hardly an intruder; he lived next door. But what on earth was he doing in her garden, half way up her birch tree? Was he some sort of peeping Tom? She looked again to see him quickly climbing down the ladder. The fact that he was in retreat emboldened her. It was an outrageous infringement of her liberty, coming into her garden with his ladder! Why on earth would he want to do that unless he had designs on her or her property? What sort of maniac was he?

Jude pulled on her jeans and T-shirt and went storming downstairs. It was either fear or anger that made her feel as if she was in a red mist; probably anger. She left the house by the front door as the back door was locked, and arrived in the garden to find Ian standing coolly at the foot of the ladder, as if nothing was wrong.

'What on earth are you doing?' Jude demanded.

'I'm sorry,' he said. 'I didn't realise that you'd be at home.

There's a parasitical creeper on the birch and it'll kill the tree unless it's removed. I've been hacking it down.'

Jude saw a mesh of branches on the grass, and guessed he was telling the truth. Not that she knew too much about trees and creepers.

'It's my tree,' she countered.

'But my view,' he said. 'Besides a tree's a tree. It needed saving.'

'You came into my garden without permission!' Jude realised she was sounding like her old form mistress at school. She could see he was beginning to resent her tone.

'I thought you weren't in. I also thought you'd be grateful that I'd done the work.' The irritation in his voice was mounting.

'Grateful?! Why grateful? Don't you think I'm capable of taking down a creeper myself? Or is it because I'm female? Living all alone, needs a man to do her heavy work?'

'As it happens, yes.'

Jude's mouth opened, but no sound came out. She was utterly incredulous. Did men like this still exist? Ought she to slap a preservation order on him? She knew she had to say something, else he would presume she *was* grateful.

'Strange as it may seem, I am perfectly capable of looking after my garden myself. Yes, even to the point of climbing ladders. I can lop off branches, I can see to fuse boxes and even change a tyre. I could probably even drink you under the table, given the chance.'

'Tonight?'

Jude could hardly believe it. He had actually interpreted her pleasantry as bait for a date. She filled with indignation and dislike. She remembered that he had seen her unclothed and her sense of vulnerability discomfited her. She didn't want to spend another moment talking to him. She hated the way he stood there so easily, one hand on the ladder, one on his hip. She turned without a word and marched back to her front door.

It was locked. With a sinking feeling Jude realised that the keys were inside. Obviously while she had been passing the time of day with her new neighbour the wind had blown the door shut, the Yale lock had snicked into place and she was marooned outside. She cursed silently.

Quickly she thought through her predicament. Her keys were in her bag, and the spare keys were in the drawer in her bedside table. There were no others. No windows were open, she was certain. She wasn't able to drive down to the locksmith in Mytholm because her car keys were in her bag too. She hadn't had lunch and the sun had disappeared behind a cloud. This time she didn't curse silently.

'Bugger, bugger, bugger!'

'Is something wrong?' Ian said.

It was all she needed. He had obviously taken the ladder round to the shed at the front of his house, and had overheard her. Jude gritted her teeth.

'I seem to have locked myself out,' she admitted.

'Why not try abseiling down the roof and hacking your way in with a sledgehammer?' There was wry amusement in his voice.

'If I had a sledgehammer now, I know precisely what I'd do with it.' She glared at him meaningfully.

'There's no need to get emotional,' he said.

'I am NOT emotional!' she screamed.

'Good. I'm pleased to hear it. As I said, there's no need to get emotional because I have a spare key to your house.'

'What on earth are you doing with a spare key?'

'I kept one on behalf of the estate agents when the previous occupants moved out,' Ian explained easily, as if they were idling away the time. 'Since the house was empty, I showed one or two people round in the evenings.'

'You should have given me back the key when I moved in.'

'It's lucky I didn't.'

Jude bristled with resentment. She knew she was right and she hated the way this man made her seem foolish to herself.

She also hated the feeling of being at his mercy. She wondered if it was worth walking to Becky's, despite the fact it would take her a good three quarters of an hour, just to save her pride. But then she would have to pay a locksmith for new locks – there was nothing for it. She would have to ask Ian for the key.

'If you give me the key now we'll say no more about it.'

'By all means; but if I were you, I'd consider giving it back to me. It's useful for a neighbour to have a key.'

'I'm quite capable of looking after myself.'

'It's remote up here.'

'I don't know what it is with you men! As soon as you think of a woman living on her own you mark her down as some sort of victim. Do you think you'd deal any better with an intruder than I would? Why should I be any more vulnerable than you? You live alone!'

'With two large dogs.'

'Who regularly harass my cats.' Jude could see this was turning into a slanging match.

'It's nature,' he said.

'So's malaria and diarrhoea.'

'Do you want your key, or are you happy to stand outside here chatting?'

Jude took a deep breath. She considered hitting him, but he was a good six inches taller than her. He crossed over into his front garden and disappeared into his house. Jude felt her heart knocking at her ribs. She had never met someone so thoroughly infuriating. That calm assumption of male superiority! It was almost laughable!

Ian returned almost immediately, bearing her key on a leather fob. He handed it to her.

'Glad to be of use,' he said.

'Don't mention it!'

Jude unlocked her front door and once in the sanctuary of her own house, she took a deep, reviving breath. He was unspeakable. Still her pulse was racing, and her legs were weak with the aftermath of the conflict. But she would not give in to the emotion. What could she do next? Her plans of a peaceful afternoon in the garden were in ruins. In fact she felt as if her house was the last place she wanted to be. The thought of sitting in her living room knowing that *he* was sitting just behind the dividing wall in *his* living room was unbearable. She had to get out.

Thank God there was Becky. And thank God as well that she didn't work, Jude thought guiltily. She was bound to be in, and Jude could off-load to a sympathetic audience. The cats sat on their haunches in the middle of the room, looking up at her inquisitively.

'The best thing I ever did was to get you two spayed,' she told them. 'I tell you, you're missing nothing!'

Jude picked up her jacket, her bag and left her house. She'd had enough of men. There were times when only a woman friend would do.

'I'd best be getting back soon.'

'But Dad, you've only just got here!' Becky felt a little hurt. She thought her father would enjoy an afternoon in her house, not to mention the ride out and back.

'Yes, but I don't know what's happening there, do I? Those lads from the estate hang around in the afternoon. Mrs Davies had her handbag taken from the kitchen table.'

'I know, but we locked up, and I checked all the windows were closed. I'm sure everything is safe and sound.'

Her father shook his head. Becky, a little irritated, felt duty-bound to make a point.

'Just think, Dad, if you were living in a rest home, you could leave your room and be absolutely certain that your things were safe!'

He looked malevolently at her. 'I wouldn't trust them nurses!'

'Dad!' she said, using the same exasperated voice with which she spoke to her daughter. She glanced at the clock. 'Amy will be home soon.'

'Oh, aye?'

'I'll have to go and fetch her from school.'

'I don't like to be left by myself.'

'It'll only be for ten minutes.'

'I'll have another slice of that madeira.'

Becky reached for the cake and began to cut a piece. There was something she ought to tell him and perhaps now was as good a time as any.

'I had a letter from Mum yesterday.'

His face was impassive.

'She's been in hospital for a hip replacement. She's made an excellent recovery, just like the Queen Mother. I didn't tell you beforehand because I didn't want to worry you.' Becky's voice was tinged with irony.

'My arthritis is bad. I can hardly walk. You saw me. I could hardly get to the door. It takes me all of half an hour to get out of bed in the morning.'

She had carried out her duty. It was right that he should know about his ex-wife's welfare. It saddened Becky that she had so little contact with her mother. She was eighteen when her parents finally divorced, as if they were waiting for Becky and her brother to grow up before they threw in the towel on their marriage. Even now Becky couldn't work out exactly what had gone wrong. There was no other woman, and no other man. It was true that her mother was overly houseproud, trapped by her own expectations of herself. True, too, that her father was just a little self-centred. Was that enough to end a marriage? For many years her parents had slept apart; her mother cited her father's snoring. Then there was the time her father sported a black eye after a night of bitter arguing. Becky even wondered if her mother had hit him, as ridiculous as that might seem.

She knew she would never find out. Becky's mother was one of the old school; children were there to be protected, and they weren't to know about adult business. She wouldn't even tell Becky the facts of life. It was Jude who had enlightened her, even to the drawing of diagrams in her precise, scientific way. Becky's mother believed that discretion was the better part of valour, and that silence and respectability were intimately related. *We never really got on.* That was the reason Becky's mother gave for the divorce. *She walked out on me.* That was her father's reason.

For a while Becky lived with her mother, feeling permanently guilty about her father. Her solution to this discomfort was to move out and live with some girls at work in a house in Moston. That worked reasonably well, and then she met Paul. A few months after the wedding, her mother left to live with Aunty Eileen in Canada.

'Have you been going to the over-sixties club, Dad?'

'Aye. They had this chappie come along, he was a whatd'y call it? A calligraphologist. He reads your handwriting. I don't hold with that claptrap.'

'Oh, I don't know. I think you can read people's character from their handwriting. It's almost impossible to tell Amy's and my writing apart now. And we have very similar personalities.'

'I can't hold a pen any more – I can't bend me wrists.'

'But you fill in your pools coupon,' she rallied him.

'It takes me half an hour.'

Becky was surprised to hear the crunch of gravel in the drive. Who could that be? It wasn't Ferguson's as their Transit was already parked outside Karen's. A visitor for her? She hoped so, although it would be awkward with her father there. She only half listened to him as he complained about his swollen knees and his bladder. It was someone for her; she could see the figure approach her back door; it was Jude.

'Hold on a minute, Dad. There's someone at the door, and I think you know her!'

Becky rose eagerly and hurried to the door to let Jude in.

'I am absolutely—' began Jude.

'My Dad's here—' Becky began simultaneously.

Jude stopped talking and looked across to the dining room table where Becky's father sat watching them. With an almost imperceptible nod of her head she acknowledged his presence.

'I'm sorry,' she said to Becky. 'I'll come round another time.'

'No, please don't. It'll do Dad good to see someone from the past. You remember Jude, don't you? You know I said we've met up again.'

'Aye,' her father said.

'Tea? Coffee?' Becky proceeded. 'I've got some madeira too. One of Dad's favourites. He's been on at me to get some Battenburg, but I can't seem to find it anywhere. These days it's all carrot cake and date-and-walnut loaf. As if they aren't as loaded with sugar as the others.'

Becky had that familiar sensation of talking into a vacuum. No one was paying any attention to what she was saying. Jude was watching her, but her face was frosty. Her father was watching Jude.

'I'm glad you've called, Jude,' Becky began again. 'I've got something rather interesting to tell you.' She glanced at her. 'Perhaps now isn't the best time.'

'Been keeping all right, have you?' Jude asked Becky's father.

'Aye. I have arthritis.'

'Pity,' Jude said.

Becky handed her a mug of coffee. 'You two stay and have a chat. I'll go and pick up Amy from school.'

Jude took the coffee and put it on the kitchen table.

'I'll get Amy from school. I know where it is.'

'Aye. And I'd best be getting home. You can take me home, Becky.'

'You do that,' Jude said, taking her car keys from her jeans pocket. 'See you later.' And she was gone.

Becky was disappointed. She had looked forward to her father and Jude meeting, but neither of them seemed very interested in the other. She blamed her father less than Jude.

If Jude had a fault, it was that at times she could come over as distant or even unapproachable. After that argument they'd had, about that boy, Becky had tried time and time again to make peace between them, and Jude had been just as curt, just as remote. Becky felt chilled.

'I want to go home now. Where's me coat?'

Becky snapped out of her reverie.

'Here it is. I'll help you on with it.'

'Be careful now. I can't bend me arm. It gets you in your joints, it does. It's me joints as is the worse. It's me joints.'


Jude left her Micra on the main road, dissuaded by driving up to the school by the quantity of traffic heading towards the gates of Mytholm High. It was a huge school, a mixture of breezeblocks, older, stone buildings, tennis courts, fields, some portakabins – Jude wondered how on earth she was going to be able to find Amy. The school gates, however, were at the end of a cul–de–sac, and she reasoned that all the pupils would have to pass through them. If she just stood where she could see them she would be bound to spot Amy.

A cool wind played with her hair now, and Jude drank in the present, the distant roar of traffic from the Halifax Road, some unrecognisable birdsong, and watched a delivery lorry back out of a courtyard, the driver frequently turning his head to check the angle of his reverse. She tried to peer in the windows of the school but all seemed quiet. Then there was the faint ring of a bell.

More and more children left the school grounds, boys with white shirts flapping loose over their trousers, sports bags slung over their shoulders; girls in twos and threes, skirts hitched up awkwardly, their voices high pitched, giggling. It brought it all back to Jude, the pungent smell of the labs, the beams in the hall ceiling, that constant pressure of striving and official approval just out of reach. She scanned the girls for Amy. She didn't want to miss her.

In a few minutes two girls came out, one of them stopping to apply some lipstick with the help of a small mirror in her blazer pocket. The girl who looked on at her doing this was Amy. Jude observed Amy's friend and thought she looked a bit brash, but she knew not to judge by appearances. The pressures on girls to conform at that age were often too strong to resist. Amy's friend had her hair up, with two tendrils deliberately escaping in front of her face. Amy walked close to her, bumping in to her as they proceeded down the drive.

'Amy!' Jude called.

Amy looked over, recognised Jude and looked surprised and glad. She came straight over to her.

'Hello! Are you waiting for me?'

'Yeah. I told your Mum I'd pick you up.'

'Oh, cool! Jude, this is Petra, my best friend.'

Petra grinned at her. There were freckles on her nose, her eyes were small, and screwed up in the sunlight. Jude reckoned she was shy.

'Petra!' Some girls shouted to her. Both Amy and Petra turned.

'See ya, Amy!' Petra said, and walked off in the direction of the other girls. Jude thought Amy looked after them rather wistfully.

'I haven't stopped you doing anything after school?' she asked.

'Oh no. I was expecting Mum to collect me anyway. Why are you here? Is she all right?'

'Fine. Only she was taking your grandad home, so I said I'd pick you up.'

Together they walked back to the main road.

'Since your mother won't be back for a bit, I thought I might take you out for tea.'

'Cool! I'm always hungry when I come out of school. Mum says I can only have fruit because I've got to watch my figure.'

'Nonsense. When you're with me, you have whatever you want. They do some excellent pastries at Clarendon's.'

'Can we go to McDonald's?'

'Are you hungry enough for a burger?'

'And large fries and a milkshake – I mean, if that's all right?'

'Will you eat your tea at home?'

''Course I will.'

'OK, then.'

Amy set about her meal methodically, dipping each of her fries into a tiny carton of barbecue sauce, as if she was baptising them. Then head first into her mouth they went. Jude settled for a doughnut, and and guiltily admitted that she was rather enjoying herself. It was years since she'd been to McDonald's. Being in charge of a teenager gave you permission to do all sorts of things that you wouldn't otherwise. Amy ate demurely, her face abstracted.

'Did you have a good day at school?' Jude asked her, to stimulate conversation.

'Not bad. The physics teacher was away and no one came to sit with us. Every time a teacher walked by we all pretended we were working. It was dead funny.'

Jude smiled. 'And is Petra in your class?'

'Yeah. We sit next to each other all the time now. I really like her. It was a bummer yesterday 'cause she was away and Sophie asked if she could sit with me and I didn't really want her to.'

'Don't you like Sophie?'

Amy looked down at her food. 'Well, yeah, I kind of still like her – she used to be my best friend – but she smells a bit – everyone says so, it's not just me – and nobody likes to sit with her.'

'Hasn't anyone told her?'

'It's embarrassing.'

'I think you've got to say something. You can either make a joke of it, or be quite direct. Tell her that you've noticed that she pongs a bit after games, and that you used to as well until you started using a deodorant. It's kinder to her to let her know.'

'I don't want to hurt her feelings.'

'You can't wrap your friends in cotton wool.'

Jude watched Amy mull this over.

'I will say something to her, but I'll be nice about it. Jude, can I ask you something else?'

'Fire away.'

'What's the right age to start snogging?'

Jude raised her eyebrows.

'Petra's had four boyfriends and she's my age. And there are other girls in our class too. I feel a bit left out.'

'Do you want a boyfriend?'

'There's nobody in our class I like – all the boys are dead stupid. But it would be kind of nice. More to talk about it than anything else. Petra said her last boyfriend wanted to sleep with her but she said it was illegal. He had a condom in his pocket and she nicked it and brought it to school to show us.'

Jude felt flattered that Amy was confiding in her like this, and wanted to live up to the role in which she had evidently been cast – approachable big sister. Her words were reassuring.

'I wouldn't believe everything you hear from the other girls. I bet it's all boasting. She probably bought a condom from the chemist to show off with.'

Amy giggled, and obviously liked the idea.

'But she's very nice to me. She lets me work on her table in art, and we go round together at lunchtime.'

'I'm sure she's a very nice girl.' Quietly Jude thought otherwise.

'I feel kind of more grown up since we've been best friends.'

Jude looked at Amy and thought she seemed very young. The fullness in her cheeks, around her chin, gave her a baby face. The milkshake sitting in front of her added to that impression. Her eyes were Becky's eyes, and had that same, winning smile.

'She said I could go and sleep over at her house.'

'I used to sleep over with your mum,' Jude told her. 'We stayed up talking half the night.'

'Oh, cool! Did you talk about boys and stuff?'

'Your mother did,' Jude said, laughing. 'I'm afraid I was as cynical then as I am now.' Amy bit into her burger and looked at Jude inquisitively. 'It seemed to me that whenever one of my friends gained a boyfriend, they lost all their individuality. All they'd go on about was the boy, as if he was the only thing that mattered. Nothing's more boring than those "he said to me" and "I said to him" conversations.'

'Do you think so?'

'And the trouble with men is that they want to take you over,' Jude continued, getting into her stride. 'Your life isn't your own any more. Do you know, my next-door neighbour took it on himself to do my gardening just because he thought a mere female wasn't capable!'

'Maybe he likes you.'

'Ha!'

Jude laughed so loudly that the family on the next table turned to find out what the joke was. 'I reckon he thinks I'm the neighbour from hell. And as for him, he's one of the most pompous, presumptuous, macho-posturing, rude, repulsive, men I've ever met.' Amy looked a little blank and Jude realised she probably didn't understand half the words she'd used. But it felt good to get it off her chest.

'Would you like a boyfriend?' Amy asked her, then didn't wait for an answer. 'I would. I think it would be nice to have someone who cares about you and treats you special. Someone you could tell all your secrets to.'

'A female friend can do all that.'

'Yes, but . . . Well, you know!'

Jude wondered whether she did know. At Amy's age she wasn't interested in boys. And afterwards, she couldn't help but wonder what their motives were. As for sex, it was overrated. And yet there was some emotion that fuelled the operas she loved, some gentle hope that made Amy look wistful now, and twist the straw of her milkshake absently, there was something that made Becky happy in her marriage, despite her awful husband. There was something Jude had missed. But she wasn't going to be maudlin. Much better to count her blessings. And one of them might very well turn out to be Amy. The girl evidently liked her, and the feeling was mutual.

'This is fun.' Jude grinned at her.

'Yeah. I like talking to you, Jude.'

'You can always talk to me, whenever you want. I can be your friend too.'

'Oh, cool! Won't Mum be jealous?'

Jude laughed. 'Women are allowed to have more than one friend. It's only men who get possessive. But don't you think we ought to be making tracks? Your mum should be home by now. I don't want her thinking I'm corrupting a minor.'

'What does that mean?'

'Never you mind. Put on your blazer and let's get going.'

# Chapter Seven

When Becky arrived back home Jude and Amy were in the lounge watching *Neighbours*. It made her smile to see them. Jude looked entirely at ease now, her black mood forgotten, and Becky was relieved.

'Look at you two,' she said, taking off her coat.

'Hi, Mum,' said Amy, not taking her eyes from the screen.

'Shhh. This is good,' Jude said.

'Stay for tea,' Becky said. 'Paul's working late tonight.'

'I'm not hungry, Mum.'

'But you only had a sandwich for lunch!' Becky hoped her insistence that Amy avoid junk food wasn't turning her into an anorexic. You read about it such a lot these days, and she knew of girls who—

'My fault, I'm afraid,' said Jude. 'I took her to McDonald's.'

Well, that was a relief.

'Come into the kitchen with me, Jude, and we can have a natter. And Amy, you know you promised me you'd only watch an hour's TV, and if you've seen *Home and Away* as well, you must get on with your homework immediately the programme's finished!'

Amy gave an exaggerated sigh. Ignoring it, Becky made her way to the kitchen, followed by Jude.

'I'm peckish. D'you want anything? I might just have some cheese on toast.'

'I'll pass. But you have something.'

'You seemed a bit taken aback to see Dad here. I thought you always got on with him.'

'Yes. I—'

'But I think I know what it was. He reminded you of your mother. I know I'm lucky, not having lost either of my parents, and I know it must be hard for you. I just want to say that I do understand.'

'Thanks, Beck.'

Becky took two slices of bread and put them under the grill. Now they were alone it was the ideal time to bring up the subject of Chris. Becky had refrained from opening the subject on the phone because she wanted the advantage of checking out Jude's response through her body language. Besides, the phone wouldn't have been half so much fun. Her father had sabotaged her first attempt at matchmaking; second time lucky.

'Jude – there was something I didn't mention to you about my writing class.'

'Go on.'

'It was—'

There was a sudden knock on the door. Foiled again! Becky turned off the grill in case the bread burnt.

'Karen!' she said.

Karen was holding several paint-spattered old sheets.

'Here we are!' She thrust them at Becky. 'I thought I'd return these. Jim finished today and we're all clear at last.' At which point Karen noticed Jude, and Becky introduced them. This time Jude was her usual self.

'Hi, Karen! Becky's mentioned you lots of time. Come in and have a chat.'

'I can't stop,' she said. 'I've left the boys on their own. But I tell you what. I've decided to have a party to celebrate getting the house straight. Just a hen party. I'd popped over to invite Becky. You come too.'

'I'd love to,' Jude said.

'Just a hen party?' Becky asked waggishly. 'What about Jim?'

Karen blushed a little.

'Jim's her builder,' Becky explained to Jude. 'And you've been seeing him out of working hours, haven't you? Denise mentioned something to me.'

'Yeah, well, I have, sort of. It's nothing serious. He's just a friend. He's gonna look after the boys during my party, so we can have the house to ourselves.'

'A party. That'll be fun,' Becky continued. 'Are you going to ask Denise too?'

'Well, I—'

'I'll tell her when I see her at the writing class. When will it be?'

'Wednesday week. Look, I must dash. God knows what Seth and Bobby will be up to.'

And Karen was gone.

Becky realised that she had provided the perfect opening.

'You remember I told you all about Karen. She's the one whose husband was violent. She vowed she'd never have anything to do with men again. But now she's seeing Jim Ferguson, her builder. Did you see the way she blushed? And he's given her a forty per cent discount on the work he's done for her. It shows you there are still some nice men around.' Becky resumed her grilling operations.

'I believe you,' Jude said. 'I read an article in the *Independent* the other day. Apparently one was spotted coming in to Ulan Bator.'

Becky decided to change tack.

'I was wondering if you'd like to come round for dinner this weekend? I feel like trying out a recipe from my pasta cookbook, and it would be wasted if it was just Paul and I who were eating.'

'I don't think I'm doing anything.'

'Oh, good. And I thought I'd also invite my creative writing tutor, Chris Scott. He's very nice. Oxford-educated, and he has a cat.'

'Is the cat coming too?'

'Jude! He's writing a novel – he's quite the intellectual. But you wouldn't guess it to talk to him. He's completely unassuming, with a lovely sense of humour, and such a sensitive teacher. All the class thought he was so easy to talk to. I think he's probably a little lonely. He lives by himself, you see, after he split with his girlfriend. But as I was saying, he's an inspirational teacher. You should have seen the way he handled the class. Tactful, firm, authoritative. And his eyes! You should have seen his eyes!'

'Two of them, are there?'

'Don't be silly. He has really attractive eyes. He's not a male bimbo, but good looking in a craggy, brooding sort of way. To be honest, I'm surprised that he's not been snapped up already.'

'He's clearly not been mixing with the right sort of croco-dile.'

'Jude – give him a chance. I wouldn't do this if I didn't think that you'd get on with him. Stop tapping your fingers on the table like that – let me finish. I feel I owe you this. I've been thinking again about that time I stood you up for that boy – you know – when we were fourteen. I realise I was wrong. I can see why you were upset. All because of that we drifted apart, and we wasted twenty years. It was my fault; I can see that now. So I'm going to make it up to you. I'm finding you a date. It's what I should have done then; I should have asked my date if he had a friend for you. So I've found you someone at last.'

'Becky, I—'

'No – don't interrupt me. All I'm asking is that you should meet him – that you should give him a chance. If you take one look at him and feel you'd rather have dinner with Quasimodo, I'll concede defeat. But for my sake, just agree to come for dinner. You might even enjoy yourself. Look at what happened to Karen! She never would have believed that just by getting her front room decorated she'd find herself a boyfriend!'

'I don't—'

'I know you don't want a boyfriend, or at least you think you don't. Commitment can be very frightening. I'm sorry – I know I'm rushing ahead. Just think, Jude, what fun it would be to have someone to go out with and make a fuss of you.'

'You sound just like Amy.'

'Just for me, give it a try. You don't have to dress up. I wouldn't wear denims, though. I love those Celtic earrings you have – the design complements your bone structure. Don't worry; I'll make sure there's plenty of candlelight because it's so much more flattering. He comes from Yorkshire, so there's no stuff or nonsense about him.'

'Look—'

'Don't say another word. I know you think I've been presumptuous, and I know how terrifying a blind date can be. But I'll be there, rooting for you. I can—'

'Becky. Will you listen to me?'

Becky saw that Jude meant business. She had her serious face on. She realised her plans had been as insubstantial as a child's soap bubbles. Jude was about to burst them all.

'I'd be delighted to come to dinner.'

'You mean . . . ?'

'What time? And should I bring a bottle? Tell me if you think my little black dress would be OK?'

'You'll meet him?'

'Why not? It's ages since I've been out with anyone. It'll probably do me good. If my next-door neighbour can go around cavorting with a girl half his age, why shouldn't I have a passionate encounter with a creative writing tutor?' Jude finished the last morsel of Becky's cheese on toast.

Becky couldn't follow her logic, but it hardly mattered. She had done it! Jude had agreed to meet Chris! She wondered what she had said that swung the balance? Or perhaps she was just an instrument of fate? Whichever, Chris would love her. If Becky experienced just the smallest pang of jealousy, who could blame her? She decided to go out first thing in the morning and buy a pasta cookbook.

'You won't regret this, Jude.'

'Is he really nice, then?'

'Oh yes! When you get talking to him, you feel as if you've known him for ever. He's that sort of man. I chatted to him for ages in the pub and he told me all about himself.'

'Does he know that you've fixed him up with me?'

Becky lowered her eyes.

'I did say that you would be there.'

'What if he doesn't like me?'

'Everybody likes you. I can't imagine anyone not taking to you immediately.'

Becky spoke these words with utter conviction. Jude possessed a charisma and individuality that Becky envied. Even when they were at school, she knew Jude was her superior. This knowledge never troubled her; she hero-worshipped her friend, and thought it was right that others should, too. Still, it was time that Jude settled down. It would inevitably bring them closer together. She would drive Jude to the ante-natal clinic; later on, Amy could baby-sit. Amy . . .

'I'd better go and check on Amy,' she said.

'Amy! Look what she's up to, Jude! She's doing her homework in front of the television and she knows she mustn't! Now either go up to your room and work, or finish watching TV.'

Amy gave a strangulated cry of 'Mum!'

Jude sat in the kitchen, thinking. There would be no harm in meeting someone, and despite Becky's optimism, it would be unlikely that anything would come of it. Jude knew she sent certain signals to men; signals that denoted a distinct lack of interest. At times she was cold with them; at other times deliberately hearty, so she could be one of the boys. That was how she managed at dental school. Other times she could be plain aggressive, but only if she was provoked. She determined not to think about Ian Fulwell again.

Perhaps she would have to learn how to flirt. Becky might

have to give her some lessons, or maybe Amy might be more appropriate. She'd seen other women do it. There was a way you could talk to men and almost hook them in like an accomplished angler. She was almost forty, and yet she couldn't remember a time when she had ever behaved like that. It was disgusting.

Though there had been boyfriends, but only at university. None were very long-lasting, but they served to make her feel more like everybody else. Then there was the night when she'd had a little too much to drink and got talking to the barman at college. He took her back to his bedsit, and Jude thought it might as well be now. She waited to see what would happen, allowed him to undress her, and then kept her eyes firmly shut. The feel of his skin against hers was not unpleasant. Then he confessed to her that he was a virgin too. In one way, she felt better about the situation, but in another, she was subtly disappointed. Nevertheless, they had soldiered on. What they did, Jude thought afterwards, probably constituted sex. Or so she told her friends the next day. She often chatted to him in the bar after that. But the understanding was that it had been a one-nighter. Both felt more worldly as a result.

Some years ago, she had been out with a man for a full six months. After a while they had made love, methodically, cleanly, but it seemed to Jude that when they started, it augured the end of the relationship. Then work became so demanding, and then her mother began with that cough.

Enough of that. Jude refused to live in the past. What she had to face now was that Becky had fixed her up with a man, and she was damn well going to make the most of it. Nervous energy made her rise from her chair and pace around the kitchen. Why not? she thought to herself. It's time I liberated my inner teenager.

Later that evening Jim Ferguson's van rumbled up the unmade

road that led to Becky and Karen's house. Jim leapt out and rapped on Karen's door.

'Your babysitter's here,' he announced when he saw her. 'Here are the keys.'

'Cheers,' she said to him. 'You're a good 'un.'

He helped her on with her sheepskin jacket. Jangling the keys to his Transit, she walked outside and got in the driver's seat. Jim and the boys waved her off.

As she drove, a box of tiles on the passenger seat made an accompanying rumble. She took the descent to Mytholm carefully, showing in her hesitation that the vehicle she was driving was relatively new to her. She slowed each time she saw an approaching car, to let it pass.

When she reached Mytholm, it was dusk. The sky was navy and flecked with dark shadows of clouds. Street lamps cast pools of light on the pavements, and the off licence and Co-op were still busy. Karen drove on.

At the canal there was a right turn over a stone, hump-backed bridge. A few teenagers in Adidas joggers and sweatshirts stood around, doing nothing in particular. Over the bridge, the houses were more modern, post-war semis, pebble-dashed, with little bow windows and covered porches by the front doors. Karen pulled up by one of these.

The house was in immaculate condition, with a miniature ornamental garden in the front complete with fishing gnomes. On the gatepost was a plaque, inscribed with the words F & J Ferguson Ltd. As Karen arrived, the front door opened. The woman who stood there bore a marked resemblance to Jim; her hair was curly too, although it was wild and unruly; both had the same, square-shaped face. She was wearing torn denims and a green checked shirt.

Karen locked the Transit and walked down the garden path. Shirley stood aside to let her pass first. Once they were both inside, Shirley shut the door.

'Is your Dad in?' Karen asked.

'No. I sent him out to the Wheatsheaf.'

The two women looked at each other for a brief instant, and smiled. Then Shirley took Karen in her arms, and they kissed, a long, passionate kiss, one that Karen wanted to go on for ever.

Denise had taken certain precautions. She'd arrived early at the flat and drunk two full glasses of Chablis. The wine made everything seem more amusing, and she almost felt that she could make love with Paul on the Manchester United bedspread again, but then, maybe not. She took it off the bed, then pulled back the duvet. She sat on the side of the bed, and placed her empty glass by the lamp. She allowed her red silk slip to ride up her legs. She had found it last night at the bottom of her underwear drawer but she couldn't remember when she bought it. It was lucky she had, however, as it was ideal for this evening. Denise sat still on the edge of the bed, and waited. She liked to have time to prepare herself, to anticipate what was to come. Unlike Paul.

Paul was the sort of man who liked instant gratification. To him, Real Sex was sex against the clock – energetic grappling and panting and thrusting over in a few minutes. She glanced at herself in the mirror again. She'd bought some red silk panties to match the slip. She felt rather odd in them as in fact she always wore plain white underwear, enjoying the virginal feel of cool cotton. But it was her intention to arouse Paul as quickly as possible, play to his need for rugby scrum sex, and then she could relax. She wondered about another glass of wine, but felt it might send her to sleep. She felt a little uneasy, sitting alone. So she checked her reflection again and pushed her hair behind her ears, decided she didn't like it that way, and shook her head to free it. Perhaps she would have some more Chablis.

She took her glass from the bedside table and carried it through to the lounge. She hoped the children were all right. Karen had promised to drop them both off at home, and Petra had said that she would look after Rowan – for a price. That made Denise smile. But she was not going to think about the children now. That was hardly the point. Children sucked you dry like leeches, with their constant demands, trumped-up illnesses – it was the way they upstaged you that was so hurtful. It had taken an enormous toll on her marriage. But she was young, and it was so unfair that her life should be over just because she'd married and had children. Really, Denise thought, as she refilled her glass, I'm quite the feminist.

And a key turned in the lock, and Paul appeared.

'Christ, Denise!' he said, dropping his briefcase and removing his jacket, exuding that familiar smell of offices and too much coffee and male sweat. He tore off his tie, pulled at his shirt, unzipped his trousers and she watched him calmly, like an infants' teacher supervising a class of little boys getting changed for gym. He lunged at her, pawing her slip, and this time surprisingly nibbled and blew in her ear, his version, she supposed, of foreplay. It made her skin prick unpleasantly. That hardly mattered. Already he had pushed her against the wall, pulled down her panties, and entered her. He stopped; was it all over? No – now he took her with him on to the floor, pushed the coffee table to one side, and was heaving on her again, muttering how gorgeous, how sexy, how – Christ! He whimpered in his climax. She let out a deep breath and braced herself as his full weight collapsed on top of her.

'Why do you do this to me?' he said, kissing her around her mouth.

I am a feminist, thought Denise, picking up her thoughts again where she had left them off, because I think I believe in the total superiority of women over men. Paul had succeeded in humiliating himself absolutely in front of her, or inside her, if she was to be entirely accurate. Men made out they were dominant, but it was women who called the tune every time – and always could do, if they had enough sense to realise the true state of affairs, as she did.

'Are you satisfied?' he asked her.

'Of course.' She wriggled from under him, and pulled her slip back over herself. 'Are you satisfied?'

'I wish I was younger, Denise. I'd have you all over again.' Denise thought it was just as well that he wasn't.

'Would you like a glass of Chablis?'

'Why not?'

She rose to pour him some. Later he had promised her that they would go out to eat. There was a new restaurant just off Deansgate that he said he liked the look of. Hopefully the wine and the food would have a somewhat soporific effect.

He sat on the settee in his boxer shorts.

'Paul,' she said, taking him his glass. 'Paul – am I better than Becky?'

He started. 'We don't have to talk about her.'

'No – I want to know. Am I better than Becky in bed?'

'Of course you are.'

'Why? Why am I better?'

'You know how to turn a man on.'

Denise was not satisfied. She felt insatiably curious. It was a strange thing; women pretended to know each other so well, and to be so much more intimate with each other than men, and they actually spoke about sex to each other, and yet she didn't have a clue about her friends' love lives – all excepting Karen, of course. She thought of Jim Ferguson, looked at Paul, and felt cheated. She returned to her original subject.

'What is Becky like in bed?'

She could see Paul looked uncomfortable.

'Tell me,' she said.

He shrugged. It dawned on Denise then that the reason he wasn't answering her question was that he didn't know. It was doubtful he ever thought of Becky when he made love to her. It occurred to her that he probably didn't think about her either. She felt a wave of solidarity with Becky. Really, they would have to talk.

'But I am better than her?' Denise made a little pout.

'Christ! I should say so. You're sexy.'

So Becky wasn't sexy. She could believe that.

'Do you think you'll ever tell her about me?'

'Are you mad?'

'Shhh, shh! It's not such a ridiculous idea. She might be quite glad. If she doesn't like sex, she might be relieved to know you have a mistress. On the continent, that kind of arrangement is quite common.' It was a tease, but Denise wanted to see how far she could persuade him.

'No.' He shook his head. 'I prefer it like this. She doesn't need to know.'

'I feel awful, Paul. Becky is my best friend, and I feel like I'm cheating on her. If it was all out in the open, it would be so much easier.' She watched him consider this.

'Forget about Becky. She's got nothing to do with you and me.'

It occurred to Denise then that she probably wouldn't have had an affair with Paul if he wasn't Becky's husband. Or rather, she would have, but it wouldn't be quite the same. Becky was a point of reference. She gave the affair meaning and colour. But she could see from Paul's awkward composure that too much talk of Becky would spoil things for him. She decided to move the conversation on.

'Have you ever had a mistress before?' She put a manicured hand on his thigh as an encouragement.

'Not a mistress exactly. The odd fling.' He looked sly.

'Am I just a fling?'

'Christ, no! You're—'

Paul was trying to frame his thoughts into words when the phone rang. Paul jumped, but then relaxed. They both turned to look at it.

'I'll get it. There was a problem about a delivery and I gave my secretary this number.'

'But I—'

Paul was at the sideboard in an instant and picked up the phone. Despite only being dressed in his boxer shorts, he assumed his work telephone manner, brisk, authoritative.

146

'Paul Howarth!'

'Is my Mum there?'

'Who's that?'

'Petra.'

'I think you have the wrong number.'

'My Mum gave me this number in an emergency and Rowan's been sick.'

Silently Paul handed the receiver to Denise.

'Hello?'

'Mum? It's Petra. Dad's not home yet and Rowan's been sick. All over the side of the settee.'

'Has he got a temperature?'

'I don't know. But he's all right now. He's playing with his Lego.'

'Look – Daddy will be home in half an hour. Go and play in another room and wait for him. Ask Rowan what he had for school dinner.'

Denise was furious at her son, and then contrite. She hoped he wasn't really ill.

'He said he had three puddings, Mum. It was a bet. And Karen bought us chips on the way home.'

So it was Karen's fault. The cow. She'd get her back for this.

'Well, if he's feeling better, I think I'll carry on with my massage. I'll be there to pick you both up from school tomorrow. Be good for Daddy.'

'The sports bag I want has "Tommy Hilfiger" written on the side. Bye Mum.'

'I know. 'Bye!'

Denise put the phone down.

'It's all right,' she said. 'He's just over-eaten.'

'Did she realise who I was?'

'Of course not. Children are never bothered about what their parents get up to. She'll have just assumed you're a client. I massage most of Mytholm Bridge, men as well as women.'

'Give me a massage.'

'Have a shower first,' she told him. Not having her oils with her, she couldn't mask his natural smells with her lavender and rosemary.

'I'll just finish my wine,' he said, up-ending his glass.

'You do that.'

# Chapter Eight

'I'll only be next door,' Becky told Paul. 'So if there are any emergencies or phone calls or—'

Paul winced to indicate that he was watching *The Bill* and she had made him lose his concentration.

''Bye!' she announced in a stage whisper, and walked into the kitchen, where she removed from the fridge a bottle of wine and an egg salad with cling film on the top.

Becky was pleased she was going out tonight. It stopped her thinking. If it weren't for Karen's party she would have been on tenterhooks all evening, waiting for a phone call from Jude. *Whatever time you come in,* she'd told her, *I want to hear from you.* Jude was meeting Chris in Hardy's Wine Bar at eight o'clock.

Something was bound to come of it. That much was obvious at the dinner party at the weekend. Both Jude and Chris had complimented her on the *pasticcio*, then chatted merrily away, and it was just as well, as Paul had woken in a bad mood from his afternoon nap, and then had too much to drink, and said very little all evening. She was annoyed with him, but as it happens, he wasn't needed. Jude and Chris really did hit it off. Becky saw the look of frank appreciation that Chris had given Jude, and Jude deserved it. She looked super in her black dress, and she had been to the hairdressers for a trim and her hair looked sleek and sophisticated. Becky could tell from observing Jude that she thought Chris was interesting, and indeed he was. He told them all about his travels in Turkey, and his experiences at a real Turkish bath, not to mention the hotel he stayed in when he'd complained to the manager that the sheets needed changing, and the next morning a cigarette-smoking Turk came into his room unannounced and took the sheets off his bed as he was lying there!

At the end of the evening Chris was quite open about asking Jude for her telephone number, and she took his too, which was possibly a little forward of her, but that was Jude. He'd rung her the very next day and they'd agreed to meet in the wine bar. Jude had forgotten about Karen's party, but Becky had forgiven her instantly. Karen had lots of friends; it was much more important that Jude should get to know Chris. A hen party was the last sort of gathering that Jude should be going to; hen parties were fine for married women like her, whose only other option was an evening in front of the TV.

She pressed Karen's bell which buzzed loudly. Karen herself answered the door, a cigarette in one hand, and planted a kiss on Becky's cheek.

'What a difference!' Becky declared.

Jim Ferguson had worked wonders with Karen's front room. He'd built a dividing wall between the dining area and the lounge in original stone, and topped it with mahogany-effect open shelving. He'd restored the original fireplace and Karen had stuffed it full of pampas grass. The old wallpaper had gone, and was replaced by off-white Artexed walls, and Karen had hung up some brightly coloured posters. The window frames were new – in fact what had formerly been a rather shabby little dwelling, was now a delightful and desirable country cottage. Perhaps, Becky thought, Jim was hoping to move in one day.

'Come and put all that in the kitchen, and then I'll introduce you to everybody.'

Some Country and Western music was playing in the background; three women Becky did not know were in the lounge.

'Put your salad on the table, Becky; we'll eat later. What can I get you? There's either red plonk or white plonk.'

'White would be lovely.'

Karen poured some wine into a plastic tumbler and handed it to Becky. She felt a little nervous, as a glance around the room revealed that she knew none of Karen's friends. It was lucky Denise was coming later. She was a little surprised Karen had not wanted to invite any men, as a party was hardly a party without the opposite sex. To her, the gathering had the feel of something that was second best. No doubt Jude would have relished it; Becky was all too aware that women were much harsher critics than men, and were weighing you up all the time.

'This is Becky,' Karen announced. 'She's me next-door neighbour, and me mate.' Becky thought Karen was a little drunk already. 'Becky, this is Gemma, and this is Wendy, who I used to work with. And this is Shirley, Jim's sister.'

Shirley certainly had a look of Jim about her. She had his wide mouth and crinkly eyes. The curly, brown hair that fell around her face gave her a roguish appearance. Becky rather liked her. Gemma was tall, with long hair and a long, equine face. Her lime-green blouse stunned Becky. Wendy was chubby with a pudding bowl haircut and was tapping her stilettos in time to the music. Shirley spoke first.

'So you live next door to our Karen?'

'That's right.'

'I bet you get cheesed off at her screaming at the kids.'

'Oh no! I've a daughter of my own and I know what it's like. I have every sympathy.'

'Do you have a little girl?' Wendy asked. 'I have a little girl. Kylie. She's three next month. I'm thinking of having a party for her with her little friends from the nursery. I'm going to see if I can make her a Barbie cake this year. She likes Barbie.'

Becky assumed an expression of interest. She knew if she

listened patiently she would be rewarded by an opportunity to talk about Amy, although she was uncomfortably aware that the subject would only be of significance to herself. Poor Amy had some sort of argument with Petra, or Petra had cut her, and she'd been moping about the house all evening, demanding sympathy and asking for advice. She'd always been a little immature when it came to making friends. Becky looked forward to her growing out of all that. It would be so much more interesting when she had boyfriends. She tried to home in again on Wendy.

'. . . and she screamed so loud when the assistant tried to get the shoes off her feet that we had to have them even though they didn't fit. And then there was the time—'

Karen came to kneel by Becky. 'Shut her up if you can. Gemma's getting upset. She had a miscarriage last month and there's no way she's over it yet.'

'All right.'

Becky floundered desperately among possible conversation topics. Politics and religion were certainly taboo; they couldn't talk about food on account of Wendy's size; it was bad form to talk about work when you were trying to enjoy yourself; even mentioning holidays might draw attention to the fact that Becky was probably wealthier than Karen and her friends. If only there was a man present, Becky thought. Men have a sense of humour and cut their way through these swathes of hypersensitivity.

'. . . and she won't go to bed without her teddy and Barbie, and she tucks them up first every night, and . . .'

Quick! She had to think of something. Was there any subject that every woman took an interest in? She had a flash of inspiration.

'How did you go on at the doctors' the other day, Karen?'

Everyone stopped talking.

'What's wrong with you?' Gemma asked her.

'She said the bleeding was caused by a cervical polyp.'

'My mum had one of those,' Gemma said. 'She had to have

it removed. They gave her an injection down below and fiddled about for ages. She couldn't feel anything, but when they told her to stand up, her legs gave way.'

'I was treated for cervical erosion last year,' Wendy interjected. 'What they do is, they cauterise you. It's all right at the time, but afterwards it hurts like hell. I couldn't sit down all evening.'

'Don't scare her,' Shirley said. 'A polyp's nothing. They just give it a twist and pull it off.'

'I knew a woman who had her fibroids removed only on local anaesthetic,' Gemma said darkly.

'Sod that!' Shirley drained her wine. 'I wouldn't want to know what was going on. I'd want to be out cold, me. Imagine watching your insides coming out.'

'My aunt's friend didn't have enough general anaesthetic when she had her hysterectomy, and she felt them removing it. She tried to tell them but no sound came out. She's going to sue the hospital.'

'Which hospital?' Karen asked Gemma.

'Beech Lane.'

'That's where I'm going!'

Everybody laughed like children at a Hallowe'en party as the story reached its delicious climax. Becky joined in, and wondered whether to follow with the tale of Amy's birth, even though Karen had heard it several times. She was about to begin when she remembered Gemma's miscarriage and careered to a halt.

'All this talk of hysterectomies is making me hungry,' Shirley said. 'Let's start eating!'

Slowly, so as not to seem too keen, everyone drifted over to the food. There were some barbecued chicken wings, potato salad, a huge bowl of crisps, some sausage rolls and Becky's own egg salad.

'Sausage rolls! I mustn't have those!' Wendy eyed them lasciviously.

'Give your diet a rest, Wendy.' Shirley picked two up and

deposited them on her plate. 'If you eat them standing up, they won't do you any harm.'

'Really?' said Wendy. 'Well, I never knew that. In that case I'll have some chicken and potato salad as well.'

Shirley winked at Becky, and at just that moment the doorbell rang loudly. Karen ran over to the door, and there was Denise in her cape. Becky thought she looked rather elegant for a girls' evening in, but then dress was very important to Denise.

'Becky!' Denise approached her immediately. 'I've not seen you for ages! I've just been to your house to see if you were still there, but Paul told me you'd gone. Karen! You look wonderful. It suits you, carrying those extra pounds. Here's a broccoli and artichoke quiche I've made. Becky – come and sit with me and tell me everything that's been happening to you.'

'There's not much to say about *me*,' she said, delighted that *her* friend had arrived. She didn't feel out on a limb any more. 'But Jude's going out tonight with Chris Scott!'

Jude stood in the middle of her living room, and looked around it for the last time.

'Oh, not again!'

She fled upstairs in the direction of the bathroom. It had been some time since she'd been bothered by her nervous stomach – all the time her mother was ill she had been fine – and it was silly and pathetic and ridiculous that a mere date with a man should bring this reaction on. Jude heartily despised herself. She hated being let down by her own body.

She came down the stairs checking her watch. It was just as well, Becky had advised her, to be a little late. Becky had phoned her yesterday evening with tips sounding as if they had been culled from an encyclopaedia of flirting. Jude picked up her bag and extracted some breath fresheners. That was another of Becky's hints, though she had told her categorically that there was not going to be any kind of physical relationship on this, their first date. No kissing, nothing of that sort! But you'll be talking to him, Becky had reminded her. And he'll be talking to you. Jude's stomach went into spasm again.

She had dressed soberly. She wore some black trousers, a white blouse and an embroidered waistcoat from an ethnic shop on Crown Street. Earlier she had put on some lipstick; then she had removed it all because her hand had been so unsteady when she'd put it on.

Ludmilla stopped in the middle of a wash, and with one leg stuck out at an angle, contemplated Jude.

'I'm not really nervous,' Jude told her.

The cat looked unimpressed.

'It's just that it's an unfamiliar situation for me. Remember how you felt when we moved here? How you went and hid under the bed? That's what I feel like doing.'

Jude fleetingly wondered what had happened to her usual composure, and tried to think of autoclaves and syringes and bridge cements. It was too late. She regretted not having used Karen's party as an excuse to get out of this evening. She thought with longing of the cosy gathering she had passed up on, the female camaraderie, the good natured acceptance that she associated with women. It was different with men. They always had another agenda.

Chris, she hoped, was slightly different. He didn't seem particularly threatening. He had treated her with a warm civility that put her at her ease. Once or twice she had even noticed him looking at her appreciatively, and that was the oddest feeling imaginable. It was possible that he liked her. Her stomach churned again.

She turned on the alarm, barely noticing the piano playing in the background. She closed the door, heard the lock click into place and walked down the path, concentrating on the here and now. If only the appointment was to remove his lateral incisor, she would have been perfectly at ease. She took a deep breath, and started the engine. She reminded herself that she was a grown woman, and had no right to be as jittery as a teenager. Even Amy would behave with more self-possession.

There was on-street parking by the wine bar, and Jude eased her Micra into a space between a Volvo and an Astra. Chris, she knew, did not have a car. At first she was worried he was going to be one of those ecologically-minded superheroes who were out to save the planet single-handedly, but he had eaten Becky's beef *pasticcio* with hearty enthusiasm, and responded knowledgeably to Paul's comments about his Mondeo. He didn't have a car because he was hard up. Jude didn't have a problem with that; she had money enough for two, and her mother had instilled into her a well-founded distrust of men with too much cash. Chris's lack of a regular income made him feel safe to her.

Apart from that, she remembered little about him. She could not even bring his face fully into focus. She had been so concerned about the impression she was making on him, that he only made the vaguest impression on her. She was flattered that he wanted to see her again, and willing to experiment further. For it was an experiment, she reminded herself. A scientific experiment. Equipment needed; one man, one woman, a wine bar, a bottle of good quality wine; method; mix slowly on a low heat until melting point is reached; observations—

She had not been to Hardy's wine bar yet, although Becky had told her it was one of Mytholm's trendiest venues. It was in the basement of an hotel, and Jude carefully walked down a few stone steps to reach it, holding on to the rail all the time, conscious of the effect she would make if she arrived head first into the room. The wine bar itself was strangely old-fashioned, with stone walls, Toulouse Lautrec posters and tables in alcoves – and no Chris. He had stood her up. It was the one possibility she had not considered.

But no. There he was, on a stool by the bar, and he turned with pleasure as he saw her. One evening in his company diluted by Becky was not enough to make him seem anything more than a stranger; a good looking, well-disposed stranger, but a stranger. She stood awkwardly in front of him, not sure whether to shake hands.

'Well, here I am!' she announced brightly.

'Me too!'

Jude felt her heart palpitating in her chest.

'Look,' he said, 'why don't we find a table?'

They both surveyed the cellar. There was a small stage, with a microphone at a forlorn angle in a stand. Most of the tables were occupied but in a far corner Jude could see one that was free. It looked frighteningly intimate. There was only one seat built into the wall which they would have to share. He waited while she sat first.

'I'll get us a bottle of something—'

'No – let me.' Jude stood again.

'I insist.'

'Well, in that case I'm going to make a contribution.' She thrust a five-pound note at him. 'Get something nice. And red.'

'A Shiraz Cabernet?'

'That's fine.'

Jude settled herself again, and followed him with her eyes as he went to the bar. He wore a navy sweater over a navy shirt, and some smart fawn trousers. His appearance gave the impression that he had made an effort. The thought made Jude even more nervous. She tried to recall Becky's advice. *Ask him about himself, men love an audience! Use plenty of eye contact, gaze at him then look away. Smile! Show you're enjoying yourself. Leave the top button of your blouse open. Compliment him! Touch him on the sleeve occasionally.* Jude had laughed long and loud at Becky when she had suggested all of this. Now, hoping no one was observing her, she surreptitiously tried to unfasten her top button. Her fingers were sweaty and she was still fumbling unsuccessfully when Chris returned. Quickly she put her hands by her side.

'They'll be bringing it over in a moment,' he said. He grinned at her. 'How've you been keeping?'

'Fine,' Jude said, smiling as brightly as the poster in her

surgery of the girl with new braces. 'And how have *you* been keeping?' She was doing well. She fixed her eyes on him, laser-like.

'Not too bad. I've been wrestling all afternoon with the third draft of my final chapter. It's good to get away from it. Is there something wrong? Have I got something between my teeth?'

Damn! She'd been staring at him for too long. She averted her eyes quickly and focused on a spot on the table.

'On the contrary! I was thinking what nice teeth you've got.'

'All the better to eat you with!' Chris quipped. Jude felt herself blush. She was relieved when the wine waiter came over with their bottle, and proceeded to pour for them. Jude took a long slug from her glass. Never had she needed a drink more. Anything to help her escape from this all-enveloping self-consciousness. She became aware that neither of them were talking. This would never do. Surely there had to be something they could talk about? Ought she to make a comment about the football? Only she remembered in time that he'd confessed to not having much of an interest in the game. What else did men talk about? Jude realised that she didn't have a clue.

She gave him a sidelong look. He was smiling at her, and she noticed now that he had the top button of his shirt open. Had Becky been talking to him as well? The thought terrified her, and she lifted her wine glass to take on board more Dutch courage. Just at that moment he reached over to touch her sleeve. She jumped; most of her wine spilled down the front of her blouse.

'I'm sorry!' He certainly looked it. 'Do you have any tissues?'

'Yes. Just a moment.' Jude fumbled in her bag, and brought out some Kleenex.

'Here, let me.' Chris took one and dabbed at her blouse, just above her left breast, where a pinkish stain was spreading, like someone had wounded her heart.

'I'm not doing very well, am I?' Chris said.

'Nor am I.'

He laughed ruefully. 'I can't believe I could be this nervous. I don't know what's wrong with me!'

'I've got the same complaint. My inner teenager's running riot tonight.'

'Have you got one too? Mine is spotty, insecure, and thinks you'll never like me as much as I like you.'

'Mine's been thinking about nothing but this date all day.'

'You seemed so super-confident to me.'

'I know. Becky says I give that impression to men and I ought to tone myself down. I've been told to listen more, smile at you—'

'Use eye contact, touch you on the sleeve occasionally—'

'So she did speak to you as well!'

'After the class on Thursday. I told her I was a little nervous.'

'But I don't see why you would be nervous. You've been in a relationship. Surely you're used to women?'

'My partner chucked me. I'm not very good at coping with rejection. I tend to blame myself.'

'That's something women normally do.'

'Men too. More than you think.'

Jude felt suitably chastened, and wanted to make amends. She would be completely honest.

'I'm nervous because I haven't been out with a man for years.'

'On purpose? Or did you not meet anyone?'

'A bit of both. You see,' she drawled, 'I'm the Greta Garbo type!'

'That's a coincidence. I see myself as a northern, working-class version of Rudolph Valentino.'

Jude laughed, and began to relax. The evening wasn't turning out so badly after all. It was possible she might even end up enjoying herself.

*　　*　　*

One advantage of going to a party next door was that you could drink as much as you wanted. Thinking that, Becky allowed Denise to fill up her glass for a second time. It was a bit cheeky of her to have brought a full bottle from the kitchen just for the two of them to drink, but Karen didn't seem to mind. Denise hadn't left her side since she'd arrived, and that feeling of being the odd one out had entirely dissipated. In fact, if anything, Denise seemed fonder of her than ever, listening to everything she said with a motherly concern. Becky found that a little disconcerting; at times the expression on Denise's face resembled that on Aida's when Becky had once seen her stalking a mouse.

'Now we can relax,' Denise said, lowering herself back on to the settee. 'The label just said "Australian Dry White". *I* certainly didn't bring it.'

It tasted all the same to Becky. Karen went over to the hi-fi and turned up the music.

'Shirley said she'd do some line dancing with us, didn't you, Shirl? I'm game, if the rest of you are.'

Karen stumbled a little as she made her way to the centre of the room. Shirley followed her and put out an arm to steady her. Becky felt herself prodded by Wendy.

'Shirley's opening that new Health Club where Bathrooms Direct used to be. She's a qualified aerobics instructor, and she does line dancing too. She's ever so good.'

Becky felt a little tempted to get up and have a go. If everyone else was joining in, there would be no one to look at her if she made any mistakes. She looked for somewhere safe to put her wine.

'Becky and I will sit this one out,' Denise announced. 'It's not my sort of thing. But you all carry on. I've never seen *real* line dancing before.'

'Where have *you* been?' Shirley said, an edge in her voice. There was something challenging in the way she smoothed down the khaki dress she was wearing, which was pulled in at the waist by a belt with a snake clasp. Becky saw that she had quite a good figure and experienced an automatic envy.

'She's drunk,' Denise whispered. 'And so is Karen. Jim and his family are a bad influence.'

'Do you think so? He's been very good to her.'

'I'm interested to hear you say that.' They watched Karen, Wendy and Gemma line up to face Shirley, who positioned herself in a corner of the room. The other three faced her. Becky and Denise had ringside seats.

'This is like having a cabaret,' Becky whispered.

'It's hardly Las Vegas.'

Which, Becky admitted, was true. Karen's living room was tiny, and despite the redecoration, Becky suddenly saw it as impoverished, she noticed the worn paisley carpet and the ordinariness of everyone there. She was worried Gemma would hit her head on the open-plan stairs that led to the bedrooms. Then Shirley began to tap her foot in time to the music and the others watched her closely.

'What *do* they think they look like?' Denise muttered.

Becky felt a little uneasy.

'That lime-green blouse! I'm sure if you turned the lights out we'd all be able to see by it.'

Denise had the ability to talk so that one could hardly see her lips move. Her voice was low enough not to be overheard, but sufficiently clear for Becky to catch every word. It felt quite wrong, quite wicked, talking about the present company in this way, but it was impossible to stop Denise.

'And the fat one! It must be years since she had a bra fitting.'

It was true. Wendy wobbled dangerously as she followed Shirley's steps. And you could see where two sections of flesh, like the tops of two cottage loaves, rose above her bra line. Becky glanced down at herself to check she wasn't coming out.

'Karen has some very peculiar friends. I think the one in the lime green—

'Gemma——' Becky interjected. It seemed kinder to talk about her by her name.

'Gemma,' Denise allowed. 'I'm sure she's the one. Karen told me that the man she lives with is a white witch.'

'What's that?'

'Well, he practises some form of magic which he says is harmless but involves using sex as a means of generating energy.'

'What do you——?'

'Shhh! They have orgies. I know she doesn't look the type, but there is a well-established coven in Mytholm that meets over the crystal shop on the Halifax Road.'

Becky was fascinated. She looked at Gemma's pained expression as she tried to follow Shirley, whose movements were becoming more and more complex.

'But don't tell Karen I told you. What do you think of Jim's sister?'

'She seems very nice.'

'She's staring at you.'

Becky flushed slightly, although she could have sworn that it was Denise that Shirley was looking at. The other women were having a break now, although the country and western music continued with Tammy Wynette's 'Stand by your Man'.

'Karen's taste in music is appalling,' Denise continued.

'Stand by your man,' Becky hummed.

'Would you?' asked Denise. 'Would you stand by your man? If he did something dreadful?'

'Like what?' asked Becky. This was better. She always enjoyed hypothetical situations. She tried to second guess the dreadful thing that Denise had in mind. 'You mean, if he was accused of fraud?'

'Yes. Fraud, or some deception like that.'

'I can't imagine Paul wanting to take that sort of risk. I'd be very shocked. But I hope I'd stay with him, and I'd try to understand what made him do it.'

'That's sweet of you, Becky. There are many, many women who wouldn't do that.' Denise looked at her fixedly again.

'I don't agree. Think about all the politicians' wives who stand by their husbands.'

'I'd stay with my husband if he was an MP, whatever he did. There'd be too much to lose if you walked out. Like money, status, influence—'

'You're too cynical. I bet love plays a part too.'

'Do you love Paul?' That look again. Just like Kaa the Snake in Disney's *Jungle Book*.

'Of course,' Becky replied automatically.

'Is he a good husband to you?'

'He's as good as anyone else.' Becky allowed Denise to fill her glass again. The conversation was taking a dangerous turn. Jude had been asking her similar questions and she had kept mum. But Denise was so much more insinuating, less easy to resist.

'Is he a kind man? I think that's the most important quality in a husband.'

'He can be kind.'

'Can be? You mean, he isn't always?'

'Not if he's stressed from work. Like most men, he has his moments. Not that he's ever hurt me or Amy.'

'I should hope not! But I imagine Paul might be cruel without realising it.' Denise's face was lit with a hypnotic concern.

'Yes; when I had the flu' last month, he came and pulled the covers off the bed because I hadn't got up to get his breakfast.' Becky laughed and hoped she hadn't been too indiscreet.

'He shouldn't have done that.'

'To be fair, I don't think he realised how ill I was.'

'Men sometimes lack imagination, don't they?'

Becky was pleased to hear this confirmed.

'Yes. That's exactly it. He reacts, but he doesn't always think how it affects me.'

'George is the same. I think sometimes you've just got to give way to husbands,' Denise commented sadly.

Tammy Wynette segued into 'Achy, Breaky Heart' as Denise refilled Becky's glass.

'It's the laws of nature,' she continued. 'You have to let them feel they're in control. They have a certain pride about their masculinity. In the same way you'd never refuse to let them make love to you—'

'Yes; even when you don't feel like it, you let them think you're in the mood.'

'That's exactly what I mean.' Denise's tongue made a brief appearance as she licked her lips. 'I think women ought to be more honest with each other about these matters. We need to compare notes.'

Jude would approve of that sentiment, Becky thought.

'How many times a week do you and Paul make love?'

Becky giggled, embarrassed by the directness of the question.

'Just on Saturday nights, as a rule. But recently he's shown a little more interest.'

'Has he?'

Denise looked taken aback. But it was true. Only the other night Paul had suddenly reached over in bed and before she knew it he was on top of her. It had taken her aback too.

'What kind of lover is he? Does he take his time with you? Does he kiss you?'

'I think it's different when you're married. You don't bother with all the preliminaries.'

'What does he say to you when you make love?'

'Come to think of it, I don't know. I don't think he says anything. It's not really the time for talking, is it?'

Denise laughed conspiratorially.

'He tends to get it over and done with rather quickly,' Denise commented. 'Though he's the sort of man who likes sexy underwear.'

'I bought some stockings and suspenders but I haven't put

them on for years. With a teenager in the house you don't like to—'

'And what about you? Does he turn you on? Does he make sure you—'

There was a loud banging at the door, and the sound of children's voices. Both Denise and Becky stopped talking instantly. Becky felt her heart palpitating. She watched Karen open the door to Jim, Seth and Bobby.

'Oh, it's you!' Karen said, in mock irritation.

'We've had an ace time!' Bobby announced. 'He's got a PlayStation and he let us go on it all night.'

'I beat you!'

'Bloody hell, they're at it again. Seth, Bobby, it's way past your bedtime and I want you straight upstairs, no questions, and wash your teeth and do a wee even if you don't want to. Did you survive?' That was to Jim.

'No sweat.' He stood looking round at the women, his eyes resting on Denise for a moment. Becky sensed his embarrassment and felt for him. Irrationally she saw him as her rescuer; had he not walked in then, heavens knows what Denise was planning to say!

With a loud click, the tape reached the end.

'I'm all in,' Shirley said. 'And I've got work in the morning.'

'We'd better be getting back then,' Jim said, a touch apologetically.

'Us too,' Gemma said. 'Thank you for a lovely time.'

Coats appeared, and Karen made hasty arrangements about returning dishes.

''Bye, love,' Shirley said, planting a kiss on her cheek. 'See ya tomorrow.'

Becky smiled to herself. Her hunch was right. Jim and Karen were serious. She was a member of their family circle now.

''Bye!'

In a moment they were gone.

'And then there were three,' Denise said. 'I'm in no rush. Let me fill your glasses again.'

'I could do with a drink,' Karen said, wiping her forehead with her hand.

'It's not just words and music. You say that because you're approaching opera from the viewpoint of the theatregoer. The two things are more than the sum of their parts. The sound and meaning marry and create an emotional impact—'

'I think poetry works in much the same way.'

'Almost, but I think it's possible to experience an opera in a foreign language that you don't understand, and still feel the full emotional impact. Would that be true of a poem?'

'It helps to understand the language. That's why I think I'd prefer to hear an opera in English.'

'Oh no! You're absolutely wrong. Operas in translation are a travesty of themselves. When you remember that an Italian tenor sings "*amore*", or a Frenchman, "*amour*" – which sounds so romantic – but the Englishman says "love" – Love. It sounds like a proprietary brand of washing powder. *I clean my undies in new, improved Luv!*'

Chris laughed, a warm, rich chuckle, which made him even more attractive. Jude was pleased to see that he didn't go on to dispute with her. She felt she had won the day.

'I'll have to take you to a foreign opera,' she said, with a victor's generosity.

'Done,' he said.

Another date! Jude realised with delight that it would be a pleasant prospect. This evening had gone very well. They had sat here finishing a bottle of wine as if they were old friends. Chris was everything Becky had promised he would be – intelligent, unpretentious, sensitive. She had been nervous for no reason at all. She toyed with the idea of suggesting they had another drink. But the truth was she wasn't thirsty, and she had drunk her quota of alcohol for the evening. Perhaps it was time to go. She looked at her watch.

'What do you make it?' Chris asked.

'Half past ten.'

'I'll have to go,' he said. 'My bus leaves at ten forty.'

'Don't bother with the bus. I'll run you home.'

'Are you sure?'

'I wouldn't have offered otherwise.'

It was the least she could do. With a common assent, they rose and walked up the steps out of the wine bar. It was chilly, and Jude pulled her coat around her tightly as she made her way to her Micra. She unlocked the passenger door for Chris.

'Where exactly do you live?'

He named a small village on the tops about fifteen minutes away, where rows of stone cottages lined the low hills. She headed off in that direction.

'Have you time to come in for coffee?' he asked.

Coffee! The old euphemism. Jude bit her lip in thought. The truth was, she would enjoy a coffee and more conversation, but could she be sure that he meant coffee? Once in his house they would be alone together. What had not developed in the wine bar could develop in the privacy of his home. Her stomach did a neat back flip and landed somewhere in the region of her rib cage.

'I wouldn't mind some coffee,' she said, throwing a light emphasis on the final word. That was all she wanted. She didn't feel ready for anything else. Besides, she hardly knew him. He gave her a few brief directions, and shortly she pulled up outside a darkened terraced cottage without a front garden.

'Are you coming in?'

'OK.'

Chris's cottage was small, smaller than hers, with a square living room, lined with books. A striped rug was thrown over a dilapidated settee and an antique-style clock sat on the mantelpiece.

'Take a seat,' he said. 'I'll put the kettle on.'

Jude eased herself gingerly on to the settee. It was rather lumpy. She licked her dry lips, and looked around her. There was a gas fire in the fireplace together with a set of fire irons, also antique, she guessed. The aroma of the house was slightly spicy, as if he'd been cooking Indian food. It was not unpleasant.

'Here we are.'

Chris returned with the coffee, and handed her a mug. So he did mean coffee, Jude thought, a little disappointed. He could have at least given her the opportunity to refuse him.

'It's been a good evening,' he said, smiling at her.

'Yes.' Jude wished her voice did not sound so reedy.

'We must do it again.'

'Absolutely.'

More silence. Real silence, the sort you can only get when there is no traffic, no birds and an electric tension in the air. Jude was scared to drink again in case he heard her swallow. He was sitting close to her, and if he wanted, he could put one arm over the back of the settee, and draw her to him. She decided she would not mind if he did that. It was only fair. She put her coffee down in preparation.

'Do you like Mytholm Bridge?' he asked her.

'I do. It's so compact.'

Chris nodded. More silence. This was embarrassing. What was he waiting for?

'I've been thinking about moving to Leeds or Manchester,' he said.

He smiled at her. She knew she had been deliberately encouraging, so why was wasn't he *doing* anything?! He hadn't moved at all. Was she that unattractive? Or were her signals too subtle? If only she'd brought a set of semaphore flags with her.

Chris drank some of his coffee, then put his mug down.

'I've got a request to make, and I hope you don't think it's too cheeky.'

'Ask away. I can only say no.'

'I think I might be having trouble with a wisdom tooth,

only I'm not sure. I don't want to go to the expense of a visit to my dentist if there's nothing wrong.'

'I don't know if I'll be able to see anything, but I'll take a look. As long as that's not the only reason you inveigled me up here.'

'Most definitely not,' he laughed.

A little apprehensively, Jude moved over to him. Her face was at an angle to his, as she tried to find a position where the light would help her to see more clearly.

'OK. Now open your mouth.'

'Make me,' he said.

Now his hand caressed her back, and she discovered that by pressing her mouth to his, it opened just a little, just enough for them to kiss. His was a gentle, tender, hesitant kiss, and she felt his hand support her back, and she turned and moved still closer to him. She came and sat on his lap. The softness of his lips surprised her. But best of all was the way he held her so close to him. She loved the way he held her, enfolding her, hugging her. She could have carried on kissing him all night, just to feel his arms around her like that. It blotted out everything, and made her feel safe. Gradually she disengaged her mouth and put her head on his shoulder, not wanting to lose contact with him.

'I hope you don't treat all your patients like this.'

'I thought you'd prefer it to the drill.'

He kissed her hair, and still held her tenderly.

'It's up to you,' he said. 'Whatever you want to do now. You have lovely skin.'

He traced a pattern on her cheek with his index finger. Jude's mind was racing. What did he mean by that last remark? *What* was up to her? Once again he brought his mouth to hers, but this time she kissed him absently. It was up to her. She had to decide what she wanted to do. It would be so easy to give into the rhythm of their bodies, but then, they hardly knew each other. As he kissed her she felt all of herself soften and yield, and then his hand moved round her back, and cupped her breast.

'No!' she said. 'Stop it!' Jude disengaged herself from him.

'It's OK.' He smiled at her.

'For some reason I don't feel ready. Look, we don't know each other yet, not properly. It's not that I don't like you—'

He kissed her lightly on the mouth. 'There's no hurry. And no need for explanation.'

'Just hold me again,' she said.

He did, and Jude felt tears come to her eyes, although she didn't rightly know why. Perhaps she was grateful to him – grateful for not being insistent, for being so understanding. She snuggled close to him, hoping she could stay a little longer, trusting she hadn't spoilt what they had begun to develop.

There was a sudden rattle at the door, and a ginger cat shot in. Jude sat up.

'It's Tom,' Chris explained. 'After T S Eliot.'

Jude got up and followed the cat to the kitchen, where she bent to stroke him, enjoying the way he flexed his back to meet her hand. He purred with a sensuous appreciation, then rolled over on to his back, looking up at her curiously, and she tickled his chest.

'He likes you,' Chris said, watching her from the doorway.

'I like him too.'

'You must introduce me to your cats.'

'I will – soon,' she said.


Denise re-crossed her legs, and took a small sip of her wine. It really was revolting stuff, with a vinegary aftertaste, but she supposed that Karen didn't mind. Apparently Becky didn't either. She had consumed nearly three glasses of that stuff, and was looking rather flushed and untidy. Once again Denise surveyed her and tried to imagine how she would react when she confessed about Paul. Becky would be upset; it was inevitable. But she would also realise once and for all – this was the important thing – Denise's superiority over her. That was what had to be established.

'You two have had a good old chinwag,' Karen said, as she came to join them. There was no room for her on the settee, so she settled at their feet.

'So Jim's not staying the night?' Denise asked.

Karen pointed upstairs to indicate Seth and Bobby.

'Tell Becky what you were saying to me over the sausage rolls,' Denise continued. 'How he had instructed you in tantric sex and you had an orgasm that lasted – how long was it?'

Karen looked from Becky to Denise. She took a large swig from her wine glass.

'Four minutes, thirty-five seconds.' Karen winked at Becky. 'Precisely.'

'Who's a lucky girl, then?' Denise was irritated. Karen was so unbearably smug, and Becky so unbelievably naïve. And didn't either of them see the look Jim had given *her* when he'd come in with the children? The way Karen went on about him, it would serve her right if – but that was not why she was here this evening.

'Come on, Becky. We can't let Karen do all this clearing up herself!'

Becky eagerly got to her feet.

'Mummy!' came a voice from upstairs. 'Tell Seth to stop getting in my bed!'

'Bloody hell!' said Karen, and ran up the stairs.

Denise and Becky began to clear the table in the dining area, bringing plates and glasses into the kitchen for washing up.

'I'm happy for Karen,' Denise said.

'Me too.'

'There's nothing as exciting as starting a new relationship.'

'Mmm,' Becky said, turning on the hot water.

'Do you ever wish you could . . . start a new relationship?'

'I'm married,' Becky said.

'I know, but it doesn't stop you thinking sometimes. In the beginning I thought you fancied Chris Scott.'

'Don't be silly. He's going out with Jude.'

'Becky, listen. I haven't told you about what happened to

me a few weeks ago, when I was shopping in Manchester.'
Denise began to tingle with excitement.

'What happened?'

'I met someone I knew, vaguely. A man. We got talking
and had lunch together. In the Café Rouge.'

'It's supposed to be nice there.' Becky put a squirt of Fairy
liquid in the sink.

'It is. We had a lovely lunch, and arranged to meet again.'
Becky did not respond. Denise could tell that she had her
attention. Her body danced with pleasure. 'I know I shouldn't
have, but I'd enjoyed myself so much. And the second time, he
told me how much I meant to him. And I felt drawn to him,
too. Oh, Becky, I know I should have told you this before, but
I was scared you'd disapprove of me.'

'No, it's all right. Go on.'

'He has a flat in Manchester, you see, and I visited him
there. I know it was silly.' Denise realised her legs were weak
with excitement. 'Once we were alone, it happened. As soon
he touched me, I knew I couldn't resist.'

'So you *slept* with him?'

Denise nodded.

'Denise!'

'It was wonderful. Afterwards, I couldn't understand how
something that felt so right, could be wrong. He said the same
thing. His marriage isn't easy, you see—'

'He's married too?'

'Yes.' It was coming. And at any moment, Karen might
come downstairs.

'You must be careful.'

'Please try to understand, Becky. I've tried to forget him,
but it's impossible.'

'Have you thought about your children?'

'Yes.'

Denise ached to reach the climax, and talking about children
delayed it.

'Does he have children?' Becky continued.

'Yes.'

'Do I know him?'

Denise took a deep breath, felt an exquisite tension, then paused. A surge of pleasure began its inexorable roll from the pit of her stomach.

'I think you—'

'Don't bother with the washing up,' Karen said, as she came down the stairs. 'Let everything soak until the morning. I'm completely knackered and I need my shut-eye. I'm kicking you two out.'

'Are you sure?' Becky asked.

'Come on. Hop it!' Karen's tone was jocular, but Denise could have kicked her. Just as she was about to confess. And yet, perhaps it was better this way. It was enough that Becky should go to bed tonight thinking about Denise and her lover, and be completely unaware that she was sleeping next to him. It made one feel just a little powerful, and created a rank order, so to speak.

She kissed Becky good night with real feeling, and told Karen that she'd see her the day after tomorrow. It was true that the party had been somewhat dire, but Denise reflected that she had managed to enjoy herself very much nevertheless. She slipped into the front seat of her Brava rather tired now, but satisfied. Quite satisfied.

# Chapter Nine

'I'll just be fifteen minutes, Eleni, and I promise to be back for the Suma delivery!'

Karen slipped out of the door of Sun Wholefoods and walked as quickly as she could in the direction of the town centre. She knew she shouldn't have presumed on Eleni's good nature, as now was one of their busiest times, but she had to speak to someone. She'd been seething with indignation all night long. Had she not come down the stairs when she did there was very little doubt Denise would have told Becky everything. She had held her tongue long enough.

She occupied herself as she scurried along the High Street, past the estate agents and the off licence, by thinking of things that she would like to do to Denise. Invite her for dinner and serve up chicken à la salmonella? Clean her toilet with her toothbrush? Borrow a delivery truck and accidentally back into her Brava? With a bit of luck, she thought, Shirley or Jim would be in the Ferguson's office. She couldn't keep all this to herself any longer.

She arrived at a little courtyard through a narrow gap between the Co-op and a pharmacy. Piled up outside were planks of wood, sacks of builders' materials and a wheelbarrow. The door to the office was slightly ajar and she saw Jim, a catalogue in his hand, consulting with a customer. She recognised him; it was Mytholm Bridge's vet – a tall, good-looking man – she couldn't recall his name. Jim glanced at her as she entered, and while waiting for him to finish she looked around the office, her eyes settling on the calendar of football fixtures on the wall, surrounded by advertisements for local firms, of which Ferguson's were one.

'I'll be up some time next week, Mr Fulwell.' She guessed the conversation was concluding. The vet shook hands with Jim, and smiled good naturedly at Karen as he departed. When he had done so, Karen shut the door.

'Is Shirley around?'

'She's down at the Health Club. They're delivering the treadmills.'

'Yeah. I should have remembered. Never mind. I'll talk to you instead. I'd better bring you up to date. You know Denise Clark, who was at my party—' Karen tried to breathe deeply to calm her anger. 'Denise who I clean for. She's having an affair with Becky's husband!'

Jim exhaled sharply.

'Yeah, and that's not the worst of it. She wanted to *tell* Becky last night.' Another deep breath. 'What a cow! No – cows are quite nice creatures. What about a rattlesnake? Or the Ebola virus?'

Jim smiled at her, then stroked his chin thoughtfully.

'I've got to say something,' Karen continued. 'But at the same time I can't tell Becky because it's what Denise wants me to do.'

'She's George Clark's wife, isn't she?'

'I reckon she's kept him in the dark as well.'

'I know George. I think I saw him the other night. I was doing the rounds, me and the lads. We sunk a pint in every pub in Mytholm.'

'Stop wittering! Can't you hear what I'm saying?'

Jim nodded.

'And I'm still working for her!'

'Once the Health Club opens you'll be—'

'Yeah, yeah. But meantime, I'm still having to clean for her.

You don't what it's like! She is so disgusting! Since she's been seeing Paul, she's even been buying all this kinky underwear – g-strings, scarlet suspenders – the lot – and hiding it in the airing cupboard.'

Jim seemed unperturbed.

'We'll sort her out, Karen. I have a bit of an idea.'

'And did you see the way she looked at you last night? As if she could eat you for dinner!'

Jim laughed. 'You're obsessed with her.'

Karen bent over and pecked him on the cheek.

'No, I'm not. You know who I'm obsessed with. If you see her before I do, tell her I'll ring her this afternoon. And do you have a fag? I'm completely out.'

He took out a crushed packet of Silk Cut from his pocket and handed her one. He lit it for her, and she hurried out of the office, back in the direction of Sun. She wondered what Jim was planning, but she was content to wait. It was a relief to get her anger at Denise off her chest. She decided to try to cheer herself up by thinking of Shirley installing the treadmills. Maybe tonight they'd take the boys over to the Club and they'd all have a go on the machines. It'd be a laugh.

Karen was happy again, completely happy, but nervous too. How would Mytholm react when she finally plucked up enough courage to tell everyone? For now, only Jim was privy to their secret. Karen wasn't ashamed, but dreaded the covert stares and the gossip. Worse still would be the trivialising of what was the best thing that had ever happened to her, when it became public property. So she decided to hug the knowledge of Shirley to herself, just for a little while longer.

She threw her cigarette on the pavement and hastily stamped it out as she saw the Suma delivery van arrive, and ran the final few yards to Sun Wholefoods.

'Dish it, Jude! I want to know all about it, right from when you arrived at the wine bar.'

'I'm hungry,' she said. 'Where are those sandwiches you said you'd bring?'

'I'm not feeding you until you tell me what happened. You haven't even said whether you enjoyed yourself yet!'

'How can I, when I haven't eaten since seven this morning?'

Becky gave an exaggerated sigh, and opened her shoulder bag to find Jude's packed lunch. When she had rung her at the surgery in the morning, Jude had insisted that the weather was far too glorious to spend her lunch break in a pub or café, and demanded a picnic. This was why they were sitting on a bench overlooking the canal, by the humpbacked stone bridge that led to the market-place. Being lunchtime, there was only one mother with a small child intent on feeding the ducks that were permanently full up on their diet of Sun's homemade wholewheat bread.

'Is tuna and mayo all right?' Becky asked Jude.

'Wonderful.' She took the sandwich and began eating immediately. 'I'm famished. I haven't had a break all morning. I had to fit in two emergencies and deal with a sales rep. Sheila's off today as well.'

'That must be difficult. Now tell me what happened.'

'What happened? Well my first patient needed a small filling in a back tooth, so we prepared the injection—'

'Jude!'

'The sandwich is delicious! Where do you buy your bread?'

'Karen fetched it for me – and I'm going to snatch it back if you don't let me know how you got on last night.'

'Can't you tell?'

Becky looked at her and saw the way her eyes danced.

'I want to know all about it!'

'There really isn't a lot to say. We met at Hardy's, drank a fruity Shiraz Cabernet, spoke about his writing, my practice, his family, my mother, contemporary literature, the opera—'

'You just talked?' Becky seemed a little disappointed.

'—the opera. And then I drove him back to his house—'

'What's it like?'

'Quite ordinary. At the end of a terrace in Birk Vale.'

'Did you go in?'

'For a while.'

'How long did you stay?'

'Damn! I should have taken my stopwatch!'

'Jude, please. Did anything happen?'

'I don't know what you mean.'

Becky wasn't sure what she meant, either. For the first time she realised that even though she'd successfully brought Jude and Chris together, she had no right to be part of their intimacy. She felt a little excluded. But what did happen last night? How much did they like each other? And what about the other thing? Both Jude and Chris were mature, and single – they might have even slept together. After Denise's revelations last night, anything was possible. Becky decided on a rather more oblique approach.

'Are you going to see him again?'

'I might.'

'Do you *like* him?'

'Yes. I do.'

Why was Jude being so laconic? Surely there was lots more to say! Becky thought that if it were she, if she had been out with Chris, she would have told Jude everything, relived every detail. It was almost unfair that she should have given Chris to Jude, and not be allowed just a little bit of vicarious pleasure.

'When are you seeing him again?' she asked.

'After the weekend. Have you forgotten – we're going to the opera on Saturday.'

'Why don't you take Chris instead?'

'Don't you want to go?'

'To tell you the truth, I haven't listened to that tape you lent me yet – I've been that busy. We can go another time. Take Chris. It would be so romantic.'

'Romantic? Do you know what *The Marriage of Figaro* is about? Lust and money.'

Becky laughed. She didn't care what the opera was about,

but a Saturday night in Manchester would be bound to advance their relationship tremendously. And then *something* would happen, and once Chris *belonged* to Jude, everything would be easier.

'I was looking forward to going with you, Becky. And you've given me the money for your ticket.'

'Treat Chris with it – I insist. You can take me to see an opera another time.' Becky pursed her lips in determination. 'If you don't take him, I'm never going to speak to you again!'

'Well, if you put it like that—'

'I do put it like that.'

Jude smiled at her. 'Since you're so insistent, I'll ring him this evening and see if he's interested.' She paused. 'I think I like him, Becky. He's kind, and . . . not pushy.'

'I know.'

'I feel happy today.'

'I'm happy for you. Despite my hangover.'

'Of course – it was Karen's party. I'd forgotten to ask how you got on. Tell me while I finish my sandwich.'

'It was fun. Shirley gave a line-dancing demonstration, and there was plenty to eat and drink. Denise was there, and maybe I shouldn't be telling you this, but then, she didn't tell me *not* to, and I know I can trust you not to spread it.'

'Spread what?'

'Jude, she's seeing someone else! She's having an affair. It's awful. I know George, her husband, and there's her children, Petra and Rowan. It was someone in Manchester, I think, not anyone we know. But that doesn't make it any better. I'm shocked at her, but on the other hand, she is my friend. Still, I wouldn't have thought it of her.'

'It's important not to judge people.'

'I know. I'm pleased you said that. But I can't approve of what Denise is doing.'

'You don't know what drove her to it.'

'But her husband, George, is such a nice man!'

'You only see his public face.'

Becky wondered about that. Yet Denise had not cited George's bad behaviour as a reason for her fling. It was typical of Jude to always blame the man. Perhaps Chris would cure her.

'Would you like an apple?' Becky asked. 'Or shall we get an ice-cream?'

'With double chocolate flakes and all the trimmings,' Jude said, getting up from the bench, and eyeing the ice cream van under the bridge.

'Aren't we wicked?' Becky said, joining her.

'I don't think I'll be able to follow this,' Chris said, frowning at his programme notes.

'It's quite straightforward. Figaro is engaged to Susanna but the Count fancies her. Marcellina wants to marry Figaro and Bartolo's in league with her because of an old grudge – and then there's Cherubino, who's in love with all the women – and they dress him up as a woman later on – and then there's the Countess and Barbarina—'

'I think I'll just listen to the music.'

Jude smiled to herself. She was confident in Mozart's power to move him, if not in her own. The safety curtain began to rise, and Jude filled with anticipation. The theatre seemed to be humming with excitement as the audience settled down. There was the rustling of programmes, a muted buzz of conversation, and then a hush and applause as the conductor walked on to the stage. Jude saw that Chris was fiddling with his opera glasses, trying them from both ends. After some discreet tuning, the overture began with gusto.

*The Marriage of Figaro* was one of Jude's favourite operas, because her mother loved it, as much for its political background as anything else. She remembered her mother explaining the *droit de seigneur* to her; Jude was only eleven, and appalled that another man should have the right to sleep with a bride before her rightful husband, just because he was rich. *That's men for you,* her mother used to say. Jude would laugh, enjoying being in collusion with her mother. And then there was Cherubino's song in praise of women. They loved that too.

She stole a glance at Chris. It was impossible to tell whether he was enjoying himself. Yet by sharing something that was so special to her, Jude realised she was being brought closer to him, almost against her own volition. No doubt Becky realised this when she had given up her ticket. She was cunning, but Jude didn't mind. When Chris put his hand softly on hers, Jude almost felt he was part of the conspiracy. She smiled contentedly to herself.

'Well?' she said, at the interval.

'The music is beautiful. I know a lot of it. And it's surprisingly easy to follow. Yes – it's good.'

Jude was delighted. 'Come on – I'll race you to the bar!'

By the time they claimed their drinks from the shelf under the window, the bar was already full. They stood in a corner under a poster advertising *Rigoletto*.

'I feel as if I need to have a good stretch,' Chris said. 'The seats are so cramped.' He rotated each of his shoulders in turn.

'That's a pity. The second half is longer still. There's the endless scene in the garden where the Countess and Susanna exchange clothes, and Almaviva gets his come-uppance.'

'And you? Are you enjoying it?'

She liked the way he looked at her. Was it Amy who'd said that it was good to have someone who cared about you? Well, she was right. Chris smiled at her as if he cared, and it was good.

'I'm enjoying everything,' she said, and smiled straight back at him.

Jude clapped until her palms were tingling.

'Doesn't the Countess remind you of Becky?' she said. 'I know she's a lot bigger, but there's something in her face.'

'I can see what you mean.'

It was true. Now that the soprano looked more natural, shyly accepting the congratulations of the audience, Jude was struck by the resemblance. That would be something she could tell her about the evening. They both rose to make their way to the exit. Jude linked arms with Chris as they joined the mass of people on the stairs. For Jude, it was always an anticlimax to leave an opera and become part of the real world. It was painful to leave the illusion that passion was possible. Opera located beauty in even the ugliest things. The truth was that ugly things were just ugly, and they had to be faced. Or laughed at.

And tonight, because she was happy, she was going to laugh.

They walked quickly through the back streets behind the Palace, to where Jude had parked her car. There was a faint aroma of Chinese cooking and the excitement of a city just coming awake. It was still warm, and gusts of steam from basement kitchens blended into the heady atmosphere.

They reached the car. Jude wondered about suggesting a drink, or even a meal, but she was aware that Chris might not have the money, and besides, there was at least an hour's drive before they were back in Mytholm. Another time, perhaps.

From Littleborough the road rose steadily on to the Pennines. The roads had been empty, and Jude was surprised by how quickly they had left the city behind. There were no street lights, and she put the car's headlamps on full beam. Dark hills massed on either side of them, and the car slowed as it began the ascent.

'This is one of my favourite parts of the world,' Chris said, after a period of silence.

'The Pennines overlooking Rochdale?' Jude asked incredulously.

'Let's stop and I'll show you.'

Jude pulled up, and they both left the car and their eyes ranged over the view. There were hundreds of street lights below them, radiating like an exuberant golden web, glowing in the surrounding darkness.

'"This majestical roof, fretted with golden fire."'

'Come on! It's only Rochdale!'

'Not from where we are.'

Jude wished she could think like him. Chris seemed to have a vision that she lacked. She was filled with envy. So when he turned to her and kissed her, she answered him hungrily, wanting whatever it was he had, wishing to bring back the colour of the opera, needing to be absorbed into the beauty that surrounded her but was tantalisingly out of reach. His kisses became more insistent too, and as they did she felt herself respond. There was a weakness in her legs, her stomach, and she felt his hands moving up and down her back.

'Will you sleep with me, Jude?' he whispered to her. 'I want you.'

'No,' she said.

'Is something wrong? Don't you like me?'

'I do like you – very much. But . . .'

He still held her, and she buried her face in his jacket, smothering herself and her words.

'What is it that's stopping you? Can't you tell me?'

He was kind, and she owed him an explanation. Perhaps it would help her to talk.

'Sex isn't really my thing. I have slept with men – not many – but I don't think I feel what I'm supposed to feel.'

'Perhaps you slept with the wrong men.'

'Yes! I've often thought that. But what if it's me? What if I'm the problem?'

'Why should it be you?'

'I always hold back. Part of me wants to lose myself, but the other part . . . finds it all rather disgusting.'

It was the truth, and it hurt her to say it.

'Disgusting? No, it isn't. Who gave you that idea?'

'Perhaps it was my mother.'

Jude knew she was lying now, but it was just as well. If she was going to break the spell tonight, she couldn't afford to face the truth. Luckily he never suspected her evasion.

'Your mother? I daresay it was to protect you. Do you still need protecting?'

'No,' she said in a small voice.

He kissed her again, and her kiss was timid, nervous.

'Let's go home,' he said.

They said little for the rest of the journey. Birk Vale was on the Mytholm Road, and Jude drove straight to Chris's cottage. When he invited her in, she said nothing but followed him. Once in the house, with the door closed, they kissed again, and Jude tried to recapture that abandonment she had felt on the moors. She clung to him with desperation.

He broke away from her.

'It's cold,' he said. 'I'll put on the fire.'

The gas fire lit the room with a bluish-yellow glow. Chris switched off the lights, and at first Jude could see little, then gradually the room, and Chris came back into focus. He pulled her to the floor and kissed her again, lingeringly, softly, until she entered into the rhythm of his kisses and it seemed quite natural when his hands began to explore her. She shivered with pleasure and the strangeness of it. The fire hissed and popped. He unbuttoned her blouse and murmured how lovely she was. She thought she ought to take off his shirt for him, and did so, fumbling a little. His skin against hers was wonderful and Jude's spirits soared. It would be all right after all.

He stood up to remove his trousers, and put on the condom. Jude stood too, and turned away from him to complete her undressing. She watched his eyes survey her body, and saw him smile. She was satisfied; it was still that same look of concern mingled with affection. He came towards her and she closed her eyes. It was better like that. He whispered her name as they approached each other.

Her throat was dry. Jude was not sure what to do. She couldn't take the initiative now, and show her near-ignorance. She knew she ought to respond by taking him, but could not.

He did not seem perturbed. He was as gentle, as considerate as she knew he would be, asking her permission, checking she liked what he was doing. And when the lovemaking began, she could hardly feel the thrusting. In her self-imposed darkness, there was just the closeness of his body, repeatedly coming nearer to her, and then a moment when he stopped, and said her name, and the lowered himself on to her, kissing her around her mouth, and tenderly stroking her breasts.

It was over, and there had been nothing to it! Now Jude was delighted, now she realised she had actually enjoyed it. She smiled, and opened her eyes.

'Thank you,' he said.

Jude sat up. She realised she wasn't in the least bit embarrassed about her nudity.

'Thank *you*!'

'Why wouldn't you open your eyes?' he asked her.

'I—' She turned her head away. 'I prefer it that way.'

'Will you stay the night?'

'If you'll have me.'

'Come on – I'll race you up the stairs!'


His bedroom was surprisingly bare. A double bed with a cream bedspread stood on floorboards; there were no curtains on the windows, but the diamond panes of glass were black with night. Jude rested her head on the crook of Chris's arm and was conscious of his leg across hers and the soft warmth from his body. She was very comfortable, despite the unfamiliarity of the room. She moved her head a little so she could look at her lover – she supposed that was the word one used now. His eyes were closed, but Jude could not tell whether he was asleep or not. She watched him a little longer, studied the faint stubble on his cheeks, the small dent in the cleft of his chin, his dark lashes and the small mole below his left eye. His strong jaw and straight nose gave him the air of a Roman consul. Some stray dark hairs grew from his shoulders, and Jude would have touched them, except she was certain now he was asleep, because of the rise and fall of his chest.

It was a very long time since she had slept in a bed with anyone else, and the novelty of it made her wide awake. Usually she read until she fell asleep, but she had no book with her. She contemplated getting up and finding one, but she was reluctant to leave the bed and the warmth of Chris's body, which almost seemed to be spreading into hers. She tried closing her eyes to see if sleep would come. Even if it didn't, it wouldn't matter, because it was Sunday tomorrow.

In the far distance, a car gunned down the hill. It had been a remarkable evening. First the opera, the drive back, and then this. It was nice, having a lover. The idea flattered her sense of herself. It was so cosy, lying in bed like this, like two children, almost. She remembered when Becky used to come and stay and her mother let them share the big bed. They'd talk most of the night, and almost always woke up at the same time and talked some more, in husky morning voices.

She smiled to herself. This was actually very different. Jude tried to recall the lovemaking that had happened to her. Now it was as if it had hardly taken place. It had all vanished, and all that remained was something like the smile of the Cheshire Cat. Then he had said to her, *why wouldn't you open your eyes?* And she had said, *I prefer it that way.* That wasn't entirely true. The explanation nudged at Jude now, only this time she didn't push it away. Chris's arm jerked from under her, and he turned and hunched into a foetal position. Jude turned too, and put her arms around him. He murmured something in his sleep.

She would let it come now. Ever since she had taken up with Becky again she had suppressed the memory, pretended it had never happened. For Becky's sake . . .

Waiting on the library steps did not bother her, even though it was dark. Jude was streetwise, always had been. She'd had no choice, coming from a single-parent family, and Phyllis was quite proud of not having mollycoddled her. It wasn't as if it was that late, and the street lights bathed everything in a yellow glow. Hundreds of street lights, all over Rochdale.

The sensible thing to do was to get the bus and go home. She had the keys to the house. She worried then in case Becky had been delayed, and would arrive and not find her. After an hour, it was obvious she wasn't coming. Jude began to walk along the street in the direction of the bus stop.

Buses were infrequent at that time of night. She guessed she'd have to wait about twenty minutes. She hoped someone would come and join her as it wasn't nice, being alone. There was a bingo hall opposite and Jude wished the women would come out. They were a funny crowd and made her laugh.

She strained her eyes for the bus. There were only cars approaching. She saw a Ford Anglia in the distance – she could tell by the two protuberant headlights like eyes on stalks. Becky's Dad drove a Ford Anglia. When she saw the number plate, she realised with a rush of delight that it *was* Becky's dad. Becky must have been late after all, and he had decided to run her to the library. She flagged him down eagerly.

Becky wasn't with him. He explained that she'd gone out with some boy. Jude was incredulous, angry, hurt. Becky's father offered to drive her home instead. She got into the front seat, trying to work out why Becky hadn't told her about this change of arrangement.

Becky's father made polite conversation. He commented on how winter was drawing in, how they were planning a one-way system for the centre of Rochdale. Jude answered absently, feeling a little awkward. She didn't know Becky's father that well, or rather, she hadn't ever spent any time alone with him.

They left the town centre. He didn't go along the main road to Shaw; she guessed there might be roadworks. He asked her if she didn't have a boyfriend too, like Becky. She said she didn't, feeling a little embarrassed.

'Come on,' he said, teasing her, 'I bet you do.'

'I don't know any boys,' she said.

With one hand on the steering wheel he seemed to fiddle with his belt. The car swerved ever so slightly and Jude kept her eyes straight ahead, too well brought up to draw attention to the fact the car wasn't holding the road properly.

'What about that disco you went to with Becky the other night?' he continued.

'The disco?'

'There must have been boys there. Did you meet anyone?'

'No.' Jude shifted towards the window.

'A pretty girl like you! You can tell me about it. What did it feel like, dancing close to a boy?'

'I didn't dance with anyone.' Jude wondered why they hadn't reached her road yet.

'You did. What did you feel, when you were close up to him? Was it hard? Did it feel like this?'

He took her hand, guided it down, and she felt something that she thought was alive, an animal? Something surprisingly warm, and a little bit sticky. She couldn't take her hand away because he was gripping her firmly. The thing under her hand quivered, leapt, stiffened. The car swerved to the verge and stopped. He groaned. There was a horrible sensation as something warm and wet oozed over her fingers. She snatched her hand away and caught sight of the dark, grotesque thing coming out from his trousers. Again and again she wiped her hand on the car seat. Her stomach heaved.

'I want to go home.' She began to get out of the car.

'I'll take you home.' He started the car again. She thought she was going to be sick. She couldn't help looking again. It was smaller now, shrivelled.

'You shouldn't have made me do it,' he told her.

Jude saw herself sitting in the car, next to him, watching the moving shadows on his face as the car turned into her road.

'You're a naughty girl,' he said. 'I wouldn't tell anyone, if I was you.'

The car pulled up outside her house. Jude ran up the front path, fumbling for her keys. Her hand was still sticky.

It smelt, too. Once inside she put on the hall lights and ran to the bathroom. She scrubbed and scrubbed her hands, breathing in the odour of the Camay soap, heaving with sobs.

She was still there when her mother came in.

*You're a naughty girl. You shouldn't have made me do it.*

Jude knew that wasn't the truth. She told her mother what he'd said, and bit by bit, explained it all. Phyllis had always been a plain-speaking woman, and she'd taught Jude to be plain-speaking too. They spoke in the language of Jude's biology text book. Penis. Erection. Ejaculation.

Phyllis had never been as angry as she was that night. Something akin to madness had entered her mother's eyes. Yet outwardly Phyllis was calm. She helped Jude into her nightdress, made her some Ovaltine. She reassured her, explained how Becky's father was probably sick. She said she had to go out. She tucked Jude into bed, and even brought her the floppy-eared bunny that used to be her security toy. Jude was surprised to see it. She thought her mother had thrown it out. Holding it tightly, Jude fell into a mindless sleep.

It was many years later that her mother told her where she had gone. She had driven to Becky's, and knocked loudly at the door. Becky's mother answered.

'It's your husband I want to speak to,' Phyllis said.

Becky's mother looked puzzled. Then her father came to the door. Phyllis was prepared. Her right hand was already formed into a fist, throbbing with tension. It landed squarely on his left eye. The force of the blow bent him double. With her right foot, Phyllis administered a hearty kick where she knew it would most hurt. He slid down against the wall.

'I'm sorry,' Phyllis said to Becky's mum. 'But he deserves it all, and more.'

In the morning Phyllis told Jude that it was all over and she never need think of the incident again. It was an order. Besides, there was a physics test in the morning and Jude wanted to do well in it. The monstrous memory was banished to the cellars of her imagination. Reality was the physics test and lunchtime hockey practice.

'And I'd avoid Becky, if I were you,' Phyllis said. 'I wouldn't give you twopence for the whole family.'

Her mother's word was law. Besides, Jude was hurt, because Becky had chosen a boy in preference to her, and didn't even bother to tell her. Avoiding Becky also meant it was easier to forget. She rebuffed her once or twice, and she could see Becky was upset. Jude tried not to care, but she was sad, because she had loved Becky. Gradually they drifted apart. It was strange to think that she'd got ninety-eight per cent for the physics test. Mrs Robinson had been delighted with her . . .

Jude's arm was numb, as Chris had been lying on it, so gently she disengaged it. He was breathing heavily now, his mouth pursed into a little pout on the pillow. Jude wondered if she had finally exorcised the memory. Perhaps she ought to tell someone, to complete the process? Chris? Possibly. There was no one else. Becky must never know. What was the point of telling her? It was lovely, the way Chris's back fitted so snugly into her body. She brought her other arm towards her, and welcomed the slow drift into the mists of sleep.

The three of them sat on the low wall of the pub car park, eating chips. Amy felt a little nervous. What if a teacher saw them? None of them had a pass out of school, but Petra said it didn't matter, they never checked. Amy picked at her chips slowly. The fear of getting caught took her appetite away, and anyway, it was too hot for chips. It was just that Petra and Dawn were having chips, so she thought she'd better. Petra was sitting in the middle, and Amy and Dawn were on either side of her. It was funny that it could be so hot when the sun had gone in. Amy couldn't think of anything to say so she stared at everyone's shoes. They all wore Kickers with laces running through the sides. At least they were wearing the same shoes. Amy's mum had been awful about the shoes, saying that they were a waste of money when her feet were growing so quickly. She didn't understand.

She didn't understand that it wasn't easy, being Petra's friend. You had to talk in a certain way and dress in a certain way. Then the rewards were great. But if you got it wrong – Amy suspected she might have been getting it wrong recently – then you were no one. And it had been so good when they were best friends. It had been really special. Then Petra had said that she needed space. Amy thought that sounded very mature. Dawn had come on the scene then, and Amy had been excluded. Only today Petra had come in and smiled at her. Then she and Dawn had asked her to have lunch with them. She was back in favour. It was worth risking getting in trouble with the teachers for that.

'Go on,' Dawn said. 'Tell her!'

Petra didn't respond.

'Tell me what?'

'Nothing.' Petra seemed unconcerned.

'You said you would.' That was Dawn again. Something was up, Amy felt sure of it. She desperately wanted to be in on the secret.

'Please tell me what it is.'

Petra gave Dawn a quick glance. 'Well, we didn't know whether to tell you or not. But in the end we thought you ought to know.'

'Ought to know what?'

Some lads walked by from year ten, and the girls stopped what they were doing. Then Petra resumed.

'You ought to know why we can't be friends any more.'

Amy felt the portcullis lowering slowly. It was agonising.

'Why can't we be friends?'

'Don't you know?'

'I haven't got a clue what you're talking about.'

'Me and Dawn thought you'd know, which is why we decided to tell you.'

'I *don't* know!' Amy was scared, and the skies seemed darker than ever, and she was hotter than ever.

'If you don't know,' Petra said, 'then we'd better not tell you.'

Did she smell, like Sophie? Maybe some lad had been badmouthing her? She didn't want to know what it was, but at the same time, she just had to.

'Petra's been very upset,' Dawn said, in a concerned, motherly voice.

'Upset about what? *Please* tell me!'

'I know something about your dad.'

'My dad? What's he got to do with it?'

'She doesn't know!' Dawn's voice was alight with mischief.

'Where was your mum last night? And your dad?' Petra asked her.

'Mum stayed in. Dad went out. To the golf club, I suppose.'

'Oh, yeah?'

'So what?' Amy's heart was thudding against her chest.

'Last week, my mum stayed the night in Manchester. And your dad was with her.'

Amy was getting confused. And hot, too. She could feel herself breaking into a sweat.

'I know because I rang my mum up when she was staying overnight in Manchester. And your dad answered the phone.'

'They're friends,' Amy said weakly.

'More than friends.' Amy heard Dawn giggle.

'Stop it!' Amy said, to both of them.

Petra went on remorselessly. 'I reckon they're having an affair.'

'Don't be stupid!'

'Petra's been really upset,' Dawn said again. 'It's all your dad's fault.'

'They're not having an affair,' Amy said. The idea was

ridiculous. Petra was making up lies so they wouldn't have to be friends.

'Your dad went out last night, right? So did my mum, only she told us she was visiting *your* mum.'

'They must have been out together,' Dawn added.

Amy felt panicky. They couldn't be making all this up, because her dad did go out last night. What if it was true? She felt very sick. She looked down at the mess of chips and tomato sauce in the cone she was holding and her stomach churned.

'It *is* true, Amy. They're having an affair. I hate your dad, I really hate him. And I hate you. No one's going to be your friend any more.' Petra gave her a sharp kick, and Amy dropped her chips, and they cascaded all over the pavement. Before she could think what to do, Petra and Dawn had picked up their bags and blazers and were off, running down the Halifax Road, back to school.

Amy stood up. The sky seemed very dark, and she felt very small and frightened. Her dad having an affair? With Petra's Mum? It didn't make sense. Only people on telly had affairs. She thought about the soaps she watched, only they weren't real. People didn't have affairs in real life. If her dad was having an affair, then her parents would get divorced. Amy's soul earthquaked. The taste of bile rose in her mouth.

Opposite her a woman cycled by, a multicoloured rucksack on her back like the shell of an exotic snail. It frightened Amy. The world she knew was breaking up. Petra hated her, and Petra was spreading lies about her dad. But they might not be lies. Large, warm drops of rain landed on her cheeks, her school shirt, and she saw other kids making their way back for afternoon lessons.

She couldn't go back to school. Amy wanted to be at home, nestling in her mum's lap, being hugged by her, and being told that everything was just as it was this morning, that she was safe. She wanted to run to her dad, her big, strong dad, only *he* was the one who was causing all this. A wild panic caught her in its grip. She picked up her blazer and bag and began to walk quickly in the direction of town. The sky grew darker still as bigger drops of rain splashed on to the pavement. Amy began to trot. This is the worst day of my life, she thought. She began to imagine what it would be like if her parents divorced. She would have to choose which one to live with. She would have to stand in a court and say which one. She couldn't do that. Terror convulsed her and she began to run as fast as she could to leave it all behind. Her bag swung wildly at her back, hitting her repeatedly.

Amy didn't care. She wanted to get home to her mum. She could get the bus from town. And then she could tell her all about it. But what if she didn't know about Dad? She would be upset too. It was a dreadful thought. No – Mum would just tell her it was all a lie. And she ran and got wetter and wetter, and hardly noticed. Behind her she heard the swish of a bus approaching, and she carried on running. It was her bus. She was ages away from the bus stop, and there wouldn't be another for an hour. The unfairness of it staggered her. The bus smoothly overtook her and vanished into the distance.

Now Amy began to cry, because of the bus, because of Petra, because of what she said about her dad. She cried with great, breathless sobs as she ran towards the town centre. The streets were empty on account of the rain. A flash lit up the sky, and then there was the long, slow rumble of thunder as if the world was ending.

'Help me!' she cried.

The centre of Mytholm Bridge looked deserted too. Amy stopped and looked up Crown Street. She didn't know what to do now. She was trembling. If she tried to walk up the hill she would be soaked, and probably get ill, and die. Most of all she wanted to talk to someone. She didn't feel well. She slowed down to a walk, and passed Crown Street, glanced up it, and remembered when she had gone to see about her brace. And she thought of Jude. Jude would know what to do. The image of Jude filled her thoughts, and she started running again, this time in the direction of the surgery. There was only a little further to go, past the wine bar, the Chinese takeaway, the menswear shop, and then the newsagent. Push open the door with Jude's name on the wall, up the stairs to the reception desk, and there was someone — not Jude.

'Can I see Jude please?'

'Do you have an appointment?'

'No.' Amy sniffed back the tears. Surely they weren't going to stop her seeing Jude?

'Hold on a moment, love.'

The lady in the white coat disappeared. Amy wiped the wet from her face and realised that her hair was dripping rain on to the shoulders of her blazer. No one came. She read the posters about cleaning your teeth properly and looked at the roll of stickers reading 'I've had my teeth checked'. Still no one came. Amy felt as if she was suspended in time. Nothing was real any more. She didn't properly understand what she was doing here. Her blazer dripped on to the green carpet.

Jude strode across the waiting room, Amy turned to greet her and saw the concern in Jude's face and it made her feel very sorry for herself. It made her want to cry again.

'Amy! Are you in trouble?'

She answered with gulping sobs.

'Sheila! Finish off for me. I'll take her into your room.'

Amy felt herself propelled into what looked like another dentist's surgery.

'You're soaking wet,' Jude said. 'Why aren't you at school? Does your mum know where you are?'

'No. I bunked off.' She gave a big sniff.

'Something's happened, hasn't it?'

Between sobs, Amy told her. 'It's Petra. She said she hates me, and she said . . .' Amy faltered. 'She said my dad was having an affair with her mum.'

'She said that?'

'It's not true, is it?'

She felt Jude's arm around her. 'She sounds a nasty piece of work to me. You're better off without her.'

'It's not true about my dad, is it?'

'I feel like I'm cuddling a sponge,' Jude said, laughing. 'First of all I'm going to give you a good towelling down, a cup of tea, and then we'll ring your mum.'

So it was all right after all. Jude was behaving the same as usual. She wouldn't do if her parents were really in trouble. But there was something she had to say to Jude first. Something very important.

'I don't drink tea. Have you got a Coke?'

'I'll send Sheila out for one immediately,' Jude said.

# Chapter Ten

Nothing concentrated the mind quite like root-canal therapy, Jude decided, as she locked up the surgery after her last patient. For the last three quarters of an hour she had forgotten about Amy and Becky. It had been a relief. Now work was finished, she returned to them, picking over again the bones of the situation.

When Becky had arrived at the surgery, Amy had rushed to her, told her she'd had a dreadful row with Petra, and had said nothing about the other business. Becky had been anxious and reproachful, told Amy off for leaving school in the middle of the day, but promised to explain to the Head of Year tomorrow. Then Jude had another patient, and had to leave them.

She dropped into second gear as she ascended the hill. What she had to establish was whether Paul really was the one having an affair with Denise. She could believe it of *him*, certainly. If only she had seen him with Denise, then she would have known. Becky had suggested they all got together on several occasions, but it had never happened. Becky's main agenda with Jude had been to get her paired off with Chris.

Chris! She had promised to ring him during the afternoon, and the business with Amy had put that clean out of her mind. He would be bound to understand when he knew. But back to Denise. Her lover could *not* be Paul, else she would have never told Becky about her affair. She should have realised that earlier, and saved herself this gnawing anxiety. In the distance was her cottage and, yes, there was the Discovery in her parking space. Men! Except Chris, she added as an afterthought. Leaving her Micra further down the lane, she walked over to her house, uncomfortably conscious that her neighbour was in. At least the storm would prevent them from wanting to use their gardens; last night both had sat on deckchairs and read, Jude being aware of his presence on the other side of the hedge. She'd jumped every time he'd turned a page. What was interesting was that the cats sedulously avoided him. They seemed to dislike him every bit as much as she did.

Jude took herself to task for digressing. She had to decide what to do about Becky. She opened the door and Aida and Ludmilla walked towards her, tails high in greeting. She stroked them absently. She could not possibly repeat Amy's belief to Becky; it was the slander of a schoolgirl, utterly baseless. She wandered over to where a bottle of Gordon's gin stood on a shelf and walked with it to the kitchen. As she opened the fridge the cats pushed against her legs, and kept her in sight as she took some tonic, and put together her drink.

She hadn't liked Paul from the beginning. Such a self-centred, arrogant bore. And slimy too. She remembered that first evening she met him, when she'd come back for her coat, and quickly he had replaced the receiver and looked so guilty. So guilty . . .

Aida jumped on to the draining board to lick at the tap. Ludmilla watched her, in case this was the prelude to an assault. He *is* having an affair with her! Jude concluded. Every instinct she had persuaded her it was true. She took her gin into the lounge, placed it on a table by the side of the settee, sat down, crossed her legs, propped her head in her hand, and thought.

She had no proof. None whatsoever. There was Petra's accusation, an interrupted phone call and Paul's general unlikeability. It would never convince a jury. And if it was true, then what? What do you do when you suspect your best friend's husband is cheating on her? Do you tell her? She wouldn't thank you for it. Do you speak to the husband? Jude tried to imagine how she could get Paul alone, broach the subject of his love life, and then tell him to lay off Denise? Utterly and inconceivably impossible.

Ludmilla landed on her lap, and began to purr insistently. Aida jumped on to the table and sniffed the full gin and tonic, and retreated quickly, wincing with discomfort. To do nothing, Jude thought, was a dereliction of duty unworthy of a true friend. Becky would have to face up to the fact of Amy's suspicions. As Amy's mother, she had to know. Then she could put her daughter's mind at rest, or . . .

The worst thing was, Jude felt such a hypocrite. How easy for her to tell Becky what a ratbag her husband was, while she was swooning over Chris. What a reversal there had been! She couldn't do it. Aida began to nip Ludmilla's legs, who turned and hissed at her. Then she leapt down and the cats began a frantic chase around the room. She would have to do it. Becky deserved no less than the truth. It was a failure to tell the truth that ended their friendship, and Jude refused to let that happen again.

As she got up, the cats raced into the kitchen. Jude only went as far as the telephone.

'Becky? How's Amy? Good? Listen – I'd like you to come round tonight. OK, later, then. No, nothing's wrong. See you soon.'

So the die was cast. Jude reached round and rubbed the back of her neck in perplexity. This wasn't going to be easy. She remembered her gin, and was about to claim it, but there was Chris to ring, and the cats needed her too. She had not fed the cats. Chris would have to wait a few minutes. She entered the kitchen amid joyous miaows.

They hugged each other, and Becky began talking immediately.

'I don't think she was well, Jude. That was why she did it.

I feel awful not having listened to her more. I didn't realise that her fall-out with Petra was so serious. But we had a good talk after dinner, and I left her in bed. Luckily Paul's in tonight, so—'

'Do you want something to drink? Tea? Coffee? Something stronger?'

'I won't sleep if I have coffee, but I'm driving so I can't—'

'I'm going to make you some tea. I'll have some with you.'

'Who's playing the piano?'

'My delightful next-door neighbour. Mr Macho Discovery.'

'He's rather good. Isn't that the theme tune from *Casablanca*?'

'I'm surprised you recognised it.'

Jude was grateful for the diversion. It gave her time to adjust to her delicate task. Becky made herself comfortable on the settee and picked up Jude's *Private Eye* and began to flick through it.

'What a day!' she said.

Jude returned quickly with the tea, and joined Becky on the settee. It would be better not to beat around the bush.

'There was something else Amy was upset about.'

'Was there?'

'Mmm. Though I'm sure it's just one of these cases of malicious gossip. You know what kids are like.'

'Are they spreading rumours about her?'

'Not about her. Actually, Petra mentioned Paul, of all people. She said that it was Paul who was having the affair with Denise'

'Paul! How ridiculous!' Becky laughed. 'He wouldn't have the time nor the energy. Paul?'

'As I said, you know what kids are like.'

'And Amy believed her?'

Jude nodded.

'Oh dear! I'll have to have a word with her. *The Return of the Native*? What's that about?' Becky picked up a book from the floor. 'Ah! It belongs to Chris. He must have lent it to you. That's nice. We had a good session last week, on getting to know our characters. We had to—'

'Becky – why do you think Petra said what she said?'

'Said what?'

'About Paul and Denise.'

Becky looked uncomfortable. Jude felt as she often did when drilling the cavities of a nervous patient, knowing she was causing pain, but being duty-bound to do it.

'I don't know.'

'Apparently she told Amy that she had rung Denise in Manchester, and Paul was with her.'

'No, he was at Clive's flat. That's where he was staying. He's been frantically busy at work . . .'

Through the walls came the melody, 'Ain't misbehavin''. Neither Jude nor Becky were aware of it. Becky was quite still, quite without motion. Then she raised her hand to her mouth and left it there. Her eyes were wide with disbelief. Jude flinched as if someone had hit her too. The pianist next door stopped in the middle of a bar, and ran his hands over the piano, bringing the tune to a dissonant end.

'No,' Becky said.

Jude said nothing.

'What shall I do?'

Jude put an arm around her. 'You ought to find out what's really going on. It might not be as bad as you think.'

As Jude said that, she knew it was every bit as bad as it could be. She would have given anything to change Becky's situation, anything. She prayed silently to a God she had given up on in her teens.

'I'd better speak to Paul.'

'Yes. You do that.'

'But not tonight. I can't do it tonight, because of Amy. There might be a scene.'

'I'll ask Amy to spend the night with me tomorrow.'

'Thank you.'

'Don't thank me.' Jude realised there were tears in her eyes. She was about to cry, and Becky was not. Becky was white and drawn, but that was all.

'Jude – I can't believe that Denise would do this. We're friends. She's known Paul for years.'

'Some women are like that.' Jude's voice dripped with distaste.

'Perhaps she threw herself at him, and you know what men are like – he couldn't say no, could he?' The thought seemed to cheer Becky.

'Perhaps.'

'I'd better find out.'

'Oh, God, he's been sleeping with both of us!' Becky laughed again, a shade hysterically. 'We're almost related! But as long as he doesn't prefer her to me.'

'That doesn't make it any better,' Jude suggested.

Becky smiled at her weakly. 'I don't know what I'm saying. I suppose I'm in shock. Like Amy. Poor Amy. Shall I keep her off school tomorrow?'

'No. I think school's the best place for her.'

'I'll have a word with her teacher.'

'Yes. Tell her to walk over to the surgery after school.'

'Paul will be late, but when he comes home, I'll speak to him.'

'You've got guts, Becky.'

'Do you think so?'

Jude nodded and Becky attempted a smile.

'For Amy's sake,' she said.


Denise parked her Brava in an empty bay outside a modern brick-built business unit. On the wall was the familiar logo of Paul's company. So this was where he worked. Denise was a little disappointed. She hoped that by agreeing to meet him at the helm of his ship, so to speak, she would recapture some of the dynamite in their relationship. Failing that, at least she'd get a decent dinner out of him. Then she would go straight back to Mytholm; she had made a point of stressing this to Paul.

She got out of the car, noticed her sun dress had creased, and smoothed it down over her stomach. She thought with satisfaction that no one would ever guess that she had had two children. Having spent the morning at the tanning salon, her legs were attractively bronzed, and so she had dispensed with stockings, and wore some leather sandals with her toenails painted scarlet.

There was a door marked 'Reception', just as Paul had said, with an intercom panel. She pressed the button he had mentioned. There was a crackle and buzz and Paul's voice. 'It's me,' she said. A click indicated that the door had been released. She entered, and ascended the staircase in front of her. Going up the wall were framed photographs of the personnel. She scanned them, looking for Paul. It was odd how few truly attractive men there were. She found Paul's portrait, and he was smirking. She allowed herself to shudder just a little.

Along the corridor was a door, which she opened to reveal his secretary's office, its computer screen dark now. The door to Paul's inner sanctum was open. He was sitting at his desk, his brow stern with thought, looking over some papers. Denise immediately saw through this studied pose. Men were such little boys.

'Have I caught you at a busy moment?'

He looked up at her and gave a lascivious wink.

'Nothing that won't wait.'

He rose from his chair, pulling off his tie. Denise froze. Surely he wasn't going to leap on her again, and here of all places? An office! With a map of Great Britain on the wall, filing cabinets, and overlooked by Parcelforce. But no. They would not be overlooked by Parcelforce because Paul had deftly closed the vertical blind and the room was now dim and shady.

In a moment he had approached her, and began to paw her, his hand pushing her dress up. Denise's eyes were wide open, and she studied his empty chair with his jacket slung over it.

The chair was one of those director's chairs, with a substantial head-rest, in sage-green leather. Hopefully Paul would give her nothing but this quick grope, and then they could go out for dinner. His hand began to pull at her panties.

'No, Paul!'

He was breathing heavily. 'What's wrong?'

'Just give me a little time,' she said.

He removed his hand, but carried on nuzzling her. Denise felt entirely unaroused. This was getting beyond a joke. There ought to be more to a relationship than sex.

'I feel awkward here,' she told him.

'No one can see us.'

'It's not that. You're just . . . so sudden.'

'Because you turn me on.' He carried on feeling her, kissing her neck, and thrusting himself against her, in what he obviously thought passed for foreplay. Denise closed her eyes. This was almost as bad as George. The only way she'd been able to tolerate George's inept lovemaking had been through fantasy, and it was probably a good idea to use some now. Over the past few years she had been to bed with Kevin Costner, Liam Neeson, Hugh Grant, and the whole of the Manchester United football team. In fact she'd worn them out. Time for someone new. Unbidden, the thought of Jim Ferguson came to mind. She remembered the litheness of his body, and that studied look he gave her at Karen's. Why should Karen have all the fun? She said she was in love with him? They certainly didn't act as if they were in love. In fact, he'd seemed much more interested in Denise, thus demonstrating his innate taste, despite the fact he was only a builder. Jim Ferguson . . .

*Jim squeezed her bottom, and began to kiss her, forcing open her mouth with his tongue. Jim's hand delved into her sundress and seized on her breast. Jim pulled down her panties and told her how wonderfully sexy she was, and when she opened her eyes she would see his young, muscular body waiting to do her pleasure . . .*

'I've had an idea,' Paul said.

She could have kicked him! She was just beginning to enjoy

herself. Paul, however, had broken away from her, and was now taking off his trousers and Y-fronts, but leaving his shirt and tie on. Denise was beginning to feel as if she was starring in some French farce. Paul went back behind his desk and to her surprise sat on his chair again.

'Come and sit on my lap,' he instructed her.

'Paul!'

'I've told you once. Come and sit on my lap.'

She didn't like the tone in which he spoke to her. What a fool he looked, sitting on his ridiculously pompous chair, with no underwear on, his stubby little penis a purplish red against his flaccid, pale skin. She gave a little laugh. He laughed back, obviously thinking that she was amused by his powers of sexual invention.

She advanced towards him, and he swivelled the chair round at an angle to his desk. No, she couldn't possibly do this.

'Sit on me,' he insisted.

She perched on the edge of his knees.

'Move up.' His voice was unattractively croaky.

'Sorry, Paul. I can't.' She stood up, feeling absolutely sickened. All sorts of perversions distressed her, and straddling Paul on his director's chair struck her as falling into that category. 'I'm really not in the mood tonight.'

He didn't look very pleased.

'It must be because my period's about to start. Any minute,' she added.

'I don't care about that.'

'And it's Becky,' she said, desperate now. 'I can't help thinking about Becky, and how devastated she would be if she knew. I need time to think.'

'What do you mean by that?'

'I have to be sure we're doing the right thing.'

Paul left his chair and came towards her. She thought how ridiculous he looked, and found it hard not to laugh.

'I can't live without you,' he muttered, and put his arms around her.

'Don't be so silly,' she admonished him. She kissed him lightly on the cheek. 'Now go and get dressed like a good boy.' She turned and knelt down to retrieve her panties. Thank God she had managed to avoid him. She really would have to think about their whole relationship. Paul was starting to get on her nerves. The idea of Paul Howarth was so much better than the reality. And the idea of Jim Ferguson was considerably better than the idea of Paul Howarth.

'Shall we go out for a drink?' Paul asked her.

'No. I was going to tell you – but you didn't give me a chance – you wild beast,' she prodded him playfully, 'that I can't stay. I haven't done my homework for my writing class. I promised the class I'd present them with chapter three of my novel. I'll ring you soon.'

'Stay with me a bit longer. You promised me—'

'I know I'm awful. I'm ever so sorry.'

Denise stroked the door handle. A smile played on her lips. She hoped that Paul interpreted it as teasing and ambiguous. In fact she couldn't wait to get back to her car and explode with laughter. Standing in the middle of his office in just his shirt, tie and navy socks he cut a truly pathetic figure.

She ran down the stairs lightly, and as she lifted the catch and walked into the sunlight she decided that she couldn't possibly let him make love to her again. The only problem was that she needed a hero for her bestseller. It was so much easier if one could act it out. Paul was too old for a hero, anyway. Women liked men who were young, strong, virile. Yes. Jim Ferguson was wasted on Karen.


Paul heard Denise close the door of the outer office. He stood still for a moment, his trousers still over the back of a chair. An unpleasant feeling stole over him, composed of disappointed lust, a sense of being made to look a fool, and fear. He was scared that she was going off him.

To Paul, fear was weakness. He swore to himself, and began

to dress. He reasoned that Denise was simply being a tease, like all women. Her refusal to play along with him was her way of keeping his interest. This thought cheered him, and under its influence, he ran a comb through his hair, donned his jacket, locked up, and made his way to his Mondeo.

Being behind the driving wheel made him feel better too. The feel of the responsive gear stick in his hand, and the way the car slid smoothly on to the road comforted him. He turned on his Meat Loaf tape. There was an indefinable tension in his body which he associated with a lack of sexual fulfilment. He was rather angry with Denise, and felt he had every right to be angry.

He accelerated down the slip road of the M66. The motorway was unusually busy. He changed lanes a few times to escape from the lumberingly slow lorries, and finally got to a clear stretch in the fast lane, and then was impeded in his progress by some stupid woman in a silver Renault. He came up close behind her, indicating right, flashing his headlamps. She seemed completely oblivious of him. He felt himself fill with rage. He couldn't undertake as a Transit was coming up in the middle lane. All his muscles tensed with anger at women who ventured on to motorways when they didn't have a clue about driving! It seemed ages to him before she dropped back, and he shot her a look of venom as he overtook, accompanied by a choice gesture. Still she didn't acknowledge him. The incident left him tingling with irritation.

It was a feeling which didn't let up as he approached Mytholm Bridge. He'd had a bloody awful day, come to think of it. There was the order to Chesterfield that had gone astray, his secretary leaving early and the confusion that caused, and this business with Denise. He felt cheated now, and next time they met he'd certainly tell her she couldn't play him around like this. If there was a next time. As he left the car he felt a little disturbed, very angry, stiff with tension, and full of self-righteousness. He needed a drink. Or two.

He unlocked the front door.

★ ★ ★

Becky heard him. He was earlier than she'd anticipated. Perhaps it was as well to settle the business now. All day she had been unable to eat, unable to get on with anything, and despite the number of times she'd thought through what she was going to say, she had still not decided how to broach the subject. Broach it she must; she could not live another day without knowing the truth. It was still possible that it was all a dreadful mistake, or a sick fantasy cooked up by Amy's friends.

He walked straight into the living room, tossing his case on to the floor, and made for the drinks cabinet.

'Hello,' Becky said in a small voice.

'Bloody awful day,' he muttered, preparing himself a drink.

'Can we talk?'

'Talk?' He sounded as surprised as if she'd suggested they scale Mount Everest.

'I think we should have a talk.' He sighed dramatically, and turned with his drink, still standing, and looked at her, suggesting that he was waiting for her to get it over and done with. She felt uneasy in his gaze.

'Come and sit down.'

'I hope it won't take that long. Where's Amy?'

'At Jude's.'

He lowered himself into the armchair, and took a sip of his whisky. She looked at him, unwilling to begin. What Pandora's box might she open? Yet seeing him like that, just as he was nearly every evening, gave her courage. He couldn't possibly be sleeping with Denise. And to be truthful for a moment, how could *she* want to sleep with him? Feeling encouraged, she opened with a prepared statement.

'Have you seen Denise lately?'

He paused, his glass halfway to his lips. It was then that she knew. The room seemed to close in on her.

'No,' he said. 'Why should I? She's your friend.'

'I just wondered.'

Becky felt herself retreating, as someone might who has

inadvertently approached a cliff edge with a vertiginous drop. She watched Paul in silence for a few moments. He drained his glass, then handed it to her.

'Get me a refill.'

Becky did so, but the peremptoriness of his command roused her. She took him his drink, and stood in front of him.

'It's just that Amy was upset the other day. Petra told her that you and Denise were having an affair.'

'Don't be so bloody stupid.'

He didn't look at her.

'Switch on the telly,' he said.

'Not yet. Can you promise me it isn't true?'

'Ask her, since you're so matey. I can't be doing with this after the sort of day I've had.'

'She told me she was having an affair – with someone.'

Paul swivelled his eyes round to look at her, in alarm. 'With someone? Who?'

'I don't know. That's why I'm asking you.'

'What did she tell you? Is there someone else?'

'Someone else? It's true – you are seeing her.'

She watched Paul grow redder, either with shame or anger. She didn't know which. She didn't care. She was adjusting to this new reality. She had only been able to cope with Jude's bombshell because it might not be true. Realising it was true was as bad as hearing it all for the first time.

'Get off my back,' he said to her.

'So you are seeing her.' Part of Becky still wanted him to deny it.

'Yes I bloody am!'

The man who was her husband had transformed into something monstrous and alien. Yet in a way his anger reassured her. He was often angry; the normality of this helped her to navigate the next part of the conversation.

'Why? I mean, how did it happen?'

He remained mute, but Becky's need to understand was even stronger than her distress, and it drove her forwards.

'Tell me how it happened.'

'Like it always does. So what else do you want to know? What we do in bed together?'

His face was white and pinched with suppressed anger. She had seen him like this before, and she knew what it boded. Normally she would back down. Tonight it was impossible.

'What about us? What about our marriage?'

He rolled his eyes in exasperation.

'Are you going to leave me for her?'

'Twitchy, are you?'

Becky hated him then. But stronger than her hate, was her fear. The little world she had built for herself, for Amy, the fragile little edifice called home, was in danger of being dashed to the ground after all because of this man's bull-headed stupidity. Despite his anger, she had to make him see what he was doing.

'Paul.' She took a deep breath. 'I want to you give her up.'

'Yeah, yeah.'

Frustration was mounting in her. It was his refusal to engage in any communication that was making her mad. She felt as if she had to find some way to pierce his armour.

'If you don't give her up, she'll give you up. At least, she will, when she knows you like I do.'

She was blinded as the whisky from his glass met her eyes. Then she jumped to her feet, and rubbed at her blouse, where the rest of the whisky had landed. Paul thumped his glass down on the table.

'Now lay off!'

'I can't. I've got to know where I stand.'

Paul rose to his feet too. 'Listen to me. I said, listen! Denise is my mistress. You get that into your head.'

He was close to her, his breath was on her face. Hot, whisky-sodden breath. She was revolted by him and it made her brave.

'I don't know what she sees in you!'

'Do you want to know? Do you want me to show you?' His arm was around her. The shock prevented her from reacting. At first she thought he was going to kiss her and that he had come round. Then he tugged at her skirt, and she was afraid. She didn't understand what he was trying to do. He was much stronger than her, and her attempts to push him off had no effect.

He dragged her down on to the floor and quickly she pushed the coffee table to one side, afraid she would bang her head on it. He was on top of her. Now she thought he was going to kill her. Rage and hatred distorted his face.

'No!' she shouted.

He pulled down his trousers, her underwear, and then she realised what he was about to do. She was paralysed with fear and horror. But he was her husband. She had no right to stop him. She felt a searing pain as he entered her. She was being torn apart. With loud puffs and grunts he lunged at her repeatedly, crushing her with his weight. What used to give her pleasure was now being used to wound her, it was a weapon; he no longer loved her; he wanted to hurt her. The horror of this revelation was greater than the pain. With the force of his thrusts she was being moved nearer and nearer the coffee table, and soon her head was jammed against one of its legs, and it cut uncomfortably into her. She tried to concentrate on that only. It'll be over soon, she told herself; it'll be over soon.

He groaned as he reached his climax. Then he gave a small laugh. He withdrew from her, and rolled over by her side, then laughed again. His chest rose and fell as his breathing regained its natural rhythm. Becky took the opportunity to rise, pick up her clothes, and leave the room.

She lay on Amy's bed. She didn't know where he was. Afterwards, he had banged about the house, gone into the kitchen, she had heard the microwave ping, and later the sounds of the television. She had gone to the bathroom to shower. It was surprising that he had not damaged her, as far as she could see.

Later on he had climbed the stairs and presumably gone to bed. He did not come to find her. What did that portend? That he was intending to leave her? At no point during their argument did he say he would do that. It was her one ray of hope. It was possible that her marriage was stronger than his infatuation with Denise. This could all be just a dreadful episode that would run its course. And then they could arrange to see a counsellor at Relate. They should have done that ages ago. And then all would be well.

He had raped her. That was the truth. Brutally and deliberately. She knew she ought to leave him. She should take Amy and find somewhere else to go. He was no good, and she'd known that all along.

But what do you do when you leave your husband? Becky didn't know. There were women's refuges, of course, but she could not bear the idea of taking Amy to a hostel, and of leaving her own home. Could she stay here? Only it was Paul's home too, and he had the keys. And how would she support them both? She thought of Karen, who had been through something similar. She used to pity Karen, suspecting that she might have brought her troubles on herself. Now she knew different.

It was a small amount of relief to Becky to recall that Karen had it worse than her. Her husband had beaten her. Paul had not done that. Never. He had thrown things, but not at her. Even tonight, it wasn't clear why he had made love to her in the way he did. It hadn't really been rape. Rape was something that happened at gunpoint. She and Paul were a married couple, and for some reason just then he wanted her badly. Too badly to stop and ask.

Looking at it in this logical way calmed Becky. It was important – for Amy's sake – that she did not overreact. The fact was that even if Paul continued to see Denise, it might not be the end. Many men had mistresses; on the continent, apparently, it was quite the done thing. A man supported his family, and often another woman too. It might not be so bad after all.

But everyone would know. Karen and Jude and Chris and everyone. She would be the talk of Mytholm Bridge. She would be utterly humiliated. There was no choice; their marriage was over. And what freedom to be away from him, just her and Amy! But what would they live on? Like a needle stuck in a groove, her thoughts repeated themselves endlessly.

Then it occurred to her that Jude would want to know all that happened tonight. She couldn't possibly tell her. Partly it was the shame of what happened, but it was more than that. Jude would leave her with no choice. She would insist Becky walked out. Perhaps Karen would understand better? Except Karen would react just like Jude. And there used to be Denise . . . Once again the enormity of the betrayal sickened her. Her friends would tell her to leave Paul, but what if she didn't want to? Was there anyone she could speak to who would truly understand her predicament?

Yes. There was someone, someone who had suffered a similar indignity, and would know just how she felt. Becky remembered her father. She thought of him now, not as the querulous old man he'd become, but as the gruff, silent, strong man of her childhood. He would protect her. The thought of him calmed her. She would go to him in the morning, first thing. She would explain what had happened and ask for his advice. It was as well to keep this in the family. She ought to see him first, before anyone else. It was only right. She pulled Amy's duvet over her, and hoped that sleep would come. And then, in the morning, she would see Dad.

# Chapter Eleven

His curtains were still drawn. That did not surprise Becky, as she knew her father often didn't get up until later on. His arthritis could be quite bad in the morning. She pounded again on the front door. He really ought to have a proper doorbell installed. Still no response. Becky smiled at an Indian lady who walked past, in a bright orange sari. It helped, coming over to Rochdale. The drive had made her feel normal again. The art of handling a crisis, she'd discovered, was simply to do one thing at a time. There was no point in thinking about the future. You just put one foot in front of the other. She banged on the door again.

It took her aback when her father suddenly appeared. He was in his pyjamas and maroon dressing gown, tied round his waist with a cord. He looked slightly bewildered.

'Are you all right, Dad?'

'I weren't expecting you.'

'I know. Can I come in?'

He stood aside and Becky entered, trying not to inhale the musty, sweet aroma of her father's house. She would have to open a window. She walked into the front room and pulled the curtains to.

'Hold on there. I'm not dressed yet!'

Becky ignored him. She yearned for some light. Then she turned and faced him, and saw he was a little, shrivelled man, frail and worn. She felt dreadfully sorry for him, and wondered if she was right to come to him for help. Yet who else could she turn to?

Feeling a little weak, she sat on a wooden chair by the table, where a folded copy of the *Rochdale Observer* lay open at the sports reports.

'I've had a bit of a shock, Dad.'

'Oh aye?'

He came to sit at the table with her, not taking his eyes from her face.

'Yes. It's Paul.' Becky took a deep breath because she was afraid that she was going to cry, but she didn't want to pause too long, lest she worry her father. 'Paul's seeing another woman – a friend of mine. I found out last night.' She cried for a few moments, then wiped her eyes with the back of her hand. 'I never suspected anything.' Becky glanced up at her father to see his reaction. He looked at her solemnly.

'That's a bad do,' he said. She was grateful for his sympathy, and also relieved that he had taken it so calmly.

'He was very angry when I confronted him. He . . . he was violent to me. Dad – I'm not sure what to do.' She started to cry again, and hated herself for being so out of control. It was saying out aloud what had happened that brought it all home to her. She let the tears have their course. She felt her father watching her, and she wished he would come over and hug her. Instead he sat very still.

'Shall I make us both a cup of tea?' she asked, trying to pull herself together.

'Aye. A brew is a good idea.'

She hurried through to the kitchen and the remains of his last night's supper. She rinsed some cups which had not been washed properly. The activity calmed her. The worst was over. She brought the tea to her father, who was still sitting at the table.

'I haven't had me breakfast yet,' he told her.

'Shall I fry something for you?'

'Aye.'

Becky returned to the kitchen. Soon some bacon was sizzling in the pan. There was just one egg in the fridge, she cracked it and watched the white congeal and its garish yellow eye harden. Her stomach turned. She concentrated on the cooking, pushing the bacon around, freeing the base of the egg from the pan. She was glad to have this time to think. If she gave his house a thorough spring clean, and re-decorated, might it be possible to live here? Amy could have the box room, and she could sleep on a put-u-up in the lounge. At least for a time. She flipped the breakfast on to a plate and carried it through to the living room. Her father licked his lips.

She waited until he'd finished eating. She made no comment as he wiped his mouth with the edge of the tablecloth. For her own sake, she had to continue her tale. 'The woman he's seeing is one of my best friends. That's the worst of it. I don't think he'll finish with her, and I don't think I could bear to live with him, knowing that.' She picked up a blue biro on the table and played with it. 'Should I leave him?' She would not look at her father.

He sucked his teeth for a while. 'And where would you go?'

'Could we stay here? Just until I found something better?' She looked around the room. There was dust on the mantelpiece, and the wallpaper was peeling in the corners. She could not possibly bring Amy here.

Her father belched. 'I'm not moving out of my room.'

'But Dad, how can I stay with him?' Becky's voice was desperate.

'I've not got room here, you know. And don't think you can come marching in and put me in some home!' He gave her a mean look, then seemed to repent. 'Don't worry, lass. You'll sort it out.'

'He was so awful to me last night, Dad. He shouted . . . and other things. I'm frightened of him. I can't go back.'

Her father adjusted his teeth. 'Same as I said, it's a storm in a teacup. You get married for better or for worse. Aye, for better or worse. Your mother never realised that. But you've always been good to me. That's what you have a daughter for, to take care of you in your old age.' Then he put a hand on her shoulder. 'You can put up with him, lass. He's a good husband to you. He's never kept you short, has he?'

'No, but . . .'

'Ah, same as I said, he's never kept you short.' Her father seemed to be cheering up. 'And if he's one for the ladies, well . . .' He chuckled. 'It's only natural. Forgive and forget, forgive and forget. Don't be like your mother, sitting in judgement on me. This bacon keeps repeating. I don't know what you've done to it. I'd go to the Legion tonight but I paid the window cleaner and I've not enough to see me through. It's a good thing you've called.' He belched again.

Despair clutched at her. Years ago her father might have done something; now it was too late. She had no right to expect this arthritis-ridden old man to help her. Yet coming here had achieved one thing; it had shown her the sheer impossibility of moving in with him. She would have to rent somewhere; she had money because theirs was a joint bank account. But what if Paul cleared it out? It was a chilling thought. Money and a home were essential.

In an unexpected way, her father had helped her after all. From Amy's point of view, from her father's, the best thing would be if she could swallow her pain, and pick up the pieces of her marriage. It was the only practical alternative. If she never referred again to the events of last night, if she spoke to Denise and asked her to stop seeing him . . . Yes. She would not have to leave Paul. It was dreadful, that he should love another woman, but with effort she might be able to come to terms with the situation. Some women had to put up with far worse. Anything but step into the void where there was no one there for her at all. At one time her father might have been the one, but not now. He was her dependant, and she was responsible for him, and for Amy too. She had no choice but to swallow her pride.

'I've been silly, Dad,' she said.

'Aye.'

'I'll stay with him.'

He grinned at her in approval. This felt better. She was certain now she was about to do the right thing.

'You wouldn't have a fiver on you?' he asked.

'I can probably do better than that,' she said, opening her handbag.


Where could she be? Jude wondered. She drummed her fingers on the steering wheel of the stationary Micra. It hadn't surprised her to discover that Becky's house was empty; she had been ringing all morning and there had been no reply. It was lucky that her two o'clock had cancelled, as it gave her time to find out for herself what was going on. As yet, she was none the wiser.

She couldn't think where Becky might have gone. And what about Amy? Jude suspected Amy knew that something was afoot. She had asked her a couple of tricky questions, and it was lucky, on reflection, that Chris had popped round unannounced. It distracted all of them, and they had played Trivial Pursuit with Amy as question mistress. Jude had been tense, waiting for a phone call. None had come. Suddenly she was alert. There was the sound of a car engine. She looked in her mirror and saw Becky's Fiesta turn the corner and pull up in front of the house. At last!

Jude leapt out of the Micra, and waited for Becky as she emerged. Becky seemed calm, but tired too. There was a slackness in her face, a lack of resistance. She was not wearing any make-up. Was that why she looked pale?

'What happened?' Jude said.

'Let's go inside.'

Jude followed Becky into the house, which also had a

dishevelled, frowsty appearance, unlike its usual self. The washing up had not been put in the dishwasher.

'Did you talk to him?'

Becky walked straight into the dining room and took a chair.

'Yes. It's true.'

What does one say now? thought Jude. *I knew it all along?*

'I'm sorry.' That sounded inadequate. 'Where have you been? I've been ringing all morning.'

'I've been at my father's.'

'Right. Look, I'm starving, and you must be too. Shall I find some food?'

'It's all right, Jude. I'll get something for you.'

'No you won't. You're going to have to put up with my cooking today.'

'I'm not very hungry.'

Jude found her appetite was diminishing too.

'Let's skip lunch. Think of all those calories we'll save.' She attempted a smile. 'Shall we go into the lounge?'

'No,' Becky said quickly. 'I'd prefer to stay here.'

'All right.' Jude was puzzled. Had something happened in the lounge? Why on earth did Becky shudder at the mention of it? She felt increasingly uneasy.

'Do you want to tell me about it?' Jude asked, feeling her way gently.

'There's not a lot to tell. He conceded fairly quickly that the rumours were true, I provoked him, he lost his temper – all in all, it was a bad night.'

'And now what?'

Becky shrugged. 'I guess I'll speak to Denise. I think I'll have to. Now they've been discovered, I can't see it carrying on. It's all a bit of a mess. But we'll pull through, as we've always done.'

A miasma of defeat seemed to surround her. Jude struggled to understand how she could be so resigned, and failed.

'You're talking as if *you're* somehow responsible. You're not. Aren't you angry?'

'What's the point?'

'But you *were* angry. You said you provoked him. What did you do?'

'I told him he had to finish with her. I insisted on hearing the details.'

'And then what? What did he do?'

Becky hesitated, just enough to arouse Jude's suspicions.

'*What* did he do?'

'It . . . it was strange. I thought he was going to hit me – not that he ever has, not exactly. But he . . . we—' Becky made a gesture in the direction of the lounge. 'I don't know. I don't know why the argument should have had that effect.'

'I don't understand. What did he do?'

'He forced me . . . to sleep with him.'

'You mean he forced you to have sex with him?'

Becky nodded.

'Oh my God!' Silence, now. Jude's soul flinched in revulsion. So Paul had raped her. First he had betrayed her, and then he had raped her. What a dreadful way for a marriage to end! Jude tried to think what she knew about injunctions and separation orders. She decided she'd offer to go with Becky to the solicitors, and tried to visualise where she'd put the telephone number of the agency that could find her a locum. They might even be able to get things under way before it was time to get Amy. But now, Becky simply needed sympathy. Jude reached out and stroked Becky's arm.

'Where is he now?'

'At work, I suppose.'

'I'm not sure quite what the procedure is, but we can start by going down to the police station. I think we can take out an order to stop him coming home, and we can change the locks the next day.'

'Change the locks?'

'So that he can't get in.'

'It's all right. He won't do it again.'

'You mustn't give him a chance.'

'I managed him before, and I can manage him now. I pushed too hard last night. He'll feel remorseful when he comes home, and we'll take it from there.'

'You mean you're not leaving him?'

'No. Why should I?'

Jude felt as if she had been winded. Becky had been subjected to the ultimate humiliation by a man who'd cheated on her, who bullied her, ignored her, abused her – and she was staying with him. She felt as if Becky was standing on the other side of a chasm, a helpless, lone figure, almost out of reach. It was vital that Jude do something.

'Becky, this is no good. You can't stay with a man like that. He raped you.'

'He's my husband.'

'That doesn't mean he has the right to force himself on you.'

'I know. It was a mistake.'

'A mistake! Some mistake! He's cheated on you. You've got to see that. I know I'm being horrible and that you don't want to see this, but he's no good. He – is – no – good!'

Becky lifted her eyes to Jude, not in anger.

'He's a man, Jude. Men are like that. It's the way they are. Marriage is about making compromises—'

'He's got to make them too,' Jude interjected.

'And more often than not it's the woman who makes them. You don't end a marriage as lightly as that.'

'Lightly! There's no virtue in humiliating yourself.'

Up until now, Jude had tried to stay calm. She wanted to inflict no more violence on her friend. Now, however, it was a case of fighting fire with fire. Becky needed desperately to have her eyes opened.

'There's no humiliation, Jude. We can hush everything up. I'll tell Amy the rumours were unfounded, and soon everything will be back to how it was. I'm not putting Amy through the trauma of a separation.'

'Don't you think Amy is affected by the way he bullies you?'

'Bullies me?'

'And ignores you and takes you for granted? Yes, it's true, and you know it's true. I would be the less your friend if I pretended otherwise. I think you'd be better off without him. Much better off. I've thought that right from the first time I met him.'

'I know how he might seem to you,' Becky gently remonstrated. 'And I admit, I've had my disappointments. But we're *married*. That counts for something.'

'That's tosh! Sentimental tosh! He raped you. He's been sleeping with Denise.'

'Stop it!'

Electricity flashed in the air. Jude felt her pulse racing, but it was partly with the excitement of success. It was important to get Becky angry. Now it was a matter of channelling that anger in the right direction.

'You can't shut out the truth. You've got to get rid of him.'

'No, I can't – I mean, I won't. I . . . I've been speaking to my father this morning. I told him all about it. We had a talk, and he also feels I'm better off seeing this through.'

'Your father!' Jude could not prevent herself from voicing her distaste.

'Yes, my father. Who else should I turn to?'

'There's me,' said Jude, feeling a little hurt.

'He's my family,' Becky said simply.

Jude was silent.

'I didn't mean to hurt your feelings, Jude. But I did think I ought to go to him first. Not just because he's my Dad, but he's experienced a broken marriage. I don't want history to repeat itself. I was never sure that my mother did the right thing by leaving him.'

'She did do the right thing.'

'How do you know?'

Jude could have kicked herself. She had said too much. How could she extricate herself from this situation? She had promised her mother that Becky would never know any of this. But her mother was dead. Becky needed to know that her father was the worst possible person to advise her. And what about Amy? She was almost the age that Jude was, when her eyes were so brutally opened. Above all, Becky's father had to be discredited, and discredited now. Becky had to have her eyes opened too. Jude took a deep breath.

'Do you know why your mother left your father?'

'They never really got on.'

'Do you know why they never got on?'

'Different personalities,' Becky said. Her mouth was dry.

'Your father wasn't very nice.' She could say no more, and regretted having got this far. She pricked with guilt.

'What do you mean, not very nice? He was nice to you. He liked you. He always asked if you were coming round.'

Jude found she was wringing her hands.

'He wasn't nice to me. That night you – the night he picked me up from the bus stop. He tried something.'

'Tried something? What?'

'It doesn't matter.'

'No, what did he try? Tell me.'

'He made me touch him.'

'Touch him? I don't understand.'

'He exposed himself, and made me touch him.'

'You're disgusting. You're more disgusting than Denise.'

'No. I wasn't the one who was disgusting. I was fourteen, just a year older than Amy.'

'I don't believe you. You're making this up.'

'I'm not. I told my mother. She went straight round to your house. She gave your father a black eye.'

Becky was silent now. All the colour had drained from her face. Jude was eaten with remorse.

'Becky, I'm sorry. Don't stare at me like that. I daresay he couldn't help it. It's a sickness, isn't it? I'm sorry, but I had to be honest with you. Becky, forgive me, please.'

'Get out.'

'Write to your mother – she'll confirm what I say. I didn't want to hurt you. But you must stand on your own two feet. You—'

'Jude – I'm not listening to you any more. Now get out. I don't want you here. Not ever again.' Becky's face was rigid with anger.

'But Amy's left some of her clothes at my place and—'

'Drop them off at the school office. Go. Go!'

Jude turned and made for the door.

'I'm sorry. Oh, what's the use!' She ran to her car, got in, started the engine, and backed up noisily on to the road. Tears ran down her face, but whether they were of relief or fear or self-hatred, she did not know. Everything was now revealed, all the layers of deceit and illusion. Maybe their friendship would not survive. It was a dreadful possibility. Yet worse was Jude's suspicion that what she had done was partly for herself. It galled her that Becky never knew about the real events on the night she was stood up. Why should it have been Becky who was protected, and Jude whose innocence had been well and truly lost? Now the tables were turned, and the funny thing was, it didn't help at all. Jude felt worse than ever.

At first Becky thought it must have been some misunderstanding, because her father was not capable of doing what Jude had suggested. Becky brought him to mind as he was this morning, old, pathetic, utterly harmless. It was Jude who was sick, not him.

Her father was a nice man. Becky used to wait for his steps coming up the garden path, and run to meet him. He'd swing her in his arms, and then she'd go to fetch him the evening paper. She felt proud to be able to minister to his needs. Her mother never did; it was a shame. Becky knew how to make her father smile; with her mother, it was more of a hit and miss affair.

Her mother never explained anything to her; her father showed her how the football league tables worked, and let her choose one of his horses on the Saturday. Her mother didn't explain the black eye, either. Becky recalled being dropped off at her house by her date, her mother appearing, white and silent, closing the door of the lounge behind her, and telling Becky to go straight upstairs. Then there had been shouts, bangs, noises that curdled the atmosphere, and merged in Becky's consciousness with the rather disappointing evening she'd just had.

It was in the morning she saw that someone had given her father a black eye. It was around that time, too, that her mother moved into the box room, and she even put a bolt on the door. She'd put a bolt on Becky's bedroom door, too, because, she'd said, you can never be too careful. Becky had thought she'd meant about burglars.

The truth permeated her mind like a black dye. Just suppose that her father was capable of what Jude had suggested. Then his moods of sulky withdrawal, the barely concealed disgust with which her mother had treated him had reasons, were not just what all married couples came to in the end. Becky shuddered as she thought how she always sided with him, always believing that she could have been a better wife to him than her mother. She had mythologised her father, told herself stories about him that weren't true. Jude, however, never lied. What she'd said, had happened.

As yet, Becky could not bring herself to focus on the details. She sat, very solemn, very still, her hands folded on the table. She was past tears. She didn't know if it was possible for a woman to withstand all that had happened to her in the past twenty-four hours. Yet she was still sitting here. She was not hysterical; she was utterly calm. More than that, she felt as if the core part of her was floating free of all this, utterly detached.

She wondered if she felt as Jane Eyre did, when she had discovered the existence of the first Mrs Rochester. Becky had her own monster in the attic now. Oddly, the thought comforted her, and dispassionately she thought about what Jane did afterwards. So what if it was only fiction? Jane didn't go back to Mr Rochester, not for some time. Instead she left everything, and went away. And then she lost what few possessions she had, and ended up sleeping rough. With nothing.

And the funny thing was, whenever Becky read that part of the book, she always envied Jane. Imagine having no ties, nothing. Imagine how free that would make you feel. Becky swallowed, and the physical action brought her back to herself. Jane survived. It was possible to survive. The most unlikely people turned out to be strong.

Becky looked at her hands, still young, yet with fine little lines under the surface of the skin. Hers were large, strong hands. She opened her palms, and considered her wedding ring, a plain gold band, and she could see her head reflected in it, distorted into a tiny oval. Above was her engagement ring, with three proud diamonds. These were not part of her hands. She twisted them and they moved easily. As she pulled them she could see where there was a permanent, pale groove on her finger. Would that ever go away? She slipped the rings back on her finger.

She could not bear to think about her father yet. Trying to decide what to do about Paul seemed the easier option. The trouble with Jude was that she saw everything in such simple terms. A man was cruel to you – you left him. Only marriage was supposed to be for keeps. Even her parents struggled on for a few more years . . . Perhaps she would leave Paul, but not yet. It was important not to rush into things, not to be impetuous. She knew she had to take one step at a time, and be sure of her footing.

It was cruel what Jude did – she told her about her father to push her into leaving Paul. She had no right to do that. It was bossy, opinionated, unforgivable. Jude, moreover, now seemed tainted by the story she had told. Some friend! Rather than comfort her, she had struck her as brutally as Paul had. Becky began to feel a little sorry for herself. She wished someone was there to make her a cup of tea, and to tell her that everything would be OK. Someone like her mother.

The worst part of all of this was feeling so alone, and so unloved. Paul did not love her, and possibly never did. He had just allowed her to love him. Amy loved her, of course, but with a child it was different. You had to be there for them; they were not meant to be there for you. Her father used her . . . There was no one else. Paul had Denise, Jude had Chris . . . She was alone, and could only depend on herself.

It was wrong, and she knew it was wrong, but she couldn't help thinking of documentaries she had seen on television, of refugees fleeing war zones, women with all their possessions on their backs, holding a child in one hand, marching on with blank faces. She felt like that. She thought of Amy at school and the sense of her vulnerability moved and frightened her. The tears came to her eyes, and she decided to let them out, because later there would be no opportunity. She would have to be strong; it was her only option. The only direction was forwards. She lay her head on her hands and sobbed.

That was why she didn't hear Karen banging at the door. Only when she raised her head because she really needed to get a tissue did she hear the noise. She jumped involuntarily with fear. Her first thought was that it was her father, come to exonerate himself, or worse still, Paul. Then she heard Karen's voice. She rubbed her eyes in a vain attempt to hide her tears, and made for the door.

'Becky? You all right?'

'No, not really.'

Karen stood stock still, looking serious.

'D'you want to talk about it?'

At first Becky thought it would be better to say nothing.

Then she remembered the hard times that Karen had been through, and how, not so long ago, she had sat in Karen's front room while Karen had sobbed. Karen, unlike Jude, would understand. There was no point in having false pride.

'It's Paul,' she stated calmly. 'He's having an affair with Denise.'

Karen didn't look surprised at all. It made Becky wonder if she was the last to know.

'They're both scumbags,' Karen declared.

'Did you know about them?'

Karen smiled nervously. 'Not for long. But I couldn't bring myself to tell you. For some bizarre reason I thought she *wanted* me to tell you, and I'd be doing her a favour if I did. God, I hate that woman!' Karen made her hands into two fists and shook them. It made Becky smile, despite herself.

'I only found out last night.' Becky sat down again, and Karen followed her. 'It was awful. Paul was pretty angry.'

'I bet. Did he hit you? I thought I heard something going on.'

'It was worse than that.' Becky didn't know how much more to say.

'Did he rape you?'

Becky let silence answer for her.

'Yeah' said Karen. 'I've been through that one, too. It's tough, kid. You all right now?'

Becky nodded. It was an exquisite relief to tell someone who understood. It occurred to her now that Karen might be a better authority on failed marriages than Jude.

'Do you think I should leave him?' Becky was asking herself as much as Karen.

'You can spend the night with me, if you like. And Amy too. I've got a put-u-up.'

'I might do that. I need time to think. I feel I ought to speak to Denise. It would help me decide. If she loves him—'

'Pardon me while I laugh.'

'You can laugh all you want. It makes me feel better. As

I was saying, if they love each other, then I'll have to leave him. If not – but it's early days. I don't know.'

Karen looked serious. 'Don't let anyone take liberties with you, Beck. You're worth a hundred of them. Just hang on to your self-respect.'

Becky filed those words away. She felt very close to Karen just then.

'Denise has actually been writing a novel about a love affair, which she's been reading aloud in our class.'

Karen gave a low whistle.

'Not that it helps me understand why all this happened. I'll have to speak to her.'

'I wish I could be a fly on the wall.'

'I'll let you know what happens.'

'She is such a tart,' Karen suddenly exploded. 'Once I changed her bed linen, and stuffed in one of the pillows was a scarlet basque and suspenders.'

'My God! For Paul?'

'Oh no! It was before all this started. I reckon she has some kinky fantasy life. Sad, isn't it? Stupid bitch.'

'You sound as if you hate her more than I do. What if it was Paul who seduced her?'

'And the earth is flat, and I'm not really sitting here, and—'

'I know, but don't you think I'd better start packing? I'll have to get clothes for both me and Amy, and I'll need to collect her from school.'

'What are you going to tell Amy?' Karen asked.

'I don't know,' she said.

Amy threw her school bags in the back of the Fiesta and began talking immediately.

'Petra and Dawn are still ignoring me. But it was all right. We had French and I'm not in their set for French and I sat next to Sophie. She's had her hair cut and it's dead nice. Everyone likes it and Rachel says she's going to have her hair cut like that too. What's for dinner tonight?'

Becky started the engine and began to manoeuvre out of the parking space. 'I don't know.' Her voice was level. 'We're having dinner with Karen.'

'Karen? Oh, cool! I can play with Seth and Bobby.'

'When you've done your homework.'

'Oh, it's all right, I haven't got any. The teachers can't be bothered because it's the end of term. Why are we having dinner with Karen? What about Dad? Is he coming too?'

'No.'

'But I haven't seen him for ages.' Amy's voice was plaintive.

Becky suddenly turned left between a pine furniture shop and an off-licence. She stopped the car. She couldn't concentrate on her driving and think about how to explain to Amy at the same time.

'Why are you stopping here? Is there something wrong with the car? Mummy, you're scaring me.' Becky ruffled her hair affectionately. The first thing was to stay utterly calm, because Amy would pick up her mood, and it would govern her reaction. The second thing was to support Amy.

'There's absolutely nothing to be scared about. Daddy and I had a bit of an argument last night, and I just think it's best if we spend some time apart.'

Amy stared uncomprehendingly.

Becky continued. 'Karen said we could spend the night with her.'

'So he is having an affair.'

Becky wanted to deny it, wanted to make everything all right for her daughter. Would a lie be more kind? No, there could be no more lies.

'Yes, Amy,' she said. 'He is.' Her daughter's face convulsed. 'But – ssh – don't worry. It doesn't mean he doesn't love you. People do clumsy, silly things sometimes. Ssh.'

She leant over to hug the sobbing Amy. This was worse

than she had imagined. She felt illogically as if it was all her fault; she hated to have to be the one to tell the truth. But now it was just a matter of withstanding Amy's grief. It will pass, she told herself. This will pass. A lady walked by the car and glanced in, curious.

'What will I tell everyone at school?'

'There's only one day left of term.'

'Why did you let him do it?'

'Ssh, Amy. I didn't know about it, just like you.'

'I hate him!' Amy screamed and sobbed. Becky could hardly bear it, but did nothing. She knew there was nothing she could say that would make it better. It was agony.

After a time, Amy's passion subsided. Her crying stopped, and she stared blankly in front of her. Becky started the engine again, putting on the de-mister. It whirred noisily.

'Can I go home and get my things?' Amy asked.

'I've done that for you. They're in the boot.'

'And teddy?'

'Of course.'

'Where will I be sleeping?'

'We'll have to see. Karen will work something out.'

'Can I ring Sophie?' Amy thought for a moment. 'Her dad left her, you know.'

'Yes. You ring Sophie.'

'She said that when he went, it was better. Her mum was a lot happier. You'll be a lot happier too. He was awful to you sometimes. I did notice, even though I pretended not to. Don't cry, Mum. Look, I've stopped crying now. I can even smile.' Amy pulled a ridiculous face. 'So go on. What are we having for dinner?'

'I tell you what. I'll go down to the Lucky Moon and treat us all.'

'I'd like that,' Amy said.

There was a red-hot pain in Karen's chest. She knew what it

was – the deadly combination of Silk Cut and high impact aerobics. She signalled to Shirley that she'd had enough, walked to the back of the dance studio and unscrewed the top of the bottle of water she'd brought with her. She took a quick slug, and the pain began to subside. She knew what she could with now. A cigarette.

She made her way to the changing rooms. They still smelt of new wood and fresh paint. Shirley was keen to get some of the classes underway before the whole club was open, just so she could start getting in some revenue. Karen was giving her support by attending the classes and twisting the arms of her mates. Eleni was there, Gemma and Wendy, and a couple of other acquaintances.

The only place Karen could think of to have a quiet smoke was the loo. She locked herself in the cubicle and lit up. As the nicotine charged her veins she relaxed, and even smiled to herself. She felt like a walking MI5, chock-full of secrets. First off, as soon as the club was up and running, she was going to be the receptionist. Full-time, and at last she'd be getting a half-way decent income. She'd arranged with Shirley to start in September, when the boys were back at school.

It was only superstition that stopped Karen telling her mates about it. The job was almost too good to be true. Also she didn't want there to be too many lines connecting her to Shirley, at least not yet. Perhaps by September she'd be ready to let people know. But then again . . . She inhaled slowly on her cigarette. It helped matters that she'd kidded Gemma and Wendy that she was going out with Jim. It was a good cover. It was so good, she'd even used it on Becky.

Not that she felt happy about it. It seemed deceitful, somehow, having spent a night with Becky, slagging off Paul and Denise, having heart to hearts, and not mentioning Shirley. As she thought of Paul, she filled with rage. Men disgusted her. When she thought what he did to Becky, she shook with indignation, and took another drag, inhaling deeply. No punishment was bad enough for him.

Then she heard footsteps and realised the others were on their way to the changing rooms. She flushed her ciggy down the loo and left the cubicle.

Gemma and Wendy were already sitting on the benches, Gemma pulling on some surprisingly skimpy knickers, while Wendy had her back to them, struggling to keep her towel round her while putting on her underwear. Shirley was bent over double, rubbing her damp hair vigorously.

Wendy turned round, having managed to get into her bra and knickers. Karen couldn't help looking at all that wobbly flesh on her thighs, the consistency of cottage cheese. Not that Gemma was any more appealing. She was in desperate need of someone pruning her bikini line, and her thighs were almost concave. Her small breasts sagged, and Karen almost wished she had a bicycle pump to inflate them for her. Dumpy Wendy, on the other hand, had breasts to die for. Life just wasn't fair.

'Shirley?' Wendy began, a little sycophantically. 'How many calories do you think we've burnt up in that session?'

'Not so many that if you have some chips now, you'll undo all the good work.'

'I wasn't going to!' Wendy sounded indignant. 'Actually, I'm back on my diet. Well, not a diet. I know you're not supposed to diet these days. I'm eating healthily – you know – cutting out all junk food and fried food and pudding and pies, and eating lots of fruit and vegetables and cottage cheese and lettuce and sugar-free jelly and that.'

'Sounds dismal,' Karen remarked.

'No, it's not. We're going away in a few weeks and I want to look good.'

'You mean you want the fellas to fancy you.'

'Shut it, Karen! What would Darren say?' Wendy let off a flurry of giggles as she twisted round to zip up her skirt.

'Well, it's true, isn't it? Why else do you put yourself through all this torment?'

'I'm off now,' Shirley remarked. She had already changed

into a fresh leotard. 'I've got my intermediates in the dance studio.'

'See ya!'

Shirley swung her sports bag over her shoulder and left the room. Karen watched her disappear.

'I don't know why we bother,' Gemma said. She picked up her aerosol body spray and applied little, aggressive puffs of Citrus Sizzler to various parts of her body.

'Bother with what?' Wendy asked.

'All this hard work and depriving yourself and suchlike, when the fellas never appreciate it.'

'You're dead right. Here we are, with our lip liners and mascara wands, and what do they do for us?'

Gemma replaced her spray in her bag, and picked up her T-shirt. 'If you're lucky, they remember to change their underpants at least once a fortnight.'

'My Darren's socks are as stiff as cardboard with sweat at the end of the day.'

'And I wouldn't mind if they knew how to work the damn washing machine – they can take apart a car engine but can't tell the difference between a boil wash and the wool cycle.'

'He thinks all his bad habits are what makes him lovable—' Wendy continued.

'When I ask him to stop whistling he carries on for a few moments longer at twice the volume – he can't bear to be told what to do.'

'But they're quite happy to sit in the front seat of the car and tell you there's a parked lorry ahead when you've seen it five minutes ago.'

'And when I tell him what I like in bed he goes ballistic – like I'm depriving him of his masculinity.'

'My Darren insists on kissing me when he's had a take-away curry.'

'I'm never letting Mike make love to me again after my three-bean casserole.'

Wendy snorted with laughter. 'And there's my Darren

apologising for his premature ejaculation, and there's me dead chuffed it's all over, because the truth is, once you get through the foreplay, sex is boring.'

'Give me the washing up any day. But what about you, Karen? Here we all are slagging off our menfolk, and you've been as quiet as a mouse. Doesn't Jim get on your nerves sometimes?'

Karen was taken by surprise.

'No, not really.'

Gemma raised her eyebrows. 'He's unusual, then.'

'Yeah, well, he is,' Karen continued quickly, justifying herself. 'There aren't many like him around.' She knew she was being unconvincing. This wasn't like her. Love had addled her brain.

'Actually,' she said, 'he's *very* unusual.'

'Do tell!' Wendy demanded.

'I shouldn't. Really I shouldn't. He'd kill me if I let it out.'

'*We* won't tell a soul, will we, Wendy?'

'Honest. Go on, Kaz. Why he is so unusual?'

'It's something . . . well, it's to do with his trouser department.'

Gemma and Wendy were listening attentively.

'I don't know how to to say this, but . . . he had an accident.'

Karen hoped Jim had a good enough sense of humour to ride this one out. She crossed her fingers behind her back.

'It was when he was no more than a lad, you see. He had this girlfriend – dead posh, she was – and her parents were never supposed to find out. So she used to let him in through her bedroom window to do the dirty deed. Then one night, he was there, right in the middle of it and everything, and the parents arrived home. Big panic. He throws on his clothes and opened the window and there they are, getting out of their BMW below him. So he climbs on to the roof, and edges along. It was dark, they didn't see him. So he's at the edge, holding on to the coping. Once the parents are inside, he wonders, should he jump down? He can't see a thing. He doesn't want to set off the intruder light, so he decides to aim for the side of the house. What he's forgotten is that there's a fence there, with razor wire at the top, to keep cats out. So he jumps, and the razor wire comes up right between his legs!'

The story was punctuated by screams of horror and amazement. Karen was immensely gratified; it was something to be able to make up stories. For some reason the thought of semi-castration pleased her. It dawned on her then that it wasn't Jim she was mutilating, but somebody else. Somebody whose name began with a P . . .

'He struggled off, and he didn't know it, but his willy was just hanging by a thread. And would you believe it, he walked all the way home like that. Then he fainted at the front door. He was rushed to hospital and they tried to stitch it back on. It hurt like hell.' Karen spoke those words slowly, with relish. 'He was in hospital for three weeks. They had to completely re-arrange him down below. He can't pee without using something. And he can't get a hard-on, at least, he has this special pump like a tiny bellows what he inflates himself with. Well, what with that, and the appearance of it – Shirl says he's thinking of auditioning it for a bit part in the *X-files* – it's put him right off. He's quite happy just going around with the lads, following the football and all the rest of it. Only he doesn't want anyone to know about him and his injuries, see, and the other lads had been ribbing him about not having a girl. That's where I come in. With me being off men, I'm quite happy to make do with Jim – or something like him.'

Wendy and Gemma's mouths were open in astonishment.

'He's good to me, and looks after the boys, and they all spend ages on his PlayStation. I'm telling you, I've fallen on my feet.'

Wendy and Gemma were still lost for words.

'Now don't either of you breathe a word of this, or I'll

let your blokes know what you've been saying about them. Was it premature ejaculation, Wendy?'

Wendy nodded.

'Oh no! Look at the time!,' Karen declared. 'I'm not even showered yet.'

She picked up her towel and headed for the shower, feeling much, much better.

# Chapter Twelve

Although she had been expecting the phone to ring, when it did, Jude jumped. She left the bowl of cat food on the kitchen work surface, and as she went to the lounge to answer the call, Ludmilla and Aida jumped up and began eating.

'Hello? Becky?'

'It's Chris.'

'Oh. I just thought it might be Becky.'

'Sorry to disappoint you.'

'That's OK.' Jude bit her lip in anxiety. It was a torment not knowing what Becky was thinking, or what was happening to her.

'Do you want to come out for a drink tonight?'

'No. I've got to stay in.'

'Shall I call round and keep you company?' Jude shrugged in reply, then realised Chris would not be able to pick that up on the phone.

'Probably not. Oh, I don't know. But can you get off the phone, as I'm expecting a call?'

'No problem.' Jude heard the click of the receiver. Perhaps Becky needed time, and then they would be reconciled. And meanwhile, what was she doing? Would she have been composed enough to collect Amy from school as if nothing had happened? How would Paul treat them both when he arrived home? What if there was another scene? Jude yearned to protect her friend, would have donned armour, and ridden to her house on a white charger, if that would help, and behead the tyrant Paul.

She wandered back into the kitchen. She was hungry now. Something smelled good. She glanced at the work surface with interest and saw the cat food. No, that would never do. She placed the bowl on the floor, and as she did so she decided she would ring Becky once again.

The phone rang once, twice, and this time there was a reply. Jude took a deep breath.

'Hello?' barked Paul.

'Is Becky there? It's Jude.'

'Do you know where she is?'

'I wouldn't tell you if I did.' Jude itched to give him a piece of her mind. On the one hand, she knew she ought not to interfere in other people's marriages; on the other, what they had could hardly be called a marriage.

'Are you sure you don't know where she is?' snapped Paul, evidently suspicious.

'I'll tell you what I'm sure about. I'm sure that you're not worth the dirt in her little fingernail. You're a self-centred bully.' Jude's anger was gaining force. 'I hope Becky's found the courage to walk out on you for good. You disgust me. You're selfish, you're as low as they come. You're worse than an animal. You deserve—'

She heard him slam the phone down. Jude was filled with the terror of victory. He had to know that Becky had friends who would stand up for her. Solidarity, that was the thing. It was a word that was often on her mother's lips. She looked at the photograph of her mother on the mantelpiece, and this evening her mother looked rather stern, no-nonsense. She would have been pleased to have heard her speak to Paul like that. When the doorbell rang, Jude jumped again. It must be Becky and Amy. Thank God! They could stay here as long as they wanted.

She opened the door.

'Chris!'

'Aren't you going to let me in?'

Jude apologised for her rudeness, and Chris entered and kissed her. She submitted.

'Is something wrong?'

'Yes.'

'Is it something I've done?'

'Oh, no. You don't need to look so anxious. It's to do with Becky.'

'Is she in trouble?'

Jude weighed up whether to let him into her confidence. Was it a betrayal of trust? No, she decided. Chris would never abuse any knowledge he had of Becky, and now she needed all the friends she could get. Besides, Chris was her man, her resource. It was up to him to make her feel better.

'It began with Amy,' she said.

As Chris eased the pasta into Jude's saucepan, he remembered Becky as he'd seen her last week, in the last session of term. She was a little shame-faced, because she hadn't got on very far with her romantic novel. She had pleaded lack of time as an excuse. He had jokingly reprimanded her by telling her that Sylvia Plath woke up early every morning to write, and Becky had recounted by saying, look what happened to her! Chris smiled at the memory. He'd enjoyed teaching Becky, and couldn't understand how anyone could be cruel to her. Rage filled him as he thought over what Jude had just said. He felt fiercely protective of Becky, shocked, angry – how could a man do something like that? He thought of Becky again, laughing at one of his jokes, or running her hand through her hair as she struggled with one of his less successful writing exercises. He could not bear to think of what had happened to her.

The spaghetti bent and softened and lay curled in the bubbling water. The bigger cat nudged his legs and purred with shameless abandon. Chris reached down to stroke its head.

Jude had put some music on, something rather mournful. A soprano was keening with grief. He felt desperately sorry for Jude too. To be the victim of a pervert when she was only young. And that the man should be Becky's father.

How would Becky feel, now that she knew about her father? *I had to tell her*, Jude had said, *I had to shock her into leaving Paul.* Of course Becky needed to know the truth, and yet . . . Chris asked himself if he would have had the strength to tell her. Probably not.

In the cupboard were a tin of tomatoes, some tomato purée and some tuna. He would try to make a sauce from that.

Chris realised then he was a little in awe of Jude. Few people were governed so strongly by their convictions. Jude decided what was right, and acted accordingly. There was something fine and uncompromising about her. It pleased him to think she had spoken so strongly to Paul. He thoroughly deserved it. Jude was an exceptional woman. She had true courage, but it had a distinctive quality. It was the courage of the adolescent, the sort that belonged to someone who'd not yet recognised that life was full of compromises and half-truths. It made her seem naïve at times.

Thoughtfully he stirred the sauce he had created. No, not naïve. That wasn't what he meant. It was another quality. He still found it strange that for all her self-assurance, when it came to sex she was so hesitant and shy, almost unresponsive. She had never taken the initiative; it was always up to him to arouse her. It had made him think that there was something missing. Was it his fault? Hers? Was it Becky's father's fault? Perhaps now he would reach the core of her. He wanted to achieve that; Jude attracted him powerfully; there was nothing to stop them making a go of it, nothing at all. Yet he was aware of a space between them, like the gap between two words on a page. She intrigued him, but frightened him a little. She . . .

'Chris?'

Jude had entered the kitchen.

'Chris, turn that off. Come here. I want you to hold me.'

Chris did as he was told. She clung to him with determination. She kissed him now, and he knew she needed the reassurance that he would never be cruel, would never deceive her, as Becky had been deceived.

'Stop me thinking about her,' Jude murmured.

He ran his hands down her body and felt the pressure of her against him.

'Shall we go upstairs?'

'Yes, please,' she said.


Jude lay with her head on his chest, hearing the thump of his heart, grateful to him for the few moments of oblivion he had given her. And yet it was disgusting of her to want to make love, not knowing where Becky was, or what she was suffering. Jude hated herself. She was selfish, not at all the good friend she intended to be. Usually, after sex, she felt high, as if she had achieved something. Now she felt unutterably sad, as if all she had done was to prove the pointlessness of everything. She could have cried. Chris put an arm around her back.

'I shouldn't have told her about her father, should I?'

'I don't know.'

'I was mean. I think I wanted her to suffer too.'

As she spoke, Chris gently stroked her back.

'I've been selfish,' she said. 'And cowardly. It was her father I should have confronted, not her.'

'Don't be so harsh on yourself.'

'Don't be nice to me. Tell me how awful I am.'

'I won't do that.'

Jude closed her eyes for a moment. Chris could be so frustrating at times. He was so fair-minded she could scream. He was almost maternal. Of course she was extremely fond of him. It was odd, but on occasion he reminded her of Becky. He was a gentle man. Yes, she thought, a true gentleman.

'And you can cook too,' she said musingly. 'Shall we go

and sample your pasta now? Unless the cats have polished off the tuna.'

'There's something I want to do first,' he whispered, and kissed her slowly, lingeringly. He was good at kissing, Jude thought, but she was feeling a little impatient. Dinner was waiting, and besides, Becky might call at any moment.


Since it was such a glorious Sunday afternoon, Denise decided that it was a good opportunity to work on her tan. It was far too hot for a session on the stepper that she had persuaded George to buy her last week. She would work out and tone tonight; now she would just bronze herself gently. Those women who said that appearance didn't count only meant that theirs didn't count. Denise was aware of the fact that her looks were her greatest asset. They had brought Paul to his knees, and with a little fine tuning, they should have a similar effect on Jim. It was really very sweet of George to agree to having a conservatory built. Becky had a conservatory, and so did her sister, in fact everyone had a conservatory! He conceded this readily enough, and she had chatted on about Karen, and how satisfied she'd been with the services of Ferguson's. Tomorrow she planned to ring for a quotation.

The tanning lotion was in the bathroom cabinet, and Denise mounted the stairs to fetch it. A song she recognised came from Petra's bedroom, no doubt one of those recycled by one of the current batch of adolescent boy groups. For a moment, Denise was aware of the passage of time. Petra was growing up, and she'd come home from school the other day clutching leaflets on contraception and sexually transmitted diseases. Her own daughter, who still hadn't thrown away her Barbies! Next year Denise would be celebrating her fortieth birthday. Forty wasn't old, especially if you looked after yourself. She had demeaned herself, going with Paul.

All over the weekend Denise had wondered why it was she had succumbed to him? He was fat, uncouth, old. She could hardly bear to think of him now. When he rang her again, she would tell him straight out that their affair was over, that it had all been a dreadful mistake, that she was terrified of George finding out. That they must never breathe a word to anyone. When she had stretched out on the lounger in the garden she would script it all, so that she would not be lost for words. He would be utterly distraught. Yet Becky would be there to pick up the pieces, and so there would be a happy ending for all of them. She stopped at the door of the bedroom and caught sight of the exercise book in which she was writing her novel. She decided to take it to the garden with her. There was something so gratifying about the neighbours seeing one at work on one's novel.

As she reached out for it she heard a ring at the doorbell. She paused.

'Petra!' she shouted. 'Someone at the door.'

She heard Petra's door open, and her daughter scamper downstairs.

'It's for you, Mum,' she shouted up. 'It's Becky.'

Becky? Denise wondered why she had called. Usually she rang first. Curious, she ran down the stairs. Becky stood in the doorway, large dark glasses shadowing her face.

'Since it's such a lovely day, Denise, I thought we might go for a drive.'

'A drive?' Denise was a little taken aback.

'Yes. I need to do some research – on my novel. I need a romantic setting and I thought I'd like to go over to Haworth. I fancied some company.'

Denise weighed this up. Her own garden had its attractions, but Rowan was out there kicking a ball around, and George was threatening to mow the lawn. It might be fun, going out with Becky. She couldn't think of anything better to do.

'OK. Give me a few moments to get my things together. Petra, tell Daddy I'm going out and there are some oven chips in the freezer and you know how to grill fish fingers, don't you, love? Just wait while I get my notebook –

I'd like to do some research too. I'm in need of some inspiration.'

Beyond them lay the vast sweep of West Yorkshire, its fields divided by a crisscross of dry-stone walls. Becky's eyes were drawn by the stark white wind generator overlooking Haworth and the steady revolution of its three immense blades which slashed at the air. This road was one of Becky's favourites. The open moors made the countryside seem never-ending, and yet the little dots of sheep and stone houses that seemed to have grown out of the fields made it human and friendly. There was the hint of something more exciting, too; here the Brontës had lived, and the thought never failed to awe her. She only knew a little about them, and always confused Charlotte with Jane Eyre, thinking of them as by and large the same person. But there was a father in the case, she remembered, as they ascended the road to the car park. She had some fellow feeling with Charlotte.

Concentrating like this on where she was, and where to park the car helped her to cope. One step at a time, she told herself. Only when she felt ready would she confront Denise. The last thing she wanted was a fight, or any sort of emotional scene. She was quite drained of feeling. Every scrap of her emotional energy had been used in comforting Amy. It didn't help matters that Paul could be heard moving around next door, and that she'd been reduced to hiding her car in Ferguson's yard so she could remain undetected. It all seemed so unreal.

So did Haworth, that fiction factory, full of tourists and cars and day trippers, intent on finding out the truth about the Brontës. Becky was in search of truth as well. She was determined to hear Denise's side of the story. The only way to get this situation under control was by discovering the height, breadth and length of it. Her desire to know overpowered her, and even now, as she returned to the car with her pay-and-display sticker, she was aware of its gentle pressure.

She would not give way just yet. Being away from her own village was a blessed relief, and she was going to drink in the otherness of Haworth. She wanted to be somewhere else, and be someone else. What was interesting was that Denise was entirely at ease with her. Evidently Paul had not contacted her to say they had been discovered. Or else she was utterly shameless. Becky watched her get out of the car and was surprised to discover that she did not hate her. She felt detached from the situation, almost as if she was a scientist, about to perform an interesting experiment. Perhaps she was just numb.

'We were lucky to find this space,' Denise said.

She was right. The car-park was full, and several coaches filled the far bays. Together the women made their way into the village, past compact stone cottages with low doorways, and over the setts to the small square at the centre of Haworth. Shops with bottles of old-fashioned sweets and lace mats and tablecloths stared each other out.

'Let's go and look at the parsonage,' Becky said to Denise.

They ascended some stone steps and skirted the side of the church along a small lane with a dark school building on one side. Becky thought how narrow the confines of the Brontë existence were – church, home, school. It must have been unbearably claustrophobic. When they reached the parsonage, they knew they would never get in. A large party of gaudily dressed foreign tourists decorated with cameras, maps, guidebooks and other impedimenta queued at the entrance. Becky glanced at the dark, imposing building, and bade it a silent farewell.

'Let's walk on,' she said to Denise.

'Not too far. These sandals aren't ideal for tramping round the countryside.'

But Becky had to get away. She followed a footpath that took her by the side of some allotments and greenhouses, and there, at last, was the view she craved of hills, and of space. The blue sky, with only a suggestion of clouds, arched over them. In the distance the outlines of hills shimmered like a mirage, and Becky wished she was there, and beginning her life anew. She leant on the wooden gate in front of her and thought how much more important the future was than the past. She had a momentary sensation of freedom, and then heard some people walk past her speaking a language that was either German or Czech. Denise tugged at her arm.

'Come on, Becky! Since we're here we might as well look around. I've brought my notebook!'


Denise did not fully understand why Haworth was full of so many people. The Brontës were only writers. It amused her to think that perhaps in later years Mytholm might be similarly full of people seeking her home, after the soaraway success of her novel. Mytholm was prettier than Haworth, for a start. She glanced at the grim stone wall of the school building they were walking past, saw the soft olive colour of the lichen, and the tired green weeds between the setts and thought the place was nothing special. Why couldn't they have gone instead to that wonderful designer kitchenware emporium in a mill in Bradford, which was open on a Sunday. If she didn't feel slightly beholden to Becky for the loan of her husband, she would have insisted they go there instead.

'Shall we look in the shops?' she asked her.

'If you like.'

She thought Becky seemed rather quiet. Perhaps she needed cheering up. They went to look in the window of a little gift shop with Branwell's Bric-a-Brac in copperplate handwriting in the window.

'Do people actually buy these things?' Denise commented. There were rows of resin figures of teddy bears and pink pigs and cats with impossibly sweet expressions. There were porcelain Brontë thimbles, floral tea towels, cloisonné earrings, Haworth mugs, and fridge magnets.

'I can just imagine Charlotte saying to Emily, "I'm just nipping out for a fridge magnet,"' said Denise archly.

Becky smiled and she was encouraged.

'Wouldn't you just love a bone-china verse plaque about motherhood? Just the thing for your conservatory!'

The word 'conservatory' gave her a pleasant tingle. All afternoon she had kept to herself the knowledge of her growing infatuation with Jim. Knowing what she planned to do excited her, made her preternaturally aware of her surroundings, of other men, and most of all of her own attractiveness. It was true that Karen was younger than her, but Karen lacked class. There was a certain coarseness about her. Denise did not doubt that when she indicated to Jim that she might be available, he couldn't fail to be interested, especially not someone as highly sexed as him.

How she wished she could tell all this to Becky! As they wandered down the hill, looking at yet more gift shops, more pottery, more scented candles, more blank-eyed teddies and more blank-eyed tourists, Denise realised how her brief fling with Paul had actually brought them closer together. They had shared a man, in the same way that one might share a slice of a particularly rich cheesecake in a tea shop. One would take turns with one's fork. And then it was all finished, and they shared the guilt as well as the sweet aftertaste. Partners in crime. Denise reflected that she had always liked Becky, right from the time their babies crawled around on the floor together while they drank coffee and discussed potty training. Denise almost felt tempted to link arms with her in a gesture of togetherness.

'Shall we turn around now?' Becky asked her. 'We'll regret it if we don't, because this is some steep hill.'

As Denise began to ascend the hill, she realised Becky was right, so she did link arms with her. They climbed past the second-hand bookshop and arrived back at the steps leading to the church. It was a small and rather tacky little village. No wonder the Brontës decided to write bestsellers as a way out.

'What shall we do now?' Denise asked.

'I'd like a drink,' Becky said.

'We passed a tea shop on the way up.'

'No, I mean a real drink. There's something we've got to talk about.'


The pub that Becky had walked into at random turned out to be almost empty. She had to adjust her eyes to its shade after the dazzling sunlight outside. On the window ledges were candles stuck in old wine bottles, and the food on offer was scrawled up with fluorescent ink on a black background. Becky walked up to the bar.

'What are you having?'

'A spritzer?' suggested Denise.

'A spritzer, please, and a double gin and tonic.'

Becky took the drinks to a table in the corner. Denise was observing her warily. She took a seat next to Becky, and lifted her glass to her mouth. Becky noticed the rather mottled appearance of the skin above her cleavage, and thought that the pale green of her sun top didn't suit her. She rather despised Paul for his taste.

Now for it. She took a gulp of her gin.

'I gather you've been sleeping with Paul,' Becky said, quite matter-of-fact.

Denise gave a slight start.

'You don't have to deny it. Paul's told me himself.'

Denise's face was a mask of horror.

'Do you want to tell me all about it?' Becky suggested peaceably. 'How did it begin? I want to hear about it from your point of view.' She was surprised at how even her voice was.

'It's over,' Denise said. She was barely audible.

'Over? You mean, now that I've found out, it's over?'

'No. It was over before that. I'm sorry, Becky. I really am. It was a dreadful mistake.'

'A mistake? How can you make a mistake about something like that? Did you mistake him for someone else?'

'No, of course not, but I shouldn't have done it. I don't know what got into me!'

Now Becky experienced a strange sensation of power which was not unpleasant. It was good to see Denise squirming like this. There was something to be said for sadism, after all.

'Becky, you must hate me, really hate me, and I don't blame you at all. I can't imagine what you must be thinking. But I couldn't help it.'

'Do you love him?'

'Heavens, no! I mean, I suppose I must have, you know, in the beginning, but I don't love him. I realise that now.'

'So why did it happen?'

'He ... I ... We met up in Manchester a few times – just as friends. He began propositioning me – I expect he was having a mid-life crisis!'

'And you? Are you having a mid-life crisis too?'

'Certainly not!' Denise looked offended. 'I know I shouldn't have given in to him. I know I should have spoken to you. But I didn't want to. How could you tell your best friend that her husband had made an advance? Oh, Becky – you know what it's like. You grow up, you get married, have children, and then it's as if it's all over. There's nothing more to do. Every day is like the other. I think I just craved excitement, and there was Paul, and that's what he was offering. I envied you, you see. I've always thought of you as so much the better mother, and better wife. It was as if Paul was giving me a chance to *be* you. Perhaps that was why I did it?' Some tears formed in Denise's eyes. 'How could I have been so foolish?'

It was an exquisite performance, Becky thought. She couldn't help but admire Denise. Imagine having the ability to re-arrange the facts so that you were always in the right!

Denise put her beautifully manicured hand on Becky's arm. Becky could not help but think how intimate that hand had been with Paul. It was all rather incestuous.

'Becky, listen to me. I know you're not going to believe the next thing I'm going to say. I care about you much, much more than I ever cared about Paul. Friends are infinitely more important than lovers. How many years have we been friends? Nearly fourteen! I can't imagine life without you being there. I don't want this terrible mistake of mine to spoil that. We'll always regret it, if you do. Men come and go, but women should always be there for one another.'

It was an affecting appeal. Becky thought she must be a very hard character not to be moved at all.

'Say something to me. I can't bear your silence. You have every right to be furious with me. You can hit me if you like. But let's talk this through. I know I've done a dreadful thing, at least according to the world. But people make so much of sex, don't you think? It's made to symbolise so much, but what is it?' Denise gave a little shudder. 'One bit of his body touching a bit of yours. That's all. It's silly. All that fuss about nothing.'

'Was that what sex was like with Paul?'

'Becky! I never thought I'd hear you talk like that!' Denise risked a laugh. 'To be truthful, the earth didn't move. He was rather intent on his own gratification.'

Becky registered this as a criticism of her husband. She knew she ought to defend him. Yet what Denise had said was quite perceptive. That was Paul all over. Intent on self. This was interesting. Denise was a good judge of character and underlying motive, probably because she was so devious herself.

'Did you talk a lot to him?' Becky asked.

'Talk? No. But I listened. I can tell you all about the insole factory in Leicester and the chap who cut him up at the roundabout.'

'And how he solved the staffing problem in small electricals?'

'Naturally. And I know all about the deliveries manager—'

'Who he trained from a tea-boy—'

'Becky, I felt as if I was some sort of glorified receptacle for him, his conversation, his self-importance, and his ridiculously little – Becky, I'm sorry! You're the last person I should be talking to like this!'

'No, go on. You're helping.'

'Am I?' Denise looked pleased. 'I thought maybe he's so full of himself because he's developed a compensating personality. Just like fat people are jolly, Paul's tiny dick gives him an inflated ego!'

Becky laughed now.

'How can we both have been so stupid!' Denise declared. 'What's wrong with women that they can be taken in by all that macho posturing? Why don't we realise that all we really want is tenderness, and sensitivity . . . and youth.'

'Do men like that exist?'

Denise looked rather coy. 'Karen seems to have found someone.'

'True,' said Becky.

'Only I've been a little worried about her. She's seemed a bit distant with me recently. You don't think they're having problems? Perhaps he's cooling. Karen has such a tongue on her, and a sensitive man might easily be distressed.'

Becky pretended to listen, but her mind was elsewhere. First Jude, then Karen suggested that she left Paul. Now Denise had revealed her opinion of him quite frankly, and Denise ought to know best of all. Becky knew she ought to loathe Denise, and yet felt utterly dispassionate. Instead she felt as if she'd had her eyes opened. She had made herself believe for fifteen years that Paul was worth staying married to. In fact she had committed one of the Great Errors of the Twentieth Century. The truth was that despite the exuberance of Seth and Bobby and having to sleep on the floor of the lounge, she and Amy had never been so relaxed as they'd been this weekend. It was bliss to be able to behave exactly as she wanted, not be constantly wary of how Paul might react. Being without him was better than being with him. Could she go back to her house now, and exclude him from it? She certainly had grounds. Only her house was polluted for her now, both because of what had happened there, and because she had lived effectively as a prisoner for so long, just like the first Mrs Rochester. The mad woman in the attic.

'I'm having a conservatory built!' Denise announced suddenly.

'That's nice.'

'I'm ringing Ferguson's tomorrow.'

Yes, she would leave him. It was the right thing to do. Terror and excitement surged through her. Only she would not tell Denise, as grateful as she was to her for being the catalyst. Karen deserved to know first, particularly as she would have to extend her hospitality a little longer. And there was also Jude.

Becky did not exactly feel remorseful about her curt dismissal. Even now the memory of Jude accusing her father gave her pain. It was a pain that had been inflicted by a surgeon's knife; it was sharp, it was an outrage, but now she could see it had been intended to do her good. Tough love, some people called it. She didn't want to be without Jude's support, especially not now. Jude and Amy were fond of each other, and Amy would need all the love she could get. Luckily it was early July; the school year had finished and by the time Amy returned, the worst would be over.

'Are we still friends?' Denise interrupted her.

Becky snapped out of her reverie.

'Of course, Denise. We're as much friends as we've ever been.'

'Becky – you are the sweetest person I know! And I promise never to keep a secret from you again. Let me get you another drink.'

'I'm driving. But you can sock me a meal. A turkey sandwich and chips,' she said, glancing at the board.

'I'll just have a salad. I want to look my best tomorrow.'

'Why's that?'

'My little secret!' she said.

Jude knew she had every right to feel despondent. A tricky root canal, followed by a woman terrified of needles and a bridge prep with a lady who wouldn't stop talking. She wouldn't have minded any of them normally, but Chris was away for a few days tutoring on a writer's course, and still she hadn't heard from Becky. She would give her a week, and then make contact. It was unthinkable that this really was the end of their friendship.

Jude decided she would grovel to her, apologise unreservedly, even admit that she could understand why she might want to give her marriage another go. Anything, so long as she was forgiven and re-admitted to their sisterhood. Even with Chris by her side, she was aware of a profound lack. In the short time they had been together as adults, Becky had become essential to her, as confidante, substitute mother, matchmaker, audience – her rock. And Jude had marched in and stripped her of her illusions as calmly as if they were wallpaper. She had been a cad. People needed illusions, she could see that now. Was it so dreadful if Becky had continued to believe in her father? He was an old man, not the same person who'd behaved so repellently. Forgive us our trespasses, as we forgive those . . . From now on she would behave with sensitivity and a true concern for others.

The Discovery was parked in her spot again. Jude wondered how easy it would be to let down its tyres? So who's perfect? She crossed the road and walked to her front door, opened it, scooped the letters from the mat, greeted Aida and Ludmilla and checked the answerphone. No messages.

She craved something sweet and creamy and comforting to

eat. There was a tin of rice pudding in the cupboard, and if she heated it up and added some jam, it would do as her tea. There was no one around to see her eat it. If she was hungry later, she could always ring the new pizza takeaway. They'd posted a menu through her door last week, and they sold ice cream, too. Genuine Italian tutti-frutti. Or butterscotch and rum . . .

Jude changed into some comfortable leggings and a T-shirt, noticed it had a stain of something on it, and dabbed at it with a damp finger. She fed the cats, and prepared her rice pudding. Her mother used to serve rice pudding nearly every evening, Ambrosia rice pudding. The food of the gods. Spiritual sustenance.

Curled on the settee, Jude began to dig in. A globule of jam dripped on to her T-shirt, and she flicked it off. Mmm. The sweet creaminess soothed her. And she took another enormous spoonful.

A ring at the door. Jude was startled, and dropped the spoon back into the dish. Who could that be? She put her bowl down, and Aida appeared to investigate the contents. Jude opened her front door.

There was Ian Fulwell, holding an enormous bunch of flowers wrapped in cellophane, tied with a peach coloured ribbon.

'For you,' he said.

So he was going to apologise! About time too. And the flowers were lovely, and it was going to be so much easier to be nice to him, now that she had Chris. She smiled warmly at him, and could see now that he had quite a distinguished, even sexy, face.

'Thank you!' She took them, and then remembered the state of her T-shirt, and held the flowers against her chest. Ought she to ask him in? If he could be gracious, so could she. She checked the state of her lounge, where Aida was calmly finishing off the rice pudding.

'The messenger boy left them with me because you were out,' he explained.

'Oh, so they're not—'

'From me? Sorry to disappoint you. I'll send you some if you like.'

The cheek of it! Jude's dislike of him just then was so acute it made her tingle. She collected herself to her full height and lifted her chin haughtily. 'What would you send me? Deadly nightshade?'

'They're berries, not flowers. But it doesn't matter. I saw you more as the venus fly trap sort myself.'

'I'm afraid I can't stand here all evening talking the language of flowers. I'm in the middle of dinner.'

He glanced at the cat. 'I think you'll find there's not much left,' he remarked. 'I'll see you another time.' And he closed the door gently.

Jude was incensed. Her appetite had entirely gone. But someone had sent her flowers! Chris? It must be his way of telling her he was thinking of her. She fumbled to open the card that was attached to the bouquet. She wondered what it was he wanted to say to her.

'I'm sorry,' read the card. It was from Becky, and there was a telephone number, a local number. So she was forgiven! Jude was wild with joy. She buried her face in the flowers for a moment, then hurried to the kitchen, filled the sink with water, and propped the bouquet in it. Then she raced to the phone. Becky might not need her, but she was beginning to realise that she certainly needed Becky.

# Chapter Thirteen

Gently Jude came to consciousness, aware of her limbs cocooned by the duvet, and then her face buried in the pillow. The brightness of the bedroom told her it was well and truly morning, another hot and humid August morning. She opened one eye to look at her bedside clock; it was just before seven. She could afford to stretch out and relax because there would be time enough to shower and breakfast. Ten glorious minutes in which to do nothing. Ten glorious minutes of solitude.

She didn't object to the fact she'd slept in the spare bedroom for the past month. Even though it was next door to the bathroom and she could hear every time Becky got up in the night, it made sense for her to sleep here, and for Becky and Amy to share her bedroom, which was much bigger. The spare bedroom – box-room, really, – was so cosy she could lie in bed and reach over to turn the main light on or off. Outside some birds set up a desultory conversation.

When Jude had discovered that Becky and Amy were holed up at Karen's, she had insisted they come straight to her. They could hardly live next to Paul and hope to remain undiscovered. It was an honour to have them, Jude had insisted. She even confessed she felt lonely by herself and would love their company. She was flattered by Amy's evident wish to take her up on her offer, and she yearned to help Becky, to be the rock she leaned on, to do something to atone for her selfish behaviour.

In the beginning it was tiring, but rewarding. Becky needed to talk, and talk they did, late into the night, sometimes with wine, sometimes without. There were times when Becky wavered, and considered having him back; at other times she would hesitantly tell Jude of occasions when he had treated her badly. Once, after an argument, he'd locked her out, and Amy had only been two at the time, and she could hear her crying in her cot. During another tantrum he'd cut up one of her dresses. Yet she had persevered in the marriage, always pretending to herself that the worst had to be over. She honestly believed that it was up to her to control his behaviour, and that all men were probably like Paul. Jude listened, incredulous. Denial in the lion's den, she remarked to Becky.

Becky had laughed, and that was a breakthrough. Jude had chuckled too, and there were some tears, of course, but from that moment Becky's spirits seemed to lighten. There were difficult times, and Jude had failed to persuade Becky to go and live in her own home, rather than leave it to Paul. Becky's point – and Jude could understand it – was that her old home was filled with bitter associations. She wanted desperately to make a new beginning, anywhere. She had found a solicitor and had spoken about a divorce; she had visited the Jobcentre and looked at employment opportunities. Jude was all for her training to be a dental nurse and coming to work in her surgery. Becky had conceded that this was a possibility.

She'd had one fraught meeting with Paul, where he had tried to cajole her, then threatened her, then begged her to come back, promising he'd change. When she'd refused, he'd cursed at her violently. Once or twice he had met Amy in Mytholm, but she had come back distressed by the visits, and they had been temporarily discontinued. If only Paul had decided to go and live in Manchester, but for reasons best known to himself, he had not. According to Karen, he spent every night in, watching the television. Jude rather hoped he'd find another woman. Only then could she be sure that they'd heard the last of him.

Slowly Becky and Amy began to pick themselves up. Sophie came round for a day, and Amy was beside herself with joy. Karen insisted on taking Becky to her aerobics class. And every night Jude came home to the warmth and chaos of a ready-made family, and two over-fed cats. Aida had put on quite a bit of weight recently, Jude thought, placing her hands underneath her head. Becky would insist on putting little titbits in her bowl, and Amy fed the cats each time they miaowed, believing it was cruel to do otherwise. Jude smiled to herself. Her delicately built Aida, with her rich chestnut fur, was developing a little pot belly.

Yes, it was good to be of use to Becky and Amy. Jude allowed herself a little glow of satisfaction as she slowly flexed her legs, preparing to get up and shower. Then she heard some soft footsteps, and the snick of the bathroom door. Damn! Becky had got there before her. She listened intently. Had Becky remembered that she needed to leave at eight this morning? Jude wriggled out of her duvet and crept to the bathroom, putting her ear against the door. Yes, Becky was having a shower!

'You won't be long, will you?' she shouted through the door.

'What was that?'

'I'm running late,' Jude bellowed, and then hoped she hadn't woken Amy. It was unlikely; a herd of buffalo stampeding through the garden would not wake Amy. She was rarely up before eleven, and then spent the next hour or so sitting in her nightdress watching morning television, while eating bowl after bowl of cereal.

Jude decided to complete her morning routine in reverse, and padded downstairs to the kitchen to switch the kettle on. Ludmilla was there washing herself, but there was no sign of Aida. Jude deliberately rattled the cutlery drawer, and shook the door of the fridge so that the cat would hear the familiar feeding noises. It worked, as it always did. Aida shot through the cat flap.

The kitchen smelt of something funny. Was there something that had gone off? Jude opened the fridge, but it wasn't in there. She opened the pantry, only to discover that someone – Amy? Becky? – had left an open tin of cat food there overnight. Jude screwed up her nose in distaste, dropped the can in the overfull swing bin, noticing traces of food on the lid, that someone – Becky? Amy? – had carelessly thrown away. Was it too much to expect them to respect the basic rules of hygiene? Jude reprimanded herself for being so irritable. She had no excuse. The weather was glorious and Chris was coming round tonight.

Which, in itself, presented a problem, Jude thought, sipping her coffee. Their sex life was now confined to his place, and was public property. She could not look Amy in the face when she said she was going to spend the night with Chris. Worse still was Becky's knowing smile. She was conscious she'd been ignoring Chris's needs in the past few weeks, and had shown little interest in his writing and the possibility of the contract at York, where they were hoping to set up a creative writing MA at the university. He seemed happy, so she could safely ignore him. Becky and Amy needed her, and so she had focused on them.

Becky came downstairs in her dressing gown.

'Sorry,' she said. 'I thought you'd been in already. Has the kettle boiled? Good! I'll make a pot of tea, coffee's far too strong for me in the morning. I'll need to get some more tea, and some flowers too if Chris is coming over tonight. Is there anything I can get for you as I'm taking Amy into Halifax? Does your suit need cleaning?'

'No. I'd better get washed.'

Jude beat a hasty retreat. She loved Becky, but she did witter at times, and Jude was not a morning person. Conversation before 8.00 a.m. grated on her sensibilities. She sought refuge in the bathroom, where there were four toothbrushes by the sink. Four? Not to mention two varieties of toothpaste, and Becky's flannel lying over the side of the bath. In the corner of the bathroom, just by the door, was something else. Jude probed it with her bare toes. Amy's knickers, discarded after her bath last night. She shook her head in wry amusement.

Jude turned up the shower as hot as she could bear it. That's for you, she told herself, for being so curmudgeonly. You ought to be pleased they're here. You're getting too set in your ways, that's your trouble. I'm sure that having an adopted family is doing you a power of good. It's making you more tolerant, for one thing. Jude remembered how she made herself say nothing when she caught Becky frantically scrubbing the base of her cast iron saucepan with an old Brillo pad, because she'd burnt some baked beans. How on earth can you burn baked beans? It demands a certain sort of genius.

Jude began to soap herself vigorously. It was disloyal, she knew, but she needed to get away. The idea of a short break from all of them was immensely appealing. She'd noticed that the travel agent's was only round the corner from her surgery. She might just pop in during her lunch hour. Yes, she might just do that . . .

Denise blamed the children. If it hadn't been for the children, Jim would have done something, or said something at the very least. When he came to size up the job – and Denise covertly sized him up, and it looked good, very good – when he came to size up the job, Rowan had been there, watching Children's BBC, and he had tousled his hair and Rowan had grinned at him. Encouraged by his friendliness, when Denise had inveigled Jim into the garden to discuss how much lawn they might lose, Rowan had followed them out, and kicked a ball towards Jim, who dribbled with it and then lobbed it back.

Nevertheless, Denise had not been too discouraged. She herself had looked ravishing; the postman had certainly noticed her when he'd delivered the mail. The crop top that she'd nicked from Petra's wardrobe was a little tight, of course, but that was precisely the idea. Her bronzed stomach was more or less irresistible. Jim's stolid lack of reaction could only be attributed to the presence of the children. And the school holidays had just begun.

Thus it was that Denise discovered she couldn't possibly come to a conclusion about which tiles to use for the conservatory floor unless someone was there to help her choose. George was so hopeless about these things, and preferred to leave such decisions to her. She could hardly ask Becky, she confessed to Jim, now that she had no home of her own, and Karen had recently increased her hours at Sun, as the summer tourists were creating a mini-boom. Could Jim possibly come with her? She would pay him, of course And he'd agreed.

She parked her Brava across the entrance of Ferguson's yard, since she was only stopping to pick Jim up. She hooted twice, then checked her reflection in the rear mirror. The Rayban sunglasses were a stroke of genius, and the scarlet lipstick gave her the air of a forties' Hollywood vamp. Young men, she knew, were immune to subtlety. One had to lead them on. She thought of Anne Bancroft in *The Graduate*, taking down her stocking in front of an entranced Dustin Hoffman. She would be Anne Bancroft.

And here was her quarry. Jim crossed the yard in his denims and a black T-shirt which accentuated the broadness of his chest and his fine, small waist. Denise was entranced. She candidly admitted to herself that this was so much better than those foolish escapades with Paul. Paul, if you like, was a trial run, a sample package. She knew she had the front to get what she deserved. Now she was aiming for the real thing.

'Rightio, then,' Jim said, getting into the Brava.

'Rightio,' Denise repeated, caressingly.

She headed out of Mytholm towards Colne, where Jim had told her of a discount tile shop in an old mill. Colne was not the most romantic setting, a charmless, old-fashioned industrial town, but around it was some rather pretty countryside. And in the back of the Brava was a picnic basket with wine packed in a cool bag, a quiche, some sausage rolls and strawberries. It was her way of saying thank you to Jim for giving up his time.

'Lovely weather,' she remarked to him, as they ascended the road to Colne.

'Oh, aye.'

Denise tried again.

'If this is global warming, I like it!'

Jim nodded. Wasn't he shy?! Denise thought that was rather sweet. Rather than force him to talk to her, she decided she'd go with the intimacy of silence. She herself refrained from conversation, and concentrated on the road ahead, only glancing across occasionally at the firm young thighs on the passenger seat of her Brava.

He directed her to Tile World, which occupied the ground floor of a red-bricked mill. They left the car and walked towards the entrance, shared with a low-cost shoe warehouse. As they entered the tile showroom Denise wondered if the assistants would think they were married, or at least an item. She decided to walk quite close to Jim, to give that impression. The envy of others was a sauce to her appetite for him. And, yes! the sales assistant did look at Jim twice, and Denise moved still nearer to him.

Choosing the tiles was, in fact, a fairly straightforward affair. Denise knew that she wanted the most expensive ones. It was just a matter of justifying her choice convincingly. 'Plain ones are so dull, don't you think, and the Italians have such a sense of style. How difficult is it for you to lay these diagonally?' she asked Jim.

He looked at them, narrowing his eyes. 'Could do,' he said.

'You're an angel,' said Denise, linked her arm with his for a moment, and gave him a squeeze. He seemed a little surprised, but it had broken a barrier. She removed her arm, and continued talking quite naturally.

'Yes. I'll think I'll go for these, if you approve. I love the creamy glaze of the light blue tiles, and the mosaic border of the patterned ones. It will break the floor up, don't you think, and that's important in a conservatory, where there'll be so much glass. And blue is such a cool colour. I think I'm certainly set on blue.'

She stood close to him and could feel the warmth of his body. How tempting just to reach one hand out and squeeze his left buttock! Perhaps if she did it very lightly he might not even notice. But no, it was too early. They must begin by simply being friends. So she continued to look critically at the Italian tiles, Medici, they were called, in the ice-blue colourway, and thought of Jim's denim-clad behind and its proximity to her, and she knew that for ever afterwards she would not be able to think of her conservatory floor without thinking of Jim Ferguson and his firm derrière. He signalled for an assistant, and Denise prepared herself for the business part of the morning.

They were approaching the Widdop reservoir when Denise deliberately broke the silence.

'Are you hungry?'

'Getting.'

'How do you fancy a picnic?'

'A picnic?'

'Just my way of saying thank you.' She pulled into a lay-by overlooking the reservoir. 'You had no other plans for lunch, did you?'

'Well, no. I was going to get started on the wall by your—'

'Good. I think you've been working far too hard and you deserve a break. Come and help me get the hamper out of the boot.'

So far, so good. She saw Jim smile to himself, and he got out of her car – as he turned she saw those buttocks again! – and together they lifted the wicker hamper out of the boot, and Jim carried it while they walked down towards the reservoir.

Meanwhile Denise surveyed the countryside, looking for a secluded spot.

'If it gets windy,' she said, 'we don't want to be too exposed. Let's try the field on the left. There's a little sign saying Public Footpath, so we must be all right.'

Jim followed her and she climbed on to the stile by the side of a dry-stone wall, glad she had backed up the sun bed with some self-tanning lotion. When a little breeze played with and lifted the hem of her sun-dress, she did not attempt to pull it down.

'Over here,' she shouted, settling by the trunk of a large horse chestnut. From where she was, the reservoir glistened in the distance. They seemed not to be overlooked by anything. It was perfect. Denise's spirits soared. She waved at Jim as he walked over with the picnic hamper. This was utterly idyllic.

He sat by her, his arms round his knees, and watched with interest as she unfastened the hamper, and brought out the various items of food she'd wrapped lovingly that morning, once George had gone to work.

'Cheers,' he said, taking a sausage roll and biting into it, flaky crumbs of pastry adhering to the sides of his mouth.

Denise poured them some wine in two clear plastic tumblers. She took a sip of hers. As she cut some quiche for herself she decided the time had come for some conversation.

'Do you enjoy your work, Jim?'

'Enjoy it? Oh, aye.'

'Why? What do you find satisfying about it?'

Jim coughed on his sausage roll, so he washed it down with some wine.

'I don't rightly know.'

'I suppose it must be very fulfilling to see a house you've built or converted, and think, "I did that!"'

'Yes. I suppose I do.'

'It must take a special sort of talent to be able to conceptuate a design and put it into execution.'

'Come again?'

'What I'm trying to say is, it must be wonderful to be so good with your hands.'

Jim reddened slightly. Denise was encouraged. He was clearly recognising their increasing intimacy.

'Have some quiche,' she said, cutting him a large slice. 'It's lovely to see someone appreciating what I cook. George is rarely at home at mealtimes.'

Jim shot her a quick glance. So he's picked that up, she thought.

'It's wonderful to be out in the open air like this. I just love the silence. There's never any at home, what with the children, and George shouting at me. But no – I'm not going to spoil this perfect day by thinking of any of that!'

Denise brought a finger to the side of her eye, so that Jim could think she was wiping away an imaginary tear. She'd got him down as the sort of man who liked helping damsels in distress. It was the only explanation she could think of for his interest in Karen. Ought she to make herself cry? Was her mascara really waterproof? Difficult questions. She sniffed appealingly instead.

'Let's talk about you. Any sign of wedding bells?'

'Wedding bells?'

'You and Karen!' Denise said archly.

Jim chuckled. 'No, I don't think so.'

'Why? Do you mean to say that you've also heard . . . ? No. I mustn't say anything. It's only a rumour.'

'What rumour?' Jim said. He stopped eating.

'That there might be someone else on Karen's horizon.' This was risky, but Denise enjoyed playing for high stakes.

'Who else?' Jim asked. It was good to get this show of fire from him.

'I gather Eleni's brother has come back from Cyprus,' she said. 'He's helping out at Sun too.'

A broad grin spread over Jim's face. 'Oh, aye. I've heard of that.'

Denise was puzzled. He seemed to have lost interest in

Karen's philanderings. So, in that case, they might not be so attached to each other. In that case, he might be willing to stray as well.

'Some women are never satisfied,' she said, finishing her wine. Now she prised open the Tupperware box of strawberries she had brought from the freezer that morning. She lifted out a tiny one, shaped like a nipple, and held it between her thumb and forefinger and brought it towards Jim's mouth.

'Here. Taste this,' she instructed. He opened his mouth, and her fingers brushed the side of his lips. Soft but firm lips. She watched him bite on the strawberry.

'Can I get you some more?'

'Not at the moment. I think I'll have a fag.' From his pocket he took out a crushed packet of Silk Cut. Denise wished she had some matches to light the cigarette for him. Instead she wriggled on to her stomach, propped her face in her hands and gazed up at him. She knew the top of her sun-dress would expose her cleavage.

'I'm going to be politically incorrect. I think smoking is sexy.'

'Do you want a fag?'

'No. I'll just watch you.'

He smoked in silence. What a wonderful change this was to Paul's pushy self-importance! Jim was exquisite, like a Greek God. Yet still he had not responded to her. What could be holding him back? She was running out of signals to send him. Denise felt as if she was playing a particularly tricky game of chess, and was at a loss to devise her next manoeuvre. Asking him to rub in some suntan oil was just too obvious and crude.

'I'm scared I'll burn in this sunshine,' she said to him. 'I've got some sunscreen here. You wouldn't rub it in, would you?'

She handed him the bottle she had prepared earlier, and pulled down the straps of her sun-dress. Her knees felt deliciously weak. She came to kneel in front of him. Obligingly he put out his cigarette and jerked out some lotion on to his large, rough hands, and began to massage it into her shoulders.

Eye contact now, she thought. She raised her eyes to his. No use. He was intent upon making a good job of the suntan lotion. She shuddered with pleasure. Her mouth ached for a kiss from him. She closed her eyes, hoping he would surprise her.

'I had a drink with George last night,' he said.

She opened her eyes.

'After his bridge evening?'

'Bridge? Oh, aye, yes.' Jim's hands left her shoulders. Denise felt thwarted. Why was he being so awkward? What was coming between them? She had never wanted anything so badly as him, and always she had been able to get what she wanted. This wasn't fair. She could have cried with frustration. She squeezed her eyes, and did cry, just a little.

'What's wrong?' he asked her.

'I feel so lonely,' she said.

'Well, you're not alone. There's me — and, look — here's another picnic party!'

Sure enough, two young women in multicoloured harem pants and tie-dyed T-shirts with a brood of half-naked children came scampering down the hill. Denise let out a deep breath. Just as she was beginning to get somewhere!

'Do you want to be getting back?' he asked her.

'I suppose so,' she said wanly. Surely he would take pity on her! She felt so sorry for herself, because she couldn't have him. If only he would feel sorry for her too.

'Come on, then!' He began to pack the picnic things away. Denise watched him. Rage and disappointment contested in her. What ought she to do? Give up, and take the opportunity of slagging him off to all her friends? Or persist with her campaign? If she didn't, if she gave up on him, then she would be left with George. Peaceable, undemanding, unimaginative, terminally boring George. Unthinkable.

Only she could not do this one alone. She needed assistance. Who would know best how to break this man down? The answer was obvious. Karen knew him best, and she was at home this afternoon. Dare she? Dare she not? She watched Jim walk up the hill in front of her, carrying the picnic hamper back to the car, his buttocks for the moment enticingly out of reach.

Karen placed a brightly coloured canvas deck chair outside her house, in preparation for an afternoon doing nothing. She had filled a paddling pool for the boys, and Jim had brought up a bag of sand for the sand pit. She'd put lashings of sun protection cream on the boys, pulled them wriggling into their bathing shorts, and surveyed them now, arranging their plastic boats in a convoy. Things were looking good.

Having all of the lane to herself, Karen decided this was as good a time as any to take just a tiny peek into Becky's old house. She was unbearably curious about Paul. What did he do every night? He never went out and he never had visitors; Denise was keeping a wide berth. For once, Karen guessed she was telling the truth. She really had finished with lover boy. So the delectable Paul had been ditched by both his women. It served him bloody well right.

It was easy to walk round the side of the conservatory. Karen did so, while listening with one ear to Seth and Bobby's chatter. Well, well, well! It was an absolute tip! The conservatory itself wasn't too bad, except for a litter of newspapers, but the door to the living room was open, and Karen could see glasses and mugs that had not been put away, and some clothes lying on the floor. To think he didn't lift a finger even when there was no one to slave away for him! And yet he still drove off in the Mondeo every morning, keeping up that silly façade. He was scary. He gave her the creeps. Becky did right to get rid.

Karen made her way back to her deck chair, and settled herself into it. The boys were deep into some role play where they both seemed to be fleet commanders. Bliss! A rare moment of peace. She closed her eyes, and let a delicious feeling of satisfaction roll through her. Two years ago she could never have imagined feeling so happy. Now she was loved again, loved unselfishly – it was wonderful! She cast her mind back to the previous night, and could not resist smiling to herself, still with eyes closed. And the Clough Hall Health Club was having its grand opening in two weeks' time, and finally Karen would be installed as the receptionist. The boys' chatter provided a gentle counterpoint to her contented mood. Then a louder noise rose above their voices – a car's engine – and Karen opened her eyes, alert and curious. Denise's Brava came into view.

Karen itched to know how the tile expedition had gone, and guessed that this visit might be the aftermath of it. For once she was rather glad to see Denise, and she got up to greet her with more than a show of pleasure. There was something that she'd been planning to tell her.

'Karen! Hi! Isn't it a glorious day?'

'Not bad.'

'I thought I'd call round for a chat. We don't seem to have spent time together for ages!'

'Take the deck chair,' Karen said. 'I can sit on the door-step.'

'Are you sure?'

'Oh, yes. Sitting on stone helps to firm your back-side.'

'Does it?'

Karen saw that Denise was stashing the tip away. Shows how naïve some people could be. Karen had made it up just that instant.

'Your boys,' Denise said, gesturing to them. 'So sweet!'

Karen said nothing.

'But it's a bind, these long summer holidays. It's all right for the teachers, though. Six weeks' holiday on full pay. I'd do anything for a break from the kids. You haven't thought of taking up child-minding, have you?'

'You mean you'd like me to look after Petra and Rowan for you?'

'Would you? Tomorrow? I'll pay you the same hourly rate as when you clean.'

'I'm glad you mentioned that,' Karen said. 'There's something I have to tell you.' She paused to extract every gram of pleasure from her next statement. If only she'd set Becky up with a camcorder or something! 'I've been offered another job. Not cleaning but receptionist work. Full-time. So I won't be able to do for you any more. You'll have to find yourself a new cleaner.'

'Oh, Karen! I'm devastated!'

But Denise didn't look devastated, Karen thought. That was worrying. Things weren't going quite according to plan.

'What will I do without you?' Denise declared.

'Will you do your own cleaning?' Karen asked nervously.

'Oh, no! I'm afraid it's a very low priority for me. I'll advertise for someone.'

'Because I don't want to leave you in the lurch. I do happen to have a friend who's looking for work. She's very good, very dependable, and all that.'

'Does she have references?'

'Oh, yeah. And she knows where you live, knows it well. Shall I ask her to call and see you?'

'Yes, all right. We'll arrange something. But will you have the kids tomorrow?'

'Why? What are you doing?'

Karen observed Denise's momentary hesitation.

'I'm not doing anything to speak of, but Jim's hard at work on the conservatory and Rowan tends to get under his feet.'

'Rowan does, does he?'

'Little boys, and bricks and mortar!' Denise stroked her finger along the wooden strut of the deck chair. 'Jim's so fond of you, isn't he?'

'Oh, yes!'

'And yet he's so shy! A rare quality in a man. It must have been hard work to get him to notice you. I didn't mean that to sound rude, Karen! But you must have had to push things along in the beginning.'

'What woman doesn't?'

Denise gave a silvery laugh. 'You're so right. We're all manipulative at heart.'

'We're all two-faced.'

'Absolutely!' Denise pressed on. 'So go on – tell me. How did you hook him in?'

'Do you really want to know?' Karen lowered her voice so the boys wouldn't hear. 'The point about Jim is that for all his good looks, and his brilliant performance in bed, he's got to feel wanted.'

'He's got to feel wanted.'

'Yes. And he's not very bright. Very loving, if you know what I mean, but not very bright. So you have to be fairly obvious.'

'I thought so.'

'And not having had much of an education, you might have noticed that he's not the world's greatest conversationalist.'

'I have noticed.'

'So just supposing someone set out to get him – not that they would now, of course—'

'Of course!'

'—Just supposing, then. It's best not to say too much. If you come across as clever it makes him feel inadequate. And being shy, he needs privacy to bring out the demon in him.' Karen sighed. 'Like a bedroom with the curtains drawn. And then you signal through what you're wearing – or not wearing – then he'll understand what's on offer. And he'll respond in kind.'

Denise extended her fingers, then contracted them as if she was about to grip something. Karen wondered if those were false nails she was wearing.

'Are you still going out together?' Denise asked.

'Oh, yes. He's the love of my life.'

'But he hasn't proposed to you?'

'Not yet, Denise, but fingers crossed, eh?' Karen hoped she didn't sound too coy.

'He has a bit of a reputation, Karen. I don't want to be the one to sound the warning note, but can you trust him to be faithful?'

'No,' Karen said candidly. 'But with a libido like his, who cares?'

She watched Denise inhale, then exhale slowly. She pushed her hair behind her ears, where a bead or two of perspiration had collected.

'It's hot, isn't it?' she said.

'Anyway,' Karen said, leaning back on the step, 'who are we to talk? Women are every bit as bad as men, if the truth were known. I've read that whereas a man comes to his sexual peak when he's quite young, a woman reaches hers as she approaches forty.'

'I've a way to go then!' Denise lied.

'I've also heard that women are meant to be unfaithful. Natural selection, and all that. We have to find the most successful sperm. It's in our instincts,' Karen concluded.

'So you're saying that we can't help it?'

'I am, sort of.'

'Isn't science wonderful? I'm sure what you're saying is right. It's so good to sit here and admit to these things,' Denise confessed. 'Women are so rarely honest.'

'Yes. Because, when it comes down to it, we're in competition. Competition for survival of the species!' Karen was enjoying herself.

'I suppose it's why we have this inbuilt distrust and jealousy of each other. I'm sure every women secretly feels she's better looking than the next! I have to say I wonder whether two women can ever truly be friends.'

'Except for us, of course!' Karen laughed.

'Except for us!' Denise cleared her throat. 'So, Karen, will you have the children tomorrow?'

The cheek of her! When Denise was finally out of her life,

she would miss her, in a way. She was so splendidly awful. But for now, it was back to business.

'Not tomorrow. The boys have an appointment with Jude. But I'm reasonably free at the end of next week. I'll take them for a day, if you like.'

'Karen, I don't know what I'd do without you!'

'Shall I speak to Gina – she's the friend I told you about, who's looking for a cleaning job?'

'Yes, you do that.'

'Because I'd like to help her out. She's been having a hard time lately. Her partner's been cheating on her, you see.'

'Poor love. You arrange a date for her to pop up and see me.'

'Will do.' Only with iron self-control did Karen prevent herself from exhibiting her delight. The old cow had fallen for it, hook, line and sinker. Jim was an out-and-out genius.


It was Karen's own fault, Denise thought, as she headed back home. Fancy being so careless about one's boyfriend. Loose talk costs men. She deserved to lose him. So it was that Denise felt absolved of any moral responsibility. No, she could go even further than that. She was actually doing Karen a favour. It would teach her not to take people for granted, and not to be so cynical. Mind you, it was good to hear another woman state what she had always suspected. Women were not as good at bonding as people supposed. Karen admitted that she was also underhand and competitive. Denise suspected that all women were like that. She certainly was. It was a shame that in pursuing Jim she might forfeit Karen's friendship, as she and Karen understood each other very well. The truth was that women were good friends with each other as long as they could be mutually useful. And only then. Like is repelled by like. It was nature. Karen had said so.

Karen wasn't going to clean for her any more, but she had served her purpose. Her inside information was invaluable. And with a bit of luck, she'd soon be possessed of the same inside information. Inside information. Denise was surprised at how aroused the thought of Jim could make her. It was impossible that she could feel so much for him, and he should feel nothing for her. Sexual attraction didn't work that way. If she removed any scruples he might have about Karen, and then leave him in no possible doubt whatever . . . Desire flashed through her. She always got what she wanted. Always. And with Karen's advice, she was bound to get him. But how on earth was she going to wait over a week?

Well, she'd waited long enough already. In comparative terms, sexual ecstasy was just around the corner. Karen would be her stepping stone, and take her to where she ought to have been all along. In just over one week. It was going to be the longest week of her life.

# Chapter Fourteen

Becky cursed herself for having forgotten to defrost the chicken for the stir-fry. Not that it was a major disaster – they had invented microwave ovens specifically for people like her, and Jude's microwave stood there in its antiseptic splendour. Becky put the three chicken breasts on a plate and switched the oven on. In the short time it took her to do that, the rice boiled over with a sizzle. A cascade of bubbles swept down the side of the saucepan. If it had been her own kitchen, Becky would have left it, but she knew that if Jude saw the tiniest speck of spilt food on her cooker, she'd be attacking it with the Dettox. So Becky felt obliged to try to clean it. Jude's meticulous house was a constant reproach to her. How lovely it would be to have a place of one's own to mess up! Her own house was still tainted for her; Becky began to dream instead of a small terraced cottage for her and Amy, and perhaps, in a real home of her own, she might even manage to run things smoothly. If only there was a small cottage she could rent, and if only she could find the money to rent it with.

Jude, she knew, would lend her, or give her the money. She had often said so. She'd been perfectly frank about the cash she'd inherited from her mother, and how Phyllis would like to think it was being used to help Becky. At which point Becky had felt something akin to irritation. The present purpose of her existence seemed to be that Jude and Phyllis should save her. Jude turned her into as much of an object as men were supposed to do to women. She wanted to be able to make her own decisions, to do things her way. Yet every time she tried to make a start, she was beset by legal obstacles, financial obstacles and Jude, who always knew better.

She slashed furiously into a row of spring onions, deftly beheading them. Only Jude did not know what she had been up to this afternoon. Having dropped Amy off at Sophie's, she'd driven to Rochdale, put her protesting father in the car and taken him to Heathfields, where a very nice but very forceful care assistant had shown him round, and taken him to the little bedroom with its floral wallpaper which would be his, if he agreed to move in.

Her father had been positively rude, muttering about everybody wanting to rob him of his money and his independence. *What about my independence*, Becky had asked him? He had tried to look forlorn then, and accused Becky of abandoning him. She'd replied that she wasn't abandoning him; she would try to visit every week, but until she was settled it might be difficult. He told the nurse that Becky had always been selfish, and came out with his familiar refrain, *what did you bring daughters up for if it wasn't to look after you in your old age*? Becky felt quite remote from him, as if he was somebody else's father. She left it to the nurse to explain the advantages of the home, the regular meals, the entertainments, the social life. When a rather attractive black nurse walked past, her bottom swinging seductively from side to side, she saw her father's eyes follow her. After that he seemed rather more resigned, although he still muttered about undutiful daughters and having his pride, but his eyes ranged over the room acquisitively, and Becky felt the same kind of relief she felt when she'd walked in with two heavy bags of shopping and finally put both down. She had never confronted him about his past; the scene would have been unbearably sordid and ugly. Some things were best forgotten.

And yet, if it wasn't for the way Jude had rewritten her

history, she'd have never found the resolution to face up to her father. Of course she was grateful to Jude, and she tried to show it. She'd cooked and cleaned to the best of her ability, and tried to anticipate her wants. If only she didn't feel so much of a dependant! It wasn't Jude's fault. She never patronised, never made Becky or Amy feel unwelcome. In her brash, rough way she was one of the kindest people Becky knew. And Chris was kind too, she mused. He had a genuine empathy, so that when he listened to her she knew for that moment he *was* her. She rationed the time she spent talking to him because, after all, he was Jude's. Remembering that she had brought them together helped to make her feel that they were even after all. They had each done a good turn for the other. Becky glowed with satisfaction. How could she have ever known that Chris would turn out to be such a catch? The more she got to know him, the more charming he seemed. He obviously loved Jude, was so at ease with Amy, and so kind to her. He was a lovely man. It was rather, she thought, grating the ginger and her finger, as if she'd got Jude a lottery ticket, which turned out to have six winning numbers! Perhaps she had an instinct for bringing people together. She could always open an introductions agency. With all the divorcees in Mytholm Bridge, she'd be sure to make a killing.

It didn't surprise her when she heard Jude open the door and Chris arrive. It seemed natural that by thinking of him, he should appear. Besides which, he had promised to come for dinner – hence the stir-fry. Becky checked her assembled ingredients – baby sweetcorn, onions, ginger, bean sprouts – it was just a matter of rescuing the chicken from the microwave.

'Hello, Becky!' Chris popped his head into the kitchen. 'Can I put this in the fridge?' He held a bottle of something wrapped in green tissue paper. Becky quickly hid the chicken breasts, which had begun to cook around the edges.

'It's looking good,' he said. 'Do you want a hand? And

don't scoff – I know quite a bit about Chinese cooking. I heard Ken Hom once, at a Waterstone's reading.'

'Everything's beautifully under control. You can go and join Jude.'

'She's deep into some soap opera. I wouldn't dare.'

Becky unwrapped the bottle. 'Champagne! Are we celebrating?' She turned to look at him. There was a boyish excitement in his face that was infectious. 'So we are celebrating! What's happened?' Her pulse beat fast as she guessed that he might have come in to tell her of his and Jude's engagement.

'I've been offered a job.' He grinned mischeviously at her.

'You mean the post at York – as creative writing tutor!'

'Yes – they rang me this afternoon. I start in October. It's initially for a year, but if the course takes off, the contract is renewable. And there's some academic teaching too, which means the post is virtually full-time.'

'Chris – that's wonderful!' She was so happy she hugged him impulsively, and he hugged her back with enthusiasm. He squeezed her so tightly she could hardly breathe.

'Does Jude know? Oh, I understand! It was you who was trying to call today! Then you heard my voice and put the phone down, because you were waiting for Jude!'

'No?' Chris looked puzzled.

'Oh. It's just that someone rang once or twice. So it wasn't you. Have you spoken to Jude yet?'

He shook his head, a little apprehensively, she thought. Becky understood why. This job brought everything to a head. Chris could not live in Mytholm and commute to York. Either he would have to see Jude infrequently, tacitly admitting that their relationship was not important, or she would have to go with him, or he would have to turn down this job. This match was her handiwork. She felt fully involved in this new development. The news ought to be broken gently to Jude.

'You'd better speak to her as soon as possible,' Becky said.

'Take her home with you tonight and tell her then – when you're alone. We'll save the champagne.'

Chris nodded.

'Are you sure I can't help you with the cooking?' he asked.

'I'm sure. Why don't you pour us all a drink instead? This is supposed to be a dinner party.'

'I'll get you something. Jude and Amy have already opened some wine.'

'Amy?'

Becky left Chris in the kitchen and hurried into the living room.

'Amy! How much wine have you had?'

'This is only my second glass, and it's a tiny one!'

'Jude. She mustn't drink! She's only thirteen.'

'Then it's legal,' Jude said, her eyes still on the screen. 'You can have alcohol at home once you're over five. Anyway, it's better she should learn to drink with us than experiment with her friends.'

Becky was speechless. She looked at Amy, whose cheeks were suspiciously pink.

'You're not to have any more,' she said firmly. 'That glass will have to last you all through dinner.'

'Oh, Mum!' Amy whinged.

Chris came in. 'Jude, you've not been corrupting minors again? Amy, do what your mother tells you. I've sliced the chicken but I've put it back in the fridge away from the cats.' He sat himself next to Jude on the settee, and put an arm around her. Becky was grateful for his intervention, and returned to the kitchen. This was the last straw. Jude had no idea how difficult it was to bring up a teenager; the next thing, she'd be showing her how to put a condom on a cucumber! The oil sizzled in the pan. What Becky did not articulate to herself was a creeping jealousy of Jude. Amy often seemed to prefer her, and at times seemed to play one of them off against the other. So much so that she was being held up as the fussy, neurotic mother, and Jude as the cool, streetwise, big sister. She had spent thirteen back-breaking years trying to turn Amy into a half-way decent human being, and now Jude was marching in, undoing all her good work, and then taking the credit!

Becky knew she was being ridiculous. The point was she needed to get away. If only she could think of a way of doing so. She moved the chicken and vegetables round and round with a spatula, not noticing some baby sweetcorn slipping out and joining the bean sprouts under the wok. There had to be a solution.

Chris sat back on the settee, one leg over the other, a glass of wine by his side.

'Watch that glass,' Becky said automatically to Amy, as she got up to put her empty ice-cream dish in the kitchen.

Amy tossed her head in a gesture of defiance, and Becky sighed. It was so difficult to have to act out the pantomime of their relationship in front of an audience. Becky's thoughts were interrupted by Jude clearing her throat.

'I've got something to tell you guys,' she said.

Becky and Chris gave her their attention.

'I called in at the travel agent's this afternoon. I've booked myself a long weekend in Paris, leaving next Friday. It's a really good deal, though I've got to take the train to London and make my own way to Waterloo for the Eurostar.' Her voice trailed away.

Becky glanced quickly at Chris to see how he took that. What was Jude playing at? Didn't she know he'd just been offered a job? Of course not, not yet. Then it occurred to Becky that she would have three days free of Jude and her heart sang. Then immediately she felt guilty. Jude had obviously had enough of her, and not only that, she had once again taken the intiative and done something about it. Becky was trumped. Amy returned from the kitchen.

'What did you say, Jude?'

'I'm going to Paris next weekend. Just me.'

'But you can't! You promised the four of us could go to Blackpool, and you said I could bring Sophie!'

'Oh, shit!'

'Jude!' Becky said warningly. She had a habit of using bad language in front of Amy.

'Look, we can go another time. I've paid for this already. There's a performance of *Aida*, and I'm trying to get a ticket.'

Becky did not so much think to herself that Jude was being selfish as that she failed to take others into consideration. And what about Chris? He didn't seem to be reacting at all. What was he thinking? How dare she treat him like that!

'No, Jude, we can't go another time because I've already asked Sophie, and her Mum said I could sleep over with her afterwards, and then the next week they're going on Eurocamp!' Amy's voice assumed its characteristic wail.

'You can all go without me,' Jude said, in a jolly voice.

There was an uncomfortable silence.

'Can we, Mum?'

'Well, all right. Will you come, Chris?'

'Don't mind if I do.'

That should teach her a lesson, Becky thought, still indignant on Chris's behalf. She hoped her invitation didn't come across as too spiteful. It wasn't meant to be. She simply wanted to stop Chris feeling rejected by everyone. And anyway, they would be chaperoned by two teenage girls. She eyed Jude to gauge her reaction, but she seemed as unconcerned as ever.

'I'll give you some spending money, Amy,' Jude said. 'No, Becky! I insist! It's partly guilt money, and partly wages, because I want Amy to look after the cats while I'm gone.'

'Oh, cool!'

Becky pursed her lips. Jude had done it again. She'd managed both to let Amy down and remain her hero. She envied Jude for being so effortlessly selfish. Perhaps I ought to be more selfish, she thought.

'Paris,' said Chris, thoughtfully.

'Yes,' Jude lifted her chin slightly. 'It's one of my favourite cities. Not that my French is up to much, but I get by.'

'I'll lend you a phrase book,' Chris said. 'Come back with me tonight, and I'll root around and find it for you.'

Becky was alert to his tone, which was uncompromising. She noticed Jude stiffen fractionally. She would have to learn that you couldn't treat a lover like that. You can't just run off to the world's most romantic city without him. Or was she playing a game? Was this her clumsy attempt to bring him to a proposal? The silence in the room was palpable. Only Amy was unaware of it, having picked up a Point Romance to flick through.

'Shall we go now?' Jude asked. Her eyes were directed at the floor.

Chris got up.

'I'll just get some things,' Jude said, and ran upstairs.

'This is a surprise to me,' Becky explained, hoping Chris didn't think she was party to it.

'Typical Jude,' he said, noncommittally.

'I'm going to go to Paris one day,' Amy said.

'Do you want your bottle of champagne back?' Becky asked Chris.

'No,' he said. 'You keep it.'

Jude reappeared with a small overnight bag.

'See you,' she said. 'Say goodbye to the cats for me.'

Ridiculous, thought Becky, the way she treats those animals.

'I will,' she said.


'Paris,' Chris said again as he followed Jude into his house.

'I know. What can I say? It's not to get away from you!'

'I'm pleased to hear it.'

'Don't be like that.' She turned and placed her hands on his shoulders. 'Look at me. It's not to get away from you. It's just a bit claustrophobic at home, and it'll do us all good if I leave them to their own devices for a bit. And *Aida* was on at the Opéra. And, OK, I was a bit of a coward. I thought you wouldn't like me to pay for you, and I know you don't have the money. So I thought I would go by myself.' Jude reached up and kissed him on the side of his cheek. He didn't seem to respond. She was a little apprehensive. She thought he would understand completely why she had to get away. They were adults, after all. Theirs was a free, untrammelled association. Now she felt a little remorseful. Chris had only recently experienced rejection by a woman. She would have to make it clear that she wasn't doing the same.

'I wish you could come with me,' she said. 'I'd enjoy it more. One day we'll go together and I'll take you to Père Lachaise and we'll walk among the gravestones.' She nuzzled his chest, and felt its firmness under his T-shirt.

'I've got the job,' he said.

'The job?' Jude was momentarily disorientated.

'At York. I'm teaching on the MA in Creative Writing. In October.'

'Chris – that's great!' Jude was overjoyed. She knew how much he'd wanted it. Gently he disengaged himself from her. She watched him go to the settee and sit down, knees apart. Quickly she went to join him and took his hand, stroking it a little.

'This is such good news! It's just the opening you needed. So they got the funding after all.'

'Yes. I'm very pleased.' But he didn't sound pleased, Jude thought. Was it because she was jetting off to Paris?

'When I'm in York, we won't be able to see as much of each other,' he said.

Jude stopped stroking his hand. What was he trying to say? That he didn't want to see as much of her? Or was he getting his own back for her sudden holiday? She wished she had Becky with her to interpret, to guide her through the conversational quicksand. She held on to his hand tightly, unwilling to let him go.

'Don't you want to see as much of me?' she asked.

'Of course I do.'

A silence. What was she supposed to say next?

'Good. I don't want to see any less of you.'

He took her face in his hand and lifted it, and then his lips lightly made contact with hers, and he kissed her, experimentally at first, and then gaining force. Jude held back a little. If she was to kiss him back, what was she saying? He stopped the kiss.

'So what will happen to us?' he asked.

Jude shrugged. 'Kiss me again.'

'No. We've got to talk. Sometimes I feel I'm not very important to you, as if I'm part of your life, not all of it.'

Jude blushed. 'No. You're very important! Chris – I love you!'

'And you love your cats, your job, Becky and Amy, and . . .'

'Yes, but—'

'Would you come with me to York, if I asked you?'

Jude was paralysed with fear. Did he understand what he was saying? If she came with him, she would be committing herself absolutely. Besides, there was her practice. He knew she couldn't leave that.

'This isn't a fair question. There's my job. Can't we wait and see?'

'How long? Neither of us are that young.'

Jude had to remind herself to breathe. The tension had made all her muscles seize. What ought she to say or do now? She was certain she didn't want to lose him, absolutely certain, but she couldn't give up her new life to follow him. It was too much to ask. She bit her lip anxiously.

'We could see each other every weekend.'

Chris nodded slowly.

'And speak on the phone.'

Chris looked at her steadily and there was something so intense and penetrating in his gaze that she felt quite abashed.

'So you don't want to finish with me?' he said.

'Heavens, no! Whatever gave you that idea?'

It was Paris, Jude realised. She had been rather thoughtless, she could see that now. What could she do to make it up to him? Her eyes travelled down his body. Perhaps she would initiate some lovemaking. She moved closer to him so she could brush her lips against his. She took one hand and pushed it up his T-shirt. making contact with his warm, firm flesh. She wanted him now, quite badly. It was with relief that she felt him begin to respond. The last thing she wanted was to hurt his feelings. She was really very fond of him. It was her last conscious thought as she felt his kisses grow more and more searching.


Afterwards Chris sat on the floor, propped up against the settee. It was too hot to dress again, and he contemplated the hair growing on the surface of his legs. Jude sat next to him, her head resting on his shoulder. Their lovemaking had done nothing to reassure him. It had been almost automatic, each of them making the expected moves. It hadn't been enough. He had wanted more Was it something missing in him? She claimed to love him, but now he wondered if he could claim to love her. He realised he could contemplate going to York without her, just as she could happily come to terms with him leaving. Jude could do without him, and he could do without her. The realisation made him sad, despite his good news, and the sadness made him lonelier than ever. He wished he had not come home with Jude, and had stayed instead in her house, with the champagne, and Becky. He hoped she was drinking it now, and was feeling his happiness for him, as no doubt she would. She was a good friend. She had seemed so glad for him when he had interrupted her in the kitchen, presiding over all those vegetables. Thinking of Becky was like moving from the shade to the sun; he was warmed. The thought of her cheered him and brought him out of his silence.

'Bed?' he asked Jude.

'Mmm,' she said. 'I'll go to Montmartre and get my portrait done for you.'

'I'd like that. But come on, else I'll fall asleep down here.'

'OK,' she said.


'Can we go to the Pleasure Beach?'

'Not yet, Amy. We've got all afternoon for that.'

Becky watched Amy consult with Sophie. Sophie seemed a nice girl, and it amused Becky that she wore a pair of white, knee-length dungarees, while Amy sported an identical black pair. Sophie had recently had her hair cut, and it was now in a fashionable bob. She'd let Amy try some synthetic-smelling perfume she'd bought with her pocket money. Becky was amused. The body odour problem was obviously being tackled. Out of their school uniform, both girls looked a lot older. They were almost grown up.

'OK,' Amy said. 'We'll leave the Pleasure Beach for now. But what shall we do?'

Here was the whole of Blackpool, and Amy didn't know what to do. How typical of Amy! Always needing her mother to think up some entertainment. She wondered if it was warm enough for the beach and so she went to join Chris, who was standing on the promenade looking over the sands. Already parties of holiday-makers were erecting deck chairs and windbreaks, and some hardy children were stepping into the water in the distance. To Becky, the sands looked rather grubby, and besides, she felt as if she wanted to keep moving. The seaside affected her like that. It was an exciting place to be, and she wanted to do as much as possible, sample all its delights, just as she did when she was young. Chris was quite silent. He was obviously thinking about Jude. Becky decided to bring him out of his reverie.

'Is there anything that *you* want to do?' she asked him.

He turned and smiled at her. 'No. I'm entirely at your command. What about the girls?'

'They'd spend all day on the Pleasure Beach, but I'd like to wander on to the pier.'

Chris addressed Amy and Sophie, who were fingering some cheap pendants on a stand in a beach shop.

'We're going on the pier,' he announced.

The four of them made their way through the turnstile, Becky and Chris hanging back so that the girls could go on in front. Each had a miniature rucksack on their back like a tiny hump. There was a distant haze of cloud and a cool wind, and Becky hoped that it would remain dry. They passed elderly couples sitting on sheltered benches, looking puffed out but pleased to be there. Seagulls wheeled above, and a tang of salt in the air stung Becky's nostrils. It woke her up. She was glad she'd decided to come out today, and felt determined to have a good time. Jude's absence was sauce to her appetite. No doubt she was living it up on the Champs Elysées. Becky needed a break from routine too. She glanced at Chris who sauntered by her side. He was looking around him observantly, and she guessed he was storing it all away for his novel.

'Do you know, you've never told any of us what your novel is about?'

'Haven't I?' He turned to smile at her, the way he did in class whenever she asked a question. It was a smile that made her feel as if she'd pleased him in some way. 'That's probably because it's not very interesting.'

'Why don't you tell me now?'

He gave a little laugh, as if he was laughing at himself. They passed a man and his sons fishing off the end of the pier. Becky couldn't help but look at the tin of squirming maggots by their side. 'It's about cultural conflict. North and south, rich and poor, male and female—'

'So there's a love interest?'

'In a manner of speaking.'

'I thought serious, literary novelists like you looked down on romance,' she said teasingly.

'Not at all. It's more a question of how it's treated.'

'No clichés?'

'That's right.'

'And no happy endings?'

He laughed. 'Are there ever happy endings? You tell me.' The sudden intimacy of his tone surprised her.

'What's your heroine like? Like Jude?' She emphasised that last word.

'No. Actually, she's African. A refugee.'

Becky was silent. As they arrived at the amusements, Amy and Sophie were waiting for them.

'Can we go on the rides, please?'

Becky nodded her assent. 'What about you, Chris?'

He shook his head. 'I get motion sickness.'

'Me too.' It wasn't true, but Becky couldn't afford for them all to go on the big wheel. Besides, she felt inclined to keep Chris company. She watched the girls get their tickets and queue at the turnstile.

'And you,' Chris said to her. 'How have you been?'

The way he asked the question made her certain that he was referring to Paul. She felt a little self-conscious, but was glad of the opportunity to speak. 'OK. I cope by not thinking of the past – I can't bear to. Perhaps I will one day, when I'm more settled. And there's so much to do – with solicitors and money and everything. I can't afford to be self-indulgent when there are so many decisions to be made. Jude's been wonderful,' she said loyally.

'She's very practical.'

'Absolutely. Oh my God! Look at the girls!' They were hanging precariously at the top of the big wheel, waving so hard Becky was scared the whole thing would unbalance. Chris waved back.

'I like Amy,' he said.

Becky felt as if he had complimented her, and warmed even more to him.

'Yes. She's a lovely girl. She's coped remarkably well in the past few weeks. I only hope it won't have a permanent effect on her.'

'She's enjoying herself today.'

The wheel jerked round as more customers climbed in.

'Do you know what I fancy?' Chris said suddenly. 'Candy floss!'

'Oh no, you mustn't! My mother always said it made your teeth go black and fall out,' Becky said.

'Well, let's see if she's right.' Chris took her arm and guided her to a stall where a plump woman with dyed blonde hair was supervising a steel vat of candy floss. Chris ordered a large one, and Becky watched the woman spin it round the wooden stick. Pink, sticky mass of sweetness – a forbidden pleasure. Chris took it from her and pulled off a strand.

'Open your mouth,' he said.

'It's bad for your teeth!'

'So don't tell Jude!' She opened her mouth and Chris filled it with candy floss, which crystallised against her tongue and the roof of her mouth. Experimentally she bit on the cloying sweetness, and felt its grittiness. It was all gone. She wanted more.

'Nice,' she said.

'Help yourself!'

Amy looked down over the tiny pier, and the toy town of Blackpool and its tower, and thought that it was funny, but the Eiffel Tower, where Jude was, looked just like the Blackpool tower really, when you thought about it. And Blackpool was brilliant and they would go on the Pleasure Beach later and do all the rides and stuff. And Sophie said they were really best friends, and tonight she thought she would tell her all about Petra, and she knew Sophie would understand. Sophie's dad left them too, that was why. It was good to have a friend like Sophie.

'Amy? Is Chris your mum's boyfriend?'

'No, don't be daft. He's Jude's.'

'He's nice.'

'Yeah.' It was funny to think of her mum having a boyfriend. She wouldn't, anyway. She wasn't like that. For a moment Amy tried to understand how her mother must feel, now she didn't have Dad any more. It must be funny. But Mum had her to look after, and that kind of made up for it. It would give her something to do. Mums didn't need that much excitement, anyway. It was different when you were thirteen. It was brilliant being her age, she thought. You had everything to look forward to.


'Please can we go round on our own?'

Becky looked apprehensively at Chris. 'But what if you get lost?'

'It's all right, Becky,' Sophie said. 'I know the Pleasure Beach really well. We come here a lot.'

'Oh, Mum!' pleaded Amy. Becky still hesitated. If they went off again, she would be alone with Chris for the second time. She felt a little awkward. It had begun in the fish and chip shop when the assistant was processing their orders and told her to let her husband wait at the counter as the chips wouldn't be a minute, love! Then Becky had realised that probably everybody thought they were married. What impression were they giving? She blushed a little and didn't dare look at Chris. They had sat together, almost too close for comfort, in a small booth at the back of the shop, and Chris had made himself a chip butty with lashings of ketchup, and Becky had teased him about that. For the rest of the lunch he assumed a thick

Lancashire accent, much to the girls' amusement. She had to smile too.

'Tell you what,' Chris said. 'Be back here at the entrance to the Pleasure Beach at three thirty. That gives you half an hour. Then if you're good, you can have another half an hour.'

'Cool!' Amy and Sophie linked arms and walked off towards the Big One.

'And you're not going on the Big One!' Becky called after them.

Suddenly Chris took her hand. 'Come here,' he instructed her. She allowed herself to be pulled along, noticing the physical contact, reminding herself that he meant nothing by it. Nothing at all.

'This is what I like,' he said, as they arrived at a stall where ten metal horses stood at a starting post, and two large, red-cheeked men were exhorting passers-by to try their luck. Chris took a seat and paid his money. The object of the exercise, Becky knew, was to throw balls into the highest scoring slots, thus moving a horse along.

And they were off. She stood behind Chris, watching him throw and bounce the wooden ball along into the scoring hatches at the top, willing his horse on, not daring to glance at the horses moving in fits and starts along their trajectories. Yes! A six! Chris's horse careered ahead. Then number eight caught up. Becky was lost in the excitement of the game. Chris threw a two – not good enough. Number eight moved ahead. Come on! she thought to herself. She willed Chris on, knowing he would win – it was up to her. And then he threw a five, and then another five. He was streaking ahead. Nothing could catch him now. And the bell rung, and yes! Chris had won. He turned and smiled at her triumphantly.

One moment of bliss, and then Becky realised she had been rather silly, getting as involved. It was only a game. The winner's ticket that Chris was handed was a tacky little thing, and when they went to look in the prize show-case, the contents were rather rubbishy. Chris selected a luminous green elephant, and then handed it ceremoniously to Becky.

'For you!' he declared. She smiled, but knew it was all a game.

Then they strolled about, looking at other stalls, Becky again uncomfortably aware that neither of them had much money to spend. She felt it incumbent on her to keep talking. She had not imagined they would be thrown together as much as this, and when they were silent the intimacy seemed to grow. She told herself that they were just good friends, nothing more.

'I bet Jude's having a good time,' she said.

'Yeah. She was thrilled about getting the ticket for *Aida*.'

'I'm sure she's missing you.'

'Yeah,' Chris said absently.

Becky was concerned. 'She will be – it's just that Jude's so used to being on her own that she needs time to learn how to be part of a couple.' Talking on behalf of Jude made her feel easy again.

'You're right,' he said suddenly. 'Do you fancy a game of bingo?'

'Why not?'

At half past three Becky and Chris were back at the entrance to the Pleasure Beach. Becky searched the knots of holidaymakers for the girls, but she couldn't see them. She sighed impatiently. Amy never had any sense of time. She scanned the faces that came towards her. No Amy.

'They're late,' she said to Chris, a little redundantly.

'It's to be expected.'

Becky was angry, nevertheless. She had treated them as grown-ups by letting them go off on their own, and they had abused that trust. It was now twenty to four. Even assuming they were on a ride that took longer than they'd estimated, they should be back now. There was still no sign of them, and her watch told her it was nearly a quarter to. Were they lost?

Was Amy even now distraught, wondering how on earth to get back to her mother? Or had someone led them away from the Pleasure Beach, some stranger? Panic swept through her.

'I'm going to go and look for them.'

'You'll never find them, Becky. It's best to stay here.'

'No – you stay. I must find them.' Becky hurried off, her eyes darting everywhere. She was possessed of the idea that something dreadful had happened. It was the only explanation. She could not bear the thought of losing Amy. But where could she be? The Pleasure Beach was huge, and Chris was right. It was silly to try to look for them. Ought she to get a message put out over the tannoy asking where the two lost children were?

At that moment she heard Chris calling her. There was something in the tone of his voice that expressed relief.

'Becky! Come here!'

He took her by the arm and led her to the back of a refreshment booth, where Amy and Sophie, oblivious that they were being watched, were talking earnestly to two boys. Becky looked on with relief, anger and above all, a sense of surprise. That was Amy, and she was flirting! She was much too young, and she didn't know this boy!

Chris put a restraining arm on her.

'Let them finish,' he said.

Becky turned away. It was wrong to watch. 'I don't know what she thinks she's up to! I'll have to go and get her.'

'No, leave them. I'm sure you did the same sort of thing at their age.'

She laughed a little guiltily. 'Come to think of it, I was probably worse. I was the biggest flirt going.'

'I can imagine that!'

Becky was horrified. Had she been flirting with him subconsciously? She certainly hadn't meant to.

'I don't flirt any more. I'm a married woman. Or I was. Look where all the flirting got me.' She allowed herself to be bitter for a moment.

'It's not your fault,' Chris said.

'In a way it is. I should have never married Paul. Only I've always done what other people expected me to, always. That's why I admire Jude so much. She's always gone her own way.'

'Now you have the chance to go your own way.'

'Yes,' Becky said, sadly.

'What do you want now?'

Becky thought seriously, the throb of the music from the rides, the reek of hamburgers retreating for a moment. *Freedom*, she thought. *And someone like you, with whom to share it.* As a friend, she added quickly to herself. The truth was, Chris was every bit as much her best friend as Jude. She'd always thought it was impossible for a man and a woman to be platonic friends, and maybe that was what was wrong with her. The new, grown-up Becky would be able to be friends, uncomplicated friends, with a man. She had no reason to be troubled by her growing intimacy with Chris. They were obviously good for each other. He could talk about Jude to her. He could interpret male behaviour for her. He was her best friend's man, and therefore as effectively out of reach as . . . as Paul had been to Denise.

Amy and Sophie approached them.

'What time do you call this?' Becky demanded.

'Sorry, Becky,' Sophie said. 'We didn't realise what the time was.'

'I think I can guess why,' she said. The girls looked at each other in consternation. 'Still, it's none of my business. Except you were late, and I'm not letting you out of my sight again.' They hung their heads. 'We're going to look round the shops, all together!'

Becky could not recover her equilibrium. Somehow the innocence of their day had evaporated. Perhaps it was the way the girls had been openly pursuing those two boys. It admitted certain possibilities. And what did Chris think of them all? It was awkward and embarrassing, to say the least. Now he was looking at a display in a joke shop, with the girls by his side. Becky felt as if Amy's behaviour had exposed her in some way. She wished she could explain to Chris that *she* was not like that. As they dispersed from the shop window, Amy came to join her, and linked arms.

'He was really nice, Mum' she said. 'His name was Damon.'

'I know, but you must be careful. You knew nothing about him.'

'I was finding out,' Amy said defensively.

Becky squeezed her daughter's arm.

'Good for you,' she said. 'You've got to start somewhere.'

'How old were you when you had your first boyfriend?'

'Not much older than you. And here's some advice. When you have your first kiss, make sure you remember to breathe. The first time I was kissed, I thought I was going to be asphyxiated.'

'What does that mean?'

'Here's Chris. Ask him.'

Chris emerged from the joke shop with Sophie in tow. In his hand he had a multicoloured tinsel wig, and quite coolly, he put it on his head. The shock of his action made Becky start to laugh.

'I think it suits me,' he said, absolutely straight.

'Tell him to take it off! Tell him to take it off!' Amy shouted.

Becky couldn't. She was in the grip of an adolescent-style fit of giggles. It was almost cathartic. And Chris persisted in walking down the promenade in this ridiculous wig. It was just like Mr Rochester, when he dressed up as a gipsy. If anything, the contrast between the glittering wig and the undeniable masculinity of his face . . .

'I was getting a bit self-conscious about my thinning hair,' he interrupted her.

The girls were wild with laughter. Eventually Amy tugged it off him, and she tried it on, and so did Sophie. They giggled all the way back to the car. Soon the girls, who were in the back, started to sing together some song that was in the charts. Their young voices harmonised beautifully, and the love song they were singing had an elegiac quality. The evening sunlight was soft and balmy, and it warmed the vegetation in the fields they passed.

Becky began to realise that she had enjoyed herself. Despite the dramas of the day, she had been happy. She seized on this unlooked-for happiness, and held it tightly to herself. For the first time in months, she loved the world she lived in, the person she was, and the people with her. Yet as she turned the happiness around she became aware of its transience. They were going home. It was all nearly over. Amy would be spending the night with Sophie, Chris would be going home, and she would be all by herself. Her brief moment of happiness had gone, as if a cloud had just blocked out the sun.

No – that was silly. Why let thoughts of the future spoil what she had now? Becky was learning to live in the moment, and she was determined to enjoy the moment. She hummed the tune the girls were singing, and then Chris joined in too. She would have him with her for a little longer yet.

Chris wondered why the song made him feel so sentimental. Perhaps it was the tune, the way it recalled his own teenage years. No, it wasn't that. It was a different feeling. Sitting here in the car, singing like this, was the thing that had eluded him so far. He wanted to be part of a unit, as he was now, the girls in the back of the car, and he and Becky together in the front. At the thought of Becky he felt an exquisite pain. He allowed himself another glance at her, saw the way the fading evening sunlight enriched her hair, and watched her lips open and close as she joined in the song. Her voice was low. She fascinated him. He accepted the dawning, certain knowledge that it was

Becky he cared about, right from the beginning. He'd been foolish to pursue a relationship with Jude just because Becky told him to, when it was Becky he wanted all the time. Now it was too late. He was unworthy of her, because he had been blind, and because he had lacked courage. As the singing faded, he knew that there would never be an evening like this again. He would be going to York; he would have little or no reason ever to see her again. He was Jude's. Jude and Becky were as close as sisters. She was so near to him on the car seat he could reach out and touch her. Lines of poetry came into his mind, where lovers had begged the heavens to stop the passage of time, so that they could stay together. Chris felt like that now, except Becky was not his, nor ever could be. And what was she thinking? When he put the candy floss in her mouth, and wanted to kiss her so much, would she have responded if he had? He could not focus on Jude at all, although he knew he ought. Becky filled his whole horizon. She *was* the sun setting.

Since they were running late, it made sense to take Amy straight to Sophie's. Out of politeness, Becky asked Chris if he was in a hurry to get home, as she would be perfectly happy to drop him off first. He was quite adamant that Becky should drive directly to Sophie's house. Becky was glad, because she didn't want Sophie's mother to worry that anything had happened to them.

Chris stayed in the car while Becky escorted the girls to the door, and exchanged a few words with Sophie's mother. Becky was glad to see that Sophie's house looked quite untidy – no having to keep up with the Joneses there. She considered kissing Amy goodbye, but realised that might be seriously uncool. Instead she feigned extreme casualness and walked back to the car.

Once again a feeling of anticlimax began to pervade her. It was the end of a lovely day, but it was the end of the day.

Time now to take Chris home, and then slowly come down to earth. Except she was filled with a perverse sense that she didn't want the day to be over, and she wondered if it was possible to extend it in some legitimate way. She had to pass Jude's house on her way back from Sophie's.

'Are you hungry? Would you like me to make us something to eat?'

The question was posed lightly, as if the answer didn't matter.

'That's not a bad idea. I like your cooking.'

'Astonishing!' Becky said. 'I'll see if I can spoil some fish fingers, specially for you.'

'Don't put yourself down, Becky.'

'I have to face the truth. I'm hopeless at cooking and housekeeping and—'

'Perhaps because your heart hasn't been in it,' he suggested.

'Maybe.'

Becky was quiet for a while. As they approached Jude's house she noticed that the Discovery, belonging to her next-door neighbour, was no longer there. Jude had told her if that was to happen, she was to occupy the space directly outside the house. It was all part of some battle, a hundred years' war, that Jude was playing with him. She confided this to Chris, who seemed a little surprised. Obviously Jude had said nothing about her neighbour to him. Odd, really, as Jude was irritatingly preoccupied with him. Putting that thought to one side, she pulled up obediently in the allotted space.

The sky was full of a soft radiance now, and a light breeze rustled the trees. The cats appeared as she unlocked the door and they shot in ahead of her. It was strange being in Jude's house alone with Chris. But it was of no account. They were just good friends, and more than that, he was her teacher. They had a professional relationship, although it occurred to her, not for the first time, that he might not be coming back to lead her fiction class.

'Once you start at York,' she asked him as he poured them both a gin, 'you won't be carrying on with the Mytholm Bridge class, will you?'

'Alas, no,' he said.

'I'll miss you. I enjoyed the class. It was one of the things that kept me going.'

'You have talent, Becky.'

'Nonsense. I couldn't write, and you knew it. I was full of ideas, but I didn't know what to do with them.'

'It's possible to learn how to write.'

'Not for me. I'm not even sure I want to any more. I need to earn money, and as soon as possible.'

'What will you do?'

'I'll have to retrain, or brush up on my typing. Jude wants me to be a dental nurse. But I don't know. I wish I had the luxury to take the time to decide what it was I do want to do.'

'Have you thought about teaching?'

'I don't really like children.'

'You don't have to teach children.'

'I don't know anything worth teaching.'

Chris shook his head slowly. 'That's where you're wrong. You have a habit of underestimating yourself. You have a lot of self-knowledge and wisdom too. Have you thought of counselling?'

'I wouldn't be able to be a counsellor. I can't give advice, and I have a habit of seeing things from everybody else's point of view.'

'In which case, you'd be an excellent counsellor.'

Becky thought for a moment. It was true, what Chris had said. Counselling was a good idea. It would be a way of making sense of her own broken marriage, and if she was strong enough to help others in a similar predicament, that would not be a bad thing. She mused silently for a while, covertly watching Chris sip his drink. As painful as it had been, she had learned the lesson of honesty. It was something she could apply to any situation. She could apply it to herself now. She was sitting here with Jude's lover, but the truth was, that she found him attractive too – but only in the way one found a painting attractive. It was an objective sort of admiration. Who could help but be attracted to him? His body was still quite lean and he sat back with an enviable self-possession. Dark lashes made his eyes soft and sensuous, and his strong eyebrows gave him a brooding look. She recalled when he bent over her work during their class, how his eyes were purposeful and serious. Explaining some abstruse point, he was playful and teasing. Now it was impossible to know what he was thinking. Perhaps he seemed a little sad. She was used to seeing him smiling, but now his mouth was still. She would have liked to touch his mouth, lift its corners, make him smile. Embarrassed by her train of thought, she tried to look away, but found her eyes were drawn to him, which was not surprising, as they were in the same room together. She felt the necessity to put some distance between them.

'I'll go and see what's in the kitchen,' she said, and got up from the armchair. The ploy didn't work. He followed her out.

'So you've cut loose from Paul now,' he said.

'Yes. I won't see him alone. I have a . . . sort of aversion to him.'

'I know why. Jude told me.'

'Told you?' Becky was alarmed. 'What did she tell you?'

'Just about everything, Becky. I just want to say, don't judge other men by him. He's a bastard.'

'I've come to terms with that. But it'll be a long time before I think of other men.' She knelt down to look in the freezer. 'There's nothing in here, I'm afraid. I can only offer you cheese on toast.'

'Well, in that case I'll have to go.' Chris made as if to leave.

'Stop it, you! You'll eat what you're given!'

★    ★    ★

The film was finally over. It was Chris who had noticed that *Jane Eyre* was being broadcast, and it was the decision of a moment for him to stay and watch it with her. Becky had curled up on the settee, while Chris had lounged in the armchair. She was tired now, having been thoroughly absorbed by the film, and was grateful to Chris for not leaving her alone.

'Shall I drive you back now?'

'You'd better,' he said. 'I can't offer to get the bus, because I've missed the last one.'

Becky stood up, and grinned at him. 'Well, let's be having you.'

Chris rose too, and as he approached her she was suddenly aware of him again, and for no apparent reason her pulse began to race. Perhaps it was the way he stopped and looked at her, almost quizzically. And they hadn't spoken about Jude all evening. She'd better do so at once.

'Jude ought be seeing *Aida* just about now.'

'So she should.'

Chris picked up his jacket, and they left the house. It was dark now, but the darkness had the thin consistency it did in summer. They got in the car, and Becky started the engine. As she tried to accelerate, the car lurched and stopped. There was a loud, grinding sound.

'Whatever's that?'

Becky tried the engine again, but the same thing happened. Chris leapt out of the car, and examined the wheels.

'Someone's let all your tyres down!'

Becky was stunned. Why on earth her? And there weren't any hooligans up here on the tops. It was why the middle classes chose to live up here.

'Are you sure?'

'Come and see for yourself.'

Becky got out of the car. Her tyres were not so much let down as slashed. It was awful. She felt herself quiver with rage and fear. Worst of all was the random anonymity of the attack. Surely if they knew who she was, they wouldn't have done this! She felt Chris put an arm around her.

'I can't believe this!'

'I know. It's hard to understand vandalism.'

'Who could have done it?' she asked.

'Jude's neighbour?'

Becky thought for a moment. 'The one she has the parking dispute with? Yes – there's his Discovery over there! Oh, my God! How awful for her! To live next door to someone like that!'

'Has he ever damaged Jude's property before?'

'She told me some story about a tree, but I didn't pay much attention.'

'It's chilly out here,' Chris said. 'Let's go back inside.' He guided her back to the house. Becky found she was still in a state of shock. She couldn't stop talking. 'I'm grounded now. I won't be able to pick Amy up tomorrow and I don't know if she's left me Sophie's number. And I can't drive you home, and you can't walk all that way!'

'I'm getting you a gin,' Chris said. 'And don't worry. I can walk over and get Amy in the morning. I've a good mind to call on Jude's neighbour too.'

'No – don't, Chris. What if it isn't him?' Becky hugged herself. She was shivering. 'I don't want things to get any worse. He might have been drinking. Please stay here.'

She sat down on the settee, shaking slightly. Chris came to sit next to her with a drink for them both.

'How are you going to get home?' she asked him.

He shrugged. 'Shall I stay the night?' he suggested. 'I don't like to think of you alone with someone prowling about.'

'Yes, stay.' It was so kind of him. She felt much safer with Chris there. She brushed away a tear that had formed in her eye.

'Becky – are you crying?'

'No. Yes. It's just the shock.'

He put an arm around her shoulders, and hugged her.

How she wished she could be enfolded by him. If he was her brother, she would have accepted his embrace. Being Jude's partner, really he was as good as her brother. So why would she not let him hug her as closely as she wanted?

'Jude will be livid when she hears of this,' Becky said, disengaging herself.

'I'm sure she will.'

'She can't stand the man next door at the best of times. She—'

'We don't have to talk about Jude all the time.'

Becky swallowed hard.

'I know, but if we don't . . .'

'Tell me. What will happen if we don't? What were you going to say?'

Becky was struck dumb. She had forgotten all about the tyres. Something odd had happened. It was as if someone had shaken a kaleidoscope, and everything had formed a new pattern. She was alone with Chris, and he was the man that she wanted. She knew now that she had felt like this since she first met him, that her gift of him to Jude was only a ploy to keep herself safe, and now that she was free, and Jude was in Paris . . . Colour flooded her cheeks. She was certain that he knew what she was thinking. She was certain because he had always known what she was thinking. He knew everything about her. She knew that at all costs she must not look at him.

He took her hand. 'Becky?' he said questioningly.

'No,' she said, summoning all her resolve. 'Think about Jude.'

'I am thinking about Jude,' he said. 'Shall I tell you what I'm thinking? I'm thinking that she wants to be without me, and that I don't mind that. I like Jude very much, and I always will—'

'She loves you,' Becky said.

'No. She needed me for a while, but I'll tell you what I've realised. I wasn't so much her lover as her therapist. I helped her get over something. Jude will be fine now, without me. Becky, it's you I want.'

She still didn't dare to look at him because everything that was happening was wrong, and she would regret it, and in Jude's house too! Yet he wanted her! How could she say no?

'Don't be shocked. I care about you, Becky. I want you to know that. I know I shouldn't be telling you this, with all the things that have happened to you. I'm sorry; I know I'm being selfish. You're angry, aren't you? Look at me, Becky. Please look at me.'

Becky did so, and his eyes held her with an intensity and hunger that made her afraid. With one finger he stroked her cheek. It was as if his finger was a flame that scorched her.

'Do you want me, Becky?'

What could she say? She moved her face to one side, to kiss his finger. The desire she had for him overwhelmed her. It was like nothing she had ever experienced before.

'Becky,' he said softly. 'Do you want me?'

She took his hand and covered it with hers.

'Most truly, sir,' she said.

Then he was kissing her, and their mouths fused together, and Becky felt as if she had come home. Their lips fitted just right, and their bodies did too, and it was almost enough to kiss like that, and then, after a time, it wasn't. Her clothes and inhibitions were abandoned. She joined with him in an intimate and secret dance, which she never wanted to end. At that moment of climax she looked at him. This was Chris! Chris Scott, who had made love to her. The knowledge transformed her to someone better than her best self, someone worthy of him.

He gently rested himself on her.

'The Elizabethans called orgasm a little death,' he said.

It amused her that he should try to be intellectual at a time like this. She smiled to herself, utterly content. Chris kissed her neck, and she turned her head so more of it was exposed, opened her eyes, and as she did so she caught sight of a large tabby and white cat glaring reproachfully at her. It was Ludmilla. She had witnessed them. All the time they had been making love, they had been observed. Becky became possessed of the idea that the cat would tell Jude everything.

The thought was crazy, but now with a dawning horror Becky began to take stock of the situation. She was lying on Jude's carpet, in the middle of Jude's living room, having just made love to Jude's man. And there was a photo of Phyllis Jackson, looking savagely down at her. It was 12.15 a.m. The clock said so. Her clothes were everywhere; so were Chris's. How could she have done all this? Becky was under no illusions; *she* had done it, not Chris. It had been her choice. What Denise had done to her, she had done to Jude. She and Karen and Jude had sat around reviling Denise as if she was the devil herself, and yet here was Becky Howarth, and she had done the same thing.

'Hey, Becky, you're quiet,' he said to her.

'What have we done?'

'Made love. I think that's what the books call it.'

'Chris – I'm thinking of Jude.' She was quite winded by her guilt.

'I know,' he said. 'If it helps, I probably feel as bad as you. It's going to be tough when we tell her.' Becky tried to interrupt him. 'Shh! We must tell her, and as soon as possible. I want to make a go of this.' Chris sat up, and gestured to include the both of them. 'I've never cared about anyone as much as you.'

'It's going to destroy her, Chris. You see, she's not as strong as you think. She's needy too, probably more than me. I don't know what she'll do when she finds out.'

'I'll explain to her,' he said.

'No. Let it be me.'

'Are you sure?'

'Oh, yes. Jude's *my* friend, and it's up to me to tell her the truth.'

# Chapter Fifteen

Coming down from Montmartre, the streets were hot, dusty and empty. This was the Paris of August, a city almost asleep. It suited Jude. She idled along, her mind moving almost as slowly as her legs. Although she knew Paris was supposed to be a city for lovers, she put that down as travel-agent talk. To her, the square lines of its buildings, its grand assumption of majesty had more to do with pride and with empire building. Here, however, in the more Bohemian quarter of the city, there was a greater sense of human interest. In an alleyway between some houses, a musician with an accordion began to play. Jude stopped to listen.

The song was instantly familiar, and it made her smile. She had some association with it she had temporarily forgotten, some pleasant association. She was able to hum along with it, and walked the few steps necessary to throw a few centimes into the accordionist's cap. The music added colour to the tired afternoon. 'Ain't Misbehavin'', that was what it was. Jude hummed it for a while as she sauntered on a little further, deciding that she had to stop and get a drink. Ahead of her was a large and busy square, and she was sure there would be a café. She still had not read the English Sunday paper that she had found on a news-stand, and she relished the idea of resting her feet. Tonight she had a ticket for a piano recital – all of Rachmaninov's preludes; in the morning she would be taking the Eurostar back to London. There she would extend her holiday by one day; there was a cousin who lived in Battersea who was happy to put her up. Then it would be back to Mytholm Bridge.

She would not think about that now. Here was a café, with some tables in front, where two or three couples sat, engaged in conversation. Jude found an empty table and thankfully sat down, stretching out her legs. In front of her she could see all of the crossroads. It would be good just to watch the passers-by. A lady walked in front of her with a small chihuahua on a lead. Soon a waiter materialised by her side.

'*Un café au lait, s'il vous plaît. Et une eau minérale.*'

He vanished without a word, and shortly re-appeared with her coffee and Perrier. The water was ice-cold, and Jude drank it slowly, enjoying the way it refreshed her. She placed her glass back on the cast-iron table. A seductive languor stole through her. This was all she'd ever wanted in life – to be able to sit alone in Paris, just being part of it, and not having to think, or do, or plan. Just be. She closed her eyes for a moment.

When she opened them, nothing had changed. The traffic still made its way noisily across the junction, and Parisians strolled by. Coming towards her was a rather attractive man, with heavily-lidded eyes and a top lip that protruded just a little way in the beginning of a pout. He had real Gallic charm and she could not help but gaze at him. Then he smiled, a smile that lit up his face, and he came towards her. Quickly she cast her eyes down, alarmed and excited. When she looked up again, he was greeting the couple who were sitting behind her, babbling in excited French. It was them he had been smiling at. Jude felt a little annoyed with herself, but amused too. What had she been thinking? That some gorgeous Frenchman would see her sitting alone, and be compelled to join her? What planet was she living on?

Just remember who you are, she told herself. Plain Jude Jackson, successful dentist, but never a romantic heroine. They're cut from a different cloth. She thought of *Aida* last night; now there was a romantic heroine, who preferred to suffocate to death in a tomb with her beloved than live without him. Jude wondered what it would be like, shut up in a tomb with Chris. A nightmare! There would be no sanitary facilities, no privacy, and no doubt he would drum his fingers on the wall of the tomb, which would drive her insane.

She hoped he wasn't too upset that she had come to Paris by herself. She had meant nothing by it. Now she began to wonder whether there may have been more in her gesture than she realised. Was she trying to indicate to him that there were limits to her commitment? That she wanted to demonstrate her freedom, and her rights? She needed to get away and be alone, and he would have to respect that. Similarly she would be more than happy for him to do the same. His new job in York was in some respects ideal. It would put just the right distance between them. From Monday to Friday she could be alone – except, of course, for Becky and Amy, until they found somewhere suitable to live.

That way she could have all week to help her to look forward to seeing Chris. She sipped her coffee reflectively. One thing had certainly changed. She had begun to enjoy sex. For the first time, she could see why there was such a cultural interest in it. Watching *Aida* last night, it occurred to her that even opera was raw sex. Most things were. The whole rhythm of life was essentially sexual. Chris was a good lover and she thought with anticipation of their reunion. In some ways, it would be quite nice to have him here, or at least in her hotel. But not here now; she enjoyed solitude too much. She hoped that he was essentially like her. She was certain he was the sort of man who needed space; from what she had heard, writers were solitary individuals. She remembered how awkward she felt when Becky had first introduced them, and how she had grown to feel so much at ease with him. She trusted him absolutely. Yes; she was very fond of Chris.

Perhaps it was time to put their relationship on a firmer footing. If only one could issue one's lover with a set of terms and conditions, so he knew exactly where he was. Chris was a very important part of her life. Her mind strayed back to when he had claimed that was all he was – a part of her life. There was the subtle implication that he wanted to be more to her than that. No. She could give no more of herself than she had already done. She loved him, in the sense that she was very enthusiastic about him. But the blinding, passionate love that some people apparently felt was beyond her. She could never love like that. It was all so clear in her mind now, and she wished she had Chris there to explain it all to him. Only he had a habit of looking mulish and stiff when she said something he didn't like. If only he could be as reasonable as she.

Jude's coffee was finished. She wondered whether she wanted another one. None of the waiters seemed to be about, so she decided to stay a little longer without getting another drink. Two drivers were having an altercation with their horns. Jude thought of Becky now and the distance made her more kind. It was perfectly natural that living at such close quarters would make them intolerant of each other. It took time for people to be able to live together, time, and strong motivation. She guessed Becky might feel a little too beholden to her, and she resolved to be kinder to her when she got back. Apart from a few distant uncles and aunts, she had no close relatives left that were hers, and Becky and Amy were her real family. If they argued, it meant nothing. Whatever Becky did, Jude knew she would forgive her. Once she was back in Mytholm, they would redouble their efforts to find her somewhere to live. According to her solicitor, Paul had still not put their house on the market. Someone would need to speak to him and get things moving. Jude was resigned to the fact that it might have to be her.

The priestesses' chorus from *Aida* ran through her mind. It was a beautiful, haunting tune. If she was Aida, Jude thought, she would have given up Radames to Amneris, her rival. He wasn't worth the trouble. Talk about daft, thinking he could both defeat the enemy and marry his daughter *and* live happily ever after! It was naïvety that caused most tragedies. At all costs one had to know oneself, and then the important thing was to be true to yourself. That was her philosophy, and she would defend it against all-comers. Even against Chris. The waiter re-appeared.

'*L'addition, s'il vous plaît!*'

A curl of paper on a pink porcelain dish was placed on her table. Jude read the amount, and deposited some coins in payment. She would walk a little more and then go back to her hotel to freshen up. One had to be clear-headed for Rachmaninov.

Denise stood at her bedroom window and looked out over the ribbon of road that ran past her house. Along that road, from the direction of Mytholm Bridge, in about ten minutes or so, Jim Ferguson's Transit van would be approaching. She licked her dry lips. Everything was ready for him, and it couldn't have worked out better.

He himself had indicated last evening that he could not start work until the afternoon because he had to collect some materials from Halifax. That gave her all morning to prepare. She had dropped the children off at Karen's and bribed Petra to the hilt to be good. Then it was off to the sun bed. She had come home, showered, massaged herself with Fendi body lotion until she was as soft as a peach. She had applied a light make-up, so not too much of it would come off on the sheets. And of course she had changed the sheets, and subtly rearranged her bedroom so that it did not speak too loudly of her married life. She was almost tempted to give it a clean, as no one had pushed a Hoover around it for a couple of weeks. She would have cursed Karen for letting her down like that, had she not come up trumps by offering to take the children. And tomorrow she was interviewing the new cleaner, Karen's friend. One advantage of having a new cleaner was that she did not have to pay her quite so much to begin with.

Gently she brought her mind back to the present. At last she and Jim would be alone. She was certain there was an unspoken bond between them, unspoken being the operative word. Sometimes in the last week she had stood at the door of the conservatory and watched him work, watched his tanned body crouched on the floor, and seen the muscles ripple in his chest, row after row of subtly defined, firm muscles. He knew she was there and there was tension in the atmosphere. She said nothing; he said nothing. It was rather like one of those late-night foreign language films. She gazed at the tight, curly hair at the back of his solid neck and how it shone gold in the sunlight. She looked at the curve of his denim-clad bottom and tried to visualise it without the denim. Did he wear Calvin Kleins? Or more traditional boxer shorts? Or perhaps he wore no underwear at all. The thought excited her so much that she took a deep, calming breath.

Denise had never felt like this before. In all of her previous flirtations she had been aware of playing a game in which men were purely tokens. Now it was different. She lusted after Jim, wanted *him*, no one else. She would deal with the fall-out from Karen afterwards. It was of no account; men were far more important than women. Karen understood that.

Denise walked over to the wardrobe mirror to check her appearance again. Even she gasped at the cheekiness of the dress she had found in Manchester last week. Its black, silky material was semi-transparent. In the shop Denise had worn her bra beneath it, but not now. Now the curves of her breasts and the outlines of her nipples were clearly visible. For decency's sake, she wore a pair of white briefs, but that was all. She worried that the dress looked too much like a slip, but the high, polo neck and the deliberately asymetrical hemline gave the lie to that. Two hundred pounds was a perfectly reasonable price to pay for such a fashion item. She would account for it to George by explaining that there were unforeseen extras that Jim needed for the conservatory, and in fact, that was not a lie. The dress

JUST GOOD FRIENDS

was a direct result of having the conservatory built. It was a perk for the builder.

She pushed her hair behind her ears, then thought she looked a little severe, and brought it forward again. Was her lipstick a little smudged? She sat at the dressing table and traced around the outline of her mouth with her lip pencil to give her lips more definition. Waiting for Jim to come was almost unbearable. Her body was tense with desire. Once again she thought her plan through. He would arrive, to an apparently empty house. He would call out, 'Hello, anyone around?' She would answer from upstairs. *Jim, you couldn't possibly come up here? I want you to look at something!* He would mount the stairs, enter her bedroom and she would indicate her dress and ask him if he liked it. If he did, she could easily take it from there. If he didn't, she could always take it off.

Her watch was lying on the dressing table – she didn't want it to scratch him in the abandon of her passion. She noticed it was two o'clock. At any moment he would be here. There was the sound of a car approaching along the road. All her senses were concentrated on the sound of the engine. Then it faded. It was not Jim's van.

What could she do to pass the time? Perhaps she could make the room even more inviting. Stealthily she crept along the landing to Petra's den, and removed her oil burner from her bedside table, taking a bottle of musk oil too. This she quickly set smouldering. Dark musk was so sensual. There was something else she had noticed in Petra's room, too – a double cassette tape, entitled *The Love Album*. She went back to borrow it, along with her cassette recorder. She turned Celine Dion's voice down low. This was better still.

He was late. Nothing to be worried about. It was impossible to give an exact time of arrival as the traffic could be bad, he could have been detained at the supplies depot, anything could have happened. It was of no account; they had all afternoon. She realised that as she walked the dress rode up, and so she pulled it down over her behind. She hugged herself, feeling the silky material, thinking of Jim's hands running down her body. Where was he? He'd said two at the latest! Irritation and anxiety fused together.

She stepped over to the window again. The road was empty. Ought she to ring Ferguson's? What if he wasn't coming? Unthinkable. Still no van. She left the window, closing the curtains, and sat down on the bed again. This was dreadful. He had stood her up. Except he could not have stood her up, because he didn't know what she was planning. That thought cheered her. If he knew, he would be here like a shot. Oh, how she wanted him! She could have cried with lust and frustration.

She heard another engine. She placed her hands on her chest to still her beating heart. The engine slowed and – yes! – it stopped, right outside her house. It was all about to happen as she had planned. The excitement was almost too much to bear. There was a rapping on the door.

'It's open!' she cried.

She heard him come in. There was Jim's usual silence. Probably he was looking for her. She imagined him in his denims and checked shirt, looking around the hall, puzzled.

'I'm up here, Jim, in the bedroom! Can you come up and look at something, please?'

Would he? Yes; she could hear footsteps ascending the stairs. It was going to happen precisely as she'd imagined. She felt something akin to stage fright.

'In here!' she called, directing him.

The bedroom door opened. There was a woman Denise had never seen before. She wore a brick-red miniskirt with black stockings, a sky-blue halter neck T-shirt, and had permed blonde hair, a pair of thick framed glasses and heavy make-up. Instinctively Denise crossed her arms over her chest.

'Who are you?'

'Gina, love. Your new cleaner. Didn't you say Monday?'

'No, Tuesday.' Denise was paralysed with horror. Any moment Jim would arrive and he would be greeted by the pantomime of her in a see-through dress and this brassy blonde cleaner. And what was the cleaner thinking? That this was some exclusive bordello? Denise flushed red-hot with embarrassment.

'You've mistaken the day,' Denise stuttered. 'I'm doing something else. I think you'd better go.'

The woman stood there gormlessly, not attempting to move. Denise was about to lose her temper, but then the phone trilled from the bedside table. She picked up the receiver.

'Is that Denise? It's Jim here. I'm on my mobile. I've got a collapsed ceiling to deal with down at Hebden Royd. I'm not going to be able to get up to you today. I'll see you in the morning.'

'But it'll be too late!'

'Too late?' he asked. Denise was aware of being watched by this ridiculous woman. Why didn't she go away? Couldn't she see when she wasn't wanted?

'There was a special reason,' she began.

'Sorry, my Dad's getting in the van. I must be off.'

Denise put the phone down slowly. This couldn't be true. All her carefully laid plans had come to nothing. He had abandoned her, and instead of an afternoon of passion with Jim, she was left with this . . . this. She looked up at her would-be cleaner, bereft.

'That's a nice dress you've got on,' said the cleaner.

Denise attempted to recover her self-respect. 'It's a Vivienne Westwood.'

'I bet that cost a packet!'

'I didn't see much change from three hundred pounds. But don't tell my husband!' She laughed gaily. 'We have a function shortly, and I was just trying it on. Rather see-through, don't you think?'

'It is quite revealing. Lovely material, though.'

'But chilly.' Denise opened her wardrobe door and found an old navy sweatshirt which she quickly put on. The cleaner still showed no signs of going. Denise felt impatient. She needed to be on her own to take stock of what had happened. It was hard to adjust to the fact that what she had been looking forward to for so long was not going to take place. She felt dislocated and numb. It was better to feel numb. She knew when the disappointment came, it would be so bitter that she would be able to taste it. Meanwhile, here she was, sitting in her bedroom with some old slapper from a terraced house in Mytholm Bridge, who had come in search of a cleaning job. Her lust was turning to disgust.

'Have you been stood up? You can tell me,' her visitor wheedled.

Denise gave her the once over. The temptation of getting some female sympathy was hard to resist. The woman's eyes were kind, and she certainly looked as if she'd been around a bit. A woman's company was better than nothing, although it was a poor second to Jim's. However, it was just as well to be discreet.

'I was expecting a visitor,' Denise said. 'A friend.'

'A male friend, was it?' Gina surveyed the room knowingly. 'Go on. You can tell me.'

The desire to boast was just too strong. 'He rang just now. He can't make it. He was devastated.'

'Men!' Gina said. 'Come downstairs, and let me make you a cup of tea. It's not quite the same, but it'll be better than nothing.'

Her voice was a little husky, probably from too many cigarettes. Denise thought she seemed a little patronising too. She had no right to be. She remembered Karen saying she'd been cheated on. She disliked being an object of charity. She followed Gina down the stairs, determined to prove herself.

'It's quite peaceful to have a break from him. Usually he's quite insatiable. Just like my last lover.' This little game of one-upmanship helped to repair her damaged self-esteem. If Gina spread rumours, she could always deny them. Denise watched her enter the kitchen and begin to prepare tea. She seemed to know instinctively where everything was, as if to the manner born. She sat by the table and watched her.

'I've always thought,' Gina said, 'that it's a pity that men aren't more like women.'

'Oh no! I can't think of anything worse.'

Gina brought over two cups of tea. Really, she looked awfully common. Even more so than Karen. And that blue eye shadow was a disaster, almost as much as her dress sense. No wonder she'd been cheated on.

'Tell me about yourself, Gina. Do you have any references?'

'I've not done any paid cleaning before now. To be honest, I'm moonlighting. I've got to take on a little bit more work to pay for my partner's spending habits. Oh! So you're having a conservatory built!'

'Yes. It was that, or move to a larger house.'

'You do have a glamorous life, Denise. Everything is just like Karen said. To be confidential for a moment, I think she's a little bit envious of you. Your money, and all the men in your life.'

Denise thought of Jim. 'There's only one man in my life.'

'Then you're like me. I'm also a one-woman man.'

Denise smiled at Gina's slip of the tongue. None of Karen's friends were very educated, or had her command of the English language ... Perhaps she might mention the novel she had nearly finished. She'd sent some chapters to a few agents and publishers and had a very good response. None of them had rejected it on account of the quality; instead, all of them had said it was not suitable for their lists. It was the only reason they had turned her down. Maybe she would not tell Gina that, yet. This woman obviously didn't have a great deal going for her. Looking at her now, Denise could see that she was distinctly unattractive. Her wrists were thick and her arms had a light covering of hair. Denise was surprised she hadn't had them waxed. She was also a little too broad around the shoulders.

The halter neck top was a sad mistake. Here was a woman who needed advice and sympathy. She would begin by correcting her English.

'You mean a one-man woman, dear.'

'No – a one-woman man.'

Denise looked at her again. Something wasn't right. It wasn't cigarettes that had made her voice so husky. Surely that wasn't stubble growing around her chin?

'Do you mind if I take this off?' asked Gina. 'It's too hot for a wig.'

Gina did so.

'George,' Denise said, with what voice she had left.

'You recognised me at last.'

Denise was transfixed. Here was her husband, in blue eye shadow and lipstick, and falsies – they must be falsies – in a red miniskirt – she looked down at his legs – they were indubitably his legs – what was going on?

'George – what on earth are you playing at?'

'I should be asking you the same question.'

Denise blanched with horror at the thought of what she had confessed. Had George dressed up like this purely to exact that confession from her? And was Karen party to the deception?

'I think it's so low of you to deceive me like this!'

George said nothing.

'And get rid of those silly clothes.'

'Not this time,' he said. 'It's been too much of an effort hiding all this from you. I wanted you to find out; I even left some of my garments lying around, but it was Karen who found them. Karen and Jim persuaded me to make a clean breast of it.' He looked down at his falsies and smiled.

'I don't understand,' Denise said.

'I cross-dress,' George continued. 'Have done for years.'

'I don't believe you. And take those ridiculous things off.'

'They are rather ridiculous. But some of my wardrobe is quite tasteful.'

Denise stared at him, open-mouthed.

'So we both had our little secrets. It's much better now that everything's out in the open.'

'Our marriage is a sham!' she cried.

'Only because you've made it so. I'm prepared to give it another go. I think you'll find there are advantages in being married to a cross-dresser. We can borrow each other's clothes, for one.'

'No, George, I can't stay married to you, knowing this!'

'A pity, as I still find you very attractive. And business is booming at the mill. I even think we can afford your new dress – as long as I can wear it occasionally too.' George drained his coffee, then got up to see if there were any biscuits. 'So it's up to you. If you can't accept me as I am, I'll understand. But I'm sure we could learn to be friends again. And think of the fun we'll have on our girls' nights out!'

Denise did not move. For once she was incapable of any calculation. The sweatshirt had slipped to one side, and the neck of her silk dress was peeping through. Without a bra, her breasts sagged. George's, however, were pert and shapely. Really, it was enough to make a girl green with jealousy.

'Hello, everyone! I'm home!'

Becky heard Jude's voice and closed her eyes for a moment. She summoned up all the strength she possessed. Despite the many conversations with Chris she realised she still didn't know precisely what she was going to say. She placed the two bowls of cat food on the floor, and Aida ran to them. Ludmilla made her way over in a more stately fashion. Becky left the kitchen.

'Did you have a good time, Jude?'

'Where's the reception committee? What have you done with the cats?'

'They're eating.'

'And Amy? I've bought her some presents. Things to wear, and some Rive Gauche perfume.'

'She's out.'

'Out? With Sophie?'

'No. Chris has taken her to the pictures.'

'Charming! I go away for a few days and my boyfriend runs off with another woman! I'm knackered after that journey. And I need to stretch my legs. But first I'll have something to drink. Six o'clock isn't too early, is it?'

Becky felt as if she was paralysed. She watched Jude walk over to her bottle of gin and prepare a drink. She looked far more relaxed than when she'd departed, and there was a healthy glow to her skin. It would not be there for long.

'Can I pour you one, Becky? And then you can open your presents. There was a wonderful shop just selling scarves. I thought—'

'Jude — I have to tell you something.'

'What?' Jude sat down on the arm of the sofa, her face all concern. 'Has Paul been causing trouble?'

'It's not about him. It's something else we have to talk about.'

Jude's brow furrowed. Becky could see that she was trying to anticipate what it was.

'Remember before you say anything, Becky, I like having you here, despite any appearances to the contrary. I don't want you to go. Now I've had a break I'm ready for the fray. Did you enjoy Blackpool?'

Becky realised why it was she could not tell Jude what had happened. It was completely contrary to her nature willingly to hurt anyone. What she was about to tell Jude would wound her. She could not plunge the knife in. She could not speak, could not move. Jude was still sitting on the arm of the settee, in denims and a black T-shirt. Her legs were crossed at the ankles, and Becky noticed she had kicked off her sandals. Her feet were bare, and and the red varnish on her toenails was slightly chipped.

'Becky? Why aren't you saying anything? You just told me you have some news.'

She clasped her hands tightly together.

'Becky? What's happened?'

'I've done something dreadful. You're going to be very upset.'

'I doubt it. Even with your genius for domestic disasters, I doubt whether you could have destroyed anything I really care about.' Saying that, Jude glanced at the portrait of her mother. It was intact, even if it seemed more ferocious than usual.

'It's about Chris,' Becky ventured.

'No sweat. He's not breakable.'

'Jude – be serious! It's to do with me – and Chris.' Becky waited. Jude would guess now.

'You and Chris. Can I have another clue, please? Or is it like Consequences? Becky met Chris at the Pleasure Beach, he wore a panama hat, and she wore a ball gown, and he said—'

'Jude! Can you hear what I'm trying to say?'

'You . . . and Chris . . .'

It was coming now. Becky felt physically sick. She saw the dawning comprehension on Jude's face. This was worse, a thousand times worse than she had imagined. Jude would hate her for ever after. Nothing she had ever done or said to Jude was as bad as this. Until now, she hoped their friendship might survive. Now she knew it wouldn't.

'Look, Becky, I'm imagining all sorts of things. Just explain very clearly what it is you're trying to say. And sit down. You're making me nervous.'

Becky sat down. 'While you were away, we went to Blackpool. And when we got home, someone had slashed my tyres. So Chris stayed with me a while. And we . . . talked. We talked about the way we felt about each other. Jude – do I have to tell you any more?' There were tears in Becky's eyes.

'So how do you feel about each other?'

'I love him.'

'Oh, shit!' Jude breathed out deeply. 'And don't tell me. He loves you too. And the consequence was, he stayed the night. And the world said – where do I fit in to all of this?'

'I'm sorry.'

'I'm sorry too.'

Jude was utterly impassive. Becky could not imagine what she was thinking. Aida came in and approached Jude curiously. She did not put out her hand to stroke the cat. Instead she put her drink on the floor, and Becky could see that her hand shook slightly.

'I said, look after my *house*, not my boyfriend.' Her voice was toneless.

'I'm ready to move out,' Becky said. 'I've found a bed-and-breakfast place.'

'I always thought you were the most selfless person I knew. But you're not. You're just like the rest of us.'

Becky hung her head. There was nothing she could say. It was true.

'And you wouldn't talk to me for ages just because I told you about your father. And now *you* tell me *this*.'

I deserve it all, Becky thought.

'So we're even.'

Becky said nothing.

'Shall we call a truce now?' Jude asked.

'A truce?'

'Yes. We're each as gloriously bad as the other, which is quite liberating. I think I like you more than ever. I still want to give you the scarf I've bought, and what's more, it's for keeps. I have no intention of taking it back, despite your appalling track record for reclaiming gifts. Or perhaps I ought to, to show you what it feels like.'

Becky was uncertain, but thought she detected a note of something like amusement in Jude's voice.

'Aren't you angry with me?' she faltered.

'Absolutely livid. Pistols at dawn, and all that sort of thing.' Jude gave a small smile. 'Becky! I ought to be furious with you, but I'm not. No, I'm not even mildly angry. I feel more

as if you've relieved me of something. Of Chris. I don't feel
bad about this at all. I should, shouldn't I? But while I was in
Paris, I began to realise that I didn't love him. I loved the sex,
but that's hardly enough to support a relationship. I wasn't sure
how I was going to tell him, but now I needn't say anything.
I'm the victim, not the villain. I can quite see the attraction.
You don't have to do a thing and everybody feels sorry for
you!' Jude laughed properly now.

'Are you telling me the truth?'

'Don't I always?'

'Do you want me to move out?' Becky almost wished
that Jude would punish her in some way. She felt as if she
deserved it.

'Do I want you to move out? Not in the slightest. Look.
Read my lips. I – don't – care. In fact, I'm pleased. Invite Chris
over, and we'll have an official disengagement ceremony. I'll
hand him over formally. Oh, my God! Whatever is Amy going
to think?'

'I shouldn't worry about Amy. She's capable of springing
her own surprises.'

'It sounds like I need to have a word with her. The least
you can do is pour me another drink.' Jude got off the arm of
the settee and walked over to the mullioned window, and stood
with her back to Becky. 'So he stayed the night.' She turned.
'Becky – you didn't sleep with him?' A pause. 'Becky?'

She nodded.

'Now that does make me feel strange. You didn't . . . you
didn't talk about me, did you?'

'Of course not!'

'I don't think anyone ought to be comparing notes here.'

'Absolutely!'

Jude made as if to feel her pulse. 'Do you know, I think
I'm going to pull through! I can even contemplate you going
to bed together without getting too incensed. In fact, I can
see that you might suit each other very well. You're both as
soft as they come. Look at you now! There's nothing to cry

about. Anyway, it's me who should be crying and in actual fact I'm starving hungry. Is there anything in the fridge?'

Becky dried her eyes. Was Jude sacrificing her own interests purely out of friendship, or did she really not care about Chris? Since it was impossible to contemplate anyone not caring about Chris, Becky concluded that Jude was being so brave just for her. Becky was so moved she did not trust herself to speak.

'I said, is there anything to eat in this establishment?'

Becky recovered herself.

'Amy and I made some chocolate mousse earlier.'

'Excellent. I don't see why we shouldn't share that too!'

# Chapter Sixteen

It was no use. Jude was wide awake. She rested her head on the palms of her hands, and tried to remember if she had been able to sleep at all that night. Perhaps she had managed to drift off once or twice. She must have done, as she felt remarkably clear-headed now. Almost up to a particularly tricky filling, she told herself.

It was not surprising she had not been able to sleep. The abrupt change in her circumstances had winded her, she knew that. Everything had happened so suddenly. It was the suddenness that threw her, not the situation itself. She *was* relieved to be rid of Chris and was able to admit to herself that sooner or later they would have parted. She told him as much last night, and he had agreed. Not only that, she was delighted for Becky. She could not see what had happened as a betrayal; she knew both Becky and Chris too well to think that either of them would be capable of real betrayal. In some ways they were both as innocent and as good as each other. Now Becky could deal with the problem of what to do when Chris went to York, not her. Last night all three of them had discussed this new turn of events with that degree of rationality commensurate with being mature adults. Jude mentally congratulated herself. So why was it she felt so bereft?

She stared at the ceiling. She ought to be able to work this problem out. Perhaps with her mother dying comparatively recently, she was prone to feeling lonely. Chris and Becky clearly loved each other; she was the odd one out. No one liked to be the odd one out. Jude felt herself becoming unusually emotional. She stopped these thoughts in their tracks. She reminded herself that she was perfectly accustomed to being single and would have no difficulty in simply going back to the state she was in before. Except she was better off than she was before. She now had Amy to care about. She had always secretly wanted a daughter. And if Becky could share her lover, Jude could always claim part ownership in Amy.

Jude smiled to herself. Things were not so bad after all. Thinking of Becky's happiness helped her. She felt no real jealousy, just a vicarious pleasure that things had turned out so well for her. Jude congratulated herself again, this time on her own magnanimity. Did it matter that her loss was Becky's gain? She could accept that and she would accept that. Part of her screamed that it wasn't fair, but Jude, who had always been good at visualisation, took one of the sharpest drills from her armoury in the surgery, and began to drill around her resentment, until it was quite loose, and then she flipped it out. There would be a little bit of bleeding, but she would feel much better afterwards. Becky's continued friendship was the most valuable thing of all, and it was worth any amount of pain to save it.

Feeling a little lonely, a little heroic, Jude decided to get out of bed. It was foolish lying here with such an active mind. Besides, the cats would appreciate an early breakfast. Since Becky and Amy had moved into her room, she had taken the cat basket downstairs. She looked forward to entering the kitchen and seeing Aida and Ludmilla curled up together in the basket, their sleepy eyes blinking curiously at her. The morning sunlight was clear and fresh – Jude could not stay in bed a moment longer. She crept down the stairs quietly, so as not to wake Becky and Amy.

She entered the kitchen. Ludmilla was in the basket, deeply

engaged in cleaning her fur, and only gave Jude a cursory glance. Aida was obviously out. Jude was a little disappointed. She bent down to stroke Ludmilla, but she was the more phlegmatic of the two cats. Aida, the younger one, was the live wire, and responded ecstatically to Jude's caresses. So she proceeded to feed them, knowing that the sound of the cat bowls being washed would bring Aida shooting through the cat flap. With half her attention, she listened for her. She heard a noise outside which at first Jude could have almost sworn was footsteps, although the milkman never normally arrived until eight. It must be the cat. However, she did not arrive. All was quiet again. Jude placed the food on the floor, and Ludmilla strolled over to proceed investigations. The key was in the back door, so Jude decided to open it and call Aida. Although she only had her pyjamas on, she was respectable enough for the world to see her.

'Aida!' She waited for the rustle of a cat through the undergrowth. No sound. This was strange. Aida always came when she was called, especially if her stomach was empty. Jude called her again, a little more loudly. Still no response.

Jude walked through the house, crooning softly.

'*Celeste Aida, forma divina . . .*'

She did not come to her signature tune. Jude opened the front door.

'Aida!' She called her name more loudly, with a note of urgency. She began to walk down the garden path, surveying the tangle of wild plants, still crooning her name. At last she reached the road. Jude could hardly bear to look. She breathed a sigh of relief. The road was clear in both directions. Aida had not been run over. Having laid her worst fear to rest, Jude felt a little calmer, and padded in her slippers round the side of the house to the back garden, to look there.

'Aida!'

That was when she saw him. A male form, crouching at the end of her garden. He was in track suit bottoms and a pullover, and was bending over something. It was Ian Fulwell. She made her way over to him, her slippers getting damp as she walked through the long grass.

'Get out of here at once!'

'Shhh!'

She looked down. There was Aida, immobile on the grass. Horror swept through her. Aida was dead! What had he done to her? She half-remembered Becky's story of her car. Was he now attacking her cats?

'Tell me what you've done!'

'Nothing,' he said, his voice low, serious. 'I came out because I thought I heard an intruder. There was someone, but then I found your cat.'

'What's wrong with her?' Jude was trembling with fear.

'At a guess, I'd say she has a broken rib or two. Look, her eyes are moving. She's terrified, and in a lot of pain, I should imagine. Whoever it was who was prowling around your garden has kicked her, I'd say. Kicked her pretty hard.'

Jude was appalled. What sort of vicious bully would kick a defenceless animal?

'Would you like me to take her down to the surgery and get her X-rayed?'

'The surgery?' Jude was confused. Did he mean her surgery?

'My surgery. I'm the vet.'

A vet! Of course! She looked at the gentle and knowledgeable way he handled the cat, who looked up at him mournfully.

'Do you have a travelling box?' he asked her.

'I'll get one straightaway.'

Jude dashed into the house and made for the cupboard under the stairs, where the travelling box was. She stopped to scrawl a note for Becky. Grabbing her bag she was out of the house in an instant, then realised she was still in her pyjamas. But what did that matter when Aida was in trouble?

Ian lifted the cat and put her in the box.

'Will she be all right?'

'There's a chance the ribs will have punctured the heart or lungs. I can't tell just from feeling her. It's why we need the X-ray.' Ian stood up and checked his pocket. 'I have my car keys. I'll drive you.'

In a few moments Jude was seated in his Discovery, the travelling box on her lap. Aida let out a faint miaow of protest, which encouraged Jude. The cat always hated travelling in cars, and she was sure the smell of Ian's dogs did nothing to put her at her ease.

'I can't believe anyone could do this to an animal!'

'You'll be surprised at what people do. But I saw the man who did this. At least, I saw him getting into a Mondeo and driving away. A tall, rather stocky man. Anyone you know?'

'Paul,' Jude said, dully.

'Who's Paul?'

'Becky's husband. Becky is the friend who's staying with me. She's just left her husband. He must have been the one who slashed her tyres, and now he's done this!'

'Have you contacted the police?'

'I will. I suspected it was Paul who vandalised her car, but I had no proof, and other events took over. I still can't quite believe this. He's been out to get his revenge on both of us. But to attack my cat!' Jude realised she was shaking. Ian continued talking to her in an even voice.

'Lucky there's not much traffic on the road at this time. I won't have a nurse, of course, so you might have to give me some assistance. I won't disturb my daughter, and she wouldn't get here in time. She lives with her mother over in Ripponden.'

'Your daughter?'

'Yes. She works with me. You've seen her, haven't you? She calls in quite a lot.'

'Your daughter,' Jude repeated.

'Who did you think she was?' Jude thought that Ian seemed to smile.

'Here we are,' he said. He pulled up outside the surgery,

which occupied the ground floor premises of a row of shops just coming in to Mytholm Bridge.

'It doesn't have your name on it,' Jude remarked.

'No. It's one of a group of practices. I'm not the owner.'

He opened the door and switched on the light. There were benches around a small reception area and posters of different sorts of dogs. Jude followed Ian into the back, while reassuring Aida. She placed the box on the black surface of the examination table.

Ian was scrubbing his hands at the sink.

'I'll have to give her some anaesthetic, but these modern anaesthetics are good, they work their way out of the system very quickly. That's it, take her out of the box.'

'She's not responding when I stroke her.'

'She's probably in a lot of pain. There'll be fluid on her lungs. Right. Just hold her while I insert the needle – she won't feel this – good! You wait here. I'll take her through for the X-ray.'

And Jude was left alone in the surgery. It was a bare room, with pale green walls, a sink, various dressings and instruments and a poster about inoculations. It was naturally more basic than her own surgery. There was no chair. On the surface of the examination table were a few stray hairs from Aida. Jude listened hard, but could hear nothing. She could hardly bear not knowing whether the cat would live or die. All her consciousness was focused on that one thing. She couldn't carry on, if that cat was to die.

She tried to make herself think of something else. She considered what Ian had said about his daughter and was amused at her error. But she could not hold on to her amusement. She thought about Aida again. To stop herself she began to look at the poster, and then began to read each word backwards, just to stop herself imagining what Ian was doing. He was taking ages. Was that a good sign, or a bad one? So Paul had been prowling round their house, and had been taking his revenge in the most cowardly way. The contempt she felt for him was beyond expression. No – she would not think about that either. She returned to the inoculation poster.

Ian entered. 'It's developing now. Are you all right?'

'No. Not really.'

'Would you like to ring someone? Your friend, or your boyfriend?'

'I don't have a boyfriend.'

'So the man who visits you is your son?' The teasing tone in his voice made her smile.

'No. He *was* my boyfriend. Look, you can go back to my cat. I'd prefer to wait by myself. No one cares about Aida like I do. People think I'm a bit silly, the way I go on about my cats. Typical repressed spinster.' Jude attempted a laugh.

'I don't think you're silly at all. No one can give you the unconditional love an animal can.'

She looked up at him. 'That's right. I think that too.' They were both silent for a moment. Jude decided she had misjudged him. He was a kind man, concerned for her and Aida. She glanced at him. He was a little older than her, perhaps in his late forties. There was a distinguished touch of grey in his hair. If he was a little old-fashioned at times, it was understandable. Their eyes met in a moment of unlooked-for intimacy. She was glad he was there. In fact, she couldn't think of anyone else she would prefer to be with her right now.

'I think the X-ray might be ready,' he said, after a while.

Jude was left alone. Suddenly she felt very tearful. The full enormity of what had happened in the last twenty-four hours hit her with unstoppable force. Chris had left her for Becky. And Aida might die. For the moment, she didn't know which was worse.

Ian returned, holding an X-ray sheet.

'Look,' he said, showing it to her. She held one edge and he held the other. 'There's the fracture; there are two, possibly three ribs broken. But if you can see, the heart and lungs are intact. There's the fluid on the lungs which will take a little time to disperse. I'd keep her in for a while, and you ought to try to stop her jumping for a few weeks. But otherwise—'

'She won't die?'

'I'd say she was at least two down on her nine lives, but no. She'll be fine.'

Jude filled up with sunshine. She gave Ian a radiant smile.

'Thank you!'

There was nothing for it. She would have to hug him. She was desperate for some physical contact, and she was so grateful. Words weren't enough. She didn't care what he thought.

He strained her to him. 'It's going to be all right,' he murmured. She felt him stroking her hair. Why was he doing that? This was only a hug between chums. It was lovely, the way he stroked her hair. She decided to say nothing. Aida was all right – everything was all right. Then it occurred to her she was still in her pyjamas.

'Ms Jackson,' he said. 'Do you like me better now?'

'Yes.'

'Are we friends?'

'Kind of,' she said, her head still against his chest. He held her so tightly, it felt as if he wasn't going to let her go. Now he kissed the top of her head, so gently she thought she had imagined it. She thought she'd better check.

'Did you just kiss me?'

'It's something I've wanted to do for ages.'

Jude clung to him even more tightly because if she didn't, she would not be able to stand. A tidal wave of excitement threatened to submerge her.

'Me too,' she said.

It was enough. Their mouths met, and Jude was astonished at the sensation his kiss unleashed in her. His hands moved down her back gently, but it was Jude who pulled him closely to her, realising in a flash that the antipathy she'd had to him had gone. Had it been an antipathy after all? She neither knew nor cared. And goodness knows what she would have done next, there and then in the surgery, were it not for a pitiful, small miaow from a distant room.

'Aida!'

'She must have come round,' Ian said.

Jude broke away for a moment. 'Do you need to strap her up or anything?'

'No, we'll just let nature take its course.'

'Good idea,' Jude said, and they embraced once more.


Becky was the first to arrive outside the Marabar Balti House. She sheltered in the porch, as the October wind was rather chilly and damp. This was not the sort of restaurant she would have chosen for a night out with Jude and Karen, but Karen had insisted, and it was her treat. Since working at the Clough Hall Health Club she'd had a lot more cash to spare and as Karen had told Becky, if anyone damn well deserved to enjoy herself, it was her.

Jude arrived next.

'So here it is! I've been all the way round Halifax trying to find this place. It's a pity there isn't an Indian restuarant in Mytholm. But since Karen's paying . . . Why are we standing outside?'

'I was waiting for somebody else to turn up.'

'I'm here now. Let's go in.'

Jude pushed open the door of the restaurant. It was just as they had both expected. Indifferent paintings of elephants and mountains adorned the walls, some sitar music played in the background and the seating and carpets were in the traditional dusky maroon. There was a small bar area near the entrance, and a young Pakistani waiter with a unusually large forehead ushered them to it. Jude ordered drinks while Becky nibbled absently at the Bombay mix in a silver dish in front of them.

'You won't eat your dinner,' Jude said warningly.

'Stop it! You sound just like my mother!'

Jude laughed. 'I do, rather. She still watches what you eat.

I saw her doing it the other day. Still, I reckon you'll miss her when she goes back to Canada.'

'I think we all will. But Chris reckons we might be able to afford to fly over there in the summer.'

'You'll find it hard to say goodbye to her.'

'I know. But I'm going to have to get used to saying goodbyes.'

Becky was quiet for a moment. In a few days she was going to York. The university had managed to arrange accommodation for both her and Chris. There had been a difficult time when Amy had refused to go with them. Her terror of having to start a new school and leave her friends was insuperable. Jude had stepped in once more, and offered to have Amy during the week, and send her to York for weekends. Just for a year, she had said, so that Amy could adjust to the transition. At first Becky was dead set against it, reluctant to leave Amy behind, and not wanting to put any impediments in Jude's relationship with Ian. Jude, however, was adamant. She insisted she had no intention of moving in with him and claimed she had what every woman secretly wanted – passion, but a place of her own as well. That way she'd never have to come to terms with Ian's irritating habits, or even find out what they were. And so it was that Becky was facing a triple farewell; from her mother, from her daughter, and from her best friend.

Tonight, however, was not the place for sentiment. Tonight they were both Karen's guests. Becky noticed the two waiters behind the bar observe them curiously. They probably assumed they were waiting for men, and Becky was pleased that was not the case. She enjoyed a night out with her friends, all the more so because where she was going, she would have to make new friends, and just like Amy, she felt more apprehensive than anyone would guess. The thought of being weighed up by all the new women she would meet!

And in burst Karen. She was dressed up to the nines, in a silver lurex dress with a black leather jacket to protect her from the weather. She'd put her hair up, except for two tendrils that framed her face. There was glitter on her eyelids.

'Hiya!' she shouted. The two waiters were transfixed.

'Sorry I'm late but Bobby cut his head open on Seth's toy tractor and we had to wait until it stopped bleeding. And then Jim was late because he had to finish a job. And, look, Shirley's come too!'

She entered behind her, shaking off an umbrella. Obviously it had started to rain. Shirely was dressed in a long skirt with large flowers on it, and a brown bomber jacket.

'Can we go straight to a table?' Karen suggested. 'Nothing's passed my lips since lunchtime, and then I only had an egg butty.'

The waiters rushed to do her bidding, simpering at her, and showing them all to a table in a booth by the wall. Becky and Jude sat facing Karen and Shirley.

'Right, girls!' Karen declared. 'Why don't we order loads of different dishes and mix and match?'

'The original Spice girl,' Shirley remarked.

'Shut up, you! Becky, what will you have? I like a veggie balti, me, and Shirl is anyone's for a tandoori chicken.'

They spent quite a few minutes working out the order while both waiters hovered at a respectful distance. Pointing her finger at the dishes they had chosen, Karen ordered the meal.

'Oh, and four poppadoms to start with, with all the stuff on the side. And a pint of lager for me, mineral water for Shirley, and what will you two have?'

Becky and Jude consulted with each other, and opted for lager too.

'Do you mind if I smoke?' Karen asked.

'I do,' Shirley said. 'You told me you were giving up.'

'Yeah, well, I am. I'm just doing it gradually. This is only my third today.' Karen winked at Becky. 'So you're finally off! I can't believe it.'

'Everything's booked now,' Becky said.

'Another couple came and looked at your old house last night. I showed them round. Did the estate agents contact you?'

'No. That's interesting, Jude.'

'There's been quite a lot of people coming up. Have you heard from that old bastard you used to be married to?'

Becky shook her head. 'The solicitor's been very good. After the warning from the police, he moved to Manchester. Collyhurst.'

'Strangeways would be more appropriate,' Shirley said.

'And so you're off next week!' Karen made a pout as if she was about to cry. 'All these changes. Becky going, and Jude almost shacked up with her James Herriot lookalike.'

'I'd say he was more the Robert Redford type,' Jude suggested.

'And what about you, Karen?' Becky said, rather boldly. For all Karen's big talk, she was rather coy about herself. 'You've not said much about Jim lately. Are you still an item?'

'Oh, great! Here's the poppadoms!'

The waiters descended once again, with frisbee-sized poppadoms and little bowls of relishes, yogurt dotted with slivers of cucumber, finely chopped onions scattered with paprika and gooey mango chutney.

'Yum, yum!' Karen said, spooning generous quantities of each on to her plate.

'Because I'm curious, Karen,' Becky persisted. 'You've been going out all this time. And you've told me you were so much in love, and he's obviously very fond of the boys. And he's done up your place so beautifully.' Karen looked more coy than ever. 'So when are you going to become Mrs Ferguson?'

Becky saw Shirley nudge Karen under the table. The poppadom trembled in her hand.

'Not ever, Becky. He's been great, and that, but, to be honest . . . well, he's just not my type.'

Now it was Jude who kicked Becky underneath the table. Now why would she want to do that?

Karen continued, colour stealing into her face. 'We're good mates, always have been, but it's his sister who I fancied. It was just that my own feelings took me by surprise a bit, and I didn't want people to talk, so he kind of covered up for us. Shirley's moving in with me soon, and then it'll be all over Mytholm. But what the hell? A girl's gotta do what a girl's gotta do!'

'So congratulations are in order!' Jude said, and raised her glass of lager.

'And from me,' said Becky rather belatedly. Delight and astonishment were jostling for supremacy.

'Yeah, well, I'd had it up to here with men,' Karen said. 'And I've never been happier. This is my coming out party, isn't it, Shirl?'

'Any excuse for a knees-up,' Shirley remarked dryly, but her eyes were shining.

'But I don't understand,' Becky went on. 'If Jim was never going out with you, why on earth was it that he'd have nothing to do with Denise? I met your friend Wendy the other day in the Co-op, and she said something about an accident he'd had, but I didn't believe her.'

'You did right,' Karen said, breaking off bits of poppadom as she spoke. 'Wendy's got that vivid an imagination! No, I'll tell you the truth now. Jim's engaged, though he kept it rather quiet. Has been for the past nine months to a friend of Shirley's, but she's working over in Holland. Big girl, lifts weights. I won't tell you what she's threatened him with if he steps out of line. So he promised he'd be faithful, and he is. He got friendly with me only because he wanted a bit of female company with no strings attached, and we've got along since we were kids. He invited me round to his place and Shirley was there. The rest is history.' Karen gave Shirley's hand a squeeze. 'But enough of me. Shirl, show them your photo of Jim and Kelly!'

Becky studied it. Kelly, Jim's fiancée, was a stringy, muscular blonde, a little taller than him, but what was most noticeable was how lovestruck Jim was, and how determined

Kelly looked to keep it that way. Becky handed the photo to Jude.

'She doesn't say a lot either,' Karen added.

'Unlike you,' Shirley commented.

'Unlike me,' Karen admitted happily. 'But what's the point of having girl friends if you can't spin them a good yarn from time to time? Which reminds me, I've got to tell you about Gemma, the postman and the parcel she'd ordered from the Ann Summers shop which came undone in the van. She kidded him the vibrator was a device for cleaning out the insides of honeydew melons. But let me start at the beginning . . .

# Brighton

WHAT'S NEW | WHAT'S ON | WHAT'S BEST

www.timeout.com/brighton

# Contents

**Published by Time Out Guides Ltd**
Universal House
251 Tottenham Court Road
London W1T 7AB
Tel: + 44 (0)20 7813 3000
Fax: + 44 (0)20 7813 6001
Email: guides@timeout.com
www.timeout.com

**Managing Director** Peter Fiennes
**Editorial Director** Ruth Jarvis
**Business Manager** Daniel Allen
**Editorial Manager** Holly Pick
**Assistant Management Accountant** Ija Krasnikova

Time Out Guides is a wholly owned subsidiary of Time Out Group Ltd.

**© Time Out Group Ltd**
**Director & Founder** Tony Elliott
**Chief Executive Officer** David King
**Group Financial Director** Paul Rakkar
**Group General Manager/Director** Nichola Coulthard
**Time Out Communications Ltd MD** David Pepper
**Time Out International Ltd MD** Cathy Runciman
**Time Out Magazine Ltd Publisher/Managing Director** Mark Elliott
**Group Commercial Director** Graeme Tottle
**Group IT Director** Simon Chappell

Time Out and the Time Out logo are trademarks of Time Out Group Ltd.

**This edition first published in Great Britain in 2011 by Ebury Publishing**
A Random House Group Company
Company information can be found on www.randomhouse.co.uk
Random House UK Limited Reg. No. 954009
10 9 8 7 6 5 4 3 2 1

Distributed in the US and Latin America by Publishers Group West (1-510-809-3700)
Distributed in Canada by Publishers Group Canada (1-800-747-8147)

For further distribution details, see www.timeout.com

ISBN: 978-1-846702-15-0

A CIP catalogue record for this book is available from the British Library.

Printed and bound in Germany by Appl.

The Random House Group Limited supports The Forest Stewardship Council (FSC), the leading international forest certification organisation. All our titles that are printed on Greenpeace approved FSC certified paper carry the FSC logo. Our paper procurement policy can be found at www.rbooks.co.uk/environment.

Time Out carbon-offsets all its flights with Trees for Cities (www.treesforcities.org).

# Brighton Shortlist

The **Time Out Brighton Shortlist** is one of a new series of guides that draws on Time Out's background as a magazine publisher to keep you current with what's going on in town. As well as Brighton's key sights and the best of its eating, drinking and leisure options, the guide picks out the most exciting venues to have recently opened and gives a full calendar of annual events. It also includes features on the important news, trends and openings, all compiled by locally based editors and writers. Whether you're visiting for the first time, or you're a regular, you'll find the Time Out Brighton Shortlist contains all you need to know, in a portable and easy-to-use format.

The guide divides central Brighton into four areas, each of which contains listings for Sights & Museums, Eating & Drinking, Shopping, Nightlife and Arts & Leisure, with maps pinpointing all their locations. At the front of the book are chapters rounding up these scenes city-wide, and giving a shortlist of our overall picks in a variety of categories. We include itineraries for days out, plus essentials such as transport information and hotels. There is also a section to suggest day trips out of town; in this chapter we have included nearby Lewes, Littlehampton and the South Downs.

Our listings give phone numbers as dialled from within Brighton. To dial them from elsewhere in the UK, preface them with **01273**; from abroad, use your country's exit code followed by 44 (the country code for the UK), 1273 and the number given.

We have noted price categories by using one to four pound signs (**£-££££**), representing budget, moderate, expensive and luxury. Major credit cards are accepted unless otherwise stated. We also indicate when a venue is NEW .

All our listings are double-checked, but places do sometimes close or change their hours or prices, so it's a good idea to call a venue before visiting. While every effort has been made to ensure accuracy, the publishers cannot accept responsibility for any errors that this guide may contain.

Venues are marked on the maps using symbols numbered according to their order within the chapter and colour-coded according to the type of venue they represent:

**1** Sights & Museums
**1** Eating & Drinking
**1** Shopping
**1** Nightlife
**1** Arts & Leisure

| Map key | |
|---|---|
| Major sight or landmark ........ | |
| Railway station ................. | |
| Park ........................... | |
| Hospital/university .............. | |
| Pedestrian Area ................. | |
| Dual Carriageway ............... | |
| Main road ...................... | |
| Church ......................... | ✚ |
| Area ........................... | HOVE |

# Time Out **Brighton** Shortlist

**EDITORIAL**
**Editor** Daniel Neilson
**Copy Editors** Ben Lerwill,
    John Shandy Watson
**Listings Editor** Judy Kneen
**Travel Intern** Carla Bradman

**DESIGN**
**Art Director** Scott Moore
**Art Editor** Pinelope Kourmouzoglou
**Senior Designer** Kei Ishimaru
**Designer** Lucy Tiller
**Group Commercial Designer** Jodi Sher

**Picture Editor** Jael Marschner
**Acting Deputy Picture Editor** Liz Leahy
**Picture Desk Assistant/Researcher**
    Ben Rowe

**ADVERTISING**
**New Business & Commercial Director**
    Mark Phillips
**International Advertising Manager**
    Kasimir Berger
**Advertising Sales (Brighton)** Gail McKay,
    Stephen Modell, Gabriella Parrish,
    Gemma Still

**MARKETING**
**Sales & Marketing Director, North America
    & Latin America** Lisa Levinson
**Senior Publishing Brand Manager**
    Luthfa Begum
**Group Commercial Art Director**
    Anthony Huggins
**Marketing Co-ordinator** Alana Benton

**PRODUCTION**
**Group Production Manager**
    Brendan McKeown
**Production Controller** Katie Mulhern

**CONTRIBUTORS**
This guide was researched and written by Sarah Bolland, Ruth-Ellen Davis, Stuart
Huggett, Richard Leighton, Anna McNaught-Davis, Adam McNaught-Davis, Adam
Monaghan, Daniel Neilson, Cat Scully, Rowan Stanfield, Bella Todd.

**PHOTOGRAPHY**
All photography by Adam Monaghan (www.adammonaghan.com), except: pages 28, 32,
59, 72, 74, 98, 103, 104, 108, 112, 113, 114, 122, 123, 126, 129, 133, 136, 138,
141, 142, 143, 144, 150, 161, 165, 166, 167, 172 Daniel Neilson; page 40 Paul
Kondritz; pages 24, 39, 52 Rowan Stanfield; pages 35, 132 Dean Chipp-Smith;
pages 68, 97 Jessica Eccles; pages 100, 101 Andy Wood, page 128 Mike Burnell.

The following images were provided by the featured establishments/artists: pages 18,
70, 78, 91, 94, 105, 111, 121, 131, 169, 170, 174, 176, 178, 180, 182.

Cover photograph: Red striped deckchair on Brighton Beach with the Palace Pier in the
background, Sussex, England. Credit: Photolibrary

**MAPS**
JS Graphics (john@jsgraphics.co.uk).

## About **Time Out**

Founded in 1968, Time Out has expanded from humble London beginnings into
the leading resource for those wanting to know what's happening in the world's
greatest cities. As well as our influential what's-on weeklies in London, New York
and Chicago, we publish nearly 30 other listings magazines in cities as varied as
Beijing and Mumbai. The magazines established Time Out's trademark style: sharp
writing, informed reviewing and bang up-to-date inside knowledge of every scene.

Time Out made the natural leap into travel guides in the 1980s with the City Guide
series, which now extends to over 50 destinations around the world. Written and
researched by expert local writers and generously illustrated with original photography,
the full-size guides cover a larger area than our Shortlist guides and include many
more venue reviews, along with additional background features and a full set of maps.

Throughout this rapid growth, the company has remained proudly independent,
still owned by Tony Elliott four decades after he started Time Out London as a single
fold-out sheet of A5 paper. This independence extends to the editorial content of all
our publications, this Shortlist included. No establishment has been featured because
it has advertised, and no payment has influenced any of our reviews. And, for our critics,
there's definitely no such thing as a free lunch: all restaurants and bars are visited
and reviewed anonymously, and Time Out always picks up the bill.
For more about the company, see www.timeout.com.

# Don't Miss

Brighton Royal Pavilion p83

# Sights & Museums

The city of Brighton & Hove exists for one reason alone: the sea. It permeates all life here, shaping the city's soul and defining its atmosphere. Just witness the beach on a warm summer evening: thousands wander down after work to watch the red sun set over the skeleton of the West Pier – a broodingly beautiful spectacle.

When the Prince of Wales (the future King George IV) came down for his first 'season' in 1783, Brighton's fate as an upper-crust seaside resort was sealed. Satirical novelist William Thackeray once wrote, 'It is the fashion to run down George IV, but what myriads of Londoners ought to thank him for inventing Brighton.' Indeed, before the Prince and his entourage came, there was little of note here.

A cursory wander around the city today, through the narrow 17th-century Lanes, past the great Royal Pavilion and down to the seafront, doesn't unearth too much history prior to the 1600s. That's mainly because, unlike Chichester or Lewes, Brighton was never historically a significant city, county seat or strategically important base. Yet the fashion among the upper classes for visiting Brighton from the mid 18th century led to a grandiose building spree that defines Brighton's character today: Georgian buildings such as the Old Ship Hotel (p172) mix with whitewashed Regency and early Victorian townhouses with characteristic bow windows.

## Of lanes & a laine

Architectural styles and characters shift swiftly as you explore the neighbourhoods of Brighton.

Directly below the train station is North Laine (a laine was an open plain divided into sections for farming). The area was once Brighton's worst slum; today, it's the city's bohemian quarter, full of bars and independent shops.

The modest housing of North Laine jars with Brighton's most iconic building, the unmissable Royal Pavilion (p83). Opulent in the extreme, the Prince of Wales's seaside home is an extravagant mix of Chinoiserie, Baroque and Gothic revival, designed by John Nash. Nearby, the Brighton Dome (p102) complex, once the Prince's stables, now houses the Corn Exchange, Pavilion Theatre and Concert Hall. Also in the building is the Brighton Museum & Art Gallery (p83). This area is known – officially, at least – as the Cultural Quarter.

Crossing gentrified North Street and heading down narrow Meeting House Lane, you'll arrive in the Lanes. Jewellers, fashion boutiques, restaurants and pubs occupy the labyrinthine area. This is medieval Brighthelmstone – Brighton's Old Town. The Town Hall, built in 1827, houses the Old Police Cells Museum (p104), a small museum charting Brighton's crime-fighting force. It's also worth noting the Cricketers Arms (p105), a pub set in a typical 17th-century building.

To the west is the city centre. The Jubilee Clock, commonly called the clock tower, was built in 1888 to commemorate Queen Victoria's Golden Jubilee (a year late) and is today a common meeting spot. From here, it's a short walk to Churchill Square. Frankly, this part of Brighton is an unattractive area, although the shopping centre has made the best of the location and is pleasant inside. Beyond Churchill Square are the grand squares, including Regency Square, now home to several boutique hotels.

**DON'T MISS**

## SHORTLIST

**Quirkiest museums**
- Brighton Toy & Model Museum (p87)
- Mechanical Memories Museum (p78)

**Most impressive**
- Royal Pavilion (p83)

**Best parks**
- Preston Park (p137)
- Queen's Park (p114)
- St Ann's Well Gardens (p69)

**For old-fashioned fun**
- Volk's Electric Railway (p115)

**Best for families**
- Brighton Pier (p78)
- Sea Life Centre (p114)
- Hove Museum & Art Gallery (p148)

**Best for history**
- Booth Museum of Natural History (p137)
- Brighton Museum & Art Gallery (p83)
- Old Police Cells Museum (p104)
- Preston Manor (p137)

**For quiet contemplation**
- St Bartholomew's Church (p138)
- Woodvale Cemetery (p138)

**Best views**
- Devil's Dyke at sunset (p166)
- Ditchling Beacon (p165)
- West Pier at sunset (p60)

**Best unsung attractions**
- Brighton Fishing Museum (p78)

**For living history**
- The Lanes (p103)

Western Road is the main thoroughfare to Hove, and is lined with many interesting shops. But the most impressive architecture is on the streets above Western Road.

## Beside the seaside

The seaside is, of course, the city's most important attraction. On arriving at the seafront, eyes inevitably are pulled towards the skeletal remnants of the West Pier (p60), which burnt down in 2003, having stood since Victorian times. It's a strangely poignant reminder of Brighton's past. Jutting out into the English Channel to the east, meanwhile, is Brighton Pier (p78), formerly Palace Pier. It's a study in bright lights, garish amusement, kiss-me-quick hats, toffee apples, candyfloss and haunted houses. Its enduring popularity owes nothing to irony – hordes still arrive with gay abandonment, and why not?

Between the two piers is a wide lower esplanade that gives access to pebble beaches and an array of shops, pubs, bars and clubs that inhabit the King's Road Arches. They were built in the late 1800s as fishing huts, boat-builders' sheds and other businesses that were geared to the entertainment of visitors to the coast.

Fittingly, the fascinating Brighton Fishing Museum (p78) occupies several of the arches and offers a glimpse into the life of Brighton's long-lost industry. Each May, the area is still the focus for the annual Mackerel Fair and the Blessing of the Nets, and there are a couple of shellfish and oyster bars here.

The King's Road Arches are also home to one of the city's oddest attractions, the Mechanical Memories Museum (p78), which celebrates the glory days of one-armed bandits, clairvoyant

St Bartholomew's Church p138

machines, horse-racing games and vintage amusements.

Further east are the Sea Life Centre (p114) – now the oldest operating aquarium in the world – and an attraction with a similar superlative: the world's oldest operating electric railway. Volk's Electric Railway (p115) has been shuttling tourists between the pier and what is now Brighton Marina (p159) since 1883.

## Neighbourhood watch

Directly inland from the railway is Kemp Town, Brighton's gay quarter – earning it the sobriquet Camp Town. This is the area for boutique hotels, bars, and shops that sell everything from bespoke art to clothes for dogs. It's also interesting for the architecture of its Georgian buildings. Although Kemp Town originally referred to the terraces east of Eaton Place, these days (and in this guide) the

name is generally used for the entire area east of Old Steine, with the main drag being St James's Street. Further inland is Hanover, a residential area notable for the pleasant Queen's Park (see box p114) and some great pubs.

The area to the west of Lewes Road is trickier to define – for the purposes of this guide we've labelled it as the New England Quarter & Preston. New England is largely a redeveloped brownfield site east of the train station, while Preston Circus has the venerable Duke of York's (p144) arthouse cinema and some good pubs.

A little further in this direction is peaceful Preston Park (p137) – not quite so serene when the Gay Pride march ends there once a year – and Preston Manor (p137), allegedly one of Britain's most haunted houses. The Booth Museum of Natural History (p137) is a museum as its Victorian curator envisaged – a private collection of the pickled, stuffed and bizarre; don't miss the merman, a hybrid of fish, monkey and mermaid.

The area of Hove has (or so many of its residents would have you believe) grown up separately to Brighton. Noticeably more laid-back, Hove stretches westwards from around Norfolk Square and is less an upmarket oasis than a quieter area popular with students and the odd rock star (Nick Cave, Norman Cook and, apparently, Paul McCartney all have houses here), who relax in cake shops, organic eateries and gastropubs.

## Into the future

As in much of the UK, many large-scale projects have been put on hold due to the recession. We are assured, however, that Brighton's most exciting new venture, the i360 (see box p60) – dubbed the Brighton Eye – will be going ahead. At the foot of the West Pier, the i360 is set to be taller than the London Eye and will be able to hold up to 200 people, rising 150 metres above the seafront in a pod. It's scheduled to open in 2012.

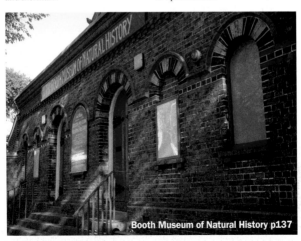

**Booth Museum of Natural History p137**

# Eating & Drinking

Brighton offers an incredible variety of dining possibilities for a city of its size, with more than 500 cafés and restaurants. Not all, of course, are great. Many might woo the visitor in with a stylish interior or superb location only to serve up a mediocre coffee or an overpriced meal; but there are dozens that value substance over, or at least as much as, style. That makes the special places – of which there are still plenty, we hasten to add – all the more notable.

New restaurants and cafés, while garnering interest, don't enjoy the immediate buzz that new eateries experience in faster-paced cities. In Brighton it takes time to become established. Many of the most popular, and best, restaurants have been open for what seems like ages. They remain perennially popular, as others ebb and flow.

Being a young, cosmopolitan and trendy city, there is a sincere café culture here. Adverts for trained baristas hang in the windows – roles commonly filled by coffee-lovers from the antipodes – and, given Brighton's large media and freelance work demographic, the sight of people nursing a flat white while tapping on a Mac laptop in a café is a common one.

For the same reasons, Brighton has a healthy drinking scene, with some truly great pubs. Many fall into the 'pewter tankards above the bar' type rather than the gastropub, and that's no bad thing – many neighbourhood pubs have a true community feel: Dover Castle (p116) even has a daily local food market in its car park. And while there is a profusion of pubs opening Thai food concessions (occasionally at the expense of some previously good food), others, such as the Hop Poles (p106) and the Lion & Lobster (p64) continue to serve a high standard of traditional pub fare.

## Vegetable patch

As is fitting for a city where an entire neighbourhood (Hanover) is nicknamed the Muesli Mountain and where worthy enterprises such as the Brighton & Hove Organic Gardening Group (www.bhogg.org) and Infinity Foods (p91) enjoy real success, Brighton caters for vegetarians incredibly well. In fact, a couple of Brighton's nationally respected restaurants – Food for Friends (p106) and Amanda Powley and Philip Taylor's Terre à Terre (p109) – are vegetarian, but this is almost secondary to their status as fine dining options. Committed meat-eater AA Gill wrote of Terre à Terre, in his idiosyncratic way: 'This is most probably the best vegetarian restaurant in Britain, but it's also better than that ghetto accolade. It is singularly and eccentrically marvellous.'

## Fine dining

There are, of course, plenty of good restaurants for meat-eaters who are willing to spend decent money on a decent meal. Several of these top-end choices are in hotels. The Restaurant at Drakes (p116), under chef Andrew McKenzie, is collecting AA stars at a rate that has put it on the national radar for its Anglo-French cuisine served in intimate surroundings. Blanch House (p115) has also been earning plaudits for its well-executed, locally sourced food, while the Hotel du Vin (p107) has a very good bistro.

Michelin stars have so far eluded Brighton's restaurants, but several have been awarded Michelin's Bib

## SHORTLIST

**Best for fine dining**
- Gingerman (p63)
- Meadow (p152)
- Restaurant at Drakes (p116)
- Terre à Terre (p109)

**Time for tea**
- Metrodeco (p118)
- Tea Cosy (p123)

**From the sea**
- Bardsley's (p139)
- Due South (p79)
- Fishy Fishy (p106)
- Regency Restaurant (p80)

**Cocktail time**
- Blanch House (p115)
- Medicine Chest (p158)

**Best for vegetarians**
- Food for Friends (p106)

**Best local boozers**
- Basketmakers Arms (p87)
- Greys (p117)
- Sir Charles Napier (p123)

**For wholesome fodder**
- Farm Café & Market (p88)
- Infinity Foods Café (p91)

**Best pub grub**
- Hop Poles (p106)
- Ginger Dog (p117)

**Best gay pubs**
- Bulldog (p130)
- Charles Street (p130)

**The finest coffee**
- Coffee@33 (p87)
- Marwood Coffee Shop (p107)
- Redroaster Café (p120)

**Bistro bites**
- Blenio (p59)
- Hotel du Vin (p107)

Gourmand badge for 'good food at moderate prices'. In addition to Terre à Terre, restaurants in this bracket include the Meadow (p152) in Hove, which has a strong local-produce ethos supplemented by touches of Mediterranean French and Italian cuisine.

The local Gingerman group of restaurants is another with a superb reputation among both residents and critics. The Gingerman (p63) on Norfolk Square opened in 2000 with a seasonally changing menu offering dishes such as pistachio-coated venison loin with savoy cabbage, red currants and sloe gin. Seven years later, the group opened the Ginger Pig (p150) gastropub in Hove, for which it was awarded a Bib Gourmand for its classic British food with, yes, a contemporary twist. For its third offering it moved out of town to Hurstpierpoint to open the Ginger Fox pub, before shifting back to Kemp Town to the Ginger Dog (p117), which has a more traditional approach.

## Seafood & eat it

Given Brighton's proximity to the sea, it's somewhat surprising that there aren't many truly great seafood restaurants. Notable exceptions are Due South (p79) in the King's Road Arches, which provides suitably nautical views, and Riddle & Finns (p107) in the Lanes, a champagne and oyster bar. The menu is full of classic seafood dishes – half a dozen oysters will set you back around £10 – and the restaurant itself is lively, with some bar seating. There's also a wet fish shop.

Brighton's most renowned seafood restaurant is the Regency Restaurant (p80), in place since the 1930s. Applauded by Rick Stein for its no-nonsense fish and chips, it has a reasonably priced menu featuring locally landed seafood.

For traditional fish and chips, the most respected outlet is Bardsley's (p139) on Baker Street, which has been frying since 1926. It's a little way from the seafront, but given the quality and price of many of its competitors, the walk up to Preston Circus is worth it.

The latest seafood restaurant to open is Fishy Fishy (p106), owned by TV presenter Dermot O'Leary. Located in a small pleasant area in the Lanes enhanced by outdoor seating, it has a reasonably priced menu and has drawn a fair amount of local acclaim.

## Café culture

You'll need all of 15 minutes to notice Brighton has a vibrant café scene. If you're in search of a caffeine boost, a pit stop or just somewhere to while away the day (it rains occasionally too in Brighton), there are dozens of options. Many are centred around the pedestrianised North Laine, allowing cafés to spill out on to the pavement on sunny days and giving a continental feel to the area. Cafés such as the Dumb Waiter (p88) and the diner-style Rock Ola (p95) serve good café food in quirky surroundings.

Bridging the café/restaurant gap in North Laine is Lewes import Bill's (p87). It's a deliciously decked-out grocers with communal tables that serves fresh, homely food. It's always busy, there's often a queue – and it couldn't be more 'Brighton' if it had stripy tights or a pork-pie hat. Nearby, Farm Café & Market (p88) offers a similar experience, with organic sausages, home-made bread and a good amount of produce hailing from its own farms.

If eating organic granola seems a little too angelic, rise against muesli with the ultimate decadence at the Bar du Chocolat (p105). Run by the world-famous chocolatiers at Choccywoccydoodah (p109), this small café serves up the finest hot chocolate, quite possibly in the world, along with vast chocolate cakes, again probably unrivalled on the planet. Or maybe that award goes to the brownies at the Marwood Coffee Shop (p107). Along with Coffee@33 (p87), it serves the best coffee we've tried in Brighton.

Meanwhile, in Kemp Town, the Redroaster Coffee Company (p120) was one of the first 'sit down and relax' coffee shops in Brighton; its own-roasted coffee is superb. In Hanover, Home (p118) has recently transformed into a great little café. If tea is your tipple, then head to the frankly bizarre Tea Cosy (p123); this shrine to royalty serves up Charles & Camilla Elevenses and is kitsch to the extreme. And if you have a dog, it's to the art deco antique shop and canine-friendly café Metrodeco (p119) you go.

## Trad pubs & trendy bars

There's no shortage at all of great boozers in Brighton: the city excels in the homely neighbourhood pub. Just take a crawl through the pubs along Southover Road in Hanover –

among them, the Greys (p117), Dover Castle (p116) and the Sir Charles Napier (p123) – if you require any convincing.

Other superb pubs include the Lion & Lobster (p64), the Cricketers (p105), the Windmill (p71), the Evening Star (p62) and the Hop Poles (p106), all in central Brighton, and the Basketmakers Arms (p87) in North Laine.

There's been a recent movement towards cool bars – something Brighton once lacked. Koba (p64) was long the cocktail drinkers' favourite venue; it's been joined by a number of bars where the mixologist (yep, mixologist) can blend the perfect drink. The ultra-stylish Merkaba (p92) in Myhotel is one of Brighton's flashier venues, and Hotel du Vin (p107), Blanch House (p115) and Drakes (p116) are among the hotels who have also spent money on good bar staff. Try a Tuaca cocktail: launched in Brighton, it's the nearest the city has to its own drink, and is almost cult among Brighton drinkers. The most exciting bar is the Medicine Chest (p158), a speakeasy-style bar that makes its own elixirs and mixes a flawless martini.

Restaurant at Drakes p116

North Laine p82

# Shopping

Brighton is a city that shuns the mainstream and embraces counterculture. No surprise, then, that it's also home to a laid-back but fiercely independent shopping scene, encompassing flea markets, art galleries, jewellery shops, top-drawer delis and idiosyncratic boutiques – perfect for any amount of browsing and café-hopping, and at a pace unthinkable in London. Low-ish rents in North Laine, Kemp Town and along Western Road have encouraged entrepreneurs with quirky ideas or a discerning eye to establish individual and inspiring shops; the area around Seven Dials and off Dyke Road is also gathering pace.

With branches of many of the more interesting national chains, Brighton comes close to being the perfect shopping destination, held back only by a lack of high-end designer stores, for those who care about such things – and it seems churlish to, with so much native creativity on offer.

## Boutique bonanza

Head left out of the station and you're plunged into a colourful pick-and-mix of bijou boutiques, independent record shops, bookshops and cafés. This is North Laine, and the discerning shopper's first port of call. Three main shopping streets thread through its heart – Sydney Street, Gardner Street and Kensington Gardens – though forays into the terrace-lined back streets can also reap rich rewards. Brightonians clearly love a bric-a-brac fix, and tat and treasures abound in the well-known

# CHURCHILL SQUARE
## BRIGHTON'S SHOPPING CENTRE

# BECAUSE YOU LOVE SHOPPING

Churchill Square Shopping Centre is Brighton's premier shopping destination. Situated in the heart of Brighton, it has over 85 leading high street stores all under one roof. Spoilt for choice, you will find all of the latest fashion offers with stores such as **Hollister**, **Urban Outfitters** and **Zara**. Alternatively, if you are looking for something for the home, then you will find inspiration in **Debenhams**, **Habitat** and **BHS**. Other big names include **Apple**, **H&M**, **Miss Selfridge** and **River Island** and much much more. The spacious, innovative design of the centre makes it a perfect destination for a day out, whether shopping, browsing or meeting friends. With regular events and promotions, you will always find a reason to visit Churchill Square.

Open 7 days a week with Late Night Shopping til 8pm on Thursdays. The Car Park is open 24 hours with over 1600 parking spaces available.

SEE WHAT'S GOING ON AT THE CENTRE churchillsquare.com

BRIGHTON'S PREMIER SHOPPING CENTRE

FOLLOW US ON FACEBOOK AND TWITTER: twitter.com/churchillsquare

CHURCHILLSQUARE.COM

Snooper's Paradise (p99). Squeeze through the turnstile to browse its myriad stalls, crammed with everything from bags of buttons and Bakelite telephones to stylish 1960s lamps. Hidden away on a side-street, North Laine Antique & Flea Market also offers good pickings, whether you're in search of ceramics, costume jewellery or a statement chandelier. For vintage clothes, head for Sydney Street's To Be Worn Again (p100) or the super-stylish Hope & Harlequin (p98). Dirty Harry (p97) is one of the oldest second-hand clothes shops in town, and still one of the best, especially for those with a penchant for the *Dukes of Hazzard* look.

If the allure of vintage starts waning, Tribeca (p100) has a beautifully edited selection of womenswear labels. For a more quintessential Brighton look, drop by Vegetarian Shoes (p101) or try a kitsch Mexican skull-print frock on for size at Get Cutie (p97). And in a city so synonymous with dirty weekends, it also seems only right to drop by chic sex toy boutiques Lust (p99) or Tickled (p110).

East of the Old Steine is Kemp Town, Brighton's gay area, home to an enticing jumble of antiques shops and eccentric boutiques. The best shopping here is along Upper St James's Street, where Brighton Flea Market's (p125) neon sign is a beacon for bargain-hunters. Antiques and vintage shops cluster along the street: for furniture, lighting and ceramics, try In Retro Spect (p127) or Metrodeco (p118) – Kylie paid a visit when she was in town. For vintage clothes, check out the charming Margaret's at 30A (p127). You can also pick up diamanté collars at Doggy Fashion (p125), devoted to dog grooming and camp canine couture.

A little further on, the street turns into St George's Road;

## SHORTLIST

**Best markets**
- Brighton Farm Market (p83)
- Brighton Street Market (p82)

**For musicians**
- Guitar, Amp & Keyboard Centre (p98)
- Resident Music (p99)
- Rounder Records (p110)

**Fine design**
- Get Cutie (p97)
- Hope & Harlequin (p98)

**Most eccentric**
- Arka Original Funerals (p71)
- Cyber Candy (p97)

**Best for books**
- City Books (p155)
- Lmnop (p73)

**For a dirty weekend**
- Lust (p99)
- Tickled (p110)

**For retro clothing**
- Beyond Retro (p96)
- To Be Worn Again (p100)
- Wardrobe (p75)

**Crafty things**
- Handmade (p125)
- Purl (p143)

**Best for curio hunting**
- Snoopers' Paradise (p99)

**Best for interiors**
- Kate Langdale (p72)
- Rume (p157)
- Sixty Seven (p74)

**Best jewellers**
- Jeremy Hoye (p109)

**Chocolate heaven**
- Choccywoccydoodah (p109)
- Montezuma's (p110)

DON'T MISS

at no.17, Andrew Fionda (07875 852926 mobile) is a lovely, polished vintage boutique. Run by one half of design duo Pearce Fionda, its stock is expensive but exquisite, with some beautiful bridal pieces and the occasional bargain.

## Town jewels

South of North Street lies the tangle of the Lanes – Brighton's labyrinthine jewellery quarter. As you'll inevitably get lost, the wisest approach is to browse the glittering window displays with no fixed plan, imagining the stories behind antique engagement rings and exquisite diamond bracelets. There's beautiful contemporary jewellery at Fidra (p109) and Jeremy Hoye (p109), whose designs are worn by Dido and Katie Melua and include unique Brighton bracelet charms. On Duke Street, Jewel Thief (p109) is one of the newest additions to Brighton's jewellery scene – and dangerously close to heavenly local chocolate

shops Montezuma's (p110) and Choccywoccydoodah (p109).

## Boys' toys

Yes, men like chocolate, yes, men wear jewellery, and yes, men like furniture. But sometimes only a record shop will do. There are two great, great record shops in Brighton. Resident (p99) in Kensington Gardens has a superb selection of music and is a good place to get gig tickets. It's a proper music shop where staff make knowledgeable recommendations from current stock and the back catalogue. Rounder Records (p110) in the Lanes is another record shop that people travel distances to reach. It holds a carefully curated selection of CDs alongside the city's largest collection of vinyl, in all genres. Rounder makes a point of promoting local bands, and offers gig tickets for most venues.

If you want to experience Brighton's mod vibe, Jump the Gun (p99) is nirvana for anyone who owns a Fred Perry shirt (or has ever had designs on a Lambretta – there's one parked outside). For the pork-pie hat to complete the look, try Mad Hatters (p99), which stocks all manner of hand-made headgear.

## Chain talk

The mainstream high-street shops, are ranged along Western Road and North Street. The two roads meet at Churchill Square Shopping Centre (p71). It's not the kind of place to get the pulse racing, but its owners are doing well at attracting interesting brands such as Urban Outfitters, Habitat and Hollister Co. It also stages fashion events.

Upmarket chains, such as Jack Wills, L'Occitane, Cath Kidston and All Saints, have been moving into the pleasant East Street area at the south end of the Lanes.

## Market value

There are several good markets in Brighton. As ever, it's North Laine that leads the way. The most significant is the Brighton Farm Market (p83) on North Road, drawing farmers and producers from across Sussex to sell barrows of fresh vegetables, alongside cakes, fish, meat, bread and flowers. The organisers have also started a Brighton Sunday Market on the same premises, with around 25 stalls selling items 'made and found' in Brighton. There are jewellers, leathercraft workers and ceramic artists. The Brighton Street Market is held every Saturday along Upper Gardner Street from 9am and is the place to pick up curios, old designer lamps, records, books and fresh produce.

Over in Hanover, the Dover Castle (p116) has a daily market in its car park with edibles and bric-a-brac. Down on London Road,

the Open Market (p143) has food and some art stalls.

## Food & drink

One of Brighton's most famous shops is Infinity Foods (p98), often credited with starting the organic food boom in the city. It opened a small shop in 1971, but today, in much larger premises on the corner of North Road and Gardner Street, it stocks a range of organic fruit and vegetables, and an array of wholefoods, confectionery and organic beer and wine. There's a bakery on site, but it faces stiff competition from the Real Patisserie (p99). For takeaway food, nearby Hell's Kitchen (p89) is a Jewish New York-style deli that sells latkes, bagels and salt beef sandwiches.

A favourite among Brightonians for its eclectic selection of world cuisine is Taj, now with four outlets. The most convenient for beach picnic goods are on Old Steine (p128) and Western Road (p75).

There are few better ways to finish a day's shopping in Brighton than heading down to the seafront and watching the sunset, as many residents do throughout the summer. To do it in style, pick a bottle of wine from the new Wine Shop & Tasting Shop (p95). It stocks wine from boutique bodegas around the world, including Sussex.

## Time to shop

High-street shops follow usual UK opening hours of 9am to 5.30pm from Monday to Saturday; the larger ones also open on Sunday until 4pm. The independent shops in Kemp Town, North Laine and the Lanes may open at 10am or as late as 11am, closing at 5.30 or 6pm. Nearly all open between 11am and 4pm on Sunday.

**Latest Music Bar p130**

# Nightlife

Pier, promenade, pavilion, pah! Partying is what brings so many down to Brighton from London and the regions – a fine tradition upon which the town's very development depended in the days of the foxy Prince Regent (George IV).

A gay hub, a major international student town, and child-friendly with it, Brighton still welcomes ravers, nudists, discerning vegetarians, surfers, sun-seekers and wastrels. It practically invented the dirty weekend. Leisure and pleasure? It has them in spades.

## Clubs

The key to Brighton's successful shift from seedy post-pub discos to cosmopolitan, quality nightspots has been the city's dynamic and influential gay community – often marginalised in lesser seaside towns – as well as the nationwide move

away from super-clubs, largely as a result of altered licensing laws.

Nothing hides the fact that gangs of pissed-up hens in dog-eared devil horns invade the city centre every weekend. West Street at chucking-out time is not a pleasant place to be of a Friday night, with young shavers and squawky girlies heading for the bright lights of Tru (p76) and the like. But move away from West Street and you'll find grown-up venues that stand out.

The intimate, tunnel-like Funky Buddha Lounge (p82) and the vast, high-profile, mainly mainstream Honey (p82) both offer potential reward. Nearby is the marvellous Audio (p128), an eclectic venue with its digit somewhere near the pulse. If you have one night in town, spend it here.

For something classier, the three-storey Oceana (p76) is the top choice. It has a fabulous sound system and a cool upstairs cocktail bar that attracts world-class DJs into town on a regular basis.

There are plenty of bars with late licences, DJs and dancefloors. The Ink Bar (p110) has a popular student night, but weekends are given over to commercial house and R&B. The new Lola Lo (p110) is a small Tiki bar and club. Heist (p75), set in a former Turkish bath, gets suitably lairy on Fridays and Saturdays. An indie classic is the Pavilion Tavern (p112), known widely as the Pav Tav. Other bars that ramp the music up on weekends include the Duke of Norfolk (p61), the Hope (p75) and the decadent Madame Geisha (p110).

## Lucky dip

It's not just the dedicated clubs that have great club nights. The recently reopened Brighton Ballroom (p130) has regular events most nights. They're invariably interesting, ranging from Indian-themed club night Bombay Jazz Café to glam Parisian-themed disco La Bistrotheque. There's fancy-dress karaoke every Sunday, hosted by flamboyant Brighton institution Boogaloo Stu. The Ballroom is one of several venues that offer a plethora of activities from live music to comedy, and the bizarre and naughty. It's a result of the open-minded owners, who are happy to hand over the venue to creative organisers and promoters. It's in these types of venues where the best nights in Brighton's are often to be had.

The Basement (p102) offers one of Brighton & Hove's more eclectic programmes. Supporting a community of local artists, events include live performance art, experimental theatre, dance, cabaret, comedy and concerts. Also in North Laine is one of the most

# SHORTLIST

**For underground sounds**
- Caroline of Brunswick (p139)
- Cowley Club (p140)
- Prince Albert (p95)

**Best for gigs**
- Audio (p128)
- Concorde 2 (p130)
- Latest Music Bar (p130)

**For funky sounds**
- Funky Buddha Lounge (p82)
- Honey (p82)

**After-hours fun**
- Heist (p75)
- Ink Bar (p110)
- Madame Geisha (p110)

**For the unexpected**
- Brighton Ballroom (p130)
- Hydrant (p143)
- Komedia (p102)
- Pav Tav (p112)

**Big beats**
- Oceana (p76)
- Tru (p76)

**Best gay venues**
- Bulldog (p130)
- Charles Street (p130)
- Legends (p118)
- Revenge (p130)

**Best comedy**
- Nightingale Theatre (p77)
- Quadrant (p67)

**For big-name bands**
- Brighton Centre (p77)
- Brighton Dome (p102)

**To sing your heart out**
- Lucky Voice (p110)

**Cocktail classics**
- Medicine Chest (p158)
- Merkaba (p92)

# Get the local experience

Over 50 of the world's top destinations available.

established venues in Brighton: Komedia (p102), on Gardner Street. Krater Comedy Club takes over one of its floors two or three times a week with a bewildering array of comedians. Komedia is also one of the city's best live music venues – there's something happening every night. The Nightingale Theatre (p77), Quadrant (p67) and Temple Bar (p68) also have regular comedy nights. The humour is ramped up at venues across the city during the Brighton Comedy Festival (p38), held in October.

## Gay disco

Most of the above clubs put on at least one gay night (look out for Wild Fruit at Oceana), but that's only the tip of the iceberg. Landmark Kemp Town pubs and clubs such as the sleek Charles Street (p130), with its pool club upstairs, and the trashier but mega-popular Revenge (p130) are two of the biggest gay clubs on the south coast.

For a few drinks before a night out on the tiles, Marine Parade, now lined with trendy new gay bars, is always a good bet. Legends (p118), a bar, nightclub and hotel, is great fun at any time in the evening.

## Live music

Brighton rocks to its own beat. The bands that have come out of the city are testament to a vibrant and well-promoted scene. Promoters such as Melting Vinyl (www.melting vinyl.co.uk) and Lout Promotions (www.loutpromotions.co.uk) are at the forefront of bringing cult, indie and just-about-on-the-radar bands to Brighton, as well as giving a break to home-grown talent. Current Brighton bands making waves are British Sea Power, Blood Red Shoes, Brakes, the Maccabees and the Go! Team – all play regularly in the city.

Thanks to the relaxing of licensing, the number of venues that put on music in Brighton is astonishing. Check websites such as East (www.eastmagazine.co.uk) and free magazines such as *XYZ* for listings. Also pop into Rounder Records (p110) or Resident Music (p99) for tickets and a glance at what's coming up (and pick up a CD of the band you are going to see).

Many of the pubs listed in this guide put on music throughout the week. The most proactive pubs include Caroline of Brunswick (p139), Greys (p117), Quadrant (p67), Poets' Corner (p153) in Hove and the unmissable Prince Albert (p95) in North Laine.

Pretty much every vaguely popular guitar band from the UK or US has played at the Concorde 2 (p130) at one time or another, often several times over. It's a superb and intimate venue – suitably dark and sweaty. It's also home to a good, and reasonably priced, bar.

Audio (p128), which doubles as a club across its three floors, has an eclectic mix of more experimental bands. Komedia is another spot that always has interesting music. A relative newcomer on the live-music roster is Latest Music Bar (p130), but it has very quickly built up a packed programme.

There's only really one option for the larger alternative bands, and that's in one of the Brighton Dome (p102) venues, which should be applauded for hosting a great mix of world music, classical music, comedy and rock and pop. The Concert Hall is bigger than the Corn Exchange. It is also the principal venue for the Brighton Festival (p35), which it organises, although events are held across the city. For the next Take That or Madness tour, or big-name comedians, meanwhile, you're looking at the Brighton Centre (p77) behemoth.

Brighton Dome p102

# Arts & Leisure

One of Britain's youngest cities and England's most popular tourist destinations, Brighton is host to the nation's biggest annual arts festival outside Edinburgh – the Brighton Festival – and the vast Brighton Fringe during May. And while the festival is the centrepiece in the cultural calendar, Brighton's arts scene is nevertheless thriving all year round. The city's most important arts venues, such as the Brighton Dome (p102), Duke of York's Picturehouse (p144) and Fabrica (see box p111) have eclectic programmes to rival any in Britain.

Art and music stream from Brighton's theatres, art galleries, boutiques, cinemas and, not least, through its very streets. Stepping off the train and heading into North Laine, you could run into a string quartet of student musicians or a street performer, a rock 'n' roll band, quiffs and all, or perhaps a theatre troupe entertaining shoppers. And that's all before you spend any money.

## Festivals

Brighton's month-long annual May shindig (see box p39) is England's largest arts festival, bringing a host of renowned authors, actors, comedians and musicians to the city. In 2010, Brian Eno curated a cast of thousands to make the festival the most successful yet. The diverse programme includes dance, theatre, music and literary events attended by participants from around the world.

The festival has its Fringe (p35) element too, every bit as inventive and popular as the main event.

In 2010, the Fringe hosted more than 3,000 artists performing at 675 events (with 145 free of charge), and more than 100,000 tickets were sold, making it the third largest fringe festival in the world. The Fringe is open-access, which means anyone can stage an event and be included in the programme.

Crucially, the festival period also provides a showcase for creative Brightonians: local artists are put on display, along with their artistic efforts, in the Artists' Open Houses Festival (p35), which sees many a boho Brightonian residence opened to the public.

The Great Escape festival (p35) also takes advantage of the spike in visitor numbers in May. It's billed as Britain's South by Southwest Festival and takes over most of the city's pubs and music venues for three days, with a great line-up of acts, as well as industry workshops and talks. Musically, it's rivalled only by Brighton Live in October – although the bands at the latter are much more underground.

## Classical & opera

The multi-faceted Brighton Dome has the most substantial classical music and opera programme in the city. Events are usually held in the acoustically brilliant Concert Hall. It's also home to the highly respected Brighton Philharmonic Orchestra (www.brightonphil.org.uk), which puts on at least one performance a month. The London Philharmonic and Royal Philharmonic Orchestras are regular guests. During the Fringe (and throughout much of the year), churches such as St Paul's, St Michael & All Angels and St Bartholomew's also hold events.

Opera fans are less well catered for, but some events do nonetheless take place at the Brighton Dome,

## SHORTLIST

**Best venues**
- Brighton Dome (p102)
- Fabrica (p112)

**Best for cineastes**
- Duke of York's Picturehouse (p144)
- Odeon (p77)

**Best festivals**
- Brighton Festival (p35)
- Brighton Fringe (p35)
- Great Escape (p35)

**Best small festivals**
- Artists' Open Houses (p35)
- Kite Festival (p37)

**For sports fans**
- Falmer Stadium (p32)

**For sporty types**
- Sussex Beacon Half Marathon (p33)
- Preston Park (p137)
- Prince Regent Leisure Centre (p102)
- Yellowave Beachsports (p115)

**Most innovative venues**
- Basement (p102)
- Cowley Club (p140)
- Fabrica (p112)
- New Venture Theatre (p77)

**For alternative drama**
- Brighton Little Theatre (p77)
- Nightingale Theatre (p77)

**Best for laughs**
- Komedia (p102)
- Quadrant (p67)
- Temple Bar (p68)
- Theatre Royal (p103)

**Best spas**
- Treatment Rooms (p103)
- Uniquely Organic Eco Spa (p158)

DON'T MISS

the Brighton Centre (p77) and, occasionally, at the Theatre Royal (p103). Operas are pretty much guaranteed during the Brighton Festival. One of the highlights for classical music lovers is the Brighton Early Music Festival in late October, in which renowned groups such as Red Priest and the Sixteen share the programme with local performers.

## Theatre & dance

There are plenty of dance events during May's festival season, whether at the Fringe or as part of the main Brighton Festival schedule.

One of the most proactive dance venues is the Nightingale Theatre (p77). Forgive, or take relish in, the fact that it's above the Grand Central bar by the train station – events can be as unconventional as the location, but under the stewardship of Steven Berkoff, it has earned widespread acclaim for its dance productions. The Nightingale's principal focus is, however, theatre, and it's now well established as one of Brighton's circuit venues, with pre- and post-Edinburgh shows. Events such as Scratch offer performers a 10- to 15-minute opportunity to read through first drafts of new work, while the audience can pay what they like.

Elsewhere is the news that dance troupe Stomp, which started in Brighton, has bought the Old Market on Upper Market Street, Hove. No details as to their plans for the space were available as this guide went to press.

The New Venture Theatre (p77) is a community theatre that has put on amateur productions since 1956. It has since added two more floors to its premises, including the cabaret-style venue of the South Hall. It has a full calendar of events, so it's always worth seeing what's on.

The Brighton Little Theatre (p77), established more than 70 years ago, is a lively company that stages around a dozen productions a year – expect plays by anyone from Alan Bennett to Shakespeare.

One of the city's largest venues is the Theatre Royal, a lovely Grade II-listed building constructed in 1806. This is a more traditional seaside theatre that is just as happy to lend its venue to Bjorn Again, panto and Peppa Pig's Party as to touring comedy, ballet and theatre. Creative alliances with the Rambert Dance Company, the Shakespeare Theatre Company and the Royal National Theatre have seen the number of performances ramped up.

## Film

Brighton has a rich history of cinematography – the first film show in Brighton took place in 1896. It sparked an interest in filmmaking, especially in Esmé Collings, who photographed the train station and other city views. He is also credited with making the first erotic film, in Brighton, called *Woman Undressing*. His friend, William Friese-Greene, built a 'chronophotographic camera' which, when unveiled in 1889, was one of the first cinema cameras. By 1900, Brighton had weekly film shows of 'animated photography', with many of them made in a dedicated film studio in St Ann's Well Gardens (see box p69). It was a vibrant period, one which led to the filmmakers being described as part of 'the Brighton School'.

The fate of what was once a two-dozen-strong collection of Brighton cinemas is rather less impressive. There are only three cinemas now: Cineworld in the Marina, the Odeon (p77) and the Duke of York's Picturehouse (p144). The latter, however, goes a long way to making up for the loss of all the others. The Duke of York's, which celebrated its centenary in 2010, has received acclaim over the last decade for its innovative programming. It includes annual Metropolitan Opera seasons (including live performances), National Theatre Live events, arthouse seasons and even gigs – fittingly, Tim Robbins played here.

## Sports & leisure

Talk sport in Brighton and it's Brighton & Hove Albion, and, more precisely, the club's stadium, that dominates. The Seagulls have bounced from League One to the Championship and back. But it's

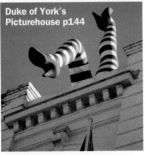

**Duke of York's Picturehouse p144**

the stories off the pitch that have garnered as much interest, especially regarding the fate of its home. For the 2011/12 season, the team will move from their temporary ground at the Withdean Stadium to the brand new Falmer Stadium (or, to give its official title, the American Express Community Stadium), near the University of Sussex, just outside the city.

If it's the sound of leather striking willow that appeals more, head to the Sussex Cricket Ground in Hove, which fields the county's first division squad. With buildings dating from 1872, and some recent stand additions, it's a charming mix of old and new. Captain Michael Yardy is a regular in the England one-day squad.

The popular Sussex Beacon Half Marathon (p33) has been established for more than 20 years and is held every February along the seafront. It'll be joined in 2011 by the first ever Brighton Marathon (p35), which will take place every April.

For participatory sports, Preston Park (p137) has eight tennis courts, four football pitches, three bowling greens, two cricket pitches and a softball pitch, plus a 500m velodrome. The Yellowave Beachsports (p115) venue has a beach volleyball and football pitch in a sandy setting – there's also a bar and regular barbecue nights. To rest weary muscles, meanwhile, there are several good spas, such as the Space at Neo Hotel (p77).

## What's on

Arts and leisure events can usually be found on venue websites. The Brighton Dome's own www.brighton ticketshop.com has tickets for all its events and many more besides. Free magazines such as *XYZ*, or the online www.eastmagazine.co.uk, have comprehensive events listings.

# Calendar

**Pride in Brighton & Hove p38**

The following are the pick of the annual events that take place in Brighton. Further information and exact dates can be found nearer the time from the tourist information centres and at the websites given. The major venues have their own programmes that can be picked up across the city.

## January

Late Jan **Brighton Tattoo Convention**
Brighton Racecourse
*www.brightontattoo.com*
All manner of painted body work.

## February

Mid-end Feb **Brighton Science Festival**
Various locations
*www.brightonscience.com*
Discuss sustainability issues during a week devoted to all disciplines of science.

Mid Feb **Sussex Beacon Half Marathon**
*www.beaconhalf.org.uk*
2011 marks the 21st anniversary of this annual charity race.

Late Feb **See Festival**
*www.seefestival.org*
The Brighton Documentary Film Festival features screenings and talks.

## March

Early-mid Mar **Sussex Beer Festival**
Hove Town Hall
*www.sussexbeerfestival.co.uk*
Great beers, good food, friendly staff and a fantastic atmosphere.

Mar-mid May **City Reads**
Various locations

*www.cityreads.co.uk*
Annual city-wide reading initiative.

## April

Ongoing City Reads (see Mar)

Early Apr **Spring Harvest
Food Festival**
*www.brightonfoodfestival.com*
Such is the popularity of the Brighton
Food Festival in September, organisers
have recently started this spring event.

Early Apr **London to Brighton
Jaguar Run**
*www.brightonrun.co.uk*
One of several classic car rallies.

2nd week Apr **Brighton Marathon**
*www.brightonmarathon.co.uk*
A new race, whose 26-mile course takes
in the best of the city.

## May

Ongoing City Reads (see Mar)

Throughout May **Brighton Festival**
*www.brightonfestival.org*

An impressive programme of theatre,
dance, music, books and debate, plus
outdoor spectacles kick-started by the
now famous Children's Parade. A
guest curator is invited each year.
See box p39.

Early-late May **Brighton Fringe**
*www.brightonfestivalfringe.org.uk*
The third-largest Fringe Festival in
the world offers cabaret, comedy, classical concerts, club nights, theatre,
exhibitions and street performances.

Weekends in May
**Artists' Open Houses Festival**
Various locations
*www.aoh.org.uk*
Free arts event with more than 1,000
artists opening their homes and studios.

Mid May **Great Escape**
Various locations
*www.escapegreat.com*
Music festival featuring new, local,
national and international bands.

Late May **Royal Escape Race**
Brighton Pier to Fécamp,
Normandy

**London to Brighton Jaguar Run**

# Discover Britain's natural beauty...

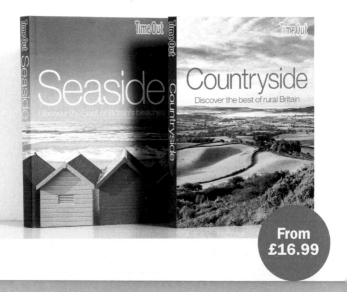

From
£16.99

*www.royalescaperace.co.uk*
Around 100 boats compete in this cross-Channel event commemorating the escape of Charles II to France from Cromwell and his forces.

## June

Early June **Springwatch Festival**
Stanmer Park
*www.brighton-hove.gov.uk*
Celebrating and promoting local wildlife and wildlife-friendly living.

2nd week in June **Brighton Fashion Week**
*www.brightonfashionweek.co.uk*
A catwalk show accessorised by great parties and a fashion emporium showcasing new designers.

Mid June **London to Brighton Bike Ride**
*www.bhf.org.uk/london-brighton*
The annual 54-mile bike ride from the capital to the coast in aid of the British Heart Foundation. It's the UK's largest charity bike ride, with 27,000 riders taking part.

## July

Early July **Paddle Round the Pier**
*www.paddleroundthepier.com*
This free festival features the best in beach culture, urban and street sports, live music and family fun.

2nd week in July **Kite Festival**
Stanmer Park
*www.brightonkiteflyers.co.uk*
A family event, that has been flying high for 33 years.

Mid July **Soundwaves Festival**
Various locations
*www.soundwaves-festival.org.uk*
Dip into an alternative world of cutting-edge new music, sound-art and participatory experiences.

## August

Early Aug **August Festival**
Brighton Racecourse

# Loud & proud

As a city that wears its gay heart on its (pink sequined) sleeve, it's hardly surprising that **Pride in Brighton & Hove** (www.brightonpride.org) is the biggest in the UK, and a major event on the local calendar. Usually taking place on the first Saturday of August and flavoured with a different theme each year, the Pride parade sets off from Madeira Drive at 11am and is watched by thousands of residents as it sashays through the city centre and out along London Road, before arriving at Preston Park.

The park itself undergoes a transformation into a free-entry festival, with fairground rides, market stalls (selling everything from pet accessories to sex toys), food vendors, bars and entertainment tents offering DJs, cabaret and more.

When the park antics tail off in the early evening, festivities continue at pubs and clubs throughout the city.

Full-on hedonists will head for big clubs such as Revenge (p130) and Tru (p76), while the more alternative crowd can be found thronging St James's Street (aka the gay village), focused on the Bulldog (p130) and nearby Charles Street (p130). Anyone still standing come Sunday will find sanctuary at post-Pride events such as Sundaylicious at Madame Geisha (p110).

Aside from the main festival, the Pride in Brighton & Hove charity organises other events throughout the year, including a dog show and fundraisers.

*www.brighton-racecourse.co.uk*
Watch the races, sip champagne and admire all the hats on Ladies' Day.

Early-mid Aug **Pride
in Brighton & Hove**
*www.brightonpride.org*
The biggest and best free Pride festival in the UK celebrates everything LGBT in a week of events and parties culminating in a spectacular parade through the city to Preston Park
See box p37.

Mid Aug **Brunswick Festival**
Brunswick Square
*www.brunswickplaceresidents.org.uk*
Annual festival in celebration of the diverse community around Brunswick Square offering a mix of food, street theatre and live music.

# September

Throughout Sep **Brighton & Hove
Food & Drink Festival**
*www.brightonfoodfestival.co.uk*
A celebration of the best food and drink available from across Sussex. Stalls fill New Road, by the Brighton Dome.

Mid Sept **National Speed Trials**
Madeira Drive
*www.brightonandhovemotorclub.co.uk*
Britain's oldest motor racing event, first staged in 1905.

Mid Sept **Ace Café Reunion**
*www.ace-cafe-london.com*
40,000 motorbikes descend on the seafront in celebration of biking and the original Ace Café on London's North Circular Road.

Mid Sept **Brighton Art Fair**
Corn Exchange
*www.brightonartfair.co.uk*
The largest art exhibition on the south coast brings together the most talented national painters, printmakers, photographers, sculptors, artist groups and Sussex-based galleries.

# October

Early-late Oct **Brighton Comedy
Festival**
Brighton Dome & other venues
*www.brightoncomedyfestival.com.*
Laughs are provided by top-quality comedians at venues across the city.

**Brighton Tattoo Convention p33**

# The big one

The Brighton Festival and numerous fringe events
light up the city each May.

**Brighton Festival**

Arrive in Brighton & Hove at any
time of year and you'll generally
find plenty of cultural diversions.
But come in May and you'll
witness an explosion of arts
events, in the shape of the
**Brighton Festival** (p35). Founded
in 1966, Brighton Festival is the
biggest multi-artform festival in
England, attracting more than
500,000 people to 200-plus
events. You can expect to see
theatre ranging from Shakespeare
to cutting-edge, classical and
other concerts, modern dance,
and talks and readings by leading
authors and thinkers.

In 2009, Indian sculptor Anish
Kapoor became the festival's first
guest artistic director, a role that
has added an even more high-
brow dimension to an already
sophisticated event.

While most of the main festival's
events take place in the formal
surroundings of major venues
such as the Brighton Dome,
Corn Exchange, the Old Market
and the Theatre Royal, the more
down-to-earth **Brighton Fringe**
(p35) utilises virtually every other
space available, from pub function
rooms and church halls to street
corners and temporary structures
– past years have included a
Spiegeltent and a giant upside-
down purple cow. Regular features
include the flamboyant Lady Boys
of Bangkok, who return every year
to their temporary pavilion in
Victoria Gardens, and Bom-Bane
Restaurant's (p115) *The Musical*,
a show where the meal is the star,
in Brighton's most eccentric little
restaurant.

Another popular component is
the **Artists' Open Houses Festival**
(p35), which gives punters the
chance to snoop inside more
than 200 private homes on the
pretence of appreciating art.
If you're genuinely interested in
perusing and possibly purchasing
works by local artists, then set
aside a weekend in May.

Not strictly part of Brighton
Festival, but nonetheless a big
contributor to the city's festival
atmosphere since 2006, is the
**Great Escape** music festival
(p35), which takes place in the
second week of May. As well as
involving established acts, it's
also a major showcase for new
talent, managing to squeeze
in 350 gigs across the city
over three days and offering
a fantastic way of discovering
up-and-coming artists from the
UK and overseas.

**Brighton Fringe p35**

Late Oct **White Night**
*www.whitenightnuitblanche.com*
An array of night-time cultural events take place across the city to mark the end of British Summer Time.

## November

Early Nov **London to Brighton Veteran Car Run**
*www.lbvcr.com*
This annual event commemorating the Emancipation Run of 14 November attracts hundreds of vehicles from the UK and abroad.

Mid-late Nov **MADE**
Corn Exchange
*www.brightoncraftfair.co.uk*
This friendly, accessible and high-quality design and craft event is firmly established. It attracts more than 100 artisans selling their creations.

Mid Nov-early Dec **CineCity Film Festival**
*www.cine-city.co.uk*
This event is the south coast's best celebration of film, featuring premières, previews, installations, talks, workshops and special events.

## December

Ongoing CineCity Film Festival (see Nov)

Weekends up to Christmas
**Christmas Open Houses Festival**
*www.aoh.org.uk*
Explore more than 100 houses across the city, where you can see and buy the work of local artists or simply enjoy a mince pie and mulled wine.

Late Dec **Burning the Clocks – Winter Solstice Parade**
*www.burningtheclocks.co.uk*
This truly spectacular sight – as flames and fireworks light up the seafront, culminating in a giant bonfire – celebrates the winter solstice. You can join in by carrying paper lanterns through the city and burn them on the beach, or just watch the flames and fireworks.

# Itineraries

Brighton Royal Pavilion

# Decadent Brighton

Decadence is Brighton's *raison d'être*. Ever since the profligate Prince of Wales swaggered down in 1783 with his entourage of gamblers, drunks and lovers, Brighton's reputation for sybaritic pleasures has been cemented.

This half-day walk takes you on a journey from Brighton's role as the Prince's playground to its current status as candidate for one of Britain's hippest cities, via the inns, hotels and bathing machines of the Regency period, the cheap tattle of the Victorian day-trippers, the gangs of the 1930s, the mods and rockers of the 1960s and the cheap thrills of the kiss-me-quick and candyfloss era – not forgetting the city's enduring potential for a dirty weekend (after all, the first ever blue movie was shot in Brighton – in 1896). The walk could take much longer – depending on how much time you indulge in Brighton's historic hostelries.

The route begins at Britain's most extravagant and opulent regal residence: the **Brighton Royal Pavilion** (p83). The Prince Regent's palace – Indian on the outside, dragon-festooned Chinese inside – was transformed into an extravagant party pad when George became regent in 1811. He had John Nash create a no-expense-spared oriental fantasy, an opulent, camp and endlessly spectacular series of rooms recently restored in a £10 million refit. The banqueting room alone, with its extraordinary chandelier, is worth the admission fee. Elsewhere, tiny royal beds are embellished with lacquered dragon patterns, and the ballroom and music room exude regal style. The twin exotic gateways, bulbous domes, turrets and minarets are all Nash's interpretation of what Eastern architecture was meant to be. George invited the nation's creative, beautiful and ambitious young things to join him for a life of drinking, riding, bathing, womanising and gambling – and foppish Londoners followed in droves. All at a time when poverty in Britain was worsening.

After you emerge from the Royal Pavilion, walk through the landscaped gardens towards the pedestrianised New Road. The Prince celebrated his 33rd birthday here in 1795 with a vast firework display; in 1802, an exploding 'Mount Vesuvius' was built.

Straight ahead is the **Theatre Royal** (p103), which opened in 1807 with a performance of *Hamlet* starring Drury Lane favourite Charles Kemble. On the right is the **Brighton Dome** complex (p102). Once the stables for 60 horses and the quarters of the Prince Regent's grooms and stable boys, it's now one of the city's most important cultural venues, encompassing the Corn Exchange, Concert Hall and Pavilion Theatre. It's also the centrepiece of the Brighton Festival (see box p39), held each May. Trot back past **Fitzherberts** (p88), a pub named after the Prince's first lover, and the **Mash Tun** (p92) – both popular pre-gig drinks venues – down to Pavilion Parade and the Old Steine. It's here that Brighton society would parade in their finest, attempting to catch the eye of royalty. It's also from here that the Master of Ceremonies, common to spa towns, would direct the social events of the 'season' that lasted from spring to autumn.

On summer days, modern visitors still like to relax around the Victoria Fountain, built in 1846, and from here you can see the reason Brighton exists: the sea.

Although a fishing village has existed in this area since at least the 12th century, it was the fashion for spas and sea bathing that led the Prince of Wales to come to

Brighton, 'the Queen of the Watering Places'. The nobility had previously derided bathing in the sea, but after the publication of snappily titled pamphlets such as *Dissertation of the Use of Sea Water in Diseases of the Glands* by Lewes physician Dr Richard Russell in 1750, all that changed. Bathing took place out of bathing machines – wooden coaches that were drawn into the sea by horses. These coaches were controlled by 'dippers', mostly female, who touted for business along the Steine. Some men chose to bathe nude, although they were fined if seen without clothes (today, a nudist beach exists further along Madeira Drive). The most famous dipper was Martha Gunn (1726-1815), who was favoured by the Prince himself.

Using the defence that 'taking water' (up to 14 pints of sea water was recommended) was an antidote for wanton living, London society would decamp to Brighton for the 'season'. It was, of course, an excuse for wanton living; spending three months by the sea, gambling, drinking, partying and parading. With the visitors came coffee houses, inns and lodging houses.

During the first 20 years of the 19th century, Brighton's population tripled to 24,000 as development spread east to Kemp Town and west towards Hove. Hotels sprang up along the seafront, as did the first ever example of that peculiar Victorian engineering feat: the pleasure pier. The first of three in Brighton, the Royal Suspension Chain Pier, was opened in 1823 with a firework display. Its attractions included souvenir stalls and a camera obscura, but it lasted only until 1896, when it was brought down in a storm.

Walk on to **Brighton Pier** (p78), previously called the Palace Pier.

ITINERARIES

To the west you'll see the haunting remains of the **West Pier** (p60), burnt beyond repair, under suspicious circumstances, in 2003. It once had a concert hall, theatre and amusement arcade, but despite its elegance the pier was beset with problems for most of its 150 years.

Brighton Pier itself was always a more populist affair. Opened in 1889, it initially hosted a theatre, a bandstand and – later – a big wheel. Entertainment included freak shows, and haunted houses with mock executions. Today, its gaudy entertainment still provides the archetypal seaside experience.

By the time the trains arrived in 1841, the Palace Pier was Brighton's most popular tourist destination. Queen Victoria, however, wasn't a great fan of the city – she stripped down the Pavilion and took the furnishings to London. A stern statue of Victoria still overlooks the building in disapproval.

After exploring Brighton Pier, re-cross Grand Junction Road and turn left, before taking a right into East Street. Capitalising on the decadent vibe of the 21st century is **Madame Geisha** (p110), a fun cocktail bar that often has burlesque dancers swinging over the bar. Next door is **Lola Lo** (p110), a new Tiki bar, and also the **Platinum Lace** 'Gentleman's Club'. Eagle-eyed *Quadrophenia* fans will recognise Pool Passage, a grotty alleyway where Jimmy and Steph consummated their brief relationship during the film's riot scenes. Fans arrive from all over the world stop to photograph this alleyway. Walk through it yourself, reading the graffiti, on to Little East Street. In front of you will be the Town Hall, home to the **Old Police Cells Museum** (p104). This modest museum highlights Brighton's decadent and criminal

past. It tells the story of how the Chief Constable himself, Henry Solomon, was killed by a prisoner in 1844. You'll also see graffiti from the imprisoned mods and rockers who fought in front of Palace Pier during the 'Battle of Brighton' in 1964, although Brighton's decline into a seedy seaside destination – an image it has since shaken off – began even earlier.

By the beginning of the 20th century, Brighton was tired. The Royal York Hotel on the Old Steine was derelict, after once holding opulent balls, recitals and readings from the likes of Charles Dickens. The *Daily Mail* called Brighton an 'unenterprising, unattractive and outdated holiday resort.' This was the Brighton that Graham Greene portrayed in his book *Brighton Rock*, published in 1938 and first made into a film in 1947. The opening salvo of the film stated: 'Brighton today is a large, jolly, friendly seaside town in Sussex, exactly one hour's journey from London. But in the years between the two wars, behind the Regency terraces and crowded beaches, there was another Brighton of dark alleyways and festering slums. From here, the poison of crime and violence and gang warfare began to spread, until the challenge was taken up by the Police.'

After leaving the Old Police Cells Museum, walk along Prince Albert Street to the **Cricketers** (p105). This lovely pub was used for a scene in Greene's novel – the author himself was a friend of the landlord, and correspondence between the two can be seen in the upstairs Greene Room. Yet, its past is even more debauched than the one Greene portrayed. There's been a pub on the site since 1547, when the first landlord, Deryk Carver, was burnt as a martyr (the Bonfire Night celebrations in Lewes

Cricketers

commemorate him and 15 others). It also reputedly once housed Jack the Ripper, who was partial to prostitutes, a demographic familiar with the pub in the Victorian age. There were more than 100 brothels in the city during the mid-1800s, and the original booths they used to hide behind can be seen in the courtyard of the Cricketers. The landlords, who live in the building, are still convinced it's haunted, but that didn't stop drinkers such as Laurence Olivier and his friend John Gielgud visiting.

You're now in the heart of medieval Brighton – the Lanes. Take time to get lost among the narrow twittens that once housed Brighton's fishing community. Continue along Prince Albert Street and turn right down Ship Street. On the left is **Tickled** (p110), one of Brighton's 'erotic gift shops' for women, and further down the road, heading down Ship Street Gardens to the right, is its sister store, **She Said**, at no.11.

It was during the 1950s and '60s when Brighton's reputation moved on from being a gangland (somewhat over-exaggerated by Greene's novel) to being a cheap holiday destination. One of the key marketing features of the time were the Promettes, who appeared in newsreels across the world. Six women each year were chosen to be a Promette. One newspaper described them as 'walking information bureaux with sex appeal.' They were a great success.

The post-war period in the UK was the first time regular workers could make the most of the Holiday with Pay Act, and people came to Brighton in droves. It was the era of candy floss and clairvoyants, donkey rides and dirty weekends. Mods and rockers regularly caused a fracas. The most notorious battle happened in 1964, but incidents happened over Bank Holiday weekends into the 1980s.

Emerging from Ship Street Gardens, you'll be met with decadence of another type, this time cocoa-fuelled: the **Bar du Chocolat** (p105). Its cakes and hot chocolate – made by the same team behind **Choccywoccydoodah** (p109) – are rich and sublime. After a sugar hit, walk up Middle Street to Duke Street where you'll find the flagship store and, almost opposite, another tempting Brighton chocolatier, **Montezuma's** (p110).

Hotfoot it through Churchill Square and down onto Russell Square for some liquid refreshment. There are dozens of great pubs all across Brighton, but a couple of the best are hidden in the town centre, such as the **Evening Star** (p62) and **Lion & Lobster** (p64). One of the most beguiling pubs is the **Regency Tavern** (p67). It dates back to the 1700s, having been both a coffee house and then the Gatehouse pub, charging a toll for anyone walking through the twitten to parade around Regency Square. (A sign read: 'This gateway hangs well and hinders none. Refresh and pay from travel on.') Today, the decor lies somewhere between opulent and kitsch, with gold cherubs, crimson drapes and a disco-ball in the loo. It's a suitable last stop in our decadent history of Brighton, showing how the glamour of the past 300 years continues well into the 21st century, and for years to come.

And why, exactly, has Brighton's decadent reputation endured to the present day? We turn again to *Brighton Rock* for the final word:

*Rose: People change.*
*Ida: I've never changed. It's like those sticks of rock. Bite one all the way down, you'll still read Brighton. That's human nature.*

# The Perfect Family Day Out

Garish rock shops, an aquarium (with sharks!), a pier with a rollercoaster overlooking the sea, and even a toy museum – Brighton is one huge, brightly lit, high-octane playground for children. Although sandcastles prove tricky on the pebble beach (a stone fort or names written in white rocks will suffice), the waterfront is still the most enticing attraction in Brighton – and it's free. There are, of course, plenty of places to part with a pound or two; and mostly worth the money. This itinerary picks out a tried and tested agenda (almost) guaranteed to keep the little ones attentive, and offer parents family-friendly places for a caffeine boost.

If you're planning a day's worth of under-age entertainment, start off at a familiar point of reference, where you can release your own inner child, **Brighton Pier** (p78).

With a funfair, an arcade dome and kiosks selling mini-doughnuts and cotton candy, the pier will whisk you back to your childhood while embedding future nostalgia in your offspring.

Five quid lighter from the arcade claw, it's time to head east along the seafront to take a ride on **Volk's Electric Railway** (p115), the oldest of its kind in the UK. The linear but endearing route goes to the Marina and back every 15 minutes. The railway only operates in the summer, so if you're looking to get out of the rain in November, visit the nearby **Sea Life Centre** (p114). Inside, there's an underwater tunnel, an interactive rock pool where children can touch various robust sea creatures and, most exciting of all, a chance to see live sharks (they're not among the touchables).

Sea Life Centre p47

Moving on from skipping stones and chasing seagulls, make your way up to **North Laine** (p82). Yes, it's the stomping ground of hip students and musos, but don't let their skinny jeans and spiky hair intimidate your young family – you'll see there are just as many fashionable toddlers as twenty-somethings, and the state-of-the-art **Jubilee Library** on Jubilee Street is a godsend for parents looking to distract quizzical minds while having a chance to savour a cup of coffee. The library hosts a range of daily drop-in activities: take part in 'baby boogie', a twice-monthly musical jam session for tots or join the Sunday morning craft time. Keeping the kiddos amused in a productive way is the name of the game here.

Stomachs starting to grumble? The neighbourhood is filled with cafés and restaurants, yet finding one that fits a pram or provides highchairs isn't always simple. **Brighton Dome**'s café (p102) is popular with yummy mummies and their brightly dressed toddlers, as is **Jamie's Italian** (p107) over in the Lanes. If the sun is shining,

a more pleasant option is to grab some fruit and cheese at **Bill's** (p87) and have a picnic in the gardens of the **Royal Pavilion** (p83). Chomp on a sandwich and lap up the free entertainment in the form of buskers and bongo players. The kids can also gaze in amazement at the extravagant Royal Pavilion itself. The inside tour might be a stretch for kids, but you can tell them a spoiled young man named George had it built for fun.

If pester power begins to take hold, nip across North Street to **the Lanes** (p103), which is home to many excellent independent shops, including **Brighton Bead Shop** (p96), where children can make their own necklaces and bracelets. Another favourite for kids and their parents is **Cyber Candy** (p97), a sweet shop selling a wide assortment of nostalgic and kitsch brands of all things sugar-coated. (For something a touch more constructive, you can always head off-route to the **Lego Store** at **Churchill Square Shopping Centre** (p71), but perhaps you're better to save this as a final treat before going home.)

Head back to North Laine along Bond Street, which becomes Gardner Street, where **Komedia** (p102) is one of Brighton's most frequented gig venues. Once a month on a Sunday, however, the popular Baby Loves Disco takes place, a 'rave' for kids who get to shake their booties to real DJ sets as their amused parents look on.

Keep heading north and west towards the station, where you'll find the **Brighton Toy & Model Museum** (p87). Exhibits of old toys spanning back 100 years will give some insight to your little one as to what life was like pre-Xbox.

Just outside the train station, catch the number 27 or 27A bus; a ten-minute ride will take you to the **Booth Museum of Natural History** (p137), a wonderful little attraction that's often overlooked by visitors. There are thousands of specimens on display, including a thorough collection of British birds and some exciting dinosaur bones. Admission is free and it provides interactive activities for kids to learn about fossils and the natural world.

In front of the Booth Museum is one of Brighton's nicest parks. **Dyke Road Park** has clear views of the sea and a safe designated children's play area. It's a quiet green space, ideal for letting your kids run amuck while you take a breather at the park's café.

Continue across the park to Old Shoreham Road and hail a taxi to the **Hove Museum & Art Gallery** (p148). Of note here is the 'Wizard's Attic', a gallery where toys come to retire (kind of a hokey year-round version of Santa's business premises). The museum also has a cinema room screening fascinating short films of the Hove area at the turn of the 20th century.

Take Church Road east to the city centre, making sure to stop at the **Book Nook** (First Avenue, Hove, 911988, www.booknookuk. com) on the way. This children's bookshop stocks quality books for babies to teens, including dual-language books and curriculum-specific literature. The reading ship in the middle of the store is fun for kids, and there's a café for parents.

**ITINERARIES**

Brighton Pier p47

Hotel Pelirocco p52

# Brighton Rock Music Tour

Brighton & Hove has spawned a glittering line of local bands and artists, and provided inspiration to many visiting ones. One of the best ways to get into the spirit of the city is to immerse yourself in its music. Here, then, is a walk around some of its musical hotspots, with accompanying playlist.

Start any time after noon by heading down from the rail station along Trafalgar Street, where you can't fail to notice a massive portrait of John Peel on the side wall of the **Prince Albert** (p95) pub. Like the legendary late DJ, the Albert is a dedicated proponent of unsigned bands; browse hundreds of old gig posters inside to discover which stars played here before they were famous. The Albert is also adorned with the notorious Banksy work, *Kissing Coppers*, which you'll find to the bottom right of John Peel.

A little further down Trafalgar Street is **Adaptatrap Percussion** (p95). In addition to stocking an impressive range of unusual instruments from around the globe, this shop's a favourite hangout for Brighton & Hove's spirited world-music community. (A leading light among them is klezmer virtuoso Merlin Shepherd, whose *Never Enough Cilantro, My Dear* will galvanise you to continue your wander around North Laine.)

Turn right on to Sydney Street, then take the second left, Gloucester Road, where you'll discover the intimate **Basketmakers Arms** (p87). Best accompanied by a pint of Harveys, the Miserable Rich's *Somerhill* describes the sometimes claustrophobic experience of living in a city where degrees of separation are minimal and secrets hard to keep. Investigate the contents of the tins around the walls as you listen out for a reference to your surroundings.

Retrace your steps back up Gloucester Road and take a left on to Kensington Gardens, where record shop **Resident** (p99) sits halfway down on the left. The knowledgeable staff will be only too happy to discuss hot local bands and their favourite new music. While you're at it, ask them when the next in-store gig is coming up – some fairly well known bands have played acoustic gigs here, promoting new albums. At the end of Kensington Gardens, turn right to detour along North Road to the well-stocked **Guitar, Amp & Keyboard Centre** (p98).

Otherwise, cross over to Gardner Street for **Jump the Gun** (p99), where mod culture – encapsulated in that iconic Brighton-based film, *Quadrophenia* – is alive and well. Listen to the title track of the Who's 1966 rock opera as you browse the shop's vintage wares. (Rockers will be wishing they had dropped into bikers' haven **Ampwitch**, back by Adaptatrap at 22 Trafalgar Street).

A few doors along on Gardner Street is one of Brighton's top music and arts venues, **Komedia** (p102). Pick up a programme as you wander past, or stop for a coffee and a cake in its cosy café while you find out what's on. Especially recommended are the regular alternative club and cabaret nights hosted here, including Rockabilly girls' night Born Bad, and Spellbound, 'an '80s night for people who hate '80s nights.' For a taste of Brighton's dark burlesque musical underbelly, listen to local band Birdeatsbaby's *I Always Hang Myself with the Same Rope*.

At the end of Gardner Street, turn left on to Church Street, past two notable music venues, the **Brighton Dome** (p102) and

the **Corn Exchange** (p102). Familiarise yourself with two notable Brighton bands as you cross at the lights over the Old Steine and turn right, then left, on to Edward Street. Brakes' 2005 hit *All Night Disco Party* will get you in the mood for a Brighton (or Hove) night out, or if you're planning a more sedate evening, the Mummers will soothe you with *Nightbus*. Second-hand record collectors can buy and sell vinyl, CDs, tapes and games at **Replay** (179 Edward Street, 673200), while guitar aficionados will enjoy **Aguilera Guitars** (673200, www.aguilera-guitars.co.uk), a few doors down at no.175.

Continue up Edward Street, then take a right down George Street. A little way along, at no.24, is **Bom-Bane's** (p115), a tiny little restaurant and music venue run by eccentric folk singer/songwriter Jane Bom-Bane. Stay for a drink or dinner and you might be treated to some spontaneous music from the woman herself. Failing that, choose some of Jane's partner Nick Pynn's acclaimed fiddle music from your playlist – *The Devil Went Down to Georgia* is recommended.

At the end of George Street, you'll find yourself in the heart of Brighton's gay village: St James's Street. Turn right then left into Manchester Street, home of the **Latest Music Bar** (p130), which has enjoyed many incarnations as a successful music venue – with artists from Amy Winehouse to Herbie Flowers having played here. From Manchester Street, turn right on to Marine Parade, which turns into Grand Junction Road past the pier, and then King's Road. As you wander past the hotels and B&Bs along the front, listen to Queen's *Brighton Rock*, which tells of an illicit love affair conducted in Brighton over a public holiday.

**ITINERARIES**

A bimble around the quirky winding alleyways of the Lanes is best accompanied by some of Brighton's more esoteric local music. Try Nic Dawson Kelly's *Mr Musician* and Salter Cane's *People Get Lost* as you turn right up East Street, left into Bartholomew Square, left down Meeting House Lane (which then spikes off to the right) and right again into Brighton Square. Pop into Brighton's longest established independent record shop, **Rounder Records** (p110), for more band recommendations and all the latest gig listings.

Wiggle your way out of the Lanes again, via Ship Street, Duke Street, Middle Street and Boyce's Street, which will bring you out on the distinctly insalubrious West Street. The only reason for coming here is to listen to *Rumble in Brighton Tonight* by the Stray Cats. If you're here on a Friday or Saturday night, it'll make even more sense.

Nick Cave at Brighton Centre

Turn left down West Street towards the sea, then right at the end along King's Road, where you can't miss the ugly, atmosphere-free **Brighton Centre** (p77) – sadly, the only venue with the capacity for hosting major bands in Brighton & Hove. Recent acts have included Gorillaz, Nick Cave, Vampire Weekend and Jeff Wayne's spectacular, *War of the Worlds*.

Two of the city's most famous musical imports are Nick Cave and Norman Cook (aka Fatboy Slim), both of whom currently reside in Hove. Cross the road at the lights just past the Grand Hotel and make your way down on to the beach, where, in 2002, Fatboy Slim's Big Beach Boutique II became one of those 'were you there?' events, as 250,000 revellers (more than the population of the city) piled into Brighton to see the DJ do his thing.

Once you've got over this startling prospect, take a walk west along the promenade towards Hove, spurred on by Cave's *Dig Lazarus, Dig!!!* and Cook's classic *Right Here, Right Now.* Cross at the pedestrian crossing opposite Preston Street and double back to Regency Square. Your final destination is **Hotel Pelirocco** (p171), a boutique hotel and venue themed around pop subculture, with rooms designed by Primal Scream's Bobby Gillespie (who had a legendary party here) and members of Asian Dub Foundation. Primal Scream's *Autobahn66* is featured on the *Hotel Pelirocco: Music from the Legendary Hotel* compilation, which you should be able to buy at reception.

Wherever you're heading from here, take local songstress Martha Tilston with you and listen to her *Brighton Song*, which proclaims 'nothing can stop us, we're effervescing.' Hopefully by now you'll know where she's coming from.

# Brighton by Area

# Central Brighton

Central Brighton has many faces. **North Laine** and **the Lanes** are together the creative, culinary and eccentric heart of Brighton, ticking playfully along in a fantastical bubble where niche shops solely selling bonsai trees, comics or vegetarian shoes do a thriving trade, and 'organic' and 'vintage' are the buzzwords du jour. The North Laine section of this guide is where you'll also find the Cultural Quarter – a small district surrounding the **Royal Pavilion** and the **Brighton Dome** complex.

It seems strange to say, but the **City Centre** area is often culturally under-appreciated. The Lanes might have their chic boutiques and North Laine remains custodian of Brighton's hippy soul, but turn an unassuming corner or climb a steep residential hill and you're in a different, less visited world, with many of the best pubs in the city, several small independent theatres and galleries

and plenty more unusual shops. The **Seven Dials** area up Dyke Road is one of Brighton's most up-and-coming areas, with new shops, restaurants and bars opening at a fair rate. The seven streets running off the roundabout are attracting many new ventures.

Brighton's principal attraction, though, is the **seafront**. Running west from the gaudy **Brighton Pier** alongside the beachfront promenade are the **King's Arches** – occupied by art galleries, museums, shops, restaurants and pubs. It's also where Brighton comes out to play in the summer, spending the days reading on the expansive beach or playing sports until the sun sets spectacularly over the strangely stirring skeleton of the **West Pier**.

For this guide, we have divided the Central Brighton chapter into four subheadings: City Centre, Seafront (p78), North Laine (p82) and the Lanes (p103).

## City Centre

There's a tendency to misconceive the city centre, within a ten-minute walk of the clock tower, as just the commercial zone around the crowded shopping areas of Western Road and Churchill Square, plus the clubbing destination of West Street, a vortex of hen parties where the smell of Lynx Pulse seems to steam up from the pavements.

This is far from true, of course. Step one street to the left or right of the crowds and Brighton's city centre reveals plenty of character. There still remain some interesting shops that, although often pushed out of the main arcades, are worth hunting out. And some of the most beautiful buildings in Brighton (including the cartoonishly gothic Wykeham Terrace, a refuge for 'fallen' women in the 1830s), as well as quirky cafés and innovative art galleries, can be found here too.

The Clifton and Montpelier conservation area is a living museum of sparkling white Regency and Victorian architecture, and even has its own festival (www.cmpcaonline.org.uk) every summer, with music and literary events based around two historic churches: **St Nicholas** on Dyke Road, and **Saint Michael's & All Angels** on Victoria Road, famed for its stained glass by William Morris. Clifton Terrace also offers one of the most striking views of the sea – framed by high rises Chartwell Court and Sussex Heights – as do the quiet rose gardens and playing field up at Dyke Road park.

**Seven Dials** (a quaint name for what is essentially a roundabout) is a compact alternative shopping spot full of independent gift shops and delis. Meanwhile, Upper North Street (and its westerly extension, Montpelier Place) is gradually developing into its own artists' quarter. The modest little row of shop fronts now accommodates various studio stores, including bag-makers **Steve & Alistair** (p74) who searched all over London and Paris before choosing a little room on this back street to set up shop.

The section between Western Road and the sea is home to most types of eaterie, from fish restaurants overlooking the West Pier to atmospherically wind-swept cafés and the international takeaway joints of Preston Street.

## Eating & drinking

### Bankers

*116a Western Road, BN1 2AB (328267, www.bankers-restaurant. co.uk). Bus 1, 2, 5, 6, 20, 46, 49, 52.* **Open** 11.30am-10pm daily. **££**. **Fish & chips**. **Map** p57 A4 ①

A standard order averages around £8 at this large, old-fashioned chippy, but then they do have a chandelier. Takeaways (many destined for the beach straight down the road) queue to the right, while eat-in diners sit at wooden tables and can choose from a fair-priced wine list or a bar selling bottled beers, liqueurs and Irish coffees. On Saturday evenings, it's a chink into another time as OAPs in tweed suits linger over jelly puddings.

### Barry at the Tureen

*31 Upper North Street, BN1 3FG (328939). Bus 1, 2, 5, 6, 20, 46, 49, 52.* **Open** 7pm-late Wed-Sat. **££**. **Classic English**. **Map** p57 D4 ②

Barry Would be chef, waiter and host at this tiny restaurant, which dates back to 1964 and has had the same kitsch Liberty print seating (and many of the same customers) since he took over two decades ago. The intimacy and English menu (pan-fried calf's liver) all add to the sense of dining in someone's front room.

BRIGHTON BY AREA

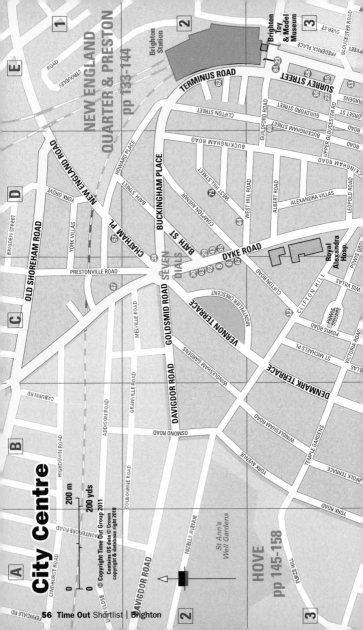

# City Centre

NEW ENGLAND
QUARTER & PRESTON
pp 133-144

Brighton
Station

Brighton
Toy
& Model
Museum

TERMINUS ROAD

SURREY STREET

CLIFTON STREET

BUCKINGHAM ROAD

GUILDFORD ROAD

GUILDFORD STREET

BUCKINGHAM STREET

UPPER GLOUCESTER RD

GLOUCESTER ROAD

FREDERICK PLACE

OVER ST

TERRACE ROAD

STROUDLEY ROAD

NEW ENGLAND ROAD

YORK GROVE

HOWARD PLACE

BUCKINGHAM PLACE

CHATHAM PL

BATH STREET

BATH ST

SEVEN
DIALS

WEST HILL STREET

COMPTON AVENUE

WEST HILL ROAD

ALBERT ROAD

ALEXANDRA VILLAS

LEOPOLD ROAD

DYKE ROAD

CLIFTON ROAD

Royal
Alexandra
Hosp.

POWIS ROAD

BRIGDEN STREET

YORK VILLAS

OLD SHOREHAM ROAD

PRESTONVILLE ROAD

CABURN RD

HIGHDOWN ROAD

MELVILLE ROAD

GOLDSMID ROAD

WINDLESHAM GARDENS

MONTPELIER CRESCENT

VERNON TERRACE

CLIFTON HILL

WIS VILLAS

ST MICHAELS PL

POWIS ROAD

VICTORIA ROAD

POWIS
SQUARE

ADDISON ROAD

GRANVILLE ROAD

DAVIGDOR ROAD

OSMOND ROAD

WINDLESHAM ROAD

DENMARK TERRACE

TEMPLE GARDENS

YORK AVENUE

NORFOLK TERRACE

COLBOURNE ROAD

MONTEFIORE ROAD

NIZELLS AVENUE

St Ann's
Well Gardens

DAVIGDOR ROAD

FURZE HILL

YORK ROAD

HOVE
pp 145-158

LINDHURST ROAD

FERNDALE ROAD

CLOSE

## 200 m
## 200 yds

© Copyright Time Out Group 2011
Contains OS data ©
Crown
copyright & database right 2010

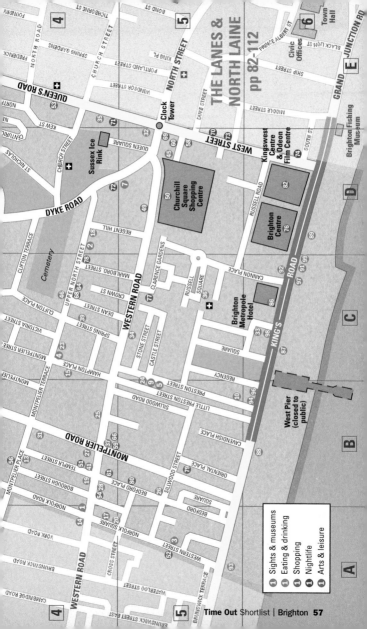

# THE LANES & NORTH LAINE
## pp 82-112

FOUNDRY

FREDERICK ROAD

QUEEN'S ROAD

FOUNDRY ST

TICHBORNE ST

BOND ST

SPRING GARDENS

CHURCH STREET

NORTH ROAD

FREDERICK ST

NORTH GARDENS

SPRING GARDENS

WINDSOR STREET

KING PL

PORTLAND STREET

NORTH STREET

Sussex Ice Rink

QUEEN SQUARE

Clock Tower

DUKE STREET

WEST STREET

Churchill Square Shopping Centre 50

CLARENCE GARDENS

RUSSELL SQUARE

RUSSELL ROAD

Kingswest Centre & Odeon Film Centre

Brighton Centre 76

82

Brighton Fishing Museum

Town Hall

Civic Offices

BLACK LION ST

SHIP STREET

MIDDLE STREET

SOUTH ST

GRAND JUNCTION RD

PRINCE ALBERT ST

SHIP STREET

DYKE ROAD

ST NICHOLAS

CHURCH STREET

KEW ST

NORTH

CENTURION

CLIFTON TERRACE

Cemetery

REGENT HILL

MARLBORO STREET

UPPER NORTH STREET

CROWN ST

CLIFTON PLACE

VICTORIA STREET

DEAN STREET

SPRING STREET

WESTERN ROAD

STONE STREET

CASTLE STREET

CANNON PLACE

Brighton Metropole Hotel

King's Road

KING'S ROAD

MONTPELIER STREET

MONTPELIER TERRACE

HAMPTON PLACE

MONTPELIER

MONTPELIER ROAD

MONTPELIER PLACE

TEMPLE STREET

BOROUGH STREET

BEDFORD PLACE

NORFOLK ROAD

NORFOLK SQUARE

YORK ROAD

BRUNSWICK ROAD

CAMBRIDGE ROAD

WESTERN ROAD

CROSS STREET

WATERLOO STREET

BRUNSWICK STREET EAST

PRESTON STREET

LITTLE PRESTON STREET

SILLWOOD ROAD

SILLWOOD STREET

CAVENDISH PLACE

ORIENTAL PLACE

BEDFORD SQUARE

WESTERN STREET

REGENCY SQUARE

West Pier (closed to public)

Brighton Metropole Hotel

- Sights & museums
- Eating & drinking
- Shopping
- Nightlife
- Arts & leisure

# The travel apps city lovers have been waiting for...

## Apps and maps work offline with no roaming charges

Search for 'Time Out Guides' in the app store

**timeout.com/iphonecityguides**

## Bedford Tavern

*30 Western Street, BN1 2PG (739495). Bus 1, 2, 5, 6, 20, 46, 49, 52.* **Open** noon-midnight Mon-Thur, Sun; noon-1am Fri, Sat. **Pub**. Map p57 A5 ❸

This 200-year-old pub has kept many original features, including exposed beams, a fireplace and, if the numerous ghost stories are to be believed, even some of yesteryear's clientele. Following a period in the doldrums, it has been restored to glory as a straight-friendly, mainly gay and lesbian local. Think country pub – with weekly drag acts.

## Billies Café

*34 Hampton Place, BN1 3DD (774386). Bus 1, 2, 5, 6, 20, 46, 49, 52.* **Open** 8.30am-4pm daily. **£**. No credit cards. **Café**. Map p57 C4 ❹

A cosy crush of blue checked tablecloths and wasted clubbers, this small corner café is a hangover institution thanks to its extensive hash menu. You can look forward to a giant slab of fried potato and onion topped with everything from guacamole, salsa and sour cream (the 'Mexican') or variations on a full English breakfast.

## Binari

*31 Preston Steet, BN1 2HP (567004, www.binarikorean.co.uk). Bus 1, 2, 5, 6, 20, 46.* **Open** 11.30am-11pm daily. **££**. **Korean**. Map p57 B5 ❺

Authentic Korean restaurant where dishes such as *jjigae* (a spicy tofu stew, here served with brown rice) and *bibimbap* (mixed rice with vegetables and various seasoned meats) arrive in stone bowls, and homemade ice-cream comes in flavours such as plum or ginseng. Six set menus, each of which is a mini-education in the cuisine, all come in at under £20.

## Blenio

*87-93 Dyke Road, BN1 3JE (220220, www.bleniobistro.com). Bus 50, 56.* **Open** noon-3pm, 7pm-close Wed-Sat; noon-9pm Sun. **££**. **Modern British**. Map p56 D3 ❻

Blenio is a modern bistro where the limited menu (six seasonal mains for lunch and dinner, and only one vegetarian option) is testimony to the freshness of the food. Piles of breads and herbs lend a homely feel, while exposed brick and candlelit tables set the scene for rustic romance. A strong wine list supports dishes such as Rye Bay skate with caper dressing.

## Café Arcadia

*15 Imperial Arcade, BN1 3EA (326600). Bus 1, 2, 5, 6, 20, 46, 49, 52.* **Open** 8am-6pm Mon-Sat. **£**. No credit cards. **Café**. Map p57 D5 ❼

Holding its own against the encroaching Starbucks, Costas and Caffé Neros, this small independent tearoom has its entrance in the Imperial Arcade, though a plant-edged window winks invitingly out onto Dyke Road. Fried breakfasts, baked potatoes and other homely snacks are served by waitresses you nostalgically imagine spending their earnings on the pier.

Billies Café

# Towering over the past

A futuristic 180-metre high observation tower on the seafront, at the head of the derelict West Pier, is set to become Brighton's newest attraction.

The **West Pier** (www.westpier. co.uk) has become the city's most controversial icon. It was built in 1866, and by the start of the 20th century had become the place to be for the middle classes, with a bandstand, a pavilion and a large concert hall with glass panelling giving its distinctive profile.

By World War I, the West Pier had become one of the country's leading pleasure piers, and it continued to thrive until after World War II, when changing holiday habits caused it to fall into neglect. It closed in 1975, but proposals for demolition were obstructed by thousands of demonstrating Brightonians, who cherished it as a landmark of seaside architecture. In the 1980s, it was sold for £100 to the newly formed West Pier Trust,

which pleaded for funding to repair it right up until the storm of 2002 and fire of 2003 that left it in a state of permanent ruin.

To give new life to the site, the Trust submitted plans in 2006 for the **Brighton i360** tower, scheduled to open in 2012. This striking attraction, set to be taller than the London Eye (and from the same architects, Marks Barfield), will afford visitors 360-degree views from 490 feet (150 metres) above sea level. They will reach these dizzying heights not in an elevator but in a ring-shaped pod that will travel up and down a slender stem, carrying up to 200 passengers at a time. Dramatic, certainly, but locals are divided over whether the i360 will be eyesore or icon.

As for the West Pier itself, the Trust says that 'a new pier remains the goal', but the skeletal remains of the original – far beyond restoration and likely to be left to the elements – suggest that it may be a distant one.

## Café One Ten

*109C Dyke Road, BN1 3JE (737310).*
*Bus 50, 56.* **Open** 8.30am-5pm
Mon-Sat. **£**. No credit cards. **Café**.
**Map** p56 A5 ⑧
This little roadside café must sell more
breakfasts and lunches than all the
other Seven Dials eateries put together,
and not just because it neighbours
Ladbrokes. Smoothies, toasties, crispy
BLTs on granary and pasta-based spe-
cials are all cheap, homemade and
quick out of the kitchen.

## Casalingo

*29 Preston Street, BN1 2HP (328775,*
*www.casalingo.co.uk). Bus 1, 2, 5, 6,*
*20, 46, 49, 52.* **Open** 5-11pm Mon-
Thur; 5-11.30pm Fri, Sat. **Italian**.
**££. Map** p57 B5 ⑨
The red painted arches and a wall of
approving customer graffiti lend
Casalingo a casual air, but this cosy
Italian takes its cooking seriously. The
à la carte menu is divided into familiar pasta and risotto, meat and fish
options, while chef's specials have
included calf's liver in Frascati wine
and artichokes with fontina cheese.

## China Garden

*88-91 Preston Street, BN1 2HG*
*(325124, www.chinagarden.name).*
*Bus 1, 2, 5, 6, 20, 46, 49.* **Open**
noon-11.30pm daily. **££. Chinese**.
**Map** p57 B5 ⑩
A 150-seat Chinese restaurant just off
the seafront, whose harsh black
frontage gives way to a warm, carpeted
space framed by sofas and filled with
the tinkling of a piano. Try squid
cakes and turnip paste from the imaginative dim sum menu between noon
and 4pm, or East Sussex-sourced Ying
Yang Dover Sole for dinner.

## Cocoa

*48 Queens Road, BN1 3XB (777412,*
*www.cocoabrighton.co.uk). Bus 6, 7, 14,*
*27, 47, 50.* **Open** 8am-6pm Mon-Fri;
9am-7pm Sat; 9am-5pm Sun. **£££**.
**Café. Map** p56 E3 ⑪

Cocoa is a French pâtisserie run by
Raymond Blanc-trained chef Julien
Plumart, making the sort of puddings
that have you reaching surreptitiouly
for your camera phone. They use
French 'Grand Cru' chocolate and
sprinklings of gold dust, producing
beautiful little mousse cakes, eclairs
and fruit tarts. If you eat in, you can
have a glass of fruity wine while
you're at it. There's a big savoury
menu too, but that's hardly the point.

## Crescent

*6 Clifton Hill, BN1 3HL (205260,*
*www.crescentbrighton.com). Bus 50,*
*56.* **Open** noon-11.30pm Mon-Thur,
Sun; noon-midnight Fri, Sat. **Pub**.
**Map** p56 C3 ⑫
Since the smoking ban, the good-sized
beer garden and new, fresh food menu
have elevated this backstreet local into
a popular meeting point. It can get quieter in the evenings, though not on
Tuesday's quiz night.

## La Cucina

*4a Montpelier Place, BN1 3BF*
*(202206, www.lacucinabrighton.co.uk).*
*Bus 51, 82.* **Open** 4-10pm Mon-Thur,
Sun; 4-11pm Fri, Sat. **££. Pizzeria**.
**Map** p57 B4 ⑬
Italian sausage, artichokes, pesto
sauce, fresh rocket, king prawns and
caramelised red onions... the toppings
list at this Italian takeaway says it all.
Choose from 20-plus thin-crust pizzas
(and the odd pasta dish) or design your
own for around £8 for 11-inch or £13
for 15-inch pizzas. There's even a
'Bambinos' pizza for £3. Sides include
pink coleslaw and feta salad, with
tiramisu on the dessert menu.

## Duke of Norfolk

*113-114 Western Road, BN1 2AB*
*(0872 148 6385). Bus 1, 2, 5, 6,*
*20, 46, 49, 52.* **Open** noon-1am
Mon-Thur, Sun; noon-2am Fri, Sat.
**Pub. Map** p57 A4 ⑭
The over-21 policy makes this book-
lined pub a welcome refuge from its

rowdy Western Road neighbours for anyone wishing to enjoy a game of Scrabble and a posh pie along with their draught beer at one of the large wooden tables. Cocktails and shots raise the energy on Friday's DJ nights.

### Estia

*3 Hampton Place, BN1 3DA (777399, www.estiabrighton.com). Bus 1, 2, 5, 6, 20, 46, 49, 52.* **Open** 6pm-late Mon-Sat. **££. Greek. Map** p57 C4 ⑮
This upmarket Greek-Cypriot restaurant is a popular place for parties, with fairy lights behind its white cottage windows and a range of traditional Greek dishes (you'll pay between £10-£13 for chicken souvlaki in a herby marinade or swordfish skewers).

### Evening Star

*55-56 Surrey Street, BN1 3PB (328931, www.eveningstarbrighton.co.uk). Bus 6, 7, 14, 37, 47, 50.* **Open** noon-11pm Mon-Fri, Sun; 11.30am-midnight Sat. **Pub. Map** p56 E3 ⑯

A rustic haven for real-ale types, with Hobbit-friendly ceilings and occasional live music. This independent microbrewery (the fabulous Dark Star) has 10 hand-pumps and a host of unpronounceable Flemish brews by the bottle. Seasonal ales include the Winter Meltdown (Sept-Mar), brewed with chocolate in a cask conditioned with ginger, while the acclaimed Hophead and American Pale Ale are among the regulars on offer.

### La Florentina

*50 Norfolk Square, BN1 2PA (774049). Bus 1 2, 5, 6, 20, 46, 49, 52.* **Open** noon-3pm, 6-10pm Tue-Sun. **££. Italian. Map** p57 A4 ⑰
Holding out barnacle-like against the tidal wave of fast-food joints and estate agents along this stretch of Western Road, this tiny Portuguese-run Italian restaurant has a loyal clientele of couples who enjoy the intimacy and the menu, featuring peach melba and things wrapped up in parma ham.

62 **Time Out** Shortlist | Brighton

## Florist

*22-23 Upper North Street, BN1 3FG (325491). Bus 50, 56.* **Open** noon-midnight Mon-Thur, Sun; noon-1am Fri, Sat. **Pub. Map** p57 D4 ⑱

Formerly the lesbian-friendly PV (Princess Victoria), this is one of the few pubs in the neighbourhood that hasn't turned to serving food. Instead, it offers fresh and airy surroundings (now augmented by a green and white paint job, a fairylight-framed fireplace and wooden tables) in which to sample from its superior wine list.

## La Fourchette

*104-105 Western Road, BN1 2AA (722556, www.lafourchette.co.uk). Bus 1, 2, 5, 6, 20, 46, 49, 52.* **Open** 10am-3pm, 6-10.30pm daily. **£££. French. Map** p57 B4 ⑲

Formal French restaurant where everyone seems to be conducting a business lunch or is meeting their partner's parents for the first time. Mains – such as crispy confit of duck leg, pot-au-feu of mixed fish with coriander cream and rosti turbot with spinach and star anise – leave the kitchen under the watchful eye of Stéphane Frelon and average around £15 (there are also set menus at £10-£15 earlier in the week). The next-door bar has a more limited menu, and serves two-for-one cocktails for £6.50.

## Gingerman

*21a Norfolk Square, BN1 2PD (326688, www.gingermanrestaurants. com). Bus 1, 2, 5, 6, 20, 46, 49, 52.* **Open** 12.30-1.45pm, 7-9.30pm Tue-Sun. **£££. Modern British. Map** p57 A4 ⑳

The original Gingerman (the family also owns three local gastropubs) is a 32-seat restaurant specialising in modern British dishes, set in an elegant town house. The lunch menu is best value, at £18 for three courses or £15 for two. Indulgent dinner options include cumin-spiced lamb rack with black cardamom followed by plum tarte tatin with amaretto ice-cream.

## Grand Central

*29-30 Surrey Street, BN1 3PA (329086). Bus 6, 7, 14, 27, 47.* **Open** 11am-midnight Mon-Wed, Sun; 11am-2am Thur-Sat. **Pub. Map** p56 E3 ㉑

This is the first sight to greet your eyes as you exit Brighton Station, which explains why it's always busy, and why the prices are some of the highest in town. There's an abundance of seating, an impressive row of pumps, gastropub food between 11am and 8pm, and even a fantastic theatre – the Nightingale (p77) – upstairs.

## Grocer & Grain

**NEW** *1 Surrey Street, BN1 3PA (823455). Bus 6, 7, 14.* **Open** 8.30am-8pm daily. **Café. Map** p56 E3 ㉒

Local fruit and veg is piled artfully in crates outside, grains and oils such as Sussex Gold line the shelves, and there's organic shandy in the chiller cabinet. Fresh bites include homemade soup through the colder months (served with a chunk of chewy brown bread for £2.50). In a happy hangover from the previous business here, DVDs are stocked.

## Hampton

*57 Upper North Street, BN1 3FH (731347). Bus 50, 56.* **Open** noon-1am Mon-Thur, Sun; noon-2pm Fri, Sat. **Pub. Map** p57 C4 ㉓

Plenty of seating, a heated beer garden and a good roast make this large pub a popular spot for Sunday lunch. Following a recent refurbishment, books and picture frames have joined the sports screens and games machines, and a weekday menu has ideas slightly above its station (the burger comes with homemade tomato relish – and you pay for it).

## Kitchen Bar

*36 Preston Street, BN1 2HP (no phone). Bus 1, 2, 5, 6, 20, 46, 49, 52.* **Open** varies. **Bar. Map** p57 C5 ㉔

More the size of a kitchen cupboard, this tiny bar offers 'proper' drinkers a

Lion & Lobster

welcome alternative to the nearby shot-bars and is so secretive it refuses to give out a telephone number or opening times. It's just big enough to accommodate someone's record collection (a shelf to the right groans with vinyl) and every liquor you could want.

## Koba & Café Koba

*135 Western Road, BN1 2LA (720059, www.kobauk.com). Bus 1, 2, 5, 6, 20, 46, 49, 52.* **Open** 8am-1am Mon-Fri; 8am-3am Sat, Sun. Kitchen 8am-10pm daily. **££. Café/bar. Map** p57 B4 ㉕

This once-secretive cocktail joint has now expanded into a four-tiered café-bar in exposed brick, steel and wood, with six seating areas, from the communal picnic tables out front to the private upstairs rooms. The modern, locally sourced dishes are almost as good as the superb Union coffee and renowned £8-plus cocktails, including a perfect bloody mary spiced according to your liking and the rum-based Berry Spiced with plump raspberries.

## Lion & Lobster

*24 Silwood Street, BN1 2PS (327299, www.thelionandlobster.co.uk). Bus 1, 2, 5, 6, 20, 46, 49, 52.* **Open** 11am-1am Mon-Thur; 11am-2am Fri, Sat; noon-midnight Sun. Kitchen 5-10pm Mon-Fri; noon-10pm Sat, Sun. **££. Pub & restaurant. Map** p57 B5 ㉖

Three floors of cosy backstreet pub (think deep red walls and paintings of hunts) now incorporate a restaurant on the first floor and a takeaway service (10pm-1am Sun-Thur and 10pm-2am Fri, Sat), televised sports throughout the week and a live jazz jam every Sunday. Food ranges from pub grub, such as chips and gravy to Alaskan salmon fillet in the restaurant. The Lion & Lobster is one of the most popular pubs in Brighton – and rightly so. It fills up after work, spilling out onto the pavement on summer days. The party then moves to the roof-top terrace. It manages to suit real-ale fans, late drinkers, lingering lunchers, and everyone for the Sunday roasts.

### Mad Hatter

*38 Montpelier Road, BN3 1AP (no phone, www.themadhattercafe.co.uk).* Bus 1, 2, 5, 6, 20, 46, 49, 52. **Open** 8am-7pm Mon-Sat; 9am-6pm Sun. No credit cards. **£. Café** Map p57 B4 ㉗
Hippyish corner café (downstairs from an acupuncture clinic) where New Age flyers pile up on the shelves and astrologists with laptops solicit custom. It's a popular breakfast spot (their muesli with fresh fruit is healthy and tasty) though it's best known for the Alice In Wonderland-'themed' toasted ciabatta sandwiches (£4.80 with salad). Other mains include houmous salad and goat's cheese tart.

### Mascara

*101 Western Road, BN1 2AA (278185, www.mascara-restaurant. co.uk).* Bus 1, 2, 5, 6, 20, 46, 49, 52. **Open** 5pm-late daily. **£££. North African.** Map p57 B4 ㉘
This North African restaurant (with wine menu and drapery to match the cuisine) has remained something of a secret despite its tempting recipe of hookahs, belly dancers and good food. You can indulge in richly spiced tagines, featuring ingredients such as monkfish or lamb shank.

### Moorish

*84 Dyke Road, BN1 3JD (777765).* Bus 50, 56. **Open** 10am-3pm Mon-Fri. **££. North African deli.** Map p56 D2 ㉙
Your rewards for negotiating the infuriatingly short opening times of this tiny deli are tagines and other North African-influenced dishes you won't find to take away elsewhere in Brighton. Sit among pink and gold cushions while they make you up a combination box.

### Murasaki

*115 Dyke Road, BN1 3JB (326231, www.murasakirestaurant.co.uk).* Bus 50, 56. **Open** 12.30-3pm, 6.30-10.30pm Tue-Sat; 12.30-3pm, 6.30-9.30pm Sun. **£££. Japanese.** Map p56 C2 ㉚

# Out in the city

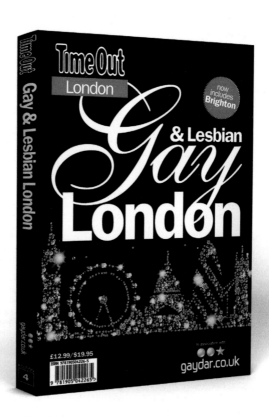

This small Japanese restaurant tucked just off the Seven Dials is intimate and authentic, though better suited to couples than large parties. Approach the large menu tapas-style and order crab tempura, pumpkin rosti or delicately dressed green beans as you go. Prices are fair (raw fish of the day with rice and miso is £6.50).

## Prompt Corner

*36 Montpelier Road, BN1 3BA (737624, www.promptcorner.com). Bus 1, 2, 5, 6, 20, 46, 49, 52.* **Open** 6pm-late Mon-Sat; 1-3pm Sun. **£££. Traditional British**. Map p57 B4 ③①

A favourite post-show haunt for Theatre Royal actors, this characterful basement restaurant just off Western Road has been in the hands of owners Alan and Ken since 1978 – and they have some tales to tell. The British menu is heavy on the fresh fish and steaks, though it always includes vegetarian and gluten-free options.

## Quadrant

*12-13 Queens Road, BN1 3FA (733238). Bus 1, 2, 5, 6, 20, 46, 49, 52.* **Open** 10.30am-midnight Mon-Thur; 10.30am-2am Fri, Sat; 11am-midnight Sun. **Pub**. Map p57 D5 ③②

A grade-II listed pub opposite the Clock Tower, dating back to 1864 and recently refurbished with outdoor tables and a low-ceilinged upstairs lounge that's host to comedy, jazz and blues, and open-mic nights. Dark and masculine, it's popular with real-ale drinkers as well as shoppers breaking for a quick refresher.

## Queensbury Arms

*Queensbury Mews, BN1 2FE (328159). Bus 1, 2, 5, 6, 20, 46, 49, 52.* **Open** noon-11pm Mon-Thur, Sun; noon-midnight Fri, Sat. **Pub**. Map p57 C6 ③③

The smallest pub in Brighton (it just has room for a plaque) is a very cosy, gay-friendly retreat for theatrical types – the bar is lined with signed black and white photos, and legend has it Sir Laurence Olivier once drank half a bottle of champagne here in disguise. There are two small rooms, but it's a pleasant place to have a quick drink. It's 'other' name, the Hole in the Wall, refers to when Royal Fusiliers were served through, yes, a hole in the wall.

## Recipease

NEW *72 Western Road, BN1 2HA (311338, www.jamieoliver.com/ recipease). Bus 1, 2, 5, 6, 20, 46, 49, 52.* **Open** 8am-8pm Mon-Sat; 8am-6pm Sun. **££. Café**. Map p57 C55 ③④

Jamie Oliver's food and kitchen shop opened at the same time as his Italian restaurant on Black Lion Street (p107), and is valued more for its great breakfast menu (the £7 'best beans breakfast' has a chilli kick that's great for hangovers) and bargain £2.50 takeaway lunch deal than for the shop selling branded dressing shakers, and his other endorsed products.

## Red Rooms

*8 Queens Road, BN1 3WA (746705). Bus 1, 2, 5, 6, 20, 46, 49, 52.* **Open** 10pm-2.30am Mon-Thur, Sun, 10pm-3.30am Fri, Sat. **Bar**. Map p57 E4 ③⑤

The Red Rooms, with its blood red bar, furniture, walls and velvet drapes is an overwhelming sight at first, but it won't take you long to settle in to the bordello vibe. As it is, the narrow basement, with its red banquettes and DJ booth, is a swankily claustrophobic spot for a well-mixed cocktail. Please just don't order campari – it'll clash horribly. The music gets a bit hard house on Saturdays.

## Regency Tavern

*32-34 Russell Square, BN1 2EF (325652). Bus 1, 2, 5, 6, 20, 46, 52.* **Open** 11am-midnight Mon-Sat; noon-10.30pm Sun. **££. Pub**. Map p57 C5 ③⑥

Where else could you find six real ales on tap *and* a disco ball in the urinal? Tucked in the twitten between two squares, this Shepherd Neame pub (that once used to operate as a toll for people promenading around Regency Square) is a pocket of seaside baroque, with striped silk wallpaper, gilt mirrors and gold cherubs. It comes into its own at Christmas, when the owners go somewhat over the top with the decorations. The weekly meal deals – steak Tuesday, fish and chips Wednesday and curry Thursday – are popular.

## Rock 'n' Roller

**NEW** 95 Western Road, BN1 2LB (710014, www.rock8roller.co.uk). Bus 1, 2, 5, 6, 20, 46, 52. **Open** noon-midnight Mon-Thur; noon-1am Fri; 9.30am-1am Sat; 10am-midnight Sun. **££. Bar/restaurant**. Map p57 B4 ③⑦

Sink a few balls along with a beer or cocktails at this American-themed restaurant and pool bar. Five tables named after US cities, booth seating and a huge screen showing old movies all contribute to the slick stateside vibe. Downstairs, the restaurant does good business with its huge homemade burgers with a choice of Swiss, blue or Monterey Jack, and locally smoked ribs. The pulled-pork burger is excellent and filling. There are several beers on tap, but it's the kind of place cocktails go down best. It's open for breakfast on weekends.

## Seven Dials Restaurant

1 Buckingham Place, BN1 3TD (885555, www.sevendialsrestaurant. co.uk). Bus 27, 50, 56. **Open** noon-4pm, 6-10pm Mon-Sat; noon-4pm Sun. **£££. Modern British**. Map p56 C2 ③⑧

Perched right on a corner of the Seven Dials with tall windows letting in elegant shafts of light, this wedge-shaped restaurant is beginning to attract a regular crowd for dishes such as fillet of local brill, wilted spinach and celeriac puree, or confit duck leg, garlic creamed potatoes, French beans and cranberry jus, accompanied by a good wine list The heated terrace has its own posh nibbles menu but is as popular for afternoon drinking.

## Shakespeare's Head

1 Chatham Place, BN1 3TP (329444). Bus 27, 50, 56. **Open** 4-11.30pm Mon-Thur; 4pm-12.30am Fri; noon-12.30am Sat; noon-11.30pm Sun. **Pub**. Map p57 C4 ③⑨

There are candlelit tables and Elizabethan-style paintings on the walls, the service is some of the friendliest in Brighton, and the back room is perfect for a board game. But it's really all about the sausage and mash here: choose from up to 20 chalked-up types of sausage (including several veggie options) and two accompaniments, from homemade gravies and mashes to ratatouille and salad. Can't decide? Simply say: 'Pork and leek, red wine gravy, four cheese mash.'

## Sussex Yeoman

7 Guildford Road, BN1 3LU (327985). Bus 27. **Open** noon-11pm Mon-Thur; noon-midnight Fri, Sat; noon-11.30pm Sun. **Pub**. Map p56 E3 ④⓪

Poll the city on its favourite Sunday roast, and the Sussex Yeoman could well come in on top. A black and cream corner pub in one of the steep residential roads to the right as you exit the station, its speciality is traditional pub grub served to very high standards, and without the usual exponential decrease in portion size.

## Temple Bar

121 Western Road, BN1 2AD (721501, www.templebarbrighton.co.uk). Bus 1, 2, 5, 6, 20, 46, 49. **Open** 11am-midnight Mon-Thur; noon-2am Fri, Sat; noon-midnight Sun. **Pub**. Map p57 B4 ④①

After an unsuccessful spell as the Star and Sailor, this pub has regained its buzzing atmosphere. It's a winning mix of grand and cosy, with green and gold decor and mismatched stools and armchairs, and both Thai and classic pub menus. The characterful upstairs room is often used by comedy promoters Laughing Horse. There's a great selection of beers, all from Sussex brewers such as Dark Star.

# Park life

Take a breather in the lungs of the city.

For breathing space away from the seafront hordes, Brighton & Hove's parks offer a different side to local culture and a chance to participate in a broad range of outdoor activities.

Just inside the Hove border and a short walk from the city centre, **St Ann's Well Gardens** is notable for its impressive range of native and exotic trees – as much a point of interest for shade-seekers as for nature-lovers.

If sports are your thing, then **Preston Park** (p137) is the place to head. The city's largest urban green space, it's equipped with football and cricket pitches, bowling greens and even a cycling velodrome. Horticultural features include a walled rose garden and the largest municipal rock

garden in Britain, which sits across London Road opposite the main park on the other side of The park is at its most alive on the first Saturday of August when Brighton Pride (p38) fills the grounds.

Hidden away in the back streets between Hanover and Kemp Town, **Queen's Park** is one of the most peaceful places in the city. Originally a Victorian pleasure garden, the landscaped park today has a duck pond, tennis courts, large playground, wildlife garden and a café.

**Stanmer Park** is a sprawling country park next to the main Sussex University campus on the Lewes Road (bus 24 or 25). Deer, badger and several species of bat can be found in its woods, which are carpeted in bluebells in May. As well as having an 18th-century stately home and village church, the park is also home to England's first Earthship (www.lowcarbon. co.uk), a passive-solar building constructed from natural and recycled materials.

Not the most salubrious of Brighton & Hove's parks, **the Level** (p137) is nevertheless a good people-watching spot and has the only outdoor skate park in the city centre.

Perhaps the most unexpected feature of any of the city's parks, however, is the miniature steam railway in **Hove Park**, open to the public in summer.

If you want green space within striking distance of the beach, take a picnic on **Hove Lawns**, an expanse of grass that runs parallel to Hove's elegant esplanade.

Rock 'n' Roller p68

## Tin Drum

*95-97 Dyke Road, BN1 3JE (777575,*
*www.tindrum.co.uk). Bus 50, 56.* **Open**
10am-midnight Mon-Sat; 10am-10.30pm
Sun. **££. Modern British/Café.**
Map p56 C2 **42**

The original of the city's three Tin
Drums (all of which draw ingredients
from the Radtke family's own farm),
this restaurant-café can have a rather
split atmosphere – with couples eating
à la carte to the rear, young parents
relaxing over a coffee and paper on a
window sofa and office workers drinking out front. It all comes together well
over an interesting brunch menu or the
£11 Sunday roast.

## Tutti Frutti

*92 Dyke Road, BN1 3JD (326147).*
*Bus 50, 56.* **Open** 7.30am-3pm Mon;
7.30am-6pm Tue-Sat; 9am-3pm Sun.
**££. Italian.** Map p56 D2 **43**

This small Italian deli is a popular
breakfast spot (on sunny mornings,
get there early to bag one of the two

'alfresco' tables tottering on the curb)
thanks to the knowledge you can get
a proper espresso with your classic or
veggie cooked breakfast. A zigzagging
counter's worth of fresh meatballs,
lasagne, salads, antipasti and Italian
desserts keeps the custom trickling in.

## West Hill

*67 Buckingham Place, BN1 3PQ*
*(748849, www.thewesthill.co.uk). Bus*
*7, 14, 27.* **Open** 5pm-midnight Mon;
5pm-1am Tue-Thur; 4pm-3am Fri;
1pm-3am Sat; 1pm-midnight Sun.
**Bar.** Map p56 D2 **44**

Perched on the hill between the station
and Seven Dials (not for nothing was it
once called the Belle Vue), this com-
muter's oasis makes up for in kooki-
ness what it lacks in cushioned seating.
It has one of Brighton's few bar bil-
liards tables, a 'lover's seat' in the tiny
courtyard, a risotto of the week and
some genuinely cutting edge Friday
and Saturday night DJ sessions. There
are regular acoustic music sets.

### Western Front

*11 Cranbourne Street, BN1 2RD (725656). Bus 1, 2, 5, 6, 20, 46, 49, 52.* **Open** 11am-1.15pm Mon-Wed, Sun; 11am-2am Thur-Sat. **££. Pub. Map** p57 D5 ㊺

A catch-all city centre pub just off Churchill Square, with two floors, lots of outdoor seating and a menu of pub classics including sausage, chips and beans, and scampi and fries for just over a fiver. Happy hour runs from 5pm to 8pm Sunday to Friday, and there's a popular free indie disco on Friday and Saturday nights.

### Windmill

*69 Upper North Street, BN1 3FL (202475). Bus 1, 2, 5, 6, 20, 46, 49, 52.* **Open** noon-midnight Mon-Thur, Sun; noon-1am Fri, Sat. **Pub. Map** p57 C4 ㊻

This excellent back-street local has one of the broadest clienteles in Brighton, drawn by a sun-trap beer garden out front and a dark, low-ceilinged section at the back. The pub food has a Mexican slant.

### Xuma

*108a Dyke Road, BN1 3TE (0872 148 6334). Bus 50, 56.* **Open** noon-1am Mon-Thur, Sun; noon-3am Fri, Sat. **Bar. Map** p56 C1 ㊼

Successfully straddling several identities, this art gallery and bar draws custom for both its cocktails and its pizzas, its live jazz or DJ nights and its contemporary paintings and photography (often by local artists). The red sofas and low, candle-lit tables are good for intimate chats. The bar staff are jolly and prevent it from tipping into anything pretentious.

## Shopping

### Arka Original Funerals

*39-41 Surrey Street, BN1 3PB (766620, www.arkafunerals.co.uk). Bus 6, 7, 14, 27, 50, 56.* **Open** by appt. **Map** p56 E3 ㊽

Quirky coffins? How about caskets made from woven willow or bamboo, urns made from environmentally respectful materials or ecopods and cardboard coffins that friends and family can help to paint themselves? One of two funeral parlours in the city run by three local women intent on ensuring Brightonians (and visitors) get a funeral befitting their beliefs.

### C&H Fabrics

*179 Western Road, BN1 2BA (321959, www.candh.co.uk). Bus 1, 2, 5, 6, 20, 46, 49, 52.* **Open** 9am-5.30pm Mon-Sat. **Map** p57 D5 ㊾

Three floors' worth of craft materials, homeware, upholstery, handbags, fancy dress outfits, ornamental gifts, board games and wedding hats, plus an in-store café Victoria Wood would enjoy. This old-fashioned department store, one of eight across the South East, is an Englishwoman's castle.

### Churchill Square Shopping Centre

*Russell Place, BN1 2TD (722308, www.churchillsquare.com). Bus 1, 2, 5, 6, 20, 46, 49, 52.* **Open** 9am-6pm Mon-Wed; 9am-8pm Thur; 9am-7pm Fri, Sat; 11am-5pm Sun. **Map** p57 D5 ㊿

Despite the seagulls and emos engaged in a turf war on its forecourt, this two-storey mall has something for most shoppers, with more than 80 shops, including two big department stores (BHS and Debenhams), a large Habitat, Schuh and Zara, plus a food court whose tenants range from McDonalds to the Italian-styled Café Giardino. Urban Outfitters' takeover of the old Borders site may skew things further toward the teen fashion sector, though there's also a farmers' market every Wednesday.

### Dance 2

*129 Western Road, BN1 2AD (220023, www.dance2.co.uk). Bus 1, 2, 5, 6, 20, 46, 49, 52.* **Open** 10am-6pm Mon-Sat. **Map** p57 B4 (51)

Regency Square

A specialist vinyl store and leading equipment supplier, where DJs can pick up the latest drum 'n' bass releases and have a protracted conversation about slip mats with the expert staff. There's a wide range of audio equipment.

### Dancia

*8 Western Street, BN1 2PG (719001, www.dancia.co.uk). Bus 1, 2, 5, 6, 20, 46, 49, 52.* **Open** 10am-5.30pm Mon-Fri; 9.30am-5pm Sat. **Map** p57 A5 ⑤²
This is the flagship store for renowned dancewear and shoe stockists Dancia International. Always a magnet for little girls thanks to its shelves of ballet shoes and a bright pink window full of lurid tutus, it's also found older custom thanks to the popularity of *Strictly Come Dancing*.

### Fair

*21 Queens Road, BN1 3XA (723215, thefairshop.co.uk). Bus 50, 56.* **Open** 10am-6pm Mon-Sat; 11am-5.30pm Sun. **Map** p57 E4 ⑤³
A fair-trade boutique for shoppers who care about design and where things come from. The emphasis here is on women's fashion – funky banana-fibre frocks and chunky jewellery made from recycled magazines – though they also stock Little Green Radicals kids wear and toys.

### Flower City

*102 Western Road, BN1 2AA (770966, www.florist4flowersbrighton.co.uk). Bus 1, 2, 5, 6, 20, 46, 49, 52.* **Open** 10am-7pm Mon-Sat. **Map** p57 B4 ⑤⁴
Fabulously unpretentious urban florist where the narrow concrete floor is home to a great selection of plants. You can buy a bunch of daffs for a quid, or give £25 to one of the friendly staff and they'll assemble a big, varied bouquet.

### Kate Langdale

*84 Dyke Road, BN1 3JD (07944 756277, www.katelangdale.com). Bus 50, 56.* **Open** noon-6pm Tue; 10am-6pm Wed-Sat. **Map** p56 D4 ⑤⁵

This is the showroom for floral and interior designer Kate Langdale, who uses vintage fabrics to make pretty lampshades, soft furnishings, nightwear and baby toys. Lovers of country garden style will feel as at home as her sleepy little dog, which lounges on the re-upholstered armchair.

## Lmnop

NEW *17 Montpelier Place, BN1 3BF (911288, www.lmnopshop.com). Bus 1, 2, 5, 6, 20, 46, 49, 52.* **Open** 11am-7pm Wed-Fri; 11am-6pm Sat. No credit cards. **Map** p57 B4 ⑤

A new shop and display space complements the recent boom in self-publishing, showcasing work by some of the city's illustrators, typographers, comic book writers, card makers and even etchers. Owners Stuart and Alison are designers themselves, and have combined a 21st-century shop concept (check out their list of planned events) with a retro love of print.

## Magdusia

*20-21 Chatham Place, BN1 3TN (203920). Bus 27, 50, 52, 56.* **Open** 8am-10pm Mon-Fri; 8am-11pm Sat, Sun. **Map** p56 D1 ⑤

'The first and best Polish shop in Brighton', according to their sign, is still the city's biggest. Its popularity, which admittedly leaped at first on some excellent beer offers, is proof that the Polish community has really taken root in Brighton. The curious chocolates, fruit dumplings and other vivid-looking desserts make this a colourful (and great value) alternative to the usual supermarkets.

## Modelzone

*37 West Street, BN1 2RE (326790, www.modelzone.co.uk). Bus 1, 2, 5, 6, 20, 46, 49.* **Open** 9.30am-6pm Mon-Sat; 11am-5pm Sun. **Map** p57 D5 ⑤

The original showroom for the UK's largest model retailer is the place to expand your Scalextric track or Action Man collection, buy a radio-controlled power boat to test out on Hove Lagoon, or build a Spitfire, At-At Walker, or the starship *Enterprise*.

## Music Shop

*90 Western Road, BN1 2LB (775607, www.musicroom.com). Bus 1, 2, 5, 6, 20, 46, 49, 52.* **Open** 9am-6pm Mon-Sat; **Map** p57 B4 ⑤

The Brighton outpost of this world-wide chain has an impressive selection of sheet music, tuition books and music software, as well as every kind of instrument (and every colour of guitar) from squeezeboxes to harps. The vibe is specialist, though many are the unmusical passers-by who've been lured in by the £20 yellow uke.

## Octopus

*16-17 Cranbourne Street, BN1 2RD (774078). Bus 1, 2, 5, 6, 20, 46.* **Open** 9am-6pm daily. **Map** p57 D5 ⑥

This quirky gift store sells designer luggage alongside novelty umbrellas and handbags, snake-shaped bike locks and bizarre kitchen implements.

## Permanent Gallery

*20 Bedford Place, BN1 2PT (710389, www.permanentgallery.com). Bus 1, 2, 5, 6, 20, 46, 49, 52.* **Open** 1-6pm Thur, Fri, Sun; 11am-6pm Sat. No credit cards. **Map** p57 B4 ⑥

It's easy to miss this tiny but innovative alternative gallery and bookshop, concealed in the bottom floor of a townhouse. The gallery has hosted live electronica and reading events, and the shop is great for alternative gifts, such as Matilda Huang's screen print *Love Story of a Jellyfish* or Brighton 'zine *Matter*.

## Record Album

*8 Terminus Road, BN1 3PD (323853, www.therecordalbum.com). Bus 6, 7, 14, 27.* **Open** 11am-4.30pm Mon-Sat. No credit cards. **Map** p56 E2 ⑥

Want a copy of the folio to *Raiders of the Lost Ark* complete with rumbling

Heist

boulder? This tiny corner store behind the train station has been selling original film soundtracks and other vintage records since 1948, and should be on the radar of every vinyl geek in the country. The window display always seems to change according to which films are on TV that week.

## Sixty Seven

*67 Dyke Road, BN1 3JE (735314, www.shopatsixtyseven.co.uk). Bus 50, 56.* **Open** *10.30am-5.30pm Mon-Sat.* **Map** p56 C2 ⑥③

As the vintage lip-sofa in the window suggests, Sixty Seven has more style than your average card and candle shop – including the odd piece of 1960s Ercol furniture. Think high-end gifts such as organic chocolate fish for kids, friends and lovers.

## Steve & Alistair

**NEW** *47 Upper North Street, BN1 3FH (777523). Bus 1, 2, 5, 6, 20, 52.* **Open** 11am-5pm daily. **Map** p57 C4 ⑥④

Newly arrived from Covent Garden via Lyme Regis, Alistair McCready and Steve Ridout are an old-fashioned outfit who prefer to spend their time sourcing and creating than announcing their own existence. McCready sits making shoulder bags at his sewing machine among piles of rugs imported from rural Iran and Afghanistan.

## Taboo

*2 Surrey Street, BN1 3PA (263565, www.tabooshop.com). Bus 7, 14, 27, 50.* **Open** 9am-8pm Mon-Sat; 11am-5pm Sun. **Map** p56 E3 ⑥⑤

In contrast to the seductive furnishings of She Said, opposite, and the high street brassiness of Ann Summers, there's something old-fashioned about Brighton's most famous sex shop, with its small misted-out window, down a slip-road to the train station. But that doesn't preclude a pleasant welcome, whether you're after DVDs, the latest adult toys, sexy lingerie or perhaps just a 'spank me' ruler.

## Taj

*98-99 Western Road, BN1 2LB*
*(325027). Bus 1, 2, 5, 6, 20, 46, 49.*
**Open** 9am-9pm daily. **Map** p57 B4 ⑯
Seasonal vegetables spill out on to the pavement, unusual cereals, pulses and puddings line the shelves, and bhangra music fills the aisles at this Middle Eastern and organic grocery emporium. A more soulful (if occasionally pricier) alternative to the nearby supermarkets, Taj has recently expanded its deli counter offerings, and now serves home-cooked Lebanese and other interesting dishes to take away.

## Three Angels

*86 Dyke Road, BN1 3JD (711009,*
*www.threeangels.co.uk). Bus 50, 56.*
**Open** 10am-5pm Tue-Thur; 10am-6pm Fri, Sat. **Map** p56 C2 ⑰
The smaller of two interiors stores (the other's in Hove) selling antique French furniture – pretty dressing tables, painted folding screens and elegantly distressed chests of drawers – along with similarly chic small gifts to elevate any bedsit into a boudoir.

## Wardrobe

*51 Upper North Street, BN1 3FH*
*(202201). Bus 1, 2, 5, 6, 20, 46,*
*49, 52.* **Open** 11am-5pm Mon-Sat.
**Map** p57 C4 ⑱
A vintage clothing corner shop that's hardly bigger than Carrie Bradshaw's walk-in closet, Wardrobe has rails of tea dresses, cascades of second-hand jewellery, and shoes and hats to match. The proprietor's more than happy to advise on which flowery tea dress to pick for a 1940s-themed party or how to wear those pearls with that 1920s ball gown – a more special, and specialised, experience than your usual vintage store.

## Waterstones

*71-74 North Street, BN1 1ZA (0843*
*290 8181, www.waterstones.com). Bus*
*1, 2, 5, 6, 20, 46, 49, 52.* **Open** 9am-7pm Mon-Fri; 9am-6pm Sat; 11am-5pm Sun. **Map** p57 D5 ⑲

Four floors' worth of books, including a bumper classics section, larger than average New Age section, themed promotional tables with great recommendations for, say, international reads, and labels flagging up local authors. Grab a Patrick Hamilton (or a Nick Cave) and head for the Costa café on the fourth floor.

# Nightlife

## Heist

*57 West Street, BN1 2RA (822555,*
*www.heistbar.co.uk). Bus 1, 2, 5, 6,*
*20, 46, 49, 52.* **Open** 4pm-1am Mon-Thur, Sun; 4pm-3am Fri; noon-3am Sat.
**Map** p57 D5 ⑳
This building has been a Turkish baths and a cinema, but never, to our knowledge, the power base of the Masters of the Universe. That hasn't stopped the current owners opting for a faux-Gothic look (complete with imposing grey frontage and giant eagle perched on the bar), despite serving up a West Street-friendly mix of cheapish cocktails, fresh pizza and funky house. There's a diverse range of DJs on Friday and Saturday – with the latter leaning more to funk and Friday being more of a party night.

## Hope

*11-12 Queens Road, BN1 3WA*
*(325793). Bus 6, 7, 14, 27, 47.* **Open** noon-midnight Mon-Wed, Sun; noon-2am Thur-Sat. **Map** p57 E4 ㉑
A little bit of Camden in Brighton, with touring indie bands playing in the small and sticky 90-capacity room upstairs, skinny indie kids sprawling on the leather sofas downstairs, and everyone pretending they're too strung-out to be interested in the contents of the pizza oven.

## New Hero

*11 Dyke Road, BN1 3FE (236635,*
*www.newherobrighton.co.uk). Bus 50,*
*56.* **Open** 7pm-4am Wed-Sat. No credit cards. **Map** p57 D4 ㉒

The Saturday night hordes have been slow to cotton on to the existence of this intimate, independently run club in a former church slightly hidden away off Western Road.

## Oceana
*Kingswest, West Street, BN1 2RE (0845 296 8590, www.oceanaclubs.com/ brighton) Bus 1, 2, 5, 6, 20, 46, 49, 52.* **Open** 9pm-3am Mon, Wed-Sat. **Map** p57 D5 73

The biggest of the seafront clubs dutifully pulls in the big-name acts (Paul Oakenfold, Taio Cruz and, er, S Club…) as well as the odd big-league footballer. Seven themed rooms attempt to recreate the atmosphere of a 'Ski Lodge' or a 'Parisian Boudoir'.

## Tru
*78 West Street, BN1 1AZ (321628, www.trubrighton.com/brighton). Bus 1, 2, 5, 6, 20, 46, 49, 52.* **Open** 10pm-2.30am Tue; 9pm-2.30am Fri; 9pm-3am Sat. **Map** p57 D6 74

Formerly Creation, this three-room nightclub is a fixture on the Saturday night circuit, complete with bouncers and a cattle-market atmosphere. The main club has a capacity of 1,200, while the Retro and Chill rooms are smaller. It has also been hosted by the likes of Calvin Harris and 2 Many DJs.

## West Hill Hall
*66 Compton Avenue, BN1 3PS (www.myspace.com/westhill). Bus 7, 27, 50.* **Open** varies. **Map** p56 D2 75

More Girl Guides than Whisky a Go Go, this tiny village hall (where the stage is lit by an old-fashioned standard lamp) is one of the more intriguing assets of Brighton's music scene. Mary Hampton recorded her stunning debut album here, John Peel's favourite UK songwriter, Liane Hall, is the venue's caretaker, and the Miserable Rich launched their 2010 album *Of Flight and Fury* with a mini residency. The gigs aren't particularly well publicised, so check the hall's MySpace site.

# Arts & leisure

## Brighton Centre

*King's Road, BN1 2GR (290131, www.brightoncentre.co.uk). Bus 11.*
**Map** p57 D6 ⑦⑧

The Brighton Centre has a standing capacity of more than 5,000 – easily enough to bring most of the big mainstream touring acts. But this venue and conference centre is still waiting for a planned £400 million redevelopment. Until then its ugly concrete exterior (as if cast from a multi-storey car park by Rachel Whiteread) will continue to provoke resentment among locals, though its size allows the city to host events such as the Labour Party Conference.

## Brighton Little Theatre

*9 Clarence Gardens, BN1 2EG (777748, www.the-little.co.uk). Bus 1, 2, 5, 6, 20, 46, 49, 52.* **Map** p57 C5 ⑦

Lively amateur theatre company the BLT has just celebrated its 70th birthday. It continues to programme everything from Shakespeare to Agatha Christie at its premises in a former church just off Western Road, putting on around 12 productions a year.

## Magnum Opus Tattoos

*33 Upper North Street, BN1 3FG (271432, www.magnumopustattoo. com). Bus 1, 2, 5, 6, 20, 46, 49.* **Open** 11am-6pm Tue-Sat. No credit cards. **Map** p57 C4 ⑦⑧

A bespoke tattoo parlour (that word doesn't rankle here) that triples up as an art gallery showing work by guest artists and a shop selling T-shirts, books, prints and paintings. Six tattoo stations are run by practitioners with names like Bob Done and Luci Lou.

## Neo Hotel

*19 Oriental Place, BN1 2LL (711104, www.neohotel.com). Bus 11.* **Open** by appt. **Map** p57 B5 ⑦⑨

This boutique hotel set in a Georgian townhouse has its own stylish therapy room, run by Elle Macpherson's former masseuse, which is open to non-guests. Slip into a kimono before enjoying an aromatherapy massage or organic facial (both £45 an hour), with the option of staying for a cocktail at the sleek little bar afterwards.

## New Venture Theatre

*Bedford Place, BN1 2PT (808353, 746118 box office, www.newventure. org.uk). Bus 1, 2, 5, 6, 20, 46.* **Map** p57 B5 ⑧⓪

This community theatre has been putting on amateur productions of popular works since 1956, and recently has taken to programming more experimental work in the smaller, downstairs studio space (unfortunately, the gorgeous 100-seat proscenium theatre upstairs is currently closed, awaiting funding). Quality is varied, but you can have fun listening in on the luvvies in the bohemian saloon bar. It sometimes hosts cabaret performances.

## Nightingale Theatre

*Above Grand Central pub, 29-30 Surrey Street, BN1 3PA (702563, www.nightingaletheatre.co.uk). Bus 7, 14, 27, 47.* **Map** p56 E3 ⑧①

This fantastic pub-theatre has Steven Berkoff as patron and Steven Brett (formerly of Ballet Rambert and London's experimental Spill festival) as its new artistic director. Catch some of the best local and international fringe theatre (as well as comedy, dance, poetry and works in development) in an intimate setting. Some performances make use of the surrounding rooms.

## Odeon

*Kingswest, BN1 2RE (0871 224 4007, www.odeon.co.uk). Bus 1, 2, 5, 6, 20, 46, 49, 52.* **Open** varies. **Map** p57 D6 ⑧②

This eight-screen cinema shows all the big blockbusters, as well as some indie releases. It also hosts parent-and-baby screenings and occasionally beams in special events such as Euro tournaments, as well as opera.

## Sights & museums

### Brighton Fishing Museum

*201 King's Road Arches, BN1 1NB (723064, www.brightonfishingmuseum. org.uk). Bus 11.* **Open** 10am-6pm daily. **Admission** free. **Map** p85 B6 🥉

The hub of Brighton's fishing quarter down in King's Road Arches, the modest Brighton Fishing Museum features an interesting chronology and documentation of the town's maritime history. Among the exhibits are letters, photographs and film clips.

### Brighton Pier

*Grand Junction (609361, www.brighton pier.co.uk). Bus 1, 2, 5, 6, 20, 46.* **Open** 10am-9.45pm Mon-Fri; 10am-11pm Sat, Sun. **Map** p85 D6 🥉

Whereas the bare frame of the ruined West Pier is a lonely, starkly beautiful local landmark, brash, brassy Brighton Pier is a riotous welter of flashing fairground rides, candyfloss kiosks and hook-a-duck booths, where kids play on the dodgems and Elvis croons softly in the background. There's a rollercoaster, the Super Booster, at the end of the pier, which goes from 0 to 60 in less than three seconds. At dusk, linger by the seaside to watch flocks of starlings swarm around the pier. There are three bars on the pier and plenty of takeaway stalls.

### Mechanical Memories Museum

*250c King's Road Arches, BN1 1NB (www.mechanicalmemoriesmuseum. co.uk). Bus 11.* **Open** weekends & school holidays – times depend on the weather. **Admission** free. **Map** p85 C6 🥉

Mechanical Memories is a working museum that offers a charming diversion from the mass of seafront tack in the vicinity, paying homage to the automated entertainments of yesteryear. The vintage slot machines date

from the early 1900s until around 1960; buy old fashioned pennies to play on the likes of fortune-tellers, horse-racing games and one armed bandits. Kids can stamp their name (or anything else) on to aluminium strips (like dog tags), and giggle at the saucy What the Butler Saw machines.

## Eating & drinking

### 106 Bar

*Metropole Hotel, 106 King's Road, BN1 2FU (775432, www.hilton.co.uk). Bus 11.* **Open** noon-11pm Wed-Sun. *Restaurant noon-7pm Wd-Sun).* **£££**. **Spanish/bar**. **Map** p57 C6 🥉

The Hilton hotel's terrace bar extends back into a large, light, arch-framed room with a long bar and some rather uninspiring brown leather seating. The menu is Spanish tapas. It's a quiet place to grab a snack away from the busy seafront.

### Birdcage Bandstand Café

*King's Road Arches, by West Pier (227194, www.bandstandcafe.co.uk). Bus 11.* **Open** 8.30am-6pm daily. **££**. **Café**. **Map** p57 C6 🥉

Raspberry mocha latte for the grown-ups, white chocolate cocoa for the children and homemade pastries courtesy of French restaurant La Fourchette (p63), all in a recently refurbished Victorian bandstand. The café also has a patio from which to enjoy the music of the bands programmed.

### Bucket Beach Café

*26-28 King's Road Arches, BN1 2LN (220222). Bus 11.* **Open** 9am-5pm daily (weekends only during winter months). **£**. **Café**. **Map** p57 B6 🥉

One of the best seafront cafés in terms of value for money, with cute arched windows affording clear views of the sea while you eat fresh baguettes, big bowls of veggie soup and cakes. It's a favourite with families thanks to the boxes of children's books and its playground and paddling pool.

Due South

## Due South

*139 Kings Road Arches, BN1 2FN
(821218, www.duesouth.co.uk). Bus 11.*
**Open** noon-3.30pm, 6-10pm daily. **£££**.
**Modern British**. Map p57 D6 ⑳
Few spots are more romantic than the
table by the arched upstairs window at
this seafront restaurant, where contemporary art lines the walls and mains
such as pan-roasted Court Garden
lamb cost around £17. A great selection of dessert wines can lead you to
fork out more than planned.

## Fortune of War

*156-157 Kings Road Arches, BN1 1NB
(205065). Bus 11.* **Open** 11am-11.30pm
Mon-Thur, Sun; 11am-late Fri, Sat. **Pub**.
Map p85 B6 ⑳
The ancient mariner of Brighton drinking establishments (it's been there
since 1882) is ship-shaped in design
more than in upkeep. Down a few pints
of Portuguese beer Sagres and you
may well feel you're out at sea as you
wobble past porthole windows down

the roped stairwell to the slimy toilets.
Its old reputation as a live music venue
is currently being re-established.

## Gemini

*127 King's Road Arches, BN1 2FN
(327888). Bus 11.* **Open** *Summer*
noon-11pm. Map p57 C6 ⑳
This alfresco drinking behemoth has a
500-seat seafront patio and live band
spot. It's open until 2am during the
summer. If you spend time in Brighton
in July, a night drinking cocktails from
jugs and dancing to reggae under the
stars here is pretty much inevitable.

## Grand Hotel

*97-99 King's Road, BN1 2FW
(224300, www.devere.co.uk). Bus 11.*
**Open** varies. Map p57 C6 ⑳
The daddy (or, rather, rich maiden
aunt) of the seafront hotels has a good
restaurant serving elegant, predominantly classic dishes. But the Grand is
most associated with its Sussex Cream
Tea, three groaning tiers of perfectly

triangular sandwiches, scones and cakes served in the long Victoria Lounge overlooking the promenade. For people watching and accent-sniping, grab a leather armchair and a cocktail at the Grand Bar.

## Meeting Place Café

*Promenade, King's Road, opposite Western Street (206417). Bus 11.* **Open** 7am-7pm daily. No credit cards. **£. Café. Map** p57 A5 ⓺⓷

Ice-cream, toasties, baked potatoes, coffees and eccles cakes the windswept way. This seafront café sits bang on the seafront between Brighton & Hove, right by the peace statue and affords one of the best views in the city.

## Melrose

*132 King's Road, BN1 2HH (326520, www.melroserestaurant.co.uk). Bus 11.* **Open** 11.30am-10pm daily. **££. Seafood. Map** p57 B6 ⓺⓸

Although not as prestigious as the Regency Restaurant (see below), probably because of the 1970s-style decor, this seafood restaurant is just as good as its neighbour and picks up much of its overspill. A more narrowly drawn menu makes it the first choice for many fish connoisseurs.

## Ohso Social

*250a King's Road Arches, BN1 1NB (746067, www.ohsosocial.co.uk). Bus 11.* **Open** 10am Mon-Thur, Sun (closing time varies, depending on weather); 10am-1am Fri, Sat. **££. Café. Map** p85 C6 ⓺⓹

As a place for a casual seaside lunch, this café/bar can be a little on the steep side, but it is a top spot to enjoy a cuppa while taking in some beachy views. There's a snack menu too with burgers and platters.

## Regency Restaurant

*131 King's Road, BN1 2HH (325014, www.theregencyrestaurant.co.uk). Bus 11.* **Open** 8am-11pm daily. **££. Seafood. Map** p57 B6 ⓺⓺

A deserved reputation for serving the best seafood in Brighton, while catering for veggies and kids, means this red and cream fronted restaurant on the corner of Regency Square is always heaving. The menu changes according to the locally caught catch, served with chips, new potatoes or salad. The sirloin steak is also a house speciality.

## Santiago

*143-144 King's Road Arches, BN1 2FN (710031, www.santiagorestaurant.biz). Bus 11.* **Open** noon-4pm Mon-Fri; noon-5pm Sat, Sun. **££. Mexican. Map** p57 C6 ⓺⓻

Currently open for lunch service only (with plans to open Saturday evenings soon), this Mexican-focused seafront restaurant is just the place to warm up after a windy stroll along the beach, with chorizo and butterbean cassoulet (£12) and a dark chocolate mousse with triple sec packing a particularly flavoursome punch.

## Steki

*127a King's Road, BN1 2FA (730202, www.steki.co.uk). Bus 11.* **Open** noon-11pm daily. **££. Greek. Map** p57 C6 ⓺⓼

Steki is a traditional Greek taverna concealed in a basement on the main seafront road. Try the *frikasse* (lamb casserole with spinach, lettuce and herbs), or a big bowl of *fasolakia* (green beans in tomato sauce with a chunk of bread) for a cheaper meal. They have one other restaurant in Portsmouth – a clue to the freshness of the daily fish dish. Take-away is available too – handy for beach picnics.

## World Famous Pump Room

*121-122 King's Road Arches, BN1 2LN (no phone). Bus 11.* **Open** 9am-6pm Mon-Fri. **Ice-cream. Map** p57 C6 ⓺⓽

This seafront pit stop is adept at blowing its own trumpet, but the 22 flavours of farm-made ice-cream (including ginger and honey), fresh coffee courtesy of St James's Street's excellent Redroaster

Brighton Pier

Coffee House (p120), and location just opposite the volleyball court, are hard to argue with. They serve homemade lemonade and acai berry smoothies too.

## Shopping

### Castor & Pollux

*165 King's Road Arches, Lower Promenade, BN1 1NB (773776, www.castorandpollux.co.uk). Bus 11.* **Open** 10am-4.30pm daily. **Map** p85 A6 ⓴⓿⓿
Small linocuts start at around £36 at this superb little gallery, which showcases printmakers and illustrators – though prices climb for established names such as Rob Ryan. Alongside the changing exhibitions, a shop sells arty cards, books, jewellery and toys.

## Nightlife

The night clubs here are often taken over by promoters who set their own opening times, so check the websites or call for details about specific nights.

### Coalition

*171-181 King's Road Arches, BN1 1NB (772842, www.brightoncoalition.co.uk). Bus 11.* **Open** varies. **Map** p85 A5 ⓴⓿①
Enthusiastically celebrating the start of the week, the popular Trash Mondays at Coalition are a student-friendly mash-up with super-cheap drinks, chart tunes and free entry before 10.30pm. Saturday nights are also big, where you can keep going until 7am if you have the stamina.

### Funky Buddha Lounge

*169-170 Kings Road Arches, BN1 1NB (725541). Bus 11.* **Open** varies. **Map** p85 B6 ⓴⓿②
Stylish folk do seem to love the Funky Buddha. The underground feel and friendly party atmosphere makes this decidedly less hardcore than other seafront clubbing options. As the name suggests, funk is the main music of choice, with a good helping of R&B.

### Honey

*214 Kings Road Arches, BN1 1NB (202807, www.thehoneyclub.co.uk). Bus 11.* **Open** varies. **Map** p85 C6 ⓴⓿③
A Hed Kandi regular, the extensive Honey Club is a nightspot catering to the masses, with five rooms providing lots of dance-inducing beats. The beachfront terrace offers an escape from the party throngs, and during the week there are drinks promotions.

## North Laine

Wide-eyed crowds descend from the station to North Laine's rainbow maze of quirky cafés, rack upon rack of alt-fashion-friendly attire, brimming record stores and some great coffee shops. Café diners enthusiastically chowing down on falafel wraps and superfood smoothies spill across the pavement, interspersed with street stalls, shoppers and the odd hairy musician.

The main shopping area lies between Trafalgar Street and North Street, a district of quirky character where you can find yourself in possession of a hippo outfit, tartan top hat and neon playsuit quite effortlessly. The evenings here, meanwhile, enjoy a spectrum of music. You'll find big international names at the **Brighton Dome** (p102), alternative, world and folky tunes at the **Komedia** (p102), and rocking local talent at the **Prince Albert** (p95).

It wasn't always like this. Once an expanse of farming plots – the word 'laine' means an open field – the late 1700s and early 1800s saw the area evolve into a pocket of dilapidated urban sprawl. Where today sit retro-clad hipsters sipping organic ciders was formerly slums and slaughterhouses, despite its proximity to the Royal Pavilion.

On Saturdays, bargain hunters head to the Brighton Street Market,

North Laine

an eclectic range of stalls on Upper Gardner Street wavering between a car boot sale and an antiques fair; you can buy books, records, knick-knacks and curios. For free-range meat, organic dairy and produce, head to North Road's Brighton Farm Market (9.30am-4.30pm) on Saturday; on Sunday, it becomes the 'Made in Brighton' craft market, open between 10.30am and 4.30pm.

No buses run in North Laine. We have listed buses that travel along Gloucester Place or from the train station down Queen's Road.

## Sights & museums

### Brighton Museum & Art Gallery

*Royal Pavilion, 4-5 Pavilion Buildings, BN1 1EE (290900, www.brighton-hove-rpml.org.uk). Bus 1, 2, 5, 12, 17, 22, 24, 40, 50.* **Open** 10am-5pm Tue-Sun. **Admission** free. **Map** p85 D4 ⓐ

Located in the Royal Pavilion gardens, the Brighton Museum houses a variety of galleries and exhibitions. View pottery, fine art, and contemporary paintings, as well as galleries dedicated to fashion and performance art. The shop sells an interesting mix of souvenirs and gifts, and the gallery café is on hand for a caffeine hit.

### Brighton Royal Pavilion

*4/5 Pavilion Buildings, BN1 1EE (0300 029 0900, www.royalpavilion.org.uk). Bus 1, 2, 5, 12, 17, 22, 24, 40.* **Open** *Apr-Sept* 9.30am-5.45pm daily. *Oct-Mar* 10am-5.15pm daily. **Admission** £8.30. **Map** p85 D4 ⓑ

The illicit love nest of the Prince Regent was designed by John 'Marble Arch' Nash between 1815 and 1822. His assemblage of minarets and balconies is far from being an exact copy of any one Oriental architectural style, freely mixing Indian, Chinese and Gothic notes in the pursuit of ornate excess;

# The Lanes & North Laine

200 m
200 yds

**CITY CENTRE**
pp54-82

MICHELL ST

DORSET PL

HIGH ST

MARGARET ST

CAMELFORD ST

DORSET GDNS

GEORGE ST

BROAD ST

ST JAMES'S STREET

MADEIRA PL

WILLIAM ST

JOHN

Police
Station

County &
Law Courts

University of
Brighton

CHARLES ST

MANCHESTER ST

PRINCES ST

STEINE ST

Sea Life
Centre

Brighton
Pier

Sights & museums
Eating & drinking
Shopping
Nightlife
Arts & leisure

OLD STEINE

213

Brighton
Museum &
Art Gallery

Royal
Pavilion

195

POOL VALLEY

84

179

104

105

D

Dome

178

EAST ST

200

210
212

85

Mechanical
Memories Museum

95

131

117

182

131

NEW ROAD

181

NORTH STREET

207

183

214

197

199

C

GRAND JUNCTION ROAD

103

137

BOND ST

Theatre
Royal

153

198

186

203

209

Town
Hall

183

184

132

Civic
Offices

KING PL

194

PRINCE

ALBERT

190

STREET

187

BLACK LION ST

191
211

215

205

204

SHIP STREET

208

201

192

PORTLAND

WINDSOR

202

206

DUKE ST

185

MIDDLE STREET

191

SOUTH ST

90

102

100

83

101

Clock
Tower

THE LAKES

Brighton Fishing
Museum

Churchill
Square
Shopping
Centre

WEST STREET

Kingswest
Centre
& Odeon
Film Centre

Brighton
Centre

RUSSELL ROAD

4

5

4

5

6

Royal Pavilion p83

the Prince Regent's outlandish country farmhouse-turned-mock-Mughal palace never ceases to amuse and amaze. The interiors are equally intriguing; if anything, their lavishness even exceeds the minarets and towers of the exterior. Chinese-style decorations jostle with magnificent furniture and furnishings, columns topped with palm fronds, gilded dragons and imitation bamboo staircases illuminated by a slosh of vibrant colours.

## Brighton Toy & Model Museum

*52/55 Trafalgar Street, BN1 4EB (749494, www.brightontoymuseum. co.uk). Bus 5, 6, 7, 14, 17, 22, 26, 27, 40, 47, 50.* **Open** 11am-5pm Sat. **Admission** £4; £3 reductions. **Map** p84 B1 **106**

Take a wander through the past at this modest museum tucked in beneath Brighton Station. Wistfully see the playthings of your childhood, and even your grandparents' childhoods, like wooden puppets, model ships and rare dolls.

## Eating & drinking

## Basketmakers Arms

*39 Cheltenham Place, BN1 4AB (689006, www.thebasketmakersarms. co.uk). Bus 5, 6, 7, 14, 17, 22, 26, 27, 40, 47, 50.* **Open** 11am-11pm Mon-Thur; 11am-midnight Fri, Sat; noon-11pm Sun. **Pub. Map** p84 D2 **107**

One to lovingly tickle the belly of beer enthusiasts, the Basketmakers stocks a comprehensive selection of cask ales. The other passion here is whisky, with over 100 different bottles on offer. Best pub in Brighton? Quite possibly.

## Bill's Produce Store

*The Depot, North Road (692894, www.billsproducestore.co.uk). Bus 5, 6, 7, 14, 17, 22, 26, 27, 40, 47, 50.* **Open** 8am-10.30pm daily. **££. Café. Map** p84 D3 **108**

At Bill's organic deli-cum-restaurant, diners feast amid baskets of fresh

leafy vegetables, and breathe the aroma of warm baked goods. During the day, long communal tables are packed with regulars tucking into pancakes, salads and hearty brunches. In the evening, the menu expands with colourful vegetable heavy dishes such as Thai spiced pumpkin and coconut curry. Queues can be long, but the food is deserving.

## Bodega D Tapa

*111 Church Street, BN1 1UD (674116, www.d-tapa.com). Bus 5, 6, 7, 14, 17, 22, 26, 27, 40, 47, 50.* **Open** 6-11pm Tue; noon-11pm Wed-Sun. **£££. Spanish. Map** p85 C4 **109**

An intimate Spanish restaurant serving a rich and juicy selection of tapas dishes. While sister eaterie Solera (42 Sydney Street) is more suited to parties laden with shopping, Bodega's proximity to the Brighton Dome complex makes it ideal for a pre-gig snack and cheek-warming swig of Rioja.

## Brighton Tavern

*99-100 Gloucester Road, BN1 4AP (680365). Bus 5, 17, 22, 26, 40, 50.* **Open** noon-midnight Mon-Thur. Sun; noon-2am Fri, Sat. **Pub. Map** p84 C2 **110**

The hulking Brighton Tavern is a large and lively gay-friendly pub sat just outside the path of the shopping hordes. Inside, it's a pretty standard watering hole – chairs, tables, bar – but you can expect welcoming staff and a convivial atmosphere.

## Coffee @ 33

**NEW** *33 Trafalgar Street, BN1 4ED (462460). Bus 5, 6, 7, 14, 17, 22, 26, 27, 40, 47, 50.* **Open** 7.30am-6pm Mon-Fri; 9am-6pm Sat; 10am-4pm Sun. **Café. Map** p84 C1 **111**

Hop off the train, then trot down sloped Trafalgar Street for a comfortable and unpretentious coffee house, with thick cushioned window seating and chirpy staff. Try a hunk of lemon and poppyseed cake with the sublime coffee.

## Dorset

*28 North Road, BN1 1YB (605423, www.thedorset.co.uk). Bus 5, 6, 7, 14, 17, 22, 26, 27, 40, 47, 50.* **Open** 9am-11pm daily. **Pub. Map** p84 C3 ⓬

Chatter emanates from this North Laine favourite, from mid morning right through to the small hours. Coffee taken on the streetside seating is a pleasure (weather depending), and the Dorset can proudly claim an accomplished food menu as well as an attractive venue: dishes such as Thai-style mussels with lemongrass, chilli, ginger and coconut milk and a diverse range of other snacks.

## Dumb Waiter

*28 Sydney Street, BN1 4EP (602526). Bus 5, 6, 7, 14, 17, 22, 26, 27, 40, 47, 50.* **Open** 9am-6pm Mon-Sat; 10am-4pm Sun. No credit cards. **Café. Map** p84 D1 ⓭

In refreshing contrast to its more polished peers, the Dumb Waiter is a shabby-chic greasy spoon with a decor and menu that appears to have been cobbled together by hungover students. Stodgy comfort food makes for a cheap feed – try signature dish Dumb Huevos: pan-fried potatoes, onions, garlic, peppers and chorizo topped with poached eggs and chilli sauce. On a sunny day munch alfresco in the yard at the back of the restaurant.

## E Kagen

*22-23 Sydney Street BN 1 4EN (687068). Bus 5, 6, 7, 14, 17, 22, 26, 27, 40, 47, 50.* **Open** 11.30am-2pm Tue, Wed; 11.30am-3.30pm, 6.30-10pm Thur, Fri; 11.30am-4pm, 6.30-10pm Sat; noon-4pm Sun. **£££. Japanese. Map** p84 C2 ⓮

Look up when passing the Yum Yum Oriental Supermarket on Sydney Street, and you'll see a modest Japanese cantina serving sea-fresh sushi at a wallet-friendly price. From the many dishes, it's the simple freshness of the sashimi that impresses, as does the crispy chicken *katsu*. E Kagen's first-floor

position hides it from many passers-by – a shame, as those willing to sacrifice the gloss of other sushi joints will think it a top little find.

## Earth & Stars

🆕 *26 Windsor Street, BN1 1RJ (722879). Bus 5, 6, 7, 14, 17, 22, 26, 27, 40, 47, 50.* **Open** noon-1am Mon-Thur; noon-2am Fri, Sat; noon-11pm Sun. **Pub. Map** p84 B3 ⓯

Feel smugly virtuous as you sit and sip at the Earth & Stars: this cosy pub is one of Brighton's most eco-conscious, with the roof sporting a solar panel, and its bar stocked with organic tipples and locally produced beer.

## Farm

🆕 *99 North Road, BN1 1YE (623143, www.farmsussex.co.uk). Bus 5, 6, 7, 14, 17, 22, 26.* **Open** 9am-5pm Mon-Sat; 9.30am-4pm Sun. **££.** No credit cards. **Café. Map** p84 C3 ⓰

Another Brighton establishment squinting in the light of its own halo, Farm not only uses local and organic produce, but many ingredients come from its own or associated farms. They can say with absolute authority that their sausages have a blissful pre-sausage existence, and you can scoff guilt-free (unless you're veggie). Start your day with a cracking Breakfast Royale: smoked salmon and golden scrambled eggs on a muffin.

## Fitzherberts

*25 New Road, BN1 1UG (682401). Bus 5, 6, 7, 14, 17, 22, 26, 27, 40, 47, 50.* **Open** noon-midnight Mon-Wed, Sun; noon-1am Thur-Sat. **Pub. Map** p85 C4 ⓱

Filed firmly under the 'cool places in which to enjoy a Brighton pint' bracket, Fitzherberts is frequented by musos, students and a smattering of other social groups partial to skinny jeans. The crowd generally has a rollicking good time, and in fine weather spills out on to a seated section on pedestrian-friendly New Road.

## Foundry

*13-14 Foundry Street, BN1 4AT
(697014). Bus 5, 6, 7, 14, 17, 22, 26,
27, 40, 47, 50.* **Open** noon-midnight
Mon-Thur, Sun; noon-12.30am Fri, Sat.
**Pub. Map** p84 C2 **118**

A fabulous wintertime pub, the
Foundry is extremely tiny (more than
20 people and it's a squash), with a real
fire and deep red sofas. A good roast
makes an appearance on Sunday.

## Great Eastern

*103 Trafalgar Street, BN1 4ER
(685681). Bus 5, 6, 7, 14, 17, 22, 26,
27, 40, 47, 50.* **Open** noon-midnight
Mon-Sat; noon-11pm Sun. **Pub.
Map** p84 D1 **119**

Scuffed wooden tables and teetering
shelves of books fill a low-ceilinged,
cramped but cosy interior, and the long
bar counter buzzes with chat and willing eye contact. Thursday and Sunday
are live music nights, typically a mix
of blues and jazz. Sunday roasts
include vegetarian options.

## Heart & Hand

*75 North Road, BN1 1YD (683320).
Bus 5, 6, 7, 14, 17, 22, 26, 27, 40,
47, 50.* **Open** noon-11pm Mon-Thur,
Sun; noon-midnight Fri, Sat. **Pub.**
Map p84 C3 **120**

A classic rock 'n' roll bar, this green-
tiled beauty sits regally on a street
corner alongside the commercial bustle of North Laine. As a vibrant neighbourhood local, it's festooned with
tatty flyers and posters for past and
future gigs and a battered jukebox
plays old vinyl records. A pizza oven
can nearly always be called into action,
and, until about 5pm, nearby café
Capers supplies burgers and baguettes
for drinkers – ask at the bar.

## Hell's Kitchen

*4 Gardner Street, BN1 1UP (604925,
www.hellskitchendeli.co.uk). Bus 5, 6,
7, 14, 17, 22, 26, 27, 40, 47, 50.*
**Open** 9am-5.30pm Mon-Sat; 11am-
5pm Sun. **££.** No credit cards. **Deli.**
Map p84 C3 **121**

Rock Ola p95

# Chocolate street

For those in need of a bit of a pick-me-up, Brighton & Hove has no shortage of alternative therapies – yoga, pilates, massage, meditation and… chocolate. On Duke Street, the main thoroughfare linking Brighton's modern Churchill Square with the more old-fashioned Lanes, is to be found a chocolate lovers' nirvana in the shape of two illustrious independent Brighton confectionery emporia.

Named on the drunken evening on which its founders decided to start a chocolate shop, the entertainingly titled **Choccywoccydoodah** (p109) is famous for its similarly outlandish bespoke chocolate cakes. But it also makes all manner of other chocolate creations – from kitsch puppies and gothic skulls to great slabs of rich Belgian chocolate embedded with marshmallows.

Christine Taylor, the shop's creative director and its main

designer, explained to *Time Out*: 'Brighton has a decadent vibe and Choccywoccydoodah taps into that.'

Even for the less cocoa-addicted, a peek into the shop window is a feast for the eyes.

Crafted entirely from chocolate (no icing, no marzipan – just chocolate), the elaborate cake decorations are made by a small team of highly trained chocolatiers using methods kept closely under wraps. The cakes themselves (chocolate, naturally) are made to traditional family recipes passed down from the owner's grandmother.

Around the corner from the main shop, on Middle Street, Choccywoccydoodah's **Bar du Chocolat** (p105) serves Belgian hot chocolate, chocolate cake and chocolate milkshakes, among other treats. Should you feel so inclined, you can hire it out for a chocolate-guzzling session.

Less outwardly ostentatious but equally devoted to 'chocolate as religion' is **Montezuma's** (p110), another Brighton institution that has achieved national recognition for its innovative products. Its offerings are more conventionally bar-and-truffle shaped than those of its flamboyant neighbour, Montezuma's subversive streak lies in its unexpected flavour combinations, among them chilli and lime, orange and geranium and peppermint and vanilla.

And just to add to the cocoa theme, further down Duke Street is an outpost of the national chain of chocolatiers **Hotel Chocolat** (www.hotelchocolat. co.uk) at no.11, with **Ben's Cookies** the next door along.

A sandwich bar and deli jam-packed with everything nibble-able. Bagels and latkes (potato pancakes) give the place a pronounced New York accent, and chunky sandwiches such as the hot chorizo and melted cheese ciabatta are enough to satisfy the most ravenous of shoppers.

## In Vino Veritas

*103 North Road, BN1 1YW (622522, www.invinobrighton.co.uk). Bus 1, 2, 5, 12, 17, 22, 24, 40, 50.* **Open** 11am-2am Mon-Sat; 11am-10.30pm Sun. **£££. Modern European. Map** p84 D3 ⓬②

An attractive menu of Anglo-French dishes is merely the supporting act for In Vino Veritas's bulging wine list. Portions are on the small side, but quality is high, and at least you'll have enough room left to justify ordering another bottle.

## Infinity Foods Café

NEW *50 Gardner Street, BN1 1UN (670743, www.infinityfoodscafe.co.uk). Bus 5, 6, 7, 14, 17, 22, 26, 27, 40, 47, 50.* **Open** 10.30am-5pm Mon-Fri; 10am-5pm Sat; noon-4pm Sun. **££. Café. Map** p84 C3 ⓬③

The cooked breakfasts at this organic and vegetarian café are immensely tasty, as are such saintly sandwich medleys as houmous, spinach, carrot, beetroot and alfalfa. Head round the corner to the associated Infinity Foods store (p98) for further inspiration.

## Inside Out

*95 Gloucester Road, BN1 4AP (692912). Bus 5, 6, 7, 14, 17, 22, 26, 27, 40, 47, 50.* **Open** 8am-5pm Mon-Fri, Sun; 8am-6pm Sat. **Café. Map** p84 C2 ⓬④

Tuck into a pancake stack speckled with berries, a full English or a wedge of homemade cake in this teeny café. With only a few tables, dining at Inside Out can often involve a bit of a wait, but its delicious brunch menu and small street-side patio make it a lovely place.

## Iydea

*17 Kensington Gardens, BN1 4AL (667992, www.iydea.co.uk). Bus 5, 6, 7, 14, 17, 22, 26, 27, 40, 47, 50.* **Open** 9.30am-5.30pm Mon-Sat; 10am-5.30pm Sun. **££. Café. Map** p84 C2 ⓬⑤

This reasonably priced and speedy canteen-style café does a roaring trade: once you've picked your main course (potato, spinach and red pepper tortilla, say, or a crisp mushroom and broccoli filo pie), your plate is stacked with seasonal salads and vegetables.

## Lick

*19 Gardner Street, BN1 1UP (945102, www.lickbrighton.com). Bus 5, 6, 7, 14, 17, 22, 26, 27, 40, 47, 50.* **Open** 10am-6pm Mon-Sat; 10am-5pm Sun. **Ice-cream. Map** p84 C3 ⓬⑥

Choose between a scoop or shake made from creamy fat-free frozen yoghurt or ice-cream, then add your toppings of choice – whether it be pineapple and passion fruit, peach and mango, or an indulgent sprinkle of white Belgian chocolate with cookies and cream.

## Lord Nelson

*36 Trafalgar Street, BN1 4ED (695872, www.thelordnelsoninn.co.uk). Bus 5, 6, 7, 14, 17, 22, 26, 27, 40, 47.* **Open** 11.30am-11pm Mon-Sat; noon-10.30pm Sun. **Pub. Map** p84 C1 ⓬⑦

Kick back in this 'proper pub' for a no-nonsense swig of real ale in easy reach of the station. Food-wise, it's your typical pub fare: sandwiches, and a roast on a Sunday. The Lord Nelson is quirkier than it would have itself think, however, being one of the only decent pubs in Brighton to show sport.

## Mange Tout

*81 Trafalgar Street, BN1 4EB (607270). Bus 5, 6, 7, 14, 17, 22, 26, 27, 40, 47, 50.* **Open** 9am-4pm Mon-Wed, Sun; 9am-4pm, 7-10pm Thur-Sat. **£££. French. Map** p84 C1 ⓬⑧

Mange Tout is an animated bistro offering well-executed French café fare during the day, and opening in the evening three times a week. From a sterling eggs Benedict to a fiendishly moreish charcuterie platter, the menu is clean and classic. For a quick fix, pop in for an applaudable coffee and buttery croissant.

## Mash Tun

*1 Church Street, BN1 1UE (684951). Bus 5, 6, 7, 14, 17, 22, 26, 27, 40, 47, 50.* **Open** noon-midnight Mon-Thur, Sun; noon-2am Fri, Sat. **Pub.** **Map** p84 C4 **129**

A laid-back student haunt with bags of character, the Mash Tun serves a hangover-busting pie-and-mash focused menu and remains one of Brighton's best-known pubs among the younger community. You can hardly miss the turquoise exterior, but your ears may get there first, as music and animated conversation blares out into the evening. It's not the sort of place that sells bowls of olives.

## Merkaba

**NEW** *Myhotel, 17 Jubilee Street, BN1 1GE (900300, www.merkababrighton. com). Bus 5, 6, 7, 14, 17, 22, 26, 27, 40, 50.* **Open** 5pm-midnight Mon-Thur, Sun; 5pm-2am Fri, Sat. **Bar.** **Map** p84 C3 **130**

With a strapline 'where spirituality meets hedonism', you may think Merkaba is a bit on the pretentious side. And, well, it is. But that doesn't stop it from being one of the few places in town capable of whipping up a proper cocktail. Its drinks are premium, with a fine selection of spirits worthy of any specialist bar.

## El Mexicano

*7 New Road, BN1 1UF (727766, www.elmexicano.co.uk). Bus 1, 2, 5, 12, 17, 22, 24, 40, 50.* **Open** noon-2.30pm, 7-10.30pm Mon-Thur; noon-11pm Fri, Sat; noon-10.30pm Sun. **Mexican.** **Map** p85 C6 **131**

A popular Mexican restaurant, especially for pre and post events at the Dome or Theatre Royal. The menu is what you would expect from a Mexican eaterie, and tasty and abundant. There are also some Spanish-style tapas to share. Upstairs is Bar Valentino, open from 5pm to late.

## Moshi Moshi

*The Opticon, Bartholomew Square, BN1 1JS (719195, www.moshibrighton.co.uk). Bus 5, 6, 7, 14, 17, 22, 26, 27, 40, 47, 50.* **Open** noon-10.30pm daily. **£££.** **Japanese.** Map p85 C5 **132**

Highly regarded sushi chain Moshi Moshi serves a steady stream of fishy delights from its conveyor belt and menu. Some locals claim standards have slipped in recent times, but the restaurant still pulls in plenty of sashimi-loving punters. The Brighton branch is housed in an eye-catching structure, going under the Bond-like title of the Opticon, which gives a nod to Japanese shoji screens.

## Office

*8-9 Sydney Street, BN1 4EN (0872 148 6071). Bus 5, 6, 7, 14, 17, 22, 26, 27, 40, 47.* **Open** noon-midnight Mon-Sat; noon-11pm Sun. **££. Bar/Thai.** Map p84 C2 **133**

Grab a cold one and tuck into some very acceptable Thai food, or relax in the courtyard space out back. A thoroughly mixed bunch walk through the Office's door, and the place gets so full at lunchtime and then again with the post-work crowd, that finding a seat becomes a treasure hunt.

## Pinocchio's

*22 New Road, BN1 1UF (677676, www.pinocchio.co.uk). Bus 5, 6, 7, 14, 17, 22, 26, 27, 40, 47, 50.* **Open** 11.30am-11.30pm daily. **££. Italian.** Map p85 C4 **134**

North Laine is peppered with cheery Italian eateries serving a similarly reasonable standard of budget eats, but Pinocchio's warmth and character (it's like dining in a big homely kitchen) puts it on top of the pile. Pizzas are their forté – there's a selection of meat

North Laine graffiti

# A taste of Brighton

Recreate your favourite dishes with two new cookbooks.

'We wanted vegetarianism that had more to do with indulgence than abstinence,' writes Amanda Powley in the preface to **Terre à Terre**'s (p109) recent cookbook. Flicking through the pages of this sumptuously photographed tome, the restaurant's trademark playful nature and its sophisticated culinary imagination are immediately apparent. What looks like soft-boiled eggs with soldiers is actually – deep breath – a mango crème diplomate and passion-fruit yolk, topped with meringue and served with fat pineapple soldiers.

The joviality also comes through in the names of the dishes, which regulars will recognise from the menu, such as Eely Good (salsify goujons with aubergine jelly eels, miso mashed potatoes, parsley liquor and lemon sage salt).

Many of the dishes are not the sort to knock up for lunch (pop into the restaurant for that)

and some of the ingredients will take a little tracking down, and as Amanda (who owns Terre à Terre with Philip Taylor) suggests: 'The recipes aren't set in stone – they're simply a starting point and the finished product is entirely in your own hands.'

The release coincides with that of a cookbook from another of Brighton's fine – and long-established – vegetarian restaurants, **Food for Friends** (p106). Its recipe book, like the restaurant, is a simpler affair. Written by owners Jane and Ramin Mostowfi and head chef Kalil Resende, *Food for Friends: Modern Vegetarian Cooking at Home* draws from its global menu. The dishes are more rustic than Terre à Terre's, with offerings such as sweet potato, garlic and rosemary gratin with red pepper sauce.

Both books are available from the respective restaurants and from City Books (p155).

dishes but this probably isn't the place for a life-changing steak – and the clean and simple bowls of pasta are pretty good for a quick break from shopping.

## Prince Albert

*48 Trafalgar Street, BN1 4ED (730499, www.myspace.com/theprince albert). Bus 5, 6, 7, 14, 17, 22, 26, 27, 40, 47, 50.* **Open** noon-midnight Mon-Thur, Sun; noon-12.30am Fri, Sat. **Pub. Map** p84 C1 ⑬

A rampantly busy and beloved music-led pub that has been made all the more infamous thanks to Banksy spraying two kissing policemen on its side. Valued as much for its music venue credentials as its bar, the Prince Albert is constantly pounding with regular gigs and events.

## Red Veg

*21 Gardner Street, BN1 1UP (679910, www.redveg.com). Bus 5, 6, 7, 14, 17, 22, 26, 27, 40, 47, 50.* **Open** 11.30am-6pm Mon, Tue; 11.30am-9pm Wed-Sat; noon-5pm Sun. No credit cards. **£. Café. Map** p84 C3 ⑬

Veggie burgers take centre-stage at this militant looking vegetarian café on trendy Gardner Street. There's no tofu on the menu, just really tasty meat-free food. Red Veg specials such as the spinach burger with tahini and pesto, and a divine mushroom burger with Swiss cheese, prove that a meat-free burger can be a mighty fine burger indeed. Should you feel you need more, you can go large for £1.

## Riki Tik

*18a Bond Street, BN1 1RD (683844). Bus 5, 6, 7, 14, 17, 22, 26, 27, 40, 47, 50.* **Open** noon-2am Mon-Wed, Sun; noon-3am Thur-Sat. **Bar. Map** p85 C4 ⑬

Knocking back shots, shooters and a rainbow of cocktails are the main activities to be had at Riki Tik, where leather booths populate a deceptively large space, and beats massage the eardrums of the late-night crowd.

## Rock Ola

*29 Tidy Street, BN1 4EL (673744, www.rockolacoffeebar.com). Bus 5, 6, 7, 14, 17, 22, 26, 27, 40, 47, 50.* **Open** 10.30am-4.30pm Mon-Sat. **££. American diner** p84 C1 ⑬

Fun-filled Rock Ola is a colourful and kitsch diner-cum-coffee bar on the corner of residential Tidy Street. Plastered with 1950s memorabilia including a large free-play jukebox, and serving breakfast loaded with such morning treats as hash browns and buttermilk pancakes, this chirpy family-run diner is a sheer pleasure.

## Wine Shop & Tasting Room

NEW *9 Jubilee Street, BN1 1GE (567176, www.tengreenbottles.com). Bus 5, 6, 7, 14, 17, 22, 26, 27, 40, 47, 50.* **Open** 11am-7pm Mon-Sat; noon-7pm Sun. **Wine bar. Map** p84 C3 ⑬

A dynamic Brighton newbie specialising in European wines from small producers, including a fair chunk of English offerings. Pop in to pick up a bottle for dinner or, for a flat £5 drink-in charge, screw dinner and enjoy it in the comfort of their premises. Nibbles are available, and the menu is set to expand to larger plates.

## Shopping

## Adaptatrap Percussion

*26 Trafalgar Street, BN1 4ED (672722, www.adaptatrap.co.uk). Bus 5, 6, 7, 14, 17, 22, 26, 27, 40, 47, 50.* **Open** 10.30am-6pm Mon-Sat. **Map** p84 C1 ⑭

Flying in the face of forbidding 'Do Not Touch' signs everywhere else, this music shop is packed with percussion instruments of all persuasions that browsers are actively encouraged to give a good old clang, clatter and bash. Adaptatrap is lined with djembe drums, kettle drums, recorders, pan flutes, xylophones, clappers, cymbals, tambourines, singing bowls, bells and whistles. Pop in and make some noise.

**BRIGHTON BY AREA**

## Angelic Hell

*2 North Road, BN1 1YA (697681, www.angelichelltattooworld.co.uk).* Bus 5, 6, 7, 14, 17, 22, 26, 27, 40, 47, 50. **Open** 11am-6pm Mon-Sat; noon-5pm Sun. No credit cards. **Map** p84 D3 **141**

While you may not be wholly comfortable with the word 'Hell' featuring in the title of somewhere that is about to start poking you with a needle, be reassured that Angelic Hell has been successfully ink-pricking for 12 years.

## Beyond Retro

*42 Vine Street, BN1 4AG (671937, www.beyondretro.com).* Bus 5, 6, 7, 14, 17, 22, 26, 27. **Open** 10am-6pm Mon-Wed, Fri, Sat; 10am-7pm Thur; 11am-5pm Sun. **Map** p84 D3 **142**

Delve into a kaleidoscope of clothes and accessories in this warehouse stocked with all that is vintage and retro. Whether you're looking for fancy dress or an unusual gift, this is a fun and eye-popping shopping experience.

## Bluedog Gallery

*20 Gardner Street BN1 1UP (622440, www.bluedoggallery.co.uk).* Bus 1, 2, 5, 12, 17, 22, 24, 40, 50. **Open** 11am-5.30pm Mon-Fri; 11am-6pm Sat; noon-5pm Sun. **Map** p84 C3 **143**

Hailing from Eastern Europe, Bluedog is a contemporary and quirky gallery with a pronounced sway towards Polish artwork. You'll find vivid colours and abstract shapes on sculpture, design posters, ceramics, glass, paintings and jewellery.

## Bonsai Tree Shop

*45 Sydney Street, BN1 4EP (621743, www.bonsai-ko.co.uk).* Bus 5, 6, 7, 14, 17, 22, 26, 27, 40, 47, 50. **Open** 10.30-5.30pm Tue-Sat; noon-6pm Sun (not open every Sun). **Map** p84 D2 **144**

Yes, a whole shop dedicated to the tiny bonsai tree. How enough people purchase mini-trees for it to stay in business is one of the great mysteries of North Laine. Worth a browse, even if just to make yourself feel like a giant.

## Brighton Bead Shop

*21 Sydney Street, BN1 4EN (675077, www.beadsunlimited.co.uk).* Bus 5, 6, 7, 14, 17, 22, 26, 27, 40, 47, 50. **Open** 10am-5.30pm Mon-Sat; noon-5pm Sun. **Map** p84 C2 **145**

Those violently opposed to beads should probably give this shop a miss. But anyone who is even slightly partial to creating will rejoice in this rainbow of glinting, shiny beads.

## Brighton Sausage Company

*28a Gloucester Road, BN1 4AQ (676677).* Bus 5, 6, 7, 14, 17, 22, 26, 27, 40, 47, 50. **Open** 11am-7pm Mon-Fri; 10am-7pm Sat; 11am-5pm Sun. **Map** p84 C2 **146**

The name doesn't lie: sausages are the focus at this specialist butchers. You'll find a yummy selection that includes some exemplary sausage rolls, as well as a deli counter that's stocked with fine-looking meats, cheeses and olives.

## Bromptons

*32 Gardner Street (697711, www.bromptonsofbrighton.co.uk).* Bus 5, 6, 7, 14, 17, 22, 26, 40, 47, 50. **Open** 9.30am-5.30pm Mon-Fri; 9.30am-6pm Sat; 11am-5pm Sun. **Map** p84 C3 **147**

If all opticians were as cool and accomplished as Bromptons, everyone would be speccing-up. Choose from thick preppy lenses, traditional shapes and colourful statement pairs.

## Crane Kalman Brighton

*38 Kensington Gardens, BN1 4AL (697096, www.cranekalman brighton.com).* Bus 1, 2, 5, 12, 17, 22, 24, 40, 50. **Open** 10am-6pm Mon-Sat; 10.30am-4.30pm Sun. **Map** p84 C2 **148**

Championing photography as a collectable art form, this popular gallery offers a selection of affordable prints and beautiful photos. Exhibitions change regularly, and are usually of an international standard. Local artists exhibit here too.

## Cyber Candy

*15 Gardner Street, BN1 1UP (08458 380958, www.cybercandy.co.uk). Bus 5, 6, 7, 14, 17, 22, 26, 27, 40, 47, 50.* **Open** 10.30am-6.30pm Mon-Sat; 11am-6pm Sun. **Map** p84 C3 ❿

The folk at Cyber Candy have travelled the world, snaffling up all the best treats so we can fill up on confectionery spanning continents and decades.

## Cyberdog

*13 Sydney Street, BN1 4EN (677961, www.cyberdog.net). Bus 5, 6, 7, 14, 17, 22, 26, 27, 40, 47, 50.* **Open** 10am-6.30pm Mon-Sat; 11am-5pm Sun. **Map** p84 C2 ❿

Aiming to please even the most adventurously dressed raver, Cyberdog glows with eye-catching neon rave and club wear. If silver spandex hot-pants rank high on your wish list, then Cyberdog's clobber will be right down your brightly lit street. There's even a children's range for your little raver. The accessories (headphones, watches) might be more accessible. Also makes good gifts for the eccentric cyclist.

**Wine Shop & Tasting Room p95**

## Dave's Comics

*5 Sydney Street, BN1 4EN (691012, http://davescomicsuk.blogspot.com). Bus 5, 6, 7, 14, 17, 22, 26, 27, 40, 47, 50.* **Open** 10am-6pm Mon-Wed, Fri; 11am-7pm Thur; 9.30am-6pm Sat; 11am-5pm Sun. **Map** p84 C2 ❿

An intriguing treasure trove of comics, graphic novels and manga titles awaits. And if you just don't get what all the fuss is about, the shop's blog gives insight into comics and graphic novels.

## Dirty Harry

*6 Sydney Street, BN1 4EN (607527). Bus 5, 6, 7, 14, 17, 22, 26, 27, 40, 47, 50.* **Open** 10am-6.30pm Mon-Sat; 11am-5.30pm Sun. **Map** p84 C2 ❿

Dirty Harry may have been surpassed by other old-school clothing joints in the style stakes, but this was one of Brighton's first vintage outlets to establish itself, and it's still a worthy destination for a rummage as they get a regular stream of stock.

## Get Cutie

*33 Kensington Gardens, BN1 4AL (688575, www.getcutie.co.uk). Bus 5, 6, 7, 14, 17, 22, 26, 27, 40, 47, 50.* **Open** 10.30am-5.30pm Mon-Thur; 10.30am-6pm Fri; 10am-6pm Sat; 11am-5pm Sun. **Map** p84 C2 ❿

Nab a black halterneck adorned with ladybirds or a strapless dress sporting skulls and red roses at this female-focused fashion boutique. Short dresses in bold prints are the mainstay, but a clutch of male shirts is just enough to keep his attention.

## Guarana Company

*36 Sydney Street, BN1 4EP (621406, www.guaranaco.com). Bus 5, 6, 7, 14, 17, 22, 26, 27, 40, 47, 50.* **Open** 9.30am-6pm Mon-Fri; 10.30am-6pm Sun. **Map** p84 D2 ❿

From a shot of fresh wheatgrass to superfood smoothies and shakes, Guarana Company has products claiming to keep eyes bright and coats glossy. As well as being a stocker of natural substances – such as bee pollen and goji berries – it's a seller of legal and herbal highs, making it popular with clubbers.

## Guitar, Amp & Keyboard Centre

*76-81 North Road, BN1 1YD (665142, www.guitarampkeyboard.com). Bus 5, 6, 7, 14, 17, 22, 26, 27, 40, 47, 50.* **Open** 9.30am-5.30pm Mon-Sat; 11am-4pm Sun. **Map** p84 C2 **155**

A memorable sight in North Laine, GAK's garish yellow front brandishing a giant guitar can be seen down Gardner Street. There's a comprehensive choice of electric instruments, guitars and audio equipment.

## Hope & Harlequin

*31 Sydney Street, BN1 4EP (675222, www.hopeandharlequin.com). Bus 5, 6, 7, 14, 17, 22, 26, 27, 40, 47, 50.* **Open** 10.30am-6pm Mon-Sat; noon-5pm Sun. **Map** p84 D2 **156**

Specialising in top-quality vintage and in-depth style advice, Louise Hill's tiny boutique oozes old-school glamour: think cashmere jumpers, sweet 1950s lace frocks and lovely swing coats. There's a good collection of jewellery.

## Infinity Foods

*25 North Road, BN1 1YA (603563, www.infinityfoodsretail.co.uk). Bus 5, 6, 7, 14, 17, 22, 26, 27, 40, 47, 50.* **Open** 9.30am-6pm Mon-Sat; 11am-5pm Sun. **Map** p84 C3 **157**

Way before organic veg-munching was given the celeb thumbs-up, workers cooperative Infinity Foods were championing the delights of organic vegetarian and vegan eating. This large shop sells whole food, confectionery, fruit and vegetables, and bread from the on-site bakery.

## Irregular Choice

*38 Bond Street, BN1 1RD (777120, www.irregularchoice.com). Bus 5, 6, 7, 14, 17, 22, 26, 27, 40, 47, 50.* **Open** 10am-6pm Mon-Sat; noon-6pm Sun. **Map** p84 C4 **158**

Jump the Gun

Footwear as quirky and unique as North Laine itself, Irregular Choice's fantastical creations come straight from some kind of dream world. Their charcterful treads are no flimsy one-wear wonders – they are built to last.

## Jump the Gun

*36 Gardner Street, BN1 1UN (626333, www.jumpthegun.co.uk). Bus 5, 6, 7, 14, 17, 22, 26, 27, 40, 47, 50.* **Open** 10am-6pm Mon-Sat; noon-5pm Sun. **Map** p84 C3 ⓯⓽

Sharpen up with Jump the Gun's slick range of mod clothing. Claiming to have the skills to truly 'Mod-ernise' the shabby man, this male boutique is the place to pick up crisp trousers, 1960s-cut raincoats or a classic felt trilby.

## Lust

*43 Gardner Street, BN1 1UN (699344, www.lust.co.uk). Bus 5, 6, 7, 14, 17, 22, 26, 27, 40, 47, 50.* **Open** 11am-7pm Mon-Fri, Sun; 10.30am-8pm Sat. **Map** p84 C3 ⓰⓪

Light-hearted novelty sweets, chocolates and gadgets will amuse initial browsers, plus there are sex toys and lingerie. Discreet staff will explain the ins and outs of any items in question.

## Mad Hatters

*89 Trafalgar Street, BN1 4ER (688488, www.madhattersandfriends.co.uk). Bus 5, 6, 7, 14, 17, 22, 26, 27, 40, 47, 50.* **Open** 10.30am-5.30pm Mon-Fri; 10.30am-6pm Sat; 11.30am-5pm Sun. **Map** p84 D1 ⓰⓵

The headgear here includes feathery fascinators, tweed flat caps and crisp Stetsons. All are hand-made and fitted.

## Punktured

*35 Gardner Street, BN1 1UN (688144, www.punktured.co.uk). Bus 5, 6, 7, 14, 17, 22, 26, 27, 40, 47, 50.* **Open** 10.30am-6pm Mon-Sat; noon-5pm Sun. **Map** p84 C3 ⓰⓶

Take the plunge at this professional and hygienic piercing studio, where friendly and experienced staff and a light and relaxed space will put worried minds at ease. These guys will make a hole in pretty much anywhere on your body you choose.

## Real Patisserie

*43 Trafalgar Street, BN1 4ED (457019, www.realpatisserie.co.uk). Bus 5, 6, 7, 14, 17, 22, 26, 27, 40.* **Open** 6.30am-5.30pm Mon-Sat. **Map** p84 C1 ⓰⓷

The artisan breads and sweet treats from this established pâtisserie are extremely popular – no wonder given its quality – the chewy brown loaf won't disappoint.

## Red Mutha

*92 Trafalgar Street, BN1 4ER (603976, www.redmutha.com). Bus 5, 6, 7, 14, 17, 22, 26, 27, 40.* **Open** 10am-6pm Mon-Sat; 11am-5pm Sun. **Map** p84 D1 ⓰⓸

Not one for the faint fashion-hearted, Red Mutha trades in one-off and customised clothes ensuring you'll pick up a truly original piece. A team of designers produce a selection of styles, and they'll also customise items.

## Resident

*28 Kensington Gardens, BN1 4AL (606312, www.resident-music.com). Bus 5, 6, 7, 14, 17, 22, 26, 27, 40, 47, 50.* **Open** 9am-6.30pm Mon-Sat; 10am-6pm Sun. **Map** p84 C2 ⓰⓹

This is *the* place to go for gig tickets and concert information in Brighton. An independent record store run by serious music-lovers, Resident is piled high with CDs and some vinyl spanning all genres. Check on the walls for the staff's recommendations.

## Snooper's Paradise

*7-8 Kensington Gardens, BN1 4AL (602558). Bus 5, 6, 7, 14, 17, 22, 26, 27, 40, 47, 50.* **Open** 10am-6pm Mon-Sat; 11am-4pm Sun. **Map** p84 C2 ⓰⓺

Paradise indeed: lose an afternoon at this busy flea market, amid Snooper's joyous jumble of retro coffee tables, antiques, random clothes, royal memorabilia mugs and tarnished trumpets.

**BRIGHTON BY AREA**

Upper Gardner Street Market

## To Be Worn Again

*12 Kensington Gardens, BN1 4AL (687811). Bus 5, 6, 7, 14, 17, 22, 26, 27, 40, 47, 50.* **Open** 10am-6pm daily. **Map** p84 C2 167

Typifying North Laine's penchant for retro fashion, To Be Worn Again's three stores (there's another branch on Sydney Street, and a third just outside the Lanes, at Providence Place) are carpeted with a jumble of 1960s and 1970s get-up. They specialise in high quality and well preserved gear, rather than a jumble of old clothes.

## Tramp

NEW *22 Trafalgar Street, BN1 4EQ (687968, www.trampvintageclothing. com). Bus 5, 6, 7, 14, 17, 22, 26, 27, 40, 47, 50.* **Open** 10am-6pm Mon-Sat; noon-5pm Sun. **Map** p84 D1 168

Tramp is a classic, high-end vintage boutique catering for women looking for items from the art deco 1930s to the glam rock 1970s. The shop is relaxed and uncluttered. Shoes, hats, jewellery, belts, hoisery and vintage wedding dresses are also for sale. Staff can also try to hunt down any requests.

## Tribeca

*21 Bond Street, BN1 1RD (673755). Bus 5, 6, 7, 14, 17, 22, 26, 27, 40, 47, 50.* **Open** 10am-6pm Mon-Sat; noon-5pm Sun. **Map** p84 C3 169

Beautifully cut, understated pieces from the likes of Isabel Marant, Vanessa Bruno, Erotokritos and Bi La Li fill the rails here – along with iconic Spring Court sneakers and a handful of hip jeans brands (Sass & Bide, Acne and Earnest Sewn). Tribeca stocks top quality designer clothes, and they are comensurately priced.

## Two Feathers

*11 Kensington Gardens, BN1 4AL (692929, www.twofeathers.co.uk). Bus 5, 6, 7, 14, 17, 22, 26, 27, 40, 47, 50.* **Open** 10am-6pm Mon-Sat; 11am-6pm Sun. **Map** p84 C2 170

Striking jewellery and 100 per cent wool blankets are the top picks from this specialist Native American store. Jewellery pieces are handmade and come directly from tribes in the United States, while quality fringed suede and leather jackets are more substantial purchases.

## Upper Gardner Street Market

*Upper Gardner Street, BN1 4AN
(www.brightonstreetmarket.co.uk). Bus
5, 6, 7, 14, 17, 22, 26, 27, 40, 47, 50.*
**Open** from 9am Sat. **Map** p84 C2 **171**
Upper Gardner Street has been used for
market-trading for over a century.
From fruit and vegetables to eclectic
cutlery, there are always interesting
items here for Saturday perusal. The
road is closed to traffic at the weekend,
so pedestrians are free to wander.

## Vegetarian Shoe Shop

*12 Gardner Street, BN1 1UP (685685,
www.vegetarian-shoes.co.uk). Bus 5,
6, 7, 14, 17, 22, 26, 27, 40, 47, 50.*
**Open** 10am-6pm Mon-Sat; 1-6pm Wed.
**Map** p84 C3 **172**
This signature Brighton store stocks a
large array of shoes 100 per cent free
of anything animal. While 20 years ago
the vegetarian shoe was one of the
most dowdy and plain items to tread
the Brighton pavement, these days it
takes vibrant and fashionable forms,
including sturdy boots and brightly
coloured sandals.

## Vintage Magazine Company

*37 Kensington Gardens, (671812,
www.vinmag.com). Bus 5, 6, 7, 14,
17, 22, 26, 27, 40, 50.* **Open** 10am-
6pm Mon-Sat; noon-6pm Sun.
**Map** p84 C2 **173**
This Kensington Gardens shop stocks
an enormous array of vintage magazines plus retro fridge magnets, shopping bags, T-shirts, keyrings and
more. Not everything is particularly
tasteful, but the vintage Brighton
travel posters make for wonderful
holiday keepsakes.

## Yoma

*39 Gardner Street, BN1 1UN
(571455, www.yomauk.com). Bus 5,
6, 7, 14, 17, 22, 26, 27, 40, 47, 50.*
**Open** 10am-6pm Mon-Fri; 10am-6.30pm
Sat; 11am-6.30pm Sun. **Map** p84 C3 **174**
At its core Yoma is a shoe store, but it
also stocks some bags and simple
clothing. Yoma has distinct style, with
round-toed chunky shoes adorned with
flowers being a staple. Prices are reasonable, so you can treat yourself to
something a bit different.

**BRIGHTON BY AREA**

## Zoing Image

*1 Sydney Street, BN1 4EN (686568, www.zoingimage.com). Bus 5, 6, 7, 14, 17, 22, 26, 27, 40, 47, 50.* **Open** 11am-6pm Mon-Fri; 10am-6pm Sat; 11am-5pm Sun. **Map** p84 C2 **175**

Zoing Image has a great selection of iconic Brighton images printed on canvas. Its coasters, fridge magnets and clocks make great souvenirs and there is a full range of Lomography products.

## Nightlife

### Komedia

*44-47 Gardner Street, BN1 1UN (0845 293 8480, www.komedia.co.uk). Bus 5, 6, 7, 14, 17, 22, 26, 27, 40, 47, 50.* **Open** varies. **Map** p84 C3 **176**

This is a quirky and daring venue that provides a platform for a wealth of quality fringe and alternative acts. An array of gigs, cabaret, child-focused events and a steady stream of touring comics, plus Komedia's own resident comedy nights, ensure a thoroughly entertaining selection.

## Arts & leisure

### Basement

*24 Kensington Street, BN1 4AJ (699733, www.thebasement.uk.com). Bus 1, 2, 5, 12, 17, 22.* **Open** varies. **Map** p84 C2 **177**

Performance art at its most eclectic, The Basement is a thoroughly creative space for boundary-pushing performance art. Regular night Supper Club sees a range of performers strut their stuff as the audience tucks into some edibles – the only catch is that sometimes no one knows what the night entails until it's begun.

### Brighton Dome

*12a Pavilion Buildings, Castle Square, BN1 1EE. Box office 29 New Road, BN1 1UG (709709, www.brighton dome.org). Bus 1, 2, 5, 12, 17, 22, 24, 40, 50.* **Open** varies. **Box office** 10am-6pm Mon-Sat. **Map** p85 C4 **178**

A dedicated music and arts complex with three venues in one, the Brighton Dome is the key player in Brighton's mainstream music scene (and, just for a bit of pub quiz trivia, it is also where Abba won the Eurovision Song Contest in 1974). Big names and large-scale productions impress in the Concert Hall – now a grand space, but initially intended as stables for the Prince Regent's horses. After being transformed into a concert venue in the mid 1800s, the Concert Hall became one of the most fashionable places in the UK to take in a show.

Also in the complex you'll find the Corn Exchange (see below) and the Pavilion Theatre, putting on everything from dance and musicals to bands and comedy.

The Brighton Dome also runs the acclaimed Brighton Festival (p35), an annual arts extravaganza in May. There's a new café in the large foyer of the Dome, which is due to increase its profile soon with a food menu.

### Corn Exchange

*12a Pavilion Buildings, Castle Square, BN1 1EE. Box office 29 New Road, BN1 1UG (709709, www.brightondome.org). Bus 1, 2, 5, 12, 17, 22, 24, 40, 50.* **Open** varies. **Map** p85 C4 **179**

Tucked to one side of the Concert Hall, the Corn Exchange – previously a museum – attracts alternative music fans of all ages with a regular stream of bands, as well as popular comedians. It's in this venue, smaller than the Dome or Concert Hall, where the most interesting acts can be found.

### Prince Regent Leisure Centre

*Church Street, BN1 1YA (685692). Bus 1, 2, 5, 12, 17, 22.* **Open** 7am-10pm Mon-Fri; 9am-6pm Sat; 9am-10pm Sun. **Map** p85 D4 **180**

For a dip in a family-friendly pool, the Prince Regent Leisure Centre is a functional option. There's a selection of

Komedia

pools and it has a gym, sauna and steam room that can be used for one-off sessions by visitors.

### Theatre Royal

*35 Bond Street, BN1 1SD (0844 871 7627, www.ambassadortickets.com). Bus 1, 2, 5, 12, 17, 22, 24, 40, 50.* **Open** varies. **Map** p85 C4 ⓭
The Theatre Royal is one of Brighton's more mainstream venues, but certainly not shy of some alternative comedy or controversial productions. The theatre is a particularly prolific venue during the Comedy Festival in October (p40) when the big name comedians arrive.

### Treatment Rooms

*21 New Road, BN1 1UF (818444, www.thetreatmentrooms.co.uk). Bus 1, 2, 5, 12, 17, 22, 24, 40, 50.* **Open** 9am-8pm Mon, Fri; 9am-9pm Tue-Thur; 9am-6pm Sat; 11am-5pm Sun. **Map** p85 C4 ⓮
Indulge yourself from a lengthy list of facials and an assortment of half-day treatment programmes, all promising to preen, polish, tighten, moisturise and lift. This urban day spa has a loyal following and can get busy.

## The Lanes

Sitting pretty by the sea, the Lanes twinkle with silver jewellery and clothing boutiques. The teeny alleys, or twittens, of the historic quarter are a real squeeze at busier times – so be prepared to plough through a throng of shoppers steaming up the windowpanes and eyeing up trinkets old and new.

The Lanes date back to the 16th century, and grew up as pathways between allotments and gardens. Many of the buildings that you see today were built later, but some pubs, such as the **Cricketers** (p105), are original.

Food is at the forefront, with stacks of global fare; innovative vegetarian restaurants **Food for Friends** (p106) and **Terre à Terre** (p109) lead an ever-increasing herd of meat-free eateries, and sea-gleaned delicacies range from the offerings at shellfish stalls to Pernod-soaked rock oysters at **Riddle & Finns** (p107).

Sweet relief can be found at choc fanatics **Choccywoccydoodah** and

BRIGHTON BY AREA

**Jeremy Hoye p109**

their café **Bar du Chocolat** (p105). If the upmarket seafood joints are a little above your budget, visit quality chains such as Vietnamese vendors **Pho** (p107), and **Jamie's Italian** (p107) for affordable dining options. A post-dinner boogie can be had at one of the several seafront clubs, the best being under the King's Road Arches rather than on the busy West Street – and if you make it until dawn, the seaside sunrise is a corker.

For most Lanes venues, we have listed the main buses that go along North Street – the main thoroughfare through the town centre. Nothing listed here is more than a ten-minute walk from North Street.

## Sights & museums

### Old Police Cells Museum
*Town Hall, Bartholomew Square, BN1 1JA (291052, www.oldpolice cellsmuseum.org.uk). Bus 1, 2, 5, 12, 17, 22, 24, 40, 50.* **Open** *May-Nov* by appt Tue, Thur, Sat. **Admission** free. **Map** p85 C5 **183**

Under the Town Hall are the police cells which were used between 1830 and 1967. The museum charts the history of the police in Brighton with colourful stories of the murder of the chief constable in 1844, to some of the mods and rockers who were briefly incarcerated here after violence on the beaches. There are items and uniforms from the police force, and cells in which to take the obvious photos. It's not going to win any awards, but makes for a good rainy-day activity.

## Eating & drinking

### Aguadulce
*10-11 King's Road, BN1 1NE (328672, www.aguadulce-restaurant.com). Bus 1, 2, 5, 12, 17, 22, 24, 40, 50.* **Open** 3-11pm Mon-Fri; 1-11.30pm Sat. **££**. **Spanish**. **Map** p85 C6 **184**

With the owners coming directly from Almería in Spain, it's clear Aguadulce is an authentic tapas bar and restaurant. There's a bar area, where you can sit with a glass of wine and some calamari. If you opt for the main restaurant try the lamb cutlets, paella or today's catch – just like in Spain.

## Bar du Chocolat

*27 Middle Street, BN1 1AL (732232, www.choccywoccydoodah.com). Bus 1, 2, 5, 12, 17, 22, 24, 40, 50.* **Open** 10am-6pm Mon-Fri; 10am-6.30pm Sat; 11am-5pm Sun. **Café**. **Map** p85 B5 185

Settle down to superlative chocolate at connoisseur Choccywoccydoodah's (see box p90) indulgent little café outlet. The chocolate dipping pots are particularly scandalous: melted Belgian chocolate served with sugary dippers that include marshmallows, Turkish delight and fudge. If you want to take some home with you, head up to the main store on Duke Street (p109).

## Chilli Pickle

*Brighton House, 42 Meeting House Lane, BN1 1HB (323824, www.the chillipicklebistro.co.uk). Bus 1, 2, 5, 12, 17, 22, 24, 40, 50.* **Open** noon-3pm, 6.30pm-10.30pm Wed-Sun. **£££**. **Indian**. **Map** p85 C5 186

Nepalese and Indian street food are the inspiration for Chilli Pickle's menu, where classic dishes take on a western twist – try tandoori-spiced quail, or curried mussels infused with coconut.

Daytime cuisine is designed for snacking, while evenings feature heartier meals, such as pork belly vindaloo, and the acclaimed oxtail madras.

## Cricketers

*15 Black Lion Street, BN1 1ND (329472, www.goldenliongroup.co.uk). Bus 1, 2, 5, 12, 17, 22, 24, 40, 50.* **Open** 11am-11pm Mon-Wed, Sun; 11am-midnight Thur; 11am-1am Fri, Sat. **Pub**. **Map** p85 B5 187

This cosy and historic pub invariably accommodates locals, clusters of shoppers and local employees on their lunch breaks – as well as the odd solitary, literary soul, attracted by mention of the place in *Brighton Rock* by former regular Graham Greene. It has a wonderful and, in parts, bizarre interior, plus a courtyard. Beware of the ghosts.

## Donatello

*1-3 Brighton Place, BN1 1HJ (775477, www.donatello.co.uk). Bus 5, 6, 7, 14, 17, 22, 26, 27.* **Open** 11.30am-11.30pm daily. **££**. **Italian**. **Map** p85 C5 188

The location for Donatello could hardly be better. In the heart of the Lanes, this large restaurant spills out

**Terre à Terre p109**

BRIGHTON BY AREA

The Lanes

on to the pavement on sunny days. It's run by an Italian family who cook up a menu of antipasti, pizza, meat dishes, pasta and some great ice-cream. Dishes include veal escalope in breadcrumbs. The set menus are great value. A fun, affordable option.

### Fishy Fishy

NEW *36 East Street, BN1 1HL (723750, www.fishyfishy.co.uk). Bus 1, 2, 5, 12, 17, 22, 24, 40, 50.* **Open** 9am-11pm daily. **£££. Seafood.** **Map** p85 C5 189

Owned by TV presenter Dermot O'Leary, this 'seafood brasserie' has earned a good reputation for no-nonsense seafood dishes, such as baked lemon sole with herb and parmesan crust or hot smoked mackerel with artichoke salad. All the seafood is from sustainable sources and most of it is caught off the shores of Sussex. The prices for the main dishes are very reasonable, especially for this location, unless you splash out for the oysters, champagne and lobster combination. There's outside seating that's lovely when the sun shines.

### Food for Friends

*17-18 Prince Albert Street, BN1 1HF (202310, www.foodforfriends.com). Bus 1, 2, 5, 12, 17, 22, 24, 40, 50.* **Open** noon-10pm Mon-Thur, Sun; noon-10.30pm Fri, Sat. **£££. Modern vegetarian.** Map p85 C5 190

The vibe is laid-back and the globally influenced food excellent at this renowned vegetarian restaurant. The warm halloumi and mango salad is a crowd-pleaser, given a hot edge by wasabi-roasted cashew nuts. Dishes are stuffed with fresh local produce, with plenty of vegan and gluten-free options to suit all. The wine list includes organic varieties.

### Hop Poles

*13 Middle Street, BN1 1AL (710444). Bus 1, 2, 5, 12, 17, 22, 24, 40, 50.* **Open** noon-midnight Mon-Thur, Sun; noon-1am Fri, Sat. **Pub.** Map p85 B5 191

For a clean, cold pint in a charming pub, you can't go far wrong with the Hop Poles. A changing menu keeps food options fresh, with sausages, hefty burgers, Italian dishes and roasts.

## Hotel du Vin

*2-6 Ship Street, BN1 1AD (718588, www.hotelduvin.com). Bus 11X.*
**Open** noon-2pm, 7-10pm Mon-Thur; 12.30-2pm, 7-10.30pm Fri, Sat; 12.30-2.30pm, 7-10pm Sun. **£££. Bistro.**
**Map** p85 B5 192
This chain gives equal weight to food and accommodation, making a point of offering reliable if unchallenging French food and thoughtfully selected wines alongside its well-specced rooms. The bistro here follows the formula but draws on local suppliers to furnish the ingredients for such dishes as pork rillettes, steak tartare and stuffed rabbit leg. Mood and decor are informal with a leather-and-brick clubbiness.

## Jamie's Italian

NEW *11 Black Lion Street, BN1 1ND (915480, www.jamieoliver.com). Bus 1, 2, 5, 12, 17, 22, 24, 40, 50.* **Open** noon-11pm Mon-Sat; noon-10.30pm Sun. **££. Italian. Map** p85 B5 193
The Brighton branch of Mr Oliver's affordable string of Italian eateries is everything you'd expect from Brand Jamie: bright, slick and radiating with good cheer. Plump green olives chilled on a bed of ice are wonderfully smoky, and even the simple bowls of spaghetti bolognaise are aromatic and comforting. Jamie's Italian doesn't take bookings, but a short wait will be rewarded.

## Marwood Café

*52 Ship Street, BN1 1AF (382063, www.themarwood.com). Bus 1, 2, 5, 12, 17, 22, 24, 40, 50.* **Open** 9am-8pm Mon-Sat; 10am-8pm Sun. **Café. Map** p85 B4 194
If it was for the coffee alone, it would be worth walking across the city – the baristas turn out carefully brewed cups, with antipodean-style flourishes – but we'd probably walk even further for its brownies. The decor is a kitsch mishmash of junk, art and 1970s album covers. Free wireless, comfy seating and a relaxed vibe make it a favourite for laptop-tapping creatives and shoppers.

## Mock Turtle Tea Shop

*4 Pool Valley, BN1 1NJ (327380). Bus 1, 2, 5, 12, 17, 22, 24.* **Open** 9am-6pm Tue-Sun. **Café. Map** p85 D6 195
Holding its own amid the flurry of trendy cafés churning out superfood smoothies, the Mock Turtle Tea Shop is the kind of traditional teatime place your nan would rave about. Choose from cream teas and over 30 homemade cakes, omelettes and fish dishes. It's traditional but not stuffy. And not an acai berry in sight.

## Pho

*12 Black Lion Street, BN1 1ND (202403, www.phocafe.co.uk). Bus 1, 2, 5, 12, 17, 22, 24, 40, 50.* **Open** noon-10pm Mon-Thur, Sun; noon-10.30pm Fri, Sat. **££. Vietnamese. Map** p85 B5 196
After four successful branches in London, Vietnamese street-food specialists Pho have popped up Brighton with their biggest restaurant yet. Here, you'll find big steaming bowls of pho (Vietnamese noodle soup), and a host of rice-noodle based dishes. For something more tangy, try the Bun Tom Hue – a hot and spicy prawn soup.

## Rasa

*2-3 Little East Street, BN1 1HT (771661, www.rasarestaurants.com). Bus 1, 2, 5, 12, 17, 22, 24, 40, 50.* **Open** noon-3pm, 6-10.30pm Mon-Sat; 6-10.30pm Sun. **££. Indian. Map** p85 C5 197
Don't be put off by the saccharine-pink exterior; this restaurant (an outpost of the national chain) serves a thoroughly decent spread of spicy South Indian fare inspired by the south-western Indian state of Kerala.

## Riddle & Finns

*12b Meeting House Lane, BN1 1HB (323008, www.riddleandfinns.co.uk). Bus 1, 2, 5, 12, 17, 22, 24.* **Open** noon-midnight Mon-Thur, Sun; 9.30am-1.30am Fri, Sat. **£££. Seafood. Map** p85 C4 198

**BRIGHTON BY AREA**

Marwood Cafe p107

At Riddle & Finn's ambitious and accomplished champagne and oyster bar, tucked down an alleyway off North Street, diners share marble-topped tables as the staff pair immaculately presented seafood with glasses of fizz. Oysters come hot or cold, rock or native, with spinach, Pernod, horseradish or vodka.

## Scoop & Crumb

*5-6 East Street, BN1 1HP (202563). Bus 5, 6, 7, 14, 17, 22, 26, 27, 40, 47, 50.* **Open** 10am-6pm Mon-Fri, Sun; 10am-7pm Sat. **Ice-cream**. **Map** p85 C6 ➒➒

A short two-minute stroll from Brighton beach and you can get your mouth around such tasty concoctions as white chocolate ice-cream or coconut sorbet. Scoop & Crumb's retro-style ice-cream parlour has a wealth of enticing flavours, and if one just isn't enough, then why not create the sundae of your dreams?

## Terre à Terre

*71 East Street, BN1 1HQ (729051, www.terreaterre.co.uk). Bus 1, 2, 5, 12, 17, 22, 24, 40, 50.* **Open** noon-10.30pm Mon-Fri; noon-11pm Sat; noon-10pm Sun. **£££. Vegetarian**. **Map** p85 C5 ➋⓿⓿

Inventive vegetarian cooking in relaxed surroundings is the hallmark at Terre à Terre. The globally inspired menu encompasses everything from blue cheese soufflé with watercress cream to fragrant aubergine jungle curry. This boundary-bashing eaterie continues to have praise heaped liberally upon it, and most certainly warrants an evening's attention. See box p94.

## Shopping

### Brighton Body Casting

*7 Ship Street Gardens, BN1 1AJ (07961 338045, www.brightonbody casting.com). Bus 5, 6, 7, 14, 17, 22, 26, 27, 40, 47, 50.* **Open** 10am-6pm daily. **Map** p85 B5 ➋⓿➊

You know that moment on a seaside break, when you realise that the only way to truly commemorate the experience is by getting a cast of your naked body? Well, Brighton Body Casting is the place to head. The studio is open every day, but warns 'it's worth phoning in case I'm bunking off.'

### Choccywoccydoodah

*24 Duke Street, BN1 1AG (329462, www.choccywoccydoodah.com). Bus 5, 6, 7, 14, 17, 22, 26, 27, 40, 47, 50.* **Open** 10am-6pm Mon-Sat; 11am-5pm Sun. **Map** p85 B4 ➋⓿➋

See box p90.

### Fidra

*47 Meeting House Lane, BN1 1HB (328348, www.fidra.co.uk). Bus 1, 2, 5, 12, 17, 22, 24, 40, 50.* **Open** 10am-5.30pm daily. **Map** p85 C4 ➋⓿➌

Fidra's Edwardian and Victorian treasures can range from delicate gold necklaces of seed-pearl-studded swallows to show-stopping diamond and pearl brooches.

### Jeremy Hoye

*22a Ship Street, BN1 1AD (777207, www.jeremy-hoye.com). Bus 1, 2, 5, 12, 17, 22, 24, 40, 50.* **Open** 10am-6pm Mon-Sat; 11am-4pm Sun. **Map** p85 B5 ➋⓿➍

The Lanes jewellery quarter is stuffed with jewellers selling glittering rings. But Jeremy Hoye's contemporary collection (and setting) has attracted attention the world over, and among celebrities. It also does a nice line in Brighton-related charms such as a deckchair and a little golden copy of Graham Greene's *Brighton Rock*.

### Jewel Thief

*26 Duke's Lane, BN1 1BG (771044, www.jewelthiefgallery.com). Bus 1, 2, 5, 12, 17, 22.* **Open** 10am-6pm Mon-Sat; 11am-5pm Sun. **Map** p85 B4 ➋⓿➎

Sneak into this shop for statement-making jewellery executed with flair and finesse. Star turns include Tina

Lilienthal's luscious, resin-cast cherry necklaces (as seen in *Vogue*) and Tufi Patah's chunky agate rings. Prices vary, but Bena's gold fox, silver skull and wooden brooches are more affordable.

## Montezuma's

*15 Duke Street, BN1 1AH (324979, www.montezumas.co.uk). Bus 1, 2, 5, 12, 17, 22, 24, 40, 50.* **Open** 9.30am-6pm Mon-Sat; 11am-5pm Sun. **Map** p85 B4 **206**
See box p90.

## Rounder

*19 Brighton Square, BN1 1HD (325440, www.rounderbrighton.co.uk). Bus 1, 2, 5, 12, 17, 22, 24, 40, 50.* **Open** 9.30am-6pm Mon-Sat; 10.30am-6pm Sun. **Map** p85 C4 **207**
A huge selection of vinyl is Rounder's USP, with in-store turntables to boot – pretty much what you'd expect from Brighton's oldest record store. Rounder continues to hold its own with a great selection of old and new, and the staff are clearly well versed.

## Tickled

*59 Ship Street, BN1 1AE (628725, www.tickledonline.co.uk). Bus 5, 6, 7, 14, 17, 22, 26, 27, 40, 47, 50.* **Open** 10.30am-6pm Mon-Sat; noon-5pm Sun. **Map** p85 B5 **208**
This female-focused boutique sells cuffs, whips and sex toys of every description (and dimension). Tickled's saucier stock is hidden downstairs – off-limits to unaccompanied gents.

## Nightlife

## Ink Bar

*54-55 Meeting House Lane, BN1 1HB (207040). Bus 5, 6, 7, 14, 17, 22, 26, 27, 40, 47, 50.* **Open** 9pm-1am Mon-Thur; 9pm-4am Fri, Sat. **Map** p85 C4 **209**
A modern, multi-level bar tucked away in the Lanes, Ink is home to some of Brighton's scene-savvy dance and urban events, plus student club nights.

## Lola Lo

NEW *Unit 2, 75-79 East Street, BN1 1NF (777904, www.lolabrighton. com). Bus 5, 6, 7, 14, 17, 22, 26, 27, 40, 47, 50.* **Open** 9pm-3am Mon, Tue; 8pm-late Thur; 8pm-3am Fri, Sat. **Map** p85 C6 **210**
A slightly twisted Tiki bar, Lola Lo offers you clubbing experiences in a kitsch South Pacific environment. The Polynesian decor welcomes a weekly mix of club nights aimed at students and the city's more stylish hedonists. Lola Lo prides itself on its cocktail, rum and champagne menu, with private booths and table service available. Wednesday and Sunday nights are usually set aside for private events.

## Lucky Voice

*8 Black Lion Street, BN1 1ND (715770, www.luckyvoice.com). Bus 5, 6, 7, 14, 17, 22, 26, 27, 40, 47, 50.* **Open** 6pm-2am Mon-Fri; 3pm-2am Sat, Sun. **Map** p85 C6 **211**
Secretly gagging to demonstrate you still know all the lyrics to 'Ice Ice Baby'? Well, here's your chance – grab a group of mates and belt out some karaoke classics. Get into character with the help of the dressing-up box, and knock back some confidence-enhancing drinks in the bar downstairs. It's half-price karaoke on Thursdays.

## Madame Geisha

NEW *75-79 East Street, BN1 1NF (770847, www.madamegeisha.com). Bus 5, 6, 7, 14, 17, 22, 26, 27, 40, 47, 50.* **Open** 11am-late daily. **Map** p85 C6 **212**
The vibrant Madame Geisha packs art exhibitions, club events, live music and pan-Asian cuisine (including tapas and a speciality teas menu) into its three labyrinthine levels throughout the week. Geisha's twisted stairwells, transparent floors and secret terraces also conceal a private karaoke suite. The venue regularly hosts parties for media, music and fashion circles, so some negotiation may be needed.

# Divine inspiration

A former church is Brighton's finest gallery space.

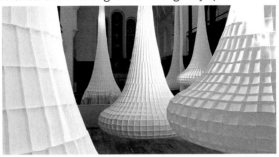

Religion and art always had a synergy. Grandiose places of worship often provide a more ethereal space in which to place art than a sterile gallery. Even when the church is deconsecrated and the art secular, the space can add a gravitas and context to the art. **Fabrica** (p112) is based in Regency-period Holy Trinity Church, in the heart of the Lanes. Its austere façade gives way to an open and multi-use space, which provides a backdrop for artists of all media.

Opened in 1996, Fabrica was set up to focus on contemporary visual art and to commission site-specific work. It has since become one of the most important art galleries in the city, and has achieved a high level of access and education for visitors.

'Our mission is to bring contemporary visual art to a wider audience,' says communications director Laurence Hill. 'It's free and in the centre of town. And we have a group of 60-80 volunteers who can talk to visitors about the shows.'

Alongside the static displays, Fabrica often commission exhibition-specific workshops, activities and, recently, a dance. 'Its about exploring the exhibition,' Laurence adds. 'It gives people a different way to understand it. We try to engage in a different way.'

Fabrica has also embraced social networking with a Twitter account and a Facebook presence that offers a behind-the-scenes insight into the workings of the gallery. There's also an artists' resource centre, designed to help artists find funding, exhibition space and studios.

There are four main shows a year, some independent, but many working in partnerships with, for example, the Brighton Photo Biennial and the Brighton Festival. During the 2010 festival, it hosted Brian Eno's *77 Million Paintings*, a kaleidoscopic light installation, seemingly inspired by stained-glass windows, on high-definition video screens with an ambient soundscape – an exhibition that took full advantage of the former church architecture.

## Royal Pavilion Tavern

*7-8 Castle Square, BN1 1FX (735819, www.pavtav.com). Bus 5, 6, 7, 14, 17, 22, 26, 27, 40, 47, 50.* **Open** noon-2am Mon, Wed; 11am-3am Tue, Thur-Sat; noon-1am Sun. **Map** p85 D5 **213**

More commonly known as the Pav Tav, this lively student pub has occupied the same premises since the early 19th century. Reputedly haunted, the Pav Tav is more genteel in the daytime, with decent pub grub available. The nights are very much the preserve of Brighton's youth, with regular alternative club nights and local rock bands playing in the sprawling, low-beamed upper storey. The drinks prices are suitably student friendly all night. And those no longer of the student demographic, it'll bring back some great memories, particularly at Snap, Crackle & Britpop, held on the last Saturday of the month.

## Arts & leisure

### Aloka

*14 East Street, BN1 1HP (823178, www.aloka.aura-soma.net). Bus 5, 6, 7, 14, 17, 22, 26, 27, 40, 47, 50.* **Open** 10am-9.30pm daily. **Map** p85 C5 **214**

This urban wellness centre might not be your grand bells-and-whistles sanctuary, but the day spa's selection of massages offer harmonious and stress-busting indulgence to round off a day trawling the shops. The treatments also include a 15-minute Aura Cleanse; intriguing, if nothing else. For something more tangible, try the vegan and raw food restaurant – the cheesy chips are actually cashew cheese coated kale chips – and the café serving Fairtrade and biodynamic coffee and organic teas.

### Fabrica

*40 Duke Street, BN1 1AG (778646, www.fabrica.org.uk). Bus 5, 6, 7, 14, 17, 22, 26, 27, 40, 47, 50.* **Open** 9.30am-5.30pm Mon-Fri. **Map** p85 B4 **215**
See box p111.

The Lanes

Hand in Hand p117

# Kemp Town & Hanover

These days, Kemp Town is defined as being the area east of the Old Steine. It used to refer just to the buildings designed and funded by Thomas Read Kemp further to the east – luxury townhouses which, when built in the first half of the 19th century, attracted visitors such as Charles Dickens and Lewis Carroll. Two centuries on, Kemp Town remains a lively area, centred now on the long and colourful stretch that is **St James's Street**.

The district is, famously, home to Brighton's gay quarter (or the 'gay village'), where expression of sexuality pulse from shops, restaurants and bars and form the foundation of the nightlife. You'll find strings of cosy cafés and coffee shops, enticing delis, informed gay lifestyle shops, unabashed bars

(including Brighton's oldest gay boozer), welcoming pubs and stylish restaurants. The stretch along the seafront attracts the larger gay clubs and bars, and there's even a naturist beach hidden in the shingle. The vibrant gay village merges into the sleepy calm pace of Kemp Town village, to the east, a laid-back district.

From Upper St James's Street through to St George's Street, planted in between mews of Victorian townhouses with art deco influence, there's a trail of interesting vintage shops all with their own eclectic mix of finds from different eras. With true Kemp Town style, the pubs, eateries, tearooms and bistros tend to show kitsch or vintage influences.

Further into the residential area, the founder of Kemp Town,

Thomas Read Kemp, has been immortalised in the magnificent buildings of Sussex Square, Arundel Terrace and Lewes Crescent, the largest crescent in Britain. If you're looking for somewhere to stay, there are a number of boutique hotels dotted in and around the seafront, each one with its own unique edge.

Further north is the residential district of **Hanover**, fondly called the Muesli Mountain due to its perceived hippyish vibe. (In reality, there is little to distinguish its demographics from other parts of Brighton.) The 15-acre **Queen's Park** is the focal point for the active Hanover community; Charles Barry, architect of the Houses of Parliament, designed the two entrance arches. The area is known for its excellent pubs, and the 'Southover Shuffle' pub crawl up steep Southover Street – stopping in the **Greys**, **Dover Castle** and **Sir Charles Napier**, among others – is a classic route.

For this guide, we have included the seafront east of the Brighton Pier, and along Madeira Drive. This includes the **Sea Life Centre**. Madeira Drive eventually reaches the Brighton Marina (p159). The road is all but pedestrianised, and is often used for events such as car rallies and antique fairs and car-boot sales. There are a handful of bars down here, plus Concorde 2, a great Brighton live-music venue.

Old Steine, Grand Parade and Lewes Road form the westernmost boundary of this chapter, and Elm Grove the northern boundary.

## Sights & museums

### Sea Life Centre

*Marine Parade, BN2 1TB (604234, www.sealifeeurope.com). Bus 12, 14, 27, 37.* **Open** *10am-5pm Mon-Fri; 10am-6pm Sat, Sun.* **Admission** *£15.50; £10.60 reductions; online discounts available.* **Map** *p116 B4* ❶
The world's oldest operating aquarium, the Sea Life Centre is one of the city's premier family destinations. There's a rock pool, an underwater tunnel with sharks, and other displays with sea-horses, piranhas and poison dart frogs. Top billing among the sea creatures, however, goes to Lulu, a giant sea turtle.

A glass-bottom boat, which floats on top of the main tank, has been recently introduced here. There are feedings (Tuesday, Thursday and Saturday), and tours throughout the day.

## Volk's Electric Railway

*Aquarium Station, Madeira Drive (www.volkselectricrailway.co.uk). Bus 12, 14, 27, 37.* **Open** (trains run every 15mins) 10.15am-5pm Mon, Wed, Thur; 11.15am-5pm Tue, Fri; 10.15am-6pm Sat, Sun. **Tickets** (return) £2.80; £1.40 reductions. **Map** p116 B4 ②

Since 1883, Volk's Railway has trundled between the pier end of Madeira Drive and near what is now Brighton Marina. The 'world's oldest operating electric railway' was designed by pioneering British engineer Magnus Volk, himself a Brighton resident. It's best seen as a quirky way to travel to the Marina, or something to take the kids on when you're at a loss. It only stops at Halfway Station near Yellowave (see below) en route.

## Yellowave Beachsports

*299 Madeira Drive, BN2 1EN (672222, www.yellowave.co.uk). Bus 12, 14, 27, 37.* **Open** *May-Sept* 10am-10pm Mon-Thur; 10am-8pm Fri-Sun. *Nov-Feb* 10am-9pm Tue-Thur; 10am-6pm Fri-Sun. **Map** p117 E4 ③
See box p121.

## Eating & drinking

## Black Dove

**NEW** *74 St James's Street, BN2 1PA (671119). Bus 1, 2, 7, 14, 27, 37.* **Open** 4pm-midnight Mon-Thur, Sun; 4pm-1am Fri, Sat. **Pub. Map** p116 C4 ④
This recent addition to the Kemp Town drinking scene is one of the most singular and sophisticated. It's decorated with ordinary junk, interesting junk and bespoke artwork, including a phenomenal urban canvas that's a mirror image of the bar in some crazy alternate reality. The selection of drinks is

huge, and includes hard-to-find beers, spirits and ciders, as well as good organic wines.

## Blanch House

*Blanch House Hotel, 17 Atlingworth Street, BN2 1PL (603504, www.blanch house.co.uk). Bus 1, 2, 7, 14, 27, 37, 47, 52.* **Open** 7-10pm Wed-Sat. **£££. Modern British. Map** p116 C4 ⑤
The stark white basement interior of this boutique hotel and restaurant reflects the reassuring brevity of its well-conceived seasonal menu. Starters might include a duo of quail with beetroot, horseradish purée, aged balsamic and parsley oil; followed by one of the five mains on offer, such as roast breast of Barbary duck with celeriac and truffle purée, fondant potato and beetroot and thyme jus. Delicacy is applied to the desserts, such as amaretto parfait with blackberries, kirsch syrup and almond tuille.

## Bom-Banes Restaurant

*24 George Street, BN2 1RH (606400, www.bom-banes.co.uk). Bus 1, 2, 7, 14, 27, 37, 47, 52, 73, N99.* **Open** 5-11pm Tue-Wed; 12.30-11.30pm Thur-Sat; 12.30-11pm Sun. **Pub. Map** p146 C3 ⑥
Run by musicians Jane Bom-Bane and Nick Pynn, this quirky little café and restaurant serves an interesting menu that ranges from Scandinavian-style venison to bresola. The food is excellent, but the decor is not to be missed: harmoniums and a theremin are packed in, alongside numerous other bits and bobs. A meal here can be an utterly bewitching experience.

## Brighton Rocks

**NEW** *6 Rock Place, BN2 1PF (601139, www.brightonrockspub.com). Bus 1, 2, 7, 14, 27, 37, 47, 52, 73, N99.* **Open** noon-11pm Mon-Wed; noon-midnight Thur; noon-1am Fri, Sat; noon-10.30pm Sun. **Bar. Map** p116 C4 ⑦
Under new management, this narrow intimate bar with indoor and heated outdoor seating offers pleasantries,

good food and sparkling cocktails. Brighton Rocks looks like returning to its former glory. A lovely pub.

## Dover Castle

*43 Southover Street, Hanover, BN2 2UE (688276). Bus 37.* **Open** noon-11.30 Mon-Thur, Sun; noon-12.30am Fri, Sat. Food served 12.30-3pm, 6-9pm Mon-Fri; noon-9pm Sat; noon-8pm Sun. **££. Pub.** Map p119 B2 **8**

The welcoming Dover Castle is a hangout for young Hanoverians in search of a community atmosphere. The daily Muesli Mountain Market (www.mueslimountainmarket.co.uk) is open 9am-4.30pm Mon-Sat in the pub car park, and it has recently opened a café in the pub (9am-3pm). By evening, the pub's dimly lit interior is unassuming, but the vibe is effortlessly cool. It's a Shepherd Neame pub, with a choice of four ales on tap, plus some interesting bottled beers. The food is upmarket pub grub: think local bangers and mash, and chilli made with dark chocolate.

## Drakes

*43-44 Marine Parade, BN2 1PE (696934, www.therestaurantatdrakes. co.uk). Bus 12, 14, 27, 37, 47.* **Open** 12.30-2pm, 7-10.30pm daily. **£££. Modern British.** Map p116 C4 **9**

Occupying one of Brighton's best boutique hotels (p177), the Restaurant at Drakes carries the quality of the residence into the intimate basement dining room. Plaudits continue to pile up and it's likely to be on the radar of Michelin inspectors before long. Chef Andrew Mackenzie conjures a menu that is a mix of English seasonal food with French stylings, incorporating dishes such as porc noir de Bigorre on celeriac purée with braised pig's cheek.

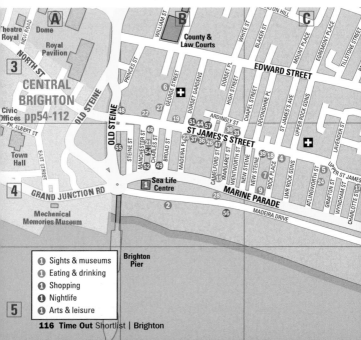

## Ginger Dog

NEW *12 College Place, BN2 1HN
(620990, www.gingermanrestaurants.
com). Bus 1, 2, 7, 14, 27, 37, 47, 52,
73, N99.* **Open** noon-2pm, 6-10pm Mon-
Thur; noon-3pm, 6-10pm Fri; 12.30-3pm,
6-10pm Sat; 12.30-4pm, 6-10pm Sun. **££**.
**Pub. Map** p117 E4 ➓

The Ginger Dog is the latest addition
to the Gingerman's group of four
premises: one fine restaurant and three
gastropubs in and around Brighton.
The menu reflects the gastronomically
aware owners, with dishes such as
slow-braised pig's cheek or partridge.

## Greys

*105 Southover Street, Hanover, BN2 9UA
(680734, www.greyspub.com). Bus 37.*
**Open** 4-11pm Mon-Wed; 4-11.30pm
Thur; 4pm-12.30am Fri; noon-12.30am
Sat; noon-11pm Sun. **££. Pub.**
**Map** p119 B2 ⓫

The Greys is a gorgeous little pub
along Southover Street, well known for
its exceptional music programme.
Concentrating on high-quality acoustic
and folk, it has attracted musicians
from Nashville, Memphis, Vancouver
and Chicago, as well as home-grown
talent. Head along for the Monday gig
night – you may even catch a member
of the E Street Band or a legendary
roots or folk musician. Entrance is usually £10. The rest of the time, it's a popular pub with Harvey's on tap and
excellent food from Piglet's Pantry. Its
menu offers the likes of parmesan and
rosemary polenta with roast courgettes
and pan-fried bream.

## Hand in Hand

*33 Upper St James's Street, BN2 1JN
(699595). Bus 1, 2, 7, 14, 52.* **Open**
noon-11.30pm Mon-Sat; noon-10.30pm
Sun. **££. Pub. Map** p117 C4 ⓬

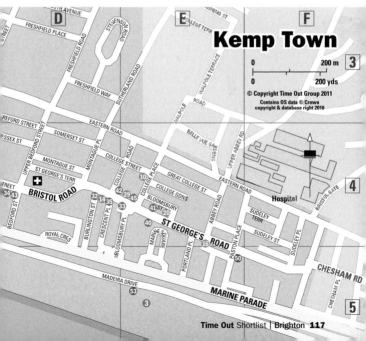

This traditional boozer deep in Kemp Town attracts a more mature, discerning clientele thanks to its outstanding range of ales. The most appropriate choice here would be the ale brewed on the premises in the microbrewery (named after its place of birth, Kemp Town). The interior is fitting and homely without any pretence. But there are enough quirky additions that you can spend a while looking at the various items displayed on the walls.

## Home

NEW *32 Egremont Place, Hanover, BN2 0GA (674456, www.home brighton.co.uk). Bus 1, 2, 7, 14, 27, 37, 47, 52.* **Open** 10am-5pm daily. **Café**. Map p119 B4 ⑬
Home has recently transformed (from Cafe 32, and before that, Bennett's) into a rather swanky deli/café, a bit like a mini Bill's (p87). As well as all-day breakfasts and excellent coffee, it offers a variety of Mediterranean dishes – frittatas, roasted vegetarian salads and the like, not to mention a selection of hearty home-made cakes. It's a good place to take kids, who are well catered for with crayons, high chairs and a big jar of sweeties to keep them quiet. It's also opposite the entrance to the park.

## Kemp Town Deli & Bistro

*108 St George's Road, BN2 1EA (603411). Bus 1, 2, 7, 14, 27, 47, 52.* **Open** 9am-3pm Mon-Sat; 11am-3pm Sun. ££. **Deli**. Map p117 D4 ⑭
On the crammed shelves of this delicatessen are a seductive selection of regional cheeses and fresh produce. There's not too much capacity in the cosy bistro upstairs, but people rotate in and out quickly enough and there's extra seating downstairs away from the street if needed. Sandwiches and potato rostis are available in a few variations, including halloumi and roasted vegetables, while fallback options include eggs Benedict, English breakfasts and a friendly cuppa.

## Legends

*31-34 Marine Parade, BN2 1TR (624462, www.legendsbrighton.com). Bus 1, 2, 7, 14, 27, 37, 47.* **Open** 11am-5am daily. **Bar**. Map p116 B4 ⑮
As well as being 'Brighton's largest gay hotel' (p178), Legends is also a popular gay club and bar. The terrace bar has views over the sea and Brighton Pier, and serves hot sandwiches and salads between noon and 5pm. It's stylish enough, with a café vibe throughout the day, before cocktails replace coffees in the early evening. On Friday and Saturdays, the Basement Club wakes up, and on Sundays there's an afternoon cabaret.

## La Marinade

*77 St George's Road, BN2 1EF (600992). Bus 1, 2, 7, 14, 27, 37, 47, 52, 73.* **Open** noon-3pm, 6-11pm Tue-Sat. ££. **French**. Map p117 E4 ⑯
This petite restaurant offers a French-inspired menu with both classic and innovative dishes for a reasonable price. The concise yet thoughtfully devised menu offers starters such as pan-fried baby squid in mixed herbs and white wine, and mains including fillet of 28-day hung Scottish beef with sautéed wild mushrooms, crispy french fries and mixed leaves.

## Metrodeco & Maltea

*38 Upper St James's Street, BN2 1JN (07878 508719, www.metro-deco.com). Bus 1, 2, 7, 14, 27, 37, 47, 52, 73, N99.* **Open** 10am-6pm daily. No credit cards. **Café**. Map p117 D4 ⑰
This 1930s-styled tearoom and basement antique shop mixes passion and eccentricity together to create a one-off environment. Shop for collectables and furniture, largely from the beginning of the 20th century, then sit, relax and drink in-house tea infusions while indulging in a piece of moist home-made cake. All are instantly welcome, especially if you are of the canine persuasion: an extensive doggie menu is offered. Kibble Bakewell Tart? Woof!

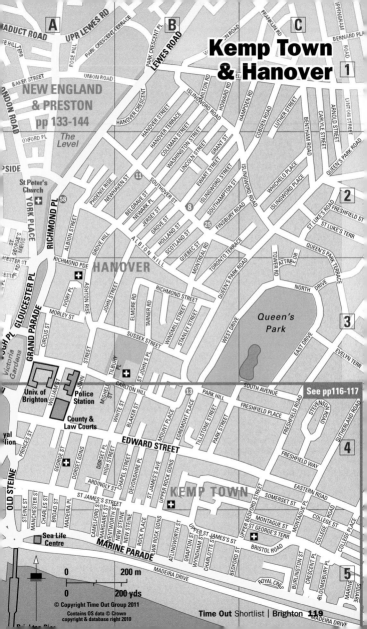

# Kemp Town & Hanover

**A**    **B**    **C**

**1**

**2**

**3**

**4**

**5**

VIADUCT ROAD

UPR LEWES RD

LEWES ROAD

FRANKLIN RD

IPPINGHAM

BERNARD PLA

ROSE HILL

PARK CRESCENT TERRACE

PARK CRESCENT PL

UNION ROAD

LINTON RD

ROAD

NEW ENGLAND & PRESTON
pp 133-144

BAKER STREET

LONDON ROAD

OXFORD PL

The Level

HANOVER CRESCENT

HANOVER STREET

HANOVER TERRACE

COLEMAN STREET

WASHINGTON STREET

LINCOLN STREET

EWART STREET

GRANT ST

ISLINGWORD STREET

ISLINGWORD ROAD

MILTON RD

HOWARD RD

HAMPDEN RD

COBDEN ROAD

LUTHER STREET

BENTHAM ROAD

CARLYLE STREET

ARNOLD STREET

QUEEN'S PARK ROAD

St Peter's Church

YORK PLACE

St George's

RICHMOND PL

PHOENIX RISE

NEWHAVEN ST

BELGRAVE ST

NEWARK PL

JERSEY ST

GROVE ST

SOUTHOVER ST

HOLLAND ST

SCOTLAND ST

QUEBEC ST

SOUTHAMPTON ST

FINSBURY RD

ISLINGWORD PLACE

WHICHELO PLACE

ST LUKE'S ROD

FRESHFIELD ST

ST LUKE'S TERR

QUEEN'S PARK TERRACE

**11**

**58**

**8**

**25**

ALBION STREET

RICHMOND PDE

RICHMOND STREET

GROVE HILL

ALBION HILL

HANOVER

GLOUCESTER PL

GRAND PARADE

Victoria Gardens

CIRCUS ST

IVORY PL

ASHTON RISE

JOHN STREET

MORLEY ST

ELMORE RD

TARNER RD

WINDMILL STREET

STANLEY STREET

MONTREAL RD

TORONTO TERRACE

QUEEN'S PARK ROAD

WEST DRIVE

Queen's Park

NORTH DRIVE

TOWER RD

BEATTIE

EAST DRIVE

EVELYN TERR

SUSSEX STREET

TILBURY

ST JOHN'S PL

CARLTON HILL

SOUTH AVENUE

See pp116-117

Univ. of Brighton

Police Station

County & Law Courts

WILLIAM ST

MIGHELL ST

WHITE ST

BLAKER ST

MOUNT PLACE

EGREMONT PLACE

PARK PLACE

PARK HILL

TILLSTONE STREET

PARK STREET

FRESHFIELD PLACE

STEVESON RD

CROLL RD

SUTHERLAND ROAD

**13**

EDWARD STREET

FRESHFIELD WAY

OLD STEINE

PRINCES ST

GEORGE ST

DORSET GDNS

DORSET PL

HIGH STREET

CHAPEL STREET

DEVONSHIRE PL

ST JAMES'S AVE

UPPER ROCK GDNS

EASTERN ROAD

SOMERSET ST

COLLEGE RD

KEMP TOWN

Royal Pavilion

STEINE ST

MANCHESTER ST

CHARLES ST

BROAD ST

MADEIRA PL

ARDINGLY STREET

CAMELFORD ST

MARGARET ST

WENTWORTH ST

NEW STEINE

ST JAMES'S STREET

ROCK PLACE

WM ROCK GDNS

UPPER ST JAMES'S ST

GRAFTON ST

WYNDHAM ST

CHARLOTTE ST

UPPER BEDFORD STREET

ST GEORGE'S TERR

MONTAGUE ST

MONTAGUE PL

BRISTOL ROAD

BEDFORD ST

COLLEGE PL

COLLEGE RD

BURLINGTON ST

CRESCENT PL

BLOOMSBURY PL

Sea Life Centre

MARINE PARADE

ATLINGWORTH ST

MADEIRA DRIVE

ROYAL CRES

MADEIRA DRIVE

0    200 m

0    200 yds

© Copyright Time Out Group 2011
Contains OS data © Crown
copyright & database right 2010

## Muang Thai Restaurant

*77 St James's Street, BN2 1PA
(605223, www.muangthairestaurant.
com). Bus 1, 2, 7, 14, 27, 37, 47, 52,
73, N99.* **Open** noon-3pm, 5-11.30pm
daily. **££. Thai. Map** p116 C4 ⑱

Easy to locate even in colourful Kemp
Town with its vibrant purple and pink
exterior, this long-established restaurant
creates reasonably priced dishes, all
freshly prepared with authentic Thai
spices. You'll find a satisfactory selection of noodles, rice, chicken, beef,
seafood, salads and soups, plus a few
specialities such as Massaman curry,
all at reasonable prices. They're accompanied by an interesting wine list.

## Nasza

*22 St James's Street, BN2 1RF
(622770). Bus 1, 2, 7, 14, 27, 37, 47,
52, 73, N99.* **Open** 11am-10pm Mon-
Thur; 11am-11pm Fri, Sat; 1-10pm Sun.
**££. Polish. Map** p116 B3 ⑲

In this cosy Polish restaurant there's a
buffet with a wide range of traditional
dishes, mostly consisting of various
stewed meats and vegetables. Seat
yourself in a booth out the back for a
more intimate experience, or take a
sunny view of the busy street for a spot
of people-watching.

## Pizzaface

*35 St George's Road, BN2 1ED (699082,
www.pizzafacepizza.co.uk). Bus 1, 2, 7,
14, 27, 37, 47, 52, 73, N99.* **Open**
noon-2.30pm, 5-10pm Mon-Thur; noon-
2.30pm, 5-11pm Fri; 5-11pm Sat; 5-10pm
Sun. **££. Pizza. Map** p117 E4 ⑳

This is not just your average pizzeria.
Pizzaface only offer takeaway or delivery, but their far-from-average ingredients are likely to seduce you to stay in
for the night anyway. Order from the
inspired in-house pizza suggestions
such as grilled courgettes, red onion,
sautéed mushrooms and rocket, or create your own from the wide range of
interesting toppings such as truffle oil
and oyster mushrooms. Salads and ice-
cream can also be ordered.

## Pomegranate

*10 Manchester Street, BN2 1TF
(628386, www.eatpomegranates.com).
Bus 1, 2, 7, 14, 27, 37, 47, 52, 73, N99.*
**Open** 11am-3pm, 5-11pm daily. **££.
Kurdish. Map** p116 B4 ㉑

A small Kurdish restaurant open for
lunch and dinner providing a good
selection of traditionally inspired
starters and mains. Examples include
fried aubergine with yoghurt, mint and
garlic for a starter, with grilled sirloin
steak served with mushroom, pistachio
and dolcelatte cheese sauce being a
popular main. Many dishes are sprin-
kled with pomegranate seeds, honour-
ing the Kurdish national fruit.

## Redroaster Coffee House

*1d St James's Street, BN2 1RE
(686668, www.redroaster.co.uk).
Bus 1, 2, 7, 14, 27, 37, 47, 52, 73,
N99.* **Open** 7am-7pm Mon-Fri; 8am-
7pm Sat; 9am-6.30pm Sun. **Café.
Map** p116 B3 ㉒

This independent coffee house has been
supplying Brighton's hangovers with a
motivational kick for more than 10
years. Because of its popularity, it
expanded in 2008 with a new local
roastery to fulfil demand from neigh-
bouring hotels, restaurants and cafés.
Frequently busy, it offers coffees in a
wide variety of beans, styles and blends
to drink in, take away or purchase by
the bag. For lunch, try the sandwiches
made with organic ingredients. It holds
literary and musical events; see the
café's Facebook page for details.

## Saint James

*16 Madeira Place, BN2 1TN (626696).
Bus 1, 2, 7, 14, 27, 37, 47, 52, 73, N99.*
**Open** noon-11pm Mon-Thur; noon-
midnight Fri, Sat; noon-11pm Sun.
**Pub. Map** p116 B4 ㉓

This is a traditional pub that, though it
doesn't stand out for its selection of ale,
more than makes up for it with a passion for rum. If the home-made spiced
rum doesn't pull you in off the street
then perhaps the conversation will.

# Sets in the city

The sun is always out at Britain's first dedicated beach volleyball court.

Playing beach volleyball on Brighton's lumpy pebbles is more of an exercise in masochism than a sport. Thank the sun, then, for **Yellowave Beachsports** (p115), Britain's first dedicated beach sports venue... and all on sand.

In the summer sun, the facility's six beach volleyball courts fill with Brightonians bouncing volleyballs, keeping up footballs, hurling Frisbees and throwing rugby balls. It's not exactly quiet when it's cloudy either – in fact, catering for sturdy types, Yellowave Beachsports is open all year around, and such is the addictive quality of beach volleyball that fanatics have played in the snow.

Yellowave was opened in 2007 by Katie Mintram and her family. Brighton-born Katie was one of the top ten beach volleyball players in the country and, after stints in California, decided that the UK needed a beach sports venue.

Yellowave is along Madeira Drive, just past the Concorde 2. As well as the sandy area that alternates as volleyball courts or a football pitch, there's a bouldering wall and a café serving homemade soups and salads.

Courts can be hired for £20 an hour – cheaper than tennis courts – but there are also drop-in sessions, coaching programmes for all levels, league games, kids' clubs and taster sessions. And the Yellowave philosophy goes beyond the sports, with monthly barbecues and live acoustic music throughout the summer.

'We've created a community,' Katie says. 'People just come down and hang out, meet friends and have a drink here.' As their mission statement says: 'We bring the surf culture to sand, offering an alternative active beach lifestyle. Yellowave is all about getting out there and having a go – getting sandy and having fun.'

Beach volleyball looks set to receive greater attention thanks to featuring in the 2012 Olympics, and it is hoped Yellowave will be an official training venue. If you've never played before, why not plug into the beach vibe and have a go? There's one guarantee: it's more comfortable than pebbles.

**BRIGHTON BY AREA**

Metrodeco & Maltea p118

metrodeco

SPECIALITY TEAS

...ONLY £1.50 A CUP T/AWAY

DELICIOUS CAKES

......£3 A SLICE

DELUXE DOGGY TREATS

## Sidewinder

*65 St James's Street BN2 1PJ
(679927). Bus 1, 2, 7, 14, 27, 37, 47,
52, 73, N99.* **Open** *10am-1am Mon-
Thur, Sun; 10am-2am Fri, Sat.* **Pub**.
**Map** p116 C4 ㉔
Located towards Kemp Town village,
this large bar thrives at night but also
offers a place to relax during the day,
especially in summer with its two
large heated beer gardens, both well
furnished with plenty of seating.
There are quiz nights, live musicians
and open-mic evenings, while on
selected nights DJs fill the bar with
indie to jazz.

## Sir Charles Napier

*50 Southover Street, Hanover,
BN2 9UE (601413). Bus 37.* **Open**
*4-11.30pm Mon-Thur; 3pm-12.30am
Fri; noon-12.30am Sat; noon-11pm Sun.*
**Pub**. **Map** p119 B2 ㉕
This unpretentious Victorian boozer is
a welcoming pub. The staff are excellent, and the ales, all from Fullers, are
well kept. There are pewter tankards
hanging from the ceiling – memories
of gone but not forgotten locals – and
an eclectic mix of wall decorations.
There's basic pub grub too.

## Street

*101 St James's Street, BN2 1TP
(673891). Bus 1, 2, 7, 14, 27, 37,
47, 52, 73.* **Open** *9am-4pm Tue-Sun.*
**££**. No credit cards. **Café**.
**Map** p116 B4 ㉖
There's certainly no shortage of cafés
in Brighton, each trying to stand out
more than the next. Street achieves this
with raw urban-style decor while
retaining everything you'd need from
a good-standard café; tea, coffee, breakfasts, and a selection of baguettes,
sandwiches, hot lunches of pasta and
chilli, and a choice of indoor and outdoor seating.

## Tea Cosy

*3 George Street, BN2 1RH (www.
theteacosy.co.uk). Bus 1, 2, 7, 14,*
*27, 37, 47, 52, 73.* **Open** *noon-5pm
Wed-Fri, Sun; noon-6pm Sat.* **Café**.
**Map** p116 B3 ㉗
Tongue-in-cheek etiquette (no clank-
ing of teaspoons or biscuit-dunking,
please) applies at this diminutive tearoom, which, decor and menu alike, is
dedicated to the Royal Family: think
commemorative china and tea-towels
on the walls, and Charles and Camilla
Elevenses, and Princess Margaret and
Diana Memorial Teas on the menu.
The latest addition is the rather grand
Wills and Kate High Tea: a selection
of sandwiches, including smoked
salmon with horseradish and crème
fraiche and a choice of sweets.

## Terraces

*Madeira Drive, BN2 1AY (545250,
www.the-terraces.co.uk). Bus 12, 14,
27, 37, 47, 52, 57.* **Open** *10am-11pm
Mon-Thur, Sun; 10am-midnight Fri, Sat.*
**Grill & bar**. **Map** p116 B4 ㉘
Located in a fabulous position above
the Sea Life Centre, Terraces has wonderful views over Brighton Pier and
along the coast to the Marina. The bar
serves jugs of cocktails, while the grill's
menu has a range of Mediterranean
dishes, including sea bass and Greek
salads, as well as a selection of lighter
bites. Friday and Saturday nights are
given over to dinner and dancing deals.

## Thomas Kemp

*8 St George's Road, BN2 1EB
(683334). Bus 1, 2, 7, 14, 27, 37,
47, 52, 73, N99.* **Open** *11am-midnight
Mon-Thur, Sun; 11am-1am Fri, Sat.*
**Pub**. **Map** p117 E4 ㉙
The Thomas Kemp, named after the
founder of Kemp Town, is a large and
inviting rustic bar with a sunny beer
garden for summer drinking. Burgers
and other standard pub grub are served
into the evening, and popular roasts are
available on Sundays. At the weekend,
it livens up with eclectic DJ sets. A new
unplugged open-mic music night has
been added on Thursdays and there's a
pub quiz on Mondays. The decked out-

door seating area is heated, but if it's really cold, huddle around the log fires.

## Shopping

### Acoustic Music Company

*39 St James's Street, BN2 1RG (671841, www.theacousticmusicco. co.uk). Bus 1, 2, 7, 14, 27, 37, 47, 52, 73, N99.* **Open** 10.30am-6pm Tue-Sat. **Map** p116 B4 ㉛

This vendor represents more than 40 guitar and mandolin luthiers (that's instrument-makers to you and me). Picking the right instrument, we're told, can take hours, if not days, especially when you can choose from new and used guitars and mandolins – or pick a bargain from 'the dusty corner', long-forgotten instruments in need of a loving home.

### Bramptons Butchers

*114 St George's Road, BN2 1EA (682611, www.bramptonsbutchers. co.uk). Bus 1, 2, 7, 14, 27, 37, 47, 52, 73, N99.* **Open** 7am-5pm Mon-Fri; except 7am-1.30pm Wed; 6.30am-1.30pm Sat. No credit cards. **Map** p117 D4 ㉜

Brush up on some history while selecting award-winning sausages or a cut of South Downs lamb from the recent winner of Sussex Butcher of the Year. The shop dates back to 1902 and has been training butchers and selling naturally reared meat ever since.

### Brick-a-Brick

*17 St George's Road, BN2 1EB. Bus 1, 2, 7, 14, 27, 37, 47, 52, 73, N99.* **Open** by appt Mon, Tue; 11am-6pm Wed-Sat; noon-5pm Sun. **Map** p117 E4 ㉝

There's a genuinely friendly reception at this vintage furniture, lighting and art shop that surprisingly shows no sign of musty fragrance or dust from other eras. Don't see what you want? The owners are happy to go hunting.

### Brighton Flea Market

*31a Upper St James's Street, BN2 1JN (624006, www.flea-markets.co.uk). Bus 1,* *2, 7, 14, 27, 37, 47, 52, 73, N99.* **Open** 10am-5.30pm Mon-Sat; 10.30-5pm Sun. **Map** p117 D4 ㉞

A bright pink hub filled with curious collectables, antiques and furniture, centrally located just between the gay village and Kemp Town village. The nmerous stalls filled with globally hunted-down treasures are spread over two floors. The challenge is to leave without buying something.

### Brighton Framing Gallery

*103 St George's Road, BN2 1EA (696221, www.brighton framing.com). Bus 1, 2, 7, 14, 27, 37, 47, 52, 73, N99.* **Open** 9.30am-5pm Tue-Fri; 10am-5pm Sat. **Map** p117 D4 ㉟

This is an independent framing workshop that has a contemporary art gallery showing meticulously selected original art ranging from metalwork to handmade art books and innovative paintings and prints.

### Doggy Fashion

*98 St James's Street, BN2 1TP (695631, www.doggyfashion.co.uk). Bus 1, 2, 7, 14, 27, 37, 47, 52, 73.* **Open** 9am-5pm Mon-Sat. **Map** p116 B4 ㊱

Apparently, not only humans feel the calling for Brighton chic – designer dogs can dress to impress too. Perhaps your pup needs a spritz of perfume, a rainbow lead or a hand-beaded collar? If not, work through the selection of kitsch and classic harness designs, Hadley hoodies and Barkley coats for pampered pooches of all sizes.

### Handmade

*106 St James's Street, BN2 1TP (http://handmadeshopbrighton. blogspot.com). Bus 1, 2, 7, 14, 27, 37, 47, 52, 73, N99.* **Open** 10.30am-6pm Tue-Sat; 11.30am-5pm Sun. **Map** p116 B4 ㊲

This creatively passionate co-operative gives local artists an opportunity to showcase and sell their handiwork.

Hand in Hand p117

Each of the Brighton-based artists rents a space from the non-profit shop, which leaves the full artistic license with the creators, offering customers the chance to grab a one-off gift or souvenir. There are unique hand-made cushions, lampshades and badges, with new stock from new artists arriving all the time.

## In Retro Spect

*37 Upper St James's Street, BN2 1JN (609374). Bus 1, 2, 7, 14, 27, 37, 47, 52, 73, N99.* **Open** 11am-6pm Thur-Sun. **Map** p117 C4 ㊳
The beauty of the Kemp Town antique trail is that each vendor has an area of interest and unique quality that makes the experience consistently absorbing. This shop specialises in 1960s and '70s original interior design; mostly furniture, with some glass, ceramics, textiles and lighting. The owner ensures that even the music matches the furniture.

## Inka Tattoos

*80c St James's Street, BN2 1PA (708844, www.inkatattoos.co.uk). Bus 1, 2, 7, 14, 27, 37, 47, 52, 73, N99.* **Open** noon-6pm daily. **Map** p116 C4 ㊴
There are seven skilled in-house artists here, each with different specialities, including one who does 'scarification'. Inka was opened by Barbara Allen and has decorated Brighton residents and visitors for more than 10 years.

## Kemptown Bookshop & the Bookroom Café

*91 St George's Road, BN2 1EE (682110, www.kemptownbookshop. co.uk). Bus 1, 2, 7, 14, 27, 37, 47, 52, 73, N99.* **Open** 9am-5.30pm Mon-Sat. **Map** p117 E4 ㊵
This independent bookshop takes great pride in its 10,000 titles, all carefully chosen. If the books themselves haven't quenched your thirst for knowledge, the bookshop hosts events and courses – primarily of a literary nature – through which to engage the radical minds of Brighton. Buy a book

from the list of recommended reading or head upstairs to the café for a panini, bagel or other snack.

## Kemptown Trading Post & Coffee Shop

*28 St George's Road, BN2 1ED (698873, www.kemptowntradingpost. co.uk). Bus 1, 2, 7, 14, 27, 37, 47, 52, 73, N99.* **Open** 9am-5pm Tue-Fri; 10am-5pm Sat; 11am-4pm Sun. Credit cards over £50 only. **Map** p117 E4 ㊶
A large showroom of ever-changing vintage and mid century modern furniture and collectables where you will find lovingly selected eclectic items that range from 1950s Coca-Cola machines and rare Scorsese film posters to vintage pearls and gnomes. Once you've tired of the antique hunt, there's a café based in the showroom for coffee and cake (they also serves sandwiches and wraps), with indoor and outdoor seating.

## Love Frankie

*3 St George's Road, BN2 1EB (07940 421812, www.lovefrankie.com). Bus 1, 2, 7, 14, 27, 37, 47, 52, 73, N99.* **Open** 9.30am-5.30pm Mon-Sat; 11.30am-5pm Sun. **Map** p117 D4 ㊷
Within this shop is Jo Franks' studio, where she creates or adapts bespoke lampshades, cushions, kids' clothes, aprons and accessories, kitchen paraphernalia, gifts, wall hangings and furniture. It's a lovely shop.

## Margaret's at 30A

*30A Upper St James's Street, BN2 1JN (681384). Bus 1, 2, 7, 14, 27, 37, 47, 52, 73, N99.* **Open** 11am-5.30pm Thur-Sat. **Map** p116 D4 ㊸
Brimming with treasures, this tiny vintage emporium is a favourite with fashion designers in search of inspiration. Fur hats perch precariously on drawers overflowing with dainty, paper-thin leather gloves, belts and doilies, while the rails are crammed with studded leather jackets, antique lace slips and floral 1940s utility frocks.

## Nice 'n' Naughty Adult Store

*32 St James's Street, BN2 1RF (626442, www.nicenaughty.co.uk). Bus 1, 2, 7, 14, 27, 37, 47, 52, 73, N99.* **Open** 10am-8pm Mon-Sat; 11am-6pm Sun. **Map** p116 B3 ⓐ

Even the most self-conscious browsers will find themselves welcome here. The general concept of the shop is for the encouragement of unabashed, healthy, happy sex lives. This is created with guidance and extensive online and in-store advice towards, for example, reigniting a lost spark, expanding horizons or choosing your first sex toy. The staff are discreet and very helpful, and there's a wide range of stock, whatever your fantasy.

## Pardon My French

*15 St George's Road, BN2 1EB (694479, www.pardonmyfrench.co.uk). Bus 1, 2, 7, 14, 27, 37, 47, 52, 73, N99.* **Open** 10am-5pm Mon-Sat. **Map** p117 E4 ⓐ

This French-inspired boutique stocks silk and cotton cushions, nightwear and bed linen, as well as hats and scarves, jewellery, pillow perfumes, vintage-style calendars, enamel door signs and labels (in French), eau de toilette and sweets. Don't overlook the selection of day and evening bags including unique shopping totes with glossy photographic prints of traditional French shops. There's even some stylish French packing tape to finish of the gift wrapping.

## Prowler

*112-113 St James's Street, BN2 1TH (683680, www.prowler.co.uk). Bus 1, 2, 7, 14, 27, 37, 47, 52, 73, N99.* **Open** 11am-7pm Mon-Sat; noon-6pm Sun. **Map** p116 B4 ⓐ

There are only three branches nationwide of this gay lifestyle shop, and of couse Kemp Town has one, offering a wide variety of sexually encouraging toys, enhancements and bondage accessories, aromas, magazines and books, gifts and clothing, including designer briefs, hats and scarves.

## Spiral

*103 St James's Street, BN2 1TP (667999, www.spiraljewellery.com). Bus 1, 2, 7, 14, 27, 37, 47, 52, 73, N99.* **Open** 9.30am-6pm Mon-Sat; 10.30am-5pm Sun. **Map** p116 B4 ⓐ

Spiral has an impressive array of sterling silver jewellery in a range of simple and classic to loosely ethnic and modern designs, with or without stones. If you're looking for everyday carefree jewellery or a small birthday present, then head here.

## Taj the Grocer

*13 Old Steine, BN1 1EJ (325027). Bus 1, 2, 7, 14, 27, 37, 47, 52, 73, N99.* **Open** 8.30am-9.30pm daily. **Map** p116 B3 ⓐ

Family-run grocers can often lack the more commercial approach many customers look for, yet this very well-established semi-supermarket has the layout, precision and efficiency of any big chain, with the added benefit of fresh vegan, vegetarian and organic produce. It specialises in Asian, Oriental and Far Eastern ingredients and has some ready-to-eat take-away products for a snack.

# Nightlife

## Audio

*10 Marine Parade, BN2 1TL (606906, www.audiobrighton.com). Bus 12, 14, 27, 37, 47, 52, 57.* **Open** varies. **Map** p116 B4 ⓐ

Once the site of the popular Escape Club, Audio opened its doors in 2005 as a nightclub and live music venue. Its programming is a mixture of bands on their way up but not yet big enough to fill Concorde 2 (past acts include the xx, Hot Chip and Friendly Fires). The downstairs club space is known for its quality and international guests. They could be playing anything from breaks to drum 'n' bass, soul to techno classics, or indie tracks. There's an excellent cocktail bar too. This is one of the best and most eclectic venues in Brighton.

Concorde 2 p130

## Brighton Ballroom

**NEW** *83 St George's Street, BN2 1EF (605789, www.brightonballroom.com). Bus 1, 2, 7, 14, 27, 37, 47, 52, 73, N99.* **Open** *7pm-2am Tue-Sat.* **Map** p117 E5 **50**

There are plenty of cabarets and burlesque shows in Brighton, but none are quite like those put on by the Brighton Ballroom. The venue, run by Proud of London, attracts well-known event organisers to create vintage glamour nights. The retro concept of the Supper Club mixes a three-course meal with live entertainment such as Broadway Musical Cabarets or White Mink Nights, described as 'electro swing versus speakeasy jazz'. Also staged here are 1930s cocktail parties, We Love Pop nights and La Bistrotheque: a Parisian-inspired evening of red wine and cheese, transitioning into disco.

## Bulldog

*31 St James's Street, BN2 1RF (696996, www.bulldogbrighton.com). Bus 1, 2, 7, 14, 27, 37, 47, 52, 73, N99.* **Open** *11am-2am Mon-Wed; noon-3am Thur; 24 hrs Fri, Sat; noon-2am Sun.* **Map** p116 B3 **51**

The lively design on the façade isn't the only thing that makes the Bulldog stand out. It's one of the longest established gay bars in Brighton – in business for more than 30 years – has 24-hour opening at weekends and doesn't charge admission during Pride weekend. All are welcome, although it primarily caters for men.

## Charles Street

*8 Marine Parade, BN2 1TA (624091, www.charles-street.com). Bus 12, 14, 27, 37, 47, 52, 57.* **Open** *noon-11pm Mon; noon-midnight Tue, Wed, Sun; noon-3am Thur-Sat.* **Map** p116 B4 **52**

This bar is owned by a chain that knows how to create an enticing gay-friendly atmosphere – there's usually a nice mix of LGBT Brighton residents and weekenders. With two floors, the bar can hold a good crowd and offers a simple menu with bar snacks, pizzas, sandwiches and classic pub food. There's an outdoor terrace on the ground floor, and club nights and cabarets are held on the second.

## Concorde 2

*Madeira Shelter Hall, Madeira Drive, BN2 1EN (673311, www.concorde2. co.uk). Bus 12, 14, 27, 37, 47, 52, 57.* **Open** *varies.* **Map** p117 E5 **53**

The venerable Concorde 2 is one of Brighton's premier music venues. Glance at any month in its listings and there'll be high-profile indie bands, top-end DJs, club nights and world music gigs – it's become a key stop-off on the countrywide tour circuit. Acts have included Femi Kuti, Mudhoney, Yeasayer, the Fall, Libertines and the larger bands at the Great Escape Festival. The venue itself is Victorian, becoming a notorious bikers' cafe in the 1960s, then an amusement arcade, before re-emerging in 2000 as this now-respected venue.

## Latest Music Bar

*14-17 Manchester Street, BN2 1TF (687171, www.thelatest.co.uk/musicbar).* **Open** *6pm-2.30am Mon-Wed; noon-2.30am Thur-Sun.* **Map** p116 B4 **54**

The latest incarnation of this music bar has very quickly established itself on the touring circuit for interesting bands. Some of the artists that have played here include Amy Winehouse and Don Letts, as well as jazz stars such as Herbie Flowers, Larry Adler and local diva Liane Carroll. It also presents out-of-the-box theatre productions and some fun club nights, including a weekly lesbian party and the monthly 'Charity Chuckle' night. Keep an eye on the website for upcoming events.

## Revenge

*32-34 Old Steine, BN1 1EL (606064, www.revenge.co.uk). Bus 1, 2, 7, 14, 27, 37, 47.* **Open** *11pm-3am Tue; 10.30pm-4am Thur; 10.30pm-5am Fri, Sat.* **Map** p116 A4 **55**

# Murder he wrote

Brighton provides the mysterious backdrop
for Peter James's crime thriller series.

The villain had been on the run
for two years when the detective,
driving through Brighton city
centre, spotted him. Jumping
out of his car, he gave chase.
They threaded through the Lanes,
the detective closing in on the
suspect. By the clock tower,
in the heart of town, the officer
rugby-tackled his target and
arrested him. 'It's just like a
Peter James novel,' the criminal
said. The policeman emailed
Peter James to tell him.

Give or take a murder or two, the
fictional Brighton of Peter James
is painstakingly accurate to the
Brighton of fact. The six bestselling
Roy Grace crime novels (so far) are
set in the city, detailing the parks
and the pubs, the courts and
the criminals, with uncanny detail.
Even the protagonist is based on
a real, high-profile policeman, who
reads the drafts.

'I go out, on average, once a
week with the police,' James tells

*Time Out.* 'Whether on a drugs
raid, with the dive teams or just
to the briefing in the morning,
I'm closely involved with Sussex
Police and its detectives.'

In the preface to his first
book, *Dead Simple*, he explains:
'Writing is always regarded as
a solitary occupation, but for me
it is a team effort.'

James was born and brought
up in Brighton. 'I'm steeped in
its criminal culture,' he says.
'It's become a hip, cool city, but
it was quite edgy. And I firmly
believe the most interesting cities
have an edge: look at Chicago,
New Orleans or Melbourne.'

'Brighton started as a
smuggling village. And then the
railway came in 1841, all the
villains came down, bringing
cockfighting, prostitution, loan-
sharking and gangs. By the
1930s, Brighton was the murder
capital of Europe.'

He reels off a list of reasons,
given to him by the city's police
chiefs, why Brighton is the perfect
place for criminals: a major seaport
on both sides, an airport in
Shoreham, miles of unguarded
coastline, Brighton Marina, the
Eurotunnel, and Gatwick '25
minutes away in a fast car.'

For a writer highlighting the
underbelly of the city, the tourist
board seems to enjoy the
publicity – there are currently
plans for a Roy Grace tour.

■ Signed copies of Peter James's
latest books are usually available
from City Books (p155).

Brighton's leading gay nightspot, established back in 1991, Revenge – and sister venue the R-Bar (5-7 Marine Parade) – holds a crucial place in the city's LGBT scene. In 2010, Revenge expanded further, adding the vibrant Box Bar to their venue. Revenge hosts many of Brighton's longest-running club nights, (including Lollipop and Kinky Dangerous), with regular celebrity guest PAs and DJs, and has been a prime mover behind Pride in Brighton & Hove in recent years.

## Volks Bar & Club

*3 The Colonnade, Madeira Drive, BN2 1PS (682828, www.volksclub.co.uk). Bus 12, 14.* **Open** varies. **Map** p116 B4 ⓹⓺

For more than 10 years, the Volks Bar & Club has, literally, offered an underground clubbing experience. The club nights are varied but reassuringly no-nonsense – outside promoters put on psy-trance, hip hop or breaks nights, but there's not a hint of cheesy techno. It's open during the day for beer and pizza, and there's a popular roots and reggae night every Monday. Keep and eye on the website for constantly updated listings.

## Zone

*33 St James's Street, BN2 1RF (682249). Bus 1, 2, 7, 14, 27, 37, 47, 52, 73, N99.* **Open** 10am-midnight Mon-Thur, Sun; 10am-12.30am Fri, Sat. **Map** p116 B3 ⓹⓻

This laid back pub – think low sofas and free wireless – attracts a regular gay clientele. Things liven up in the evenings, with karaoke or drag queen shows several times a week to entertain the crowds – and when the lights are low, it can feel a bit like a boudoir. They serve light daytime meals.

## Arts & leisure

## Phoenix Brighton

*10-14 Waterloo Place, BN2 9NB (603700, www.phoenixarts.org). Bus 5, 25, 49, 50.* **Open** 11am-5pm Tue-Sun. **Map** p118 A2 ⓹⓼

The Phoenix Brighton gallery has been at the centre of the city's arts scene for two decades. Occupying a huge building on Waterloo Place, this not-for-profit organisation provides studios for more than 100 artists. There are regular events and courses, as well as various exhibitions at any one time.

**London to Brighton Jaguar Run p35**

Preston Park p137

# New England Quarter & Preston

Although the name New England Quarter – after New England Road, upon which it is centered – is a relatively new term, it's a moniker that has been readily accepted by Brightonians. In this chapter we have also included the area up to Lewes Road to the north-east, and Preston Circus, with Preston Park and Preston Manor, to the north-west.

Since construction work began in 2004, the redevelopment of the **New England Quarter** has drastically altered the landscape of the centre of Brighton. This narrow strip of hillside immediately east of Brighton Station had housed locomotive and goods yards (built in 1840). After they closed in 1964, areas of the land remained derelict apart from some high-density housing developments, small businesses and car parks. It took until the late 1980s for the first

serious proposals to be put forward for redeveloping what was the city's largest brownfield site. Brighton & Hove City Council finally gave planning permission for the development in 2002, and any tourist who has been away from the city in the intervening years will be amazed at the number of striking new buildings.

Adjacent London Road, the southerly end of the A23, is gradually shedding its low-rent, pound-shop image as a smattering of attractive bars, cafés and restaurants establish themselves. London Road's old Co-op building, with its notable, curving 1930s façade, is also ripe for careful redevelopment, but in the meantime it has become a sought-after space for art exhibitions and site-specific theatre productions. The renowned **Duke of York's Picturehouse** (p144) sits, as it

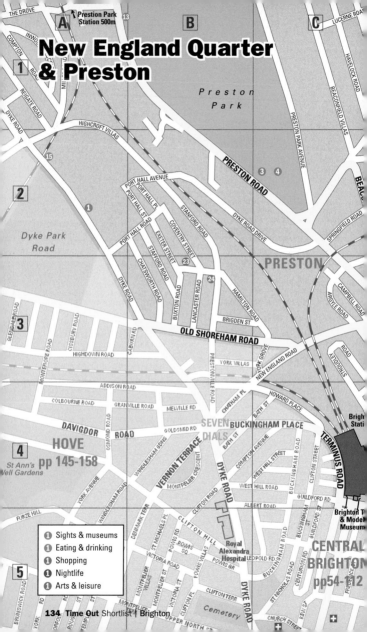

# New England Quarter & Preston

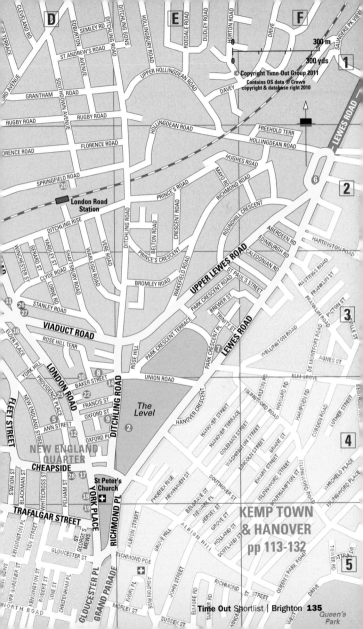

# Silver screen

Duke of York's is still in the limelight after 100 years.

The **Duke of York's Picturehouse** (p144) opened its doors to the public over one hundred years ago, on 22 September 1910, and has remained open in this capacity ever since. The first film shown was *Byways of Byron*, by local filmmaker George Albert Smith, and the cinema retains close connections with the city's creative community to this day.

Now part of the nationwide Picturehouse chain, the Duke of York's remains a respected arthouse cinema, counting among its patrons such well-known residents of the city as comic actor Steve Coogan, musician Nick Cave and director John Hillcoat. The venue's recent centenary, marking it as Britain's oldest continuously operating cinema, was celebrated with the screening of many classic and rarely-seen films shot in the city over the preceding 100 years, and the publication of the definitive story of the building: *The Dukes at 100*, by historian Allen Eyles and film agency Cine-City.

Part of its great charm is its relatively unchanged appearance across the years. The rear of the auditorium predates the cinema itself, formed by the walls of the Amber Ale Brewery that previously stood on the site. Less dated are a giant pair of can-can dancer's legs on the roof – the work of sculptor John Buckley.

Today, the cinema has a fully licensed café-bar on the first floor, leading on to a movie-heaven balcony where film fans can stretch out on sofas, armchairs and plush cinema seats to enjoy the action.

Regular special screenings at the Duke of York's include Late Nights (on Fridays), Silver Screen (for seniors), Big Scream (for parents and babies), Kids' Club, autism-friendly and access screenings for the hard of hearing. It also hosts numerous musical concerts, live satellite links to other arts venues, and Q&A sessions with directors, actors and other crew. Manager Jon Barrenechea keeps a regular blog (http://splendorcinema.blogspot. com), where he discusses issues affecting his workplace, as well as films worldwide.

has done for more than a century, at the top end of London Road overlooking Preston Circus.

Further north, below the huge Grade II-listed London Road viaduct (now colourfully illuminated from beneath in the evenings), is Brighton's largest urban park, the beautiful **Preston Park**, with **Preston Manor**, open to the public as an Edwardian museum, at the far end. West of London Road and the New England Quarter stretches Dyke Road, home to the **Booth Museum of Natural History**. Dyke Road leads upwards to the South Downs beauty spot Devil's Dyke (p166).

## Sights & museums

### Booth Museum of Natural History

*194 Dyke Road, BN1 5AA (03000 290900, www.brighton-hove-rpml.org.uk). Bus 14, 27.* **Open** 10am-5pm Mon-Wed, Fri, Sat; 2-5pm Sun. **Admission** free. **Map** p134 A2 ❶

Wonderfully old-school, 'dead things in glass cases'-style museum built to house the collection of Victorian ornithologist (and gun enthusiast) Edward Booth. Behind the small red doors you'll find over half a million insects, animal skeletons, and stuffed birds posed – rather ghoulishly to modern eyes – in re-creations of their natural habitats. A favourite with local children, artists and ironists, its most popular exhibits include the 'Merman' (a Victorian fake cobbled together from a fish and a monkey) and the 140-million-year-old bones of a Sussex dinosaur.

### The Level

*St Peter's Place, BN1 4SA (www.brighton-hove.gov.uk). Bus 26, 46, 50.* **Map** p135 E4 ❷

To the north of the landmark St Peter's Church lies the great flat triangle of the Level, a formal recreational space since the late 18th century, and in use for public gatherings for many years before that. The Level currently contains a large children's playground, skate park, toilets and café at its southern tip, while the northern side, bordered by many 19th-century elms along Union Road, is popular with both picnickers and street drinkers. Funfairs still come to the Level, as they have done for over a century.

### Preston Manor

*Preston Drove, BN1 6SD (03000 290900, www.virtualmuseum.info). Bus 5, 17, 40.* **Open** 10.15am-4.15pm Tue-Sat; 2.15-4.15pm Sun. Closed Oct-Mar. **Admission** £5; £3-£4 reductions. **Map** p134 C2 ❸

Allegedly one of Britain's most haunted houses, Preston Manor has been preserved as an example of Edwardian life, with an *Upstairs, Downstairs* mix of elegant reception rooms and bedrooms contrasting with workaday kitchens and servants' rooms. During the summer, visitors are escorted around the manor during daylight hours, while the nights are left to the spooks and spectres: regular late-night ghost tours can be booked throughout the year.

### Preston Park

*Preston Road, BN1 6HL (www.brighton-hove.gov.uk). Bus 5, 17, 40.* **Open** 24hrs daily. **Map** p134 C2 ❹

Formally opened in 1884, the expansive green spaces of Preston Park add much needed peace to the bustle of Brighton. Within its grounds are eight tennis courts, four football pitches, three bowling greens, two cricket pitches and a softball pitch, plus a 500m velodrome. As well as scented and walled gardens, the park also features the winding Rookery Rockery, the largest municipal rock garden in the country. Notable buildings in the park include the 19th-century Tile House shop and the Grade II-listed, red-brick clock tower, as well as the Rotunda Café, purchased from the 1924 Wembley Exhibition.

## St Bartholomew's Church

*Ann Street, BN1 4GP (620491, www.stbartholomewsbrighton.org.uk). Bus 5, 17, 40.* **Open** 10am-1pm, 2-4.30pm Mon-Sat. **Admission** free. **Map** p135 D4 ❺

Visible from many miles around, the towering edifice of St Bartholomew's is a Grade I-listed parish church, described by Sir John Betjeman as 'one of the great churches of the 19th century'. And St Bart's is indeed an architectural wonder – its vast red brick exterior contains the voluminous interior of the tallest parish church nave in Britain, with opulent design features in the style of the Arts and Crafts movement. Commissioned by the Reverend Arthur Wagner and designed by the Brighton-based architect Edmund Scott, the church opened in 1874. Throughout the year, St Bartholomew's hosts major concerts of classical and choral music.

## Woodvale Cemetery

*Lewes Road, BN2 4DU (www.brighton-hove.gov.uk). Bus 23, 24, 25, 49.* **Open** 9am-5.30pm Mon-Sat; 11am-5.30pm Sun. Winter closing 4pm. **Admission** free. **Map** p135 F2 ❻

Open 365 days a year, Woodvale Cemetery is a worthwhile detour for the sensitive tourist. Nestled in a wooded valley off Lewes Road, the cemetery features hundreds of specially planted trees and shrubs, landscaped lawns, rockeries, flower-beds, a waterfall and stream, and impressive 19th-century twinned Gothic crematorium chapels.

# Eating & drinking

## Aroma Spice

*4 Lewes Road, BN2 3HP (677608, www.aromaspiceindian.com). Bus 23, 24, 25, 49.* **Open** noon-2pm, 5pm-midnight daily. **££**. **Indian**. **Map** p135 E3 ❼

Aroma Spice is one of the few sit-down restaurants on the otherwise take away-filled Lewes Road. Though it covers all the usual dishes, the interesting house specialities – such as *chatga* chicken, cooked with garlic, onions, soy sauce and honey, or the chicken *shatkura*, with a medium-hot sauce utilising citrus fruit that's popular in Bangladesh – also set it apart. It's convenient for a late night after visiting the pubs of Hanover or the New England Quarter.

St Bartholomew's Church

## Bardsley's

*22-23a Baker Street, BN1 4JN
(681256, www.bardsleys-fishandchips.
co.uk).* Bus 5, 17, 40. **Open** 11.30am-
2.30pm, 4-8.30pm Tue-Sat. **££. Fish
& chips**. Map p135 D3 ❽

A fish and chips institution, Bardsley's
has passed through four generations
of the same family since it was founded
in 1926. The 65-seat restaurant is fully
licensed, and popular for both takeaway and sit-down meals (book ahead
for large groups and on busy nights).
It takes care to use seafood from sustainable sources in both its regular
menu and its seasonal specials.

## Caroline of Brunswick

*39 Ditchling Road, BN1 4SB (624434,
www.carolineofbrunswick.wordpress.com).*
Bus 26, 46, 50. **Open** noon-midnight
Mon-Thur, Sun; noon-2am Fri, Sat.
**Pub**. Map p135 D4 ❾

One of the great alternative Brighton
pubs, the Caroline of Brunswick welcomes all sorts, including biker get-
togethers, as well as hosting various
discussion groups, comic karaoke and
very silly, very filthy quizzes. The
pub's intimate function room attracts
notable alternative musicians (punk,
electronica) and stand-up comedians –
its Edinburgh Fringe preview season
punches well above its weight. The
walls of the main bar are covered in
bizarre artwork and sleeves of dozens
of cult albums; rock usually blasts out
from the sound system. There's a menu
of home-made burgers and pies.

## Chilka House

*15 Baker Street, BN1 4JN (677085,
www.chilkahouse.co.uk).* Bus 5, 17, 40.
**Open** 5.30-11pm daily. **££. Indian**.
Map p135 D4 ❿

Trading for over 25 years, the Chilka
House is one of Brighton's established
favourites (for both dining in and takeaway), focusing on traditional north
Indian and Goan food. It specialises in
a variety of fish dishes – try those with
monkfish or tilapia, such as the Goan

# Free radicals

## Harry Cowley's legacy.

Harry Cowley (1890-1971) was
a Brighton hero who dedicated
his life to social activism, helping
the town's poor and unemployed
citizens to find homes, food and
jobs. He was also a key figure
in opposing Oswald Mosley's
British Union of Fascists in
1930s Brighton and helped
to organise and establish the
original Open Market (p142).

In 2003, the **Cowley Club**
(p140) opened on London Road.
It's dedicated to carrying out
activism and campaigns, from
local to international levels,
in the spirit of Harry Cowley's
socialist beliefs. Unsurprisingly,
everyone who works at the
Cowley is a volunteer.

During the afternoon, the
club that bears his name is open
to all, with cheap vegan meals
available in the café, and a well-
stocked bookshop and library
(including free internet access)
of radical publications and
DVDs. The bookshop hosts
regular public talks on social
and environmental issues by
authors and activists from
around the world.

To avoid alcohol licensing
restrictions, the Cowley Club
becomes a members' club in
the evening, run by a separate
organisation, the 12 London
Road Social Club. So befriend
a Brightonian, as many are
members, with the ability to sign
guests in for the building's busy
programme of music, from open-
mic nights to touring bands,
alternative club events, evening
meals and film screenings.

**BRIGHTON BY AREA**

dish *chacuti*, with monkfish cooked with fresh coconut, green and red chillies, poppy seeds and tamarind. It also has several good tofu options.

## Circus Circus
*2 Preston Road, BN1 4QF (620026, www.circus-circus.co.uk). Bus 5, 17, 40.* **Open** 11.30am-11pm Mon-Fri; 11.30am-midnight Sat; noon-11pm Sun. **Bar/Thai.** Map p135 D3 ⑪
Circus Circus is hard to miss, occupying a wide curve at the head of Preston Circus. It's one of the more upmarket options in the neighbourhood, selling itself as a wine bar. Although some locals lament the loss of its admittedly down-at-heel predecessor, the current incarnation is a contemporary affair, with dark wood tables, shiny chrome fittings and long sofas. It's as much a place for a coffee as an evening drink. It also features the reasonably priced Thai Café, offering sit-down and takeaway dishes throughout the day.

## Cowley Club
*12 London Road, BN1 4JA (696104, www.cowleyclub.org.uk). Bus 5, 17, 40.* **Open** noon-4pm Tue-Fri. **£.** No credit cards. **Vegan café.** Map p135 D4 ⑫
The Cowley is a social club (see box p139), with a café and radical bookshop open to the public in the afternoon. The café offers freshly made vegan meals for under £3, alongside herbal teas and organic hot drinks. Although famed in Brighton for its wild evenings of alternative gigs and club nights, the Cowley is technically a members' club, so any guests must be signed in.

## Crown & Anchor
*213 Preston Road, BN1 6SA (559494). Bus 5, 17, 40.* **Open** 11am-midnight. **Pub/Thai.** Map p134 A1 ⑬
A spacious pub within the old Preston village, the Crown & Anchor is a good, friendly neighbourhood local, convenient if you're visiting Preston Park and the manor. It has been smartly refurbished with dark furniture and

there are with board games to entertain the children. There's regular live music throughout the week – acoustic folk on Sundays and lively plugged-in bands on Saturdays. The real highlight at this freehouse, however, is the choice of real ales from the local area, such as Harvey's and Kings & Barnes. Its location near the current Brighton & Hove Albion stadium means it gets very busy before home games.

## Druid's Arms
*81 Ditchling Road, BN1 4SD (605689). Bus 26, 46, 50.* **Open** 3pm-1am Mon-Thur; 3pm-3am Fri; noon-3am Sat; noon-1am Sun. **Pub/Thai.** Map p135 D4 ⑭
A late-night pub, and very popular with the city's students, the Druid's Arms is home to Pokky's Thai Kitchen, serving reasonably priced dishes until 10pm most nights. As with many Brighton & Hove pubs, Sunday is given over to roast dinners, with families welcomed. The pub has occasional music events, most notably the Nice Weather for Airstrikes Festival of alternative bands.

## Dyke
NEW *218 Dyke Road, BN1 5AA (555672, www.dykepub.co.uk). Bus 14, 27, 77.* **Open** noon-midnight Mon-Thur; noon-12.30am Fri, Sat; noon-11.30pm Sun. **Pub.** Map p134 A2 ⑮
Formerly the rather fearsome Dyke Tavern, this large pub has shortened its name and headed notably up-market. Its fine quality, pan-European menu, available in the afternoon and evening, is predominantly sourced from organic, GM-free and free-range suppliers – the pub refuses to use farmed fish or other intensively produced ingredients. Typical dishes include beetroot risotto with dolcelatte and watercress, and roast venison loin with wild mushroom jus and truffle mash, as well as homemade pub classics. With garden space for families, a kids' menu and an extensive wine list, it's developing a strong word-of-mouth reputation.

## Eastern Eye

*58 London Road, BN1 4JE (685151, www.easterneyerestaurant.co.uk). Bus 5, 17, 40.* **Open** *noon-9.30pm daily.* **££. Indian**. **Map** p135 D3 ⑯

Eastern Eye is considered by many to be one of the better Indian restaurants in Brighton, and is worth the trip if you've been hankering after something authentic. The key to its success is that it largely eschews the usual suspects to make space for its south Indian specialities. Its reassuringly short menu, (for an Indian restaurant, at least) includes dishes such as spicy swordfish *achari* cooked in pickling spices. The dishes are well-presented, and the restaurant itself is light and airy.

## Hobgoblin

*31 York Place, BN1 4GU (602519, www.hobgoblinbrighton.co.uk). Bus 5, 17, 40.* **Open** *noon-midnight Mon-Thur; noon-2am Fri, Sat.* **Pub**. **Map** p135 D4 ⑰

The Hobgoblin underwent a much-needed refurbishment in summer 2010, and is now one of the most pleasant places to drink along London Road. Exposed brick walls, candles in wax laden bottles, bare floor boards and junk-shop seating lend it a laid-back atmosphere. There are two elements key to its success: its extensive range of local beers – at least six on tap – and the upstairs music venue, which also occasionally hosts comedy nights. There's decking out the back, where you can enjoy the Tex-Mex cooking.

## LangeLee's Cafe Lounge

*30 York Place, BN1 4GU (684840, www.langelees.com). Bus 5, 17, 40.* **Open** *8am-5pm Tue-Sat; 9am-4pm Sun.* **Café**. **Map** p135 D4 ⑱

This family-friendly café and restaurant serves a range of café food throughout the day – jacket potatoes and full English breakfasts, for example – though the home-made burger is the

Dyke

best option. The café's decked out in pale wood tables and chairs, red sofas and modern lighting. LangeLee's has the added bonus of a garden lounge.

## Moksha Caffe

*4-5 York Place, BN1 4GU (248890, www.mokshacaffe.com). Bus 5, 17, 40.* **Open** 7am-7pm Mon-Fri; 8am-7pm Sat; 9am-6pm Sun. **Café. Map** p135 D5

This well-regarded, modern Brighton café serves own-blend coffees, smoothies, home-made cakes, sandwiches and toasties, and has wines available for an early-evening tipple. Moksha is a popular exhibition space for contemporary Brighton artists, and also hosts regular spoken-word events, open-mic evenings and the odd bit of stand-up comedy. Lingering over a coffee and newspaper is encouraged here.

## Open House

*146 Springfield Road, BN1 6BZ (880102). Bus 5, 17, 40.* **Open** noon-midnight Mon-Thur, Sun; noon-2am Fri, Sat. **Pub. Map** p135 D2

A spacious pub on one side of London Road Station (the opposite side is served by the Signalman, 76 Ditchling Rise), the Open House is a popular location for family meals, especially on Sundays. Paintings by the local Fiveways Artists Group adorn the walls, while the Open House's artistic credentials are further strengthened by its regular Safe-house Jazz and Brighton Folk & Blues Club evenings, which both attract important international musicians to the venue.

## Raj Pavilion

*16-18 Preston Road, BN1 4QF (672255, www.rajpavilion.com). Bus 5, 17, 40.* **Open** 5.30-11.30pm daily. **££. Indian. Map** p134 C3

A pleasant Indian restaurant with a broad menu (also available as take-away), including a lengthy list of specials such as *moglai murgh* – chicken in yogurt and ginger. The Raj Pavilion prides itself on preparing healthy dishes utilising many fresh ingredients, including its own herbs and spices.

Preston Park p137

and patterns needed to knit your own garments, while the window display offers tea-cosies and other kitsch gifts for sale. There are 'stitch and bitch' sessions on Thursday evenings.

## Quilty Pleasures

NEW *1b Upper Hamilton Road, BN1 5DF (563032, www.quilty-pleasures.co.uk). Bus 5, 17.* **Open** 10am-2pm Tue, Wed; 10am-5pm Thur-Sat. **Map** p134 B3 ㉔
Craft is back. Along with the opening of Purl, opposite, Quilty Pleasures has made Upper Hamilton Road a destination for anyone interested in patchwork, quilting and sewing. And like Purl, it's largely aimed at the Kirstie Allsopp or Cath Kidston fan. The manager, Liz, studied textiles at the London College of Fashion. There's an array of courses, including hand-quilting workshops, squares quilts for beginners and seasonal events – handy if you want to make a funky fabric Christmas wreath. A cute little store, it also has a good blog.

## To Be Worn Again

*51 Providence Place, BN1 4GE (624500). Bus 5, 17, 40.* **Open** 10am-6pm Mon-Sat; noon-5pm Sun. No credit cards. **Map** p135 D4 ㉕
Vintage clothing outlet To Be Worn Again has a boutique shop located on Sydney Street in North Laine, but its Providence Place hideaway is also worth seeking out. TBWA carefully sorts the clothing that comes through its doors, selecting the best groovy retro-style items and presenting them cleanly and colourfully.

## Nightlife

## Hydrant

*75 London Road, BN1 4JF (681163, www.thehydrant.co.uk). Bus 5, 17, 40.* **Open** 4pm-midnight Mon-Thur; noon-1am Fri, Sat; noon-midnight Sun. **Pub**. **Map** p135 D3 ㉖
Positioned prominently at the junction of Preston Circus, the Hydrant is a

# Shopping

## Open Market

*London Road. Bus 5, 17, 40.* **Open** 7am-1pm Mon; 7am-5pm Tue-Thur; 7am-6pm Fri, Sat. No credit cards. **Map** p135 D4 ㉒
An established daily (except Sundays) market for fresh fish, fruit and veg, meat, dairy, whole foods and suchlike, joined by the odd arts and crafts stall, flower-seller and book stall. The market has two entrances: the main, gated London Road one, and a rear one on Ditchling Road, where vibrant commissioned street art can be seen. The site has survived for more than half a century in its present form, but there are plans to redevelop it.

## Purl

NEW *17 Upper Hamilton Road, BN1 5DF (248642, www.purl-brighton.co.uk). Bus 5, 17, 40.* **Open** 10am-6pm Tue-Sat. **Map** p134 B3 ㉓
The brightest and best knitting shop in Brighton, stocking all the wools, books

Purl p143

large pub formerly known as the Hare & Hounds (the name survives on the exterior gables). Since its relaunch, the Hydrant has made itself notable as a radical music venue, attracting cult international musicians through promoters including Punker Bunker and Club Zygotic. Often featuring simultaneous shows in both the downstairs bar and upstairs function room, the Hydrant can be very loud, but is one of the most interesting venues in Brighton.

## Arts & leisure

### Duke of York's Picturehouse

*Preston Circus, BN1 4NA (0871 902 5728, www.picturehouses.co.uk). Bus 5, 17, 40.* **Open** varies. **Map** p135 D3 ㉗
The Duke of York's cinema opened to the public on 22 September 1910, and has remained in continuous operation in this role ever since, giving it a strong claim to the title of Britain's oldest cinema (see box p136). The listed building has changed little over the years, so it retains a remarkable charm, although the – now iconic – stripy legs sticking out of the roof may surprise some. Part of the Picturehouse chain of arthouse cinemas, the Duke of York's doesn't shy away from mainstream features, but gives greater prominence to international films and curios. The cinema has an enviable selection of film introductions and Q&A sessions with notable actors and directors.

### York Place Studios

*28 York Place, BN1 4GU (www.cub culture.com). Bus 5, 17, 40.* **Open** varies. No credit cards. **Map** p135 D4 ㉘
A tiny art gallery in a former shop unit, York Place Studios features irregular exhibitions from the city's young artists. Whatever is happening at any one time is usually very colourful (bright paintings and screen-printed posters), affordable and friendly, with many artists taking up residence in the gallery to create and sell.

# Hove

Hove is the home of celebrities and ladies who lunch, Regency terraces and Victorian villas, chichi boutiques and arty cafés, expensive handbags and lattes. Yet it's not all Primrose Hill-by-Sea, thankfully. For every upmarket restaurant, there's a down-to-earth boozer, for each polished fashion store, there's a ramshackle antiques shop.

Hove developed at the same time as Brighton, and has always been inextricably linked to its brasher neighbour. But when the town of Hove was merged with Brighton to form the Brighton & Hove unitary authority in 1997, residents began to complain – 'Hove, actually' (see box p149) became the call-sign for the movement. The maxim reached its zenith in 2009 when the Hove Alone website asked for signatories to the statement: 'We, the people, of Hove, have sat and seethed long enough. We are standing up and protesting against this union.'

Hundreds signed the petition, but Hove nevertheless became part of the City of Brighton & Hove.

The most interesting parts of Hove are in clusters. To the east, the shops along Western Road meld seamlessly into Brighton city centre. Further west, where Western Road turns in to Church Road, cafés and restaurants begin to dominate the main street.

Pedestrian-friendly George Street is largely a bland row of high-street shops but is the busiest part of Hove. Nearby Blatchington Road is worth exploring, not least because it leads to Poets' Corner, an area with a handful of good pubs (and watch this space – the cheap rents there are creating a bit of a buzz).

Along the seafront, as the number of holidaymakers thins, the promenade widens, amply accommodating a sparser cross-section of skaters, bikers, boarders and walkers. The pebbled coastline,

# Hove

WEST BLATCHINGTON

Hove Park

**Sights & museums**
**Eating & drinking**
**Shopping**
**Nightlife**
**Arts & leisure**

0                    400 m
0                    400 yds

© Copyright Time Out Group 2011
Contains OS data © Crown
copyright & database right 2010

colourful beach huts, sea-view restaurants and the undeniable grandeur of its proud townhouses are what Hove residents like to highlight. But Hove provides plenty more of interest besides.

The boundary between Brighton and Hove is as contentious as its union. For this guide, we have taken Boundary Passage (an alleyway parallel to York Road), and Norfolk Square and Western Street to the sea as the border. To the north, we have followed York Avenue to Goldsmid Road, into Seven Dials and up Dyke Road.

## Sights & museums

### Hove Museum & Art Gallery

*19 New Church Road, BN3 4AB (03000 290900, www.brighton-hove-rpml.org.uk). Bus 1, 6.* **Open** *10am-5pm Mon, Tue, Thur-Sat; 2-5pm Sun.* **Admission** *free.* **Map** p146 B3 ❶

Hove's own museum features exhibits of 18th-century toys (in the Wizard's Attic) and early 19th-century movie-making, as well as photos and artefacts from Hove through the ages. It's notable too for its extensive contemporary craft collection, and there's also an assortment of prints, drawings, sculpture and paintings. A local-history gallery charts the development of Hove from prehistoric times, and the film gallery shows the town's cinematic heritage. The museum is housed in an Italianate Victorian villa with an unusual Indian gate in its grounds, the latter evoking the architectural splendour of the Brighton Pavilion across town.

## Eating & drinking

### 9Bar Cafe

*118 Church Road, BN3 2PG (721838, www.9bar.co.uk). Bus 1, 6.* **Open** *8.30am-6pm Mon-Sat; 9am-6pm Sun.* **Café. Map** p146 C4 ❷

Allegedly claimed by local Nick Cave to serve the best coffee in Hove 'by far', it's no wonder they stopped worrying about dinner and went back to focusing on what they do best here: breakfasts, brunches, cakes, pastries, teas and coffees in continental surroundings. Commuters may recognise the quality of the coffee – the owners have a very popular stand at the train station.

### Ancient Mariner

*59 Rutland Road, BN3 5FE (748595). Bus 2, 46, 49.* **Open** *noon-11.30pm Mon-Thur; noon-midnight Fri, Sat; noon-11pm Sun.* **Pub. Map** p146 A2 ❸

Situated on a residential corner of the emerging Poets' Corner area, it's easy to imagine the spacious west-facing veranda bringing a sunny evening buzz to this sleepy yet salubrious nook. The pub's evening entertainment includes music and quizzes. The sausages on the menu are a house speciality.

### Archipelagos

*121 Western Road, BN3 1DB (779474, www.archipelagosbrighton.co.uk). Bus 1, 2, 5, 6, 49.* **Open** *11am-3pm, 5-11pm Mon-Fri; 11am-11pm Sat, Sun.* **Greek. Map** p147 E4 ❹

Having run a restaurant in Greece for 16 years, the owner took over this taverna two years ago. It's as authentic as you'd expect, from the blue and white colour scheme to the wine list to the warm family welcome. Classic mains such as lamb kleftiko go down a treat, but do as the loyal regulars do and opt for a selection of meze plates to share. Vegetarians are well catered for with dishes such as moussaka, saganaki, and beetroot salad with feta and garlic.

### Bee's Mouth

*10 Western Road, BN3 1AE (770083). Bus 1, 6.* **Open** *4.30pm-12.30am Mon-Thur; 4.30pm-1.30am Fri; 2.30pm-1.30am Sat; 3.30pm-12.30am Sun.* **Bar. Map** p147 E4 ❺

Noted for its arty crowd and a quirky take on cocktails, this is best described as a taste of Brighton, in Hove. Its worn leather sofas lend the place an alt-roughness that would still stand up well to your grandma's duster test. Claimed by locals to be one of the friendliest, not to mention 'kookiest', hostelries around.

## Brasserie Pascal

*6 Queens Place, 2nd Avenue, BN3 2LT (729990, www.brasserie-pascal.co.uk).* Bus 1, 6. **Open** 11am-11pm daily. **£££**. **French**. **Map** p147 D4 ⑥

Boasting a huge, although somehow understated, chandelier and positioned so it catches the evening sunshine, Brasserie Pascal channels continental France into BN3. The menu includes such classics as snails in garlic butter and foie gras, and there's a strong selection of contemporary-twist meat dishes. Mains cost from £13 and specialities for two to share from £33.

## Bow Runner

*62 Brunswick Street West, BN3 1EL (327688).* Bus 1, 6. **Open** 11am-9pm Mon-Thur; 11am-11pm Fri, Sat; noon-7pm Sun. **Pub**. **Map** p147 E4 ⑦

Small in size, big on history, the Bow Runner is claimed by committed locals to be the friendliest pub in Hove – despite the rumoured ghost, who seemingly tries to ruin this reputation by smashing glasses and making other mischief. Muscle in at the bar for a pint of cask ale and it won't be long before you get the full colourful account of someone's day or the venue's history.

## Brunswick

*1 Holland Road, BN3 1JF (733984, www.brunswickpub.co.uk).* Bus 81. **Open** noon-midnight Mon-Thur; noon-2am Fri; 10am-2am Sat; 10am-midnight Sun. **Pub**. **Map** p147 D5 ⑧

Variety is the speciality at this event-focused hub, with space given to jazz jams, comedy and anything else that needs a stage (see the website for a calendar). You'll be hard-pressed to find a night when there's nothing on.

# Hove, actually

## The genesis of the phrase.

Supposedly coined by the city's most celebrated luvvie resident, Sir Laurence Olivier, the phrase 'Hove, actually' has long been a frequent tongue-in-cheek remark used in reference to Brighton's less famous (or should that be less notorious?) neighbour. According to lore, when asked by outsiders where they live, Hovians will habitually respond 'Brighton… well, Hove, actually,' to distinguish themselves as being from the respectable end of the merged city.

On the opposite end of the spectrum are those who prefer to distance themselves from the less trendy associations of Hove by declaring themselves as being from Brighton, even though they live 'across the border'.

A walk along the seafront quickly reveals the essential difference in atmosphere between Brighton and Hove, and is as good a way as any to appreciate the cultural divide. As soon as you pass the peace statue at the Hove border, the bars and garish touristy shops of Brighton give way to Hove's esplanade, with its chic multi-coloured beach huts and the serene backdrop of Hove Lawns. Inland, as you head west you'll spot fewer hipsters, while seeing glamorous grannies pass the shops in ever greater numbers.

The truth is that, despite their apparent haughtiness, Hovians are more likely to venture into Brighton – with all its amenities and attractions – than the other way around.

## Ethel's Kitchen

*59 Blatchington Road, BN3 3YJ (203204, www.ethelskitchen.co.uk). Bus 2, 5, 46.* **Open** 8.30am-5pm Mon-Sat; 9am-5pm Sun. No credit cards. **Café**. **Map** p146 C3 ❾

Be seated (if you can find a pew) for a journey into English pantry-inspired eating and, more specifically, the larder of Grandma Ethel. 'We are not trying to recreate her traditional menu, as British food is much more international now, but we're hoping to celebrate the tradition of home cooking,' states the menu. Piled-high treats include raspberry and lavender Victoria sponge, lots of loose-leaf tea, juices, wraps and, as it turns out, a surprisingly Mediterranean lunch menu. All of the coffee here is Fair Trade and there's a good and (mostly) wholesome kid's menu.

## Gallery

*115 Church Road, BN3 2AF (777488, www.gallerybistrohove. co.uk). Bus 1, 6.* **Open** 9am-11pm Tue-Sat; 9am-6pm Mon, Sun. **Café**. **Map** p146 C3 ❿

If a Hove eaterie's output is not ethically sourced, seasonal and made from the finest local ingredients, it's going to stand out like a sore opposable, so three important ticks on this front. Where the Gallery stands distinct from the competition is with its outlook – not only does it feature local art but, where other interiors are subtle and understated, its own isn't afraid of being a splash of primary colour. The atrium out back feels summery all year round.

## Giggling Squid

*129 Church Road, BN3 2AE (771991, www.gigglingsquid.com). Bus 1, 6.* **Open** noon-4pm, 5.30-11pm Mon-Sat; noon-4pm, 5.30-10pm Sun. **££**. **Thai**. **Map** p146 C3 ⓫

Just as much thought has gone into the names of the dishes as the name of the restaurant, and it's paying off for these rustic Thai specialists: just you try not to order Sleeping Honey Duck. The two-floor establishment is one of three such diners across the region, each offering freshly prepared street food and coastal specialities.

## Ginger Pig

*3 Hove Street, BN3 2TR (736123, www.gingermanrestaurants.com). Bus 1, 6.* **Open** noon-2pm, 6.30-10pm Mon-Thur; noon-3pm, 6.30-10pm Fri; noon-2pm, 6-10pm Sat; 12.30-4pm Sun. **£££**. **Modern British**. **Map** p146 B4 ⓬

Let's face it: in Hove, if you haven't got a fat pig motif on your sign, you're nothing. In this case, the porky fellow joins a chain of animal-inspired, food-focused gastropubs and restaurants across the city and Sussex – all prefixed 'Ginger' – including the Ginger Dog in Kemp Town (p117). Expect honest food with a twist, a stylish and contemporary interior, and an appealing terrace. Mains range from £11 to £18 and include roast partridge with smoked-bacon potatoes and pickled muscat grapes. It's a recipient of a Michelin Bib Gourmand award.

## Graze

*42 Western Road, BN3 1JD (823707, www.graze-restaurant.co.uk). Bus 1, 6.* **Open** noon-2pm, 6.30-9.30pm Tue-Sat; 1-4pm Sun. **£££**. **Modern British**. **Map** p147 E4 ⓭

Surrounded by modern references to Regency Brighton, this is the place for urban grazing. Enjoy a seven-course tasting menu accompanied by a glass of specially selected wine with each course. 'We've a passion for food, wine and people,' chorus owners Kate and Mani. Dishes include cannelloni of wild mushroom; Rye Bay scallops with crispy ham and beetroot essence; and dark chocolate terrine with rhubarb and honeycomb ice-cream. Graze ticks all the seasonal, local, organic and free-range boxes. There's a two-for-one deal on two-course meals on Sundays (except holidays).

# City of words

Brighton's favourite bookshop celebrates its 25th birthday.

Will, Nick and Iain are friends of **City Books** (p155) in Hove – on first-name terms, in fact. Others will know them by their surnames: Self, Cave and Banks. It's a further sign of a terrific bookshop that *Cloud Atlas* author David Mitchell only chose two places for book readings in 2009: the Hay-on-Wye Literary Festival and City Books in Hove.

City Books celebrates its quarter-century in May 2011, and for 25 years the shop has sated Brighton's literary appetite with an intelligently chosen selection of titles, friendly service and a wide roster of interesting events – making the most of their clientele; when Hove resident Nick Cave released his book *The Death of Bunny Munro*, set in Brighton, they got Will Self to interview him.

The owners, Paul and Inge Sweetman, who met while working in WH Smiths, had long dreamed of opening a bookshop. 'We like it quiet and to feel a little like a second-hand bookshop,' Paul says. 'The chains miss out on an unbelievable amount of great titles; we like to get them in.'

City Books has an almost cult status among Brighton's readers and writers – those who regularly pop in to sign books include Peter James (see box p131), Louise Rennison and Alison MacLeod – and the shop has built a community around it. It organises some 25 literary events a year, held at nearby venues and at the Ropetackle Arts Centre (www.ropetacklecentre.co.uk) in Shoreham and the De La Warr Pavilion in Bexhill (www.dlwp.com), as well as working closely with Charleston House (p164), the Bloomsbury Group's former home near Lewes.

From the first event, which threw PD James and Sandi Toksvig together, to a recent programme that included Grayson Perry and Iain M Banks, the programme has become popular. 'We run events how we want. Our literary lunches are good fun, and the evening events are always sold out. We offer free wine too,' Inge adds with a smile. '25 years later, it's still an exciting business to be in.'

For upcoming events, check the website: www.city-books.co.uk.

## Harry's English Restaurant

*41 Church Road, BN3 2BE (727410, www.harrysenglishrestaurant.com). Bus 1, 6.* **Open** 9am-10.30pm Mon-Sat; 9.30am-9.30pm Sun. **££. Traditional British**. Map p147 D4 ⓮

Hints of seaside chic – combined with just enough attention to the decor and friendly service – make Harry's worth consideration if English is what you're after. Breakfasts, lunches and dinners created in the manner you'd expect include beef stew with mash, and grilled plaice with lemon and parsley butter, both under a tenner. If you're hungry, attack the 'pile-up' breakfast.

## Hove Place

*First Avenue, BN3 2FH (738266, www.goldenliongroup.co.uk). Bus 1, 6.* **Open** 11am-11pm Mon-Wed; 11am-midnight Thur; 11am-1am Fri, Sat; noon-11pm Sun. **Pub**. Map p147 D4 ⓯

Featuring an Italian garden at the rear, which was once part of a nunnery, this set-back public house tricks visitors into forgetting how central they are. Reasonably priced, reasonably interesting pub food, a limited wine menu and interior wood-panelling all lead towards the sense of being in a golf clubhouse – albeit quite a nice one.

## Karims

*15 Blatchington Road, BN3 3YP (739780, www.karimsrestaurant.co.uk). Bus 2, 5, 46.* **Open** 5.30-11pm daily. **££. Indian**. Map p146 B3 ⓰

Rated by the Curry Club as one of the region's strongest kitchens, Karims has been offering Indian and fusion cuisine for more than 20 years. Dishes such as Burmese coconut chicken help it to stand apart from the usual anglicised spice eatery.

## Leonardo's

*55 Church Road, BN3 2BD (328888, www.leonardo-restaurant.co.uk). Bus 1, 6.* **Open** noon-11pm daily. **££. Italian**. Map p147 D3 ⓱

Staffed by Italians, including a Sicilian chef, there's a strong sense of the authentic to dining here, enhanced by a loud weekend buzz when the sizeable space fills with an enthusiastic mix of locals and visitors. Don't go for peace and quiet; go for the seafood linguini. Mains are in the £7-£9 range.

## Meadow

*64 Western Road, BN3 2JQ (721182, www.themeadowrestaurant.co.uk). Bus 1, 6.* **Open** 9.30am-2.30pm; 6.30-10pm Tue-Sat. **£££. Modern British**. Map p147 D4 ⓲

The Meadow subscribes firmly to current trends: the menu is regionally focused and ranges from £10 to £20 for mains such as whole-baked Rye Bay plaice with swiss chard, lemon and caper butter. Head chef Will Murgatroyd certainly has pedigree, having trained under Marcus Wareing. The restaurant is large and light, mostly due to the giant window installed by its previous resident – a bank. It's the recipient of a Michelin Bib Gourmand award.

## Orsino

*141 Church Road, BN3 2AE (770999). Bus 1, 6.* **Open** 10am-11pm daily. **££. Italian**. Map p146 C4 ⓳

Orsino is an independent Italian eaterie with expansive inside seating, though you'll want to go alfresco for those long summer afternoons of people-watching. Grilled swordfish and filetto rossini (both £18) are among the authentic Mediterranean dishes.

## Poets' Corner

*33 Montgomery Street, BN3 5BF (272212, www.thepoetscorner.co.uk). Bus 2, 46, 49.* **Open** 4-11pm Mon-Thur; 4pm-midnight Fri, Sat; noon-10.30pm Sun. **Pub**. Map p146 B3 ⓴

Rebuilt after a fire five years ago, this late-1800s boozer features a log-burner, two bars and a rear yard, and has great Sunday roasts and Sussex favourite Harvey's on tap. There's occasional live music, comedy and, of course, poetry.

Real Eating Company

## Poets' Corner Café in the Park

*Stoneham Park, Stoneham Road,
BN3 5FS (736587). Bus 2, 46, 49.*
**Open** 11am-4pm daily. No credit cards.
**Café**. **Map** p146 A2 ㉑

This community-run café serves fresh coffee and offers a little bit of a green getaway (Stoneham Park) a hop and skip from one of Hove's main roads.

## Real Eating Company

*86-87 Western Road, BN3 1JB
(221444, www.real-eating.co.uk/hove).
Bus 1.* **Open** 8am-8pm Mon-Thur; 8am-9pm Fri, Sat; 8am-5pm Sun. **££**.
**Modern British**. **Map** p147 D4 ㉒

Although the company now has six outlets, Hove is one of only two full restaurants in this mini-food empire – the other is in nearby Lewes. The concept isn't new these days: locally sourced seasonal produce, etc, but it's the humility and sincerity with which it's delivered, not to mention the quality of the 'seasonal favourites with a modern British influence', that matters.

## Red Lion

*1 Hove Place, BN3 2RG (770034,
www.redlionhove.co.uk). Bus 11X,
700.* **Open** 3-11pm Mon-Thur; noon-midnight Fri, Sat; noon-11pm Sun.
**Pub**. **Map** p146 C4 ㉓

A well-stocked CD collection, pool for 50p, a heated beer garden, Sky Sports, near the beach but central, pub food, cask ales, hearty Sunday roast and occasional visits from Morris dancing sides. Could this be the perfect neighbourhood pub?

## Station Pub

*100 Goldstone Villas, BN3 3RU
(733660, www.thestationhove.co.uk).
Bus 5, 7.* **Open** noon-11pm Mon-Thur;
noon-midnight Fri, Sat; noon-10.30pm
Sun. **£**. **Pub**. **Map** p146 C2 ㉔

Part-pub, part-pizzeria and a favourite with commuters, the Station also offers cocktails and comedy to complete its curious blend. It must work, though, as the only audible complaints are that it can be too busy. It has been located next to Hove Station since 1820.

## Three Graces

*168 Portland Road, BN3 5QN
(730040). Bus 2, 46, 49.* **Open** noon-1am daily. **Pub**. **Map** p146 A3 ㉕

The Three Graces has recently replaced the well-known Volt. Dramatically bigger out than in, the snug venue delivers an adventurous pub food menu, with an express menu if you're in a hurry. The pub is eclectically designed with a mish-mash of modern art on the walls. It's family-friendly before 6pm and is carbon-neutral.

## Tin Drum

*10 Victoria Grove, Second Avenue,
BN3 2LF (747555, www.tindrum.
co.uk).* **Open** 10am-midnight Mon-Sat;
10am-10.30pm Sun. **££**. **Café**.
**Map** p147 D4 q ㉖

Did Observer critic Jay Rayner consider moving to Brighton just to be near a Tin Drum? Apparently so. One of two in the city (the Kemp Town premises recently closed, leaving only the Seven Dials branch at 95 Dyke Road), and the newest, the Hove outlet offers outside decking and a light interior perfect for world-watching on sunny days. Menus for breakfast, lunch and dinner are simple in design and give diners not just 'locally sourced' assurances, but the names of the farms too. Try the speciality Reuben sandwich.

## Treacle & Co

NEW *178-180 Church Road, BN3 2DJ (933695, www.treacleandco.co.uk). Bus 1, 6, 49.* **Open** *8.30am-5.30pm Mon-Fri; 9am-5.30pm Sat; noon-5pm Sun.* **Café**. **Map** p146 B4 ㉗

Treacle & Co have been supplying gorgeous gooey cakes to Brighton for some time, but now they have their own café. These small premises are piled high with cookbooks, old china tea sets and shabby-chic furniture, and you can sit in for a savoury lunch (noon-3pm Mon-Sat), but it's the perfect buns and cakes that are unmissable.

## Wick Inn

*63 Western Road, BN3 1JD (736436). Bus 1, 2, 5, 6, 46, 49.* **Open** *noon-midnight Mon-Wed, Sun; noon-1am Thur; noon-2am Fri, Sat.* **Pub**. **Map** p147 D4 ㉘

There is something appealing about a standalone circular bar – most likely that you rarely have to queue. Among the more traditional of Hove's pubs, the informal Wick Inn offers cask ales and interior curiosities such as a spiral staircase to the second-floor bar, which is only open when it's busy. There's a Thai food concession if you're felling peckish.

## Shopping

## Audrey's Chocolates

*28 Holland Road, BN3 1JJ (735561, www.audreyschocolates.co.uk). Bus 1, 6.* **Open** *9am-5pm Mon-Sat.* **Map** p111 B3 ㉙

The hand-dipped milk chocolate range here will appeal to fans of traditional chocolate-makers. In its 60th year, the original and award-winning Hove store is one of two in the city. Owners source ingredients from across the globe and specialise in fondant creams. Follow Prince Charles's lead – there are photos on the wall of him trying some of the products – and sample from the counter. They'll gift wrap the chocolates for you.

## Bert's Home Store

*33 George Street, BN3 3YB (732770, www.bertshomestore.co.uk). Bus 2, 5.* **Open** *9am-5.30pm Mon-Sat; 11am-5pm Sun.* **Map** p146 C3 ㉚

One of two in the city, Bert's is an independent emporium of practical and peculiar things for the kitchen and home. Launched in 2007 by friends and veteran North Laine traders Andrew Earley and Jane Stewart, the Hove shop offers everything from silicone oven mitts to polka-dotted laundry bags.

## Brass Monkey

*109 Portland Road, BN3 5DP (725170, www.brassmonkeys.org.uk). Bus 2, 46, 49.* **Open** *10am-5pm Tue-Sat.* **Map** p146 B3 ㉛

Seven independent artists toil in the workshop at the rear of Brass Monkey, while showcasing their jewellery, metalwork and silver in a small studio shop. The collective, run by Jenifer Wall and Samantha Maund, makes individual pieces themselves and also sources from some 40 UK designers. This classy shop stocks a wide range of unique pieces for all tastes.

## Canham & Sons Butchers

*48 Church Road, BN3 2FN (731021). Bus 1, 6.* **Open** *6am-5pm Mon, Sat; 6am-5.30pm Tue-Fri.* **Map** p147 D4 ㉜

One of only a few surviving Hove high-street family businesses – it's been in the same family for 25 years – Canham & Sons Butchers is now thriving, and for obvious reasons. If you can get past the queues, grab some well-presented meat or just select from the pile of excellent pasties, pies or towering clotted-cream scones.

## City Books

*23 Western Road, BN3 1AF*
*(725306, www.city-books.co.uk) Bus*
*1, 6.* **Open** 9.30am-6pm Mon-Sat;
11am-4.30pm Sun. **Map** p147 E4 ㉝
See box p151.

## La Cave à Fromage

NEW *34-35 Western Road, BN3 1AF*
*(725500, www.la-cave.co.uk) Bus 1, 6.*
**Open** 10am-7pm Mon, Tue; noon-7pm
Wed; 10am-9pm Thur-Sat; 11am-5pm
Sun. **Map** p147 E4 ㉞
La Cave à Fromage is the public front of
Premier Cheese, a well-known supplier
to the trade. The arrival of Hove's
second, continent-loving fromagerie
(after the nearby, British-focused Real
Eating Company's upstairs cheese
shop) has caused a bit of a fondue in
these parts. This south coast opening
follows a successful South Kensington
outlet, and cheese and wine evenings
in the adjacent café are planned.

## iGigi General Store

NEW *31a Western Road, BN3 1AF*
*(775257, www.igigigeneralstore.com).*
*Bus 1, 6.* **Open** 10am-6pm Mon-Sat;
11am-4.30pm Sun. **Map** p147 E4 ㉟
This shop is split into two locations.
The main branch contains the general
store itself on the ground floor; it's a
pleasing showroom full of nothing you
couldn't give a home to, such as
furniture, pottery and knickknacks –
mostly in earthy colours. While
downstairs, the menswear section has
designer brands including Albam,
Hartford from France, and Italian
designers 120% Lino. There's a café
upstairs, which serves tasty things –
such as sardines on toast, Welsh
rarebit with baby roasted tomatoes
and dippy-eggs – on chopping boards,
accompanied by Monmouth coffee.

A couple of doors down the street, at
no.37, you'll find a whole boutique
that's dedicated to carefully selected
women's labels (Nygårds Anna, Blank,
Privatsachen), again in a beautifully
designed boutique.

## JUGS

*44 Blatchington Road, BN3 3YH*
*(719899, www.jugsfurniture.co.uk).*
*Bus 2, 5.* **Open** 9.30am-5pm Mon-Sat;
noon-2pm Sun. **Map** p146 C3 ㊱
Just Unusual Gifts is a two-storey
shop with well-priced, authentic Indian
and Thai furniture. The understated
entrance is deceptive; inside, the shop
teems with handcrafted safari animal-
shaped ornaments, exotic materials,
drums and curiosities collected from
abroad. It appeals to a specific taste,
but for those who lean towards dark
wood and Eastern influences will love it.

## Poppets

*50 Blatchington Road, BN3 3YH*
*(770449, www.poppets.biz).*
*Bus 2.* **Open** 9am-5pm Mon-Sat.
**Map** p146 C3 ㊲
A long-standing family-run shop for
kids, Poppets is the answer for many a
Hove parent. Here, you'll find new and
nearly-new toys of the non-electrical
variety, as well as a large selection of
fashionable clothes for the little ones,
in a shop full of youthful energy.

## Quaff

*139-141 Portland Road, BN3 5QJ*
*(820320, www.quaffit.com). Bus 2.*
**Open** 10.30am-7.30pm Mon-Thur;
10am-8pm Fri, Sat; noon-7pm Sun.
**Map** p146 A3 ㊳
Quaff sells wine independently, coffee
thoughtfully and wedges of very good
cake selfishly. There are regular wine-
tasting courses and there's a case club.
Most of the wines are from small
boutique family-owned wineries, and
Quaff also stocks English wines from
producers in the Sussex area.

## Real Eating Company Cheese Shop

*86-87 Western Road, BN3 1JB*
*(221444, www.real-eating.co.uk). Bus*
*1, 6.* **Open** *Restaurant* 8am-8pm Mon-
Thur; 8am-9pm Fri, Sat; 8am-5pm Sun.
*Cheese shop* 10am-6pm Tue-Sat; 10am-
5pm Sun. **Map** p147 E4 ㊴

Medicine Chest p158

It's all about English produce at this lovingly crafted cheese shop, upstairs from a lovely restaurant and café. The celebrated Neal's Yard Dairy supplies the majority of cheese on offer, but it's complemented by a selection of Sussex products, much of which is exclusive.

## Rume

*54 Western Road, BN3 1JD (777810, www.rume.co.uk). Bus 1.* **Open** 9.30am-5.30pm Mon-Sat. **Map** p147 D4 ⓴

Run by second-generation designer and craftsman Richard Baker, Rume is a seriously good contemporary furniture shop. It sells two of its own lines of furniture, which are clean, edgy takes on quintessentially English styles. They sit alongside flamboyant lighting, cushions, deckchairs and the like – all with a solid, accessible style. There's also a bespoke service.

## Zamaan

*38 Church Road, BN3 2FN (727171). Bus 1, 6.* **Open** 9am-6pm Mon-Sat; noon-5pm Sun. **Map** p147 D4 ㉑

If you look past Zamaan's predictable photo frames and candles, you'll find some interesting lines in drawer handles, cushions and mirrors. There are many shops like this in Hove, but there's something different about Zamaan, perhaps best summed up by its slogan: 'for the eclectic in you'.

## Nightlife

## Freemasons Tavern

*38-39 Western Road, BN3 1AF (732043). Bus 1, 2, 5, 6, 49.* **Open** noon-midnight Mon-Thur, Sun; noon-1am Fri, Sat. **Map** p147 E4 ㉒

Once the meeting place for Hove's secret handshakers – don't miss the mosaic façade, unlike anything else in the city – the Freemasons Tavern is due for a needed refurbishment in early 2011, although it still remains a well-frequented Hove boozer. Let's hope they keep the good wine list, ales and cocktails.

# Class couture

## A revived fashion concept.

An old and largely forgotten Parisian tradition is being repackaged for the fashionable and at-leisure at Hove's **2floor** (65 Church Road, BN3 2BD, 728651, www.2floor.co.uk).

'We're bringing the French boutique apartment concept back to life,' says anglicised German clothes designer Nicole Urbanski. 'I want people to be able to come up here and know we'll lock the door so they can run around in their bra and knickers trying things on, just like they used to in Paris.'

Urbanski's own collection is supplemented by selected ranges from across Europe, including garments from France and Italy, and hats and accessories from her homeland.

'I have to be careful what I say, but the Germans tend to use the best materials, like pure wools.' Nicole arrived in the UK in 1967, aged 23, 'with a sewing machine and a rucksack.' Within six months, she'd joined the BBC as a costume designer, and during the following decade she worked alongside the likes of Jean Paul Gaultier and Paul Smith. 'We recognise that women do not like the rushed high-street experience, so I offer a bespoke service from Monday to Wednesday in relaxed surroundings. Here I can offer the time and personal attention clients want.'

If you don't want to book, you can just drop in on Thursdays and Fridays (10am-5.30pm), as well as Saturdays (10am-2pm).

## Grosvenor

*16 Western Street, BN1 2PG (770712, www.thegrosvenorbar.com). Bus 1, 2, 5, 6, 11X, 49.* **Open** 5pm-late Mon-Fri; 4pm-late Sat, Sun. **Map** p147 E5 ⑬

This lively bar on the Brighton/Hove border specialises in cocktails and attracts a large lesbian and gay contingent for themed parties and the weekly quiz night. The art deco-inspired, converted end-of-terrace townhouse, located just up from the seafront, prides itself on offering neighbourhood friendliness rare for a bar – hence the faithful clientele.

## H Bar

*16 Church Road, BN3 2FL (725890, www.h-bar-hove.com).* **Open** 5pm-2am Tue-Thur; 5pm-3am Fri, Sat. **Map** p147 D4 ⑭

Black from the outside and rainbow-lit from the inside, the H Bar claims to have brought a London-chic late-bar experience to an otherwise club-bereft part of the city. Cocktails, tick. LED wall, tick. VIP lounge, tick. Fire-throwing dancers on opening night, tick. 'Soho by the sea', although perhaps said with a tinge of irony, seems like an apt description.

## Medicine Chest

NEW *51-55 Brunswick Street East, BN3 1AU (770002, www.themedicine chest.co.uk). Bus 1, 6.* **Open** noon-11pm Mon-Thur, Sun; noon-1am Fri, Sat. **Map** p147 E4 ⑮

The newest addition to the Brighton bar scene is set to become one of the finest. This chemistry-inspired gin bar occupies a rather faultless little space below street level, just off the main drag. Mixologist Mike Mason has blended his own set of 'elixirs', using fine botanicals and fruits and cordials for the house cocktails, and serves the finest dry martini south of London. The low-lit bar has a speakeasy feel that gets buzzy as the cocktails flow. There's an interesting tapas menu and a small restaurant.

## Misty's

*116 Church Road, BN3 2EA (220302, www.mistysbar.co.uk). Bus 1, 6.* **Open** 11am-2.30am Mon-Fri; 10am-2.30am Sat; 11am-midnight Sun. **Map** p146 C4 ⑯

With a fold-back front and compact interior, this is an honest little alcove for a late-evening cocktail or late-morning french toast with maple syrup. Classic and unusual tipples are on offer, including Brighton's favourite liqueur, Tuaca, for those who like brandy-based blends.

## Ton.ik

*72 Blatchington Road, BN3 3YH (771305). Bus 2, 5, 46.* **Open** 11am-2am daily. **Map** p146 C3 ⑰

Long, thin and sparse (except for the TV monitors), Ton.ik gives the distinct impression of having been designed to be easy to clean after a busy Friday night. There are large daytime food and night-time shots menus, and free wireless internet.

# Art & Leisure

## Gwydyr Hair Salon

*Gwydyr Mansions, Holland Road, BN3 1JW (732923). Bus 1, 6.* **Open** 8.30am-5.30pm Mon, Tue, Thur, Fri; 8.30am-1pm Wed; 8.30am-4.30pm Sat. No credit cards. **Map** p147 D4 ⑱

This family-run high-street barber has been in the same location for 120 years, though the present shop's fixtures and fittings, including beautiful antique barber's chairs, are only 80 years old.

## Uniquely Organic Eco Spa

NEW *40 Church Road, BN3 2FN (726973, www.uoecospa.com). Bus 1, 6.* **Open** 10am-8pm Mon-Fri; 10am-6pm Sat; 11am-4pm Sun. **Map** p147 D4 ⑲

There's a lot to like here for the 'Hove, actually' resident and ethical visitor. The treatments include all manner of massages, facials and spa packages, all of which incorporate organic products.

Brighton Marina

# Days Out

## Brighton Marina

Brighton Marina, a 10-minute bus ride from the city centre, is the lively setting for restaurants, boutiques, bars and markets, and is not without its charm. Park Square and Mermaid Walk are appealing modern pedestrian walkways with the yachts on one side and shops overlooking them on the other.

Many visitors are attracted by the water sports on offer, but for those wanting a different brand of entertainment, a cinema, bowling alley and casino are also on site.

The marina's eastern edge contains a plush residential area of balconied flats and houses, sandwiched between colossal white cliffs and the outer harbour; many residents have boats proudly bobbing outside. Since opening in 1978, the UK's largest marina has continued to grow. By 2002, hundreds of homes had been built,

along with a further section of retail units, eateries and the **Alias Hotel Seattle** (p182) that collectively made up the Waterfront. Further commercial and residential developments are planned for the future.

Each weekend, the **Mermaid Market** takes place in Marina Square between 11am and 4pm, showcasing arts and crafts, jewellery and fresh local produce. There are more than 20 eating and drinking venues to choose from, the majority lining the upper level 'Board Walk' of the Waterfront, with gorgeous views overlooking the boat-swelled harbour.

The best placed for a scenic cocktail or meal is the **Seattle Restaurant** at the Alias Hotel Seattle (p182). Hidden in between the chains are independents such as the **Gourmet Fish & Chip Company** (18 Waterfront, BN2 5WA, 01273 670701,

www.gourmetfishandchip
company.com), who also are
the proud owners of a Hollywood-
style Walk of Fame for Brighton.
Among the 100 names to have
a star here are Sir Winston
Churchill and Chris Eubank.

For an interesting chocolate-
related experience, **Chocoholly**,
(7 Marina Walk, BN2 5WA, 07780
975068, www.chocoholly.com)
holds workshops every Saturday
and Sunday from 2pm, where you
will be able to make your own
organic chocolate.

Shoppers will find high-street
retailers juxtaposed with quaint
establishments such as **Pebble
Beech** (Unit 45, Brighton Marina,
BN2 5WA, 07594 229747, www.
pebblebeech.co.uk), which imports
a range of ethical, handmade
crafts from all over the world.
As it's quiet during the week,
several shops are only open
Friday to Sunday, including
**Fiery Foods UK** (Unit 30, Marina
Square, BN2 5WA, 01273 705606,
www.fieryfoodsuk.co.uk), whose
sole *raison d'être* would appear to
be to set your mouth on fire as it
entices you in with everything from
chilli sauce to chilli chocolate.

Water sports are brought to you
by **Brighton Dive Centre**, (37
The Waterfront, BN2 5WA, 01273
606068, www.thebrightondive
centre.co.uk), which offers PADI
training courses, children's diving
lessons, equipment hire and even
the chance to dive with sharks at
the Brighton Sea Life Centre (p115).

Rather go on, not in, the water?
**Ross Boat Trips** (Pontoon 5,
BN2 5UP, 07958 246414, www.
watertours.co.uk) can give you
a powerboat-style soaking, pier
cruises, harbour tours, stag and
hen trips and even sprinkle ashes
at sea. Fishing trips can also
be organsied on two of its boats,
holding 29 and 50 people.

## Lewes

A 15-minute train ride from
Brighton, Lewes is a handsome
county town set amid the South
Downs. Stepping off the train
you're greeted by elegant Regency
architecture and the manicured
lawns of a bygone era. But behind
this well-heeled veneer there's
a definite edge, with remnants
of Lewes's anarchic past and
independent spirit in evidence
everywhere – from the quirky
bookshops steeped in local history
to the conspiratorial pubs and
right-on artist co-operatives.

The town is so independently
minded, in fact, that in September
2008 retailers introduced their own
currency, the 'Lewes pound', with
the aim of encouraging people
to spend locally. (Appropriately,
the local 17th-century agitator,
revolutionary and founding father
of America, Thomas Paine, is the
figurehead on the notes.)

The town's behind-doors
revolutionary spirit – you feel
that locals would happily embrace
a republic of Lewes – spills out
on to the street once a year for
the infamous **Lewes Bonfire**;
a bacchanalian celebration that
draws thousands of revellers.

Start out at the **Needlemakers**,
an arty, crafty shopping emporium.
Then head up Market Street to the
High Street – perhaps stopping for
a swift half and a ploughmans in
much-fêted local pub the **Lewes
Arms** (1 Mount Place, BN7 1YH
01273 473152).

Lewes has the middle-class
foodie market sussed; there's
something for most tastes, from
upmarket chocolatiers **Bruditz**
(16 Station Street, BN7 2DB, 01273
480734) to specialist fromagerie
**Cheese Please** (46 High Street,
BN7 2DD, 01273 481048, www.
cheesepleaseonline.co.uk) and the

**Lewes Bonfire Night**

beguiling **Bill's Produce Store & Café** (56 Cliffe High Street, 01273 476918, www.billsproduce store.co.uk), stacked with colourful fruit and veg displays and rows of own-made condiments.

There are also some great antique shops, with eclectic curios and art deco lamps available from **Southdown Antiques** (48 Cliffe High Street, 01273 472439), and more fashionable, reclaimed salvage pieces at **Cliffe Antiques Centre** (47 Cliffe High Street, BN7 2AN, 01273 473266).

**May's General Store** (49 Cliffe High Street, BN7 2AN, 01273 473787) is also worth a nose around, but stick to the herbs, handmade soaps and health foods at the front – the back room is crammed with random gift items, from felt rainbow hats to Ganesha smoking pipes, that often crosses the line between idiosyncratic and plain tat. For beautifully packaged and expensive-looking gifts (such as gorgeous bath soaks), try

**Wickle** (Old Needlemakers, West Street, BN7 2LU, 01273 474925, www.wickle.co.uk) instead.

West up the high street from the war memorial, the architecture is particularly picturesque, especially if you go off-piste for a stroll in the twittens (Sussex alleyways). Head north and you'll come across antique bookshops, craft shops – such as **Tash Tori Arts & Crafts** (29 Station Street, BN7 2DB, 01273 487670, www.tashtori. co.uk) and a wealth of artists' studios and private galleries.

The fine **Hop Gallery** (Castle Ditch Lane, BN7 1YJ, 01273 487744, www.hopgallery.com) and the artist-run **Chalk Gallery** collective (4 North Street, BN7 2PA, 01273 474477, www.chalkgallery lewes.co.uk) deserve further exploration for their local art.

Reflecting the rich musical and craft heritage of the town, there are several bespoke guitarmakers in residence. Local luthier **Richard Osborne** specialises in mandolins

Lewes

and bouzoukis (Studio 14, Star Gallery, BN7 1YJ, 01273 473883, www.osborneguitars.co.uk).

A stroll up the tiny Pipe Passage, off the high street, brings you to a bijou, nameless bookshop run by the affable **David Jarman** (1 Pipe Passage, BN7 1YG, 01273 480744). It houses a fine selection of second-hand art books and fiction ranging from 50p to £100 (for a hardback complete set of Sir Walter Scott). For collectable children's literature, try the labyrinthine **Fifteenth Century Bookshop** (99-100 High Street, BN7 1XH, 01273 474160, www.oldenyoung books.co.uk).

In warm, sunny weather, buy a Winkle tartan picnic blanket, stock up on provisions at Bill's and head south down Keere Street to the postcard-perfect Southover area of Lewes. The **Anne of Cleves Museum,** (52 Southover High Street, 01273 474610, www. sussexpast.co.uk) occupying a 15th-century townhouse, is best admired from the outside, while lazing in the lush, romantic surroundings of the **Southover Grange Gardens** (Southover House, Southover Road, BN7 1TP, 01273 484999).

**Lewes Castle** (169 High Street, BN7 1YE, 01273 486290, www.sussexpast.co.uk), a striking 11th-century stone motte and bailey fortification is the centrepiece of the town. It's a perfect setting at sunset, when a hike to the top of the tower rewards you with breathtaking panoramic views across the steep sweep of the Downs stretching out to the coast.

The dominant building along the High Street is **Harvey's Brewery and Shop** (6 Cliffe High Street, BN7 2AH, 01273 480217, www.harveys.org.uk, book in advance). This is the home of Sussex's most famous real ale, and an institution in Lewes.

So much so that, when the Lewes Arms was bought by Greene King, a boycott ensued until it put at least one Harvey's ale on tap. If you can stand the smell of hops, then a trip round the brewery is a fascinating introduction not just to the brewing process but to the heritage of Lewes itself. If you miss out on the tour, check out the range of merchandise in the shop on Cliffe High Street.

For a pint of the finest Harvey's, step into the nearby **Gardners Arms** (46 Cliffe High Street, BN7 2AN, 01273 474808). This minuscule boozer has all the bonhomie of a village pub.

For a place to linger over lunch, try the **Real Eating Company** (18 Cliffe High Street, BN7 2AJ, 01273 402650, www.real-eating. co.uk). It's a slick operation, serving supremely fresh dishes. The menus and specials constantly rotate, reflecting the organic, locally-sourced credentials. The wide, light-filled space and friendly staff make this a welcoming space.

If you are planning to spend the night in Lewes, **Pelham House** (St Andrew's Lane, BN7 1UW, 01273 488600, www.pelhamhouse.com) is a good option. This converted 16th-century manorhouse is now a 31-bedroom hotel. With its tasteful decoration, period features, airy spaces and attentive service, Pelham is artful and discreet. Stop here for lunch in the impressive Garden Room, with its eau de nil walls and magnificent views across the gardens, or for afternoon tea on the terrace or dinner in the ornate Panelled Room. Another good option is the **White Hart Hotel** (High Street, BN7 1XE, 01273 476694, www.whitehartlewes. co.uk). Thomas Paine, Lewes's own radical pioneer, fortified his ideas in the 'Headstrong Club' which held meetings here. Today, its a pub and hotel with a spa and indoor pool.

## Charleston House

Five miles further east of Lewes is **Charleston House** (Firle, East Sussex, BN8 6LL, 01323 811265, www.charleston.org.uk). The Bloomsbury set's country retreat is a worthwhile excursion, although it's a bit of a trek from Glynde, the nearest train station. Countryliner service 125 runs from Lewes from Wednesday to Friday, but a car makes it an easier option from Brighton. Guided tours are available Wednesday to Saturday. On Sunday and bank holidays visitors are free to roam.

Artist Vanessa Bell set up house in East Sussex in 1916 – accompanied by her lover Duncan Grant, his lover, David Garnett, and her two children. Vanessa revelled in the rural freedom, as her sister Virginia Woolf noted: 'Nessa seems to have slipped civilisation off her back, and splashes about entirely nude, without shame, and enormous spirit. Indeed, Clive now takes up the line that she has ceased to be a presentable lady – I think it all works admirably.' Bell and Grant daubed every available surface with murals, and filled the farmhouse with textiles, ceramics and pieces of art – including works by Picasso and Sickert. The house looks as fantastical today as it did 90 years ago: a gloriously uninhibited explosion of colour and creativity.

## Littlehampton

Hopping on the train west (about 45 minutes, with a change at Hove) is Littlehampton. *Vogue* may have hailed Littlehampton as the 'coolest British seaside resort' in 2007, but many who visit may struggle to believe the hype; the place still has some way to go before it becomes Sussex's equivalent of Kent's

Whitstable. Yet, therein lies the appeal for many: with its pretty coastline, faded promenade, colourful beach huts and old-school fairground, the place still has a ramshackle charm. And, with a pair of architecturally striking, and, in the case of the East Beach Café, gastronomically lauded, seafront eateries – as well as retro chippies – it has also become something of a destination for foodies.

The fact that picnicking on the beach, lounging in hired deck chairs and building sandcastles are all favourite summer activities here means that the spot is still every bit the British seaside resort. The 'Blue Flag' East Beach is even good for swimming – particularly if you head eastward past the groynes. Best of all, the shingle fades into sand so you don't stub your feet in the shallows. It's framed by brightly coloured beach huts at one end, and a grand Regency crescent at the other. The landscape is somewhat blighted, however, by a Harvester restaurant and rows of scruffy shops off the promenade, along with a fairground that's home to a miniature log flume and bumper cars.

But what most come here for is the **East Beach Café** (Beach Road, BN17 5GB, 01903 718153, www.eastbeachcafe.co.uk), the gastronomic venue that put Littlehampton on the map. Its organic, sculptural form – designed by visionary architect Thomas Heatherwick, of Sitooterie fame – looks like a giant brown clam shell, while the interior feels more like a boutique restaurant than a beachside café. The menu runs from simple classics such as beer-battered fish to imaginative seafood dishes such as mussel, gurnard and salmon saffron chowder.

On the other side of the River Arun is the West Beach. It's more

Devils Dyke p166

rugged, with wild dunes to the rear, perfect for a spot of secluded sunbathing or sheltering from the wind on blustery days. For natural beach lovers, this is seaside nirvana – with a long stretch of unadulterated sand, free from neon clutter, and a horizon that seems to stretch on forever. The best place to eat here is the **West Beach Café** (Rope Walk, BN17 5DL, 01903 718153, www.eastbeachcafe. co.uk). Distinctly less showy than its East Beach sister, this eaterie is still a cut above your usual beachside café – it's also architect-designed. In summer, the doors open out on to the patio next to the beach. West Beach sells simple fare such as fish cakes, scampi, and good fish and chips.

Littlehampton's low-key ambience, as well as its strong winds and busy tides, have seen it become a popular destination for windsurfing and kitesurfing and, in recent years, surfers.

## Ditchling Beacon

From the vantage point of Ditchling Beacon (reached by the 79 bus from Old Steine in Brighton), the undulating contours of what Rudyard Kipling called the 'blunt, bow-headed, whale-backed downs' stretch as far as the eye can see. To the west, the **South Downs Way** (www.nationaltrail.co.uk) dips and climbs the chalk escarpment for some 50 miles, back to Hampshire; eastwards on the horizon lies the hazy blue-grey outline of the cliffs at the Seven Sisters, where the downs finally reach the sea. The Beacon, rising steeply above the villages and farmland of the Weald on one side, then sloping gently southwards down towards the sea, has its own quiet pleasures and oblique charms.

It's a landscape shaped by centuries of sheep grazing – the most profitable use for these bare, precipitous inclines, with their

**BRIGHTON BY AREA**

shallow, chalky soils. The sheep's constant grazing soon finished off any saplings or taller plants that took root on the close-cropped slopes, letting shorter, less showy species thrive. As the naturalist and novelist WH Hudson observed in *Nature in Downland*, published in 1900: 'The turf is composed of small grasses and clovers mixed with a great variety of creeping herbs, some exceedingly small.' Seen at ground level – as you stretch out at full length on the soft, springy turf – the seemingly bare hillside is a miniature kingdom, teeming with life. Most exhilarating of all, though, are the sudden steep ascents, on paths that are little more than a series of chalky footholds hewn into the sheer slope.

And at the top? No café, no toilets, and certainly no cable car: just the spirit-lifting sweep of the Sussex Weald and the white ribbon of the South Downs Way, entering its homeward straight.

For sustenance head to the **Half Moon** (Ditchling Road, BN7 3AF, 01273 890253, www.half moonplumpton.com) in nearby Plumpton for log fires and stellar British food such as warm pork pie with homemade chutney or a wild rabbit stew.

## Devil's Dyke

The Victorians, like many modern-day visitors, preferred the drama of Devil's Dyke, a five-mile walk along the South Downs Way from Ditchling Beacon (or take the 77 bus from Brighton train station). This plunging, vertiginous gulf was carved out from the chalk strata as the Ice Age snowfields retreated. In its tourist heyday at the end of the 19th century, day-trippers flocked to peer into the abyss – there was even a cable car, perilously strung across the valley. Today, it's popular with walkers, picnickers and hang-gliders.

Once at the top, admire the panorama across the Weald below. According to John Constable, the view is 'perhaps the most grand & affecting natural landscape in the world – and consequently, a scene the most unfit for a picture'.

There's a pub at the top of Devil's Dyke, but it's best to head down into the Weald, to the **Shepherd & Dog** (The Street, BN5 9LU, 01273 857382, www.shepherd dogpub.co.uk) in Fulking. This 17th-century inn is set at the foot of the downs and has low, beamed ceilings, an inglenook fireplace and a glorious beer garden.

# Essentials

Hotel Pelirocco p171

# Hotels

There are no more lumpy beds or grumpy landladies in Brighton these days. Hoteliers are tripping over themselves to convert tatty guesthouses into boutique hotels, squeezing themed rooms into the narrow confines of terraced houses in the streets that lead up from the seafront. No longer are your only options restricted to seedy B&Bs (although some still exist) and huge identikit corporate rooms.

The townhouses of Kemp Town are where you'll find most of the new 'boutique' accommodation. A consequence is that many are either gay-run, or at least notably gay-friendly (it's highly unlikely that sexual orientation will be an issue in any of the accommodation listed here, or, indeed, city-wide).

In the townhouses, owners often make up for the lack of space by offering as many services as they can possibly provide: organic breakfasts delivered to your room, luxurious bathroom products, film and music DVDs. And despite the modern facilities, many maintain a junkshop-chic look. Places such as **Snooze**, **Paskins** and **Brighton Wave** are both amply appointed and moderately priced. More upmarket boutique options in Kemp Town include **Blanch House** and **Kemp Townhouse**. Nearby **Drakes** is one of the more established venues and has earned plaudits from around the world for its stylish rooms and top-level service. It is, like Blanch House, one of the few which offer an excellent restaurant.

**Hotel du Vin**, closer to the centre, is often spoken about in the same breath. Although it's part of a small chain, the bistro and wine lounge are decorated like a Parisian restaurant and the rooms are large and characterful.

The townhouses around Regency Square are also beginning to be converted, including the **Artist Residence** or **Hotel Una**. One of the most singular properties in Brighton is **Hotel Pelirocco** – a self-styled rock 'n' roll hotel.

What Brighton currently lacks are hotels in-between the trendy guesthouse and the 200-room hotels that earn trade from conference. However, with more than 4,000 beds in the city – there's no shortage at any price range.

## Price wise

As Brighton is a popular weekend destination, all good hotels book up in advance on Friday, Saturday and occasionally Sunday nights. Also be warned that many only accept a minimum two-night stay. This does mean, however, that there are some excellent bargains to be had midweek, with discounts of up to 50 per cent.

Needless to say, the summer is significantly busier, and weekends with festivals get particularly booked up, so check what is on first. For the month-long Brighton Festival in May, Pride weekend in August and for any political party conference in September, hotels fill up fast. If you're after budget accommodation, there are still plenty of guesthouses. The Tourist Information Centre by the Royal Pavilion can make reservations for £1.50 per person per reservation on the day; £5 for advance bookings.

## City Centre

### Artist Residence

*33 Regency Square, BN1 2GG (324302, www.artistresidence.co.uk). Bus 11X.* **££.**
See box p173.

### Granville

*124 King's Road, BN1 2FY (326302, www.granvillehotel.co.uk). Bus 11X.* **££.**
Billing itself as Brighton's 'original' boutique hotel, the seafront Granville has buckets of personality and imagination. And, considering the location,

the two dozen, meticulously conceived rooms and the quality of the buffet breakfast on offer on its summer terrace, it's a bit of a bargain too. If you're feeling extravagant, opt for an elaborately carved four-poster with en suite jacuzzi; other themed rooms include the Gothic Room, the art deco Noel Coward Room and the romantic Brighton Rock Room, with its muslin-draped Victorian four-poster.

### Hilton Brighton Metropole

*King's Road, BN1 2FU (775432, www.hilton.co.uk). Bus 11X.* **£££**.
Completed in 1890, the Hotel Metropole, now owned by Hilton, is Brighton's largest hotel. In a bold departure from the white stuccoed style of other seafront properties, the red brick Metropole was mildly controversial, but nevertheless a grand proposition. Today, it's a rather more modern affair, but remains elegant if a little bland. The rooms vary quite a bit – so have a look at a couple if you can – and not all have a bath. The customer service is excellent. Internet costs extra.

### Holiday Inn

*137 King's Road, BN1 2JF (828250, www.holidayinn.com). Bus 11X.* **££**.
There's no getting away from the ugly exterior of this Holiday Inn, but once through the doors, it's a pleasant, if functional hotel, as you'd expect from the international chain. Feedback has been consistently good and if you're with a group of people, or you bag a bargain room, it's a perfectly amenable stay. There are also clear sea views from the front rooms, especially those of the fourth and fifth storeys.

### Hotel Pelirocco

*10 Regency Square, BN1 2FG (327055, www.hotelpelirocco.co.uk). Bus 11X.* **££**.
Describing itself as 'England's most rock 'n' roll hotel,' the Pelirocco harks back to the days when a weekend in Brighton was a dirty weekend – one of the rooms has a mirror on the ceiling,

## SHORTLIST

**Best for business**
- Barceló Brighton Old Ship Hotel (p172)
- Thistle Brighton (p173)

**Most rock 'n' roll**
- Hotel Pelirocco (p171)

**Friendliest welcome**
- Guest & the City (p177)
- Hotel Una (p172)

**Cheap & chic**
- Avalon (p175)
- Brighton Wave (p177)
- Snooze Guest House (p178)
- Twenty One (p180)
- Umi Brighton (p174)

**For design buffs**
- Kemp Townhouse (p178)
- MyHotel Brighton (p174)
- Oriental (p172)

**Best for pampering**
- Grand (p173)
- Lansdowne Place Hotel (p180)
- Neo Hotel (p172)

**Best for foodies**
- Blanch House (p177)
- Drakes (p177)
- Hotel du Vin (p174)

**Best breakfast**
- Five Brighton (p177)
- Paskins Town House (p178)

**Best views**
- Alias Hotel Seattle (p182)
- Holiday Inn (p171)

**Arty stays**
- Artist Residence (p170)
- Sea Spray (p178)

**Notably gay-friendly**
- Amsterdam (p175)
- Legends (p178)

**ESSENTIALS**

and sexual enhancement hampers are available. Each room is individually decorated; you may find yourself in the Rough Trade room, complete with decks and headphones; or in Betty's Boudoir, dedicated to the 1950s pin-up. There's a PlayStation 2 in each room, handy if you want to chill after a night in the bar drinking cocktails with Brighton music types. The bar also has regular DJ nights.

## Hotel Una

*55/56 Regency Square, BN1 2FF (820464, www.hotel-una.co.uk).* Bus 11X. **£££**.

Hotel Una is one of Brighton's fancier residences. Owned by architect Zoran Maricevic, the hotel intelligently melds contemporary furniture and lighting with the building's Regency history. Each of the 19 rooms is individually decorated: Danube has a ball and claw bath; the Aragon room has a sauna; and Flores has a mezzanine seating area. There are six different price structures but check the website for some good midweek specials. There's a great cocktail bar too.

## Motel Schmotel

*37 Russell Square, BN1 2EF (326129, www.motelschmotel.co.uk). Bus 1, 2, 5, 12, 14, 17.* **££**.

Motel Schmotel is an absolute bargain given its location in a five-storey townhouse on a quiet square right in the city centre. The three-star accommodation is modern, there's wireless internet in each of the 11 rooms, and each has Freeview. The breakfast is also good. There's a minimum two-night stay on weekends.

## Neo Hotel

*19 Oriental Place, BN1 2LL (711104, www.neohotel.com). Bus 11X.* **££**.

A sense of lavishness is readily apparent throughout this hotel, from the deer head on the wall overlooking the opulent Georgian furniture to the well-stocked bar. It's balanced by a certain romance in the sumptuously decorated rooms. Each of the nine rooms have been designed by the owner Steph in different styles, using vintage prints and wallpapers. Each has modern facilities and a silk kimono for lounging. Therapies are available in the hotel.

## Oriental

*9 Oriental Place, BN1 2LJ (205050, www.orientalbrighton.co.uk).* Bus 11X. **££**.

Only 30 seconds from the sea and two minutes from the bustle of Western Road, the Oriental is ideally placed in the relative quiet of Oriental Place. It's a typical Brighton Regency townhouse and features nine modern but interesting rooms over five floors, all en-suite. As one of the original boutique hotels in town, the decor is contemporary and stylish. The public areas and bar feature an ever-changing selection of art works. Excellent breakfasts are made from local produce.

## Ramada Jarvis

*149 King's Road, BN1 2PP (0844 815 9061, www.ramadajarvis.co.uk).* Bus 11X. **££**.

There are two Ramada hotels in Brighton: one in the Marina, and this city-centre branch, which is a grand Victorian hotel built in 1864. The Grade II listed building retains many of its original features, including the mirrors and chandeliers. The rooms are, however, a thoroughly modern identikit affair in dark mahogany.

## Seafront

## Barceló Brighton Old Ship Hotel

*31-38 King's Road BN1 1NR (329001, www.barcelo-hotels.co.uk). Bus 11X.* **££**.

The oldest hotel in Brighton occupies a fine position right on the seafront, squarely between the two piers and by the finest shopping area in the city. The unassuming façade belies the hotel's importance. It was established before

1600, but the current building dates from c1794, with a sensitive refurbishment in the 1960s. The assembly room and ballroom from 1761 are spectacular. There are 154 traditional but brightly coloured rooms, some with sea views.

## Grand

*99 King's Road, BN1 2FW (224300, www.grandbrighton.co.uk). Bus 11X.* **£££**.

Most certainly Brighton's grandest hotel, the Grand is a Victorian masterpiece built in the 1860s. The magnificent open-well staircase is a suitably grand introduction to the hotel, and the professional staff live up to its grandeur. The 201 spotless rooms are well-appointed and retain the Victorian styling, plus all have complimentary internet and satellite TV. There's a gym and a good restaurant serving classic English cuisine, as well as a comfortable lounge bar.

## Thistle Brighton

*King's Road, BN1 2GS (0871 376 9041, www.thistle.com). Bus 1, 2, 7, 11X, 37.* **£££**.

Located by City Hall, this hotel, run by the chain Thistle, is a conference favourite. There are 210 rooms and excellent facilities, but its central position and the good offers available on its website make it worth checking out for leisure trips too. The rooms are what you'd expect from such a hotel: clean and comfortable. The centrepiece is the vast and welcoming atrium.

## Queens Hotel

*1 King's Road, BN1 1NS (321222, www.queenshotelbrighton.com). Bus 1, 2, 7, 11X, 37.* **££**.

This large hotel is a popular choice for weekenders and conference delegates, with 94 good-sized rooms decorated in a modern, inoffensive way. Amenities include a decent gym, swimming pool and a bar and bistro with an extensive menu. The location is excellent, though the area can be noisy at night.

# The art inn

Young artists have always needed a helping hand. Enter **Artist Residence** (p170), a new hotel that offers invited artists free accommodation for two months, followed by their own exhibition. Set in the finest townhouse on Regency Square, built c1830, half of its rooms have a view over the derelict West Pier, directly opposite. It's a suitably inspiring panorama of the seafront.

Owner Justin, with partner Charlie, turned the run-down guesthouse into an arts space 'where families and young couples can enjoy the extensive art culture of their surroundings.'

The hotel is, of course, open to all, and less artistically hands-on guests can enjoy the creative atmosphere – a different painter or graffiti artist has decorated each of the 13 rooms with original works, and there's also an exhibition space.

Brighton artist Mel Sheppard has painted a bright and funky interior, while Australian Laura Krikke has opted for a mellow Japanese-inspired room with cherry blossoms. Perhaps the most high-profile artist is Pinky, a Brighton-based urban artist who has worked for Justin Timberlake and the BBC. His bold room, also with a sea view, is one of the most popular.

There are plans to offer hotel packages with workshops in screen printing, textiles, jewellery, photography, painting or furniture refurbishment – whether for overnight guests or those staying longer. Keep an eye on the website for news.

**ESSENTIALS**

Drakes p177

## Umi Brighton

*64 King's Road, BN1 1NA*
*(323221, www.umihotelbrighton.co.uk).*
*Bus 11X.* **££.**
Umi has found a niche in the Brighton
hotel scene: a stylish budget hotel. The
rooms are basic, but spotless and comfortable. There's also a good selection
of twin, triple and family rooms. The
location, with some rooms facing the
sea, is excellent, although it's on a busy
junction on the corner of West Street,
home to the big nightclubs and bars.

## North Laine & the Lanes

### Hotel du Vin

*2-6 Ship Street, BN1 1AD*
*(718588, www.hotelduvin.com).*
*Bus 11X.* **£££.**
One of half-a-dozen classy, provincial
venues in this mini chain, the Brighton
branch is set in a jumble of mock
Tudor and Gothic revival buildings.
High-quality bistro food brings many
non-guests to the restaurant, and a

carefully chosen cellar supplies an
equally popular wine bar on the first-
floor terrace; there's also a wine-tasting
room, humidor and heated 'cigar
shack'. The 49 rooms are well-specced,
and each is slightly different: regulars
return to specific rooms – so ask to
have a look around before you choose.
The suites are huge.

### Leona House

*74 Middle Street, BN1 1AL (327309,*
*www.leonahousebrighton.com). Bus 1, 2,*
*7, 11X, 37.* **££.**
Within a Regency guesthouse, Leona
describes itself, accurately, as a 'bijou'
hotel. The seven rooms are each tastefully decorated. Four rooms share a
bathroom, reflected in the cheaper
rates, but every room has a radio and
TV. There are regular midweek offers.

### Myhotel Brighton

*17 Jubilee Street, BN1 1GE (900300,*
*www.myhotels.com). Bus 5, 22, 24,*
*26, 49.* **££.**
Myhotel labels itself as 'where Freddie
Mercury meets the Maharishi,' which

## Kemp Town

### Amherst

*2 Lower Rock Gardens, BN2 1PG*
*(670131, www.amhersthotel.co.uk).*
*Bus 1, 2, 7, 37, 47.* **££**.
Located between Kemp Town and the sea, the neat, fashionable Amherst opened in 2005 and offers two types of room – Junior Suite and Luxury Double – some with sea views. Each room is individually styled and features feather duvets, Egyptian cotton sheets and widescreen LCD TVs. A full English breakfast – brought to your room – is included in the price, and there are complimentary snacks too. There's a discount for single occupancy.

### Amsterdam

*11-12 Marine Parade BN2 1TL*
*(688825, www.amsterdam.uk.com).*
*Bus 12, 14, 27.* **££**.
The sea-facing Amsterdam is a large venture with a hotel, bar and restaurant. This gay-friendly venue also has a sauna (voted Brighton's best in the 2008 LGBT Golden Handbag awards), and massage treatments. There are often events in the bar, with a regular Sunday night cabaret. A Golden Handbag was also awarded to the hotel itself – and rightly so. There is a fair variety of rooms (and rates), from a £70 room with a side view to the penthouse at around £170. Discounts are offered for two-night stays.

sums up the premises pretty nicely: styled, tranquil and very, very camp. Stark white is the dominant theme, with each floor sporting its own bright colour interjecting against the bare backdrop. Rooms decorated with rounded corners and sparkling crystals are the norm; a crystal light fixture glows in the corner of each room, slowly rotating through an assortment of colours. Myhotel is certainly fun and original, and in keeping with the creative vibrancy of the surrounding area.

### Radisson Blu Hotel

*Old Steine, BN1 1NP (766700,*
*www.radissonblu.co.uk). Bus 5, 22,*
*24, 26, 49.* **££**.
The Radisson chain took over this formerly down-at-heel hotel that was built in 1819. Past guests Charles Dickens or William Thackeray may have recognised some of the Regency elegance in the suites, but as with all of Radisson's 'Blu' hotels, most rooms are modern. There are short-stay apartments with kitchenettes; otherwise, splash out in the dining room and cocktail bar.

### Avalon

*7 Upper Rock Gardens, BN2 1QE*
*(692344, www.avalonbrighton.co.uk).*
*Bus 1, 2, 7, 37, 47.* **££**.
This traditional bed and breakfast has been widely lauded for its friendly hosts Brian, Tom and George, and the fact it welcomes dogs. In the heart of Kemp Town, the Avalon is well placed for Brighton's gay quarter. There are seven well-appointed rooms, each furnished with whatever took the owners' fancy. They're a good source of information and will loan out maps for walkers.

Hotel du Vin p174

## Blanch House

*17 Atlingworth Street, BN2 1PL*
*(603504, www.blanchhouse.co.uk).*
*Bus 1, 2, 7, 37, 47.* **£££.**

Blanch House is a wonderfully conceived hotel, cocktail bar and restaurant. Hidden behind the façade of an unassuming Georgian terrace house are a dozen rooms themed after snowstorms, roses and 1970s disco. Splendid Fogarty goose and duck down duvets and pillows, Relyon pocket-sprung beds, big plasma screens and other thoughtful touches make for a comfortable stay. There's a full range of therapies and beauty pampering, and the sleek bar is known for its cocktails. Their excellent dinner menu is mostly locally sourced, and includes dishes such as grilled Sussex lobster with crayfish tails and lemon and tarragon beurre blanc, or roast saddle of wild boar and grilled pancetta.

## Brighton Wave

*10 Madeira Place, BN2 1TN (676794,*
*www.brightonwave.co.uk). Bus 1, 2, 7,*
*37, 47.* **££.**

'Laid-back', 'funky' and 'quirky' have all been used to describe Brighton Wave. The eight rooms are tastefully decorated using solid colours and splashes of modern art. The communal areas welcome you with regularly changing art exhibitions from local artists. With late checkout and late breakfast options, the emphasis is on chilling by the sea. A good value stay.

## Drakes

*43-44 Marine Parade, BN2 1PL*
*(696934, www.drakesofbrighton.com).*
*Bus 1, 2, 7, 37, 47.* **£££.**

It's luxury all the way at Brighton's hugely popular high-end designer hotel. Snag an expansive bedroom with a view overlooking Brighton Pier and you can sink into a free-standing bath set beside floor-to-ceiling sea-facing windows. All 20 rooms have been individually created, and come with sheets of Egyptian cotton, duck-down duvets, LCD-screen TVs and broadband. The in-house restaurant is run by respected chef Ben McKellar – of Gingerman (p63) fame – so be sure to have at least one meal here. The small cocktail lounge mixes some accomplished concoctions. Drakes also offers a full concierge service. Make sure to book ahead – it's a popular place.

## Five Brighton

*5 New Steine, BN2 1PB (686547,*
*www.fivehotel.com). Bus 1, 2, 7,*
*37, 47.* **££.**

Of the converted townhouses around this arera, Five is one of the most pleasant. There's a cosy feel to this ten-room guesthouse; for instance, the superb locally sourced cooked breakfast is taken around a communal table. The rooms have tea- and coffee-making facilities and iPod docks. The knowledgeable owners will advise on their favourite pubs and restaurants.

## Guest & the City

*2 Broad Street, BN2 1TJ (698289,*
*www.guestandthecity.co.uk). Bus 1, 2,*
*7, 37, 47.* **££.**

This very popular, gay-friendly (but not exclusively so) seven-room guesthouse is lauded for its warm welcome. The loft suites, with two double rooms and a kitchenette, are suitable for families or sharing couples. We like the superior doubles, especially with the stained glass window. The superior doubles have a view of the sea.

## Gulliver's

*12a New Steine, BN2 1PB (695415,*
*www.gullivershotel.com). Bus 1, 2,*
*7, 37, 47.* **££.**

The recently refurbished Gulliver's is a classic B&B, with friendly staff and well-equipped, if unremarkable, rooms. Its locally sourced breakfast buffet – with vegetarian and vegan options – is a welcome addition. A couple of doors down, the owners have opened a French-style bistro called New Steine Bistro.

## Kemp Townhouse

*21 Atlingworth Street, BN2 1PL
(681400, www.kemptownhousebrighton.
com). Bus 1, 2, 7, 37, 47.* **£££**.
This boutique hotel has been gathering
a lot of plaudits, and is one of only a
couple of five-star small hotels in
Brighton. The accolades are well-
deserved: there are nine tastefully decorated rooms with muted colours and
spashes of brightness. They are of
varying sizes, from a 'cosy single' to
the 'four-poster feature' room with a
free-standing bath. It's effortlessly chic.

## Legends

*31-34 Marine Parade, BN2 1TR
(624462, www.legendsbrighton.com).
Bus 1, 2, 7, 37, 47.* **££**.
As the name suggests, this proudly
gay hotel holds a bit of a legendary status on the Brighton seafront.
Combining the hotel with a lively bar
and late nightclub keeps the overall
atmosphere fun and easygoing. The 38
rooms are spacious and modern and
feature flatscreen TVs and iPod docks,
and many offer great views of Brighton
Pier. At weekends, the bar and club are
open until 4am and there's a street-
level sun terrace at the front.

## Nineteen

*19 Broad Street, BN2 1TJ (675529,
www.hotelnineteen.co.uk). Bus 1, 2, 7,
37, 47.* **££**.
Thanks to minimalist decor and light
colours, the smaller rooms here feel
bright and airy. Beds sit on bases of
illuminated, coloured glass bricks, the
linen are fresh and white, and the
walls are adorned with work by local
artists. Luxurious bathrooms come
with Molton Brown products and
mouthwash, and all rooms have CD
and DVD players, with a library of
discs available downstairs. Guests
may also help themselves to Penguin
biscuits from the kitchen, and the honesty fridge filled with quality wines
and Czech beers. The courtyard room
has a hot tub.

## Paskins Town House

*18/19 Charlotte Street, BN2 1AG
(601203, www.paskins.co.uk). Bus 1,
2, 7, 37, 47.* **££**.
This immaculately kept Victorian
townhouse has 19 eclectic rooms, with
an underlying art deco vibe. It offers a
better breakfast than most – the owner
buys mainly organic produce and
makes his own veggie sausages (the
tarragon and sun-dried tomato ones
are excellent). In fact, it has been voted
vegetarian hotel of the year by the
Vegetarian Society (don't worry carni-
vores: local bacon and sausages are
still served) and all the soaps are natural and organic.

## Sea Spray

*25 New Steine, BN2 1PD (680332,
www.seaspraybrighton.co.uk). Bus 1,
2, 7, 37, 47.* **££**.
The gimmick of this newly converted
themed boutique hotel is the chance
to share your bedroom with Elvis,
Salvador Dali or Andy Warhol – but
this doesn't detract from the comfort
of the fluffy bath towels, chic bar and
airy breakfast room. Standard 'budget'
doubles are also themed – Indian or
Japanese – and most things here are
executed with a sense of fun (there's a
Hove, Actually room). There's also a
modest treatment room and you can
check-out as late as 3pm.

## Snooze Guest House

*25 St George's Terrace, BN2 1JJ
(605797, www.snoozebrighton.com).
Bus 37, 47, 52.* **££**.
This funky guesthouse has six 'super
snooze' rooms and four 'snooze light'
options for those on a budget. Each
room is individually designed, whether
Georgian chic or a 1960s-style crash
pad. The decoration could have come
from the antique and curio shops
around Kemp Town itself. There are
two suites in the 'penthouse' and they
include Freeview, iPod docking and
breakfast in bed. Snooze is a great
value place to stay.

Alias Hotel Seattle p182

Legends p178

## Square Brighton

*4 New Steine, BN2 1PB (691777, www.squarebrighton.com). Bus 1, 2, 7, 37, 47.* **£££**.

There are 10 beautifully designed rooms in Square, a handful of which have sea views. Money has certainly been thrown at the design, but its never in danger of being style over substance. Brightly coloured furniture is set against wooden floors and white walls in some rooms, while others are more muted, but often with a statement piece of furniture.

## Twenty One

*21 Charlotte Street, BN2 1AG (686450, www.thetwentyone.co.uk). Bus 1, 2, 7, 37, 47.* **££**.

The eight rooms of this converted townhouse have the modern conveniences of digital radios, iPod docks and Freeview, but the decor is resolutely antique – think distressed dressers, junk shop finds and brass bedsteads. Rooms 3 and 6 have baths. There is also a small single room for between £50 and £70. The owners can direct you to food, drink and good times.

## Hove

## Claremont

*13 Second Avenue, BN3 2LL (735161, www.theclaremont.eu). Bus 1, 6, 20, 49.* **£££**.

The Claremont is an upmarket guesthouse with 11 traditionally elegant rooms with huge beds. Although popular for weddings and other functions, the hotel also attracts couples looking for a romantic getaway. In the heart of Hove, it's one of the best places to stay away from the city centre.

## Lansdowne Place Hotel

*Lansdowne Place, BN3 1HQ (736266, www.lansdowneplace.co.uk). Bus 1, 2, 5, 6, 25, 49.* **£££**.

After a recent restoration job, this hotel near the Hove seafront has become one of the area's top hotels. Guests have

# Cheap stays

Brighton has long been on the backpacker circuit, thanks to its proximity to Gatwick Airport and London – and its fun-loving reputation. But Brighton's budget sector in the last 10 years has moved from cheap guesthouses and B&Bs to the hostel. As travellers, and those just up for partying, become more discerning, an increasing number of hostels are combining budget appeal with the cool, urban style and decor one would expect from a boutique hotel. You might still have to sleep in a room with snoring strangers, but the rest of the time you can hang out on a terrace or lounge on retro space-age chairs.

There are two **Grapevine** hostels, one by the seafront and the other in North Laine. The seafront branch (75/76 Middle Street, BN1 1AL, 777717, www.grapevinewebsite.co.uk) is smartly appointed, particularly the single rooms. The four-bed rooms are the largest. The North Laine (29/30 North Road) location has larger dorm rooms. Both premises welcome hen and stag groups, backpackers and sport teams.

**Seadragon** (36 Waterloo Street, Hove, BN3 1AY, 711854, www.seadragonbackpackers.co.uk) is one of the cosier and quieter options (well, it is in Hove), with two- or four-bed rooms. The latter have a seating area, and all the beds have duvets.

**Baggies Backpackers Hostel** (33 Oriental Place, City Centre, BN1 2LL, 733740, www.baggiesbackpackers.com), is another more-restrained hostel, with only a bohemian 'music room' to break the quiet of the square it overlooks. The Brighton branch of the **St Christopher's** chain (10-12 Grand Junction Road, Seafront, BN1 1NG, 3202035, www.st-christophers.co.uk) has views over the beach and the pier. There's a late bar downstairs – so expect some noise if you don't join in.

The largest hostel is **Journeys** (33 Richmond Place, Hanover, BN2 9NA, 695866, www.visitjourneys.com). Its bright decor comes courtesy of 'Quirky Boutique Hostels Inc' and it offers wireless internet, and has video games in the pleasant common room. The bunks have curtains around them.

been spinning through the stately revolving doors here since 1854, but now they are treated to contemporary amenities such as LCD flatscreen TVs, walk-in showers, king- or queen-sized beds and 24-hour room service. Most rooms have sea views. The rooms are modern but the Victorian heritage is reflected in the furnishings. The hotel has also invested heavily in its spa, with eight treatment rooms, a sauna, a steam room and a 'relaxation suite'. It has superb value spa day and residential packages. Guests can avail themselves of French cuisine in the Grill restaurant or cocktails in the bar.

## New England Quarter

### Jurys Inn

*101 Stroudley Road, BN1 4DJ (862121, http://brightonhotels.jurysinns.com). Bus 21, 37.* **££**.
This is the first of several proposed hotels to be built in the ever developing New England Quarter. The Jurys

Inn's 234 rooms are what you'd expect from a business chain – clean comfortable and well-equipped. There is a bar and restaurant.

## Brighton Marina

### Alias Hotel Seattle

*Merchants Quay, Brighton Marina, BN2 5WA (679799, www.aliashotels. com). Bus 7, 21, 23.* **£££**.
The Alias Seattle has been situated in the Marina since 2003, but saw a major refurbishment in 2008. There are now 70 modern and spacious rooms, with half of them facing out on to the Marina. The overall feel is professional but relaxed, and the original vintage film posters and 1960s screen prints show that someone has lavished not only money but also some passion on the place. The restaurant and bar are open to non-residents all day and feature decked areas that provide a perfect location for enjoying the glorious Brighton sunsets.

Oriental p172

# Getting Around

## Arriving & leaving

### By air

#### Gatwick Airport

*0844 335 1802, www.gatwick airport.com. 25 miles north of Brighton, off the M23.*
Brighton is, on average, a 30-minute train journey from Gatwick. Trains leave at least every 10 to 20 minutes, usually from platform 5 or 6. All are direct, although some will have more stops than others. The regular trains run from around 5am until 11.45. There are sporadic trains overnight but they can take more than an hour.

Two companies operate between Gatwick and Brighton: **First Capital Connect** (0845 026 4700, www.firstcapitalconnect.co.uk) and **Southern Railway** (0845 748 4950, www.southernrailway.com). The same ticket is valid for both services unless you purchase one marked 'FCC only' (these are only marginally cheaper, so it's not worth limiting yourself for a Gatwick–Brighton journey). A one-way ticket valid for any train costs £7.90. An off-peak day return costs £8.50; an anytime day return £10; and an open return (valid for 30 days) £15. Prices normally rise each New Year.

By road, **National Express** (0871 781 8178, www.national express.com) runs a regular coach service for £8.40 each way (from £7 booked in advance). It takes 45 minutes. Taxis will cost around £35-£45. **Brighton Airport Taxis** (01273 414144, www.brighton airportcabs.co.uk) charges £35 for up to four passengers. **Brighton Taxis** (0844 335 0705, www. brightontaxihire.co.uk) charges £38.

### Other London airports

The other London airports are much less convenient for getting to Brighton, usually requiring a transfer in central London. Direct coaches are available on National Express from Heathrow Airport for £26.10 each way and take around 2 hours 30 minutes. First Capital Connect trains connect to the shuttle from Luton Airport and take a minimum of 2 hours; fares start at £28.50 (£33.50 return) for off-peak travel.

### By coach

**National Express** (0871 781 8181, www.nationalexpress.com) operates coach services between Brighton and London (journey time 2 hours 20 minutes), and other destinations in England, departing from Pool Valley Coach Station, located just off Old Steine.

Some of the services run by **Brighton & Hove Bus and Coach Company** (p184) to destinations in the south-east – including Arundel, Bognor Regis, Chichester and Littlehampton – also depart from here.

#### Pool Valley Coach Station

*Pool Valley, BN1 1NJ (202020).*

### By train

Brighton's central station is served by two train operators. **Southern Railway** (www.southernrailway. com) operates on the main line to London (mostly to London Victoria, but some services go to London Bridge), and to other destinations along the south coast, including suburban stations (p185) in Brighton & Hove.

### First Capital Connect

(www.firstcapitalconnect.co.uk) has services to Bedford via London Bridge, Blackfriars, City Thameslink, Farringdon and St Pancras International (for direct high-speed Eurostar services to Paris and Brussels, as well as domestic connections to northern England and Scotland). Note that you can purchase cheaper tickets limited to First Capital Connect services (marked 'FCC only'), however conductors do check, and you will have to pay a penalty if you attempt to use these on Southern trains. Fares vary by time of day and cost roughly £14-£21.50 single; £17-£26 return.

The information desk at Brighton station has timetables and details of discount travel, season tickets and international travel. **National Rail Enquiries** has details by phone on 08457 484950 (24 hours daily), or check www.nationalrail.co.uk.

Some services to London from coastal destinations to the west bypass Brighton station, but stop at Hove station instead.

### Brighton Railway Station

*Queen's Road, BN1 3XP (0845 127 2920, www.nationalrail.co.uk).*

### Hove Railway Station

*Goldstone Villas, Hove, BN3 3RU.*

## Public transport

### Buses

The city and its surrounding suburbs are very well served by a comprehensive (but difficult to decipher) bus network. **Brighton & Hove Bus and Coach Company** (886200, www.buses.co.uk) runs the vast majority of bus services throughout Brighton & Hove.

Other operators are the **Big Lemon** (www.thebiglemon.com), which runs a service between the city centre, Lewes Road and the universities; and **Stagecoach** (www.stagecoachbus.com), whose Coastliner 700 route goes from Old Steine to destinations along the coast as far west as Southsea.

Several parts of the city are served by a great number of buses. We have listed individual bus services but not every variation of that route (for example, 2A, 2B). Below are the groupings for some of the most popular spots in Brighton used throughout this guide, together with a list of bus routes that serve the respective streets or areas. For full information on routes, timetables and maps see www.buses.co.uk.

There are a total of seven **night bus** routes in Brighton. Five of these are Nightclub buses operating Thursday, Friday and Saturday nights (N29, N69, N97, N98 and N99). The N7 and N25 Night Buses run nightly around Brighton and into the suburbs.

**Brighton City Centre** 1, 1A, 2, 2A, 5, 5A, 5B, 6, 7, 12, 12A, 12C, 12X, 13X, 14, 14B, 14C, 17, 20X, 21B, 22, 22A, 24, 25, 26, 27, 27B, 28, 29, 29A, 29B, 29C, 37, 37B, 38A, 40, 40X, 46, 47, 49, 49A, 49E, 50, 52, 52A, 55, 56, 57, 59, 71, 73, 77, 78, 79, 81, 81A, 81B, 81C, 81E, 273, 700, N7, N25, N29, N69, N97, N98, N99.
**Brighton Marina** 7, 14B, 21, 21B, 23, 27, 47, 52, 57, N7, N99.
**Brighton Pier** 1, 1A, 2, 2A, 5, 5A, 5B, 7, 12, 12A, 12C, 12X, 13X, 14, 14B, 14C, 17, 20X, 21B, 22, 22A, 24, 25, 26, 27, 27B, 28, 29, 29A, 29B, 29C, 37, 37B, 38A, 46, 47, 49, 49A, 49E, 50, 52, 55, 56, 57, 59, 73, 77, 78, 79, 81, 81A, 81B, 81C, 81E, 273, 700, N7, N25, N97, N99.
**Brighton Train Station** 6, 7, 12, 12A, 12C, 12X, 13X, 14, 14B, 14C, 21, 27, 27B, 37, 37B, 38A, 47, 49E, 50, 52, 52A, 57, 59, 77, 78, 79, 81A, N7.

**Hove Town Centre** 2A, 5, 5A, 5B, 6, 7, 11X, 20X, 25, 46, 49, 49A, 71, 81, 81C, 93, 95, 95A, 700, N7, N25, N98.
**London Road Shops** 5, 5A, 5B, 17, 21, 21B, 22, 22A, 24, 26, 37, 37B, 38, 38A, 40, 40X, 46, 49, 49A, 49E, 50, 55, 56, 78, 79, 81, 81B, 81E, 273, N69.

## Fares

There is a flat fare for most journeys in Brighton of £1.80. Under-5s travel free, up to a maximum of three children per adult passenger. For children ages 5-13, the fare is half the adult fare. Ages 14 and up pay the full adult fare. A single journey on the city's Night Buses N7 and N25 costs £2.20. The Nightclub buses N97, N98 and N99 are £3 and the N29 and N69 are £5. Exact change is required for all single fares.

### Visitor tickets & passes

Visitors may want to make the most of the **Short Hop fares**, which are available across the city for £1. There is also a tourist fare between Brighton Station and Churchill Square, Brighton Pier or the Royal Pavilion, also for £1.

If you're planning on making several journeys during one day, it may be worth buying a **Saver ticket**, which allows for unlimited travel on the Brighton & Hove bus network (excluding the Night Buses and Nightclub Buses). A one-day Saver ticket is available from bus drivers for £5, from the website (£3) or from newsagents (£3.30). A seven-day Saver ticket costs £16.50 if bought in advance from the website or newsagents. For more information, see www.buses.co.uk/tickets/saver.

## Trains

The city has a few suburban rail stations, including London Road, Moulsecoomb and Falmer (for the University of Sussex) to the north-east, and Hove (a five-minute walk from pedestrianised George Street), Portslade and Aldrington to the west. All can be accessed from Brighton station and are served by Southern Railway. Preston Park station, north on the main line to London, is served by both Southern and First Capital Connect trains. Single tickets for all are £2.20 from Brighton; return tickets vary depending on destination and time of day, and cost £2.40-£4.40.

## Taxis

Taxis are a quick way to get around the city and are available 24 hours a day. There are plenty of taxi ranks throughout Brighton, with the main ranks situated in East Street, Queen's Square near the Clock Tower, and outside Hove Town Hall.

There are two types of licensed taxis operating in Brighton: Hackney Carriage vehicles, which are white and aqua and can be found on one of the ranks or hailed from the street; or, Private Hire vehicles, which can only be booked prior to the journey. Private Hire vehicles will not stop if you try and hail them. Many taxis are wheelchair accessible.

The minimum fare is £2.60 and it rises in 20p increments according to how far you travel. As a guide to what your journey may cost, the first mile will be £3.80 and each subsequent mile will be £2.20. For example, Churchill Square to Kemp Town will cost around £3.80. Vehicles carrying five to eight passengers are able to charge a higher fare (equivalent to 1.5 times the normal fare). There are additional charges at night, on Sundays, on public holidays, at Christmas and the New Year, and for telephone pre-bookings.

**ESSENTIALS**

**Brighton & Hove City Cabs** *205205*
**Brighton & Hove Radio Cabs**
*204060, www.brightontaxis.com*
**Brighton & Hove Streamline**
**Taxis** *202020, www.brighton-streamline.co.uk*

## Cycling

Cycling in Brighton is quick and easy (though the out-of-shape may find the hills challenging), with cycle lanes provided across the city, notably along the seafront. For information on hiring bicycles, contact the Visitor Information Centre (p189). Alternatively, try **Go Cycle Hire** (697104), at the Marina, or **Rayment Cycles** (13/14 Circus Parade, New England Road, 697617, www.rayment-cycles.co.uk).

## Driving

Driving around Brighton is relatively easy, but like most big cities, it can become congested during peak times. On-street parking can be difficult to find but there are plenty of car parks dotted around – see 'Car parks' below.

### Vehicle hire

Most car rental firms insist that drivers are over 21 years old (at the very least), with a minimum of one year's driving experience and possess a current and full driving licence with no serious endorsements. The following car hire firms have branches in and around the centre.

**Avis** *0844 544 6042, www.avis.co.uk*
**Enterprise Rent-A-Car**
*202202, www.enterprise.co.uk*
**Europcar** *329332,*
*www.europcar.co.uk*
**Hertz** *0870 850 4882,*
*www.hertz.co.uk*

**National Car Rental** *202426,*
*www.nationalcar.co.uk*
**Thrifty Car Hire** *738227,*
*www.thrifty.co.uk*

## Car parks

All the car parks detailed below are open 24 hours a day. Rates are around £2 for two hours. For a full list (and map) of car parks, visit www.brighton-hove.gov.uk.

**Brighton Lanes (Town Hall)**
**Car Park** *Black Lion Street (294296).*
**Trafalgar Street Car Park**
*294296, www.ncp.co.uk*
**Church Street Car Park**
*0870 606 7050, www.ncp.co.uk*
**Regency Square Car Park**
*294296, www.ncp.co.uk*
**Churchill Square Car Park**
*0845 050 7080, www.ncp.co.uk*

## Clamping & fines

Always carefully check street signs to find out the local parking regulations. Most on-street parking is pay-and-display. You must pay for parking between 9am and 6pm daily. Payment should be made at the on-street pay-and-display ticket vending machines. There are lots of wardens, so its unlikely you can get away with not paying.

The fine for parking illegally is £50 or £60 depending on the infraction, reduced to £25 or £35 if the ticket is paid within 14 days. If you get towed, an additional fee of £105 is levied for removal, plus a £12 storage fee for every day the vehicle remains uncollected. If it has been impounded, you'll need to collect your vehicle from the City Car Pound.

### City Car Pound
*Sackville Road Trading Estate, Sackville Road, Hove, BN3 (0845 603 5469).* **Open** *6.45am-11.30 daily.*

# Resources A-Z

## Accident & emergency

In the event of a serious accident, fire or incident, call **999** and specify whether you require an ambulance, the fire service or the police.

### Royal Sussex County Hospital

*Eastern Road, Brighton, BN2 5BE (696955). Bus 1, 1A, 7, 14B, 14C, 23, 37, 37B, 40X, 47, 52, 57, 71, 73, 90, 94A, N7, N99.*
The city's 24-hour casualty department.

## Credit card loss

Report lost or stolen credit cards immediately both to the police and the 24-hour phone lines listed below. Inform your bank by phone and in writing.

### American Express
*696933,*
*www.americanexpress.com*

### Diners Club
*0870 190 0011,*
*www.dinersclub.co.uk*

### MasterCard
*0800 964767,*
*www.mastercard.com*

### Visa
*0800 891725,*
*www.visa.com*

## Customs

Citizens entering the UK from outside the EU must adhere to these duty-free import limits: 200 cigarettes or 100 cigarillos or 50 cigars or 250g of tobacco; 2 litres of still table wine plus either 1 litre of spirits or strong liqueurs (over 22% abv) or 2 litres of fortified wine (under 22% abv), sparkling wine or other liqueurs; 60cc/ml perfume; 250cc/ml toilet water; and goods to the value of no more than £145. For more details, see the customs website, www.hmrc.gov.uk.

## Dental emergency

If you need emergency dental care, call the dental helpline (0300 1000 899) and specify that you are in pain. They will give you an appointment at one of several practices. Outside normal working hours, phone the emergency dental service in Lewes on 01273 486444. This service is available 6.30-9.30pm weekdays, and 9am-1.30pm Saturday and Sunday.

## Disabled

For information about disabled access and accommodation in Brighton, refer to the website www.visitbrighton.com/site/tourist-information/accessibility. The majority of buses have easy access and priority seating for disabled people. For more information, visit www.buses.co.uk. For wheelchair-accessible taxis, try www.205205.com (205205).

## Electricity

The UK electricity supply is 220-240 volt, 50-cycle AC rather than the 110-120 volt, 60-cycle AC used in the US. Foreign visitors will need an adaptor to run appliances.

ESSENTIALS

# Embassies & consulates

For a list of consular offices, consult the *Yellow Pages* (118247, www.yell.com). All the embassies and consulates are in London. Most embassies and consulates (the US is an exception) do not accept callers without an appointment.

## American Embassy
*24 Grosvenor Square, W1A 2LQ (7499 9000, http://london.usembassy. gov). Bond Street or Marble Arch tube.* **Open** 8.30am-5.30pm Mon-Fri.

## Australian High Commission
*Australia House, Strand, WC2B 4LA (7379 4334, www.uk.embassy.gov.au). Holborn or Temple tube.* **Open** 9am-5pm Mon-Fri.

## Canadian High Commission
*38 Grosvenor Street, W1K 4AA (7258 6600, www.canada.org.uk). Bond Street or Oxford Circus tube.* **Open** 8am-4pm Mon-Fri.

## Embassy of Ireland
*17 Grosvenor Place, SW1X 7HR (7235 2171, 7225 7700 passports & visas, www.embassyofireland.co.uk). Hyde Park Corner tube.* **Open** 9.30am-5.30pm Mon-Fri.

## New Zealand High Commission
*New Zealand House, 80 Haymarket, SW1Y 4TQ (7930 8422, www. nzembassy.com). Piccadilly Circus tube.* **Open** 9am-5pm Mon-Fri.

# Internet

Public internet access is abundant in Brighton. Many cafés and bars offer free wireless internet access, and chain cafés such as Starbucks offer wireless access by subscription.

If you're not toting a laptop, a handful of internet cafés have computers available to rent. The best two central branches are:

## Curve Bar & Brasserie
*45 Gardner Street, BN1 1UN (603031).* **Open** 10am-10pm daily.

## Eazinet
*1st floor, 47 West Street, BN1 2RA (721995).* **Open** 10am-midnight daily.

# Opening hours

In general, business hours are 9.30am-5.30pm Mon-Fri. Most shops are open 9am-5.30pm Mon-Sat and 11am-5pm on Sun. Officially, closing time for pubs is 11pm, but most pubs have licences to sell alcohol until 1am.

# Pharmacies

There are independents on most high streets, and branches of **Boots** (www.boots.com) have a pharmacy; the branch at 129 North Street (207461, 8am-7pm Mon-Sat, 11am-5pm Sun) has an after-hours pharmacy open until midnight from Monday to Saturday.

# Police

If you've been the victim of a crime, call 0845 60 70 999.

## Brighton Central Police Station
*John Street, BN2 0LA (0845 607 0999, www.sussex.police.uk).* **Open** 24 hours daily.

## Hove Police Station
*Holland Road, Hove, BN3 1JY (0845 60 70 999, www.sussex. police.uk).* **Open** 8am-8pm Mon-Fri; 10am-6pm Sat.

# Post

Post offices are usually open 9am-5.30pm during the week

and 9am-noon on Saturdays. For the nearest branch call the Royal Mail on 08457 223344 or check www.royalmail.com. The main post office is located in WHSmiths in the Churchill Square Shopping Centre (p71).

## Smoking

Smoking has been banned in enclosed public spaces across England, including all pubs and restaurants, since 2007.

## Telephones

The area code for Brighton is 01273. International codes are as follows: Australia 61; Belgium 32; Canada 1; France 33; Germany 49; Ireland 353; Italy 39; Japan 81; Netherlands 31; New Zealand 64; Spain 34; USA 1.

## Tickets

Most venues sell their tickets through their own website or through **Ticketmaster** (www.ticketmaster.co.uk, 0870 5344 4444). The **Brighton Dome** (p102) sells tickets for its own and other venues at www.brighton ticketshop.com. You can also try **Rounder Records** (19 Brighton Square, 325440) and **Resident** (28 Kensington Gardens, 606312).

## Time

Brighton operates on Greenwich Mean Time (GMT). Clocks go forward to run on British Summer Time (BST) on the last Saturday in March, and return to GMT on the last Saturday in October.

## Tipping

Tipping 10-15 per cent in taxis, restaurants, hairdressers and some

bars (but not pubs) is normal. Some restaurants and bars add service automatically to all bills; always check to avoid paying twice.

## Tourist information

As well as the office listed below, there's an additional Visitor Information Point at the **Brighton Toy & Model Museum** (p87), on Trafalgar Street just below Brighton railway station.

### Brighton Visitor Information Centre

*5 Pavilion Buildings, Brighton, BN1 1EE (0300 3000088, www. visitbrighton.com).* **Open** 10am-5pm Mon-Sat; 10am-4pm Sun.

## Visas

EU citizens do not require a visa to visit the UK; citizens of the USA, Canada, Australia, South Africa and New Zealand can also enter with only a passport for tourist visits of up to six months, as long as they can show they can support themselves during their visit and plan to return. Use www.ukvisas.gov.uk to check your visa status well before you travel, or contact the British embassy, consulate or high commission in your own country. You can arrange visas online at www.fco.gov.uk.

## What's on

Brighton & Hove has a number of listings publications – the most comprehensive are the online **East** (www.eastmagazine.co.uk), with an East Sussex-wide remit, and the more music-oriented **XYZ** (www.xyzmagazine.co.uk), also issued monthly. For gay listings, look out for the free magazine **Gscene** (www.gscene.com).

# Index

ESSENTIALS

# TUACA

LIQUORE ORIGINALE

**PREMIUM VANILLA LIQUEUR
WITH CITRUS ESSENCES**

TUACA®
LIQUORE ORIGINALE

Cuoni&Canepa

 Find Tuaca at
facebook.com/tuacaliqueur

**START CHILLED.
FINISH RESPONSIBLY.**

for the facts **drinkaware.co.uk**